For Molly

Vicki Allen

To Anne —
Hope this makes
you laugh & smile —
& remember special
friendships!
Enjoy! (!!)
Warmest Wishes,
Vicki Allen
2/24/02

Published by Magnolia Publishing Company, Inc.
P.O. Box 770514
Oklahoma City, Oklahoma 73177
1-800-953-MAGNOLIA

ISBN 0-9674880-4-4

Manufactured in the United States of America

For Molly is contemporary fiction with southern flair, set in multiple locations around the Deep South, beginning in central Louisiana, progressing to the pristine white shores of Florida's Emerald Coast then detouring through the campus of Northeast Louisiana University before settling down in present day Oklahoma City.

It is a story of friendship, love and loss, revolving around the book's heroine Ashley Stewart. She is a typical small-town girl: feisty, strong and independent, secure in the love of her family and surrounded by a close-knit circle of lifelong friends. When a speeding truck erases the only truth she's ever known, Ashley flees her hometown, denying her past, ultimately meeting up with the one man who holds the key to her destiny.

"FOR MOLLY is the most wonderful story I've read in some time. I fell in love with the characters and just hated to see the story end. It truly touched my heart." **Janet Hall,** Alexandria, Virginia

"This is the first time in a long time that a book has been so good that it made me laugh, cry and hope with all my heart. I couldn't seem to put it down, except when my tears were blurring the pages or I was so exhausted that I could not read another word." **Darcy Jenkins,** Moore, Oklahoma

"I neglected the house, kids and husband to finish this book – IT WAS GREAT! Overall, I thought it was a great story and it kept me interested the whole way through, excited to turn the page." **Robin Wallis,** Edmond, Oklahoma

"This book brought back wonderful memories of true friendships, some of which still exist today." **Jeannine Boudreaux Nalley,** Pineville, Louisiana

"FOR MOLLY is simply the best!!! Memories, laughter and tears combined into a heartwarming story." **Carrie Cheek Roy,** Pineville, Louisiana

"FOR MOLLY is for everyone. It does not matter if you are young or old-this book is a page-turner." **Casey Posey,** Monroe, Louisiana

"Couldn't put it down." **Jeff Fenwick,** Fort Smith, Arkansas

"A charming tale of self-discovery with southern flair. This book satisfied me like a big ol' helping of Red Beans and Rice!" **Suzanne Lafargue**, Dallas, Texas.

"Great read, could not wait to find out how it ended!" **Lori Bridges,** Lawton, Oklahoma

"Perfect mix of emotions." **Tiffany King**, Edmond, Oklahoma

"Literally could not put it down. Devoured all from first to final page. Vicki Allen's eye for fine points and atmosphere made me feel I had stepped back into luscious Louisiana. Emotional, yet empowering!" **Karen McMillen**, Marietta, Georgia

"I thoroughly enjoyed FOR MOLLY and could not put it down. It took 3 nights to read it. Having grown up in the setting of the book, I feel Vicki did an excellent job in describing the town, the characters and events." **Doug Harville,** Jonesboro, Arkansas

"Vivid characters, dynamic dialogue.... great story line! I picked up FOR MOLLY and could not put it down. Vicki Allen's propensity to write captivating dialogue is the catalyst that drives this book. There's an emotional story told here and the characters are ones the reader doesn't soon forget. The details, which provide the Louisiana and Oklahoma settings, are reminiscent of the time frame when FOR MOLLY occurs. There's great writing talent here and it provides a fascinating reading experience for the person who delves into FOR MOLLY. What's the best compliment a reader can give? I didn't want it to end! **Karen Brantley** from Oklahoma City, OK

"An enjoyable read-a nice distraction from my adult life." **Stacy Allen,** Brentwood, Tennessee

"I couldn't put it down!! A fantastic first outing for this promising young author. The book is well crafted and the dialogue is extremely clever. Anyone who has ever wondered what it is like to live in Louisiana should get this book. I can't wait for the next novel from this talented author. **Chris Blevins**, DeRidder, Louisiana

"FOR MOLLY is a must for 'coming of age' teens, boys and girls alike. A true to life drama: it stirs emotions and touches the heart! A captivating book, FOR MOLLY takes you from laughter at the teenager we all were, or wanted to be, through the tears of loss, to anger at the cruelty of self-centeredness, then leaves you with the rightness of life as love does conquer all. FOR MOLLY illustrates the importance of making wise decisions. It shows the strength of character needed to live with the consequences of our decisions or, when necessary, to admit we made a mistake and ask for help! Look for strong family ties and forever friendships that truly define the word friend. **T.J. King**, Edmond, Oklahoma

A NOTE FROM THE AUTHOR

I began FOR MOLLY as a teen living in Pineville, Louisiana, writing what is now equivalent to the first hundred pages at the age of fifteen. When I left for college, I put the manuscript in a manila envelope and tucked it away in a closet at my parents' house. I married young and, as with so many other young women, later divorced, putting my dream of writing on hold to finish college and support a child as a single parent. After college, I was lucky enough to meet a wonderful man on a blind date. I married that man two years later and went on to establish a career in pharmacy practice.

Several years and two more children later, I returned to my childhood home in Louisiana to help my parents pack for their retirement move. While cleaning out closets, I came across the manuscript I had put away sixteen years beforehand. I brought it back to Oklahoma and read it, then picked up where I left off, adding and polishing until it became what it is today.

FOR MOLLY was a very special project for me, started with the innocence of a child and finished with the insight of an adult. Hidden within the pages of this tale of a determined young woman are a salute to family and friendship, a tribute to a good friend long deceased, and a reminder of the consequences of paths chosen.

I hope you enjoy FOR MOLLY and will pass it, and its message, on to others.

Warmest regards,

Vicki Allen

For my parents, who encouraged the dream

For Kent, who kept the dream alive
For Karla and Suzanne, the best pals
a girl could ever have
And for JLB, a good friend gone,
but not forgotten

For Molly

PROLOGUE

Relaxing in the sugary white sand of Florida's Gulf Coast, Ashley allowed the cool, salty waves to lick playfully at her toes. She loved this place with its crystal-clear emerald waters and snow-white beaches, fast in her belief that it was the closest place to heaven that earth had to offer. Destin had always been a haven for her.

She had spent many summers on this beach, beginning in early childhood and continuing, even now, into adulthood. As a child, she had come here to play, to splash in the warm aquamarine waves and build castles in the sugary sand. Later, she journeyed to Destin for refuge, seeking sanctuary from the chaos reigning over her life. The events of the past decade had ended the untroubled existence she had previously known and she had resolved many a crisis sitting along this shore, gazing pensively out over the waters of the gulf.

And now, she came here simply for the feeling of peace that washed over her the moment her feet sank into the cool, silky sand. It was only fitting that she returned to Destin to reflect on her life, seeing once again each joy, each loss, and each brutal mistake, contemplating, if she had to do it all again, what would she change?

At the sound of shrill laughter, Ashley turned her head, smiling at the young couple strolling past her, hand in hand, obviously head-over-heels in love. She was filled with nostalgia, reflecting back to a time when she had been so completely captivated by another. To recall him from the depths of her memory was bittersweet at best; a warm reminiscence mingled with wondering what if? Cries of anguish and tears of pain also came to mind, causing the once familiar ache to stir deeply within her heart.

Losing him had been a turning point in her life. She had done foolish things, made terrible choices and spent years suffering the consequences of her actions. She leaned back, pressing her palms deeply into the sand, closing her eyes and cringing as images from her past fought their way into the present.

She had pushed away the one who loved her most, choosing instead another. It was with greater reluctance that she remembered him. He had caused her more grief and pain than anyone she'd ever known. Getting involved with him had almost cost her life. Tormented, her conscience was filled with shouts of anger and screams of terror, the image of a taunting, distorted face, suppressed for years, suddenly clear before her eyes.

She flinched, remembering it all perfectly, yet not wanting to see.

Had it all been worth it? It was a tough question with no good answer. She never looked back. To do so only opened places in her heart and mind that she had closed off long before. She had successfully avoided facing the old ghosts for quite a few years, but now the memories refused to be repressed and she was forced to let them resurface.

CHAPTER ONE

Hearing the rev of an engine and the screeching of tires, Ashley Stewart raised her head, waving goodbye as Doug Fairchild, Mitch Guidry and Scotty Jeansonne roared away in Scotty's mustard yellow GMC pickup. They headed in the direction of Kincaid Lake to fish and drink beer; hauling behind them the old Ranger bass boat and an ice chest full of clandestinely obtained Budweiser and Miller ponies. She grinned as she watched them disappear from sight, then closed her eyes, laying back and relaxing, content just to soak up the warm rays of late August sun.

"I heard Doug ask you about the Back to School Dance. You going?"

Ashley turned her head, glancing over to where her best friend Kate Ducote floated next to her on the muddy waters of Indian Creek, lounging comfortably on her back atop a rubber raft, peeking out at Ashley from beneath drowsy eyelids.

"Dating Dougie would be almost incestuous, don't you think?" Ashley asked her lightly, her eyes dancing with good humor behind dark Ray Bans.

"You're avoiding the issue."

"There's no issue, Kate."

"Sure there is, Ashley, and you're dancing all around it."

"You're not going to start that again, are you?" Ashley sighed heavily, flopping onto to her stomach and burying her face in the crook of her tightly folded arms, muttering unhappily at the thought of another one of Kate's well-meaning lectures. "I get awfully tired of your constant badgering about my social life."

"It's more your *lack* of a social life that really bothers us." Roused from a lazy catnap by Ashley's whining, Susanna Robicheaux spoke up indignantly, lifting her head from the pillow of her raft and shading her skeptical eyes with her freckled forearm. "What is it with you, Ashley? Are you going to miss every important social event we have for the rest of your life?"

"I haven't missed all of them. I go out all the time."

"Yeah, right, maybe in a group of twenty! Why don't you break down and have a real date?"

"With who?" Ashley asked, raising an interested brow to Susanna as she rolled off her raft into the waist-deep water.

"How about one of those stud-muffins who just left for Kincaid Lake?"

"Scotty, Mitch and Doug are all like brothers to me. Just because their voices have changed and they're sporting a little more testosterone than usual doesn't mean that I want to date them." Ashley leaned down, splashing some of the murky creek water over her shoulders to cool the sun-kissed skin on her back. "Besides, it's pretty hard to see any true romantic possibilities in someone you shared a sand box with."

"They don't see it that way. They think you're just frigid," Susanna informed her in a voice loud enough to wake the dead. "They call you *The Ice Princess,* for crissakes! Jeez, Ashley, is that how you want to be remembered?"

Susanna jumped in, pushing through the water to stand next to Ashley, waving her arms wildly in the air as she illustrated her point. "I can just hear them now, 'Ashley Stewart, remember her? She was the girl so frosty that we called her the Ice Princess!' "

"Susanna, I wish you'd get your own life and leave mine alone."

"Not gonna happen, sweetheart."

"Give it a rest, Susanna," Kate intervened on Ashley's behalf, frowning at Susanna. "There's nothing wrong with Ashley. She just has high dating standards."

"Yeah, they're high all right," Susanna scowled, flopping ungracefully back onto her raft, drenching Kate with the splash of her wake. "Ashley has the dating standards of a nun."

"Now Suz, I'm not saintly. I'm just selective."

"Whatever, Ash. Just stay home with your folks and miss all the fun. See if I care."

Ashley Stewart was a true child of the South, born and bred in Louisiana, the fertile green land of rolling rivers and marshy bayous. She grew up in Pineville, a picturesque little town nestled in a thick forest of sweet-smelling pines along the banks of the Red River, and was the only child of Remy and Maggie Stewart, being hellacious enough as a toddler to prevent them from ever wanting another. From the time she was a year old, Ashley knew her parents simply as Maggie and Remy, and Maggie, being the open-minded soul that she was, saw no reason to teach her any differently.

Maggie was an Alabama beauty, outgoing and energetic, with a dazzling smile and contagious laugh, brought home to Louisiana by Remy when he graduated from Auburn University. She was a registered nurse and had worked forever for crazy Pete Gautreaux, the local family practice doc, running his office efficiently and professionally, her intuition and careful hands saving him time and time again from certain malpractice.

Remy was a pharmacist and owner of an old-fashioned drugstore on the corner of a downtown intersection across from city hall. The renovated old Walgreen's was a place of fascination for a young girl, filled with perfumes and body lotions, dime candies and Coca-Cola, and a place where Ashley spent many Saturday mornings. Bypassing both the temptations of the fountain area and the candy aisle, Ashley would head directly to the prescription counter at the very back of the store. There with the wide, adoring eyes of a Daddy's girl, Ashley would watch him work, the tall, handsome pharmacist so openly beloved by all his customers. She observed his easy smile and the kind, patient manner in which he dealt with people, absolutely convinced that her father was the smartest man in the world.

The Stewarts had lived in the same house all of Ashley's life, a two-story, white plantation-style house on four tree-filled acres right outside the city limits, with huge picture windows draped in lace, interior walls dabbled in soft pastels and antique furnishings of maple and cherry.

Just across a grassy field lived the Ducotes and Ashley's best friend, Kate. Tall, willowy Kate was a fair-haired knockout with the face of an angel and wisdom beyond her years, becoming at a very young age the exclusive keeper of Ashley's innermost thoughts and deep, dark secrets. Ashley told Kate everything, knowing that Kate would take it to the grave with her if necessary.

In kindergarten, Ashley and Kate met up with Susanna Robicheaux and the three became best friends for life, weathering the usual girlhood activities together: tap dancing and girl scouts, Barbie dolls and bicycles. They were inseparable, considering themselves to be the perfect trio.

Susanna was short, cute and freckled, notorious for both her loud voice and long, russet-colored curls. She was outspoken, opinionated and rebellious, battling continuously with her father and constantly grounded for her attitude, her grades, her smoking or any combination of the three.

Despite her loud-mouthed hardheadedness, Susanna did have some very redeeming qualities. She was lively and she was fun; her devil-may-care stance on life kept everyone around her in stitches, and, excluding the fact that she was impossibly abrasive most of the time, Susanna was, for the most part, a passionately devoted, true-blue friend.

Ashley was middle-of-the-road, the perfect complement to either Kate or Susanna, soft-spoken yet ambitious, a good listener yet vivacious and flirtatious. Despite popular opinion, Ashley wasn't an angel. She had her defiant moments, the most memorable being the three days of her eighth-grade year she spent at home after being suspended for smoking with Susanna in the girls bathroom. It was a very proud moment for Maggie and Remy, and one that they didn't let Ashley forget for a very long time.

But, unlike Susanna, Ashley wasn't purposely rebellious; her greatest downfall was her impulsiveness. Independent and stubborn, she tended to act first and think later, usually while suffering the consequences of her actions.

Pineville was small, and life was simple, yet the perfect trio always found something to hold their terribly short attention spans. Autumn brought hayrides, pig roasts and the Rapides Parish Fair, with high school football games dominating Friday nights.

Thanksgiving marked the beginning of deer hunting season and the disappearance of virtually every male in a hundred-mile radius. Attired in camouflage and fluorescent orange hunting vests, they left town for hunting camps on Friday night and returned on Sunday afternoon, too tired or hung over to be much good to anyone.

Spring and summer were sultry, long, hot and humid, officially beginning with the ear-splitting crack of the bat and sound of cheering crowds from the overflowing softball and baseball fields. Of all the seasons, summer was their favorite, and the teens of Pineville littered the lakes around town, lazily enjoying their freedom from the shackles of required education.

Ashley, Kate and Susanna retreated to Indian Creek to bask in the rays of the hot summer sun, lounging on inflatable rafts atop the muddy brown waters, slathering their bikini-clad bodies from head to toe with baby oil in an effort to become as darkly tanned as possible. It was during those Indian Creek summers that Kate and Susanna discovered boys, gladly casting aside Saturday night slumber parties in favor of pizza dinners and drive-in movies with their suddenly attractive childhood schoolmates.

Kate and Susanna were in hog heaven, dating abundantly and frequently, and after significant pressure from both of them, Ashley quickly followed suit, accepting a few invitations from well-meaning classmates, and attending the required social functions. She went through all the motions, but could not have cared less. No one really piqued her interest; she'd known them all too long for anyone to truly hold her fascination. If all had remained the same, Ashley would have been content to spend her remaining year in Pineville without establishing a romantic connection with anyone.

Everything changed the day she met Jimmy Moreau.

CHAPTER TWO

It all started the beginning of their senior year, a period of time fondly referred to by Kate and Ashley as "The Jimmy Era." Although many years had passed, Ashley could still recall vividly everything about Jimmy Moreau. She remembered that Jimmy was exceptionally handsome and charming, with a unique wit about him, and he could make her laugh more easily than anyone she had ever known. She remembered that they were wonderful together, and that she loved him a great deal. She also remembered the first time she saw him.

It was the post-disco era, the period of time just following the frenzy of *Saturday Night Fever*, and an age of Izod polo shirts in pastel hues, long madras shorts, very snug straight-legged blue jeans and canvas Nike tennis shoes. The vehicles of choice were the gas-guzzling Camaro, Firebird and Trans Am, along with gigantic pickup trucks equipped with bright yellow fog lights and huge tires for four-wheeling and mud-hogging. The airwaves were flooded with the sounds of Deborah Harry and Blondie, REO Speedwagon, Air Supply and early Duran Duran while *Urban Cowboy*, *Raiders of the Lost Ark* and an assortment of Chevy Chase/Goldie Hawn movies flashed across the movie screens.

Over the summer, following her annual trip to Florida and between trips to Indian Creek, Ashley worked as a cashier at the drugstore, inspired by the need to buy a car at some point in her life. She worked diligently all summer and finally had enough money to purchase a second-hand burgundy Toyota Corolla, her pride and joy. After purchasing the Corolla, she drove her friends everywhere, including to church each Sunday.

"Remy, I just can't ride with y'all now that I can drive!" Ashley said indignantly, appalled that he would even suggest it.

Ashley was running late that particular Sunday, having just enough time to pick up Susanna, race across the back roads into town, and skid into the parking lot behind The First United Methodist Church of Pineville just as the bells in the church tower chimed eleven. From the parking lot, they broke into a full trot, dashing into the sanctuary, with Ashley hustling to keep up with Susanna as she scampered across the back of the church and joined the eclectic bunch known as the church youth group assembled on the back two pews.

Susanna plopped down on the back row next to Scotty Jeansonne, a big teddy bear of a guy with shaggy brown hair and smoky eyes. An avid hunter, fisherman and all-around athlete, Scotty had been the object of Susanna's undying affection since the days of junior high. He seemed unaware of her feelings, although Ashley couldn't imagine how. Susanna hadn't exactly been discreet about it; but then again, Susanna wasn't discreet about anything.

On the other side of Scotty was Doug Fairchild, the once shy, tow-headed boy who had been Ashley's buddy since kindergarten. Upon reaching puberty, Doug had shocked them all by transforming into a drop-dead gorgeous young man with an outgoing personality and clever wit. His additional status as one of the most talented high school quarterbacks in the state of Louisiana left him with no lack of female adoration, with the possible exception of Ashley. Her feelings for him had not changed with his metamorphosis; she could never see him as anything other than nerdy Doug, her pal.

Seated on the pew in front of Doug was Cheryl Moreau, a sassy little thing with a halo of uncontrollable sooty curls and bright blue eyes, Pineville High School's resident genius. She had skipped kindergarten, becoming a senior at barely sixteen and outshining her older classmates at every academic turn. She could have easily progressed on to college but had been kept in high school by her mother, who was desperate for Cheryl to have some sort of a normal social life.

Ashley had just settled next to Susanna when, in a split second, her world was changed forever. Life as she knew it was never the same from the moment he walked into the sanctuary. He was tall, with a trim athletic build, hair of sandy brown and outstanding eyes the color of Hershey's milk chocolate. His dimpled smile was dazzling, his teeth brilliant white, and he was, without a doubt, the most handsome thing Ashley had ever seen.

"I've died and gone to heaven," she said under her breath, her wide, green eyes staring as he made his way down the side aisle of the church, unable to believe what she was seeing.

After recovering from the shock of beholding such a spectacular specimen of a man, Ashley nudged Susanna sharply with her elbow, interrupting her excessive chattering to Scotty Jeansonne. "Susanna, who is that?"

"Who?" Susanna glanced around curiously, following the direction of Ashley's awestruck gaze, grinning widely as she spotted him. "Oh, yeah, I forgot to tell you about him."

"How could you forget something like that? Have you taken a good look at him? Who is he?"

Susanna regarded her with a great deal of amusement. She had never seen Ashley show such interest in a guy before. They eyed him admiringly, following his every move as he took a seat next to Cheryl on the pew in front of them.

"Absolutely amazing," Ashley thought as she stared at Susanna, shaking her head in astonishment, conveying her silent message with huge, dancing eyes.

Before Ashley could wrestle more information from Susanna, the pipe organ belted out the opening notes of the first hymn, the choir rose to sing, and Maggie turned in her seat, frowning slightly, giving Ashley a look that spoke volumes. Meekly, Ashley shut her mouth and lowered her eyes, reaching discreetly for her church bulletin and scribbling furiously, "Who is he, Susanna?"

Much to her dismay, Ashley watched as Rhonda Williams slid into the pew beside the mystery man, flashing him her most winning smile. "Great," Ashley thought. "There goes that opportunity."

Rhonda Williams was in a league all her own. Ashley had known her since grade school and Rhonda had always been stunning, never having to endure the awkward stage the rest of them had. She was five-foot-eight with long, tan legs, jet-black hair and magnificent sapphire eyes, and possessed the undying devotion of every guy in town. To the male population, she was an angel. To the females, she was a bitch. Any girl with any sense at all despised her. They'd had to put up with her for too many years.

Rhonda wasn't all that intelligent, but had flirted and brown-nosed her way through school, in theory making her much smarter than she was given credit for. She had dated every guy Ashley could think of, was on the cheerleading squad and, given her unstoppable ambition, was practically a shoo-in for homecoming queen that year.

"I see he's already met the piranha," Ashley said in a loud whisper to Susanna, nodding to the bench in front of them.

Susanna smiled wickedly, appreciating Ashley's description of Rhonda, and took the pencil from her hand, scrawling across the church bulletin the answer to Ashley's burning question.

The mystery man was Cheryl's cousin, Jimmy Moreau. He and his family had moved to town two weeks earlier because his father, an electrical engineer, had been transferred to Alexandria, the neighboring city across the Red River. Jimmy was seventeen, would be in their class at Pineville High, and had already started practicing with the football team.

"How did I miss all this?" Ashley asked, frowning in disbelief, unable to imagine how, in a town the size of Pineville, she had lost out on such good gossip for almost fourteen full days.

"That's what happened when you decided to get a job. You've been working while the rest of us have been playing!" Susanna giggled.

After drawing another ominous glance from Maggie, along with one from Susanna's mother, Claire, Ashley quit asking questions and spent the rest of the service trying not to look at Jimmy Moreau, which was easier said than done. He really was exceptional. Her impressed gawking drew multiple glares from Rhonda Williams, who peered around the sanctuary, taking inventory of anyone who might be admiring her beauty. Her eyes rested on Ashley and she looked smugly down her nose, smirking at Ashley's obviously interested gaze, inching herself closer to Jimmy Moreau before turning her head to dismiss Ashley altogether.

"Overconfident wench," Ashley scowled, rolling her eyes, resisting the childish urge to stick her tongue out at the back of Rhonda's head.

After church, Ashley drove Susanna home, turning to interrogate her the minute they got into the car. "Have you met him yet?"

"What is *with* you?" Susanna pulled her sunglasses down, surveying Ashley with mocking hazel eyes. "I've never seen you get your panties in such a wad over a boy before."

"I've never seen one like him before!" Ashley said. "But I don't even stand a chance of having a conversation with him since he's already met Rhonda."

"You look as good as she does," Susanna pushed her shades up with her index finger and leaned back in her seat. "And you are a helluva lot nicer. She's such a pig."

"How do you really feel about her, Susanna?"

"Well, she is a pig, and a conceited pig at that." Susanna propped her feet up on the dashboard, tapping her toes in time to the music blaring from the car radio.

"That may be true, but men still flock to her in droves. I just don't understand it. Beauty isn't everything, you know."

"The answer is easy." Susanna stopped her rhythmic dance as she confidently educated her. "It's sex."

"Sex?" Ashley took her eyes off the road and glanced over at her, blinking in surprise.

"Yeah, you know the act of intercourse between a man and a woman. Sex."

Ashley rolled her eyes in exasperation. "I *know* what sex is, Susanna."

"I don't know how. You never leave the house."

"Don't start that again. Just tell me why you think it's sex that makes them crazy for Rhonda."

"Look, Ashley, pretty girls in this town are a dime a dozen. Pretty girls who put out aren't, which is what separates us from the Rhondas of the world. When a guy has to pick between witty, stimulating conversation or having sex, he'll pick getting laid every time. And in spite of Rhonda's holier-than-thou attitude, the girl's an easy lay."

"You have the mouth of a sailor," Ashley said, scolding Susanna and eyeing her skeptically. "How do you know that for sure?"

"Guys gossip worse than girls do, trust me. And I've heard what they say about Rhonda. She's been around more than a few times, and I don't mean around the block."

Ashley absorbed this information thoughtfully. "I refuse to believe that all guys are that way. If they were, the rest of us would never have a date."

She pulled into the Robicheaux's driveway and Susanna hopped out of the car, slamming the door behind her. She leaned back in the window, tormenting Ashley with a knowing laugh.

"Yes they are, Ashley. Our only saving grace is that we only have one Rhonda to deal with." She flashed one final grin before bounding up the front steps and into the house.

After leaving Susanna, Ashley traveled the short distance home, following a winding lane accented by tall pines, hot pink azaleas and fragrant magnolia trees to the circle drive in front of her house. She stepped inside the front door, inhaling the tantalizing aroma of Maggie's Sunday pot roast as it drifted from the kitchen to greet her. She yelled a quick hello to her folks, then dashed up the hardwood stairs to her bedroom. Her room was large and airy, located in the front corner of the house, and was her own private sanctuary with pale yellow walls and white eyelet décor, lit by sunshine streaming through windows that overlooked the lake across the street.

Still thinking about Jimmy Moreau, she squinted at her reflection in the dresser mirror, studying it critically. There was nothing special about her appearance to enable her to compete on *any* level with Rhonda Williams. Her face was interesting, but her long, straight hair was boring and mocha brown and her almond-shaped eyes ordinary, the same color green as an old Sprite bottle. Her button nose was sprinkled with a light dusting of freckles, the freckles that her father loved and she despised.

She couldn't consider herself leggy. At barely five foot three, Ashley thought she was lucky to have legs at all. She couldn't even boast about having a great figure, being scarecrow thin and having no chest size to speak of.

Sighing with resignation, Ashley stripped off her church clothes, throwing on shorts and a T-shirt, then sat on her quilt-covered bed, propping comfortably against the wrought-iron headboard and reflecting on what Susanna had said.

There had to be some way to capture Jimmy Moreau's attention, in spite of Rhonda Williams. It was so unfair that Rhonda had the sexual advantage. Surely, that couldn't always be the case. There had to be something else. At some point, good girls had to finish first.

The next morning, after stopping at Jack's supermarket for Kate's morning staple of M&Ms and a Yoo Hoo, Kate and Ashley pulled into the rapidly filling parking lot of Pineville High School.

Pineville High was a single-story, red brick structure on a shady residential street, overflowing with teachers and students all ready to meet the challenge of being thrown together for yet another school year. Kate and Ashley strolled through the front doors, cat-calling and saying hello to their long lost classmates, moving down the long corridor flooded by students scurrying like mice toward homeroom.

"Same faces as always," Ashley observed, glancing around with a grin. The only changes, if any, from the previous school year were new haircuts and different clothing.

School was a source of constant strife between Ashley and her father, Remy. It wasn't Ashley's grades that bothered Remy. It was the curriculum for which Ashley opted that got under his skin. She wasn't a Rhodes Scholar, but Ashley was bright. She simply chose not to apply herself. Instead of taking the usual college prep courses, she picked classes such as Environmental Science, a class about hunting and fishing, taught by the football coach. Not that hunting or fishing interested her in any manner, but the class was an easy A and had the cutest guys in it, thus meeting the Ashley Stewart curriculum requirements, but leaving Remy fit to be tied. Ashley didn't know what all the fuss was about. She just couldn't seem to make Remy understand that she didn't want to study. She wanted to socialize.

Ashley's one true love in her high school curriculum was journalism, the one class that she shared with Kate and Susanna. Their teacher was Marianna LeBlanc, an older woman in her mid-fifties with salt-and-pepper hair and dark piercing eyes. Mrs. LeBlanc was feared by most but loved by the journalism class, who thought she was terrific.

With her journalism students, she was lenient, pretty much tolerating anything just as long as they didn't do anything stupid. But most importantly, Mrs. LeBlanc inspired her students to write.

Kate and Susanna took their assignments to heart, penning serious papers and articles on social injustices or policy changes. Ashley preferred comedy, writing about her experience deer hunting with Doug Fairchild and Scotty Jeansonne, cruising the beach in Florida for boys, and teenage fashion woes. She never thought that anything so seemingly frivolous would fly with Mrs. LeBlanc, but surprisingly, she liked Ashley's style, frequently publishing her work in the school paper.

While Kate had aspirations of becoming a world-renowned trial attorney and Susanna dreamed of fame and independent fortune, under the persistent guidance of Marianna LeBlanc, Ashley found her destiny. Ashley wanted to be a writer.

Her third hour class was geometry, a subject Ashley had managed to elude until her final year of high school. Ashley was having an ordinary day when she slid into a desk next to Doug Fairchild, who flashed a comical smile as he greeted her.

"What are you doing in geometry?" he asked, feigning amazement.

Ashley stuck her tongue out at him. "Did you think I was a total brainless wonder?"

"Well, I wasn't quite sure, we did have Environmental Science together, you know."

Doug was a tease and a flirt and Ashley loved him. Searching for a cute comeback to his remark, Ashley's ordinary day ended. She was struck speechless when Jimmy Moreau sauntered in the door and took a desk on the other side of Doug.

"Hey, Jimmy," Doug welcomed him, obviously already well acquainted with him. "How's it going?"

"Fine, so far," Jimmy said with a friendly grin. "Just learning my way around." He glanced Ashley's way, catching her staring at him with open admiration, and Ashley felt her face grow hot, sensing that she was turning nine shades of red.

"Jimmy, this is Ashley Stewart, a good friend of mine," Doug said, introducing them. "Ashley, this is Jimmy Moreau."

"Hi," Ashley said, stammering shyly.

Noting her unusual bashfulness, Doug shot Ashley an odd look, and Jimmy smiled warmly, displaying deep dimples and perfect white teeth.

"Hi, Ashley," he said. "Didn't I see you in church yesterday?"

Oh, my God, he had actually noticed me with Rhonda sitting right beside him. Ashley nodded with wide-eyed enthusiasm, hoping to reply with something clever or witty, but their conversation was cut short by Mr. Dauzat, the geometry teacher, screeching his stick of chalk across the blackboard to get their undivided attention.

Needless to say, from that moment on, Ashley was hopelessly distracted and absorbed not one word from her first day of class, which was not good, since it lead to her total inability to understand anything that went on in geometry.

Ashley managed to squeeze in a shy "nice to meet you" with Jimmy as they strolled down the back hall toward the cafeteria before a livid Rhonda tore him away from her side. She met up with Susanna in the lunch line, then located Kate sitting at their usual table with Doug and Scotty Jeansonne. Scotty was making an observation about Jimmy and Rhonda just as Susanna and Ashley slid into their chairs.

"The way I see it," he lectured, "Rhonda has already been with everyone else in both the junior and senior classes. Mitch has been with her, and Jeff, hell even I've been with her." Scotty laughed lightly, moments away from beating his chest proudly with his fists, like Tarzan over Jane.

"You've never dated Rhonda," Susanna pointed out in a withering tone, the proverbial horns of jealousy springing from her coppery head of hair. Ashley winked at Kate, observing with humor Susanna's hostile reaction to Scotty's confession.

"Susanna, my naïve temptress," Scotty continued, with a note of teasing in his voice, "one does not have to date Rhonda in order to *be* with her. Hell, even Dougie here has probably done her."

"I've never been with Rhonda," Doug spoke up in protest. "I do have some standards, after all."

Scotty gave him a knowing look. "Cut the sanctimonious crap, Fairchild," he chuckled good-naturedly. "The only reason you haven't been with Rhonda is because she has much better taste in men."

Doug shot him a broad grin, starting a heckling session between the two of them that seemed to last forever until, finally, Scotty turned his attention back to the rest of the table. "Anyway," he said, "It's only logical that Rhonda would hook up with the new guy. She needs a new victim to weave her web around."

"Not to mention the obvious fact that he is just gorgeous!" Kate chimed in enthusiastically, sipping her soda and smirking up at Scotty with laughing eyes.

"Oh, please. What's he got that the rest of us don't?" Scotty said, casting an annoyed glance in Kate's direction.

"Plenty, believe me," Ashley declared, getting into the conversation as she glanced across the lunchroom to where Jimmy leaned against the wall talking with an enamored Rhonda. Flooded with envy, she forced herself to look away, returning her full attention to Scotty. He scowled at her while Doug grinned in amusement, lounging casually in his chair as he watched them bicker. Susanna remained unusually subdued, still sulking jealously over Scotty's confession about Rhonda Williams.

"Ashley Stewart showing an interest in a guy? What's the deal, Ice Princess?" Scotty inquired, raising his eyebrow at her suspiciously.

"What's that supposed to mean?" Ashley said, her eyes flashing with indignation.

"The rest of us have been trying for years to get you to spark up like this. I'm just amazed, that's all."

"Well that would certainly explain it," Kate said, grinning smugly at him. "Considering the fact that it has been you guys trying, you should know why she hasn't sparked up."

"Why, Kate, I'm hurt," Scotty said, pretending to pout, but not doing a very good job of hiding his comical grin.

Cheerleading practice was held during gym period, the last hour of the day. Ashley was in the locker room changing into practice clothes when Rhonda approached her. She stood with her feet planted firmly in front of Ashley, regarding her with disdain and wagging a well-manicured finger in her face.

"Hey Ashley, just what were you doing with Jimmy Moreau before lunch? You're wasting your time, Precious. He's dating me, you know."

Ashley stopped tying her white canvas tennis shoes and stared up at Rhonda impatiently, biting back the string of scathing words rising quickly in her throat. Ashley wasn't about to fight with her, remembering what Remy had taught her about people like Rhonda. Remy always said that people who behaved like pigs didn't merit the energy one had to put out to argue with them.

"Oh, for heaven's sake, Rhonda," Cheryl Moreau intervened, overhearing Rhonda's caustic remark. "You don't hold the monopoly on every man at this school, especially Jimmy. My cousin can talk to anyone he wants, including Ashley. Now come on and get changed."

She pulled Rhonda along by the arm while Rhonda glanced over her shoulder at Ashley, giving her one final withering glare.

"Great, the piranha is pissed," Ashley observed shrewdly, something for which she paid dearly a little later during practice.

The PHS cheerleading squad prided itself for its death-defying formations and Ashley perched precariously atop a human pyramid, supported, unfortunately, by Rhonda. As soon as the configuration was complete, Ashley felt Rhonda's hold on her loosen, sending her toppling from the top to land on the hard asphalt below, literally seeing stars flash before her eyes as she lay sprawled flat on her back.

"Ashley, are you all right?" Chris Alexander, their captain, ran over, bending down to offer Ashley a hand up. "What in the hell happened?" she asked, glancing sternly at Rhonda.

Ashley accepted Chris' hand and pulled herself up, wincing as she rubbed her smarting backside. "I'm fine," she told Chris, glaring at Rhonda, who was grinning ear to ear, very pleased with herself.

"Oops, she just slipped," Rhonda drawled, attempting to look sheepish but failing miserably. "I'm so sorry," she smiled menacingly at Ashley, who understood her meaning all right. Determined to keep Ashley away from Jimmy Moreau, Rhonda was out for blood.

Susanna observed the entire incident from afar and sauntered over to Ashley after practice ended. "We can arrange to have her taken out, if you know what I mean," she told Ashley solemnly.

"First you're a sailor, now you're a mobster." Ashley kidded her with a grin.

"You think I'm joking?"

"I'm not concerned about Rhonda, Susanna. What comes around goes around; she'll get her payback some day."

"I only hope I'm there to see it," Susanna said, glaring over her shoulder at Rhonda then laughing loudly as she and Ashley headed across the parking lot toward the Corolla.

Over the next few weeks, Ashley spent her days sneaking discreet glances at Jimmy, enjoying the time spent with him in geometry, then watching as Rhonda monopolized him the rest of the time. Rhonda didn't allow her to get within ten feet of him, warding Ashley off effectively with her caustic stares.

On the up side, it was nice for Ashley to be able to observe Jimmy without him knowing it. In addition to being so breathtakingly handsome, he was also very bright. At least he was a geometry whiz. Ashley was in awe of that feat alone. He had a great sense of humor, constantly making those around him laugh, and, as she got to know him, Ashley began to like the person she saw on the inside and not just his outward appearance.

After the first football game on Friday night, Ashley made her way to McDonalds on Highway 28, one of the usual weekend hangouts. There she met up with Kate and Susanna, passing them as they headed out the door with Mitch Guidry and Scotty Jeansonne. Kate winked at her, but Susanna hardly noticed her presence. Scotty and Susanna appeared completely engrossed in one another, exchanging syrupy smiles and looks of absolute admiration. It appeared that all the years of Susanna's secret devotion to Scotty were beginning to pay off. He seemed to have finally noticed that she was more than just one of the guys.

"We're going riding around," Kate called as they crossed the parking lot toward Mitch's car. Her voice broke the spell between Scotty and Susanna and they glanced back to Ashley standing alone in the doorway.

"Come with us, Ashley," Scotty said considerately. "We've got plenty of room."

"Nah, that's okay. I'm sure there will be enough people here to entertain me," she said, which was an understatement, to say the least. On game nights, there wasn't a booth or table left in the place. Ashley waved as they drove away in Mitch's 1965 red Mustang, then pushed through the crowd, navigating her way inside to get a Coke.

Cheryl Moreau strolled through the front entrance with Kimberly Seaton, one of the sophomore cheerleaders, in tow. Ashley liked Kimberly. She had a very sweet personality and Ashley had never heard her utter an unkind word about anything or anyone, making her a rarity on their squad full of catty, gossiping girls.

"Hey, Ashley, come sit with us," Cheryl called out. Ashley waved cheerfully as she inched her way through the crowded room, joining them in a booth by the window.

"Did I see your appendages leaving with Mitch Guidry and Scotty Jeansonne?" Cheryl asked, joking as Ashley slid in across from her.

"Yeah, despite popular opinion, we're not constantly joined at the hip," Ashley replied with a chuckle, leaning against the back of the booth and propping her feet up discreetly under the table.

"Could've fooled me. I don't remember the last time I saw you without them on a Friday night." Cheryl chewed the straw protruding from her cup, watching with dancing eyes for Ashley's reaction. Kimberly listened quietly, offering no opinion, dragging her French fries through the puddle of ketchup in the center of her paper-covered tray.

Ashley reached out and stole a fry from her, chewing it as she regarded Cheryl thoughtfully. "Speaking of appendages, where's your good friend Rhonda?"

"Panting after my cousin somewhere, I'm sure," Cheryl said, shaking her head in exasperation. "Poor guy can't catch his breath from running from her."

Ashley giggled at Cheryl's remark, looking up in time to see Doug dash in a side door, followed directly by Jimmy. Her heart beat a little faster. So, he wasn't with Rhonda after all.

Kimberly looked as if she might swoon at any moment, her eyes as wide as saucers. "Here comes Doug Fairchild," she whispered adoringly. "What a doll."

Ashley rolled her eyes, chuckling to herself. "If she'd only known him when he was younger," she thought, vividly remembering when Doug had been the shy little geek with his head stuck in a book.

After grabbing Cokes at the counter, Jimmy and Doug pushed through the mob of rowdy high school students and over to their booth. "Slide over, Ash," Doug said, moving into the booth to sit next to Ashley as Jimmy sat across from them with Kimberly and Cheryl.

"What's going on, ladies?" Doug asked teasingly, his big brown eyes flashing with good humor.

"Just hanging," Ashley said, sipping her Coke nervously, very aware of Jimmy's knee lightly touching hers under the table, making her tingle excitedly. However, she held her poker face and managed to maintain control nicely.

"What did you think of the game?" Doug asked her with a playful smile.

"It was great," Ashley said, beaming up at him proudly. He had played a fantastic game that evening. But then again, he always played a fantastic game.

"Ashley, do you actually watch the game or do you just socialize the entire time?" Doug rested his arm casually along the top of the seat behind them and glanced over at her with mischievous eyes.

She returned his look, sniffing haughtily. "Why would you think that I just socialize?" she said in an offended tone, turning sideways in her seat so that she might glare at him more effectively.

He grinned at her insulted stare. "Could it be all the gesturing and shouting into the crowd that you do?"

"That's called cheerleading," she smugly folded her arms across her chest, believing that she had won that round.

"Uh-huh. I particularly enjoy the cheer that starts with 'Kate!'"

"How do you have time to notice all this?" Ashley said, growling defensively. "I thought you were supposed to be playing football."

"Ignore them," Ashley overheard Cheryl telling Jimmy. "They fight this way all the time."

"That's okay. I like a girl who stands up for herself," he replied with just a hint of admiration. Ashley smiled demurely at Jimmy, flattered by what she considered to be a compliment. She noticed Doug cutting his eyes in her direction, but he said nothing.

At eleven-thirty, Kimberly slid her slim legs out of the booth. "I've got to get home," she said, a disappointed glimmer in her eyes.

Ashley glanced down at her watch, noting that it was almost time for her to leave also. She smiled deviously over to Doug. He may have won the first round, but Ashley was ready to pay him back.

"Dougie, why don't you walk Kimberly out to her car?" Her suggestion enticed Kimberly to beam fondly at Doug, while he carefully suppressed the frown meant only for Ashley.

Ashley glanced quickly at Cheryl and Jimmy. They were grinning ear to ear, trying not to laugh, entertained by Kimberly's open admiration for Doug.

"Sure, I'd love to," Doug graciously conceded to Ashley's request and guided Kimberly by the elbow out to her car.

Ashley watched out the window as Doug managed to get away from Kimberly's car without breaking her heart. She gestured for Jimmy and Cheryl to follow her as she pushed the door open to meet Doug outside.

Doug immediately presented the irritated scowl that he had been saving for her. "Was that really necessary?" he asked of his trip to the car with Kimberly.

"Why didn't you kiss her good night?" Ashley asked curiously, linking her arm through his as they walked toward their cars.

Doug blinked incredulously, staring at her with wide eyes. "She's a little girl, Ashley!"

"She's only a couple of years younger than us," she reminded him with a teasing nudge.

"A couple of years can make a big difference."

"I would've kissed her," Jimmy interjected, walking up behind them. "She's cute."

Cheryl elbowed him sharply in the ribs. "You have your hands full enough, Mister," she scolded him. "Just one girl at a time, you hear?"

With always-impeccable timing, Rhonda Williams wheeled her small silver sports car into the parking spot next to Doug's red Camaro and swung out her shapely legs. She walked toward them with feline grace, followed closely by her entourage of Chris Alexander and Scotty's little sister, Monica Jeansonne. She strutted over to Jimmy, linking her arm through his possessively. Ashley turned away, her lip curling in disgust.

Doug observed her expression quizzically. "Come on, I'll walk you to your car," he offered, taking her hand. Ashley told Cheryl goodbye and strolled to her car with Doug.

"You like him a lot, don't you?"

Ashley glanced up at Doug in surprise. She hadn't realized that her growing affection for Jimmy Moreau was that apparent. "I don't really know him that well," she covered, using a little discretion for once in her life. Word traveled fast in their small town and all Ashley needed was for the rumors to start flying about her crush on Jimmy Moreau. She would never live down the humiliation.

"Uh-huh," Doug eyed her knowingly as she dug her keys out of her purse with downcast eyes.

"Thanks for walking me to my car," Ashley teased him, mimicking Kimberly.

Doug grinned. His little buddy had certainly changed since kindergarten, he noted, glancing at her with growing appreciation as she leaned against her car in her red cheerleading uniform, her long brown hair pulled away from her pretty face in a silky ponytail.

"Now, *I'll* kiss *you* goodnight," he joked good-naturedly, leaning down to kiss her playfully on the cheek. She smiled fondly up at him and unlocked the car door.

"Are we still on for tomorrow night?" he asked, leaning back against the car. Doug and Ashley, along with anyone who cared to join them, had a standing "not-a-date" to the drive-in movie, a Saturday evening ritual that started during their sophomore year.

"Of course, I wouldn't miss it for the world," Ashley said cheerfully as she eased into the driver's seat of the Corolla. He grinned back at her before strolling back toward Jimmy and company.

Ashley honked and waved at Jimmy and Cheryl as she drove by them, laughing at Rhonda's surly expression as she surveyed her in the rear view mirror. "Thank God, I'm not that jealous," Ashley thought with a roll of her eyes. She couldn't imagine anyone being as jealous as Rhonda was.

CHAPTER THREE

On Saturdays, Ashley worked at the drugstore, restocking the candy aisle and running the cash register, from nine in the morning until Remy closed the store at two in the afternoon. She arrived every Saturday with good intentions of going straight to work, but never made it very far from the front doors. The mouth-watering smell of homemade buttermilk biscuits and sizzling bacon beckoned her, drifting like a fragrant cloud as she dashed past the fading green leather-covered booths of the old-fashioned fountain and grill. Unable to resist the temptation, Ashley always back-tracked into the restaurant to perch high atop one of the round swivel stools in front of the shiny chrome counter, beaming eagerly while Mister Eddie Thibodeaux, the grill manager, whipped up her favorite concoction, a strawberry milkshake with rainbow-colored sprinkles.

Mister Eddie was one of Ashley's favorite people, an old Cajun man who called her funny nicknames like "Ma Petite Crawfish" and pinched her rosy cheeks as he told her jokes and hilarious stories about "ol' Boudreaux and ol' Fontenot," his favorite fictitious characters. Ashley loved listening to him and would inevitably lose track of time until pulled back to reality by the appearance of Remy's full-time clerk, Frannie.

Frannie was a robust woman of Cajun-French descent, a distinction reflected in both her prominent accent and her raven black hair, worn pulled back from her comely face in a tight knot. Her olive complexion, once flawless, was now etched with laugh lines and mirthful crinkles around her raisin-colored eyes. Frannie had worked for Remy for fifteen years, starting the first day he was open for business, and was extremely protective of him, considering herself to be in charge of his well being, outranked only, of course, by Maggie.

After an unusually busy Saturday, Ashley returned home with Remy, grabbing a quick snack before intercepting Doug's call shortly after three.

"Hey, Ash! How was work?"

"Hi, Doug," she flopped down, settling back against the fluffy down pillows on her bed. "Work was good. What's up?"

"Are we still on for tonight? Or have you gotten a better offer?"

"Yours has been the best so far," Ashley said with a hint of laughter in her voice. "What flick is playing?"

"There's a triple feature tonight, *Halloween*, *Friday the 13th* and *The Texas Chainsaw Massacre*," he said slyly. "I thought if I took you to something scary, you might be forced to sit close to me."

"Doug, I can't think of *anything* scary enough to force me to sit close to you."

"A guy can hope, can't he?" Doug chuckled lightly. "I should be there about seven-thirty."

"I'll be ready," she promised as they hung up, and immediately called Kate to see if she wanted to go with them.

"Oh, that's sounds great, but I have a date," Kate said with a delighted giggle.

"Must not be with Mitch since he's going with us."

"No, Jeff Thomasee tonight," Kate answered happily. "I think we are going to the movie but not the drive-in. I'll pass on the horrorfest."

"Well, you'll be missing a good time."

"I'm sure I will," she agreed. "And I'm certain you'll tell me all about it tomorrow."

After hanging up with Kate, Ashley picked out a denim shirt and jeans to wear that night before venturing downstairs. Maggie was at the stove in their cheerful kitchen, overseeing a huge pot of red beans and link sausage. "Date tonight?" she looked over hopefully as Ashley strolled into the room.

"Just my usual not-a-date," Ashley replied, reaching into the cabinet for the dinner plates. "I'm going to the drive-in with Doug and some other people."

Maggie grinned happily. "Oh, that's so exciting!" she beamed enthusiastically. "Doug is such a handsome guy!"

"Isn't Doug that skinny little kid who used to hang around here and acted like he was scared of his own shadow?" Remy piped in from the den. Ashley noted the laughter in his voice and suppressed a smile. Remy knew how much Maggie liked Doug and he loved to give her a hard time about it.

"Remy, that was ten years ago, for heaven's sake!" Maggie snapped at him in exasperation. Her defensiveness about Doug only served to entertain Ashley more. She grinned and went about her business of setting the table.

"Well, he sure hasn't changed much." Remy continued to terrorize her. Maggie gave up with a frustrated roll of her eyes, and Ashley turned her back to hide her amused giggling.

Doug arrived promptly at seven-thirty. Ashley raced down the stairs when the doorbell rang and flung the door open. "Hi!" she said, breathlessly, flashing him a dazzling smile as Doug eyed the stairs behind her in amusement.

"Did you know I could hear you clamoring down those steps all the way out here?" he teased her and she stuck her tongue out at him.

"Come say hi to Maggie and Remy," she said, beckoning him into the living room.

"Hi, Ms. Maggie, Mister Remy," Doug greeted them affectionately. Maggie smiled broadly up at him and Remy rose from his chair to shake Doug's hand.

"Hi, Doug. Great game last night," Remy congratulated him warmly and Doug smiled, flattered.

"Thanks, sir. The team did a terrific job." Doug was very modest about his talent, constantly crediting his teammates for a good game.

"So, Ashley said you all are off to the drive-in," Maggie said, joining in on the conversation.

"Yes, ma'am. What time should I have her home?"

"Well, one o'clock at the latest. We'll let her stay out a little bit later since she is in such good hands." Maggie said, shamelessly flirting with Doug.

From where she stood behind Doug, Ashley shot Maggie an appalled look, shaking her head in mock disgust. Maggie grinned wickedly, smirking at her daughter and making a face. On her way out the door, Ashley kissed Remy goodnight, then paused to hug her mother.

"He's way too young for you," she whispered kiddingly into Maggie's ear as she embraced her.

"I can still look and dream," Maggie responded, laughing lightly as Ashley grinned at her and followed Doug outside.

Arriving at the sole drive-in movie in Alexandria, Doug backed his father's truck into one of the remaining front row spaces. While Doug, Mitch and Scotty folded out chairs and spread a blanket in the bed of the truck for optimum movie viewing, Susanna and Ashley volunteered to go to the concession stand for popcorn and cokes.

"Where's Kate?" Susanna asked as they walked toward the concession stand, their shoes crunching rhythmically across the gravel beneath them. "No, wait, don't answer that, let me guess." She held her hand up to halt Ashley's speech. "Jeff, right?"

"You got it."

"Ye gods, how fickle can one girl be? Mitch, Jeff, Mitch, Jeff," Susanna alternated lifting her hands as she said each name, symbolically juggling them as Kate did. "I wish she'd make up her mind. Her indecision is killing me."

"I don't know why it bothers you so much," Ashley said sarcastically as they approached the window of the concession stand, pausing briefly to place their order. "I hardly think that Kate's love life is any of your business."

"Now, how can you say that, Ashley?" Susanna snatched the drink tray from the counter, firing Ashley an irritated look. "You know I make everything my business."

Ashley rolled her eyes and sighed, gathering the popcorn and trudging after Susanna in the direction of their parking spot. Back at the truck, they found another pickup parked beside theirs. Jimmy, Rhonda, Cheryl and Kimberly Seaton had joined them.

Susanna shook her head, cackling evilly as she observed Ashley's thrilled expression. "Oh goody, Ashley, a night with Jimmy and Rhonda!" she spouted cynically just as they reached the group.

Ashley threw her an ominous glance, narrowing her eyes in irritation. "Shut up, Susanna," she said, shoving a box of popcorn to Scotty while Mitch stood in the bed of the truck and began bellowing to Jimmy.

"Hey, Moreau, how'd you manage to show up with a truckful of women?" he demanded loudly, eyeing Rhonda, Kimberly and Cheryl with a naughty grin.

"Just got the touch, that's all," Jimmy said with a wink. "Come join us, I'll share them with you."

Mitch vaulted out of the back of Doug's truck and hopped in the back of Jimmy's, planting himself between Cheryl and Kimberly.

"Hello, sweetie," he grinned mischievously at Kimberly, throwing an arm around her shoulder as she blushed profusely.

Ashley climbed into the bed of the truck to sit next to Doug. Scotty and Susanna settled on the blanket in front of them, just in time for the opening credits of *Halloween*. Ashley refused to watch the bloody or violent scenes and spent most of the movie hiding her eyes behind her hands, peeking through her fingers, judging whether it was safe to look or not. Doug found it highly entertaining that she was terrified, and poked her in the ribs mercilessly, making her jump and squeal.

Susanna buried her head in Scotty's shoulder to keep from watching the scary parts, or so she led him to believe. Doug put his finger to his lips to shush Ashley and slipped silently over the side of the truck. Ashley watched him, suppressing the giggles rising into her throat. Doug crawled stealthily beneath the truck and reached up to grab Susanna's foot. She screamed deafeningly and Ashley cracked up, unable to choke back her laughter as Doug stuck his head out from underneath the truck.

"Damn it, Doug!" Susanna yelled at him. "You scared the shit out of me." She glared furiously at him, both for scaring her and embarrassing her in front of Scotty Jeansonne.

Doug smiled broadly, very pleased with himself.

"Fairchild!" Mitch howled from Jimmy's truck. "What in the hell is going on over there?"

By this time Ashley was laughing so hard that she thought she'd wet her pants. Wiping the gleeful tears from her eyes, she stole a glance at the other vehicle. Rhonda and Jimmy appeared unaware of the commotion around them. Rhonda pointedly ignored their entertaining antics and curled up next to Jimmy, letting him shield her from the movie screen. "Please," Ashley thought, rolling her eyes in disgust. "She's just sickening."

During *Friday the 13th*, Cheryl joined them, crawling into the bed of the truck with Doug and Ashley. "I feel like a fifth wheel," she said, nodding toward the two couples in the other truck.

"Stay over here with us." Ashley urged her. "Doug and I are just chaperoning Scotty and Susanna."

"We could be doing more if you'd let me," Doug said naughtily, nudging her gently with his shoulder as he leaned forward to whisper in Cheryl's ear. "Is Mitch behaving himself with that little girl over there?" he asked about Kimberly, looking over Cheryl's shoulder to spy on the occupants of the neighboring pickup truck.

"I think so," Cheryl told him. "I think that they're just becoming good buddies. I heard that Mitch likes someone else." She glanced at Ashley hoping that she would give out some vital information.

"I know nothing," Ashley said innocently.

"Where *is* Miss Kate tonight?" Doug interrogated Ashley with a raised eyebrow. His eyes glowed expectantly, reflecting that he suspected something fishy about Kate's absence from the group.

"She had other plans."

"You know more than you're telling," Doug said, accusing her with just a hint of a smirk.

Ashley shrugged her shoulders nonchalantly. "Maybe I do and maybe I don't," she smiled. "Doug, I swear, you gossip worse than a girl."

"I get the best dirt that way," he said, grinning like a naughty little boy.

"It's not nice to gossip," she chided him playfully as he glanced over at her in amusement.

"I'll remind you that you said that the next time you want some juicy tidbits of info from me."

They settled back on their elbows to watch the rest of the movie and Ashley sneaked another peek at Jimmy. He was talking to Mitch, smiling broadly, his teeth flashing brilliantly in the light from the movie screen. What a beautiful smile, Ashley sighed, a dreamy look in her eyes.

"Stop that," Doug whispered, catching her staring adoringly at Jimmy. She scrunched her neck from the warmth of his breath against her ear and looked over at him, smiling sheepishly.

They left the drive-in before *The Texas Chainsaw Massacre*, trading Mitch back for Cheryl as they pulled out, bumping over the spikes covering the pavement on the exit ramp and heading back over the Red River to Pineville. After delivering Susanna and Scotty to the Robicheaux's, Doug took Ashley home, walking her to the door.

"Thanks for another great Saturday night," she said to him as they climbed the porch steps. "It was fun."

"I had fun too. Maybe we can do this again some time," Doug suggested, looking down at her with twinkling eyes.

Ashley snapped her fingers jokingly, as if he was suggesting a novel idea. "Like, maybe next Saturday night!" she said, laughing as she turned the handle and opened the door to go inside. Doug leaned against the doorframe and she paused, sensing that he had something else to say. She raised her eyebrows inquiringly at him. "What?"

"Never mind," he said, shaking his head slightly. "Good night, Ash. See you Monday." He watched her go inside and then bounded down the steps to the truck.

CHAPTER FOUR

Pineville High had four winning football games in a row before it dawned on Ashley that homecoming was right around the corner and she had no date for the homecoming dance. For the first time she was in a dilemma over a social event. For the first time she really wanted to go to a dance with someone in particular. But Jimmy Moreau was out of the question. He and Rhonda had made plans to go together to homecoming weeks ago. Ashley found herself back in the same familiar situation, racking her brain trying to come up with a suitable date, a task that wasn't easy.

The answer to her predicament came during study hall one afternoon two weeks before the dance. She was beating her head in frustration against her geometry book when Doug slid into the chair next to her. "Hey, Ash," he said, greeting her casually.

Ashley lifted her head from her book and peered up at him. "Hello, Dougie," she responded with a weary smile. Geometry was really eating her lunch and had her absolutely frazzled. She ran her delicate hand quickly through her already tousled hair, as if the gesture would help rid the throbbing headache hampering her studying.

"Want to go to the homecoming dance with me?"

As his out-of-the-blue question rang in her ears, Ashley gawked at Doug in amazement. Although she had heard rumors, she couldn't imagine that Doug didn't have a date to the dance yet. Doug was her friend and her Saturday night guy, but he was also a handsome devil with curly, blonde hair and mischievous brown eyes, highly regarded by her female classmates as a very desirable date. She was certain that there were scores of them who would jump at the chance to go to the homecoming dance with him.

"Doug Fairchild, do you mean to tell me that you don't have a date to that dance yet?" she said, scolding him. "What's the matter with you?"

"Oh hell, Ashley, who would you suggest I take?" he said, growling good-naturedly. "You're the best looking girl I know."

"You could ask Kimberly Seaton or Cheryl Moreau."

"No way. I told you, Kimberly is too young and I'm not interested in taking Cheryl." He threw off her suggestion irritably, leaning back in his wooden chair and propping one boot-shod foot on the table in front of him.

"Doug, I'm not going to the dance with you. That's stupid." Ashley rolled her eyes at him. " I've known you since kindergarten. You're like my brother. It'd be too weird."

"You've gone out with me every Saturday night for the last two years and this is the first time I've ever heard you say that it's weird."

"The movies are different. The dance is a *real* date. A real date with you would be weird."

"Ashley, it would be fun. I know I'd have fun with you, you'd have fun with me, and we look good together, so why not?" Doug thought he made a pretty decent argument. "Besides, he's taking Rhonda," he watched with a slow, appraising glance for her reaction.

"Who's taking Rhonda?" Ashley asked, batting her eyelashes at him innocently.

"C'mon, Ash, I've known you my whole life," he reminded her. "I've seen the way you look at him when you think no one else is looking."

He had her again, and she sat without reply. Doug leaned his head toward hers. "So," he breathed softly against her ear, "what's it gonna be?"

Ashley sat silently contemplating. On one hand, she could go to the dance with the great looking quarterback, be the envy of her female classmates and have a terrific time. On the other hand, she could sit home with Maggie while she pouted over Ashley turning Doug down for a date and missing the dance. Hmm, tough decision.

"Ok, Doug, you win," she conceded. "I'll go to the dance with you."

Doug grinned broadly. "Great. I'll call you." He sauntered off, whistling as he went.

As word traveled of their date to homecoming, Ashley received congratulations from jealous classmates, a pat on the back from Kate and a tongue lashing over not being appropriately excited from Susanna. Needless to say, Maggie was beside herself with glee. On Saturday, a very thrilled Maggie dragged Kate and Ashley to search for "the perfect dress." Ashley tried on what seemed like hundreds of dresses at a dozen different stores before deciding on a slim, sapphire blue gown. She dressed while Maggie danced off to pay for the dress.

"Jeez," Kate observed, "you'd think it was her date."

"Tell me about it. She's been this way for days." Ashley laughed, finding some humor in it. "I should let Doug take her to the dance. She's crazy about him."

After dropping Maggie at home, Kate and Ashley caught a movie then stopped by McDonald's to see who might be hanging out. Doug was there with Mitch and a couple of other guys, eating burgers and telling tall tales about their latest fishing expedition. He spotted Ashley and Kate as they sat down, coming over to join them. He stood at the end of the table, his hands tucked in the front pockets of his snugly fitting blue jeans.

"Hey Ash, I know you probably haven't given it a second thought, but do you have a clue about what color dress you might be wearing for homecoming?" he asked laughingly. "Ma wants to order your corsage. You want pin or wrist?"

Kate and Ashley exchanged amused glances, finding it humorous to have the very masculine Doug discussing flowers with them.

"Relax, Doug," Kate teased him with a giggle. "It's only a dance."

He grinned at her charmingly. "Only a dance, Kate?" he said mockingly. "I'll have you know that I am the first among my peers to entice Ashley Stewart out on a real date. It's much more than just a dance. It's a monumental occasion."

"Oh, I hardly think so," Ashley muttered in annoyance. "You all act as if I've been locked away in a convent or something."

"Susanna would tend to think so anyway," Kate reminded her with a smirk, laughing softly at Ashley's irritated facial expression.

"Pin or wrist?" Doug repeated the original question.

"Wrist," Ashley made the decision quickly, if only to get him off her back.

"Wrist it is, then," Doug grinned and swaggered away to rejoin Mitch. "Oh, Ashley," he remembered, snapping his fingers and coming back to the table, "we're going to double with Jimmy and Rhonda." He didn't wait around for a response, he knew better. In fact, he practically ran from the table.

"Oh, good God!" Ashley said to Kate, her eyes wide in dismay. "Now I get to double date with the man of my dreams *and* the homecoming queen. This couldn't get any worse."

"Never say never," Kate advised with a slight smile. "This is getting better all the time."

The next afternoon, Ashley stretched across her bed, trying desperately to study for the geometry test she had the next day. "I don't get this at all!" she declared in aggravation to the ceiling above her. She pounded her mattress with her fist as her phone rang. She rolled over and grabbed the receiver, praying it would be someone who could rescue her from the defeat she was suffering at the hands of her textbook. "Hello?" she answered in a pleading tone.

"Ashley?" she jumped nine feet in the air at the sound of the voice on the other end of the line. "Hi, it's Jimmy Moreau."

"Jimmy Moreau! Unbelievable," she shook her head in ecstatic bewilderment.

"Hi, Jimmy," Ashley said, trying hard to keep her breathing at a regular rate. No panting in his ear, she told herself sternly. "What's up?"

"I'm studying for the geometry test tomorrow and I had a question," he said sincerely.

"Then why on earth are you calling me?" she asked incredulously. "I don't get any part of this stuff and I never will."

"Are you serious?"

"Yes, I'm serious," she said with a heavy sigh. "I must not have a logical mind, if you can call geometry logical. I might as well write this test off tomorrow."

"Well, why don't we study together?" he suggested. "That way, I can help you understand that geometry is actually very logical and help myself review at the same time."

Ashley was floored, her wildest wish coming true. Time alone with Jimmy Moreau. Life couldn't get any better than this. "Okay," she agreed, as nonchalantly as possible. "Where do you want to study?"

"Why don't you give me directions to your house and I'll come there."

She gave him directions to the house and, after hanging up, jumped off the bed, her arms and legs flying in a thousand different directions as she tried to decide what she should do first. She raced out of her room and down the long hallway toward the stairs.

"Maggie!" she bolted down the stairs, bellowing loudly as she went. The aroma of chocolate led her directly to Maggie, who was in the kitchen baking chocolate chip cookies for Remy, a Sunday afternoon ritual.

"Ashley, will you ever learn not to yell in the house?" she asked, shaking her head disapprovingly. "What on earth are you shouting about?"

"We've got to clean this place up," Ashley said breathlessly, even though she knew the only mess in their tidy house was her own room. "I've got a study date!"

Remy strolled into the kitchen, snatching a hot cookie off the wire rack where several dozen lay cooling. "Isn't 'study date' an oxymoron?" he asked, entertained by his daughter's obvious state of disarray. "If you've got a date, you won't be studying."

"Remy, I don't have time for these games! Jimmy Moreau is coming over to teach me how to do geometry."

"I can teach you how to do geometry," Remy said, still ribbing her as he munched on his cookie, his eyes twinkling at her maddeningly.

Ashley rolled her green eyes at him, striving to maintain what little patience she had left. "That's not quite the same," she said, jutting her chin out impatiently. She looked to Maggie, hoping that she might be more helpful. "Will you help me clear a place to study in the den," she raised her eyebrows at her, "or do you want us just to study up in my room?"

"I think the den might be just a bit more appropriate," Maggie suppressed a grin at Ashley's clever insinuation and led her by the arm to clear a place on Remy's desk for studying.

Maggie poured up iced tea while Ashley raced upstairs to make herself more presentable. She scattered clothing from one end of the room to the other as she changed from T-shirt to sweatshirt and finally to a denim oxford shirt. She pulled her long hair out of the standard weekend ponytail and brushed it furiously until it fell loosely below her shoulders. The doorbell rang and she flew out of her room and down the stairs. "I'll get it!" she yelled.

Too late. Remy beat her to it, smirking up at her before swinging the door open widely for Jimmy.

"Hi," Remy greeted Jimmy in a hearty voice. "You must be Jimmy Moreau. I'm Remy Stewart, Ashley's dad." He extended his hand to vigorously shake Jimmy's.

"Nice to meet you, sir," Jimmy smiled and caught a glimpse of Ashley on the stairs where she had paused to regard him with open admiration. "Hi, Ashley."

She descended to the landing with a much grace as possible. "Hi, Jimmy," she beamed fondly at him, still not believing that he was actually standing in their entry hall. "Incredible," she sighed at the sight of him.

Maggie came out of the kitchen and Ashley introduced them. With a plate of cookies and iced teas in hand, Jimmy and Ashley went into the den to prepare for their geometry test. She forced herself to pay attention to Jimmy's tutoring, although it took a great deal of effort on her part. She would've much rather observed him instead. His thick, shiny headful of sandy hair, his expressive eyes like deep, creamy pools of milk chocolate, his long muscular legs and trim torso, they were all so hard to resist. His voice was deep, yet gentle and melodic, and Ashley lost herself in the sound of it, bewildered at how she could be so swept away by one person, one person whom she barely knew.

After an hour of lecture and illustrations, Jimmy finally managed to make her understand how to do most of the math problems.

"Well, I'm starting to get this," Ashley said, shaking her head in wonder. "I still don't see the logic in it or know where in the real world I'll ever use this stuff."

Jimmy chuckled heartily. "So you don't want to be an architect or engineer?" he teased her. "Headed down the path of a super model, are you?"

"Hardly," she laughed with him. "I'm planning on going into journalism."

"Really? Broadcast or print journalism?" He reclined in his chair awaiting her explanation while Ashley forced her gaze away from his outstretched legs to answer his question.

"I want to write. Being in front of a camera doesn't appeal to me at all." Ashley shifted, curling her tiny feet underneath her in Remy's comfy burgundy leather chair.

"What do you want to write about?" Jimmy was actually interested. Ashley couldn't believe it. She relayed to him the stories and articles that she had written for journalism class and on her own, for fun.

"You went deer hunting?" his eyebrows shot up in surprise. "With Doug and Scotty?"

She pretended to be hurt. "Why sure. What kind of southern girl would I be if I had never gone deer hunting?" she asked, using her best southern belle drawl. "I'll never go again, I can assure you. I had to go once to see what all the fuss was about."

Jimmy grinned, pleased with her explanation. "Your sense of humor is great. It's awfully nice to find a girl concerned with something other than being a beauty queen." He implicated Rhonda without having to mention her name and Ashley found this to be encouraging.

"Is that a compliment?" she flirted with him, enjoying his company immensely. This afternoon of studying was turning out to be much better than she had ever anticipated.

"Of course," he smiled playfully, leaning across the desk to help himself to another chocolate chip cookie. "Did you bake these?" he asked, pointing to his cookie.

"Good God, no! Cooking is not on my wide list of talents."

"Well, at least your mother will keep me from starving," he paused, reflecting as Ashley did a double-take over his statement. "What's your relationship with Doug Fairchild?"

Ashley cocked her head to the side and batted her eyelashes at him. "What's your relationship with Rhonda Williams?" she asked him, tongue-in-cheek. After all, turnabout was fair play.

Jimmy smiled broadly, delighted with her spirited response to his question. "You first," he challenged, leaning forward ever so slightly in his chair and gazing intently into her eyes.

She shrugged her shoulders. "Doug is my friend, and has been since grade school."

"You're only friends?" His brown eyes lit up from this unexpected discovery. "I thought the two of you were much closer than that."

"We're only friends," she reassured him patiently, her heart leaping wildly in her chest.

"Okay, so why are you going to homecoming with him?"

"Because he asked me, I like him, and we'll have fun. Now, answer my question about Rhonda."

"Well, I can't honestly say when I started *dating* Rhonda," he looked down at his hands. Ashley's face fell, until he looked back up at her with a boyish grin. "I was under the impression that she and I were only friends also."

"Oh," Ashley exhaled softly. So Jimmy wasn't dating Rhonda after all. Where was this conversation leading? Whatever the reason was behind this discussion, she didn't really care. She was enjoying every moment of it.

"So," he continued. "I'm in a little bit of a mess. I'm 'dating' one girl while I really like another one."

"How does one get out of such a mess?" Ashley asked him, hypothetically, thinking it in her best interest not to comment directly on the situation presented to her. She used an old "Kate tactic" of testing the waters before jumping in headfirst.

He scrutinized her, seeking to analyze her thoughts. Ashley prayed for a good poker face, hoping that she would give nothing away, but knowing that her eyes said it all. Every emotion she felt, every thought running through her head could always be detected in her expressive green eyes. Jimmy sensed that she returned his affections and smiled with relief that he had not made a fool out of himself.

"I guess we'll just have to make it through homecoming then play it by ear," he said with resignation. "It may be a very long two weeks."

"Tell me about it," Ashley agreed, thinking of having to watch Rhonda with Jimmy, day in and day out, for fourteen more days.

"My date is on the homecoming court, you know," he kidded her as he rose from his chair to leave.

"Yes, I know. She reminds us daily."

"I better go," Jimmy gathered his books and looked down at Ashley, still seated in her father's chair. She waited with anticipation, hoping that he might kiss her goodbye. She wasn't disappointed. He leaned down, giving her a soft kiss on the lips. "I'll see you tomorrow," he said with a smile.

Ashley rose blissfully from the chair and floated beside him to the front door. "Bye," she breathed softly, unable to say more for fear she would begin stammering like a blithering idiot. She watched him get into his green and gold Chevy pickup, returning his smile as he waved and drove away. Ashley retreated into the house, closing the door and leaning against the back of it. What in the world just happened here?

Squealing, she ran, taking the steps two at a time, to call Kate and Susanna. The phone was already ringing when she dashed into her bedroom. She threw her body across the bed and answered.

"I was driving down the road and I thought I saw Jimmy Moreau's truck in front of your house," Doug's voice rang mockingly on the other end of the line. "Must have been a figment of my imagination since he is supposed to be dating Rhonda Williams."

"Doug, are you spying on me? If you must know, we were studying for the geometry test tomorrow."

"Yeah, right!" Doug laughed at her indignant denial of the real situation. "This should make for a very interesting homecoming evening."

"I don't know what you are speaking of," she continued to dance around the truth.

"I'll protect you from the piranha," Doug offered gallantly.

"Get over yourself, Douglas," she said, scoffing good-naturedly. "There's nothing to protect me from."

"There might be if she gets wind of you two seeing each other behind her back. You know how protective Rhonda is of her playthings."

"Jimmy is not her plaything, Besides, we were only studying."

"You were studying each other," Doug taunted her, all the while maintaining the entertained hint of laughter in his voice.

"You don't know that, you weren't there," Ashley argued childishly. "Do you have anything really important to say? If not, I'm hanging up now."

"Nope, I've said my piece," Doug chuckled smugly. "I'll see ya in class."

The next day was full of challenges for Ashley. Despite sneaking numerous little peeks at Jimmy, she did manage to make it through the geometry test without losing total concentration. She was pretty confident that she had passed the test, thanks to Jimmy. After class, Jimmy and Ashley exchanged a glance and a secret smile at one another. Or so they thought.

"You two will never pull this conspiracy off," Doug whispered in her ear as they made their way down the back hallway toward the cafeteria.

"Conspiracy is a bit harsh, isn't it?" she objected, turning to look at him.

Doug shook his head. "Not in this case, sweetheart," he said with a wide grin. "This is the coup of a lifetime."

He glanced over to the table where Jimmy sat, watching as Rhonda descended upon him like a black widow spider weaving a web around her prey. Ashley scowled as Doug took her by the arm, guiding her toward the lunch line. "You had better eat lunch with me," he said. "It'll keep you out of trouble."

So they continued on toward Homecoming, with Jimmy and Ashley discreetly exchanging whispers and fond glances by day and getting acquainted over the telephone by night.

Finally, homecoming arrived.

CHAPTER FIVE

One of the most memorable highlights of their senior year was homecoming night and Rhonda Williams' fall from grace. After a fun-filled week of float building, bonfires, pep rallies, and a daylong celebration with the assembly and parade, everyone gathered for the big football game and the coronation of the homecoming queen at halftime.

They were all certain that Rhonda would be crowned queen. It was her destiny, her greatest ambition in her small, shallow existence. Susanna and Ashley stood on the sidelines, frowning and muttering to one another as the homecoming court took the field.

"Did you see that car Rhonda rode in today?" Susanna said, glancing over at Ashley.

"The gold Corvette convertible?" Ashley nodded that she had indeed seen Rhonda's car in the homecoming parade earlier that afternoon but it hadn't been Rhonda she had been viewing. As she rode through the main streets of Pineville in the back of a festively decorated pickup with the other cheerleaders, Ashley had craned her neck to stare worshipfully at the sandy brown head in the passenger's seat of the sparkly gold Corvette three cars ahead of them.

"Yeah, a classy little sports car like that was wasted on her," Susanna said with a devilish laugh. "I think Rhonda would've been much more accurately represented riding in a car with a *huge* back seat."

Kimberly Seaton stood nearby, overhearing Susanna's scathing remark. Her mouth dropped open in shock, her sweet young face flushing with embarrassment. "That wasn't very nice," she said, breathing to Susanna in a chiding voice.

Susanna raised an eyebrow and cracked up with laughter at Kimberly's naïve response to her commentary on Rhonda. Ashley, pursing her lips in annoyance with Susanna, glanced sympathetically at Kimberly.

"Nothing that comes out of Susanna's mouth ever is," Ashley told her. "So don't waste your breath scolding her over it. She'll never change."

She turned her gaze from Kimberly to the members of the court being guided to the center of the field by their football player escorts. She smiled at Kate, lovely as always, gracefully strolling to her place on the grass beside Mitch, followed closely by saucy little Cheryl bouncing gleefully to stand alongside Doug. With jealousy overpowering her senses, Ashley narrowed her eyes at the sight of Rhonda, dressed to kill in teal blue, hanging possessively onto Jimmy's arm.

"Rhonda's been so belligerent all week, I don't care who wins just as long as it's not her," Ashley said, rolling her eyes exaggeratedly for Susanna's benefit.

"Oh, hell, it'll be her." Susanna's lip curled in disgust before another idea brought a bright smile to her face. "At least there's a plus side to all this," her eyes sparkled evilly with anticipation. "I can use that glittering tiara to wring her skinny neck."

Caught off guard, Ashley sputtered and coughed as laughter choked her, and Susanna slapped her back with several firm blows to ease her gasping breaths. Wiping her teary eyes, Ashley grinned her approval of Susanna's tiara suggestion and focused her attention on the presentation getting under way in the center of the field.

Susanna and Ashley listened with dread as the names of the runners up were announced. First was Cheryl, second runner-up with Kate coming in as maid of honor, the equivalent of first runner up. Finally came queen and as the name spilled out over the loudspeaker, Susanna and Ashley exchanged looks glazed with shock, gaping at one another in stunned silence. Rhonda Williams' name was not the one echoing throughout the hushed stadium.

In the coup of a lifetime, the football team had crushed Rhonda's incorrigible vanity by choosing instead Stacy Crawford, their vivacious blond trainer who had served them so well. As they viewed Rhonda's disbelieving yet humiliated expression, the shock wore off and Susanna and Ashley embraced each other, cackling wildly while jumping up and down with devilish glee. Rhonda had finally gotten exactly what she deserved and they had been there to see it.

After the game, Ashley rushed home to get ready for the dance, with approximately thirty minutes to throw herself together before Doug, Jimmy and Rhonda came to pick her up. She drove her little burgundy Corolla through town at break-neck speed, smiling expansively every time she thought of Rhonda's stunned expression when Stacy had been crowned queen. Thank God, at least there would be no sparkling tiara upon Rhonda's head for her to compete with that night. Rhonda's presence alone was enough.

She burst in the front door, dashing hastily up the stairs to her room with Maggie at her heels, as eager as Ashley to begin the preparation and primping. Ashley shed her cheerleading uniform, tossing it carelessly across the foot of her bed and slipped on the sapphire blue dress and strappy high-heeled black sandals then lifted her hair out of the way as Maggie fastened the clasp of her grandmother's pearls around her neck. With great skill, Maggie arranged the thick weight of her daughter's long hair into a French twist then loosely curled the tendrils of hair surrounding Ashley's face.

"You look just beautiful!" Maggie exclaimed at the finished product, embracing her affectionately as she kissed her rosy cheek.

As the doorbell rang, Ashley walked carefully down the stairs, unable to race Remy for the door in her high heels. "Hello Doug, hello Jimmy!" she heard Remy's voice boom up the steps. "And this must be Rhonda. I've heard so much about you, I feel like I already know you."

"Way to go, Remy," Ashley scolded him silently, "be sure and pump up her deflated ego before I have the chance to enjoy her humiliation."

"I'm sure you have," Rhonda purred like a cat, reaching out to shake Remy's outstretched hand. Ashley noted from her vantage point on the stairs that Rhonda had changed clothes, wearing a scarlet red dress that set off her dark hair and flawless skin to perfection. The boys, dressed in their tuxedoes, came into view as Ashley reached the landing. Doug wore dove gray and Jimmy, overwhelmingly handsome in anything he wore, was attired in dark blue.

"Hi everyone!" Ashley said cheerfully, calling their attention to where she stood on the stairs and smiling as the mouths of both boys dropped open involuntarily.

"Wow!" Doug voiced his opinion. "You never played in the sandbox in anything like that, Ash. You look great, almost like a real girl." Ashley resisted the urge to scowl at him, really wanting to stick out her tongue childishly.

Jimmy said nothing, simply smiled up at her, his eyes sparkling with admiration. Rhonda glared, her eyes shooting daggers at Ashley's lovely figure. She was not having a good night and Doug and Jimmy's open appreciation of Ashley's appearance did not make her any happier.

"Thanks, Doug. You all look pretty sharp yourselves!" Ashley held out her arm, allowing Doug to slide the much-discussed corsage of velvety red roses onto her slender wrist.

Maggie bounded down the steps, snapping photos, the bright light of the flash blinding them. They endured posing for almost an entire roll of film until Ashley began to protest. "Maggie, if you don't quit taking pictures, we're going to miss the dance."

"Okay, okay, you kids have fun!" Maggie put the camera down. She winked at Doug and Jimmy and loyally ignored Rhonda. "She doesn't look too bad for a girl with a crushed ego," she whispered over Ashley's shoulder. Ashley suppressed her amused grin, casting an entertained sidelong glance at her mother as Maggie made her way to stand beside Remy.

"What time is the dance over?" Remy inquired, ready for the battle over Ashley's curfew.

"One o'clock." Her eyes pleaded pathetically with him to let her stay out just a little bit later than usual.

"Okay, have her home before one forty-five at the latest, okay, Doug?" Ashley smiled gratefully at Remy for making a small concession and kissed his cheek fondly.

"Yes, sir, I will," Doug promised. "Good night, Ms. Maggie."

Maggie beamed adoringly at Doug and Ashley winked at her as they left. "He's way too young," she said quietly as she floated by her, and could hear Maggie's amused giggle as Remy closed the door behind them.

Rhonda was oddly silent as they rode in Doug's car to the convention center. She may have looked terrific but she was significantly subdued, the wind having been completely let out of her sails. For four long years, Rhonda had let them all know in no uncertain terms that no one stood a chance of getting homecoming queen over her. She had been betrayed as the boys, most of whom she had been very involved with at one time or another, taught her a hard lesson about her arrogance and self-admiration.

They arrived at the convention center for the dance as a good-sized crowd gathered in front of the door to go inside. Ashley beheld what a perfect gentleman Jimmy was with Rhonda. He was attentive to her, though not overly so, gently soothing her wounded pride. What a good guy he is, Ashley thought as she watched them pause to talk with a group congregated by the front door. Doug took Ashley by the arm and they separated from Jimmy and Rhonda to go inside.

The normally dull convention center was transformed into a sparkling ballroom. Twinkling white lights lit the ceiling like tiny stars bright against a dark sky. Clusters of brilliantly colored balloons bobbed festively above each linen-covered table and crepe paper streamers, intertwined with tiny lights and ivy, were looped along the walls.

Ashley noted with pride what a fabulous job her decorating committee had done in spite of themselves, wishing that Kate could be there to enjoy the fruits of their labor. It just wasn't fair that Kate's religious beliefs didn't allow her to attend any of their school dances, a point that bothered Ashley much more than it bothered Kate. Ashley missed her, wanting Kate to be there, firsthand, to rejoice with them over Rhonda's worst nightmare. Telling her about it the next day just wouldn't be the same.

Doug watched her thoughtfully, guiding her by the elbow over to the line forming to have dance pictures made in front of a backdrop splashed with their school colors of red and gray. "You really do look great, Ash," he said, bending to give her a soft kiss on the lips. Ashley blinked at him in surprise, unused to Doug being so mushy with her.

"What was that for?" she asked him with wide astonished eyes.

Doug grinned widely. "A guy's got to take it when he can get it," he cut his eyes naughtily at her. "I've got to have something to fill my dreams with."

"Would you stop that!" Ashley slapped his arm lightly in kidding. "It wasn't even that great of a kiss."

"I'll make it up to you, I promise," Doug's eyes flashed with good humor as he squeezed her arm and excused himself, strolling over to compare game notes with Mitch Guidry. Ashley watched after him, smiling broadly at his off-the-cuff remark.

Susanna and Scott arrived, getting in line right behind Ashley. Scotty's large bulky frame was outfitted in a white tuxedo, reminding Ashley of a gigantic, shaggy ice cream man. Susanna looked very pretty in a white halter-top dress and matching sandals. She had subdued her riotous red curls by pulling them tightly atop her head and wore a sparkling bangle bracelet and dangling gold earrings. She could have very easily passed for a lady.

"Hey, guys!" Susanna said, greeting Ashley and Doug as he returned from male bonding with Mitch. She embraced Ashley as if she hadn't seen her in years, meaning only one thing. She wanted details about the evening.

"How are things going with Jimmy and the bitchy one?" Susanna asked in a low voice.

"So far, so good."

"You mean you and Rhonda haven't come to blows yet? I'm surprised. She's probably just a tad testy after losing the crown."

"I haven't noticed that she's any testier than usual," Ashley said with a wicked grin. "In fact she's been pretty subdued, especially for Rhonda."

Susanna nodded with a grin of her own, glancing around the room to see who else had arrived. "You know, red is such a good color for Rhonda," Susanna declared in a loud voice, spotting Rhonda chatting outside through the glass doors at the front entrance. "What is that shade called, harlot red?"

Ashley couldn't help but laugh, even as she ducked her head in embarrassment. She could always depend on Susanna to be perfectly blunt and she wondered how many people had just been graced with her opinion.

"I think she looks great," Scotty said, defending Rhonda. Susanna rewarded him with a withering stare.

"Who asked you?" Susanna said frigidly. "We didn't invite you into this conversation."

Ashley suppressed a grin. Susanna had lost all the early relationship shyness she had feigned with Scotty, speaking her mind with him also. He had to be admired simply for putting up with her. Susanna Robicheaux was the very definition of high maintenance.

After posing for their dance photo, Ashley and Doug proceeded into the ballroom to dance and socialize. After claiming a spot at one of the tables, Doug pulled Ashley out onto the dance floor, pulling her close to him as the band played the opening strains of an Air Supply favorite. They slowly circled the floor, Doug singing softly into Ashley's ear while she giggled at him.

"Having fun?" he asked, grinning down at her.

She met his gaze with eyes shining in pleasure. She was indeed having a good time. Nerdy little Dougie had certainly come a long way, she decided as she stared up into his exquisite eyes. She could certainly see why all the girls went ga-ga over him. He was truly breathtaking, especially in his tuxedo.

"Of course," she said with a brilliant smile. "Didn't you tell me I would?"

Out of the corner of her eye, she spied Jimmy and Rhonda entering the ballroom and she watched them from her secure location behind Doug's broad shoulder. Rhonda was draped possessively on Jimmy's arm and she was holding on for dear life, Jimmy Moreau being her only saving grace out of the whole humiliating homecoming extravaganza. Ashley rolled her eyes, determined to ignore the way Rhonda was enveloped around him like a second skin, and focused her gaze on Jimmy.

She gazed at him with an infatuated expression as he paused beside Mitch Guidry and began telling Mitch some animated tale, judging by his hand motions and his expansive smile. Ashley's eyes grew dreamier still as she examined him from head to toe. His lean muscular torso rippled underneath his tuxedo jacket with each movement of his arms, and his long, athletic legs seemed to stretch on forever. She sighed adoringly.

"You know, Ash," Doug spoke up. "I'd rather hoped that my beautiful date would be sighing over me instead of the guy she's been drooling over on my shoulder."

"I'm sorry, Dougie," she apologized, feeling guilty for ignoring him. "I can't help it, there's just something about him. I can't seem to take my eyes off him," she glanced up at Doug contritely before returning her gaze to the spot where Jimmy had been standing only moments before. Much to her dismay, he had disappeared from her viewing area, as had Rhonda. Darn it, she scowled silently.

"May I cut in?" Jimmy suddenly appeared beside them and, despite being in Doug's warm embrace, Ashley felt herself grow weak at the sight of him. It was Doug's turn to scowl.

"Don't you have your own date, Moreau?" Doug questioned tensely, clearly annoyed with Jimmy for cutting in.

"I do, but she's sulking in the bathroom with Cheryl and ten other girls, being consoled over being robbed of the crown. She could be there all night," Jimmy smiled broadly, displaying the dimple in his cheek, and Ashley's heart melted. "I thought I'd kill a little time and borrow Ashley for a dance."

"Why don't you kill a little time elsewhere?" Doug suggested, still wearing a cross frown.

"I would, but I can't think of any other place I'd rather be," Jimmy directed his smile to Ashley, then glanced down at Doug's arm around her waist. "Hey, do you have to hold Ashley so close?"

"Hey, bubba, she's my date tonight," Doug reminded him, marking his territory obstinately. "You made your choice."

"You can let me have one dance," Jimmy shot back at him, beginning to lose his patience with Doug's stubbornness. "It won't kill you."

"Will the two of you please quit talking about me like I'm not here?" Ashley said, growing tired of their duel-at-sunrise attitude. "Don't I have a say so in any of this?"

"No," they returned in unison as Doug handed her over to Jimmy.

"Remember, just one dance, that's it," Doug glared at him. "This may be the only official date I ever have with the girl." He strode away in the direction of the table encircled by Susanna, Scotty, Mitch and the rest of their gang.

Jimmy chuckled as Doug crossed the floor away from them. "I think he's annoyed," he commented, looking down at Ashley with laughing eyes.

"And why wouldn't he be? It's quite a sacrifice to give up time with such a witty and charming date."

"I'll say," Jimmy pulled her into his arms as they heard the opening notes of the next song. Despite all their phone conversations and secret glances, this was the first time their bodies had been this close. The electric charge his touch sent through her was jarring, like sticking her finger in a light socket. They danced slowly, gazing deeply into each other's eyes, enjoying their first official moment of togetherness, a moment that Ashley would remember forever.

"We've got to stop staring at each other like goons," she broke the silence with a giggle as she realized how lovesick they must have appeared. "People are going to start talking."

"They're already talking, I'm sure," Jimmy said, flashing a goofy little grin, his signature goofy grin that Ashley would soon regard as very endearing. He glanced back toward their table. "Just take a look at Susanna."

Ashley followed the direction of his gaze, bursting into laughter at the sight of Susanna. She was gaping intently at Jimmy and Ashley, gabbing nine hundred miles an hour to Scotty and Doug, the gusts of air from her wide hand gestures causing the balloons on the table to sway back and forth recklessly. Ashley looked back to Jimmy with a giggle.

"At least it keeps her entertained and out of trouble," she told him. "I've no doubt that she is expressing her opinion on our romantic status."

They circled the floor again, with Ashley sneaking a sneering wrinkle of her nose over Jimmy's shoulder to Susanna. Susanna stuck her tongue out in return, her mouth curving into a saucy grin.

"Well, my date is back," Jimmy's smile faded ever so slightly as he saw Rhonda saunter back from the ladies' room, surrounded by her loyal supporters.

"Has she spotted us yet?" Ashley relied on his view of the crowd around the table, as she certainly wasn't going to risk making eye contact with a furious Rhonda. "Should we go over?"

Jimmy shook his head adamantly. "Not until the song is over. Rhonda looks annoyed but that could be because Doug is attempting to entertain her with his boundless wit."

"Be nice to Doug! Not many guys would put up with what he has from the two of us. After all, I am his date."

"I could see that by that tight grip he had on you earlier," Jimmy teased lightly. "You're right, though. Doug's a pretty good guy."

The song ended and they reluctantly made their way over to the table. Rhonda picked up on their reappearance immediately, instantly casting a scolding eye upon Ashley.

"Ashley, you should be ashamed, leaving your date like that and snatching up mine," she said, drawling scornfully while flashing her nauseating, sugary smile.

"I know, Rhonda, but I couldn't help myself," Ashley rewarded her with a gooey sweet grin of her own. "Your date is so cute."

Ashley wasn't going to let Rhonda get the best of her, not tonight. She patted Jimmy fondly on the arm. "Thanks for the dance, Pumpkin," she said, batting her eyelashes flirtatiously at him, then strolled around the table to join Doug. Rhonda's eyes pierced her back like steel daggers.

"Ooh, look, here comes the homecoming queen!" Susanna called out loudly to irritate Rhonda further, as Stacy Crawford entered the ballroom, sparkling tiara upon her fair head, and was immediately encircled by the crowd expressing their sincere congratulations. Ashley stole a smug glance at Rhonda, whose surly frown reflected her feelings about Stacy's arrival. Ashley exchanged a jolly look with Susanna, each of them still basking in the glow of Rhonda's degradation.

"Let's get something to drink," Doug suggested as Ashley walked up beside him. Taking her by the arm, he navigated them through the crowd and away from Rhonda and Jimmy.

"Can we have something really strong?" Ashley asked. "Rhonda may ambush me at any moment."

"I told you I would protect you from the piranha tonight," Doug reminded her with a distracted smile. "Tomorrow, you're on your own."

"You're so generous," she said, teasing him, knowing that the first few days after homecoming were going to be rough for her. Rhonda would be livid over losing both the race for queen and Jimmy on the same night, and Ashley would catch the brunt of her anger. She'd probably be dropped on her backside quite a bit over the next several weeks if Rhonda had anything to do with it.

Later, as the crowd started thinning out, Doug glanced down at his watch, then to Ashley. "Should we gather the carpool and go home? I'd rather keep Mr. Remy on my good side, if you don't mind."

"Sure, if you're ready to go," she agreed, although she wasn't in any hurry. She was having a terrific time. Susanna was in rare form, keeping them all in stitches with her opinionated critique of homecoming while distracting Ashley from the couple carpooling with Doug and her.

They pushed through what was left of the crowd and found Jimmy and Rhonda dancing close to the bandstand. Doug strode up to them nonchalantly.

"Whenever y'all are ready," he began, but Jimmy didn't give him an opportunity to finish his sentence.

"We're ready!" Jimmy said, dragging Rhonda from the floor. She looked indignant. Ashley was amused.

Ashley was the first to be taken home and she said goodnight to Jimmy and the sullen Rhonda before Doug walked her up to the front door. "You were right. I had fun, I really did!" she told him with a happy smile.

Doug reached out and held her hands warmly in his as he returned her sentiments. "I did too, I just wish we had taken the time to do this before you met Jimmy."

"Oh, Doug, you yourself have said that I'm like a sister to you," she reminded him casually. "How could you possibly have a romantic relationship with a relative?"

"Okay, fine, little sister," he smiled broadly, "but I have one small incestuous request."

"And what would that be?" She tilted her head up to gaze directly into his eyes.

"I'd like a real good night kiss, Ash, and not one of your usual little, measly pecks on the cheek."

His request was unusually solemn and Ashley stammered with sudden shyness. "I suppose I can accommodate that small request," she said, trying to maintain a flippant attitude with him. Doug quickly leaned down to kiss her before she could change her mind. Ashley wrapped her arms carelessly around his neck and gave him a long kiss goodnight. When he released her, she was a little breathless.

"That was not very brotherly," she said with an inviting smile. "If you had done that before now, things might be different."

Doug smiled warmly. "Now you tell me," he said, squeezing her hand tightly. "See ya, Ashley."

"See ya, Doug." She winked at him and slipped inside the house. She climbed the steps to her room, stomping lightly outside her parents' room so that they could hear that she was home safe and sound.

She changed into a pair of cozy pajamas, reviewing the evening's events. How wonderful it felt to finally have Jimmy hold her. She could still feel the warmth of his hands on her bare back as they danced and the weakness in her knees from his touch. She slid between the cool sheets on her bed and turned out the lamp. It had been a very fun evening. She snuggled her head deeply into her fluffy pillow, a content smile on her blissfully happy face, and drifted off to sleep.

Some time later, she was awakened by light clicks against her bedroom window. She threw back the covers and quietly rolled out of bed to open the lace curtains covering the window. She looked down to see Jimmy standing outside, gently tossing pebbles at the window. Her face lit up with a broad smile. He was still in his tuxedo, sans bow tie, meaning, hopefully, that he was impatient to see her again.

She glanced at the closed bedroom door, quickly assessing the sleep status of her parents. Remy's snoring could be heard from down the hall and if he, the night owl, was asleep, so was Maggie. After determining that neither parent was awake, she quietly slid open the window and leaned out over the windowsill.

"What are you doing here?" she said, calling down to Jimmy in a hushed tone, her once sleepy eyes dancing vivaciously.

"Hey, homecoming's over," he said. "Why don't you come down here?" Grinning mischievously, he beckoned her with a wave of his arm.

Ashley held one finger up to him and backed away from the window, tripping over the clutter on the floor as she looked around the room to find her Keds. After successfully locating them under the bed and hastily slipping them on, she scampered back to the window and swung effortlessly out onto the rose trellis outside. She climbed down quickly yet as quietly as possible. As she neared the bottom, Jimmy placed his hands at her waist and helped her down.

"Nice pajamas," he commented on her red plaid flannel pajamas with a sly smile.

"Thanks, I wasn't expecting company at two in the morning," she said in a saucy voice, turning to face him. She was mere inches away from the warmth of his firm chest, but managed to resist the urge to reach out and softly finger the fine white shirt beneath his jacket.

"I'm glad to hear that, especially after that good night kiss Fairchild gave you," Jimmy teased, leading her by the hand to sit next to him underneath the tall magnolia tree adjacent her bedroom window.

"Oh, you saw that, did you?" she winked playfully at him, unable to resist kidding him just a little. It served him right after all the weeks she had endured watching Rhonda and him together.

"Couldn't miss it." Jimmy returned her teasing good-naturedly. "And I think you might've enjoyed it just a little."

"Maybe I did, and maybe I didn't," she giggled, leaning back on her palms to stare up into the clear night sky. It was a great night, crisp and cool, with a full moon reflecting silvery slivers of light through the thick tree branches above them. Ashley inadvertently snuggled a bit closer to Jimmy, looking back at him expectantly.

"So, Mr. Moreau, why *are* you out here in the middle of the night?"

"I just wanted to see you," Jimmy confessed with an easy smile. "I would've been here sooner but I had a devil of a time getting away from Rhonda."

"However did you manage to escape?"

"It wasn't easy, believe me. I'd probably still be there now, if it hadn't been for Doug," his eyes were merry with amusement. "He finally irritated her so badly that she practically begged us to leave."

"That's my Dougie. He lives to antagonize."

"And he's so good at it," Jimmy agreed with an appreciative chuckle. He gazed over at her, prompting her to lean forward inquiringly.

"So," she raised her eyes to him flirtatiously, "what are your plans now that you're here?"

"My mission is actually pretty simple. I came to ask you a question."

"Okay," the quizzical sparkle in her eyes bade him to continue.

"Would you like to catch a movie later tonight?"

His sincere request made her laugh out loud. "You came to my house at two in the morning and risked an encounter with Remy just to ask me to a movie?" she asked, incredulously. "That couldn't have waited until a wee bit later in the morning?"

"I wanted to make sure no one beat me to the punch, even though I understand that you have standing Saturday night plans."

"I think my standard not-a-date will understand," she said, thinking of Doug with a smile. "Okay, before I accept your invitation, answer me this. We're not going back to the drive-in, are we? I've seen enough horror to last me a lifetime."

He laughed. "No, we're going to a regular old movie theater. Mitch is taking Kate to a movie and to get a pizza afterward and asked if we wanted to go along."

"Well, if that's the case, I guess I'll take you up on your offer," she conceded casually, although her heart was leaping erratically from the very nearness of him.

Jimmy facetiously mopped his brow with relief. "You didn't make me beg quite as hard as I thought you would."

"Normally I'd make you beg on your hands and knees, but I thought I'd give you a break after having to spend the entire evening with Rhonda."

"That's awfully big of you."

"Hey, I'm just that kind of girl." She encircled her bent legs with her arms, resting her flushed cheek against her knees, gazing up at him with bright eyes. "Any other requests while I'm in such a giving mood?"

"Just one," he revealed, fixing his eyes on her full ripe lips. "A kiss to seal the deal?"

"I can go for that." She leaned forward, meeting him halfway as his lips sealed hers with a warm, stirring kiss. It began softly, but quickly grew meaningful enough to make Ashley's head spin. Her arms instinctively reached forward and wrapped tightly around his neck. She lost herself in the moment and was disappointed when he loosened his hold on her, luring her reluctantly back to reality.

"Wow," she sighed breathlessly, her eyes staring passionately into his. "Do that again!"

"I'd love to stay here and kiss you all night long, but I shouldn't stay much longer. Your dad might wake up and shoot me."

"That's a possibility, especially with me in these sexy jammies."

"Ready to scale the wall?" Jimmy indicated the rose trellis with a nod of his head, offering his hand to Ashley. She pulled herself up from the grass and impulsively leaned over to give him another quick kiss.

"I'm glad you came by," she said, her voice quiet and suddenly shy. "I had a good time."

"Me too," he agreed with a wink. "I just wish you didn't have to go back inside."

"Well, I must get my beauty sleep," she teased. "I do have a date tonight."

"Beauty sleep you can do without," Jimmy's mouth brushed her ear as he helped her onto the trellis. "You're already more beautiful than the law should allow."

She acknowledged his compliment with an embarrassed smile before stealthily proceeding up the wall toward her bedroom window. She achieved her goal, swinging her legs over the sill and hopped quietly into her room, turning once again to gaze out at Jimmy.

"I'll call you later this afternoon to tell you what time we'll pick you up," he called to her.

She nodded and gave him an okay sign, along with a flirty little wave goodbye. He sprinted up the driveway to the spot beside the road where his truck was parked and she watched from the window, leaning on her elbows and resting her chin on her hands. The exhilarated smile fixed on her mouth didn't fade, even after he jumped in his truck and sped away.

CHAPTER SIX

Later that morning, Ashley slipped downstairs to get coffee before beginning her assorted array of "morning after" phone calls. Remy had already gone to work. Luckily he had given her the day off, given the unusually late night she'd had the night before. She found Maggie in the sunny green and cream-colored kitchen, sitting comfortably in jeans and a gray sweatshirt, watching squirrels playing on the lawn outside the bay window.

"Hi!" Ashley greeted her with abnormal cheerfulness as she poured a steaming cup of coffee, shoveling heaping spoonfuls of cream and sugar into her cup while Maggie looked on in amusement.

"You get that any sweeter and it'll be syrup," she said, advising Ashley with a smirk.

"Kate said that I need to start drinking coffee to battle my black morning moods, and I can't drink it any other way," Ashley told her as she retreated through the kitchen door. "I'm going to call her and Susanna to find out how their dates were last night."

"How was the dance?" Maggie called after her.

"The dance was fun, and yes, Doug was a perfectly charming date!" Ashley voiced loudly, pausing on the stairs for Maggie's reply.

"Are you going to see him again? On a real date, I mean?"

Ashley observed the hope in Maggie's question and grinned. "Doug and I are only friends. You know that!"

She meandered back to the kitchen, sticking her head inside the door. "But if you're lucky, maybe he'll still be available when you're a merry old widow." Ashley stuck her tongue out at Maggie playfully, then bounded up the steps to her bedroom.

She phoned Susanna first, greeting her in a booming voice. "Hey, you awake?"

"Barely," Susanna grumbled, her voice gravelly with sleep.

"How'd it go last night?" Ashley curled up in the antique rocking chair near her window, covering her bare feet with a quilt that had fallen from the foot of her bed onto the hardwood floor.

"I could ask you the same question," Susanna countered, suppressing a huge yawn.

"I asked you first."

"I don't have much to tell," Susanna groaned loudly as she stretched her stiff body. "We left the dance right after you all did and came to my house. Dad made breakfast for us."

"How fun!" Ashley said enthusiastically, sipping her overly sweet coffee and irritating Susanna with her chitchat.

"Yeah, yeah, it was great," she acknowledged impatiently. "Give me the details, Ash. Any cat fighting, barroom brawling or sucking face?"

Ashley quickly filled her in on both Doug's good night kiss and Jimmy's early morning appearance beneath the bedroom window. "We're going out with Kate and Mitch tonight," she finished with a self-satisfied giggle. "So it appears that he *has* picked being with me over getting laid. Aren't you going to admit you were wrong?"

"Have you ever known me to admit I was wrong?"

"No, but there's a first time for everything."

"True, but trust me, Ashley, now is not that time," Susanna said haughtily. "You talk to Katie today?"

"Not yet, you were the first one I called."

"Aren't I the lucky one."

"Going out with Scotty tonight?" Ashley asked as she prepared to end the conversation.

"Yep," Susanna's mood lightened significantly at the mention of his name. "Maybe we'll see you all out somewhere, if you're lucky."

Kate called Ashley before Ashley could call her. "I guess it's official now," she said cheerfully. "Mitch just called me and said that you and Jimmy are going with us tonight."

"Good news travels fast. How was your night with Jeff?"

"We had fun. He was such a good sport to miss the dance and all," Kate praised Jeff Thomassee's consideration for her plight.

Kate was juggling both Mitch and Jeff, both of whom wanted to date her exclusively, but Kate could not decide which one of them she liked best. It would be a tough decision: Jeff, tall, raven-haired and ruggedly handsome, or Mitch, shorter with boyish good looks, a muscular physique and the best legs in town. Ashley was certainly glad it wasn't her call to make.

"Does he know that you're going out with Mitch tonight?" Ashley was still curious as to how Kate managed two guys at once. She'd be lucky to manage one.

"He knows I have plans. He probably knows with whom."

"I don't know how you do it."

"It's amazing," Kate laughed agreeably.

After hanging up with Kate, Ashley took a break from the phone to shower. Jimmy called right after she got dressed.

"Hi there!" she said, elated to be hearing from him so soon. She sat on the edge of the bed, towel-drying her thick hair as they talked.

"I hope I didn't call too early," he said apologetically. "I didn't want to wake you up."

"Nah, I've been up gossiping for hours."

"Why does that not surprise me?"

"What have you been doing all morning? Sleeping?"

"Not even close. I've been out bumming around with my brother, Will."

"I didn't know you had a brother. How come I've never seen him?"

"Because we never see him," Jimmy responded, laughing good-naturedly. "Will's a second-year engineering major at LSU in Baton Rouge. He's also a big time partying frat boy who never comes home. Breaks Mother's heart. She has to beg him to visit her."

"Lucky for her, she has you," Ashley said with a giggle, conjuring up a mental image of Will Moreau. She envisioned him as an older version of Jimmy except with ratty hair and a torn shirt, smelling of beer and cigarettes.

"Yeah, I'm the good son. What a consolation prize," Jimmy said, teasing her and shifting gears. "Are we still on for tonight, or have you forgotten that you saw me really early this morning?"

"How could I forget? You, me, the moonlight.."

"Your red flannel pajamas," he interjected to torment her.

"Those red flannel pajamas are our secret! I really don't want my red flannel pajamas to be the hot topic in the field house on Monday."

"Your secret is safe with me," Jimmy reassured her, entertained by her reaction. "God knows I wouldn't want any other guy to get a visual picture of you in those baggy red pajamas."

"You are too kind."

"If we are on for tonight, I thought I'd come get you a little early, then swing back by my house before picking up Mitch and Kate. My mother would really love to meet you."

"Sounds good to me. I'll look for you early."

After casually saying goodbye to Jimmy, she grabbed one of her pillows, hugging it to her chest, and squealed excitedly. Life was good. The phone rang again and she answered on the first ring.

"Did you know that your line has been busy for hours?" It was Doug.

"It's been a busy gossip morning," she said cheerfully, a happy lilt radiating in her voice. "What are you doing?"

"Just wanted to say hi and tell you again that I had fun last night."

"You're very subdued this morning, what's up?"

"It's Saturday and since I've lost my Saturday night girl, I'm going to be reduced to hanging out with Jeff and all the other guys with no date." He pretended to pout, but Ashley could hear the underlying good humor in his tone.

"Doug, you could ask someone out some time."

"If you say Kimberly Seaton, I'm throttling you," he warned her sternly.

"I wouldn't dare mention her name to you again. How about Rhonda? I hear she doesn't have a date tonight."

He snorted his rejection of her idea. "And I take it you do have a date tonight?"

"Maybe, maybe not."

"I'll ask your mother, she'll tell me. She loves me," he taunted her. "Where are you going on your 'maybe, maybe not' date?"

"I might be going to a movie and to get a pizza with Kate and Mitch."

"Well, have fun. I'll probably see you out," Doug said, preparing to hang up.

"Doug?"

"Yes, ma'am?"

"I really had fun with you last night," she told him sincerely "Thank you."

"I'm glad, Ashley. I did too. See ya."

And with that, he hung up, leaving Ashley staring thoughtfully at the phone. She simply had to find a girl for Doug. He was so adorable. She just couldn't stand for him to be alone.

Jimmy arrived right on time and Remy let him in, Ashley having refrained from racing down the steps for once.

"Hi, Jimmy. Come on in!" Remy greeted him as Jimmy stepped inside, looking absolutely terrific in a denim shirt, jeans and boots. Ashley watched from the top of the stairs, knowing that she could see him but he couldn't see her.

"Hi, Mr. Stewart. Are you getting tired of seeing me yet?"

"No, Jimmy, not yet," Remy laughed. "Actually, you're pretty entertaining. I just keep waiting to see who you might show up with."

Ashley decided that she had better get downstairs before Remy started terrorizing him about Rhonda. "Jimmy, hi!" she bounded down the steps, challenging Remy with her eyes. "Did you say hello to Maggie yet?"

She pulled Jimmy by the arm into the den where Maggie was curled up in a chair, reading. They chatted with her parents while Jimmy outlined the evening plans and after being given the standard midnight curfew, Ashley quickly kissed her folks, leaving before Remy could resume his good-natured badgering of Jimmy.

Exiting the front door, Ashley saw that Jimmy was driving a nice black BMW. "Wow, where's your truck?" she asked while admiring the car.

"Will traded me for tonight." He opened the front passenger door for her.

Ashley slid into the front seat, waiting until he joined her in the car to continue. "This is your brother's car? The party boy's?" she asked incredulously. "I like it."

"He does too," Jimmy shrugged indifferently. "It's okay, I guess. I like the truck better though."

Jimmy lived with his parents in a subdivision a few miles from Ashley down Highway 28. It was one of her favorite neighborhoods because it was very scenic, full of tall pines and sparkling lakes. The Moreaus' large, single-story house was situated on a hill above one of the lakes. She recognized Jimmy's truck in the driveway, parked alongside his mother's car, a blue Volvo station wagon. Jimmy parked behind the truck then walked around to open Ashley's door for her as she chewed her lip anxiously. She was pretty nervous about meeting his family though she didn't know why. She was usually pretty good at meeting parents.

Jimmy opened the front door for her and called out, "We're here!"

Ashley glanced around the living room admiringly. It was a large, spectacular room with a long wall of windows overlooking the lake. Painted a soft shade of pale blue, the room was furnished with a powder-blue-and-white-striped couch and a pair of denim blue overstuffed chairs, all of which were adorned with lacy accent pillows.

The room was very clean and very pretty, and Ashley wasn't truly convinced that this was the home of two teenaged boys. Doug and Scotty's houses didn't look this way. She was much more accustomed to the modern camouflage decor of their homes, and had always felt profusely sorry for their mothers for having to tolerate such messes.

Mrs. Moreau came in from the back of the house, easing into the room with a smooth, catlike grace. Ashley couldn't believe her eyes. Doug and Scotty's *mothers* didn't look this way either. None of the mothers Ashley knew looked this way, not even Maggie, and Maggie was beautiful. Jimmy's mother was absolutely stunning, remarkably tall and slender with silky chin-length, ash-blond hair and wide fawn-colored eyes. Ashley estimated that she was in her late thirties to early forties, but could have easily passed for being a full decade younger. Ashley was most impressed.

She extended her hand, taking Ashley's and squeezing it warmly. "You must be Ashley," she said with a kind smile. "Jimmy has told me a lot about you. I'm Lana Moreau."

"Nice to meet you, Mrs. Moreau." Ashley said shyly, still in a state of astonishment.

"Please call me Lana. All of the boys' friends do," Lana said, inviting her to sit down.

"Where's Will?" Jimmy asked, sitting on the arm of the couch next to Lana, his eyes conveying obvious affection for his mother.

"He's back in the den, watching the end of a football game."

"I'll be right back," Jimmy reassured Ashley before striding down the hallway, presumably to retrieve Will.

Lana smiled as she assessed Ashley. "Well, you certainly are different from Rhonda. No, dear, that's a good thing," she quickly reassured her, patting Ashley's arm as her face fell disappointedly. "I didn't care too much for Rhonda."

Ashley laughed out loud at Lana's confession. "Rhonda does tend to have that effect on women. I don't know many females who *do* care much for Rhonda."

"Except for my niece. I'm just glad that Cheryl isn't turning out just like her."

"Cheryl has too much personality, and is way too smart to be like Rhonda." Ashley glanced appreciatively around the room, enjoying the serene view of the lake offered by the wall of windows.

Jimmy returned shortly thereafter, followed by his older brother. Will Moreau didn't look at all like the wild-haired, irresponsible party boy Ashley had earlier envisioned. Much to the contrary—he was very striking, favoring his mother in both features and coloring. He was taller than Jimmy and more muscular, though not heavy. His hair was wavy and blonde, and his eyes were wide and brown like Lana's. His smile was charming and contagious, Ashley noted, as he strode over to her, giving her a big hug.

"Hello, Ashley. I'm glad to finally put a face with your name," he greeted her heartily, like an old friend. "I'm Jimmy's brother, Will."

"Nice to meet you," Ashley said with an easy smile.

Will turned to Jimmy, wearing a grin that stretched from ear to ear. "It's about time you displayed some taste in women," he kidded Jimmy good-naturedly. "Your last few choices have been questionable." Jimmy responded with a wry grin and a sound punch to Will's arm.

As she and Jimmy made their way to the front door to pick up Mitch and Kate for the movie, Ashley said goodbye to Lana and Will. "I'm really glad to have met you," she said.

"Come back again soon," Lana encouraged her with a warm smile.

"Make sure that he behaves himself, Ashley," Will's eyes danced as he warned her. "Fast hands run in the family."

Ashley giggled as Lana responded to Will's remark, slapping his arm with her delicately manicured hand, giving him a reprimanding look. Jimmy shook his head in disbelief, hustling Ashley over the threshold and to the driveway, grinning mischievously back at Will as he opened Ashley's car door.

After the movie, the foursome ended up at B.J.'s Pizza, home to what they all considered the world's finest pizza. It was a locally owned pizza parlor and another of their favorite weekend hangouts. As they pulled in, Ashley quickly surveyed the parking lot in front of B.J.'s, finding no familiar vehicles. Going inside, they found the large room crowded, even for a Saturday night, with every wooden table and booth filled to capacity. While waiting, they played pinball and studied selections on the jukebox before finally getting a booth by one of the large glass windows near the front door.

After placing the order, Kate and Ashley nabbed some quarters from Mitch to play some music. Ashley was singing along with Tom Petty and the Heartbreakers when Mitch muttered, "Uh-oh, Jimmy." He nodded toward the window beside him. "Here comes trouble."

Ashley peered out the window to see Rhonda walking in, along with Cheryl and the rest of her usual entourage. Ashley shook her head, sighing in disbelief. Great, and things were going so well. She glanced at Kate, raising one eyebrow in a questioning slant, nodding toward the girls nearing the front entrance.

"As I said before, this gets more and more interesting as time goes on," Kate said, answering Ashley's quizzical look in a soft voice meant for Ashley's ears only.

Rhonda entered the room as she always did, with a flip of her mane of black hair and the batting of her sapphire eyes. She spotted Ashley and Jimmy almost immediately. Her eyes grew wide with betrayal and Ashley thought she might scream. But she didn't. She kept her cool and strode purposely over to their table.

Cheryl watched in horror as she mouthed, "I'm so sorry," to Jimmy and looked as if she couldn't decide whether to watch the battle or cover her eyes to hide from the carnage.

"Well, well, isn't this sweet?" Rhonda said acidly as she leaned on her hands at the edge of the table. She offered Ashley a frigid stare then glanced at Jimmy. "Would you like to explain this to me?" she asked him, her eyes flashing with anger.

"There's nothing to explain, Rhonda," Jimmy said calmly, meeting her withering stare with an unwavering look of his own as he leaned casually back in the booth.

"Nothing to explain? You're obviously out with her," she jerked her thumb toward Ashley, "and there's nothing to explain?" Her voice rose hysterically.

Mitch watched Rhonda intently, his eyes blinking with incredulity and his jaw dropping in shock, his angelic impression of Rhonda instantly shattered by her unrefined display of temper. Seeing his face, Ashley almost laughed out loud, but thought better of it. Rhonda was moments away from losing complete control and Ashley didn't want to do anything to further infuriate her.

Susanna and Scotty walked in about that time and Susanna stopped dead in her tracks, staring at the scene unfolding at their table. She looked at Ashley with huge eyes and mouthed, "Holy shit!"

It was all Ashley could do not to burst out laughing. She sat with an amused look on her face, in spite of herself, while Jimmy and Rhonda continued to stare stonily at one another. Finally, Jimmy stood.

"Rhonda, let's go outside and talk about this," he attempted to reason with her.

"Why, are you protecting her?" she indicated Ashley with another jerk of her hand.

Ashley was beginning to take offense to the way Rhonda kept dismissing her as "her" and scowled her displeasure to Rhonda. Jimmy took Rhonda calmly by the arm and led her outside. Rhonda was so mad that she was practically spitting. Ashley watched them through the window, taking note of the flush of indignation spreading over Jimmy's face, sensing that he was getting an earful from Rhonda Williams.

Susanna and Cheryl scurried up to the table while Mitch excused himself to go talk to Scotty. "Nice date," Susanna said, staring out the window at Jimmy and Rhonda.

"Don't start, Susanna," Ashley warned her wearily, her eyes challenging Susanna as she seated herself in Mitch's spot next to Kate.

"I bet Jimmy is fit to be tied," Cheryl said, sliding into the booth beside Ashley. "I didn't know y'all were here, I swear," she apologized. "I looked for Jimmy's truck and since I didn't see it, I thought it would be okay to stop here."

"We're in Will's car," Ashley said, not bothering to hide her irritation with the situation.

Rhonda and Jimmy were still fighting it out in the parking lot when Ashley spied Doug's Camaro pulling into the lot. He got out with, of course, Jeff Thomasee. Ashley gawked in astonishment at Kate. "You're not going to believe this, Kate. You talk about getting better and better."

Kate glanced out the window to see Jeff sauntering across the blacktop parking lot and she sank deeply into the booth, disbelief written all over her face. She was now faced with Mitch and Jeff in the same place at the same time while she was on a date with one of them. Kate's predicament made Ashley feel a little better about her own.

Jeff stopped to converse with Scotty and Mitch by the video games while Doug strolled over to the booth, nodding toward Jimmy and Rhonda.

"What the hell's going on out there?" he asked, directing his question to no one in particular. Ashley certainly didn't feel obligated to answer him.

He dragged a chair noisily across the floor and sat at the end of the booth, leaning back with a smug look of enjoyment on his handsome face.

"Lovely, isn't it?" Susanna was only too happy to egg Doug on, enjoying the chaos that had overtaken their Saturday night.

"Thanks for bringing Jeff here," Kate interjected caustically, her look shooting daggers.

Noting her obvious displeasure with him, Doug laughed heartily. "It was inevitable that you all would end up in the same place at some point, Kate," he pointed out to her. "This is a really small town."

When the pizza was ready, Mitch brought it over to the table and they each grabbed a piece. "Should we save some for Jimmy?" Ashley asked Mitch, as she watched the pizza rapidly disappearing.

Mitch peered out at the continuing battle in the parking lot. "Why bother?" he shrugged, shaking his head in wonder.

Mitch seemed much more concerned with Jimmy and Rhonda than with his own situation with Kate and Jeff Thomasee. However, Ashley didn't buy it. She had witnessed too many stony stares exchanged between he and Jeff, as well as many longing glances at Kate. The time was fast approaching for Kate to make her decision. The natives were growing restless.

Ashley looked over at Kate. She seemed to know that the days of her juggling act were drawing to a close. She wore a forced bright smile and glanced nervously from Mitch to Jeff, trying to come to some reasonable conclusion.

They finished the pizza just in time to see Rhonda storming across the parking lot and burst angrily through the front door of B.J.'s. "I'm leaving!" she stomped over to the booth where Chris and Monica were sitting, making her announcement in a loud, shrill voice.

"But Rhonda, we just got our pizza," they protested.

"Then find your own ride home!"

She whirled around, glaring at Ashley. "You can have him. I didn't want him anyway," she spit out the words with contempt then flounced out the door, passing Jimmy on his way back in.

"Ha!" Rhonda sputtered at him and continued on to her car, striding angrily with steam practically rolling from her ears. Jimmy watched after her wearily as she roared away, then rejoined his party at the table.

"What a woman!" Mitch observed as Jimmy pulled up a chair.

Jimmy shot him an exhausted look. "You go fight with her then," he said.

"Got your hands full, Jim?" Doug kidded him, obviously entertained by the entire situation.

Ashley made no comment as Jimmy sat down next to her and didn't meet his gaze. She felt his eyes searching her face, wondering how she felt about what had transpired. Ashley couldn't say that she was surprised by Rhonda's behavior. She had expected Rhonda to cause trouble when she found out about them. She just hadn't expected her to confront them while they were out on their first date.

The original group of four left B.J.'s shortly thereafter, much more subdued than when they had arrived. It was only eleven-thirty but the evening's events had worn Ashley thin. She was ready to retreat to the comfort of her room. After dropping Mitch at Kate's, Jimmy drove next door to the Stewart house and they sat in the car, enveloped in awkward silence.

"Ashley, I'm sorry," Jimmy said finally, glancing over at her anxiously. Ashley tried to offer him a comforting smile, but was too discouraged to be of much help to him.

She wasn't mad at Jimmy but was thoroughly pissed at Rhonda, and sorely disappointed in her Saturday evening, not to mention the lovely memories she would have to treasure of her first date with Jimmy Moreau. Rhonda wasn't going to take what she interpreted as betrayal lying down. If tonight was a preview of what her dating life with Jimmy was going to be like, Ashley wasn't too sure that she wanted to continue seeing him. She'd be much better off as the Ice Princess.

"Jimmy, I'm not mad at you," she said, quietly looking down at her hands. "But maybe we should give Rhonda a little time to cool off before we see each other again."

Jimmy's eyes grew wide, his mouth set in grim determination. "Now Ashley, you've got to be kidding! After all the weeks we've waited to go public, how can you call everything off now?"

"I just think that it might be easier this way, that's all," she explained, sounding confident, but feeling blue. Defeated sadness tugged at her heart as she threw away the relationship she had spent weeks avidly pursuing. Foolishness may have been one of her strong points, but her pride was much stronger.

"You don't mean that."

"Let's just step back and see what happens over the next few weeks," Ashley suggested coolly as she opened her door and stepped from the car.

Jimmy leapt out his side, leaning between the door and the body of the car, watching as she strode purposely toward the house. "Where are you going?" he called out in bewilderment.

She stopped in her tracks, turning back to face him, offering a light shrug of her shoulders. "I'm going inside," she replied matter of factly, continuing on her course to the front door. She heard the car door slam and Jimmy bounded up the steps behind her, stopping her with his warm hand on her cold shoulder.

"C'mon, Ashley!" he said, objecting determinedly. "Don't be this way. This isn't my fault."

Ashley leaned against the front door, looking up at him. He was so irresistible but unfortunately for him, she was much more stubborn than he was charming. So, slipping one hand discreetly behind her back, Ashley turned the doorknob, easing open the front door.

"Thank you for the movie, I enjoyed it." She ignored his plea for understanding but remembered her manners at the last minute. "Good night." She evaded his puzzled stare and slipped inside the house.

Ashley spent much of the night kicking herself for her adolescent behavior and for being idiotic enough to give Jimmy Moreau up because of Rhonda Williams. How cowardly, how very stupid! She scolded herself mercilessly. She needed consolation. She wanted to phone Kate or Susanna but thought better of it. Kate would undoubtedly be sleeping peacefully, a blissful smile on her virtuous face as she dreamed of Mitch and Jeff, delighting in possessing the undying admiration of them both.

And as for calling Susanna, Ted Robicheaux would blow a head gasket if she called their house at such a late hour. So instead, Ashley was forced to suffer alone. It was going to be a very long night.

Doug ended up being the one to save the day. The next morning as Ashley was getting into her car to go to church, Doug pulled into the driveway behind her. "Hey, Ash!" he greeted her, jumping from his car. "Ride to church with me." He gestured for her to join him in the cherry red Camaro.

Ashley obliged, as her long night of tortured isolation had left her lonely for human contact and conversation. And if anyone in town knew the very latest bits of gossip, it would be Doug Fairchild.

As they rode to church, he told her what had transpired after Jimmy left her house the night before. All the guys, Doug, Scotty, Mitch, Jeff and Jimmy had ended up by the lake, drinking beer and discussing "Rhonda's Last Stand" at B.J.'s Pizza. "Don't be pissed at Jimmy, Ashley," Doug said, urging her to lighten up a bit. "He can't help that Rhonda is such a bitch."

"It's not all Rhonda's fault, Doug. Jimmy should've given her some warning about me."

"I never thought I'd hear you take up for Rhonda Williams." Doug glanced abruptly at her with wide, skeptical eyes.

"I'm not taking up for her," Ashley corrected him, offended that he could ever believe such a thing. "The way she behaved is inexcusable, but I just think that the whole thing could've been avoided if Jimmy had talked with her about it beforehand, that's all."

She turned away from him defensively and pouted as she stared forlornly out the window, watching the rapid change in suburban scenery as they sped down Old Marksville Highway toward downtown Pineville.

"Now listen, my obstinate little Ice Princess." Ashley could've been insulted by his taunting use of her nickname, but she didn't miss the underlying hint of humor in his voice. "I know that this whole 'man thing' is new to you, and I also know that you have an uncanny knack for making yourself miserable, so I'm going to attempt to help you out a little."

"What's your point, Douglas?" Ashley said, jerking her head around to regard him critically.

"All I'm saying is, give the guy a break," Doug said gently. "He's crazy about you."

Ashley dropped her sarcastic stance, her icy cold resistance about Jimmy melting away. "He is?" she questioned softly. Doug nodded affirmatively and her face brightened with pleasure. "How do you know that?"

"Jeez, Ashley, get a clue. I just finished telling that the guy cried in his beer over you all night last night. How'd you think I knew?"

Ashley grinned at him, both entertained by Doug's bluntness and immensely pleased to know that she hadn't blown it all with Jimmy. Doug took note of her enhanced receptiveness to reason and continued in his plea for Jimmy's case.

"I think you should give him another chance. After drinking beer with the guy and listening to him spill his guts, I feel more inclined to help him win you back," he said as he wheeled the Camaro into a parking spot behind the church gymnasium.

At Doug's urging, Ashley decided to give her relationship with Jimmy another chance. Strolling casually into church together, Doug and Ashley drew curious stares from the congregated youth group. Doug took her hand and led Ashley to the back pew, scooting her in next to a pensive-looking Jimmy then proceeded to take the place on the opposite side of her, presumably to block her exit if she foolishly decided to make a run for it.

Jimmy wore a pitiful look of appeal and glanced at her, seeking to read her thoughts. Ashley gave nothing away, carefully concealing the information she had received from Doug. When in doubt, playing hard to get was a girl's best option.

As the choir began to sing the opening hymn, Jimmy reached over, painstakingly scrawling a message across the creamy white parchment of the church bulletin resting atop the hymnal in her lap. "Forgive me?"

Ashley smiled slightly, her game of hard to get ending with just one look from him. "Forgiven," she wrote back, underlining the word twice for good measure.

Jimmy smiled broadly at her and she leaned against him, luxuriating in the warmth of his muscular shoulder. He peered over the top of her head to Doug and mouthed, "Thank you," to which Doug gave the okay sign.

And thus began the Jimmy Era.

CHAPTER SEVEN

The final football game was played early in November and as Ashley watched from her spot on the sidelines, she felt the familiar thrill wash over her as the team ran onto the field and the marching band blasted out the school fight song. She would miss this Friday night ritual when she left for college the following year. During the game, she danced merrily while the band played, chattering with Cheryl and Kimberly between plays. She did her usual amount of bellowing to Kate and Susanna in the student section, catching Doug's eye a couple of times as she yelled to Kate. He grinned expansively at her and Ashley had to laugh in spite of herself, remembering his terrorizing accusation that she only came to the games to socialize.

They upheld their usual post-game tradition of meeting at McDonalds and Ashley waited there for Doug and Jimmy after the game, bouncing from table to table with Susanna and Kate to gather the very latest gossip.

"Hey Ashley!" Doug called to her as he burst through the glass doors of the restaurant, "how'd you like the game?" He had asked her the same question after every football game for the last four years.

Ashley grinned and gave him the same answer that she always had. "It was great, Doug," she said, beaming at him as he strolled up beside her.

"Right on cue," he chuckled, putting his arm around her in a fond embrace.

"Hey, Fairchild," Jimmy frowned in mock irritation, noting the comfortable arm draping over Ashley's shoulder. "Just remember, she's *my* girl."

Ashley and Jimmy dated throughout basketball season, falling in love by the Festival of Lights in early December. They had a wonderful time getting to know one another, spending many evenings alone, isolated from the world around them. Ashley loved being with Jimmy more than anything. He had so much enthusiasm for life, every day was a new adventure for him and his zest for living was contagious for Ashley and all those who knew him.

Jimmy Moreau was Ashley's soul mate, both emotionally and intellectually. He found her writing fascinating and throughout their time together, she wrote many poems and short stories for him. Ashley discovered his proverbial skeleton in the closet in his extraordinary talent for painting and sketching. She was one of the few people privy to this artistic ability. Jimmy carefully kept it hidden, especially from his macho football buddies.

Jimmy became a fixture at the Stewart house, and if Remy and Maggie ever tired of finding him at their dinner table, they never said a word about it. Remy liked Jimmy's quick wit and intelligence, praising Ashley more than once over her excellent choice in a boyfriend. Jimmy endeared himself to Maggie by being crazy about her cooking and their informal dining style that Ashley said was "one step shy of paper plates." Maggie's initial goodwill toward Jimmy grew into such deep affection that he came very close to rivaling Doug for the soft spot in her heart.

Finally home from his frequent travels, Ashley met Jimmy's father, John, right after she and Jimmy got out of school for Christmas break. Will had come directly home from LSU after finishing finals, without making his usual Bourbon Street detour, and Lana wanted to have a nice dinner to celebrate. Jimmy called Ashley to issue an invitation.

"Does Lana want me there?" Ashley hesitated to accept, not wanting to intrude on a special family dinner.

Jimmy chuckled, "Yes, she does. If she didn't, believe me, I wouldn't be asking." Lana may have been the only woman in their household, but she clearly ran the show.

Ashley didn't think that jeans would be appropriate for dinner with the Moreaus, so she carefully chose a red, green and black plaid jumper and red turtleneck, adding black tights, flats and a red hair ribbon to pull back her hair from her face.

"Don't you look adorable!" Maggie said, sticking her head into Ashley's bathroom as she brushed her teeth.

Ashley spit out her toothpaste, rinsing her mouth and shooting Maggie a wry look. "Gee thanks, Maggie, but I was actually aiming more for acceptable."

Maggie suppressed an amused smile. "Well then, don't you look acceptable!" she said and exited the doorway quickly, escaping Ashley's wrath by letting Jimmy in the front door.

When Ashley arrived at the Moreaus' with Jimmy, Will greeted them at the front door. "Hello, Ashley!" he pulled her into a bear hug and swung her into the living room while she giggled with delight. "It's great to see you again. Have you been keeping my little brother out of trouble?"

"I've been trying, but it's not an easy job." Ashley joked with him as he deposited her back on her feet and beamed fondly at him, wishing that he were in Pineville more often. She liked his easy-going personality and felt an odd kinship with him.

The living room was gorgeous, Ashley noted as she gazed admiringly around the room, which smelled wonderfully of cinnamon and pine, instantly reminding her that Christmas was only a few days away. A cozy fire crackled in the fireplace, the family stockings hung on the mantle. A huge Douglas fir with perfectly coordinated ornaments and ribbons graced the spot directly in front of the wall of windows, allowing its twinkling white lights to shine out onto the lake for all to see.

Hearing the doorbell, John Moreau entered the living room. He shared the same tall, athletic build of his two sons, but Jimmy definitely favored his father in looks. John Moreau had the same thick, brown hair and rich chocolate brown eyes. He wore a warm, animated smile as he reached out to shake Ashley's hand.

"You have to be Ashley. I've heard a lot about you from these two," John nodded toward his sons. "I'm John Moreau."

"It's a pleasure to meet you, Mr. Moreau," Ashley said, smiling back at him. He instantly made her feel at ease.

"Please call me John," he said with a flirtatious wink. "I'm much too young to be Mr. Moreau."

Ashley retrieved the poinsettia she had brought for Lana then wandered into the kitchen to see if she could be of help. Lana stood in front of the icemaker, busily filling glasses with ice.

"Hi, Lana," Ashley said. "Let me do that for you." She traded the crimson red poinsettia in her own arms for the ice bucket in Lana's. "My mother sends Christmas greetings."

"What a beautiful poinsettia!" Lana said with a delighted smile, placing it on the sideboard in the decorator-perfect dining room.

Ashley observed Lana with ongoing fascination as she followed her into the dining room. Lana was beautiful in a skirt, crisp white blouse and sweater vest decorated in holly and Christmas wreaths. Her hair and makeup were perfect, as always. If Jimmy had ever wanted a woman just like his mother, Ashley felt that she wouldn't fit the bill. She would never be as flawless or graceful as Lana Moreau.

Dinner was marvelous, with everything tasting delicious, of course. In spite of the identical place settings of Christmas china, linen napkins and crystal stemware, dinner itself was very relaxed and Ashley was completely comfortable there. John, Will and Jimmy kept the conversation lively with their jokes and teasing, and after dinner, Ashley helped Lana clear the table and do the dishes, enjoying spending time with the delightful older woman. Despite her elegant appearance and mannerisms, Lana was not intimidating in the least, and clearly took pleasure from having Ashley around.

"If you're done with the dishwasher, I thought I'd steal her for a few minutes," Jimmy strolled into the kitchen, wrapping his arms around Ashley's slender waist as she stood at the sink rinsing the last of the dishes.

Lana laughingly nodded her consent and Jimmy took Ashley by the arm, leading her into the study off the living room. The study was John's, filled with an antique roll top desk and walls of bookshelves, brimming with multi-colored volumes of literature. The heather-purple walls were adorned with framed watercolors, varying in colors and sizes but definitely done by the same artist.

Ashley eyed Jimmy with raised eyebrows. "Did you do these?"

He nodded with a modest grin and she turned her attention back to the wall, studying each picture with great interest. She was constantly amazed at the quality of Jimmy's work, at the intricate landscapes, realistic herds of wildlife, the portraits of various family members.

She tore her eyes away from the pictures and beamed appreciatively up at him. "These are wonderful!" she said sincerely, as she slid her arms invitingly around his neck. "Will you paint something for me some time?"

He raised his eyebrows. "Sure I will, but only if you keep whispering to me like that. It's pretty sexy."

Ashley felt flushed under his innocently seductive gaze.

Will interrupted them by clearing his throat as he came into the room and Ashley jumped backward involuntarily. Will chuckled. "You didn't have to move away from him like that." Will said, teasing her as his eyes crinkled mirthfully. "I just wanted you two to know that I was here."

"What do you want, Will?" Jimmy glared at him, clearly annoyed with his brother for intruding on their private moment.

"Now, don't go getting all bent out of shape, little brother," Will grinned mischievously at Jimmy's irritated scowl. "I was told to come and tell you that Mother has dessert and hot chocolate in the living room. You two just take your sweet time. We'll wait for you."

He laughed heartily as he turned on heel, heading back in the direction of the living room. Jimmy and Ashley exchanged a good-humored, yet disappointed glance and followed him.

They had a nice time eating hot-from-the-oven chocolate chip cookies and drinking cocoa by the fire. Ashley delighted in listening to Jimmy and Will bicker back and forth, each trying to top the other, while she and Lana exchanged amused glances over their light-hearted heckling.

"I had fun with your family," Ashley said as Jimmy drove down the highway toward her house later that evening.

"I'm glad. My mother was really happy to have you there. I think that she gets tired of being there with just Will, Dad and me all the time. She misses having other girls around."

Ashley sat close to him, growing intensely aware of the warmth of his leg against her own and found her mind drifting back to their embrace in his father's study earlier that evening. She ached with an inner longing unfamiliar to her and glanced sidelong at Jimmy's handsome features.

"You know, we don't have to go to my house yet," she said, snuggling a little closer to his muscular physique.

Jimmy considered this thoughtfully, noting the time with a quick glance at his watch before looking over at her innocently. "What do you want to do?"

"We could park the truck by the lake and talk," Ashley grew warm, flushing at her own suggestion. Jimmy still didn't get it.

"It's kind of cold out, don't you think?" he said, reminding her that it was the dead of winter. The perfect gentleman in him had no idea what she was suggesting to him. Ashley was a little shocked herself.

"I could keep you warm," she said blatantly, uncharacteristically outspoken and sounding more like Susanna than herself.

Jimmy's eyebrows shot up in surprise. "What are you proposing?" he asked her, grinning ear to ear.

"Not *that*!" Ashley decided that maybe her suggestion wasn't such a good idea, suddenly embarrassed that she had even been the one to bring it up.

"I know you didn't mean *that*," Jimmy teased her, squeezing her hand affectionately. "I'm just amazed that you were the one to suggest parking at all."

"Well, can I help it if I just wanted to be alone with you?" she snuggled against him, beaming up at him dotingly.

"You know, it isn't really *that* cold out." Jimmy abruptly steered the truck down the gravel road leading to the very secluded lake across the road from the Stewart house.

It was still and quiet by the lake. The night was cold and clear and the moon shone its bright silvery beams across the water in a spectacular display of light. Jimmy cut the engine and turned the key in the ignition to leave the radio playing, humming softy to Journey's *Open Arms*.

Ashley sat very still, not sure what to do next. "Well, here we are," she giggled nervously, fidgeting in her seat as butterflies did somersaults in her stomach.

Jimmy smiled down at her with amusement dancing in his eyes. "You really haven't done this much, have you?"

"I haven't done this at all. Remember, I didn't even have a real date before this summer."

"I'm glad. I like the idea of being the first one to take you parking." He turned toward her, pulling her closer to him while enveloping her in his incredibly strong arms. She shivered more from nervousness than from the cold. "Are you cold?" Jimmy asked with sweet concern.

Ashley shook her head, her heart thumping with anticipation of his passionate kisses. "No."

"Are you scared?"

"A little." she said, admitting this truth bashfully. "So much for all my big talk," she thought.

"I won't hurt you, in spite of what Will says about the fast hands of the Moreau men." Jimmy flashed a naughty smile then kissed her, gently cupping her face in his hands. His fervent kiss instantly filled her with the warm feelings of desire cultivated earlier in the evening and she began to relax, kissing him back.

As their passion grew, it began to heat up in the cab of the truck and Ashley laughed as she saw the windows fogging over from their steamy breath. "My mother would have a cow," she whispered breathlessly into his ear, brushing aside a lock of his sandy hair with her lips.

"Your mother's not here," Jimmy left a trail of kisses down the length of her neck as he reminded her, unnecessarily, of the fact that they were completely alone. He nibbled playfully at her throat as she arched her neck with a throaty giggle. But as his mouth moved closer to her heaving chest, she scrambled abruptly into full sitting position.

"What time is it?" She searched for a good reason for ending their parking session. It was getting a little too heated for comfort.

Jimmy held his wrist up, squinting at his watch in the moonlight. "Eleven-thirty."

"Maybe we should start heading that way."

"We still have thirty minutes," Jimmy began kissing her again, not yet ready to take her home.

"We have to have a little time to pull ourselves back together," she reminded him. "I can't go in my house all flustered and breathless."

Jimmy threw his head back in laughter. "You're probably right, Ashley. I certainly wouldn't want to do anything to end the goodwill I've finally earned from your mother."

He turned the key in the ignition, and as the truck started, Jimmy glanced over at her, regarding her with open affection. He reached his hand out, gently brushing back from her face a lock of hair straying from its red satin ribbon. She gazed at him from beneath her thick eyelashes, her eyes echoing the adoration glowing in his.

"I love you, you know," Jimmy revealed solemnly, unsure of what she might say in return.

Ashley's heart leapt, fluttering wildly in her chest as she stared at him with huge eyes. "You do?" she asked shyly. He nodded, smiling his affirmation. "I love you too," she whispered, kissing him warmly and circling her arms tightly around his as they traveled back up the gravel road toward the house. It was almost midnight when they pulled into the driveway and Jimmy walked her to the front door.

"I better not come in since it's so late," Jimmy said, kissing her once more and Ashley felt herself becoming breathless again.

"I had fun tonight," she said, with a suddenly shy smile as she recalled their time by the lake.

His eyes sparkled in agreement. "Me too," he teased her with a boyish grin, kissing her forehead affectionately. "Good night, Ashley."

"Good night, Jimmy." She blew him a kiss and went inside, floating upstairs and tapping lightly on her parents' door to let them know that she was home. Getting into bed, she reviewed the evening's events, still glowing over Jimmy's admission of his love for her. She lay back against her pillows, smiling elatedly. With the kind of love and passion she and Jimmy shared, she knew that she would end up constantly fighting her hormones on a regular basis. And the down side to this would be what? She giggled into the darkness and rolled over to go to sleep.

CHAPTER EIGHT

Jimmy and Doug left the next morning for a long-anticipated hunting trip with Doug's father, Nick Fairchild, giving Ashley a few days to regain her composure. She used his time away wisely, Christmas shopping with Kate and a neglected-acting Susanna and helping Maggie wrap presents and bake Christmas goodies.

She learned during a brotherly phone call from Will Moreau that Jimmy and his family would be going to south Louisiana for the Christmas holiday to visit his Gram who lived right outside New Orleans. Jimmy sent a message through Will that he would be by on Christmas Eve to exchange gifts.

It was late in the afternoon when Ashley, in a bright red sweater and black leggings, lit the lights on the Christmas tree. Theirs wasn't the Martha Stewart tree that Lana had decorated, but each evergreen bough was adorned with decorations Ashley, Remy and Maggie had collected through the years, each ornament holding unique memories of many Christmases they had shared as a family. Sentimentally, Ashley preferred their tree to Lana's picture-perfect one.

Jimmy strode into the room wearing jeans, a flannel shirt and baseball cap, having just returned from three days of deer hunting earlier that afternoon. Ashley leapt ecstatically across the room and flung herself into his arms.

"I missed you!" she kissed him hard on the mouth, displaying her obvious affection for him.

"I missed you too, Sugar. Doug's not quite the kisser you are." Ashley wrinkled her nose in mock irritation at his pet name for her. Jimmy was the only person on the face of God's green Earth who could get away with calling her "Sugar."

"Did y'all have fun?" Ashley was glad that she hadn't been invited along. The one deer hunting extravaganza in which she had participated with Doug and Scotty a few years beforehand had been enough to last her a lifetime.

"Yeah, we did, even though we drank more beer than we hunted," Jimmy admitted with a chuckle. Nick Fairchild was notorious for sharing a beer or two with his son, just as long as it wasn't during football season or spring training.

They sat on the floor in front of the tree. Jimmy leaned back on his elbows and stretched his long legs out on the carpet while Ashley glanced around expectantly. "Where's my present?" she said with the voice of a small child.

Jimmy laughed, entertained by her sulky expression. "You obviously don't dig through the gifts under your tree the way Will and I do under ours. I brought your present by while you were out shopping the other day. It's been under your tree the whole time I've been gone with Doug. I can't believe you haven't found it."

"You've got to be kidding!" Ashley dove under the tree, searching wildly for her present, and finally found it buried on the far side of the tree. She pulled out the shiny red package, shaking it diligently, but no noise came from within to offer her a clue about its contents. She set the gift down and picked up the holly-green package she had for Jimmy, presenting it to him with a grin.

"You first," she told him, hoping that he would like it.

She had taken Lana's advice concerning Jimmy's present, going to the hobby shop to purchase several palettes of watercolors, coal to sketch with and a large sketchpad. Returning home, she wrote Jimmy a huge Christmas greeting on the first page of the sketchpad: "Merry Christmas, Jimmy. I'm still waiting for <u>my sketch</u>. I love you, Ashley."

"If you insist. You know you don't have to ask me twice." Jimmy tore into the package eagerly. He still had so many childlike qualities about him. That was one of the things Ashley loved most about him. She held her breath, waiting as Jimmy opened the box, pulling the art supplies out while an enormous smile lit his face.

"This is perfect," he told her sincerely. "I've been out of art supplies for weeks. In fact, I put them on my wish list for my mother." Jimmy opened the sketchpad, reading her Christmas greeting. "I'll work on your sketch in the car tomorrow," he promised. "Now open yours."

Ashley opened the package slowly while Jimmy looked on, fidgeting impatiently as she tore the paper and opened the box. Inside was a small cedar chest, its lid engraved with a delicate magnolia. Ashley eagerly lifted the cedar chest from the box and examined it in the multi-colored rays of light cast from the Christmas tree.

"Jimmy, it's beautiful," she said, her eyes shining with pleasure.

"Open it," he studied her face as she lifted the lid to discover the engraved gold locket inside, holding it up to read the inscription: "You'll always have my heart. J.M." Ashley was touched by the amount of thought he had put into this gift. She leaned over, kissing him tenderly. "Thank you, I love it!"

Jimmy reached over to take the locket from her hand. Unfastening the clasp, he put the chain around her neck then returned the clasp to its locked position. He leaned back, supporting himself on the palms of his hands to get a look at the necklace on her. "Looks good on you," he acknowledged with a satisfied nod.

Jimmy stayed until Remy came in from work, declining Maggie's dinner invitation in order to return home to celebrate Christmas Eve with Lana, John and Will. "I'll call you when we get back from Gram's," he promised as Ashley walked with him out onto the front porch.

"I can't wait until you get back, I miss you already," she said, standing on her tiptoes to kiss him goodbye. "Merry Christmas, Jimmy."

"Merry Christmas, Sugar," he laughed heartily as Ashley winced at the nickname and he pulled her close, giving her a much warmer kiss. "You make me not want to leave," he revealed his irresistible silly grin.

Ashley smiled back at him and swatted his arm. "Get going or Lana will skin me alive," she joked, waving as he pulled out of the drive in his old pick-up, honking his horn as he sped away.

By the end of the winter, Ashley had established her own place in the Moreau household. Because she considered him a second father, Ashley held the greatest respect and admiration for John Moreau, who was an older, wiser version of Jimmy. He was a kind man with a gentle soul and Ashley came to adore him almost as much as she adored his youngest son.

Ashley and Lana became fast friends, kindred spirits in their love for the Moreau men. They enjoyed afternoons of girl talk curled up in front of the fireplace, sipping cocoa or braving the warmer days lounging outside on the veranda overlooking the lake. Will often came home from Baton Rouge during breaks from class and Ashley came to love him as a brother. Underneath his clever sense of humor and devil-may-care exterior was a heart of gold and a wonderfully sentimental human being, which didn't surprise Ashley at all. Good-heartedness was a family trait.

Despite her increasing affection for the other two Moreau men, the one whom she loved with all her heart was Jimmy, and her love for him grew stronger with each passing day. One gaze from his rich brown eyes instantly filled her with an inner longing for their next moment alone, a moment when she could lock him in her warm embrace and kiss him passionately like there was no tomorrow. Their desire for one another was overwhelming. Had it not been for Doug's persistent presence, Ashley and Jimmy would have spent more time secluded alone by the lake than was healthy. Ashley spent a lot of time cursing Doug that winter, cursing him for coming between her unfulfilled passion for Jimmy but at the same time, oddly enough, thanking him for keeping them celibate.

Spring brought baseball season and Jimmy had made the high school team, becoming their celebrated third baseman. Baseball, thankfully, required no organized cheerleading so Ashley went to all the games with Doug. She sat in the stands with him, staring dreamily out onto the field, watching Jimmy play.

One afternoon as she sat high atop the bleachers adjacent the baseball field at Pineville High, gazing adoringly toward third base, Ashley felt Doug's eyes on her and glanced over at him. "What?" she asked him, lowering her sunglasses to peer curiously at him. He wore an odd look on his face and he was smiling peculiarly at her.

"Nothing," he said, his eyes still fixed on her face.

She shifted self-consciously on the bleachers and pursed her lips in annoyance. "No really, Doug, why are you looking at me like that? You're making me paranoid."

"I've just never seen you like this before."

"Like what?" It was like pulling teeth to get a straight answer from him sometimes.

"You don't look at all like the Ice Princess that I know and love," Doug smiled fondly at his reference to her former alias. "You just glow. Your eyes are all bright and sparkling, and your cheeks are so rosy. You must be in love," he said, speculating poetically.

Ashley sensed that her cheeks were growing yet rosier as she flushed under his gaze. She avoided his eyes and fidgeted, finding the end of her long braid to occupy her fingers. "I am in love," she said, responding shyly while looking over at Jimmy. Feeling her eyes on him, Jimmy glanced her way, smiling softly at her before turning his concentration back on the game.

Doug grinned as he looked from Jimmy to Ashley. "Well, at least it's unanimous," he said, observing the look in Jimmy's eyes when he gazed over at her. "You really make him happy, Ashley."

"He makes me happy too, Doug," she beamed as Doug nodded in response.

"I hope that I find what you have some day," he sighed. Ashley blinked in surprise, finding it unusual for Doug to comment on his own romantic well being. That was her job.

"Doug, you have to date before you find love," she couldn't resist teasing him, still unable to understand why Doug showed so little interest in dating. He spent a lot of time with Jimmy and her, their ever-present chaperone, keeping them away from the lake and out of trouble.

"I'll date when I find someone fantastic," Doug squared his jaw stubbornly.

"Is she going to drop out of the sky?"

Doug looked fittingly annoyed, turning his attention back on the game in an effort to ignore her. Ashley patted his arm apologetically. "Okay, okay, I'll leave you alone about women, scout's honor."

"You are such a liar!" Doug winked at her, indicating that all was forgiven. They watched the ballgame, letting the subject of Doug's love life drop.

College picks became the talk of the town, dominating every social event Ashley and her friends frequented, and Jimmy didn't hesitate in his decision to attend Louisiana State with Will. He had made up his mind long before moving to Pineville and he hoped to influence Ashley and Doug to go there also.

The football team had barely finished with its state playoff game in November when scholarship offers began flooding in for Doug. The vast number of them clearly overwhelmed him. Every school in the state of Louisiana offered to sign him, as well as several colleges in the surrounding states. Doug had made his choice shortly after Valentine's Day, choosing Louisiana State University in Baton Rouge, influenced by state loyalty and Jimmy's insistence that he join him there to party with Will. Jimmy applauded Doug's choice and looked to Ashley, stating, "One down, one to go."

Ashley started putting together stories and articles to apply for a scholarship in journalism. She hadn't determined where she would go to college, leaning toward either Louisiana State or Northeast Louisiana University in Monroe. In the spring, Ashley received journalism scholarship offers from both and naturally accepted the offer to LSU so that she could be with Jimmy and Doug. She immediately began to try to persuade Kate to come with them.

"You are coming to Baton Rouge with us, aren't you?" Ashley asked her innocently as she lay sprawled out on the Ducotes' living room floor.

Kate lay flat on her back next to Ashley, watching the ceiling fan spinning high above their heads. She glanced at Ashley, wearing an extremely patient smile and shook her head, laughing at Ashley's persistence. "No, Ashley, I've told you a thousand times that I'm going to Northeast."

"Because Mitch is going there?" Ashley batted her eyelashes, teasingly accusing Kate of basing her choice on a man.

"No, not because Mitch is going there," Kate mocked Ashley in a singsong voice with a sarcastic imitation of her question. "I'm going there because I want to go there. *I* have a mind of my own."

"I can't believe you'd go off to school without me." Ashley's next ploy was the introduction of guilt into the equation. Kate rewarded her efforts with a knowing glance, regarding her suspiciously.

"Don't try that with me," she said, intuitively aware of exactly what Ashley was trying to do. "Ashley, we're coming to the point in our lives when we'll have to go our separate ways. We're not going to be together forever, you know."

"I don't see why not," Ashley, protesting, pushed herself into sitting position. "We've been together since birth. I'll miss you, Kate."

Kate smiled affectionately at Ashley and sat up to hug her reassuringly. "You'll always be my best friend, no matter what."

"And you'll always be mine," Ashley said. "But I still don't see why you can't come to LSU with me." Kate grinned exasperatedly and punched her arm, letting her know that the discussion was officially over.

There was no way in the world that Susanna would consider going to college. "Do you honestly think that I would *pay* someone to make me study?" her face reflected the anguish the thought of studying inflicted upon her, throwing Ashley into gales of laughter with her indignant expression. "You've got to be crazy if you think I'm going to college with y'all."

"So what are you going to do? A little moonlighting at the 7-Eleven or what?"

Susanna answered with a wry smirk. "No, smart ass, I have a job, remember?" Susanna had taken a part-time job at one of the local banks and at last found her niche. She had a surprising head for figures and her supervisor at the bank had been so impressed that he offered Susanna a full-time job after graduation.

With her two closest girlfriends deserting her, Ashley resigned herself to the fact that she would have to take the luck of the draw with a roommate. She sighed with frustration, voicing her dilemma to Jimmy as she lay locked tightly in his arms on a blanket by the lake one early spring afternoon.

"That's okay," Jimmy reassured her, rolling over to face her. "You'll be with me most of the time anyway."

"Oh, you think so?" she wiggled out of his embrace, sitting up to tease him with her lighthearted laugh.

"I know so. In fact, after Will graduates next year, you can just move in with me and Doug."

"What makes you think that I want to live with you and Doug?" Ashley cocked her head to the side, her eyes defiantly flashing her independence.

"Okay, so we'll kick Doug out and you can live with me," Jimmy leaned over to kiss her lips invitingly. She returned his kiss with a good-natured smirk, laughing skeptically under her breath.

"I can see that going over well with Remy," she said, murmuring even though his mouth was still locked on hers. Jimmy gave up on kissing her and leaned back on the palms of his hands, grinning over at her in amusement.

"Jimmy, Remy likes you and all, but I can't imagine him condoning our shacking up together in Tiger Country."

"If I can't convince him to let you live with me in sin, then you'll just have to marry me," Jimmy winked at her, the extraordinary twinkle in his eyes telling her that he was completely sincere in his proposal. Ashley flung her arms around his neck with all her might, knocking him backward onto the ground and landing on top of him, kissing him enthusiastically.

The crunching gravel on the adjacent road caught their attention and they glanced up to see Doug jumping out of his car.

"I knew I'd find you two here!" he called out to them as he sauntered their way. Jimmy gave him an impatient stare.

"Doug, buddy," he said as he pushed himself up onto his elbows. "You've got to let us have a little time alone."

Doug wrinkled his brow impatiently. "Whatever for?" he chuckled heartily at Jimmy and Ashley's identical glares of irritation. "Okay, okay, I get it. But Ma sent me to find y'all. She's got a pot of crawfish etouffee on the stove just screaming out your names."

Jimmy and Ashley exchanged an eager glance. Ms. Bobbie Fairchild's crawfish etouffee was too mouth-watering to pass up, even for an afternoon of passion under blue skies and pine trees. They scrambled to their feet, snatching the blanket from the ground and tossing it into the back of Jimmy's pickup, then followed Doug as he led the way to Ms. Bobbie's Cajun cuisine.

From that day forward, Ashley Stewart and Jimmy Moreau plotted their future together. Their plans were so simple, so straightforward and so wonderful.

Ashley was ecstatically head over heels in love, having no reason not to trust that their dreams of a lavish white wedding, beautiful children and abundant grandchildren would come to pass. At that point, nothing had happened in her life to make her doubtful, cynical or afraid to believe.

But that would soon change.

CHAPTER NINE

The last big event before graduation was junior/senior prom, held the last weekend in April. Ashley slept late on prom day, resting up for the coming night since Remy had finally granted her request allowing her to stay out the entire night. She was thrilled. She didn't know what they would do all night, but there was no way that she was coming home before dawn.

She broke with tradition, wearing a short party dress to prom, a strapless black gown with a velvet bodice and full chiffon skirt. Kate came over mid-afternoon, uncharacteristically rebellious in the fact that she had elected to attend the prom that year. She'd kept her dress, a dazzling silver number, hidden in Ashley's closet for weeks. Ashley looked up from polishing her nails as Kate waltzed into the bedroom.

"Where are you telling your folks you're going tonight?" Ashley didn't know how Kate was going to get away with going to the dance. Her parents were bound to know that it was prom night.

Kate giggled as she plopped down on the bed beside her, earning an annoyed stare from Ashley for fouling up her polish job. "I came right out and told them that it was my senior prom and I was going with Mitch," she smiled broadly and Ashley jerked upright, her jaw dropping in shock.

"No way! What did they say?" Ashley could only imagine the scene that had unfolded at the Ducote home, envisioning Frank's normally kind smile hardening into a tense, disappointed pucker, and Imogene swooning dramatically onto the sofa.

Kate dashed her animated image with her answer. "They actually took it better than I thought. They gave me the speech about my being eighteen now and capable of making my own decisions," she smiled as she recalled their words. "They also said that I had better have my happy butt back in that house before dawn," she added with a merry chuckle.

"Good God, Ashley," Susanna burst through the bedroom door, her gold sequined gown draped haphazardly over her arm. "What the hell are you yelling about?" she eyed Kate and Ashley suspiciously, wondering what she had missed. Upon hearing Kate's news, she grinned naughtily, "I'm proud of you, Katie. It's about time you got some balls!" she said, ignoring Kate's pained wince at her crudity.

Doug was taking Cheryl Moreau to the prom. Remembering his resistance to dating Cheryl in the past, Ashley wondered at his choice.

"Why Cheryl?" she asked after hearing of his decision. They had been sitting alone, shoulder to shoulder on the Stewarts' front porch steps as they often had in the days before Jimmy.

"How can you go wrong with the cousin of your best friend?" he nudged her shoulder and smiled whimsically. "Besides, I consider Cheryl a pretty safe date."

"Safe? What are you protecting yourself from?" Ashley shook her head in bewilderment. The boy was a mystery to her.

"I don't want to make any attachments here before I leave for school," he said with an unconcerned shrug.

"I don't know why you think that's going to happen. You've managed quite nicely to avoid any attachments for the last four years."

"Don't start with me, Ashley," his raised eyebrows warned her not to continue down her present path. "I don't know why you are always so concerned about my love life."

"Now, Doug, don't be that way. You know I love you and just want you to be happy."

"I am happy, *perfectly* happy with things just the way they are," he said huffily.

Ashley hurriedly changed the subject, not wanting to spoil the quality time they had been sharing on the front steps. But her desire to help Doug find happiness lingered just below the surface, waiting for an opportune moment to again raise its unwanted head.

Doug, Jimmy, Mitch and Scotty rented a limousine for the evening, picking the girls up at Ashley's house a little before seven. Cheryl, whose long white dress clung to her curves in a most complementary manner, accompanied them.

Ashley commented on how terrific she looked and snidely whispered to Doug, "She might not be as safe as you thought," earning a sullen scowl for her effort. She smirked up at him before taking Jimmy's outstretched hand and rushed to the car.

Riding together in the limousine was a blast. They cranked the radio up and the eight of them shouted deafeningly over each other, driving the chauffeur insane. Ashley sat encircled in Jimmy's arms, bickering with Doug as usual. Heated debating had become great sport for the two of them and luckily, Jimmy seemed most entertained by it all.

Cheryl stared incredulously at Doug and Ashley as they argued in the back of the limousine, glancing abruptly away from them with a deeply wrinkled brow, directing her look to Jimmy, "What is it with them?"

"Nothing, they do this all the time," he reminded her with a grin. "Remember, you were the one who warned me about it when I first met them."

"And their constant heckling of each other doesn't bother you?"

"Not in the least," Jimmy playfully kissed Ashley's cheek as he answered Cheryl. "If they're not fighting, they're not happy."

After a profoundly sentimental senior prom filled with memorable dances and special kisses, they left the convention center for party rooms at various hotels around Alexandria. Arriving at the reserved suite, which was nothing fancy but a great place to party, several poker games sprang up immediately, like mushrooms after a summer rain.

Ashley circled the room, talking with the other girls deserted by their card-playing dates. She joined Kate and Susanna, finding them leaning against one wall, drinking beer and critically viewing the table full of men deeply engrossed in stud poker.

"I'm certainly glad that I fought Dad tooth and nail to stay out all night just so I could watch Scotty play poker," Susanna huffed to Kate, who nodded sympathetically in agreement. Mitch was completely absorbed in the game and, after winning the previous three hands, showed no signs of folding any time soon.

"I think it's become a custom for the senior guys to play cards on prom night," Ashley interjected, leaning up against the wall beside them.

"Well, it's a stupid custom," Susanna stuck out her bottom lip in a testy pout. "Whatever happened to the time-honored tradition of getting laid on prom night?"

Ashley suppressed a broad grin, giggling soundlessly as she slipped away to the ladies room. As she exited the rest room, a strong arm swathed in a black tuxedo jacket halted her return to the party suite. Startled, Ashley glanced up into the mischievously dancing eyes of Jimmy Moreau.

"Come with me," he whispered, taking her hand. They slipped silently from the room and Jimmy glanced cautiously over his shoulder, ushering her hurriedly down the corridor. Plucking a key from his jacket pocket, he unlocked a door at the end of the hall, yanking her quickly inside.

"What's the big rush, mister?" her bubbly laughter filled the room as she surveyed the relieved look on his face as he shut the door and leaned up against it. Jimmy grinned appreciatively.

"We had to get inside before Doug spotted us. It's a shame when I hide from my best friend to get some time alone with my girlfriend," he removed his jacket, tossing it carelessly on the bed before turning to take her into his warm embrace.

Ashley's heart thumped wildly, hammering skittishly with anticipation and naïve fear of the unknown. In all this time together, she and Jimmy had never made love and while she wanted to with all her heart, she was scared to death. His impassioned kisses filled her with wanton desire and as her expectations grew, an involuntary shudder jarred her entire body.

Jimmy stopped kissing her and gazed into her face with concerned, caring eyes. "Sugar, are you scared?"

She nodded her honest answer. "Yes," she whispered shyly.

He embraced her tenderly, kissing the top of her head affectionately. "Do you want to leave?" There was no pressure from him, only thoughts for her well being, which only made Ashley love him more.

"No, I don't want to leave," she whispered, showing no hesitation in her response.

Jimmy gave her a soft smile, cupping her small face in his hands and began to kiss her, beginning with soft butterfly kisses on her closed eyelids then moving slowly down her cheeks until reaching her waiting lips. Their kisses became more feverish and intense as they moved mindlessly from their position in front of the door and fell recklessly onto the bed, carelessly shedding their clothing as their passion grew. Then, at long last, Ashley and Jimmy made love.

Afterward as they lay with arms and legs entwined, Jimmy kissed her forehead gently. "Are you okay?" He was so sweet and concerned about her. Ashley snuggled against him, purring with contentment.

"Yes, I'm fine," she sighed blissfully. It really had been worth the wait. She settled her head on his chest and listened to the steady rhythm of his heart, perfectly willing just to lie there with him forever.

Jimmy rolled his head to the side, eyeing the clock on the bedside table. "Honey, it's four o'clock. We're going to have to go soon," he said quietly, his regret at the thought of leaving the hotel room, making their first time together become only a memory, showing in the depths of his brown eyes.

"Do we have to?" Ashley too was reluctant to return to the real world. She gazed longingly at Jimmy, silently pleading to stay just a bit longer.

He chuckled at her sad, puppy-dog eyes, struggling to remain firm in his resolve to get her home on time. "Yes, Ashley. Remy will kick my butt if I don't have you home by daybreak."

"We still have a little time left." She pulled him to her, kissing him invitingly, and they made use of the time they had left before dressing and leaving for home.

Needless to say, their relationship was slightly different after prom night. They looked for opportunities to be alone together and all but deserted Doug.

"Y'all are pitiful," he protested when they begged him to let them be alone. Jimmy pulled into the parking lot of McDonalds, hoping to pawn his best buddy off on someone else.

"Two's company, three's a crowd, buddy," Jimmy reminded him, pointing to the passenger door, silently ordering Doug out of the truck.

"Does this mean that I never get to go out with y'all again?" Doug opened the door, looking back over his shoulder at them dismally.

"This means that you may have to get your own date. I'm through sharing Ashley with you," Jimmy smiled broadly as Doug scowled at him, slamming the door shut.

Doug leaned his head back into the window, ignoring Jimmy and giving Ashley a droll look. "Traitor! And after all we've been to each other."

Ashley grinned as he turned away from them, swaggering into the restaurant. Women seemed to crawl out of the woodwork to be near him, instantly surrounding him the minute he opened the door. Ashley watched him circle the room, trailed by girls everywhere he went, shaking her head in wonder.

"I wish Doug would break down and get a steady girlfriend," she spoke aloud to Jimmy, sipping her Coke thoughtfully as she winked at him.

"I don't think it's going to happen any time soon," Jimmy said, surveying the swirling crowd of doting females enfolding his best buddy.

"Why not? There's lots of cute girls in there."

"Not gonna happen, Sugar. Trust me, none of those girls will do. He has some ideal in mind and won't be satisfied until he has her."

Jimmy's revelation peaked Ashley's interest and she regarded him with probing eyes. "What's his ideal?" she asked, foolishly thinking that, just perhaps, Jimmy might reveal all to her in a weak moment.

"I'll never tell," Jimmy said, dashing her hopes while teasing her, giving Ashley the impression that he knew much more than he was telling her. He further distracted her by whispering suggestively in her ear, "Let's dump Doug with those lucky women and go to the lake."

Ashley accepted his proposition with a playful grin and Jimmy turned the key in the truck's ignition, firing up the engine. Doug's head jerked around in their direction and he scowled unpleasantly while Jimmy waved obnoxiously to him as they pulled away.

Although momentarily distracted by Jimmy's charming ways, the very next morning Ashley became a girl with a mission. If Doug Fairchild had an ideal, Ashley would find her. She would make it her sisterly duty, wanting for him the same blissful happiness she shared with Jimmy.

Graduation, the long awaited day in every scholar's life, arrived in mid-May. Ashley donned the dove gray cap and gown the afternoon of commencement, scarcely able to fathom her reflection in the mirror. She was graduating. She thought this day would never come. She rode to graduation with her parents with Maggie, clutching a wadded tissue to her red-tipped nose, bursting into tears every time she looked at her.

"Will you have her hormones checked?" Ashley said, pleading with her father. Remy grinned mischievously, looking at her in the rearview mirror as they shared a laugh together.

"Well, I'm glad you two find this so funny. My only baby is graduating and leaving home. I have every right to cry if I want to," Maggie huffed to them, her holly-green eyes once more overflowing with tears.

From Cheryl Moreau's valedictorian address to Ted Robicheaux dancing in the aisles as Susanna received her diploma, the commencement ceremony was bittersweet, an unrealistic blur brimming with mixed emotions. Ashley was ecstatic to be graduating and to be finished with that phase of her life. However, as it drew to a close and she watched her lifelong friends toss their hats into the air with wild abandon, Ashley was filled with sadness knowing that they would never be together this way again.

After graduation, she met them in the lobby of the gym, her forever friends Kathryn Anne Ducote and Lily Susanna Robicheaux. Susanna was whooping wildly, waving above her head the cylinder of white paper tied in red satin ribbon, her proof of a diploma finally earned. She displayed it proudly to anyone who would give her the time of day.

"I did it, I did it," her repeated singsong echoed through the lobby and she gaily disregarded the fact that she looked like a blithering idiot. Kate and Ashley exchanged an entertained look, then, when they couldn't take it any longer, each linked an arm through one of Susanna's, pulling her out the doors of the gym to Scotty's waiting vehicle.

Ashley rode with Jimmy, Doug, Kate and Mitch to the graduation party Maggie and Remy were giving for all her friends and their families. They were a jovial crew, filled with celebratory adrenaline, joking and teasing one another, the sound of John Cougar crooning from Doug's cassette player providing a background for their chatter.

As they came to a stop in front of the Stewarts' illuminated house, Doug produced a beer for everyone from the ice chest behind the front seat. "A toast!" he declared. "To the graduating class of Pineville High School, may all our dreams come true."

"Here, here!" they toasted, clinking their bottles together and quickly downing their beers before going into the party. Ashley and Jimmy played doorman, welcoming their friends and families with huge smiles lighting their faces. Will arrived with Lana and John and embraced Ashley heartily, pulling her aside.

"I just wanted to tell you congratulations and that I'm looking forward to having you as a roommate at LSU," his eyes danced merrily as he kidded her. "My brother is so excited over you coming to school with him that we can hardly stand to be around him."

"You can throw me out of the apartment any time you want to," Ashley smiled brightly as she returned his ribbing.

"Who said anything about wanting to throw you out?" Will's face grew more mischievous with each passing moment, leading Jimmy to intervene. He stood in front of Will with his arms folded across his chest.

"Are you trying to pick up my girlfriend, Bro?" Jimmy said, pretending to scowl at Will, suppressing his irresistible boyish grin as well as he could.

"Well, if the girl wants to marry a Moreau, I'm obviously the better choice," Will shot back at him, displaying a devilish smile as Jimmy punched his arm.

Ashley smiled at their facetious sparring, admiring the bond they shared. She'd never seen closer brothers. Will lifted Ashley's hand to his lips, kissing it lightly.

"Until Baton Rouge, mon amour," he raised his eyebrows flirtatiously. "Then you shall see who is the better man." He whistled a jolly tune as he rounded the corner, heading toward the overflowing buffet tables that were groaning from the weight of Ms. Bobbie's delectable entrees and Lana's elegantly iced cakes.

"Come with me," Jimmy took advantage of their first moment alone, reaching for Ashley's hand and pulling her toward the stairs.

"Where are you taking me, little boy?" she teased him as she followed him willingly upstairs. He glanced back at her over his shoulder, flashing his perfect smile at her clever insinuation.

"I have something to give you," he said, causing her to raise an eyebrow at him.

"Here? I don't think my father will like that!" Ashley continued to terrorize him as they took a seat at the top of the stairs.

"Happy graduation," he said, presenting her with a small wrapped package from his shirt pocket.

Ashley blinked with surprise. "I didn't know we were exchanging gifts! I don't have anything for you."

Jimmy smiled, shaking his head reassuringly. "You're all I need." He softly kissed her lips. "Open your present." He nudged her impatiently with his shoulder and Ashley tore the paper, lifting the lid of the small black velvet box underneath. Inside was a silver band of X's and O's.

"Jimmy, it's beautiful!" her face flushed with happiness as she slipped the ring onto her left ring finger. She held her hand up into the light streaming down the hallway behind them, admiring the shining band. Jimmy reached up to take her hand.

"So you'll always remember my hugs and kisses," he explained, pointing to the X's and O's on the band.

Ashley cupped his face tenderly in her hands. "I love it!" she said, touching the tip of her nose to his.

"Just wait until you see the next ring I put on your finger," Jimmy said as Ashley kissed him passionately, enfolded in his fond embrace.

They rejoined the party downstairs before Remy sent out a search party for them. Remy pulled Kate, Susanna, Doug, Jimmy and her to one side of the room, placing a bright pink package in Ashley's hands. "We have a present for you," he said as Maggie looked on from over his shoulder, beaming eagerly.

Ashley opened it to find a shiny gold key inside and a miniature umbrella, like the colorful ones used in frozen daiquiris. She held up the key ring, glancing at Remy questioningly.

"Hot damn, a new car!" Susanna bellowed, beside herself with excitement as she gripped Ashley's arm.

"No, it's not a new car," Remy chuckled good-naturedly at Susanna's outburst. "That's a key to the condo in Florida. Maggie and I are letting you all have it all to yourselves for a graduation trip."

Kate, Susanna and Ashley squealed excitedly, jumping up and down with glee, and Doug and Jimmy grinned, covering their ears to muffle their wild shrieking. Ashley flung her arms around Remy's neck. "Thank you, thank you!" she kissed his cheek. "That's a terrific gift."

Ashley loved Destin, having been there every summer for as long as she could recall. To her, Destin was the closest thing to heaven that earth could offer. It was breathtaking, the snowy-white sand so soft and so fine, like grains of sugar, and the water, the clean blue-green water, so clear that one could see straight to the bottom. Staying there for a week, in her parents' condominium on the beach off old Highway 98 would be the perfect graduation gift for them. Seven endless days of lying in the sun, snorkeling in the surf, eating wonderfully fresh seafood and spending their evenings out dancing at the local clubs.

When the party broke up, Ashley's close friends stayed to help clean up, and after finishing, they gathered on the front porch, still chattering excitedly over the Stewarts' unexpected graduation present. "So, when are we leaving for Florida?" Susanna asked.

"Next weekend," Ashley said, balancing on the rail where she perched, swinging her legs in a carefree fashion. "Let's leave early on Saturday morning and get there in time to catch some rays."

She gazed up at Jimmy to see if he was in agreement and he smiled uneasily at her, then glanced at Doug, who nodded, urging him to say something. "Ashley, Doug and I were talking and we decided to pass on the trip," Jimmy said.

"Why?" Her eyes blinked in bewilderment as she frowned, her feelings injured by his surprise announcement.

Jimmy was quick to explain. "This will be the last trip you girls get to take together before the 'perfect trio' parts and you go your separate ways," he said. "Doug and I thought that it might be better if we stayed here and let you all go alone."

"That's so sweet of you guys," Kate said, kissing both of them on the cheek. "It's been a long time since Ashley, Susanna and I have road-tripped together. We'll enjoy having a bonding week"

"Not to mention picking up old men in Speedo's," Susanna recalled one of their favorite adolescent pastimes of critiquing men in their swimsuits and snickered devilishly at the memory.

Jimmy and Ashley spent the entire next week together, taking pleasure in their first week of freedom from the drudgeries of required education. Remy let her off work at the drugstore until after the trip to Florida. She and Jimmy goofed off during the day, swimming and going to the movies, and spent their nights shaping their plans for LSU and making love under the stars. Being with Jimmy Moreau was all that Ashley ever wanted, and she felt as if she couldn't spend enough time with him.

The Friday night before leaving for Florida, Ashley had dinner with Jimmy and his parents. After dessert, the two of them went back to her house and sat together on the front steps. It was getting late, but Ashley didn't want Jimmy to go.

"Are you sure you won't go with me to Florida?" she half-asked and half-pleaded with him, hoping to change his mind at the last minute.

"Ashley, I know it'll be tough to be apart," he said with a soft smile. "I'm dreading it too, but I really think you should spend the time with Kate and Susanna. You're going to miss them next year. Believe me, you'll have your fill of Doug and me at school."

"What are y'all going to do while I'm gone?"

"Probably just fish a lot and goof off. I have to make up with Doug. He's still pouting because we've neglected him so badly." Jimmy winked as he kidded her.

"We'll go to Baton Rouge and visit Will as soon as you get back," Jimmy promised as Ashley encircled her arms around his neck, pulling his face even with her own.

"I still wish that you would go with me. Think of all the fun we could have in the sand."

"I'll go with you the next time, I promise," Jimmy chuckled lightly, sealing his vow with an impassioned kiss. "I better go," he sighed regretfully, rising to stand in front of her.

"I don't want to let you go," Ashley said, sadness ringing true in her soft voice. Jimmy took her hands, pulling her up from her seat on the steps.

"I'll be here waiting for you when you come home on Friday. Then you're mine the rest of the summer." He smiled, kissing her again as Ashley walked him to the truck. "I love you, Ashley," he said as he climbed into the driver's seat.

"I love you too, Jimmy," she beamed up at him adoringly, bidding him a fond farewell with her vivacious smile.

"I'll call you tomorrow night," he called out his window as he drove away. Ashley waved and went inside.

The three girls hit the highway at four the next morning with Ashley's sleepy parents waving goodbye after issuing stern warning for them to be careful on the trip. Ashley sipped coffee and drove while Susanna entertained her with lively conversation and Kate dozed in the backseat. They drove the Corolla south through the bustling city of Baton Rouge and then east from Slidell, Louisiana, through the gulf-side cities of Biloxi, Mississippi, and Mobile, Alabama. After stopping for a late breakfast in Mobile, they drove speedily on to Destin, arriving shortly after noon.

Ashley surveyed her surroundings with excitement, taking in the spectacular view from atop the East Pass Bridge as she drove across. Below them, jetties and snow-white sand bordered the clear waters of the gulf, its colors ranging from the palest emerald to the most vibrant aquamarine. Ashley never grew tired of being there. Destin was as beautiful each morning as it had been the day before.

They unloaded the car at the condo then immediately threw on their swimsuits and ran to the beach like children, splashing haphazardly into the surf. After wearing themselves out in the waves, they sat under striped beach umbrellas, drinking sodas and watching the people walking along the shore.

Late that afternoon, they dragged their things indoors and showered so they could go out to dinner. Ashley gazed around the familiar interior of the condominium, its décor screaming of Maggie with its dominating pastel shades of green and pink. She phoned Remy and Maggie to let them know that she had arrived safely. Susanna and Kate had finished getting ready for dinner and were impatiently waiting for her to get off the phone. Ashley hung up with her parents and as they were leaving, the phone rang again. Susanna moaned and threw herself in a chair while Ashley answered the phone.

Jimmy's voice rang out over the line. "Hi, you all made it safely, I see. Having fun?"

Ashley smiled at the warm, melodic sound of his voice, instantly missing him and yearning to be with him. "Yes, we're having a great time. We're on our way to dinner." She indicated to Susanna and Kate that she was talking to Jimmy and they started to bellow in protest.

"We're starving, Jimmy!" Susanna yelled out.

"We've only been gone fourteen hours, Jim! Give it a rest," Kate joined in on the harassment.

Jimmy started laughing, noting their annoyance with his phone call. "I better let you go before there's a mutiny."

"That might be best, they're pretty ruthless," Ashley giggled. "I love you, Jimmy." She encircled the receiver tightly with both hands, wishing she could feel the warmth of him over those endless miles of telephone lines. Friday was forever away.

"I love you too, Sugar," he couldn't resist teasing her with his pet name, knowing that she was giving him an irritated glare even though he was hundreds of miles away. "I'll call you Monday night." They reluctantly hung up and Ashley left with the ravenous Kate and Susanna for dinner.

They spent all day Sunday at the beach. It was a fantastic day, perfect for the beach: warm, but not too hot and filled with everlasting sunshine. The girls floated on rafts in the warm gulf water, sunning themselves in jewel-toned bikinis and walking up and down the beach, taking in the marvelous sights in the form of breathtaking landscapes and muscular physiques. Sunday night was spent watching movies and making margaritas with the ingredients Ashley's folks had left behind from a previous visit. They stayed up late and slept in Monday morning before returning for another day of fun and sun at the beach.

CHAPTER TEN

Ashley, Kate and Susanna came back from the beach that Monday afternoon, tanned and laughing, without a care in the world. The only thing on their minds was what they wanted for dinner and whether to walk on the beach that evening or watch a movie instead. Covered completely with suntan lotion, sand and surf, they immediately hit the showers. Kate and Ashley finished and waited for Susanna in the living room.

"Where do you want to eat tonight?" Ashley asked, lying back on the couch, flinging her legs carelessly over its arm.

Kate shrugged indifferently. "I'm happy with anything," she smiled expansively, patting her stomach playfully at the thought of another fine meal, "as long as it's seafood."

"I don't think that's much of a problem down here," Ashley said, just as the phone rang from its place on the bar across the room. Ashley scrambled up off the couch and scampered over to answer its beckoning ring, hoping profusely that it was Jimmy on the other end of the line. She hadn't talked to him since Saturday afternoon and was starting to have withdrawals. Kate and Susanna were loads of fun but could hardly replace the constant yearning she had for him.

Ashley grasped the receiver eagerly, greeting the caller on the line with an effervescent "Hello!"

Looking back, Ashley could still hear how odd Doug's voice sounded on the other end of the phone, "Ashley?"

"Hi, Dougie! Are you missing me too?" she greeted him jovially, not missing the opportunity to trade punches with him. "It must be pretty bad there without me if even *you're* phoning."

Doug ignored her invitation to brawl. "Ashley, you have to come home, honey." Although he tried very hard to be soothing, there was something in his tone—something very disconcerting. His ordinarily feisty voice was a lifeless monotone, leaving Ashley somewhat puzzled.

"Come home?" she blurted into the phone, struggling between scorn and confusion over his unusual request. "We've only been here two days! Surely you guys can't miss us that much already," Ashley teased him mercilessly, seeking to cheer him up, to bring him out of the black mood in which he appeared to be.

Susanna bounced into the room, eyeing Ashley with amusement and Kate's bubbly laughter filled the room like tinkling chimes. Ashley grinned impishly at them, glad that, at least, they were willing to play with her.

"Ashley, let me talk to Kate, " Doug continued speaking in a wooden, distant voice, making Ashley even more concerned with his behavior.

"Is everything okay, Doug? You don't sound like yourself at all." She looked at Kate and Susanna, wrinkling her brow, conveying to them that something was definitely up with Doug.

"Kate, Ashley. Just get Kate." At least in his aggravation over her stubbornness, Doug allowed some sort of emotion to reflect in his tone.

"I don't know what's wrong with him," Ashley shrugged her shoulders, whispering loudly as she handed Kate the receiver. "I've never known him to act so strange, even in the days when he was a little strange."

Kate frowned, perplexed as she accepted the phone, placing the receiver up to her ear. "Hi, Doug," she said, somewhat hesitantly.

Those were the last words she got in. Ashley watched Kate as she listened to Doug, becoming anxious as Kate's face paled and her eyes grew wide with shock and disbelief. She cast many small, discreet glances Ashley's way and Ashley got right in her face, dancing impatiently, demanding to know what was wrong.

"Yes, Doug, we'll be home in a few hours," Kate replaced the receiver and stood speechlessly with her hand on the telephone for what seemed like an eternity. Susanna and Ashley exchanged questioning stares.

"What is it, Kate?" Susanna said, unwilling to stand being left in the dark any longer. Ashley squirmed restlessly beside Susanna, awaiting some explanation for Doug's mysterious call.

"Sit down, Ashley," Kate commanded quietly, keeping her back to them.

"Shit, Kate, don't be so dramatic. She doesn't need to sit down," Susanna scowled at Kate's back, shaking her head impatiently.

"Ashley, please just sit down," Kate repeated her request. Ashley shrugged at Susanna, who answered with a scornful roll of her eyes. Obediently, Ashley sat on the edge of the couch, fidgeting with her hands in her lap.

"All right, Katie, she's sitting down. Now, spill," Susanna said, seating herself on the coffee table in front of Ashley.

Very slowly and deliberately, Kate turned to face them. Her face was ashen, her eyes brimming with tears that threatened to spill over onto her delicate cheekbones. Ashley stared blankly at Kate, feeling a prickling sensation crawling up her spine, sensing that something was horribly wrong.

"Kate," she said, beginning to rise from her position on the couch, but Kate stopped her with a light touch on the shoulder.

"Sit down, Ashley," she said softly, her voice wavering, threatening to crack at any moment.

"I don't want to sit down," Ashley said, her voice becoming high and hysterical. "I want you to tell me what in the hell is going on!"

Kate gently pushed her to sit fully on the couch and Susanna moved beside her, looking from Kate to Ashley, questioning Kate silently through narrowed eyes. Kate took the place on the coffee table directly in front of them.

"Ashley, I stood by that telephone trying desperately to find the right words to tell you this," she said, hesitating, grasping for the easiest way to say what she had to say. She cleared her throat as her eyes misted over again. "Ashley, there's been an accident."

Ashley's eyes widened in alarm and she stared soundlessly at Kate.

"Could you be a little more specific?" Wide-eyed, Susanna urged Kate to continue.

"Is it my folks?" Ashley's tormented face begged Kate for a straight answer. She sat on the edge of the sofa, her heart pounding anxiously in her chest, ready to race to the telephone and call home, just to make sure Maggie and Remy were okay.

Kate didn't move. She remained seated, staring at Ashley through sorrow-etched eyes as she revealed the terrible truth. "No, Ashley, it wasn't your folks. It was Jimmy," she paused, wanting so much to spare Ashley's feelings but realizing that when the truth was known, her grief was inevitable. Kate took a deep breath and told all. "Ashley, Jimmy's gone. He died this morning in a car wreck."

The icy feeling that came over Ashley at that moment was indescribable. It was as if a cold fist tightened around her heart, cutting off all warmth to her soul. She could hear her own pulse roaring in her ears, and her mind reeled, vibrating at the speed of light. As the entire room began to spin, she thought she might faint. Swaying, she steadied herself by grasping the arm of the sofa.

Then she began to scream, letting out a strangled cry that rapidly rose to a hysterical shriek. "No! No, no, no!" Ashley pounded Kate with her fists. "You're lying to me. There's no way that he's gone! He's at home right now, waiting for me. I know he is."

Kate pulled her tightly against her, encircling Ashley in her comforting arms, rocking her slowly back and forth. Ashley broke down and sobbed, devastated. Susanna patted Ashley's back distractedly, standing beside her in shocked silence, the color draining from her face as she blinked back uncharacteristic tears.

Ashley wept in Kate's embrace, blocking her words from her disbelieving mind. Ashley prayed for the phone to ring, for someone to tell them that Doug had been mistaken. She waited in vain, knowing in the back of her mind that the call would not be coming.

When she could cry no more, Ashley wrenched herself from Kate's arms, staggering to the window to stare forlornly out at the brilliant sunset and the magnificent waves crashing onto the sandy shore. She was stunned, unable to grasp that Jimmy was gone and she would never see or talk to him again. Please, God, please, she pleaded silently, not Jimmy. Tell me this is a mistake, that he's not really gone.

But she knew. The dull, empty ache gnawing at her soul told her that Jimmy was forever lost to all on this earth. All their plans for a lifetime together were gone in a matter of minutes, leaving her completely shattered. A large portion of Ashley's heart died that day as she stood staring out at the gulf. She knew in that instant that her life would never be the same.

Kate phoned Maggie, telling her that they knew about Jimmy. Ashley vaguely heard her talking. "Ashley, come talk to your mother, sweetie," Kate quietly beckoned her to the phone.

Ashley wasn't ready to talk to anyone. She was unwilling to admit the truth out loud. She kept her back to Kate, staring out at the water as she shook her head adamantly in answer to Kate's request. She could hear the muffled undertones of the remainder of the conversation with Maggie but had no idea what Kate was saying. She heard only the sounds without absorbing the words.

Susanna left Ashley alone in the living room, casting one last, woeful look in her direction before obediently trudging upstairs behind Kate to help gather their scattered belongings. As they packed, Ashley slipped out the door and stumbled blindly across the sand to the water's edge. Her legs were so rubbery that she could no longer stand and she sunk, paralyzed, onto the sand. She couldn't cry anymore. She was too numb to cry. She didn't notice the salty water washing up onto her clothing or the wet sand clinging to her skin. She just sat, oblivious to it all, staring with pain-filled eyes into the clear emerald water with Jimmy's sweet face haunting her mind, making every deal she would make with God, begging him to return Jimmy to her.

She didn't know how long she'd been there when Kate found her. Kate bent down, gently pulling Ashley up out of the water. "We've got the car loaded, sweetie," she said. "Let's get you inside and put on something dry to travel in."

Taking her by the hand, Kate led her slowly back to the condominium, her heart breaking as she studied the lost expression fixed on Ashley's pale face. She wanted so badly to comfort her, to say the right words to make it better, to take some of the sting out of such a cruel blow. But there were no words that could possibly change how Ashley was feeling, so Kate remained quiet, handing Ashley a dry pair of shorts and a T-shirt. Like a zombie, Ashley changed clothes and followed Kate out to the car.

Ashley could hardly recall the ride home from Florida. She lay in the narrow back seat of her beloved Corolla, curled into fetal position, her body numb and wracked with convulsions of grief. With an aching heart, she relived every moment she had shared with Jimmy Moreau, etching him into her memory forever.

They arrived in Pineville the next morning, just as the sun was peeking its fiery head over the horizon. Kate dropped Susanna at home before wearily pulling into the circle drive in front of the Stewarts'. Kate opened the door and Ashley climbed slowly out of the back seat to stagger up the front steps of her home. Remy was in the kitchen waiting for them to arrive and the minute she saw him, Ashley fell into his arms and began to wail, heartbroken.

Remy stroked her soft hair, whispering to her soothingly. "I'm so sorry, baby. I'm so sorry," he said, holding her closely. She lay her head on his shoulder; grateful for the comfort that only her father could give.

Kate sat down in the kitchen, its cheery décor mocking her sorrow, and wearily rested her forehead on the palm of her hand. She was completely drained both from the long drive from Florida and from the terrible, heart-wrenching reality of losing a good friend.

As Ashley pulled reluctantly away from Remy's consoling embrace, he took her by the hand into the den where Doug was asleep on the couch. She glanced inquiringly up at her father. "He's been here all night, waiting for you," Remy said, patting her shoulder before leaving her with Doug.

She sat on the couch beside Doug's curly blond head as he stirred, opening his eyes and appearing momentarily confused, unsure of where he was. With a start, Doug remembered the circumstances of being on the Stewarts' plaid sofa and sat up with a jolt, rubbing his blood-shot eyes and stretching exhaustedly. He glanced over at Ashley with the saddest pair of eyes she had ever seen. "Are you all right?"

"No, I'm not all right." Her lifeless voice was strained as she lay her head wearily against the back of the couch. She really and truly did not want to talk about it but she had to know what had happened. "When did it happen, Doug?" she said, whispering hoarsely as she rolled her head to the side to look at him. "Were you with him?"

Appearing uncomfortable, Doug cleared his throat, averting his eyes before supplying her with the details. "We went fishing," he began. "We took my car to the lake just down the road from the Moreaus'. We had just settled down on the dock to fish when Jimmy remembered something he wanted to use, some special lure or something, I can't remember exactly what now."

Doug stared off into space, his eyes transfixed with shock and grief as he called forth the prominent details from his mind. "I tossed him my keys and he took off running, bellowing like a goon that he would be right back. He looked just like a little kid, running in his shorts with his ball cap on backwards, giving

me that stupid grin of his, you know, the goofy one that you loved so much."
Doug glanced over at her. Ashley nodded, envisioning Jimmy's boyish, smiling
face as he raced through the trees toward the car parked on the shoulder of the
highway.

"Anyway," Doug swallowed hard and continued, "you know how sharp that
curve is that runs in front of that lake?" Ashley nodded again, urging him to go
on, yet not wanting to hear.

"This guy in a huge pickup was hauling ass down Highway 28. I guess Jimmy
never saw him coming around that curve. He pulled across the highway right into
the truck's path. The truck hit him on the driver's side." Tears were coursing
uninhibitedly down Doug's face as Ashley reached out and numbly took his
hand. "I heard the screeching of the truck's tires and the sound of the crash. I
dropped my fishing pole and ran up to the highway." He stopped as his voice
caught in his throat. Ashley continued to squeeze his hand to comfort both him
and her. He collected himself and went on.

"Jimmy was still alive when I got to him through the passenger door. The
whole driver's side was crushed, pinning him in the car. So I just held him,
begging him to wait for the ambulance. I could hear the sirens coming in the
distance and I begged and begged him to wait, help was on the way. But he
couldn't hold on. I was holding his head in my lap when he died."

Doug clenched his jaw and stopped talking, looking so exhausted and so
heartsick. Death had claimed more than his best friend. Doug and Jimmy had
been like brothers and Doug would be forever lost without him. Ashley sat
staring into space, a stricken look dominating her features, feeling the sobs
welling up in her throat, choking her.

"Ashley, I'm so sorry that this had to happen to Jimmy and to you."

Ashley's violent sobs shook her body and Doug put his arms around her,
pulling her tightly to him. She leaned her head into his chest as Doug broke
down, crying despairingly with her. They held onto one another, seeking the
comfort that both needed so desperately.

After exhausting their supply of tears, Ashley sat up, pulling away from
Doug. "When is the funeral?"

Doug gulped, swallowing hard. "I think that it's tomorrow. I met Lana and
John at the hospital yesterday and I think tomorrow is the day they were
discussing with the funeral director." Doug was so worn out that he was
rambling.

"How's Lana taking it?" Ashley was naturally concerned about Lana. Jimmy
had been her baby, her pride and joy. She had to be beside herself with grief.

"Oh, Ash, I never thought I'd live to see Lana Moreau hysterical and out of
control. She was a mess, crying and screaming and holding onto Jimmy. I'm
betting they sent her home on a strong tranquilizer."

Ashley nodded, absorbing the details solemnly with her exhausted mind.
"And John? How was John?"

"John was a pillar of steel, like always. He didn't say much. He just stood
with a devastated look on his face."

"Where's Will?" She asked about them all, a little of her own grief overshadowed by her love and concern for her second family.

"I haven't seen him yet, but I would imagine that he is in town by now," Doug said as he closed his tired eyes, resting his head in his hands.

Maggie had slipped into the den and stood listening, her eyes wet with tears. Ashley rose from the couch and fell into her arms, letting her mother hold her close. Maggie didn't say a word, comforting Ashley with her mere presence.

Ashley heard the front door open as Ms. Bobbie Fairchild tiptoed in to retrieve her son. She kissed Ashley on the cheek and patted her shoulder, knowing that it wasn't necessary for her to verbally express her sorrow. She had adopted Jimmy as one of her own and also felt his loss.

Doug stood to leave with his mother, pausing to kiss the top of Ashley's head. "I'll call you later," he said and she nodded mutely, not trusting herself to speak.

After Bobbie and Doug left, Ashley wandered into the kitchen. Kate was nowhere in sight. "Did Kate leave?" she turned to Maggie, who nodded affirmatively.

"Yes, I sent her home to bed. She was wiped out after driving all night." She brushed her daughter's bangs back from her pale, drawn face. "Why don't you go up and lie down? You look pretty worn out yourself."

"I can't sleep."

"Well, go lie down anyway. You need some rest, even if it's just a cat nap."

Ashley obediently ascended the stairs to her room to find Jimmy's smiling face greeting her from the nightstand. She walked over and picked up his picture, stroking his cheek and holding his picture close to her heart. She lay on the bed and held it tightly in her arms, just as she wished she could hold Jimmy.

She must have dozed off because she startled, awakening as the doorbell rang. Ashley squinted at the clock beside her bed, discovering that it was almost noon. She lay very still, listening as Remy opened the front door and hearing softly muffled voices in the foyer followed closely by footsteps, beginning on the stairs and stopping outside her door.

"Ashley?" Maggie opened the door and looked in at her. "Honey, Will is here." Ashley pushed herself by her palms into sitting position and blinked at Maggie, struggling to focus her bleary eyes. "Put some clothes on, Ashley, and come downstairs. He came to see you," Maggie said, commanding her gently.

Ashley nodded silently, swinging her legs over the side of the bed. She pulled on her old gray gym shorts and a T-shirt, leaving the sanctuary of her bedroom to face Will. She moved down the stairs in a dreamlike state, gripping the handrail to steady her descent. As she reached the landing, she spied Will, noticing immediately how tired he looked, his handsome face drawn, dark shadows around his downcast eyes. He probably had not slept in two days. She stood on the stairs, not wanting to break the silence, not wanting to remember the reason behind Will's visit. However, Will sensed her presence and lifted his eyes to meet hers. Her heart wrung with pity as she saw the stricken look on his face.

"Hello, Will," she said quietly, welcoming the feel of his arms around her as he rushed to embrace her. The very familiar lump rose in her throat and she couldn't stop the tears that spilled over into scalding rivers, coursing freely down her cheeks. She didn't know what to say to him. What does one say at a time like this?

"I can't believe this is happening," she spoke aloud the thoughts rushing through her mind as she sank down onto the bottom step, pulling Will down to sit beside her. Wiping her eyes on the back of her hand, Ashley turned to look at him, hoping he would say something, anything, to ease the dull, empty ache gnawing at her soul.

Will took her hand, squeezing it comfortingly as he offered a sad smile. Ashley rested her head on his shoulder and they sat speechlessly, each drawing much-needed solace from the nearness of the other. "When did you get home?" she asked him finally, her words echoing through the soundless foyer.

"Late yesterday afternoon," he said, his voice cracking ever so slightly. "Dad called me from the hospital."

"How's Lana?"

"Not good," Will said somberly. "She's a mess, completely inconsolable. I left her with Dad at the funeral home to come for you."

"For me?"

Will nodded, brushing a stray lock of hair out of her eyes. "I thought you might want to see him before everyone else arrives this afternoon."

The surreal sensation of disbelief once again clouded her mind, leaving her lightheaded and dizzy. She hadn't begun to deal with seeing Jimmy. She didn't think that she could do it. She shook her head, both in an effort to clear the thick cobwebs and to answer Will's request. "I don't think I can, Will. I'd rather remember him the way that he was," she said, using what little strength she had left to be stubborn. "I can tell him goodbye here, in my heart," she patted her chest firmly with her closed fist.

"I know it'll be tough," Will gently squeezed her hand again, offering her an empathetic smile. "I know first hand just how very tough it really is. But you have to tell him goodbye, Ashley. You'll never forgive yourself if you don't." Taking note of her look of indecision, Will stood, pulling her up by the shoulders. "Go get your shower. I'll wait for you here."

She rode to the funeral home with Will in the little black BMW, the car that held so many precious memories for her. Ironic, wasn't it? They pulled into the drive of the funeral home, a beautiful building of red brick accented with shutters of white and carved columns along its tree-shaded porch. It should be someone's house, Ashley thought, instead of what it was, and what it would always be. To Ashley, it would always be a grand showplace of human sorrow.

Will parked beside his parents' car in back of the funeral home then opened Ashley's car door, forcing her out of her thoughts. She glanced at him uncertainly then took the hand he offered her, holding onto it for dear life as they walked solemnly into the building.

Cheryl sat quietly on a chair in the reception area, her blue eyes wide and child-like, her sorrow revealing the true naivete beneath her intelligence. Ashley stopped beside her chair, squeezing her shoulder warmly with her hand. Cheryl glanced up, rising unsteadily from her chair to embrace Ashley. "Ashley, I'm so glad you're here," she said, whispering hoarsely into her ear.

Ashley nodded and took her hand, clasping it tightly, expressing her true feelings in one simple gesture. She allowed herself to look slowly around the room, not wanting to see too much too quickly.

John Moreau and his brother, Tom, were standing solemnly in front of a window, looking out and talking quietly to one another. Ashley walked over, taking John's hand, looking up into the face so much like his son's. Only now, his handsome face was ashen and there was a wounded look in his brown eyes. "I'm so sorry," she whispered with tearful eyes.

"I'm sorry too," John said, putting a comforting arm around her shoulders. "Jimmy loved you a great deal, I hope that you know that." She nodded, accepting the solace John conveyed in his sincere words, yet not knowing what else to say to him. She had lost her lover and her best friend, but John and Lana had lost their son. Their loss was so much greater than hers.

Will came up behind her, putting his hand on her shoulder. "Are you ready to go in to see Jimmy?" he asked. Looking to her left, Ashley could see Lana in the room with Jimmy's casket. She quickly turned away, shaking her head in answer to Will's question.

"Not yet, Will," she whispered, panicked. "I don't want to remember him this way. I have my memories of him, full of life and energy. I don't know if I should go in there."

"Please go in and see my wife, Ashley," John said, pleading with her. "She's been waiting for you." His eyes influenced her and she gave in, allowing Will to escort her into the room where Jimmy lay.

Lana was talking quietly to him, standing beside the coffin with the most despairing expression on her lovely face. Watching Lana with her son, Ashley was filled with such sadness. It broke her heart to see Lana this way. Lana turned as she heard them coming toward her and reached out her hands to Ashley.

"Ashley, come here, honey," she clutched Ashley's hands tightly in hers, their eyes meeting in a mutual expression of sorrow. Neither of them noticed as Will slipped discreetly from the room, leaving them in privacy.

"Hi, Lana," Ashley held onto her hands, her eyes purposely avoiding the casket. "How are you holding up?"

Lana sighed heavily with an exhausted shrug of her delicate shoulders. "About as well as you are, I'm sure," her doe-like eyes regarded Ashley with motherly concern. Ashley glanced again in the direction of the casket, only this time Lana noticed her reluctance to approach it.

"I felt the same way about seeing him when we came here this morning," she said, her voice wavering, threatening to break into a wail at any given moment. "Go see him, Ashley. You need to say goodbye." She gave her a gentle push toward the casket.

Ashley gripped the sides of the coffin with her eyes closed and, taking a deep breath, opened her eyes to look at her beloved Jimmy. He appeared as if he were sleeping, so handsome and so young. Ashley gazed at him lovingly, knowing that she would cry.

"Hi there, Jimmy," she whispered, stroking his cheek and putting her hand on his. She stood there, the tears she thought she'd gotten out of her system coursing uninhibitedly down her cheeks. "I'm going to miss you more than you'll ever know," she told him, her own voice cracking as the force of her sobs took control. "I can't imagine my life ever returning to normal without you. We had so many plans together. You were my whole world."

She rested her head sadly against the smooth wood of his casket and wept. Lana came to her, drawing Ashley into her arms and they clung to one another, mother and sweetheart, crying together while trying to imagine their lives without him. Jimmy had been a bright, shining light in both of their lives and now that he was gone, they were left with only darkness and the emptiness of their grief.

Ashley sank onto the couch and Lana sat next to her, bending down to pick up a box at her feet. "I put together some things of Jimmy's that I know he would've wanted you to have," she said as she placed the box in Ashley's hands.

"Oh, Lana, I can't take his things from you," she said, shaking her head in protest while she attempted to return the box to Lana.

She held up her hand to stop Ashley's protest. "No, Ashley, these are things that you should have. I have many things of my own to cherish," Lana reassured her gently.

Ashley accepted the box from her but could not bring herself to open it. This was neither the time, nor the place to look at the precious collection of memories. She would wait to open it in the privacy of her room so she could relive the events that went along with each item.

Ashley became aware of the rustling sound of people arriving to express their sympathies to the Moreau family. She watched as Lana smoothed her skirt and rose to join John in the foyer area before she hastily scooped up the box and scurried from the room. She couldn't stay there. She didn't want to be there to hear people say how wonderful Jimmy looked. She simply couldn't bear it.

Slipping discreetly out a side door, Ashley settled wearily on the cool concrete steps of the stoop. She lay her head down on top of the box in her lap, drifting away in her own gloomy thoughts, seeing his face, remembering his laughter and wanting so badly to be in his loving arms. She didn't know how long she sat there before Kate found her.

"There you are," Kate sat down beside Ashley, her gentle eyes searching Ashley's face for a clue to her emotions.

"I should have never left him to go to Florida, no matter what he said," Ashley said forlornly, burying her head into the coarse cardboard in her lap and gulping back the lump forming in her throat.

"Ashley, this is not your fault. You're being here or in Florida makes no difference," she reached over to touch Ashley with a sympathetic hand. "It was Jimmy's time to go, sweetie; you couldn't have done anything to change the Lord's plan for him."

"I don't believe that," Ashley lifted her head, jutting her chin out stubbornly. "I don't believe that God gave us someone so wonderful just to take him away."

"Why? That's what he did when he gave us Jesus," Kate reminded her, a serene smile on her angelic face as she attempted to provide some solace in Ashley's darkest moment.

"That's not the same thing," Ashley said, growling skeptically at her, refusing to accept any justification for the loss of her beloved Jimmy.

"Sure it is," Kate said, as she squeezed her hand comfortingly. "The Lord gave you a wonderful gift by letting you know Jimmy. Jimmy made a difference in your life and you'll never forget him. Your life is richer for having known him."

"It doesn't feel richer now. I just feel empty and depressed."

Kate put her arm around Ashley's shoulder, allowing Ashley's head to rest on her shoulder and they sat wordlessly, soaking up the soothing warmth of the late afternoon sunlight as it streamed through the dense pine needles high above their heads.

"Doug has been looking for you." Kate said after a while.

"I don't want to see Doug," Ashley said, abruptly shaking Kate's arm off her shoulder and jumping to her feet, prepared to run and hide if necessary. Kate smiled gently, shaking her head at Ashley's skittishness.

"You can relax, Ashley. He doesn't know where you are. I left him inside with Mitch and Susanna."

"Good, I can't see him, not now. In fact, I don't want to see anybody. Will you take me home?"

Kate nodded her understanding as she rose from their seat on the stoop. "Sure, honey. Let me go inside and tell Mitch that I'm leaving." She tossed Ashley the keys to Mitch's car. "We're parked in the back. Go let yourself in."

Ashley picked up the box Lana had given her, making her way to the car without seeing anyone else. She hid inside Mitch's car, enjoying the solitude until Kate reappeared, sliding into the driver's seat and starting the car. Intuitive as always, Kate uttered not a word as she drove her home, appreciating Ashley's need for silence. As Kate pulled up next to the white columns of the Stewarts' front porch, Ashley slid out of the car, thanking Kate quietly for bringing her home, then waved goodbye before slipping into the house.

The house echoed with utter stillness. Maggie was at the funeral home and Remy was still at work. It was only Tuesday. It didn't seem possible that only four days had passed since she had passionately kissed Jimmy goodbye as she left for Florida. It seemed like a lifetime ago.

Maggie had left a pot of chicken soup on the stovetop and a note directing her to eat some of it. Ashley ladled some into a mug and carried it and the box with her to the serenity of her room. She changed out of her dress and dressed again in boxer shorts and a T-shirt. She sat somberly in the middle of her bed, sipping Maggie's chicken soup and eyeing the box. After several minutes of debating, she finally broke down and opened it.

On the very top was Jimmy's letterman's jacket, heather gray with a red "P," its sleeves filled with patches added from each of the playoff games in which he had participated. Ashley had worn that jacket a hundred times in the last year. She picked it up, hugging it tightly against her chest. It smelled wonderfully of Jimmy. She closed her eyes and thought of him, remembering the feel of his arms around her and the warmth of his loving embrace.

She peered again into the box, her eye catching the shiny gold of Jimmy's class ring. She picked it up, inspecting the ruby red stone in the center of it before sliding it on the middle finger of her left hand, next to the silver hugs and kisses band Jimmy had given her for graduation.

The rest of the box was a hodge-podge of poems, stories and letters she had written for him, photographs taken of the two of them together and sketches that Jimmy had done. Ashley began to weep inconsolably as she read the letters. The love that she felt for Jimmy Moreau leapt dramatically from each syllable she had written. The love she expressed for him in those letters was still vividly alive in her heart, but now she could never tell him, in written or spoken words, of that love again. As she sobbed, she packed the letters, poems, pictures and sketches back in the box, unable to look at any more of them. She lay down on the bed and as exhaustion finally took over, slept fitfully through the night.

CHAPTER ELEVEN

Wednesday dawned sunny and bright, although Ashley would have preferred it to be as gloomy and gray as she felt. It was still relatively early when she rolled reluctantly out of bed. Both Maggie and Remy had taken the day off for the funeral and she could hear them banging around in the kitchen but she didn't join them. She wasn't ready yet.

She stood brooding in front of her closet and pulled out a slim, sleeveless black dress, one she had recently purchased for her college wardrobe, one of her "just in case" purchases. This wasn't the type of occasion she'd had in mind when she bought it. She had been thinking more along the lines of a romantic dinner or a nice party. Never in her wildest dreams could she have anticipated the occasion for which it would be worn. She would wear the dress today and never wear it again.

Attired in the black dress and dark sunglasses, she joined Maggie and Remy downstairs, leaving for the funeral home just before noon. Lana was with Jimmy when they arrived. Ashley waited at the door, leaning against the rich maple doorframe, not wanting to interrupt Lana. She watched, her chest heavy with pity and grief, as Lana stroked Jimmy's hair, crying softly. Ashley sniffled, wiping her wet eyes with the lace handkerchief Maggie had stuffed into her pocket.

Lana turned at the sound of her crying, gesturing for Ashley to join her. She draped a graceful arm around her shoulder, kissing her cheek fondly. "I was just saying goodbye," she said, her soft voice quavering as she spoke.

"That's what I came here to do," Ashley said as Lana dropped her arm from her shoulders and touched her softly on the arm with her fingertips.

"I'll leave you alone with him," Lana said, turning to leave the room.

"Lana?" Ashley said and she stopped to look back at her over her shoulder. "Thank you for the box. I'm glad I have those memories to keep."

Lana smiled wearily, "You're welcome, honey."

Ashley noted with sadness how slumped her stance was, in sharp contrast to her normally perfect posture, and how she shuffled out of the room without a hint of her catlike grace. Lana had aged fifteen years in the past two days. Her heart was shattered into pieces and Ashley wondered soberly if she would ever recover from losing Jimmy.

She stood by the cherry wood casket and memorized every detail of Jimmy's peaceful face. In her mind, she could envision him animated, telling a story and laughing, flashing his signature grin as he kidded around with his friends. She could still see his brown eyes sparkling with affection as he told her that he loved her. She remembered the feel his warm lips pressed passionately against hers and recalled the sound of his heart beating as she rested her head on his chest. He had been so spirited, so full of life and so absolutely wonderful. She would miss him as long as she lived. She leaned over and kissed his forehead ever so softly.

"Hi, Jimmy. I came to tell you goodbye and that I love you and I miss you already," she whispered to him, her swollen eyes burning from hot, salty tears. "I hope that you can hear me. I'm certain that you are in Heaven. You were the most wonderful person I've ever known." She touched his cheek, stroking it softly, wishing, as she would for the rest of her days, that she could see him alive just one more time.

She slipped into the chapel and watched from her hiding place near the back as the room quickly filled to capacity, observing that the majority of their former classmates were there, filing somberly into the pews. She located her parents sitting near the front and quietly slid in beside them, hoping that she was incognito. Susanna and Kate joined them. Kate squeezed her hand comfortingly. Susanna was reserved and uncharacteristically reverent.

Jimmy's family filed in shortly before the service: John stoically supporting Lana, Will following a step behind them, his shoulders bowed in grief. Jimmy's beloved Gram and his cousins from south Louisiana, Cheryl and her parents. Ashley watched as Jimmy's close friends served as his pallbearers and carried in his closed casket, covered in a multi-colored spray of daylilies. Ashley viewed it all through bleak, tear-filled eyes, never hurting so badly in her entire life.

She rode in her parents' car to the graveside service, numbly staring out the window as reality started to set in. She could no longer live in denial, refusing to acknowledge the truth. As Remy drove their car through the gates of the cemetery, Ashley was forced to accept that she would never see Jimmy again.

After his burial, she received embraces and condolences from her life-long friends, thanking them graciously while inwardly she was screaming at the top of her lungs to be left alone. Finally, as her friends gathered to talk quietly, Ashley stole away with Maggie and Remy, anxious to retreat to the sanctuary of home.

After a long, hot soak in the tub, Ashley pulled on her fluffy, pink terry bathrobe and curled up on her bed, staring desolately at the ceiling, waiting for fatigue to lull her into another fitful night of sleep. As she waited, Maggie tapped lightly on the door.

"Darlin', Doug's here and he really wants to see you," she said, wrinkling her brow worriedly as Ashley gave her a weary look.

"I don't want to see him. I don't want to see anybody," Ashley rolled on to her side, turning her face toward the wall, staring miserably at the creamy white blossoms of the magnolia tree outside her window.

"I really think you should see him, Ashley," Maggie said, firmly. "I'm going to send him up." She was gone before Ashley could protest, leaving her to sigh in frustration as Doug tapped on the door.

"Come in," she pushed herself into sitting position as he crept in the door, closing it behind him as he shot Ashley a wry look.

"I never thought I'd see the day when your mother would send me to your bedroom," he said, teasing her in an attempt to cheer her up. She rewarded him with a slight smile as he sat at the end of her bed. He observed Jimmy's jacket lying on the pillows beside her but wisely chose to say nothing about it, his only reaction being the look of profound sadness clouding his handsome features. Ashley stared inquiringly at him with swollen, bloodshot eyes, waiting for him to reveal the reason for his intrusion into her private state of depression.

"I missed you at the Moreaus' this afternoon," Doug said, alluding to her absence at John and Lana's house after the funeral. "We were worried about you."

"I didn't go," she said, stating the obvious. "I just couldn't, Doug. I couldn't go to their house, Jimmy's house, and face all those memories knowing that I will never see him again."

Doug drew her into his arms, stroking the top of her head as she sobbed desolately against his muscular shoulder. When he sensed that she was beginning to gain some control of her emotions, he kindly offered her a tissue from his shirt pocket. She took it gratefully, smiling dismally as she dried her eyes.

"You've been avoiding me, Ash," he said. "I'm here to find out why."

"I've been avoiding everyone," she sighed, hugging her pillow tightly against her and burying her chin deeply into the softness of the down. "I don't want to see anybody and I certainly don't want to talk about how I feel."

"You've been avoiding me in particular," he said, staring pensively into her face. "Ashley, do you blame me for Jimmy's death?"

She gaped at him in surprise, startled by his question. "No! How could you think that?"

"It would be a logical conclusion to the way you've been acting."

"No, I don't blame you, Doug," she said. "No one is to blame. If I were to blame anyone, I would blame myself for leaving him here to go play in Florida."

"That's ridiculous," Doug said, furrowing his brow as he frowned at her.

She nodded in agreement, successfully illustrating her point. "Just as blaming you or anyone else would be," she said, her voice distant and wooden. "All I want for now is just to be left alone so I can sort out my feelings."

"You would be better off sharing your feelings with your friends, darlin'," Doug said, covering her tiny hand with his much larger one. "I need you, Ashley. I need you to help me with this. And you need me, whether you realize it or not."

"I don't need anyone," she said, snatching her hand away from his consoling touch. She didn't want him to question her or to comfort her. She just wanted him to leave her alone. "You grieve in your way, I'll grieve in mine," she folded her arms across her chest, symbolically blocking him out.

"Do you think that you have an exclusive on grieving for him?" Doug asked, his outraged eyes leaping angrily at her. She recoiled, dumbfounded by his outburst and shook her head speechlessly in answer to his question. "That's good, because you certainly aren't the only one who mourns him. I loved him like my own brother. I held his head in my lap as he drew his last breath! Do you think that I can ever forget that?" Doug leapt from the bed and began pacing the floor. "I see his face in my sleep every night and I feel so guilty for being alive when he's dead."

"Doug, you shouldn't feel guilty. You weren't driving the car," Ashley tried her best to soothe him. She'd had no idea that he felt this way. She watched as he strode in frustration to her bedroom window, pushing back the curtains and pressing his hands against the frame, leaning his bowed head against the window to gaze woefully down at the front yard below.

Memories came back to her swiftly and unexpectedly, and she smiled with nostalgia as she recalled the night she had scooted down the rose trellis to sit underneath the magnolia tree with Jimmy. "Me, you, the moonlight… and your red flannel pajamas," Jimmy had teased her playfully. She allowed her mind to drift, filled with soothing warmth at this reminiscence.

Doug turned abruptly from the window to face her, bringing her reluctantly back into the present. "Maybe your way is the right way," he said, his face softening with compassion. She gave him a puzzled look, wondering what she had missed while away with Jimmy in her daydream.

"I think that you're right. It might be best if we spent some time apart while we're sorting out our feelings," he said, regarding her carefully, hoping for a sign of protest, but spotting none in her distant emerald eyes. "I have a lot of anger about Jimmy's death, Ash, and I don't want to take it out on you." He crossed the room and kissed her affectionately on the forehead. "I'm sorry that I yelled at you just now. I had no right to deny you your feelings."

"You're forgiven, you know that," she said, teary-eyed once again.

Doug lifted her petite hand to his lips, kissing it softly, and left, leaving her feeling lost and alone.

She leaned back against her pillows, hugging Jimmy's jacket tightly to her chest, missing him tremendously. She had to fight the urge to pick up the phone to call him. She hadn't truly accepted that he would never be on the other end of that telephone line again. The void that his death left in her life was huge. Jimmy had become the center of her existence in the time they had been together.

She had already begun to imagine their life together in Baton Rouge and their probable marriage. She had vivid images of the children they would've had together and the grandchildren they might have given them. A speeding truck on a Louisiana highway erased the entire blueprint of her future.

She didn't know how she would make it through this. True, she was only eighteen years old, but her age didn't make her love for Jimmy insignificant. She would never love another the way she had loved him. Daniel James Moreau had been one of a kind. He was the one great love of her life.

The days following the funeral were among the darkest in Ashley's life. She spent most of that summer alone, avoiding everyone, even Kate and Susanna. She wanted no comfort, no kind words from any of them. She could not say once more that she was just fine, nor could she adequately explain exactly how miserable, lost and alone she felt, so it was simply easier to withdraw from them altogether.

To add to her frustration, she found her sadness over Jimmy's death compounded by Doug's absence in her life. He had been right. She did need him. But she had too much foolish pride to call him and admit that she was wrong.

Her own memories haunted her. Every place she went, every sight she saw reminded her of Jimmy. She had to leave Pineville. If she didn't, she would surely go insane.

So, with Maggie in tow, Ashley retreated to Destin, hoping to find some solace in the one place she loved most. She wandered aimlessly up and down the pearly white shoreline, the aqua waters giving her no feeling of exhilaration for the first time in her life. She was a lost soul, knowing she couldn't go on with life as she had planned, yet not knowing what she would do.

She shut the world out completely, growing more and more depressed. Will Moreau and Doug, as well as Kate and Susanna, made numerous phone calls to the condo throughout the long summer, speaking only with Maggie because Ashley refused to talk to anyone. She didn't eat. She didn't brush her hair or put on makeup and wore the same pair of boxers and the same T-shirt nearly every day. She tried to release her grief through her writing and found, to make matters worse, that she had developed one serious case of writer's block. She couldn't compose a simple sentence, much less a heartfelt expression of mourning.

Her depression was much harder on Maggie and Remy than it was on her. It nearly killed them to see their once happy-go-lucky, vivacious daughter so withdrawn and blue. Maggie had taken a brief leave of absence from her job with Dr. Gautreaux in order to spend the summer with Ashley in Destin, and alternated between worrying over Ashley and fretting over Dr. Gautreaux killing or maiming someone in her absence. Remy visited often, bearing gifts and putting forth his most jolly face in attempt to cheer Ashley while gently reminding her that one day she would have to return to the real world.

By July's end, Ashley had determined that she couldn't spend the rest of her life as a recluse in Destin, but she could no longer go through with her plans to attend LSU. She rescinded her scholarship and returned to Pineville with a new plan in mind.

Ashley was filled with delight as Maggie wheeled the car into the circle drive in front of their home and displayed one of the few smiles she had given since her high school graduation almost three months previously. She was glad to be home, though she knew she couldn't stay in Pineville long. She had struggled very hard to overcome what grief she had and those old ghosts were still there, haunting her at every turn of the twisting roads through town. After helping Maggie unload the car, she skipped her ritual of dashing upstairs to her bedroom and went instead to see Kate.

"Hello, Stranger!" Kate said, flinging open her front door in answer to Ashley's timid knock. She grabbed Ashley enthusiastically, pulling her frail little body into a huge bear hug. "I didn't know whether I'd ever hear from you again."

"Well, I couldn't stay away forever. Believe me, I tried, but Maggie wouldn't let me." Ashley said, awkwardly attempting to tease her as she stepped into the Ducotes' house. Ashley glanced around the welcoming living room where she had spent countless childhood hours, glad that something had remained constant and real in her life.

"It's good to have you back," Kate linked her arm through Ashley's, strolling casually into Imogene Ducote's prized Florida room, filled with warm sunshine and huge Boston ferns. "I've missed you."

"I've missed you too," Ashley settled onto the rose floral cushion on the white wicker divan, curling her legs beneath her.

Kate sat beside her, regarding her with a kind-hearted smile. "You doing better?" she said, cautiously optimistic.

Ashley answered with a quick nod. "Somewhat," she gave what was becoming her standard one-word answer, finding it easier to pretend to be cheerful if she didn't have to speak in full sentences.

"I wouldn't expect you to be any other way. You don't have to pretend to be jolly with me, Ashley."

"Can we change the subject? I'm not about to play 'in five hundred words or less, describe your summer vacation' with you, Kate," Ashley fidgeted uncomfortably, fearing Kate would bring up Jimmy's death and Ashley's summer of mourning. Tears were no longer on her agenda and Kate's comforting voice could bring them on in the blink of an eye.

"Sure," Kate humored her, equally relieved to talk about something else.

"Do you have a roommate for Northeast yet?" Ashley asked, anxious to reveal her unexpected decision to Kate.

"No, not yet. I was just going to play luck of the draw. Why?" Kate eyed her curiously, narrowing her eyes slightly as she began to recognize what Ashley had in mind.

"How about I go to Northeast with you?"

"I thought you were set on going to LSU," Kate said. "Doug and Will are still under the impression that you're going to Baton Rouge with them."

"That was in another life. I'm ready to start a new life and I can think of no one I'd rather be with than you," Ashley smiled fondly at Kate, her best friend of eighteen years, and Kate returned her smile as she reached out to squeeze her hand affectionately.

"I suppose I could put up with you for another four years," Kate said, kidding lightly as she flashed her grin of approval. "What do your folks think about your change in plans?"

"I haven't exactly told them yet, but I think they'll approve." Ashley said with a nonchalant shrug of her shoulders. "They'll be ecstatic just to know that I'm *making* plans."

It did feel good to be making plans, Ashley decided as she walked home from Kate's. As she climbed the front porch steps, she decided to swallow her pride and phone Doug.

He wasn't home but she talked to Ms. Bobbie Fairchild. "I'm happy to hear from you, Ashley girl. I've missed you," she said in her sassy, booming voice. "Doug's been pretty lonesome this summer."

"I've been missing you all too," Ashley said truthfully. "Where is Douglas? Is he out on a date?"

"You've got to be kidding. I wish I could get that kid to go out on a date!" Ms. Bobbie laughed heartily. "No, he's out bumming around with Scotty Jeansonne."

"Will you tell him that I called?"

"Sure, darlin'. He'll be thrilled," Ms. Bobbie told her. "Come by and see me soon, okay?"

"I will." Ashley promised before hanging up. If Scotty was out with Doug that meant there was a good chance that Susanna might be at home. She dialed her number and Susanna answered the phone.

"What's going on with you and Scotty?" Ashley asked her after getting the preliminary chitchat out of the way.

Susanna sighed in exasperation, "Well, since he's going off to Louisiana Tech in August and I'm staying here to work at the bank, we decided to call it quits."

"When did this happen?" Ashley asked, saddened by the news. She had liked Susanna and Scott together and hated to see all those years of Susanna's secret devotion thrown down the tubes.

"While you were away in your deep, black hole," she said with a little of the abrasive Susanna that Ashley knew and loved beginning to emerge.

"Aren't you sad?"

"I'm getting over it," Susanna said, brushing aside her emotions swiftly, always a master at concealing her true feelings. "Hell's bells, Ashley. Scotty Jeansonne's not worth getting all choked up over. There's other fish in the sea."

After hanging up with Susanna, Ashley wandered over to her window, staring out across the street toward the lake, which was almost completely obscured from view by tall pines and thick brush. She felt a hard tug at her heart as she thought of him and of all the times she had been down by the lake with her darling Jimmy. She was filled with an undeniable urge to venture there, to be in a spot that held so many wonderful memories of the two of them. She crept quietly out of the house, crossed the street, and strode purposely down the gravel road leading to the water.

She rested upon the huge moss-covered boulder near the water's edge, meditating on the beams of early evening moonlight reflecting off the gently lapping waves. It was so peaceful there and she hugged her knees to her chest and sat quietly reflecting.

"I heard that you were back," his familiar voice cut through the silence like a welcome ray of sunshine and she turned her head to find that Doug had joined her on her stony perch. "I thought I might find you here."

She smiled brightly at him as her heart soared with happiness to see him again. She felt as though it had been years since she had last seen Doug, instead of just weeks. He was indeed a sight for sore eyes, sitting beside her in his khaki and navy baseball cap and cut offs, his long legs tan and muscular.

He returned her smile with a playful grin of his own as he quickly scrutinized her appearance. "You look a little bit better than you did the last time I saw you," he said. "How are you?"

She frowned slightly, not wanting to ruin their happy reunion by telling him the truth. "I'm okay," she shrugged indifferently, attempting another gleeful smile. "How are you?"

He nodded slightly and shrugged as she had. "I'm making it."

"Are you ready to head down to Baton Rouge?"

Doug's face lit up with excitement. "You bet. I leave in a week to start practice with the team." His voice was giddy with anticipation over beginning his collegiate football career. Ashley beamed at him, thrilled for his continuing opportunity to show his great talent. "What about you, Ash? Have you found a roomie for LSU?"

She glanced guiltily at him, averting her eyes, staring out at the water as she broke the news. "Doug, I've decided against going to LSU," she said, her voice very faint and quiet. "I'm going to Northeast with Kate." She glanced back at him, eyeing him as she weighed his response.

He raised his eyebrows and his eyes widened in surprise. "When did this happen?"

"Tonight, I decided tonight," she said, her eyes meeting his as she attempted to fix a casual expression on her face.

"Just like that? You just changed all your plans for college with no more thought than that?"

"No, not just like that," she leaned back on the palms of her hands, kicking her legs back and forth rhythmically. "I've never put more thought into anything in my whole life and that's a promise. I can't go to Baton Rouge, Doug. There's just no way. There would be too many reminders for me of what could have been."

Doug reflected silently on her decision, not liking it but knowing that Ashley was right. He also knew that it would do him no good to argue with her at this juncture. Ashley Stewart was a stubborn little cuss and her mind was made up. There would be no changing it now.

"You mean you're going to leave me down there all alone?" Doug decided that it would be better to tease her than to argue with her.

"I'm sure that you can fend for yourself," she said, kidding him in return, relieved that Doug had broken the ice and they had moved past the awkwardness between them. "You're a big boy now."

"I won't argue with you, but I wish you would go with me," Doug said wistfully. "I was really looking forward to being with you again. I'll miss you, Ash."

"I'll miss you too, Dougie, but I'll see you over breaks, you know."

"That's not often enough for me," Doug said, frowning slightly as he pouted. "I'm used to seeing you everyday."

"You haven't seen me *every day* for almost three months. You should be weaned of seeing me by now," Ashley playfully pinched his cheek. It did so cheer her to be with Doug again, even though, in the back of her mind, she couldn't help but miss the inseparable threesome of days past.

Doug took her by the hand, pulling her from the rock to stand beside him. "Come on," he said, nodding toward the road before them. "I'll walk you home." Ashley smiled up at him in agreement and they walked hand in hand up the crushed rock road toward her house.

CHAPTER TWELVE

If losing Jimmy ended one era in Ashley's life, going to Northeast started another. Remy and Maggie approved of her plans to go to Northeast Louisiana University with Kate, and Remy was particularly pleased with her decision to follow in his footsteps and change her major to pharmacy.

"What prompted this big change?" he asked, his eyebrows shooting up in surprise. Ashley had wandered into his den, the same evening she had broken the news to Doug, and announced her intentions to her father. "What about journalism?"

Ashley plopped down on the soft leather couch beside him, leaning her head back against the overstuffed cushions. "I haven't been able to write one syllable since Jimmy died," she confessed. "It would be futile to pursue a degree in journalism if I can't even write," she finished with a disappointed sigh. Remy absorbed her answer thoughtfully before flashing a mischievous grin.

"Well I think that pharmacy is a great choice for you," he said, his eyes dancing merrily as he teased her. "I'll be needing someone to take over the business before much longer. But you know it's a tough program, Ashley. You'll really have to put your nose to the grindstone and study, something you're basically unfamiliar with. I'm afraid it might cut into your social life a little bit."

"Somehow, I don't think that socializing will be as much of a problem as it has been in the past," she said, giving a playful answer heavily laden with a solemn double meaning.

Before leaving for school, Ashley removed all reminders of Jimmy from her bedroom, placing them with care in the box on her closet shelf. If she was going to Monroe to get over Jimmy, she couldn't take any sentimental reminders along for the ride. There was one exception. The hugs and kisses band remained on her finger where it had been since Jimmy placed it there the day of their graduation. She couldn't bring herself to remove it. The little silver band held special meaning for her.

"To remind you of my hugs and kisses." She could still hear his voice echoing through her mind. As she shoved the box to the top of her closet, she blinked away her tears and tried to shake off the feeling of a dark cloud over her head. She had done it. She had literally stored away her memories of Daniel James Moreau, and now she was ready to leave for college.

Doug left for Baton Rouge just after the first of August, stopping by her house before leaving town. "I'll call you with my address and phone number before you leave for Monroe," he told her as they sat together on the front steps.

"I hope that you have loads of fun down there," she said, her eyes crinkling mirthfully as she kidded with him. "Just don't party too hearty with those wild frat boys. From what I hear, Will Moreau can be an awfully bad influence."

"We'd have more fun if you were going with us," Doug tried one final time to get her to change her mind as he rose from the steps to leave.

"Save it, Douglas," she warned him with a hint of a smile. "It's not going to work."

He nodded, giving her a hug and brotherly kiss. "You can't blame a guy for trying, can you? See ya, Ashley."

She beamed fondly at him, watching as he bounded down the steps toward his car, an old second-hand Chevy he had bought to replace the fire-engine red Camaro. "See ya," she echoed, thinking how odd it felt to know she wouldn't see Doug again for such a long while. After twelve school years together, it would be quite an adjustment not to see him every day.

She raised her hand to wave as he started to drive away. "And for heaven's sake, go out on a date every once and a while!" she called after him. He flashed a skeptical grin, waving goodbye as he pulled out of her driveway.

Saying goodbye to Susanna was even more odd than saying goodbye to Doug. With Susanna in Pineville, Ashley felt as if they were leaving her behind. She came over to see Ashley off the morning she and Kate left for Monroe.

"This is too weird, watching you load stuff into your car like this," Susanna said, regarding Ashley with probing eyes. "Are you doing okay, Ashley? You look like hell."

Ashley abruptly stuffed another box into her trunk then glared over at Susanna with a scornful roll of her eyes. "How kind of you to comment on it,

Susanna," she said, scowling unpleasantly. "Just how would you expect me to look? I've had one hell of a bad summer."

"Sorry, that was pretty stupid of me to say something like that," Susanna offered a rare apology, then continued to lament. "It'll be so bizarre around here without you and Kate. Everyone is leaving town—you, Kate, Doug, Mitch, Cheryl and Scott. I'll be so bored!"

"You could still come with us," Ashley said, her eyes twinkling as she half teased and half encouraged her to join them in Monroe.

Susanna shook her head adamantly. "Good God no, I already told you, I don't want to go to college. I never want to study again for the rest of my life."

"Oh, Susanna, it might be fun." Ashley shoved yet another box into the overly crowded trunk of the Corolla as Susanna chuckled sarcastically.

"Yeah, whatever," she said with a grin. "And you know what? In December when you and Kate are all stressed out, studying for finals, I'll be lounging on the couch, eating bon-bons and watching television. Why in the hell would I give up that kind of freedom?"

Ashley slammed her trunk closed firmly and turned with a grin to embrace Susanna. "I'll miss you anyway, you grumpy old thing," Ashley told her, and Susanna pushed her away with a hearty laugh.

"Miss me? I'll be coming to see you dogs up in Monroe!" she punched Ashley's shoulder playfully. "I expect to be given the red carpet treatment when I get there too. And you had better have one terrific date lined up for me, now that I've managed to shake Scotty Jeansonne off my coat tails." She turned to get into her car. Susanna hated mushy good-byes.

"Stay out of trouble, Susanna," Ashley waved affectionately to her as she started the engine.

"Why?" she yelled as she drove out of the driveway. "It's a helluva lot more fun being naughty!" She honked the horn and drove out of sight.

Northeast Louisiana University in Monroe was ninety miles northeast of Pineville, in a part of the state known as the Sportsman's Paradise. Kate and Ashley drove up in the Corolla, followed closely by both sets of parents who wouldn't dare miss the big move to college. They traveled Highway 165, winding their way past dense forests green with pines, and through the sleepy little towns of Pollock and Georgetown before crossing over the Ouachita River in Columbia and heading straight into Monroe.

Ashley had been to Northeast several times in the past to look around the campus and to visit friends. The grounds of the university were beautiful and well maintained. Its surrounding streets were lined with tall shade trees, and flowing down the center of campus was a gorgeous bayou. A classic symbol of Louisiana, Bayou DeSiard was crossed by either road or footbridge and was used frequently by the student body for rafting, and canoeing or feeding the ducks that flocked there in droves. The bayou soon became one of Ashley's favorite places, a lovely, quiet location where she could find some peace.

Out of a dozen or so residence halls from which to choose, Kate and Ashley were assigned to Slater Hall, an inside women's dormitory, a fact that greatly pleased both Maggie and Imogene. Shortly after lunch, they shoved their tearful mothers out the door and began settling into their tiny room on the fourth floor.

Campus life was different, a great change from what Ashley's life in Pineville had been and a change for which she had prayed. Their suitemates were Hillary Wilson, a leggy blond pre-med major from Texarkana, Texas, with a perfect body and a photographic memory, and Melissa Morgan, a dainty brunette elementary education major from Shreveport with round tortoiseshell glasses and a shy smile. Both were very friendly, although Melissa was a little timid, and seemed perfectly suited to Ashley's and Kate's temperaments and study habits.

Kate and Ashley took early morning classes, breakfasting on hot black coffee and Pop Tarts, fresh and cold, straight from the box. Their afternoons and evenings were filled with frequent trips to the library or to the Student Union for snacks and supplies.

On those numerous late nights, the four girls would rush out for pizza or Funyuns and onion dip, bringing them back into the dorm room before the front doors locked at eleven. Although their intent was to study, they often ended up lounging across the quilt-covered beds in Kate and Ashley's room, laughing and gossiping well into the night.

Their lives were filled with care packages and phone calls from home; intertwined with college football games and frequent weekend visits from Susanna, and they soon fell into a routine. Kate became a workout queen and a campus socialite who frequented parties of every kind, sometimes with Mitch in tow and sometimes with a newly found conquest.

Northeast was a great place for a college coed, except for a coed in mourning. Ashley barricaded herself from student life, content to hide within the cinderblock walls of her dorm room, determined to study while fighting her tortured mind for the ability to concentrate. Socializing above and beyond the classroom or the dorm room no longer interested her. Anyone of the male persuasion who crossed her path she immediately compared to Jimmy, a comparison unfair to her and to him. She left her room only for class, food or to walk solitarily along the bayou, stopping on the footbridge to stare forlornly out at the moss-draped cypress trees at the water's edge. She lived in a sad state of mind, but every day got a little better, just as long as she didn't go home.

Kate was very good to Ashley. She worried about her dear friend, but was patient with her chosen state of solitude. She sympathized with Ashley, understanding her private pain. After all, Kate had been the only one to see the devastated look in Ashley's eyes when she had broken the news to her that life as she had previously known it was over.

Maggie was not as patient, feeling that Ashley had her period of mourning and the best way for her to heal was to jump right into the center of the social scene. And she certainly didn't understand Ashley's refusal to come home to Pineville.

"But Ashley, we haven't seen you in over two months," Maggie said, protesting loudly over the telephone. "You really should come home soon."

"Maggie, I've got a test in the morning and I really don't want to go into this tonight. There's no reason to worry about me. I just like it here. At least here, I'm not constantly reminded of things that will never be."

"Ashley, you really need to get out and start meeting some new people," Maggie said, being very persistent, more so than usual. "Enough time has passed."

"Did you expect that I would get over losing him overnight?" Ashley questioned her irritably. "Do you think I can just push it all to the side and act like I never met him or loved him?"

"No, honey, that's not what she meant," Remy, on the other extension, attempted to smooth Ashley's ruffled feathers, rephrasing what Maggie had said. "It would just be good for you to get out a little."

"I will, when I'm ready," she said adamantly. "Until then, I just want to be left alone."

Kate was fast asleep in her bed when Ashley finally managed to get off the phone. Ashley wearily pulled on her pajamas, red flannel ones very similar to the pair she owned when she and Jimmy started dating. She smiled faintly at the memory and pulled back her lace-edged sheet to climb into bed, twisting the silver band on her finger and choking back the sobs that were trying to escape.

"No," she insisted to herself, "I will not cry." She wouldn't allow herself to slip on her self-recovery plan. No tears and no reminiscing, she sternly reminded herself as she pulled the sheet angrily over her head and rolled over to try to get some sleep.

She was prepared to spend a very lonely two days in Monroe that weekend in early November. Their normally overcrowded suite of rooms seemed extraordinarily empty with the absence of Kate, Hillary and Melissa, all of who had gone home for the weekend. Ashley remained behind, stubbornly resisting Kate's gentle urging that she ride home with her and Mitch to visit her parents.

She used her time wisely to catch up on her assignments and some research for a paper due by the end of the semester. But she could only kill so much time and by Saturday afternoon, Ashley had run out of things to do. She was contemplating scrubbing the grout around the shower tile with a toothbrush when the phone rang. She leapt up from the hard tile floor of the bathroom and scrambled across the room for the telephone.

"Hello?"

"I heard from a reliable source that you've become a recluse," Doug's voice echoed over the line and Ashley smiled broadly at the sound of it, glad to hear from him since it had been several weeks since they had spoken. She sat Indian style on the edge of her bed, cradling the receiver against her shoulder.

"Hi, Doug! How's Baton Rouge?"

"Baton Rouge is fine, just as Pineville is," he said gruffly.

"Oh, are you home this weekend?" Ashley was surprised. "What about football?"

"We have a bye weekend this weekend. So I thought *I* would grace my parents with my presence. I'm a good son." His voice dripped with cynicism and Ashley geared up for a playful brawl.

"I'm sure they're very grateful to you." The sarcasm in her voice equaled that in Doug's.

"Ash, you have to come back here some time," Doug dropped his hostile stance, allowing his tone to become gentler. "You had a life here before Jimmy and you have a life here now that he's gone."

"Doug, leave me alone about that. I'm not ready to come home. The subject is closed."

"Okay then, just get out of that dorm room. There's a whole city full of men just waiting to meet you."

"Not interested," Ashley said, her sing-song response hiding her growing irritation.

"This is going nowhere," Doug sighed in frustration. "You may have lost your will to live but you haven't lost any of that doggoned stubbornness. I'll call you tomorrow. Maybe you'll be more receptive then." He hung up the phone with a resounding click.

Ashley stared at the receiver, exasperated with Doug for his abrupt end to their conversation. She hung up the phone then rolled over on her bed, staring at the ceiling and wondering what on earth she would do with the rest of the weekend.

Two hours later, she was collecting some books to take to the cafeteria with her when the phone rang again. She tossed her books carelessly onto the bed to answer the phone.

"Hello?"

"Come downstairs." It was Doug again.

"What?" she asked, puzzled.

"Come downstairs. I'm here."

Ashley blinked her eyes in surprise. "You've got to be kidding," she laughed.

"Just come downstairs or I'll find some way to come up there," he notified her abruptly. Ashley knew Doug and knew that he was serious. She decided that she had better go down.

She raced down four flights of concrete steps then swung open the door to the lobby, slowing her pace to enter very casually. Doug was standing by the desk, dressed in jeans and a red flannel shirt, and Ashley smiled fondly at him. He returned her smile, surprisingly enough since Ashley was certain that he was furious with her. She crossed the room, tiptoeing up to give him a big hug.

"I'm glad to see you anyway," she said, her eyes twinkling mischievously.

"You are by far the most stubborn woman I know," Doug said, scolding her as he hooked his arm through hers. "You're just lucky I didn't send Susanna. She's definitely ready to give you hell."

"Thank God for small favors."

"Come on," he pulled her toward the door. "I'm at least taking you out for dinner."

"Your parents have some fund-raising dinner to attend tonight or they would be here too," Doug said as they drove through the streets of Monroe.

"You told them you were coming here?"

"Yes, I did and Ms. Maggie loves me all the more for it. She sends her love and a warning that she and Mr. Remy will be up next weekend. You've got them pretty worried about you."

"I told them that there was nothing to worry about," she rolled her eyes indignantly. "I'm just fine."

"Yeah, yeah, yeah," Doug said, scowling at her as he pulled into a parking spot in front of a little Mexican restaurant. "Tell me another one."

After being seated at a table in the soft glow of the restaurant, Doug encouraged Ashley to have a margarita. "God knows you need a drink. It might loosen you up a little."

Their college coed waitress lingered by the table, waiting for their order and staring at Doug in open admiration. Doug met her gaze and with a flirtatious grin placed their order. "Chips and salsa, please, and the lady will have a large margarita, frozen."

The girl brought their order and Ashley slurped the frosty lime concoction quickly while Doug eyed her in amusement, sipping his ice water and munching on chips and salsa. Ashley relaxed significantly and flashed Doug a brilliant smile. "See there, I told you that I'm fine," she said in sassy defiance.

"I know you're not fine, Ash," Doug said, eyeing her skeptically. "But I'm a little more understanding about why you're not. I miss him too."

Ashley may have loosened up but much to Doug's dismay, she also became teary-eyed, turning into an emotional mess and unleashing tears held back for months as she lay her head on the table and wept. "You know that's why I won't go home. It hurts too much to remember," she sobbed, while Doug stroked her long, silky hair that fell in a tumble across her face.

"Ash, you know that he'd hate to see you this way," Doug tried to soothe her. "*I* hate to see you this way. Jimmy would want you to move on."

"Knowing that doesn't make me feel any better," she wailed. "I'm not ready to move on. I don't want anyone else but Jimmy."

"Maybe I shouldn't have pushed you to have that drink," Doug said, muttering more to himself than to Ashley. "Darlin', I didn't want to make you cry. But you're asking the impossible. There's no way to get him back, you know that."

"I know," she sniffed at him, lifting her head off the table, pushing back the hair from her face and gazing at him with her swollen red eyes. Doug leaned back in his chair, hesitant to drop his next bombshell.

"Well, I was going to tell you this over the telephone before your gloom-and-doom routine forced me to make a trip here," Doug began, ignoring Ashley's fierce frown at his cynicism. "While you're already upset, I might as well tell you that Lana and John have sold their house in Pineville. They are moving to New Orleans."

"Lana can't stand the memories there anymore than I can," Ashley speculated, dabbing at her wet eyes with her dinner napkin. "When are they moving?"

"Right after Thanksgiving. I think you should muster up a little courage before they leave and go home to tell them goodbye."

"I will, I promise. I owe them that much." A guilty expression dominated her features. "I've been horrible. I haven't even gone to see them since the funeral and I've refused to take any of Will's calls. They must think I'm just terrible."

"I've seen them and they understand," Doug said, reassuringly. "They're not upset with you at all. They miss you but they're not mad at you."

With a clink of the glasses on her heavy tray, the waitress sat down another margarita in front of Ashley and Doug grinned as she gulped it down greedily.

"You *did* need a drink," he kidded her. "Would you like a cheese enchilada to go with your tequila, Ashley?" She nodded enthusiastically, sticking her fork into his plate to mooch a bite or two of his huge dinner.

"How is Will doing?" she asked between bites. "Do you ever see him at LSU?"

"You mean, William 'Animal House' Moreau?" Doug chuckled heartily. "Yeah, I see him all the time. He's made quite a name for himself on Fraternity Row."

"Is he doing okay?" Ashley leaned back lazily, propping her feet up on the edge of Doug's chair.

"He's doing as well as could be expected," Doug slid his empty plate to the side and met Ashley's worried gaze. "About the same as the rest of us."

"Tell him I said hi," she said, feeling a little tipsy at this point, but that wasn't totally unpleasant. She didn't mind having a little bit of fun. It had been a long time since she'd truly enjoyed herself.

Doug returned her to the dorm just before eleven o'clock, walking her to the double glass doors at the entrance and giving her a brotherly embrace.

"Thanks for getting me out and about. I'd forgotten what a great Saturday night guy you are," Ashley smiled up at him.

"My pleasure," Doug said, looking relieved that she had stopped crying and was more cheerful.

"Dougie, are you going to be okay driving home tonight?"

"I'll be fine," he laughed. "You're the one who drank, remember? I didn't." He reached out to push a loose lock of hair from her face. "You are going home for Thanksgiving break?" he reiterated, raising one eyebrow questioningly.

"Yes, I promise," she said, holding up her fingers to swear scout's honor before pulling open the door and stepping into the dimly lit lobby of Slater Hall. "See ya, Dougie."

"See ya, Ash." She watched him stroll down the sidewalk, smiling after him fondly.

She toddled up the stairs to her dorm room, threw on her pajamas and jumped into bed. She quickly drifted off, sleeping soundly for the first time in months.

CHAPTER THIRTEEN

True to her promise to Doug, Ashley went home when classes let out the Tuesday afternoon before Thanksgiving. Despite the sad tug at her heart as she drove through the streets of Pineville, she was truly glad to be home, having missed her hometown more than she knew. When she pulled into the driveway, Maggie's car was in the garage, indicating that she was home from work already. Ashley sprang from the Corolla, bounding up the front steps.

"Hello!" she bellowed as she flew in the front door.

Maggie met her in the hallway, hugging her as Ashley rested her head on her mother's shoulder. "Hello," Maggie said, happily. "Welcome home."

"Thanks, it's really good to be here." Ashley lifted her head to look around the house, relieved to find that not one thing had changed since August. Everything looked exactly as it had for years.

After a tasty welcome home dinner of seafood gumbo with Maggie and Remy, Ashley carried her bags upstairs to her room, pausing briefly in the doorway before going in and letting the nostalgia hit her in the face. She quickly unpacked, made a short phone call to Susanna, and then took a long hot bath before getting into bed.

She pulled the lace-trimmed floral sheet to her chin, staring in frustration at the ceiling before giving in to the urge to glance at the box on the closet shelf. It beckoned her, silently begging her to pull it down, to open it, to bring Jimmy alive again by revisiting him in her mind. No, she resisted the call of the box. Not now, not tonight. The trip to John and Lana's tomorrow would be hard enough. There was no need to reopen old wounds tonight.

The next morning, with a Thermos bottle filled with hot tea and a plate of oatmeal cookies, Ashley drove stoically down the highway to the Moreaus' house. With a heavy heart, she pulled into the driveway, parking behind the cars of Lana and Will. She sat very still, staring at the house, gathering the courage needed to face the ghosts. With a deep breath, she opened her car door, getting out to troop valiantly toward the Moreaus' front door.

She rang the front bell, fidgeting nervously as she waited. The door swung open to reveal Lana, lovely and once-again youthful, her face taking on a look of shock and delighted surprise. "Ashley! Oh my God, come in!" Lana pulled her into the house, hugging her tightly as she kissed her cheek. "I'm so glad to see you, honey."

"I'm glad to see you too," Ashley blinked away the hot tears flooding into her eyes and glanced around the sunlit living room, bursting at the seams with moving boxes and tissue paper. She looked back to Lana, relieved that the dark circles of exhaustion had disappeared from underneath her eyes, leaving only a distant flicker of deep sorrow, especially when she looked at Ashley.

"I brought tea and cookies," Ashley lifted her package. "I thought you could probably use a break from packing."

"I hope you brought enough for me!" Will's voice filled the room as he entered from the back of the house. He crossed the living room in two great strides, lifting Ashley into a fond bear hug. "Hello, ma chère," his lips brushed her cheek affectionately. "It's about time you came to see us."

The three of them picnicked on the carpet, drinking tea from Styrofoam cups and munching cookies as they caught up on the months they spent apart. "Where's John?" Ashley asked, glancing around for signs indicating his whereabouts.

"He's still in New Orleans, at his new office," Lana said. "He'll be so sorry that he missed seeing you."

"I'm sorry that I missed seeing him too." Ashley truly regretted that she wouldn't get to say goodbye to John Moreau. She loved him dearly.

"How are you liking Northeast?" Will inquired.

"I like Northeast just fine," Ashley tried to keep her tone light. "I study a lot."

Will raised a doubting eyebrow. "I can't believe that remark came out of your mouth," he said with a chuckle. "I seem to remember that studying was not your strong point."

"Will, be nice," Lana said, her eyes wide as she frowned at him.

"That's okay, Lana." Ashley said, laughing good-naturedly. "If Will didn't tease me, I'd be shocked." She turned her attention to Will. "I've changed a lot since those days."

"I was disappointed when I heard that you weren't coming to LSU," Will said, "but I do understand why you couldn't."

"Doug tells me that you're getting along just fine without my presence," she laughed devilishly as Will flashed a naughty grin, knowing exactly to what she was referring.

"Do you like the house that you're moving into in New Orleans?" she turned to Lana, who smiled hesitantly at Ashley's question.

"Yes, the house is very nice. I will miss this house, of course, but it's time for me to go," she admitted with a sad sigh. Ashley reached out, clasping Lana's hand in silent comfort, their eyes meeting in mutual understanding. Each woman still ached from her loss but knew that she had to move on with her life.

"I think I'll miss the lake the most," Will declared, gesturing toward the windows. "You can't beat a view like that one."

After a morning of catching up, Ashley reluctantly rose to leave. "I should go and let you all get back to packing," she said, her eyes memorizing the room one last time for future reference.

Will stood with her, objecting to her departure. "Don't rush off, Ashley. Stay for lunch."

"I really should go. I haven't seen my folks much this semester so I should spend some time at home."

Lana rose for a farewell embrace. "Have a happy life, Ashley," she whispered softly and Ashley felt the salty sting of tears welling up in her eyes, but didn't stop them, allowing them to cascade down her cheeks in hot, bitter streams. Lana held her at arm's length, gazing at her with woeful eyes. "I'm very sorry that I'll never have you as a daughter-in-law."

"Me too," Ashley's voice cracked as sobs choked her and she threw her arms around Lana's graceful neck. They embraced tearfully until Will broke the tension.

"Hey, don't rule me out!" he joked to lighten the mood, successfully managing to wrestle laughter from both Lana and Ashley. The two women said their goodbyes, then Will escorted Ashley out to her car.

"Keep in touch," he leaned down to kiss her cheek. "In person and not just through Doug." His eyes sparkled with good humor as he teased her.

"I will," Ashley said, sliding into the driver's seat of her faithful vehicle. "Try to behave yourself, Will Moreau," she said as she put her car in reverse. "You can't let anything happen to you, you know. We'd never survive losing you too."

Ashley blew him a friendly kiss then backed out of the driveway, heading in the direction of her parents' home, breathing a deep sigh of relief. She did it, and she was glad that she had visited them. It did her a world of good to know that the Moreaus were getting better with each passing day. It gave her hope, hope that her life might at some point return to normal, or at least something closely resembling normal.

After a dismal, lonely Thanksgiving and an equally depressing Christmas break, Ashley returned with Kate to Northeast to begin the second semester of her first year of college. With each passing day, life improved and she began to display some hints of her former vivacious personality, to the amazement of Hillary and Melissa, neither of whom had seen her out of her subdued state of mourning.

Yes, for Ashley, life was better that second semester. She welcomed care packages from home, along with weekly phone calls from Doug and frequent visits from Susanna, who was determined to leave Monroe on its ear with each visit. She occasionally ventured from the dormitory, working out at the gym with Kate or going to a movie or coffee shop with Hillary and Melissa. She felt like a new woman, almost.

But then it would happen. Just as she became confident that she would be able to go on with her life, the haunting memory of Jimmy would visit her in the night. His image in her dreams was so real, so lifelike, that she would wake the next morning with an aching heart and a pillow wet from her heartbroken tears, making her realize that she still loved him. God help her, she still loved Jimmy Moreau deeply and mourned him with every beat of her heart. The resulting melancholy brought by his entrance into her dreams lingered for days before Ashley could shake it off, forcing herself to offer a radiant smile to the rest of the world, while inside her soul wailed inconsolably.

At last, following a long semester of endless study, sleepless nights and gallons of black coffee, Ashley's first year of college was complete. After packing her things back into their cardboard boxes, she loaded the Corolla and headed with Kate back home to Pineville for the summer.

Ashley went to work for Remy at the drugstore, being promoted from the front register to the pharmacy register. She pulled up to the curb in front of the drugstore on a sunny morning in the middle of May, her first day back to work, and stepped out of the car, beaming up at the beige brick building fondly. Seeing Remy's Family Pharmacy, with its green awning over the doors and sparkling plate glass windows decorated with brightly colored sale signs was like coming home again. She pulled open the glass door and scurried in, heading directly for the pharmacy at the back of the store.

"Don't be thinkin' that you can sneak by here without sayin' hello to ol' Mist' Eddie, chère." Robust Mister Eddie Thibodeaux flashed a toothy smile from behind the chrome counter in the grill, clutching an iron skillet in one chubby hand and a silver spatula in the other. "Git yo'self in here, girl."

Grinning broadly, Ashley stopped in her tracks and turned in to the restaurant.

"Hey, Mist' Eddie. Comment allez-vous?" she approached him wearing a look of delight, happy to see her old friend.

"Hey yo'self, chère. C'mon over here and let me see what college life done to ya." As she walked toward him, he took inventory of Ashley's tiny frame, dressed in blue jeans and a button-down oxford, her brown hair plaited in a long braid hanging down to the middle of her back. "Sit yo'self down. Mist' Eddie gonna make you de finest strawberry milk shake, guaranteed to put some meat on dem bones."

Ashley perched on the swivel stool in front of him, watching as he scooped the pink ice cream into an aluminum shaker. As he mixed her shake, he filled her in on the latest gossip. "I see yo' friend Miss Susanna Robicheaux near about every day. She walks down from the bank during lunchtime," he said, his eyes dancing with amusement. "She be a feisty one, dat girl."

"That's one way to put it."

"Gonna make some man a fine wife some day."

"God forbid," Ashley grinned, accepting the frosty parfait glass overflowing with strawberry milkshake and topped with rainbow-colored sprinkles that he slid across the counter to her.

"Der you go, baby, dat'll put de rosy back in your cheeks." Grinning, Mister Eddie leaned on the counter, observing her with his wise gray eyes. "Hard for me t'believe dat yo're already nineteen," he said, shaking his silver head in disbelief. "I 'member when you was a little girl in piggy tails, comin' in here, holding tight of yo' daddy's hand. Now, yo're all growned up and in college, lookin' jus' like Miz Maggie did when yo' daddy bringed her here from Alabama, 'cept I think yo're a might bit prettier."

Ashley acknowledged his compliment with a sincere smile while Mister Eddie reached out to pinch her cheek. "Now, tell Mist' Eddie 'bout college. How many boys ya keepin' on a string?" his eyes twinkled merrily at her.

"Actually, I've haven't been dating yet," she said with just a hint of sorrow creeping into her solemn green eyes.

"Dey ain't no reason for ya to look so sad, dahlin, not a pretty, young thing like yo'self." He reached out, squeezing her hand comfortingly. "Mist' Jimmy Moreau was a fine young man and he be up der in Heaven waitin' on ya. But it gonna be a long time before ya up der wid him and I don't 'pect he'd like ya pining away over him de way ya do."

He straightened suddenly, snapping his fingers as an idea came to him. "Ya know what ya need, chère? Ya need a good coon-ass boy. Dat'd cheer ya right up."

Ashley raised an eyebrow speculatively. "A coon-ass, huh?"

"Yeah, girl, some good ol' Cajun boy with de name of Fontenot or Boudreaux. He'd show ya a good time, I guarantee it." He shook his finger knowingly. "But ya ain't gonna find one up der in Monroe, no sirree. Ya need to be in school in Lafayette or in Baton Rouge wid Mist' Doug Fairchild, dat's where ya need to be."

"Eddie Thibodeaux!" Ashley swiveled around to see Frannie standing behind them, her hands thrown firmly on her voluptuous hips, glaring at Mister Eddie sternly. "What are you doin', man? Mist' Remy up there waiting for Ashley to come to work and you got her back here, feeding her strawberry milkshake and filling her ear with your bull."

"Now, Frannie, I was jus' feedin' da girl. Look at her, she's skin and bones." Mister Eddie said, protesting her reprimand of him. "And da girl needed some advice."

"From you? Lordy mercy! What an old fool you are."

Ashley suppressed a giggle, watching with merrily dancing eyes as Frannie and Mister Eddie argued like small children in a schoolyard. It didn't surprise or shock her in the least. She had listened to the same variety of bickering from them for most of her life. She slid easily off the stool, striving to pacify Frannie by going to work.

"Bye, Mister Eddie. Thanks for the milkshake," she offered him the bright smile of a silent ally in his fight against Frannie.

"Bye-bye, dahlin'," he grinned expansively as she walked away from the counter. "Ya jus' 'member what Mist' Eddie done tol' ya now, ya hear?"

"Crazy old goat," Frannie fumed under her breath as she walked beside Ashley toward the pharmacy. "I wouldn't listen to one word he said if I were you."

May twenty-second was Ashley's Pearl Harbor, the day for her that would live in infamy. May twenty-second marked a year that Jimmy had been gone. In some ways, she couldn't believe that it had already been a year, and in some ways, she felt like he had been gone forever.

She wasn't the only one who remembered that date. She was lying across her bed, staring out the window and pondering life when Maggie tapped lightly on the door. "Hi," she smiled gently as she stuck her head in the door. "You okay today?"

Ashley nodded distractedly as she continued to gaze out the window. "Yeah, I'm okay."

"Do you want me to go with you out to Jimmy's grave?"

Ashley snapped to attention at Maggie's question, jerking her head around to stare at her mother. "I'm not going there ever again," she said determinedly. "He knows that I love him without me paying homage to a concrete tombstone."

"Ashley Stewart, you ought to be ashamed," Maggie scolded her, a look of disbelief shrouding her face. "You should go out and put some flowers on his grave at least."

"Why in God's name would I want to commemorate his death? I'd rather just continue to celebrate his life." Ashley rolled to sit on the edge of the bed, staring up at Maggie defiantly.

"You are such an odd girl sometimes," Maggie shook her head and sighed heavily, leaving Ashley alone in the solitude of her room.

"I don't know what's so odd about not wanting to go to a cemetery," Ashley mocked her statement after Maggie left, hesitating for a moment before scooping up her car keys and scooting out the front door. She drove away, in search of the one person who would understand her feelings and the one person who could offer her some solace. She went in search of Doug.

The Fairchilds lived in a rustic two-story log cabin designed and built by Nick Fairchild a few miles down Old Marksville Highway near Paper Mill Road. Ashley pulled into the driveway, searching for Doug's old car. Ms. Bobbie opened the front door and stepped out on to the porch.

"Hello stranger! You've been home a week and you're just now coming to see me?" Ms. Bobbie's booming voice hailed her as she climbed from the Corolla. Ashley grinned at her, giggling as Ms. Bobbie chided her, and strolled over casually to join her on the front porch.

Ashley was quite fond of Bobbie Fairchild and embraced her affectionately as they walked arm and arm into the house. Ms. Bobbie was an attractive woman, pleasingly plump with graying dark-brown hair and large dark eyes. Ashley had heard over the years that Roberta Comeaux had been quite a belle in her younger days. Out of the many suitors vying for her hand, Roberta had chosen Nick Fairchild and married the handsome local architect and homebuilder. From that day forward, she had let go of her frivolous teenage ways, becoming the woman known by all as Ms. Bobbie Fairchild, gladly devoting her entire existence to Nick and their only child, Douglas Shawn.

Ashley stepped inside the front door, viewing the large, open great room with warmth and familiarity. The Fairchilds' house was very different from the Moreaus' house, its best description falling somewhere between designer camouflage and homey.

The living room held a huge overstuffed tan couch with multi-colored, crocheted afghans draped over each arm and pillows thrown haphazardly upon its cushions. The big screen television, usually tuned into some sporting event, held center stage opposite the couch and two well worn recliners that had been there as long as Ashley and Doug had been friends.

On the bookshelves against the wall were trophies of all shapes and sizes; some were Mr. Fairchild's hunting and fishing prizes, but most were Doug's football trophies dating back as far as grammar school. Above the stone fireplace was the mounted head of Nick's prize deer, its glassy brown eyes staring out at Ashley as she settled comfortably on the couch.

Ms. Bobbie pulled open the glass-front cabinet above the sink, bringing down two tea glasses and filling them with iced raspberry tea. "Ashley, I've got some of those lemon squares you like so well. Want some, honey?"

"I'd love some," Ashley turned her body, leaning over the back of the couch to watch Ms. Bobbie fuss over her in the kitchen. "Where's Douglas?"

"Now, Ashley, I've never known you to ask such a silly question," Ms. Bobbie glanced over her shoulder with a broad smile. "It's summer time, girl. You should know he's out fishing with Scotty."

For an instant, Ashley was overcome by an eerie chill. Fishing, just like this day last year, she thought morbidly before shaking off the gloomy thought. "When do you think he'll be back?"

"I don't imagine that he'll be out much longer," Ms. Bobbie strolled over to hand Ashley a glass of tea and a plate of cookies. "Stay here and tell me all about Monroe."

Ashley drank iced tea and munched lemon squares with Ms. Bobbie, relating the highlights of her freshman year of college. Ms. Bobbie's dark eyes twinkled with laughter as she listened and she shook her head skeptically as Ashley finished. "Sounds pretty sedate next to Doug's year," she said. "That boy was so wild that I'm surprised that he passed any of his classes."

About that time, they heard a car door slam and the thudding sound of scrambling feet across the wooden porch before the door was thrown open with a loud bang. "Where's my Ice Princess!" Scotty's large frame filled the doorway as he stood there, grinning ear to ear, holding a line of fish in one hand.

"Scotty Jeansonne, get those fish out of my living room!" Ms. Bobbie sprang from the couch, swatting Scotty on the arm as she shooed him out into the garage. "I swear, boy, sometimes you act like you were raised in a barn!"

Ashley could hear her scolding him all the way from the living room into the garage and she giggled, glad that it was Scotty getting the tongue-lashing and not her. She glanced toward the doorway as Doug appeared, sneaking stealthily inside from the driveway.

"If Scotty sees me, he'll make me help him clean those fish," he said as he strode purposely to join Ashley on the couch. Doug looked terrific, tanned and relaxed, in shorts and a Panama Jack T-shirt, his curly blond hair hidden under his standard baseball cap. He stretched his arm casually across the back of the couch, appraising her with his lingering gaze. "Hello, Ash," he leaned forward to kiss the top of her head. "I thought I might see you today. You okay?"

"Yeah," Ashley said, her concern for him flickering in her eyes. "Are you?" She knew that Doug's memories of this day were much darker than hers. His were vivid memories of the awful sounds he'd heard and the horrible sights he had seen.

"Yeah, I'm okay," he wrinkled his brow as his temples throbbed and reached his hand up to massage them, hoping to ease the pain this day caused him. Ashley stroked his shoulder consolingly and moved closer to lay her head on his shoulder.

"I needed to be with you today," she said, her voice reduced to a faint whisper. "I'm feeling pretty down and lonely."

"Then I'm the guy for you," Doug stopped rubbing his temples, shooting her a sidelong glance as he grinned and winked.

"Is he propositioning you?" Scott demanded, marching in from the garage, noting Ashley's head on Doug's shoulder with an expansive grin.

Ashley lifted her head to look at Scotty, answering him with a saucy smile. "Nothing I can't handle."

Scotty plopped clumsily into a recliner, eyeing them from beneath a fallen lock of his shaggy hair. "Y'all want to call up some people and fry some fish?"

Doug shook his head. "Let's save it for next weekend. I think Ashley and I want to spend a little time alone tonight."

"Oh yeah?" Scotty grinned at the implication of Doug's statement. "Is there something y'all aren't telling me?" He pulled himself out of the sinking cushion of his chair, laughing at Doug's wry look as he trudged toward the front door.

"Bye Princess!" Scotty bellowed over his shoulder as he shot out the door, grinning at the aggravated look on Doug's face as he joined him outside. Ashley waved to Scotty from the window and gave Doug an expectant look as he re-entered the room.

"Call Ms. Maggie and tell her we're going out in the boat for a little while," Doug said, grabbing his car keys from the table next to the door.

They rode around Buhlow Lake for hours, letting the early summer wind whip through their hair and cool their hot faces. Finally, Doug steered the boat toward the narrow beach along the edge of the lake and cut the engine, joining Ashley in the bow of the boat, stretching out on his back to stare up at the sky. It was peaceful there, with no unwelcome interruptions, a perfect place to talk.

"Do you ever think about him?" Ashley asked curiously, turning her head to look at Doug.

"Sure I do," he spoke softly, his eyes fixed on the snowy white cumulus clouds in the sky above them. "Not a day goes by that I don't think of him in one way or another. I may not have been in love with him, but I still miss him as much as you do."

"Sometimes I think that I'll never get past this," she whispered to him. "I want to go on, Doug, I really do."

Doug looked over at her, smiling sympathetically. Ashley didn't know how he could be so patient with her. Even *she* thought that she was beginning to sound like a broken record.

"Today's not a good day for either of us," he said, taking her hand and applying a soothing squeeze, "but you've made it past the one year mark, Ash. You're going to be fine, I promise you that. I'll make sure that you have one fantastic summer and then I'll send you back to Monroe, ready to conquer the world."

Ashley squeezed his hand tightly and offered him a grateful smile. "Thank you, Doug," she said. "Thank you for being such a good friend."

Doug was as good as his word, providing Ashley with a marvelous summer; keeping her much too busy with social activities and too entertained with his charming wit and personality for Ashley to have much time to revisit the past. She kissed Doug's lips fondly as he told her goodbye the day he left to go back to Baton Rouge.

"What was that for?" he marveled with a grin, his twinkling eyes wide with surprise and delight.

"That was a thank you," she said, returning his smile. "You did it, Dougie. Mission accomplished. You're sending me back to Northeast ready to conquer the world."

CHAPTER FOURTEEN

Kate and Ashley moved back to Northeast the middle of August, opting for another year on the fourth floor of Slater Hall with Hillary and Melissa. It was good to be back in Monroe, Ashley decided as she unpacked her boxes and bags, quickly filling her tiny closet and her side of the dorm room with clothes, books, snacks and pictures. Determined to live up to her bargain with Doug and conquer the world, she shocked Kate, Hillary and Melissa by accepting their invitation to go to The Bleachers, a club near campus.

The club was packed with college co-eds checking out the romantic prospects for the new academic year. Ashley climbed on a stool at their table near the dance floor, watching, with an entertained smile, the couples gyrating to the sounds of the Go Go's, their faces speckled by the light from the spinning mirrored ball above their heads.

Having Hillary with them was an automatic man magnet. No sooner had they given their drink order to their waitress than men swarmed their table, begging Hillary to dance. Ashley watched the down-to-earth Hillary as she looked around the table with an unassuming smile, laughingly giving in to the least offending of the assembled group.

Melissa sighed. "No competition," she said. "I can't stand to be with her sometimes!" Melissa, once quite timid, had come out of her shell since befriending Hillary and was well on her way to being as obnoxious as her suitemates.

"There are plenty of men to go around," Kate noted with a sweeping gesture of her hand, taking Hillary's obvious popularity in stride. As Ashley suspected, it wasn't very long before the lovely Kate also took to the dance floor, gliding gracefully in the arms of a guy from her psychology class. Melissa leaned across the table.

"If the prospects aren't coming to our table, then I'll just have to walk around and scout out some potential victims," she said with a devilish grin, sliding off her stool and heading in the direction of the bar.

Ashley tapped her fingers in time with Prince, wiggling her shoulders as she danced in her chair. She was having fun, glad that none of the males crowding the bar had approached her. Coming to the club was fine but she didn't know whether she was ready to attempt mindless chatter with a perfect stranger.

"Hey, pretty lady," she suddenly felt the touch of a hand, "let's go dance."

"I spoke too soon," Ashley thought as she turned to face the owner of the firm hand on her shoulder. He was cute enough, she decided, although he was very intoxicated. She smiled politely at him. "I'd rather not, but thank you though," she said, shaking her head and continuing to smile at him. If she was going to dance, it was going to be with someone who might remember it the next day.

"How about with me, then?" she looked to her left to discover that he had a companion who was equally inebriated.

"No, thank you," she said, refusing firmly as her polite smile began to wane. She was beginning to tire of them and wanted them to leave.

"Do you think you're too good for us?" the first fellow said hotly, grabbing her roughly by the arm. Ashley's eyes widened with surprise and anxiety, wondering how feisty with her these little drunks might become.

"I'd rather that you didn't grab my arm that way," she said through gritted teeth, keeping her voice calm and even as she tried to pull away, but he held on tight. Ashley glared vehemently at him, narrowing her eyes in frustration.

"Let go of my arm!" she repeated her request, although it did no good, he only squeezed harder. She was ready to look around for help when a strong voice intervened.

"I believe the lady would like you to let go of her arm."

Ashley glanced up into the face of one of the most appealing men she'd ever seen. Her eyes widened in appreciation as she gazed at him, reveling in the absolute beauty of him. He was tall and lean, with thick dark hair and gorgeous eyes the shade of Caribbean waters surrounded by long, thick lashes. Ashley forced herself to blink, thinking it rude to stare at him so incredulously.

The hand gripping her arm relaxed. "Hey, I was only asking her to dance," her soused harasser said, protesting with an indignant slur.

Her handsome rescuer wrinkled his brow. "Maybe you should work on your people skills." He challenged them with a stern glare and finally the two guys sauntered away, muttering under their breath as they toddled toward the sound of the clinking glasses at the crowded bar.

"Thank you," Ashley said breathlessly, once again gazing in awe at the great-looking stranger. The depth of her immediate attraction was overwhelming. For the first time in a long time, she found her knees growing weak in the presence of a man.

"You're welcome. You looked like you could use a little assistance," he smiled, his teeth perfect and white, in a mouth that could only be described as inviting. "May I join you?"

"Of course," Ashley nodded, gesturing to the chair beside her.

He sat down, extending his hand to her. "I'm Rick LeNoir," he introduced himself, and Ashley noted a hint of southern Louisiana drawl in his voice. A coon-ass, she laughed inwardly, a good omen sent courtesy of Mister Eddie Thibodeaux.

She took his hand, shaking it firmly and noting the warmth she felt at his strong touch. "Ashley Stewart." She didn't want to let go of his hand. His touch was electrifying.

"What are you drinking?" Rick asked, indicating her glass with a nod of his head.

"Margarita on the rocks."

Rick gestured for the waitress, a bouncy young redhead from Northeast, and ordered Ashley's margarita and for himself, a beer. Ashley continued to survey him with interest. He was completely mesmerizing, with a panther-like elegance about him that fascinated her. He was obviously older, appearing to have just come from work, attired in a tailored charcoal gray suit, which he wore wonderfully. Totally GQ, she decided with an impressed smile.

"Do you go to Northeast?" he looked over at her with his marvelous aqua eyes, his face lit with enthusiastic curiosity.

"Yes, second year," she said, stammering shyly. "How about you?"

Rick chuckled slightly. "Thanks for the compliment. I graduated from Northeast three years ago."

"How old *are* you?" Ashley said, without thinking, wanting to kick herself for being so rude. Way to impress him with your natural grace and boundless charm, Ding Dong.

"I'm twenty-five," Rick seemed unaffected by her blunt question. "How old are you, Ms. Stewart?"

"Younger than you are," her eyes flirted with him as she turned to accept the drink offered by their waitress. She sipped her drink, watching Rick LeNoir intently over the salted rim of her glass.

He quickly evaluated her with an educated rove of his eye. "I would say that you are somewhere between nineteen and twenty," he declared with a smile.

"I'll never tell." Ashley giggled under his attentive gaze, feeling as giddy as a schoolgirl.

"What's your major, college girl?" he poured his beer from its brown bottle into a frosted glass as he awaited her response.

"Pharmacy."

"Ah, brains and beauty all in one package, a rare combination," his speech pattern was clipped and deliberate, as he tried to suppress his Cajun accent. Ashley wondered why he tried so hard to disguise his dialect. She thought that it would be so charming if he slipped up and ended a sentence by calling her "Dahlin'."

"I don't know if I would go that far if I were you," she dismissed his compliment casually while blushing, flustered at his flattery. "What do you do?"

"I'm a computer analyst."

"Sounds pretty impressive. What does a computer analyst do?"

"I create and evaluate computer programs for a corporation. My job is based here in Monroe, but we have several offices around the country."

"So basically, you're telling me that you're a computer nerd."

"I guess that's one way of looking at it." Noting the tenseness in his reply, Ashley hoped that she hadn't offended Rick. She had grown so used to the perverted sense of humor shared by her friends that she offered her unsolicited opinion without giving it a second thought. It worked for Susanna anyway.

"I didn't mean that in a negative way."

"No offense taken," Rick assured her with a sincere smile.

Kate returned to the table, openly admiring Rick before glancing curiously at Ashley. "Who's your friend?" she inquired with raised brows.

"Rick LeNoir, this is my best friend and roommate, Kate Ducote."

Kate extended her slender hand with casual grace, offering Rick her most lovely smile.

"Pleasure to meet you, Kate," he said, returning her smile with a captivating one of his own.

"Likewise, I'm sure," Kate drawled, pulling up a chair and shooting Ashley a congratulatory salute with her dancing eyes. She then turned to Rick and began firing questions at him in a motherly drill, determined to complete her fact-finding mission before granting Rick LeNoir permission to date Ashley. Rick answered her questions good-naturedly, aware of her motive. He was let off the hook by the arrival of Mitch Guidry, who whisked Kate off to the dance floor for the Cotton-eyed Joe.

"How long have you known one another?" Rick asked, nodding toward Kate as she whirled past their table, circling the dance floor in Mitch's arms.

"All our lives. Our parents are next-door neighbors. I'm sorry for the third degree. Kate's not usually so pushy."

"That's fine, really," he gazed warmly at her. "It's nice to know that a lovely woman such as yourself has such a good friend looking out for her."

"Now, that's a line if I've ever heard one!" Hillary plopped down on the chair next to Rick's, grinning vivaciously. "And believe me, buddy, I've heard them all."

Rick surveyed the leggy, blonde Texan, arching a brow speculatively. "I'm sure you have," he said, his tone slightly cynical.

"But I assure you, she hasn't," Hillary jerked her thumb in Ashley's direction. "In fact, Ashley, this is a first. I don't think I've seen you with a man since we've been at Northeast."

Rick swiveled his head to stare at Ashley in surprise. "I find that hard to believe," he said, regarding her inquisitively as he waited for an explanation.

"It's a long story," Ashley promptly closed the subject, giving Hillary a look that shot daggers.

After closing the bar down, Rick escorted Ashley out into the muggy night air, drawing her to the side as they approached the parking lot. "Would you mind if I called you?" he asked. "I'd really like to take you to dinner or a movie."

She nodded and smiled. "I'd like that," she said, writing her phone number down on the back of the business card Rick handed her. "Thanks again for coming to my rescue," she said as she handed the card back to him.

"It was to my benefit, I assure you," Rick smiled charmingly, lifting her dainty hand to his sensual lips and kissing it softly. He met her gaze with his magnificent eyes, captivating her with his smile. "You'll be hearing from me."

Ashley stared after him as he strolled away, feeling like she was developing symptoms of a teenage crush. She joined Kate in the back seat of Hillary's white Volkswagen Bug convertible, grinning ear to ear as she leaned her head back against the seat. Hillary whipped the little car out of the parking lot, traveling at break-neck speed toward the dormitory.

"You have the silliest look on your face," Kate said. "I haven't seen that look in a long, long time."

"What did you think of him?" Ashley asked her. With Kate, she had to ask. It was only Susanna who offered her unsolicited opinion.

"I think he's very good-looking and he seems nice enough."

"I'll tell you what," Hillary chimed in, turning down the radio as she glanced at Ashley in the rearview mirror. "He can park his shoes under my bed any time."

"He's a little old for you, don't you think?" Melissa craned her neck, peering at Ashley from the front seat to get in her two cents worth.

"I don't think so. He's only six years older than I am," Ashley challenged her defensively. "That's not that big of a difference in age."

"Only if you don't consider that when you were in sixth grade, he was a senior in high school," Melissa said, and Ashley stuck her tongue out at her before scowling in annoyance.

"Killjoy."

Kate laughed at Ashley's pouty expression. "You don't have to be so defensive, Ashley. We're not going to forbid you from seeing him."

"It would take wild horses to keep me from seeing him," Ashley said, sighing deeply as she conjured up his face in her mind. "That is, if I hear from him again."

And hear from him she did, the very next afternoon. Returning from chemistry lab, she flopped stomach-first onto her bed, resting her chin on a pillow as she clicked on the television to catch her afternoon soap. When the phone rang, she lazily stretched out her arm to retrieve the receiver from the bedside table. "Hello?" she answered casually, expecting to find Maggie or Remy on the other end.

"May I speak to Ashley please?" Ashley's heart thumped excitedly as she recognized his voice immediately.

"You've got her," Ashley said, rolling off the bed onto the braided rug in the center of the dorm room. She lay on her back, cradling the phone against her shoulder with the world's silliest smile on her face.

"Hi Ashley. This is Rick LeNoir. We met last night." He actually believed that she wouldn't remember.

"Hi, Rick. How are you?" she said, proud of herself for acting so nonchalantly.

"I'm great. How was class?"

"Class was good." She didn't trust herself with long answers, afraid that her voice might quiver with the excitement she felt.

"Would you like to see a movie tonight? We could go to the early show, so that you can still study tonight if you need to."

Ashley kicked her feet in the air, thrilled with the prospect of seeing Rick LeNoir again. She wanted to squeal at the top of her lungs but she refrained, keeping her cool. "Sure, Rick, I'd love to."

"Fantastic! I'll pick you up around six-thirty. Tell me where you live."

She gave Rick directions to Slater Hall, then, after hanging up with him, jumped up from the floor, dancing wildly around the room. She tried to study, but she was too excited. She cursed Kate for not being in from class yet, disappointed that she had not one person with whom to share the moment. She paced in front of the closet, trying to decide what to wear. She was changing into her fourth outfit when Kate finally came in from class, curiously surveying the pile of clothing at Ashley's feet.

"Going somewhere?" she regarded Ashley quizzically, her green eyes sparkling with amusement.

"I'm going to the movie with Rick!" Ashley smiled happily and peered into the mirror as she evaluated her outfit, a tan denim shirt paired with a long brown corduroy skirt and brown riding boots. She nodded with satisfaction then lifted one side of her heavy mane of hair as she glanced questioning toward Kate. "Up or down?" she said, seeking guidance over a hairstyle.

"Definitely down," Kate said as she handed Ashley a hairbrush. "All this for a movie?" she indicated the mess on the floor.

"Well, this is my first date in a very long time. I'm a little out of practice."

"And what a gorgeous date he is," Kate set her pile of books on her desk with a loud thud. "I'm proud of you for taking this first step back into the dating scene, Ashley. I know the last year has been hard on you."

"It's taken some time." Ashley put down the brush and sat on the end of Kate's bunk. "But you have to admit, Rick didn't have to twist my arm very hard to get me to go out with him."

Kate changed quickly into gray sweatpants, pulling her pale blond pageboy up into a ponytail as she prepared to hit the books for the evening. She looked at

Ashley skeptically. "Rick may be exceptionally handsome, but believe me, Ashley, he holds no special magic. You must've been ready to date again or you still wouldn't have gone out with him."

"He would've been pretty hard to resist," Ashley grinned, retrieving her purse as their bright red Mickey Mouse alarm clock on the bedside table chimed half past six. "See ya, Katydid."

"Behave yourself, dahlin'," Kate laughed as Ashley pranced out the door, glad to see Ashley playful again, at last.

She spotted Rick the moment she exited the stairwell. He was leaning against the wall, casually surveying a group of girls gathered in the sitting room adjacent to the lobby. He glanced up as she came into sight, flashing one enchanting smile. "Hello Ashley."

"Hi," she said, feeling a scalding warmth flood into her cheeks and butterflies flip-flopping deep within her gut as she stared at him. How was it possible that he looked even more gorgeous by the light of day?

"Ready to go?" he asked and she nodded, taking the arm he offered her. Rick opened the door and led her outside into the dusky August night toward his car parked at the front of Slater Hall.

"Nice car," she told him as he opened the passenger door of his black MG convertible, one of the few two-seaters in which she'd ridden. It made her poor Corolla look pretty bad in comparison.

"Thanks. I've only had it for six months. I'm still trying to get used to a car with no dings and a paint job that shines."

"I understand," Ashley laughed, thinking of her own car. Rick laughed lightly in return, closing her car door firmly as he made his way to the driver's side.

As he drove into Monroe toward the movie theater, Ashley watched the passing scenery outside her window, casting numerous discreet glances at him from beneath her long lashes, taking in his overall magnificence. His body, his face, his hair and those exquisite eyes- there was nothing unappealing about him.

Reaching the theater, Ashley and Rick thoroughly enjoyed the movie, sharing an armrest and a huge bucket of buttered popcorn. After the movie, Rick suggested stopping for coffee, to talk and to fuel Ashley with the caffeine she needed for a late night of studying.

The Campus Coffeehouse, a popular nightspot for Northeast co-eds, was packed and buzzing loudly with intellectual conversation. Ashley spotted a group of people she knew from class, nodding a casual hello to them as she followed Rick through the crowd.

"So, Rick, how long have you lived in Monroe?" she asked after placing their coffee order and settling into a corner booth in the back of the smoky room.

"I've lived here for nine years," he said. "I was born in Lafayette, living there until I was sixteen. Then I moved to Monroe with my mother and my sister, Celeste."

"What about your father?" As Rick's expression hardened, Ashley knew that with one question she had crossed from open season into No Man's land. Rick's cheerful smile vanished, taking on a sardonic twist as he turned cold eyes her way.

"My *father*, Emile LeNoir, esquire, lives in Lake Charles," he said, his tone icy. "At least I assume he does, I haven't seen or heard from him in over ten years."

Ashley could have kicked herself for prying, ruining an evening that had been going so well. She reached out, placing a sympathetic hand gently on his arm. "I'm sorry, Rick," she said, her eyes misty with regret. "I shouldn't have asked something so personal."

The muscles in Rick's jaw relaxed and he instantly offered her a lighthearted smile. "Not a problem," he said easily, placing his free hand over hers on his arm. "How about dinner Friday night?"

"Two dates with you in one week?" Ashley teased him with a pleased twinkle in her eyes. "Aren't you going to get tired of me?"

"I can't see that happening any time soon," he met her gaze unflinchingly, still holding onto her hand.

"Won't your other girlfriends be jealous?"

"There's no one else," he shrugged indifferently. "No one serious anyway."

"Okay then," she said, picking up the steaming cup of cappuccino placed in front of her by their tousled-haired waiter. "You're on for dinner Friday night."

Rick walked her to the door of the dormitory just before ten o'clock. Ashley smiled up at him, stopping just outside the double glass doors.

"Thanks for your company, Ms. Stewart," Rick said with a warm smile. "I had a great time."

"Me too, Mr. LeNoir," she tilted her face up toward his as he leaned down to present her with a light kiss on the lips.

"Until Friday night then," he opened the front door for her and she crossed the threshold, waving as she strolled toward the stairwell door. As he fell from sight, she yanked the door open and, taking the concrete steps in giant strides, bounded up to her dorm room.

"How was it?" Kate said, greeting her as she burst into the dorm room and leaned breathlessly against the door.

Ashley caught her breath then beamed at her, grinning ear to ear. "Wonderful," she said, sighing elatedly.

Kate groaned loudly, rolling her eyes and burying her head on her desk. "Oh lordy," she said, her voice muffled by the thick sleeve of her sweatshirt. "Here we go again."

After a wonderful dinner together on Friday night, Rick and Ashley began seeing one another on a regular basis. Ashley enjoyed his company immensely. Not only was Rick LeNoir charming and entertaining, but he was also highly intelligent, so clever that he was almost intimidating. He was capable of recalling minute facts and details in the blink of an eye, absorbing all knowledge thrown his way like a sponge, in many ways resembling a walking encyclopedia.

What Rick lacked, however, was a true sense of humor, finding it hard to respond to Ashley's abundant off-the-cuff remarks and witty suggestions. As she noted Rick's growing irritation with her droll sense of humor, Ashley began to curb her clever interventions into their conversations, striving to maintain a serious attitude whenever she was with him.

Ashley and Rick spent every available waking hour together, enjoying companionship in a strictly social setting at first. However, as the weeks passed, they began to hibernate in Rick's apartment off campus. Ashley liked Rick's tastefully decorated upstairs apartment, which was always immaculate, filled with antique furnishings that Maggie would die for. His inclination toward Ralph Lauren was reflected in his bed linens and draperies in patterns of paisley and plaid, hued in masculine shades of traditional navy, rich burgundy and hunter green. Ashley spent her evenings curled comfortably in the corner of his nubuck leather sofa, chemistry book in hand, while Rick pounded away at the keyboard of his computer, catching up on the work neglected in his pursuit of Ashley.

In mid-October, while Rick was away on business, Ashley spent a rare Wednesday evening in her dorm room, studying for a big exam the following day. Wearing sweats and sipping diet soda, she was beating her head into her zoology book, begging her brain to absorb by osmosis, when the phone rang. Hanging upside down off the side of her bed, she hastily grabbed the receiver, her heart beating in wild expectation, hoping that it was Rick on the other end of the line. "Hello?"

"My God, you're home," Doug's laughter rang out across the miles of telephone line separating them. "I was beginning to think that you'd been abducted by aliens."

Ashley smiled happily at the sound of his voice, excited to hear from him. "Hi, Doug!"

"Hi, Ash!" he said, sounding equally glad to talk to her. "What have you been up to? You're never home anymore."

"Nothing much," she eluded his question with a laugh as she pulled herself up onto her mattress, propping up on her stack of pillows as she prepared for a very lengthy conversation with him.

"Liar," he laughed fondly. "I can always tell when you're fibbing."

"You cannot. How's football? I've been watching the games."

"Then you've seen how badly Wexler has been playing," Doug said. John Wexler, the starting quarterback for LSU, had been playing poorly the last several games.

"Yeah, I've definitely seen him play better. What's his problem?"

"I have no idea but Coach is replacing him Saturday." Doug was chomping at the bit to tell her his news. "Ashley, I'll be starting quarterback Saturday."

"No way!" Ashley squealed so loudly that Kate dropped her book and Hillary stuck her head in from the other room, checking on her with a perplexed expression on her face. "Sorry," Ashley mouthed to them, smiling sheepishly before turning her attention back to Doug's chattering on the other end of the line.

"Yes way!" Doug was giddy with delight. "Can you believe it, Ash?"

"Well it's about time he let you show your stuff," Ashley smiled, thrilled for him. "Doug, that's terrific. I'll be watching you."

"I wish you'd come to the game, Ash. I have a little pull. I could get you tickets for this weekend."

"I can't this weekend," Ashley said, remembering that she and Rick had already made plans. "But I will before you graduate, I swear."

"So, where have you been all these nights I've tried to get in touch with you?" Doug said, casually interrogating her. "I've been trying for days now, just ask Kate."

"Well, I've been dating. Hasn't Kate told you all about it?"

"Ashley, Katie doesn't gossip, you know that. Now, if Susanna was your roomie, I'd know all about it."

"Which is why Susanna is not my roomie. If you must know, I've been dating, almost every night of the week, as a matter of fact."

"Fabulous! How many guys are you stringing along?"

"Just one," she confessed softly. "Doug, I've met someone kind of special."

"Oh yeah?" Ashley could hear the protective tone in Doug's voice. "Tell me about him."

"His name is Rick LeNoir, a computer analyst. He is nice and smart and just wonderful."

"Oh, so this guy has a real job. He's not a student and must have a college degree," Doug observed. "Just how old is Mr. Wonderful, Ashley?"

Ashley shook her head in wonder. "Just how did you get to be so intuitive, Douglas? I thought you were supposed to be a dumb jock."

"Where in that statement did I hear you mention his age?"

"Rick's twenty-five."

"Did you say *twenty-five*?" Ashley winced as Doug raised his voice. She should have known that he would get bent out of shape over the age difference.

"Yes, that's what I said," she replied. "And what's so wrong with that?"

"Can you say 'cradle robber'? What's this guy doing dating you?"

"Have you ever thought that he might be attracted to me?"

"Damn, Ashley, we're all *attracted* to you. But this Rick guy is too old to be pursuing it."

"Says you," Ashley said defiantly as she and Doug reverted to their former selves, childishly arguing the point into the ground. Kate was becoming annoyed with her for disrupting her concentration, just as Ashley was becoming annoyed with Doug for being so bull-headed about her new love interest. At a stalemate, they ended their phone conversation as she wished him luck with his big debut as LSU's quarterback.

"I love you, Dougie!" she reminded him in a sisterly fashion, hoping to hang up on a lighter note.

"I love you too, Ash," Doug sighed with frustrated resignation and he hung up the phone with a resounding bang. Ashley replaced the telephone receiver on its base and fell heavily back onto the bed, groaning in exasperation.

Kate glanced away from her lap full of class notes, viewing Ashley with amusement. "I take it Doug is none too happy about Rick," she said.

"I guess not. He seems to think that Rick is too old for me," Ashley rolled her eyes as she looked across the room to Kate. "But he'll change his mind when he meets him."

"I wouldn't be so sure about that," Kate said, suppressing an entertained smile as she pulled her book up in front of her face.

CHAPTER FIFTEEN

After her grueling afternoon exam, Ashley dragged herself into the dorm room and flopped face first across the bed. "Ugh!" she groaned loudly, burying her face into the soft comfort of the quilt covering her bunk.

"Ashley!" Kate stuck her head in from Hillary and Melissa's room, laughing as she observed Ashley's face-first position on the bed. "Are you up to going out tonight?"

Ashley lifted her head wearily to look at her. "Where to?" she asked.

"Just out to The Bleachers for a few drinks to unwind."

Ashley quickly weighed her options. Rick was still out of town and was not due back until late the next afternoon. There was no way she could face another night of studying, not after the exam she had just taken. Going out seemed like a good idea to her. "Why not?" Ashley said as she dropped her head back on the mattress. "I'm going to take a nap. Wake me up when it's time to go."

They had a great time out, returning to the club where Ashley had met Rick. After a night of dancing, gossiping and drinks, they left The Bleachers just after eleven to grab a late snack. Returning to their dorm, Ashley caught the tail end of the phone ringing as she unlocked the door to their room and looked in puzzlement at Kate.

"Who would be calling so late?" she lifted her arm into the dim lighting of the hallway to squint at her watch. "It's almost twelve-thirty."

Kate shrugged indifferently, pushing her way into the room. "Probably Doug, wanting to spar some more about your new boyfriend."

"Probably!" Ashley laughed, agreeing with her as she kicked off her loafers. "I don't think Doug's going to let that fight go too easily."

"Probably not," Kate smiled broadly as she pulled her nightshirt out of the footlocker at the end of her bed. "I've never known him to give up an opportunity to argue with you." She crawled into her unmade bunk, snuggling cozily under the covers.

Ashley threw on a gold NLU sweatshirt and plaid flannel sleep pants then jumped into bed, leaning out to click off the lamp between their beds. She wiggled around, punching her pillow with her fists, nesting until she finally got comfortable. Just as she dozed off, the phone rang again. She and Kate reached out in unison to grab the receiver, tipping the nightstand and sending the Mickey Mouse clock clattering loudly to the floor. The phone continued to jingle into the darkness until, at last, Ashley's hand found the receiver.

"Hello?"

"I can't even trust you while I'm away on business." Over the line, Rick's distinct voice dripped with bitter deliberation over her absence from the dorm room that evening. Ashley grinned into the pitch black of the room, believing at first that he was joking with her, pretending to be mad. But her smile faded as he went on and she discovered that he was not kidding around. "Where have you been, Ashley? You've been with someone else, haven't you?"

With each syllable, Rick's voice rose an octave until he was bellowing ferociously. The raw anger in his words took Ashley aback and she slumped against the wall, chewing her lip, listening as Rick continued to berate her.

Kate bounded from her bed to snap on the light, hearing Rick's screaming from her side of the room. She creased her brow, staring at Ashley with narrowed eyes. "Who is that?" She whispered loudly across the room.

"Rick," Ashley mouthed to her, blinking her eyes incredulously. Kate frowned and joined Ashley on her bed, her ear cupped next to the receiver so that she could hear what Rick was saying.

"Answer me, Ashley! Where have you been?" he said irately.

"I went out with Kate, Hillary and Melissa," she stammered, meeting Kate's wide eyes with a shocked look of her own. Ashley couldn't believe that this was truly Rick LeNoir thundering angrily on the other end of the line.

"Out? Out where?"

"We went to The Bleachers and had a few drinks. Then we went to get something to eat." Ashley was completely honest with him, having no reason not to be.

"You know that you shouldn't go out without me." An edge of impatience crept into his voice. "Don't you remember what was happening when I met you? You need me to take care of you."

Her inbred independence shone through with a vengeance. His insinuation that she couldn't look out for herself insulted her. "Look, I don't know what your problem is," she said, struggling to maintain her cool, "but I don't deserve this temper tantrum from you. I've done nothing wrong, and furthermore, I am perfectly capable of taking care of myself."

"Sure you are," he said, taunting her sarcastically. "That's why the night I met you some guy came close to breaking your arm before I stopped him. From now on, I don't want you going anywhere without me."

"I'll do exactly as I please," Ashley said hotly, clenching and unclenching her fists angrily. "You don't own me."

"Don't tell me what you're going to do!" As Rick's words grew louder, Ashley wrenched the receiver from Kate's tight grasp and hung the phone up with a resounding bang. Instantly, it began to ring again and Ashley scrambled from her bed, yanking the phone cord from the wall outlet.

"There!" she declared with satisfaction, turning to meet Kate's disbelieving stare.

"What in the hell was that all about?" Kate said, her mouth gaping open incredulously.

Ashley shrugged tiredly. "You tell me and we'll both know." She strode over to her closet, pulling out her duffel bag, into which she began stuffing clothes and personal items.

"What are you doing?" Kate leaned forward in her bed, watching inquisitively.

"I'm leaving Monroe after class tomorrow afternoon, even though I should leave right this minute," Ashley said in a huff. "I'm going home to pout to Maggie."

Her feelings were hurt and she had no intention of seeing Rick when he returned from his trip the next afternoon. She knew that if she saw his gorgeous face, she would melt and immediately forgive him for raving like a lunatic. She was too upset with him to let him get away with his behavior and she wanted him to have the weekend without her to think about it.

"Ashley, you better reevaluate this relationship with Rick." Kate said solemnly, her eyes reflecting her troubled thoughts. "If he'll go this ballistic over you going out with your girlfriends, it would be safe to say that he's very jealous and overly possessive. If he acts this way after just eight weeks of dating, he'll eventually smother the life out of you. You won't be able to stand it."

Ashley didn't answer, stubbornly turning her back to Kate as she continued to pack her bag. Kate persisted, scooting to the end of the bed so Ashley would be forced to listen to her. "Ashley, I know that I was the one who wanted you to get out and I think that it's great that you did, but I didn't expect you to get so involved with the first person you dated. Your spending every waking hour with Rick LeNoir is not what I had in mind."

Kate paused and Ashley glanced back at her, waiting with annoyance for the other shoe to fall. "Honestly, Ashley, I don't think that you are ready for anything this serious. I don't think that you're really over Jimmy."

"For heaven's sake, Kate, it's been well over a year now," Ashley said, snapping crossly, whirling around to scowl at her.

"I don't care if it's been ten years. You still grieve for him and you're still hurting," Kate reached out to place a sympathetic hand on Ashley's shoulder. "Your brave front doesn't fool me, Ashley. Do you honestly think that I don't hear you crying sometimes late at night when you think I'm asleep?"

"Why would you want to go and bring all this up? Was my night not going badly enough without you throwing in the Jimmy factor?"

"I just want you to admit the truth, if only to yourself, and give yourself some time to really and truly heal. Cool things down with Rick for now and slowly get back into the social scene before jumping head first into a serious relationship."

"I don't want to cool things down with Rick. I may be furious with him but I still like him," Ashley said stubbornly. " Besides, how can I get over Jimmy when you always want to talk about him? I get along just fine until you go dragging him out in the open."

"Sweetie, you can't get over someone by burying him deeply in your mind. You have to let him out, relive the memories and let him go."

Ashley looked up at Kate with woeful eyes and a heavy heart, tears sliding unchecked down her pale cheeks. "I can't, Kate," she confessed quietly. "I don't want to let him go."

Kate put her arms around Ashley, hoping to soothe her. "But you have to let go, honey. He's not coming back."

"I know that. But as long as I keep him inside, I'll always have him with me."

She zipped the duffel bag with a hard jerk and stood, wiping her eyes on the back of her hand and cursing herself for her moment of weakness. "Besides, Kate, this is not about Jimmy, this is about Rick. I'm going home for the weekend because I am pissed off at Rick," Ashley argued, sniffling loudly, denying her feelings about Jimmy. Ashley's brave performance proved to be nothing but wasted energy. Kate was a master at reading her mind and knew that Ashley was lying.

Ashley watched Doug's debut as starting quarterback from her parents' living room, curled up cozily with Remy on the couch, sharing a bowl of cheddar cheese popcorn and kicking herself for not being at the game. Upon her arrival in Pineville the previous afternoon, she had phoned Susanna, hoping that they could get together on Saturday to cheer Doug on.

"Sorry, Toots, I can't," Susanna told her. "*I'm* leaving for Baton Rouge first thing in the morning."

"*You* got tickets to the game?" Ashley asked jealously.

"You could've had tickets. I heard that you turned down an invitation from our illustrious quarterback himself."

"Yes I did, and don't tell me what a stupid move it was. I already know."

"I also heard that you are dating someone in Monroe *and* I heard that you think this guy is just wonderful," Susanna informed her smartly, having way too much information not to have talked to Doug. "So, Ashley, if this guy is such a prize, what are you doing here all alone this weekend?"

Ashley quickly brought Susanna up to date on Rick LeNoir, describing how they met and how attractive she found him. Then, with a heavy sigh and a brooding voice, she replayed the events of Thursday evening. "So, I'm mad, and I'm home and this is where I intend to stay until Sunday afternoon." Ashley abruptly ended her tale at the sound of Susanna's mocking laughter.

"God, Ashley. Don't you think you went a little bit overboard?"

"No, I don't think I went a little bit overboard," Ashley said defensively. "I don't even think that he has the right to be mad. I did nothing wrong. Besides, we have no permanent commitment to each other. I'll see anyone I like."

"Ashley, you are such a princess! I can't believe that you're getting all bent out of shape over a little yelling. That's nothing, honey. Scotty and I used to get into screaming matches on a regular basis."

"You did? I didn't know that."

"You didn't need to know because it wasn't that big of a deal. Welcome to the real world, my friend. Not every man is going to be like Jimmy was. You're gonna have to grow up a little bit. If Rick is such a hunk and you enjoy being with him so much, you gotta stop making such a fuss over a little yelling."

Ashley bristled, remembering Susanna's biting words of advice, frowning unpleasantly before the sound of thousands of screaming fans caught her attention. She looked up at the television just in time to see Doug, larger than life, sprinting down the center of the field at Tiger Stadium, rolling across the goal line to score the winning touchdown.

After the game, she called Doug's room, even though she didn't expect him to be there, certain that he would be out on the town celebrating Louisiana State's victory over Tennessee. As she had anticipated, she got his answering machine, and in the spirit of old times, she left him a message. "Hi, Dougie, it's Ash. Just in case you were wondering, I think you played a great game. I love you."

Doug called her back some time during the night. Ashley was unsure of the time but sensed that it was late. "Hello, sweetheart." She smiled at the sound of his voice in her ear.

"Hello, football star," she murmured sleepily. "Fabulous game today."

"Thanks!" he said enthusiastically, still pumped up with adrenaline over the huge win. "I saw Susanna tonight. She told me that you were in Pineville."

"Yes, the dog deserted me for the football game."

"You should've come down with her. You could've gone out with me after the game."

"What, and rob all those swooning women of their hero? I don't think so," Ashley smiled as she teased him, envisioning the huge grin spreading over his face at her words.

"I still wish you had come down. I miss you, Ash," Doug said, his voice softening with affection.

"I miss you too, Dougie. Will you be home for Thanksgiving?"

"Don't know yet, but I doubt it. Depends on the status of the bowl games. Hopefully I'll make it home over Christmas so I can see you."

Ashley and Doug talked late into the night and Ashley reluctantly told him about her falling out with Rick. She asked his opinion, half expecting to hear another disapproving lecture on her immaturity level. She was wrong.

"What a jerk!" Doug said tensely, his voice rumbling with repressed anger. "Where does he get off yelling at you like that? You don't have to take that crap from anyone, Ash."

"Susanna says that I'm being childish."

"Which only goes to show you how much Susanna knows. You aren't going to see him again, are you?"

"I haven't decided yet," Ashley said hesitantly. "I really like him, Doug."

"I don't care if you do like him. He's not worth it. There's plenty of other fish in the sea."

"Aren't you a fine one to offer romantic advice?" Ashley said with a light-hearted giggle. "Exactly how much experience do you have in this area?"

"Don't change the subject," Doug said irritably. "I just think, no, *I know* that you deserve better than that guy."

"And I think that he deserves a chance to explain his actions before I make up my mind."

"Look, Ash, you've never been one to take my advice, although God knows I always try," Doug said with an aggravated chuckle. "Whatever you decide to do about this guy is your choice, Ashley, but whatever that choice may be, just be careful."

He made her solemnly promise to use good judgement before he said good night, leaving Ashley smiling into the darkness before she drifted off to sleep.

Kate gave Ashley a weary look when she breezed into the dorm room late Sunday afternoon. "Thank God you're back. Rick is driving me crazy," she said, looking pointedly over the frame of her reading glasses. She gestured around the room with a wide sweep of her arm, pointing out the vases and vases of sweet-smelling flowers and bouquets of festively colored balloons taking up every available inch of extra space in their small living area.

Ashley's jaw dropped open in shock. "These are all from Rick?" she asked, looking around the room with wide eyes, turning her head slowly from arrangement to arrangement until she found herself gawking at Kate.

Kate answered with an exasperated nod and a flustered sigh. "Yes, and he has called a thousand times since Friday night. I finally gave up and moved in with Mitch for the weekend."

"Where did you tell him I'd gone?"

"I told him that you were out of town for the weekend and that I wasn't going to tell him where you were."

"Was he okay with that?"

"No, which is why I had to go to Mitch's apartment. Rick kept calling me, hoping that I would grow tired of his terrorization and tell him where you were. It was worse than Chinese water torture."

"Does he know that I'm mad at him?"

"Yes, I'm sure that he does," Kate said with a wry grin. "If he had any doubt about it, I set him straight. The last time I spoke with him, he apologized over and over again for his behavior Thursday night. I informed him that I was not the one owed the apology and that he had better lighten up if he wanted to continue to date you."

"Thanks, Kate." Ashley smiled gratefully, dropping her duffel bag to the floor and sitting on the edge of her bunk. "That's really nice to hear after Susanna's remarks on the matter."

"What did she have to offer?"

"Basically she said that I overreacted, that I was being a princess and that I'm wrong for being mad at Rick."

"Which is precisely why Susanna has such a successful and abundant love life," Kate said. "Maybe her standards aren't as high as yours are."

"I don't know, Kate. Maggie has pretty high standards and she thinks I jumped to the wrong conclusion about Rick. She actually defended him."

"You're kidding!" Kate said, breaking into incredulous laughter. "I find that so hard to believe. Ms. Maggie usually has better sense than that. Maybe she'd feel differently if she had heard his hysterical ranting from across the room like I did."

Ashley glanced at the phone setting silently on the nightstand. "Phone still unplugged?" she asked.

Kate nodded emphatically. "You bet your life it is."

"Good," Ashley said, flopping backward onto the bed, heaving a great sigh. "I'm not quite ready to negotiate a truce with Rick."

As she left chemistry lab the next afternoon, Ashley spotted Rick sitting on the hood of her car, watching her pensively as she strolled toward him, and she turned brusquely to walk in the other direction. Rick caught up with her easily, gently taking her arm while his voice pleaded, "Ah, Ashley, don't be like that."

"Go away, Rick," she said firmly, gazing into his stunningly handsome face, trying desperately to maintain her stance, knowing that all her resolve would be melted away the longer she stared into those aqua-blue eyes.

"Ashley, I was wrong. I had no right to yell at you like that. I was just so worried about you when I couldn't get you on the phone. I had no right to accuse you of seeing someone else and I certainly have no right to tell you what you can and cannot do."

"That's true," she told him curtly, cutting him no slack whatsoever. "I'd rather not have a repeat performance of Thursday night ever again."

"Does that mean that I get a second chance?" Rick asked, flashing a confident smile. He was so irresistible when he wanted to be and Ashley couldn't withstand his charm.

"Yes, I think that I can grant you another chance," she said, shaking her finger at him teasingly. "Just remember what you said earlier. No yelling and no bossing me around."

"You won't regret it, I promise," Rick said, assuring her with a brilliant smile, sliding his arm around her shoulder and escorting her down the sidewalk to her car.

For Ashley, Thanksgiving break couldn't come fast enough and she left Monroe for Pineville filled with relief. The last several days had been trying, bringing out emotions in her that she wasn't prepared to deal with, and she needed some time away to think.

Since their blow-up in October, Rick had been as good as gold. True to his promise, he no longer tried to tell her where she could go or whom she could see, but instead opted for a new strategy of divide and conquer, keeping Ashley so busy with him that she didn't have time to see anyone else.

Not that Ashley minded. Rick put out a great deal of effort to be as charming as possible, introducing her to his friends and colleagues from work, filling every weekend with parties, dinners and dances. Rick was very complimentary and attentive to her, making her feel special, like the most wonderful woman in the world, genuinely sweeping Ashley off her feet. When Rick was on his best behavior, he was a dream come true.

Ashley met his mother and sister the Sunday before Thanksgiving, traveling with Rick to his mother's quaint gingerbread house in a quiet suburban neighborhood in West Monroe. His mother, Dominique, greeted them with open arms, breezing out onto the porch as Rick and Ashley pulled into the driveway.

"It's about time you came to see yo're Ma Ma," she said, reaching up to pinch Rick's cheek, ignoring the pronounced expression of displeasure on his face. Ashley viewed their exchange through dancing eyes, thinking it refreshing to see a woman get the better of Rick.

Dominique LeNoir was a diminutive woman in her early fifties, who shared Rick's dark hair and bright blue eyes. She was attractive, but her alabaster skin showed signs of aging, marked with deep lines from laughter or sorrow, although Ashley couldn't possibly know which, and she smiled warmly at Ashley as Rick introduced them.

"C'mon in the house, chère," she put her arm around Ashley's waist, guiding her inside. "I'm so glad that I finally get to meet you. Rick talks about you so much, I feel like I already know you."

"We accused him of hiding you from us," his sister Celeste spoke up, wiping her hands on the legs of her jeans as she strode in from the kitchen.

At thirty, Celeste was older than Rick, favoring him in appearance, having the same South Seas eye color, dark wavy hair, and long, lean frame. Leaning in the kitchen doorway, she eyed Rick skeptically, seeming quite feisty and spirited in her confident stance, drawing Ashley to her immediately.

"I just wanted to spare her from hearing what a great guy I am from the two of you," Rick lounged on the plaid loveseat, flashing Celeste a cocky grin.

"I doubt very seriously that you have to worry about that, brother dear," Celeste said, rolling her eyes at him, offering him a sassy smirk. "We don't think that you're such a fine catch."

Rick laughed heartily. "Touché," he said, "you win again."

"As always."

"Oh no, not always, little sister," he said cynically, his voice slightly menacing. "It is a rare day when you top me."

Celeste glared hotly at him, prompting Dominique to run interference. She stood as a physical barrier between them, looking from Celeste to Rick, with a warning in her eyes and her hands on her hips. "I hope you're hungry," Dominique said, turning to Ashley. "I got a big dinner ready for you all, a little Shrimp Creole, a little bread pudding with rum sauce."

"That's what I was hoping for." Rick stood up, leading Ashley by the hand into the dining room. He pulled out a chair for her, seating her with firm pressure to her shoulder. "Let's eat."

After dinner, Ashley helped Celeste with the dishes while Rick and his mother went into the living room. Ashley took her place at the kitchen sink while Celeste cleared the table.

"I'm glad you gave Rick another chance, Ashley," Celeste said, leaning against the counter to chat with Ashley as she rinsed their plates. "You must make him very happy. I haven't seen Rick this relaxed in a long time."

Celeste sighed, crossing her slender arms against her well-endowed chest. "I read him the riot act the weekend you two had that huge fight. He told me all the things he said to you and I took him to the mat and told him he'd better straighten up or he'd lose you too."

"Too?" Ashley said, narrowing her eyes speculatively. She stopped rinsing the dishes, shutting off the water and turned to Celeste, waiting with bated breath for her to elaborate.

"I've warned him more than once about that monstrous temper of his. Rick inherited that jealous streak from our father. Daddy was so overbearing that my mother had to leave him. I'm hoping that Rick will learn some patience and trust before he ruins another good relationship."

"Why are you telling me all this?"

"I want you to understand that I love my brother and I think that he's a handsome and captivating little devil," Celeste said, offering Ashley a wry smile. "But Rick has a tendency to be overbearing and possessive. If you care about Rick and want a lasting relationship with him, you'll have to be patient with him. He can be extremely difficult when he wants to be."

"Is this a warning or just sisterly advice?"

"Think of it as sisterly advice," Celeste said lightly, sensing that she was frightening Ashley, brightening the mood with her conspiratorial smile. "I think Rick's main problem is that he just doesn't understand independent women. You'll be good for him, Ashley. Between the two of us, we'll straighten him out yet."

Rick wandered into the kitchen, interrupting their heart-to-heart. "You're taking forever to do those dishes," he said jovially, glancing from Ashley to Celeste, and Celeste smiled a little guiltily under his suspicious gaze. "Have you two been talking about me?"

"You are so conceited, cher," Celeste teased him, patting him lightly on the cheek. "We have better things to talk about than you."

After ending the evening with Dominique and Celeste, Rick drove back toward Monroe, his hands gripped tensely on the steering wheel. "What was Celeste telling you?"

Judging by Rick's curt tone of voice, Ashley decided it was best not to reveal what Celeste had said about him. "Just girl talk," she said, shrugging casually. "Nothing really important."

She turned her face toward the window to see Rick take the exit leading to his apartment and looked back over her shoulder at him. "Aren't we going back to the dorm?"

"I thought we'd go to my place for a while." Rick glanced at his watch. "It's still pretty early."

"We could go out for coffee," Ashley said brightly, liking her suggestion better, thinking that maybe a little jazz music at the Coffeehouse would improve his waning good spirits.

"Do you not want to be alone with me?" Rick said caustically, glaring at her with a furrowed brow. "First you have a cryptic heart-to-heart with Celeste, and now you don't want to be alone with me?"

Ashley picked up on the underlying rumblings of anger in his question. "Of course I do, Rick. I just thought that coffee sounded good." She placed her hand on his arm, offering him her most enchanting smile, seeking to smooth his ruffled feathers.

He cast her a sidelong glance, relaxing and returning her smile. "It does sound good," he agreed. "But let's stay in. I can make coffee at the apartment."

Reaching his place, Rick unlocked the door, holding it open as Ashley slipped inside. She removed her jacket, clicking on the lamp beside the couch while Rick went into the kitchen to make coffee, returning with two steaming cups in his hands. He set them on the coffee table, using carefully placed coasters, and after hanging Ashley's jacket in the closet, joined her on the sofa.

"What did you think of my mother and sister?" he asked as they sipped their coffee.

Ashley's face lit up and she smiled warmly. "I liked them a lot. Your sister is very straightforward and friendly."

"I still want to know what she told you about me."

"What makes you think that she said anything about you at all?"

"Because I know Celeste," Rick stated with certainty. "She has a bad habit of sticking her nose into matters that are none of her concern."

Sensing that Rick's mood would not be improving, Ashley placed her empty cup on the end table, peeking at the antique clock on the wall. Eleven-thirty, time to go home.

"We should get going. I have seven o'clock class in the morning," Ashley said, reminding him that she needed her beauty sleep.

Rick returned his cup to the table and reached for her, pulling her to him firmly. He lowered his mouth, kissing her warmly. "You could stay here tonight," he said, nuzzling her ear with a low, deep whisper.

"I don't think that's such a good idea."

"Why not? I think it's an excellent idea," Rick nibbled sensually at her ear, slowly inching his lips down her neck.

Ashley tried to wriggle out of his embrace but he held her tightly and she lifted her gaze, meeting the intensity radiating from his eyes with a pitiful plea from her own. "I'm not ready, Rick, not yet."

Rick ignored her appeal for leniency, kissing the base of her throat, his hot breath burning her skin. He worked his way back up to her lips, kissing her more persistently than before.

"Rick, no, I'm not ready for this yet," she insisted when he allowed her to speak. "I want to go back to the dorm."

Rick leered at her with dark and smoldering eyes. "You are ready, Ashley. I see the way you respond to me when I kiss you. You may be telling me no, but your body is telling me something else."

Before she could protest, he eased her down onto the couch, continuing his seduction of her. Ashley's body betrayed her and soon she could no longer think rationally, responding wantonly to his commanding touch. In a dreamlike state, she followed Rick to his bedroom, yielding as he lifted her onto his bed and made love to her, sending her into elated throes of ecstasy with his skillful touch.

Afterward, Ashley lay numbly in Rick's arms, listening to his breathing become more regular as he fell into a deep sleep. She didn't know what was wrong with her. She should've been elated but felt lonely and empty at best. She slipped out of his arms and padded softly across the room to the bathroom, closing the door behind her and twisting the lock. Her rubbery knees gave way and she slid down the door, collapsing in muffled sobs on the cold tile floor.

Subconsciously, she had hoped that the addition of a sexual component to their relationship would make her feel closer to Rick, but it hadn't. She didn't feel anything more for him, nor did she feel anything less. She only felt guilty, hating her body for deceiving her, and hating herself for being unfaithful to her haunting love for Jimmy.

She dried her eyes and washed her face before leaving the bathroom, retrieving her clothing from the crumpled heap on the floor and tiptoeing silently from Rick's bedroom, knowing that she would be unable to sleep in the same bed with him in her present state of mind. She dressed quickly, then huddled on the couch to wait for morning.

Rick gently shook her awake at six o'clock. "What are you doing out here?" he said, his pleasure from the night before still shining in his intensely blue eyes as he leaned down to kiss her tenderly on the lips.

Ashley yawned, stretching her stiff arms above her head. "I couldn't sleep and didn't want to keep you awake with my tossing and turning," she said, noting that he was dressed for work. She took the hand he offered her and rose sleepily from the couch.

"Come on, I'll drive you home." Rick fussed over her, helping her on with her jacket and handing her a hot cup of black coffee as he ushered her out the door.

On their short drive to campus, Rick was animated, in sharp contrast to Ashley's noticeable silence. He was immensely pleased with himself for successfully seducing her, believing that it had formed an unbreakable bond between the two of them. Ashley had other thoughts about it.

"Why so quiet?" Rick glanced over, regarding her quizzically as he turned onto the street in front of Slater Hall.

"I'm not a morning person," Ashley used the truth to her benefit, hoping that he would be convinced that was the reason behind her silence. All she wanted was out of the car and away from him for the time being. Rick pulled into a parking slot in front of the building and she pecked him quickly on the lips before leaping from the car, practically running down the sidewalk.

"I never imagined that you would be this shy about it," Rick called after her, grinning from ear to ear with amusement.

Ashley responded to him with a hasty wave and hurried through the lobby doors. She took the steps in giant strides, rushing to get her books so that she wouldn't be late for her first class. Kate had backpack in hand, ready to leave for class when Ashley charged into the room and she paused, regarding Ashley with concern. "Where have you been all night?"

Ashley scurried through the room, gathering her books from the desktop and shoving them into her bag. "I spent the night at Rick's."

"Well, thanks for calling. I thought you were dead," Kate said, not bothering to hide her irritation.

"It was a spur of the moment decision," Ashley said, following Kate into the hallway and sprinting toward the stairwell.

"Was it wonderful?" Kate asked, waiting for the details she was certain were coming.

"That's open for debate," Ashley said, shrugging indifferently, forcing a smile onto her weary face.

Kate studied her with narrowed eyes, instantly suspicious of Ashley's less than enthusiastic response. "That's not exactly the answer I expected. I would think that Rick could be quite entertaining in bed. He just seems like the type."

"Is nothing sacred?" Ashley scowled at her, wishing that Kate would stop trying to analyze her.

"Not between us. At least nothing has been before."

"I'm not keeping secrets from you, Kate," Ashley said as they paused on the sidewalk before going into their first class. "It's just not a topic I want to discuss first thing in the morning."

They finished their discussion that evening in their dorm room, after a less than satisfactory dinner in the cafeteria. Rick had called earlier in the afternoon, hoping to persuade Ashley to spend another night at his apartment. "I think I'll pass," Ashley said, declining his suggestion gently. "I didn't sleep well last night and I'd like to turn in early. Plus, I need to get some things together to take home for Thanksgiving break."

"You're still going to Pineville for Thanksgiving?" he asked, sounding disappointed. "I thought after last night you might stay in Monroe with me."

"Why on earth would you think that? Did you think that my sleeping with you would change my holiday plans?" Ashley tried to keep the conversation light, fighting to keep her increasing crankiness out of her voice.

"I thought, obviously incorrectly, that you would consider me more a part of your life now, that's all."

"I do consider you a part of my life, Rick. But that doesn't change my relationship with my family. I'm going home for Thanksgiving, and for Christmas."

"I understand," he said, although judging by his clipped tone, Ashley sensed that he did not. "I love you, Ashley."

Oh God, not now, Ashley thought, panicking slightly. Now was not the time for Rick to declare his love for her. Her own feelings were unclear. Anything she felt for Rick was shrouded in guilt and confusion, making it impossible for her to express even the smallest glimmer of affection.

"I'll see you next week, Rick," she artfully ended their conversation by simply choosing not to address it at all, hanging up the phone before he had an opportunity to protest.

Kate sat by the window in her desk chair, hugging her knees to her chest, watching in curious silence while Ashley mechanically loaded her duffel bag with various odds and ends of clothing. "Do you want to talk about it?" she asked, observing the faraway look in Ashley's green eyes.

Ashley startled, pulled out of her dismal thoughts, looking sheepish when she realized that Kate had spoken. "What did you say?" she asked, bewilderment replacing the distant expression on her face.

"Whatever's bothering you, do you want to talk about it?"

Ashley nodded, pulling a chair across the floor to sit next to Kate. "It just wasn't what I expected it to be," she said, taking up where they had left off early that morning.

"*It* would be sex with Rick, I assume."

"Yes."

"From what I understand, it rarely is," Kate said with a grin.

Ashley had to smile, in spite of herself. "*That* part was fine, I assure you," she said, laughing softly. "It's the way I feel inside that bothers me. It just doesn't feel right. I remember how making love with Jimmy left me elated and full of contentment, loving him more and more each time we were together. Last night with Rick left me feeling empty, lonely and disappointed. I couldn't wait to get away from him this morning."

"Were you ready to sleep with Rick?"

"I should've been, but I really wasn't," Ashley said, rising from the chair, pacing the floor as she sorted through her mixed emotions. "I'm really mad at myself. I should've held my ground and not given in to him. If we had waited until I was ready, maybe I would feel differently about it."

"Maybe, maybe not."

"But Rick's a great guy."

"Rick has some very positive attributes," Kate said, agreeing with Ashley with a wise nod of her head. "Even so, you don't have to keep seeing him, Ashley, not if you don't want to. Nothing is written in stone saying that you are forever committed to the guy, even if you did sleep with him. Everyone makes mistakes. You should see other people and experience life."

"I don't know," Ashley flopped backward onto her bed, reaching above her head for a pillow and hugging it insecurely to her chest. "I don't know what I want."

"I'm glad that you are getting away from here for a few days. You really need some downtime to sort out your feelings."

"Oh yeah, like going back to Pineville, the city full of memories, will really help me clear my mind," Ashley said, muttering into the pillow sarcastically.

Kate laughed, grinning cynically. "Well, at least in Pineville you won't have your hormones doing all the talking for you, you shameless hussy."

CHAPTER SIXTEEN

Fueled by Fleetwood Mac and Coca-Cola, Ashley made her way to Pineville on Tuesday afternoon, rolling into the driveway just in time for dinner. Remy waited for her on the front porch swing, sipping hot apple cider and flipping through the pages of *The Alexandria Daily Town Talk*, tossing the newspaper aside when Ashley sprang from her car.

"Hey Remy!" Ashley greeted him with an elated grin, lifting her bag from the hatchback of her car and handing it to Remy as he hustled down the front steps to take it from her.

"Welcome home, little girl," Remy said, giving her a fond kiss on the cheek, putting his free arm around her shoulder, guiding her up the front stairs and into the house. Once inside, he set her bag at the foot of the stairs as Ashley stepped into the foyer, inhaling deeply, savoring the familiar aroma of home. The smell of Maggie's homemade vegetable soup drifted enticingly to her nostrils, casting its magical spell, willing her to join Maggie in the kitchen.

Over dinner, Ashley learned that Thanksgiving would be a little different that year. "We're having a community dinner here at our house," Maggie said as she placed a heaping bowl of soup in front of her daughter.

"What kind of community dinner?" Ashley asked, looking intrigued.

"Well, Bobbie and Nick are all alone, with Doug in Baton Rouge, so we invited them over for dinner, then I decided that if I invited Bobbie and Nick, I should invite the Robicheauxs and the Ducotes too. The guest list just grew and grew until it turned into one big community dinner." Maggie took her chair across the table from Ashley, sipping her iced tea and waiting for Ashley's feedback.

"I think that's a wonderful idea," Ashley turned to grin at Remy, seated at the head of the table. "And it'll keep Remy from getting bored, having all the dads here to watch football with."

"My sentiments exactly," Remy agreed, giving her a mischievous wink.

After helping Maggie clear the table, Ashley began to tire, the last several sleepless nights beginning to take their toll on her. "Mags, do you need help with anything?" she asked, setting her empty bowl in the kitchen sink. "If not, I'm going up to bed. I haven't been sleeping too well this week."

Maggie instinctively reached out to place a hand on Ashley's cool forehead. "Everything okay, Ashley?" she questioned, wrinkling her brow in concern.

"Yes, everything's fine." Ashley hated fibbing to Maggie, wanting so much to confide in her, but she simply couldn't come up with a graceful way of telling her mother that her insomnia had been caused by her confusion over sleeping with Rick. Maggie was liberal, but she wasn't *that* liberal.

Upstairs in the frilly white sanctuary of her room, Ashley methodically unpacked her bag, hanging her clothes in her closet. Above her head on the closet shelf loomed the box, the very box she had avoided for well over a year. She eyed it as it beckoned her, wondering about the sanity of opening it. It was Ashley against the box, and in the end, the box won.

Feeling the once-familiar tug at her heart, Ashley opened the box on the soft, pastel rug in front her window, her breath catching in her throat when she found Jimmy's letterman's jacket on the very top. She hugged it tightly against her, burying her face in the gray flannel wool. It had long since lost the smell of him, but she could remember exactly how Jimmy smelled: Clean, like soap, with a hint of Polo after-shave. She pulled on the jacket, then reached into the box for the next item.

Ribbons and dried roses attached to elastic bands, her corsages from the homecoming dance and junior/senior prom. She smiled whimsically, remembering the tuxedos and frilly dresses, the music and the laughter. She laid the corsages aside and looked toward her bedroom window, her eyes taking on a distant glaze.

In her mind's eye, Ashley could see the bright slivers of autumn moonlight peeking through her lace curtains and could hear the tiny pebbles tinkling as they hit her windowpane. It was so real to her that she imagined that if she looked out the window, she would once again see Jimmy, standing on the ground, gesturing for her to join him outside. She saw herself, clad in red flannel pajamas and white Keds, scooting down the rose trellis in the soft moonlight to steal a late night kiss. She leaned against the wall, closing her eyes and feeling his alluring lips against hers and the passion of his kiss, seeing the unconditional love shining in his brown eyes when her hungry gaze met his. Her mind fast-forwarded to prom and the first night they made love, retracing every passionate detail. She was drawn to the past, lost in her thoughts of Jimmy, and that's exactly where she wanted to be.

As the scalding tears began to flow, Ashley startled, coming abruptly to her senses. "Damn it," she cursed in frustration, pulling Jimmy's jacket from her body. "What have I done?"

She shoved the jacket back into the box and slammed it closed, swiftly hoisting it back onto the closet shelf, but it was too late. The damage had been done. All her hard work, all the grueling progress she had made toward her recovery, was gone the moment she lifted the lid.

After a fitful night's sleep, Ashley awoke late Wednesday morning to find her parents already gone to work. She took a long hot shower, letting the hard stream of water pound her into wakefulness. Dressing in faded jeans and an old flannel shirt, Ashley pulled her damp hair into a ponytail and donned one of Remy's camouflage caps before leaving the house to meet Susanna for lunch.

She stole quietly into the drugstore grill, hoping not to call attention to herself. There was no sign of Mister Eddie, so she made the best of her break, sliding unseen into an empty booth next to the front window and hurriedly opening a menu in front of her face. She studied the lunch selections, unnecessarily, having long since memorized every single item on it.

She heard Susanna before she saw her, her timely arrival announced by her brassy voice echoing through the fountain area. "Eddie Thibodeaux, where you be, man?" Susanna leaned over the shining chrome counter, craning her neck as she peered into the kitchen. Mister Eddie came around the corner, his large body filling the doorway.

"Miz Robicheaux," he flashed a toothy grin her way as he dried his hands on a dish towel. "What you be wantin' ta eat today? You all alone?" he asked, glancing around for a lunch companion.

"I'm meeting someone," she flirted with a dazzling smile. "So, no lip out of you today, you hear?"

"Yeah, girl, I hear ya," Mister Eddie chuckled and turned his attention to the sizzling hamburgers on the grill.

Susanna peered around the room, spotting Ashley hiding in the corner booth. She strode over to her, yanking the menu from in front of her face. "Slumming today, Ashley?" she asked, regarding Ashley's attire with a nitpicking stare.

Ashley shrugged. "Didn't feel like dressing up today."

"Well, that's pretty obvious," Susanna said cynically as she pondered the menu for her lunch choice. Mister Eddie appeared beside them to take their order, blinking in surprise as he recognized Susanna's lunch date.

"You ought ta be ashamed, sneakin' in here wid out even sayin' hello to ol' Mist' Eddie, gal," he scolded her with a shake of his chubby finger. Ashley couldn't help but smile at him and rose to give him an apologetic bear hug.

"I'm sorry, Mister Eddie, I'm just not myself today." She kissed his cheek affectionately, hoping to make up for her aloof behavior.

With squinted eyes, he studied her, frowning slightly at what he saw. "Ya do appear ta be a lil' peaked," he said, before smiling expansively. "But Mist' Eddie know what ta do ta fix ya right up." He turned on his heel, waddling swiftly toward the kitchen, leaving Susanna staring after him with her mouth dropping open wide.

"He didn't even get my order," she said, shaking her head as she protested. "He's so aggravating when he wants to be."

"You're one to talk," Ashley said, watching as Mister Eddie returned, beaming proudly with a heaping plate of food in each hand. He set Ashley's plate before her and she smiled, touched that he still remembered her favorites. A patty melt on rye, overflowing with onions and melted cheese, and homemade fries, done to golden brown perfection. He winked at Ashley before delivering Susanna a duplicate order.

"Mister Eddie, this is *not* what I wanted!" Susanna called after him as he lumbered to the next table. She rolled her eyes indignantly. "Mister Eddie!"

"Just eat it, Susanna," Ashley suppressed her entertained giggle, knowing that he was ignoring Susanna just to be ornery. "If that's what he wants you to have, he's not about to change it."

"I hear that we're all coming to your folks' house tomorrow," Susanna gave up and begrudgingly lifted the sandwich to her mouth, taking a huge bite. The look on her face indicated that she liked what she tasted, although she would have rather died than admit it.

"That's what I hear too," Ashley said, pointedly ignoring Mister Eddie as he wandered by, clucking his tongue in disapproval after noticing Ashley apathetically pushing her food around her plate.

"I can't wait to tell Katie what a piss poor job she's doing at taking care of you," Susanna said. "Every time I see you, you're all bummed out and depressed about something. What's the crisis this week?"

"There's no crisis. I just have to sort some things out, that's all." Ashley pushed away her plate, having no further interest in eating.

Susanna regarded her suspiciously as she lifted her glass of cola. "Do these things involve Mr. Wonderful up in Monroe?"

"His name is Rick," Ashley corrected her. "And, yes, in a round about way they do."

"Who else do they involve? Douglas Fairchild?"

Ashley laughed outright at her ridiculous question. "Doug? Why on earth would you ask something so silly?"

"Because every time I've seen or talked to him in the last year, all he wants to talk about is you."

"Doug and I are only friends, Susanna, you know that." Ashley discouraged any stray thoughts that Susanna might be having. The thought of anything other than friendship between herself and Doug was ludicrous.

"Then what else could you be sorting out?" Susanna said persistently.

"Jimmy," Ashley answered softly and Susanna's eyes widened, staring at Ashley as if she had lost her mind.

"Jimmy?" she asked incredulously. "Hello? Ashley, Jimmy's dead. He's been dead a long time."

"He's not dead to me, not in my heart or in my mind."

Susanna sat back against the booth with a thud. "You are really pitiful," she stated solemnly. "I can't believe that you're messing up a perfectly good relationship with a living, breathing guy because of memories of a dead one."

"Why would I expect you to be sympathetic or even try to understand just a little bit," Ashley threw her napkin on her plate in disgust. "Remind me to never confide in you again."

"Oh Ashley, don't be mad," Susanna said, sorry that she had been so frivolous about Ashley's emotions. "I didn't mean to be such a bitch. I've just never lost anyone I loved, so I guess I don't really understand." She glanced quickly at her watch. "Ooh, I've got to go before I'm late for work."

She slid out of the booth and grabbed her purse, leaving Ashley the money to cover her meal. "I'll see you tomorrow."

Mister Eddie came over as Ashley pulled money out of her pocket to pay the tab. "Put that away, chère, ya know yo're money's no good here."

"Thanks for lunch, Mister Eddie," Ashley forced a brilliant smile onto her face as she gazed up at him with woeful eyes and slid from the booth to leave.

"Ya didn't eat nuthin'," he said disapprovingly. "Go on back and help yo're daddy and Frannie with the 'scriptions and I'll bring ya a milkshake after I git rid of the rest o' these good folks."

Remy and Frannie were working frantically to fill all the orders placed before the Thanksgiving holiday. Ashley slipped behind the counter and helped Frannie sack up the finished prescriptions and write up slips for the deliveries. She stayed for a couple hours, working diligently and sipping on the huge bright-pink milkshake hand-delivered by Mister Eddie, before returning home. It felt good to work again. It kept her mind off all that was troubling her.

Ashley smelled the beginnings of Thanksgiving dinner preparations filling the house as she breezed in the front door and she found Maggie in the kitchen, stuffing the huge turkey upon the stovetop. "There you are!" Maggie glanced over her shoulder to welcome her. "Where have you been?"

"I had lunch with Susanna at the drugstore then I helped Remy and Frannie get caught up in the pharmacy. They're really busy today," Ashley said, holding the cooking bag open for Maggie as she lifted the turkey from the countertop.

"I talked to your young man," Maggie said, beaming playfully at her.

"Pardon me?"

"Rick, I talked to Rick; he called about an hour ago."

"Oh yeah? What did he have to say?" Ashley opened the oven door and Maggie slid the giant bird in to bake.

"We talked for a long time," Maggie said, grinning ear to ear. "He's a very nice young man. Quite a charmer."

Ashley nodded in agreement. "Yes, Rick can be quite a sweet talker when he puts his mind to it," she laughed.

"When do you think Remy and I can meet him? I was hoping that you might invite him home for Thanksgiving."

"No, I need some time away," Ashley said quickly, struggling not to frown. "Maybe he can come down over Christmas break."

"Is everything all right?" Maggie asked, studying her solemnly.

"Yes and no. But it's me, not Rick," Ashley sighed, leaning soberly against the wall, her hands shoved deeply into the pockets of her worn jeans.

"What's the problem?"

"Just had a little haunting from the past, that's all," Ashley shrugged and lowered her eyes, not wanting to meet Maggie's worried stare.

"It still hurts, doesn't it?" Maggie's compassion was what Ashley needed more than anything else, and she nodded, accepting her mother's heartwarming embrace, while Maggie softly stroked her hair.

"Oh, Ashley," she sighed, tenderly kissing the top of Ashley's head. "I wish I could make all the pain you feel go away. But, honey, only you can resolve the way you feel. I only hope you can put it all behind you before you throw away happiness with both hands."

It was a welcome distraction to have a house full of company on Thanksgiving Day. The Ducotes arrived first, Frank, Imogene and Kate, along with her older sister Debbie and brother-in-law, Christopher, bearing sweet potatoes, whipped into a creamy casserole covered with miniature marshmallows, and homemade yeast rolls, piping hot and dripping with melted butter.

They were followed closely by the Robicheauxs, Ted, Claire, Susanna and her baby brother, Max, who struggled under the weight of a huge pan of cornbread dressing and a dish of tasty broccoli and rice. Last to join the party were Bobbie and Nick Fairchild, regrettably lacking a son. Ms. Bobbie handed a tray full of pumpkin pies and other delectable desserts to Max to haul to the kitchen, and then turned to Ashley for a hug.

"I haven't seen you in forever!" she scolded playfully. "Why are you such a stranger?"

"I don't mean to be," Ashley grinned at her. "You could come to Monroe to visit me, Ms. Bobbie. Monroe is a lot nicer than Baton Rouge."

"Monroe may be nicer, but Baton Rouge is where my baby is," Ms. Bobbie said with a huge grin, pinching Ashley's cheek playfully.

They all converged on the dining room, gathering in a huge group around the linen-covered table. Remy said the blessing, and then began passing bowls and platters of food around the table. They were talking and laughing so loudly that they didn't hear the persistent ringing of the doorbell.

"I hope you saved me some turkey!" Doug's booming voice filled the dining room and all heads turned to look at him.

"Boy! What are you doing home?" Ms. Bobbie bellowed across the dining room in astonishment and delight. "Your coach is going to skin you alive!"

Doug laughed heartily and slid into an empty chair between Kate and Susanna. "Coach knows where I am. He sent us all home for the rest of the week, got tired of hearing us bitch and moan."

"Douglas, watch your language," His father cautioned him sternly. "This is the dinner table, not the locker room."

Ashley hid her amused smile behind her hand and looked at Doug with dancing eyes. He met her gaze and flashed a wide smile as a greeting. Ashley watched him chat animatedly with Kate and Susanna during dinner. He was as great looking as ever and Kate and Susanna giggled at his anecdotes, matching him story for story with entertaining tales of their own. Ashley enjoyed seeing them all together again, thinking how refreshing it was to hear their laughter.

Max watched Doug with hero worship. Doug was having a golden season at LSU and Max was speechless, in awe of having Doug in the same room with him. Max had forgotten all the years that Doug had haunted the Robicheaux house as a mousy little boy. Now, all he could recall was the great football star who happened to be a friend of his sister's.

After dinner, the men retired to the den to watch football while the women cleared the table and did the dishes. Ashley listened to the shouts and cheers coming from the den, smiling as she carried a stack of plates from the dining room.

"So I hear you're dating again," Ms. Bobbie joined Ashley at the sink where she stood diligently rinsing plates.

"Yes, I've been seeing someone since August."

"You don't seem very excited about him." Ms. Bobbie leaned against the counter and eyed her speculatively, her dark eyes piercing Ashley's very soul.

"Oh, Rick's a great guy," Ashley assured her, although her face was shadowed by a touch of uncertainty. "I just have some issues to resolve before I can get excited about any man."

Ms. Bobbie nodded, patting Ashley's sudsy hand. "Honey, I understand. I loved Jimmy like my own son and I miss him every day. I can only imagine how you must feel."

"It's just so hard sometimes," Ashley felt the overwhelming urge to unload her problems on Ms. Bobbie and tried to ignore the hot sting of tears welling up in her eyes, pushing them away impatiently with the back of her hand. "I do really good most of the time but then, just when I think I'm over it, I come home and it starts all over again."

"Don't, honey," Ms. Bobbie put her warm motherly arms around Ashley, pulling her close. "I sure didn't mean to make you cry. Now, give me a smile, come on."

She tilted Ashley's chin up with her fingertips, nodding approvingly as Ashley offered her a weak smile. "That's better. It's Thanksgiving, and despite what you think now, you have a lot to be thankful for."

At half time, Doug emerged from the den. "I need to walk off some of this food," he declared, patting his stomach and sauntering over to take Ashley by the hand. "Let's go for a walk."

Ashley agreed with a keen nod of her head, grabbing her jacket from the coat rack by the kitchen door, and they slipped away, unseen by anyone. They crossed the street and followed the dirt road leading to the lake, the stillness of the woods interrupted by the crunching gravel under their feet. They journeyed to their spot, the two rocks near the waters' edge, and Ashley took her place on one of them while Doug sat facing her. She remained silent, looking out at the motionless water, appreciating the peace and tranquility of her surroundings, going back in time and hearing the sound of Jimmy's gentle laughter ringing in her ears.

"So how's the world conqueror?" Doug asked, his brown eyes twinkling with good cheer as he awaited her reply, his smile fading as he examined her face. "What's up, Ash? You seem a little blue."

"Doug, do you think that it's crazy to piss away a perfectly good relationship because of memories of a dead man?"

Doug pondered her question thoughtfully. "Well, I guess that depends on what relationship and what dead man."

"I've still been having some problems letting go of Jimmy," she admitted quietly, leaning down to splash in the water just below her feet, twirling her fingers, making ripples in the icy lake while avoiding Doug's somber gaze. "No matter how hard I try to go forward, I always come back to him."

"I know that, Ashley. I've always known."

Ashley reflected pensively, wiping the water from her fingertips down the length of her jeans. She leaned back on her palms, staring soberly up at the trees, silently watching as a few of the remaining rusty-colored leaves on the branches above them spiraled downward in the autumn breeze.

"Maybe you haven't found the right person to help you get over him." Doug suggested wisely. "I think with the right guy and a little time, you'll be as good as new."

"Maybe," Ashley shrugged her shoulders indifferently. "Dougie, do you believe in ghosts?" she asked, lowering her eyes to meet his bewildered stare.

"Ash, you're losing me here. What are you talking about?"

"I'm talking about Jimmy," she said, and Doug quietly listened to her, his eyes fixed on her lovely face. "He still visits me in my dreams, not so much now as in the past, but he still comes to me all the same. I try so hard to block him out, but he always returns to haunt me, never letting me forget."

She encircled her knees with her arms, hugging them tightly to her chest and laying her head against them, staring up at Doug with huge, sad eyes. "I'm thinking of going away, Dougie."

"Where would you go?"

"I don't know, but sometimes I think if I don't get away from here and leave it all behind, I'll go crazy."

"I've got the perfect solution for you. Just come to Baton Rouge," Doug grinned, using his best Cajun accent. "Der be lots o' Cajun men to distract ya der, chère."

"Yeah, man, dat's what I be needin'," Ashley said, lifting her head, countering with her own cocky impersonation. "I be needin' another man to complicate my life!" She giggled as they played together, the solemn moment passing as she tightly squeezed his hand, grateful for Doug's uncanny ability to cheer her as no one else could.

As the sun set and their surroundings became cooler and darker, Doug and Ashley left the seclusion of the lake, walking hand in hand back to the house. "Ashley, you're going to be okay, I promise you," Doug reassured her as they reached the front porch.

"I hope so," she embraced him tightly as he kissed her softly on the forehead.

"Just don't do anything stupid, okay? I know how you are, Ash. You're so impatient, hardheaded and so god-awful impulsive. You don't need to run away, just give yourself a little more time."

"I'm not going to do anything stupid," Ashley said, punching his arm, frowning in annoyance as she muttered to him. "Sometimes you are so irritating."

"You love me anyway," Doug said with a huge smile.

"You make it pretty tough sometimes." Ashley marched up the front steps in front of him and opened the front door, leaving it wide open for him as she strode inside.

The rest of the week flowed by smoothly and quickly. Ashley filled her remaining time at home by sleeping late, Christmas shopping, and catching dinner and a movie with Doug on Friday night. She enjoyed her break from school, but by Saturday night, she was ready to return to Monroe.

Doug stopped by on Saturday evening to say good-bye before returning to Baton Rouge. Ashley donned a warm fleece jacket and joined him on the porch. In the air, she could smell the lingering odor of burning wood and smoke from the neighborhood chimneys, the weather finally turning cool enough to tolerate a fire in the fireplace. The late November night was breathtakingly pretty and clear, with a full moon shining brightly down on Doug and Ashley as they sipped cocoa, sitting shoulder to shoulder on the front steps.

"So, how are things with you, really?" Ashley asked him. They had spent so much of their time together discussing her life that she had yet to force any detailed answers out of him.

"Things are going really well," Doug said, embracing the heat from his ceramic mug with his hands. "We've had a great season."

"I meant with you personally. You do have a life other than on the football field."

"Not much of one," Doug said, chuckling good-naturedly.

"You are dating some, aren't you?"

"A little. Between football, classes and fraternity stuff, I don't have a whole lot of time for dating."

Ashley clutched her chest mockingly. "God forbid that you should give up a frat party for some woman."

"There hasn't been one worth giving up a frat party for, yet."

"You know that you're breaking your mother's heart, don't you? She has all but given up hope of ever having grandchildren."

"I still have plenty of time before I need to present her with grandchildren," Doug scoffed with a roll of his eyes. "Unless, of course, you're willing. We could have a child together and make both our mothers happy." His eyes danced playfully and he yanked the end of Ashley's long ponytail teasingly.

"And they could take turns raising it while we finished school," she said, giggling at his proposal and continuing the banter. "I'm glad that you got to come home, Doug," she smiled affectionately at him and he nudged her with his shoulder.

"I'm glad I did too. And I'm glad that I got to spend some time alone with you. The telephone just isn't the same, you know?"

"I know. I've missed doing this," Ashley indicated sitting on the porch together with a sweeping gesture of her hand.

Doug stayed until well after midnight when, regretfully, he had to leave for home and get a little sleep before returning to school. Their coach would work them exhaustingly for the next few weeks, in preparation for LSU's bowl game appearance in December. "I'll see you some time over Christmas break," Doug promised her as he rose to leave.

Ashley stood on the top step in order to match his height, looking him flirtatiously in the eye. "Keep in touch," she said. "I'm only a phone call away!"

"You can bet on it, darlin'," he smiled charmingly, flashing his perfect white teeth.

Then, impulsively, Doug leaned forward, presenting Ashley with a warm kiss on the lips. Ashley responded by involuntarily wrapping her arms around his neck and returning his kiss carelessly. After a long, breathless moment, she came to her senses and pulled away, although somewhat reluctantly.

Doug's twinkling brown gaze met her wide-eyed green one. "Wow!" he said with a broad smile. "What a send off!" He winked at her, turning to stroll to his car, whistling jovially as he went.

"Behave yourself!" she called after him, her lips still tingling from his amazing kiss.

Doug grinned mischievously and waved goodbye, wheeling Nick's truck out of her driveway and onto the street, honking the horn as he drove out of sight.

Ashley floated into the house and ascended the stairs to her room. Now that was a kiss, she reflected as she crawled into bed. She hadn't had a kiss that turned her knees to jelly in quite some time. Rick's kisses were stimulating but they were by no means what Jimmy's kisses had been, nor were they anything like what she had just experienced on her parents' front porch. She touched her lips with her fingertips, smiling as she dropped off to sleep.

CHAPTER SEVENTEEN

Driving back to Monroe, Ashley plugged in the Eagles, turning the volume of her car stereo up loudly, hoping to take her mind off her jumbled feelings. The visit home had been wonderful, but at the same time, it had taken its emotional toll on her. Opening the box had been a mistake, a definite setback in her recovery effort. As she drove pensively down the highway, she caught the reflection of bright sunlight bouncing off the silver band on her left ring finger and her thoughts drifted back to Jimmy.

Maybe she should remove the ring as well, and hide it away with the rest of his things. She held her hand directly in her field of vision, studying the painstakingly engraved circle of X's and O's. No, removing the ring would mean letting go of him forever, and she wasn't ready for that.

Melissa had been the first of the four to arrive back at Northeast, meeting Ashley in their suite at Slater Hall. "Hi, Ashley! How was your Thanksgiving?"

"It was wonderful." Ashley hoisted her heavy duffel bag onto the foot of her bed, flashing Melissa a friendly smile. "How was yours?"

"Pretty good," Melissa ventured into the room, leaning comfortably against the brick wall. "I just got back a half hour ago myself."

"Is Hill back yet?"

"No, I don't expect Hillary until later this evening. How about Kate?"

"I would imagine that she'll be along any minute," Ashley said, finishing her sentence just as the door opened and Kate breezed in, tossing her bag onto the floor. "Speak of the devil," Ashley said with a laugh, nodding her head toward Kate.

"Hey, Melissa!" Kate said with a warm smile. "You're back early. I thought only Ashley and I rushed back to school."

"Yeah, I know," Melissa grinned. "But my folks were driving me nuts. I was ready to come back yesterday but bravely fought off the urge to bolt until this morning."

"What were your folks driving you nuts about?" Ashley asked curiously. Melissa didn't seem to be the type who would give anyone a minute's trouble.

"I don't think that they're real comfortable about me coming out of my shell," Melissa revealed with a wink. "They think that y'all are bad influences on me."

Kate and Ashley exchanged an entertained glance, bursting into laughter. "Well, this is a first. I don't think I've ever been called a bad influence before!" Kate giggled.

"Boy, do I feel like a rebel!" Ashley joined in, throwing herself carelessly onto the bed.

"That's what I tried to tell them!" Melissa said, laughing at their good-natured heckling. "But they wouldn't listen to me, so I came back early for more corruption."

"Well, I have only one thing to say about that," Kate said, with an evil twinkle in her eye. "Margaritas!"

Ashley glanced at her watch. She had made dinner plans with Rick but that was still a couple of hours away. She had plenty of time to indulge in the progressive defilement of Melissa.

"Let's go!" Ashley encouraged Melissa to grab her coat and the three set out for Cantina's, the little hole-in-the-wall Mexican café not far from campus. The late autumn afternoon was sunny and warm, so they opted to walk, trudging in a merry pack across the footbridge and toward the restaurant.

They spent a delightful couple of hours drinking margaritas, eating chips and queso and girl talking, tucked in a large corner booth of the festively decorated Cantina's.

"What did you do at home the rest of the week?" Ashley reached for more queso, turning an inquisitive eye toward Kate.

Kate shrugged and munched reflectively on a tortilla chip. "Nothing much, fought the crowds at the mall with Mom and Debbie on Friday, went to dinner with Mitch Saturday night, and came home today. What about you? Didn't I see Doug's car at your house more than once this weekend?"

Ashley nodded. "Yep, we went to the movie Friday night and he came by to say goodbye last night." Kate raised an interested eyebrow, and Ashley shot her an innocent look. "What?" she asked, and Kate grinned impishly without reply.

"Who's Doug?" Melissa asked curiously, observing their unspoken exchange.

"A friend we went to high school with," Ashley answered quickly.

"Doug Fairchild, LSU's quarterback," Kate supplied better information, by which Melissa was suitably impressed.

"I've seen him on TV," Melissa said, sitting up interestedly in her chair. "He's a cutie."

"I guess he'd do in a rush," Ashley joked, thinking of Doug's dazzling good looks and smiling dreamily, remembering the farewell kiss he had given her the night before. She knew that the kiss hadn't meant anything, but it had been a nice kiss nonetheless.

Kate watched her, inquisitively engrossed by the animated expression on Ashley's face. Ashley shook off her thoughts and looked back at Kate, flushing slightly under her knowing glance.

"Where were you just then?" Kate teased her with a huge grin.

"Nowhere that I'll be taking you," Ashley told her, using her huge margarita glass to shield her embarrassment.

"Are you keeping secrets from me?" Kate peered through the bottom of the glass, trying to see Ashley's eyes, knowing they would give the answer to her question.

Ashley just smiled mischievously and didn't utter a word.

A wave of appreciative murmuring from the male patrons of Cantina's signaled the arrival of Hillary. She glided across the room toward them with feline grace, her long legs encased in snug jeans and a radiant smile on her gorgeous face.

"I was right," she announced, sliding into the booth next to Melissa. "When I saw all the luggage scattered around the dorm room, I knew that either someone died or y'all were drinking. And I guessed right." She signaled the waiter for a drink and turned to Ashley. "Rick called for you."

Ashley's eyes darted to the chiming clock on the wall above the door. "I need to get going," Ashley told them, draining her glass and rising hastily from her seat. "I've got a dinner date."

"You drank two huge margaritas and ate a bowl of chips and queso. How are you going to manage to eat dinner on top of all this?" Melissa laughed.

"I'm going to dinner for the company not the food," Ashley informed her with a smile.

"Are you going out with Rick?" Melissa asked. "He's such a babe."

Kate rolled her eyes as Ashley grinned with delight. "Yes, I am, and yes, he is," she said. "Are y'all staying here to continue the corruption of Melissa or coming back with me?"

"Staying," they answered in unison, their dancing eyes taking note of the abundance of males in the room. Ashley dug deeply into the pocket of her jeans, leaving money with them to cover her tab, then set out for her walk back to the dorm.

She met Rick in the lobby of Slater Hall at six o'clock, her knees instantly weakening at the sight of him. He was so unbelievably irresistible, she thought, crossing the room to embrace him. "Hi ya, handsome," she said with a radiant smile, reaching her hand up to affectionately finger his thick, sooty hair.

"Hi yourself." Rick appeared to be happy to see her as well, bending to kiss her lightly on the lips. "Are you ready for dinner?"

"Sure, just lead the way." Ashley took his hand and they exited through the front glass doors. Kate and Melissa were meandering up the sidewalk as they came out.

"Hey!" Melissa called to them, a little tipsy, which amused Ashley to no end.

"Hey!" Ashley called back to her, laughing as Melissa weaved unsteadily and clutched Kate's arm for support.

"You left too early!" Melissa notified her as they came closer. "The cutest group of guys came in right after you left. So cute, in fact, that we couldn't get Hillary to leave."

Rick turned, looking questioningly at Ashley, and she returned his gaze sheepishly while Kate elbowed Melissa in the ribs. "Ouch!" Melissa cried out, giving Kate a dirty look. "What was that for?"

"Come, Melissa, before you get us all in trouble." Kate took her by the arm, guiding her past Rick and Ashley toward the building. "They really were cute!" Kate reiterated to Ashley as she sailed by, and Ashley smiled broadly, suppressing another giggle. Still pretty loose from her margaritas, she found everything to be humorous.

"What were you girls up to this afternoon?" Rick asked as they walked down the sidewalk to his car.

"We went out to celebrate our return to Monroe."

"That much I've gathered," Rick told her with a smile, opening the passenger door of the car for her. "I wish you had waited to celebrate with me."

"We can celebrate now," she said, getting into the car. She waited happily as he got in. "Tell me about your Thanksgiving," she said as he pulled the car away from the curb.

"There's not much to tell," Rick shrugged as he glanced over at her. "I went to my mother's and had Thanksgiving dinner with her and Celeste."

"How's Celeste?"

"Fine, except she's got a new boyfriend." Rick's lip curled slightly with wordless contempt.

"Don't you like him?"

"The boyfriend is acceptable, but his kids are not," Rick said, scowling and issuing a haughty laugh. "Rug rats, that's all they are. I don't understand why people insist on having them."

Ashley laughed out loud, taken aback by his clear dislike of children. "Oh Rick, lighten up," she said. "You too were once a rug rat."

"No, Ashley," he corrected her sternly. "*I* was never a rug rat."

They dined at a little Italian restaurant not far from Rick's apartment, seated at a candlelit table for two. Ashley chatted animatedly with him throughout dinner, filling him in on her trip home and her earlier outing with Kate and Melissa. Rick propped his elbow on the table and rested his head against his fist, viewing her with amusement and enjoying her prattling oration. Ashley finally stopped, reaching for her water glass and gulping thirstily.

"Did you stop to take a breath?" Rick teased her, his eyes dancing with apparent delight.

Ashley replied with self-conscious giggling. "I'm sorry to go on and on that way," she said. "I'm boring you."

"No, you're not," Rick corrected her. "As a matter of fact, I'm enjoying this. You're pretty entertaining when you've been drinking."

"Oh, so I'm not entertaining when I'm sober?"

"You're always entertaining." Rick smiled sincerely. "You are just more so right now." He took her hand. "I missed you while you were gone."

"I missed you too," Ashley admitted. "My mother is driving me insane wanting to meet you. You must have been very influential on the telephone with her."

"Your mother is a delightful woman. I enjoyed chatting with her."

"She wants you to come to Pineville over Christmas break."

"I'd love to. That was an invitation, wasn't it?" he asked, his eyes sparkling brightly as he joked with her.

"Of course it is."

"I can only come for a few days. I have to go to Oklahoma City right after the first of the year."

"What's in Oklahoma City?" Ashley perked up, her interest piqued by his unexpected announcement.

"Our corporate office. The big bosses have requested my presence at a meeting in January."

Ashley was fittingly impressed. "Wow! That's pretty exciting, isn't it?"

"Sure it is," Rick beamed. "I just wish I had a clue about the reason for my visit."

"How long will you be in Oklahoma?"

"A little over a week."

"That sounds like fun. I wish I could go with you," Ashley blurted out, refilling her glass from the bottle of wine in the center of their table.

"I wish that you could too," Rick replied wistfully. "But not this time. This trip will be strictly business."

"Bummer," she stated, draining her wineglass. Rick eyed the full entrée still on her dinner plate.

"Perhaps you'd care for a little Veal Parmesan with your wine, Ashley?" he nodded toward her plate. Ashley shook her head, giddy with drink.

"Nah, the wine is just fine, thanks."

Rick paid the check and they rose to leave, with Ashley swaying none too gracefully through the dining room. Rick steadied her, guiding her across the room by the elbow. As they stepped outside into the cool night air, her head started to spin slightly and she began to giggle. "I think I'm a little tipsy," she told Rick as he settled her into the passenger's seat.

"To say the least." Rick suppressed a smile as he closed her car door.

"I guess I've had more to drink than I thought," she murmured, laying her head back against the seat, rolling it to one side to look at Rick. "Take me home with you, Rick."

"Take me home with you and make me forget," she added silently, offering him a pair of gently pleading eyes.

"Ashley, my pet, I really have no other choice," Rick said lightly, turning the car in the direction of his apartment. "I can't get you up the steps to your room and I don't think you can make it up alone. I'll have to take you home with me and put you to bed."

"An excellent idea," Ashley slurred her words suggestively to which Rick chuckled heartily.

"Ashley, I *do* like it when you drink," he grinned, glancing over at her limp figure reclined in the passenger seat, three sheets to the wind.

After helping her out of the car and up the steps to his apartment, Rick removed Ashley's shoes and jeans as she lay sprawled in a drunken stupor upon his bed. She curled up on his pillow and Rick lay down beside her, grinning ear to ear.

"Will you call Kate and tell her where I am?" Ashley said, her sleepy voice barely audible. "The last time I stayed with you, I got in trouble for not calling her."

"Kate Ducote, your own mother hen."

"She worries about me," Ashley garbled her words, opening her heavy eyes to stare into his handsome face. "You're awfully cute." she told him, patting his cheek fondly. "Thank you for helping me to forget," she whispered faintly, blinking at him with wide, adoring eyes.

"Forget what, Ashley?" Rick said, puzzled. But she didn't answer. The last thing Ashley saw before passing out was the highly entertained sparkle in Rick's bright blue eyes.

Ashley awoke with throbbing temples and a head that felt like a bag of lead. She painfully pulled herself into sitting position and rubbed her eyes, looking around her unfamiliar surroundings. After remembering where she was, she peered around for Rick, then heard the shower running. She squinted at the clock beside his bed, noting that it was just before six in the morning. She had to get moving or she would never make it to class.

Holding her palm atop her aching head, she padded gingerly across the bedroom and tapped on the bathroom door.

"Rick, I'm going to grab a cab back to campus!" she called through the closed door. Just as she finished her sentence, Rick swung the door open, clad only in the towel draped around his waist, displaying his well-defined chest and sculpted abdomen. Ashley grinned at him as appreciatively as she could for as badly as she felt.

"If I weren't so hung over, you'd look pretty good," she said.

"I wondered how you would feel this morning," Rick smiled sympathetically. "Give me two minutes to throw on some clothes and I'll drive you back to school."

—

Rick fed her aspirin and coffee before driving her quickly back to the dorm. "This could turn into a habit," she said, smiling slightly as he pulled up in front of Slater Hall, her home away from home.

"I wouldn't mind," Rick said sincerely.

Ashley leaned over and kissed him warmly on the mouth. "Thanks for the ride," she said, swinging her legs out of the open car door.

"Can I see you tonight?" Rick asked as she started toward the door.

"Call me later and I'll see how I'm feeling." She waved a fond goodbye.

Ashley did see Rick that night and the night after that, and for all practical purposes, she moved in with him, only returning to campus for classes and clothing. She threw herself wholeheartedly into her relationship with Rick, forcing all other thoughts from her mind by centering her world on his wants and desires. Every night, she lay in his arms, studying his chiseled, Adonis-like face, wordlessly thanking him for being in her life.

After two weeks of constant cohabitation with Rick, she was forced to move back into the dormitory to study for finals. She couldn't stay with Rick during finals week. He was too much of a distraction.

Kate viewed Ashley humorously as she moved her clothes and toiletries back into their room. "Will you please call your mother tonight? I can't keep saying that you are at the library or in the shower. It's starting to look a bit suspicious."

"I'll call her, I promise," Ashley said with a naughty grin, imagining that Maggie didn't buy Kate's excuses for one minute. Luckily, Rick had worked his charm on Maggie while she had been home over Thanksgiving. Otherwise, she would probably get the lecture of a lifetime. She began unloading her books from her backpack.

"And call Doug. He has called about nineteen times this last week."

Ashley's face lit up radiantly as she whirled around to face Kate. "He has? What does he want?"

"Since when does Doug have to *want* anything? I would imagine that he just wants to talk to you."

"Where did you tell him I was?"

"I just tell him that you're out, which hasn't been an easy task since he has started calling as late as midnight," Kate's tinkling laughter filled the room. "I think that he's on to you, babe."

After dinner, Ashley first called her mother. Maggie actually bought the story that she had been engrossed in her books over in the library for the last two weeks. After all, it was almost finals. Ashley assured her that she would be home within days of finishing the semester. "What are you going to do right after finals?" Maggie wanted to know.

"I'm going to stay in Monroe for a couple days and be with Rick before I come home."

"So, I take it that all is well with Rick?" Maggie sounded pleased.

"Everything is peachy," Ashley replied truthfully, thinking of how much her definition of "peachy" had changed since her naïve youth.

She hung up with her mother and phoned Doug, who answered on the second ring. "You've been phoning me?" she asked him jovially.

"Ah, so you haven't been kidnapped by a band of desperadoes," Doug greeted her with a laugh. "I was beginning to wonder."

"No, I'm safe and sound here in good old Monroe, USA," she teased him. "I'm just getting ready to perk some Java and start hitting the books for the night."

"Me too," he paused. "So, where have you been all these nights? Or do I want to know?"

"I've been with Rick." Ashley wasn't certain why it bothered her so much to admit this to Doug. It shouldn't have been any different than telling Kate or Susanna, but somehow, it was different discussing her social life with Doug.

"Oh," he said, his tone becoming strangely hushed. "So when do I get to meet this Rick guy, Ash?"

"I think that he'll be coming to Pineville for a few days over Christmas break."

"Is it pretty serious with this guy?"

Ashley sighed. "I don't know how serious it is, Doug. I do know that I'm having a good time with Rick. Things are good with us right now."

"I'm glad to hear that," Doug's voice became significantly more tense and Ashley picked up on it immediately.

"What's wrong, Doug?" she asked softly.

He sighed heavily on the other end of the line. "I don't know, Ashley I just thought that we'd finally made a connection over Thanksgiving."

"What do you mean?" she gently prodded him to continue.

"I thought that we were making some progress toward a relationship ourselves." He was suddenly shy, much like the Doug she remembered from their childhood.

Ashley fell back against the head of her bed with a loud thud, stunned. She never in her wildest dreams would have imagined having a romantic relationship with Doug Fairchild. The thought certainly didn't repulse her, but it did frighten her a little.

"Doug, why would we want to mess up a perfectly wonderful friendship by turning it into a romance?" she inquired, trying to make light of his admission.

"Forget about it, Ashley," he snapped at her, surprising Ashley with his unusual anger with her. "I need to go. I have to study."

"Okay," Ashley said, thinking it better not to argue with him. "Good luck on your finals," she added, wanting to end the conversation on a friendly note.

Doug had other ideas for the termination of their discussion. "And Ashley," he warned her sternly. "Never kiss me like that again unless you mean it." He hung up the phone with a resounding bang.

Ashley clutched the receiver, staring at it in disbelief. Kate looked up from her notes, finding Ashley's confrontation with Doug much more interesting. "Now what?" she asked, intrigued.

"You wouldn't believe me if I told you," Ashley said incredulously, still reclining in astonishment against the head of her bed, holding the dead receiver in her hand.

"Try me," Kate urged and Ashley told her verbatim of her terse exchange with Doug.

"What do you think of that?" Ashley asked indignantly, leaning forward to hang the telephone receiver back on its base.

"I think that I've been trying to tell you that about Doug for years. Susanna and I both have tried to tell you how Doug feels about you."

"I don't want Doug to feel anything for me other than friendship."

"Why not? He's a perfect match for you."

"I like things with Doug just as they are," Ashley retorted with a great deal of frustration. Why would Doug want to complicate her life this way? Just when she thought she had it all straightened out, Doug had to pull a stunt like this.

Kate shrugged. "You asked what I thought and I told you. That's all I can do." She pulled her notes back in front of her face, pointedly ignoring Ashley's perturbed stare.

Ashley stomped in exasperation across the room to the coffeemaker and poured a strong cup of black coffee into her monster-size insulated mug. She curled up on her bed and leaned against the wall, burying her face determinedly into her chemistry book. But she couldn't focus. She was too mad at herself, and mad at Doug too.

The phone rang a little later, shattering the tense silence of their dorm room. Looking up, Ashley frowned, as she had just begun to gain some concentration. Dropping her notebook, Kate rolled over, grabbing the telephone from the nightstand.

"Hey," she greeted the person on the line. She listened for a moment, and then replied, "Yes, she's right here." She stretched out her arm to hand the receiver to Ashley. "Be nice." Kate told her with an insistent shake of her finger.

"Hello?" Ashley spoke into the telephone, her face brightening as she recognized the voice on the other end of the line.

"I can't study when I'm mad at you."

"Me either," Ashley admitted with a smile.

"I'm sorry I snapped at you."

"I'm sorry I kissed you that way," Ashley conceded, remembering her passionate response to his post-Thanksgiving goodbye kiss.

"I'm not," Doug chuckled. "I have to take it when I can get it."

Ashley laughed at his restored playfulness. "Thanks for calling me back," she told him tenderly. "I feel better already."

"Now that we are back on good terms, let's not say anymore until I see you again." Doug said. "We'll talk this out face to face some time."

"Is there anything else to say?"

"Good night, Ashley!"

"Good night, Doug," Ashley reluctantly gave up and hung up the phone.

Finals week ended on Thursday afternoon, ten days before Christmas. Ashley packed up the things she would need to take home over break and told Kate, Hillary and Melissa goodbye before heading to Rick's, where she would stay until Sunday morning. Glad to have her exams behind her, she drove to his apartment in an uplifted mood, singing Christmas carols and rejoicing over the holiday season, her favorite time of the year.

She could picture her parents' house in her mind, decked out for Christmas with fragrant garland trimmed in red velvet bows wrapped around the banister on the staircase. She could envision the tall Douglas fir, adorned with hundreds of twinkling white lights and sparkling ornaments, gracing its usual place in front of the living room picture window. Maggie would have a huge green wreath on the door by now and Remy would have lights strung from one end of the house to the other. Ashley could hardly wait to get home.

She tapped on Rick's front door, entering when she heard his voice call out to her. The heavenly aroma coming from the direction of the kitchen welcomed her and she followed the smell to find Rick chopping vegetables on the wooden cutting board. "What are you doing!" she laughed, coming up behind him and wrapping her arms around his waist.

"I'm making your dinner," he informed her. "How does seafood gumbo sound to you?"

"Sounds wonderful. I'm glad that one of us can cook," Ashley confessed with a giggle. "I can't boil water."

Rick lifted a skeptical brow. "Well, jump in here," he said. "It's high time you learn." He guided her through the dinner preparations like a pro, giving her instructions and helpful hints and Ashley found that she was enjoying it, in spite of her past aversion to anything domestic.

"How did you learn to do all this?" she asked Rick over dinner.

"My dear Ma Ma wanted to be sure that I could take care of myself," Rick told her. "She taught me to cook, sew, do laundry, basically the works."

"You'll make a fine wife to someone some day," Ashley teased him, receiving a wry stare from him in response.

"Cute," he rose from the table. "I cooked, you clean."

"That's not fair!" she protested. "I helped you cook."

"I did most of it," he reminded her as he kissed her on the cheek. "Besides, I need to work for just a little while this evening."

Rick retreated to his computer and Ashley heard him pounding away on the keyboard. She sighed, pouting just a little. She wasn't used to not being the center of Rick's attention and it made her a little fussy. She clanged the dishes together loudly in protest but it did no good. Rick basically ignored her.

He left for work early the next morning, leaving Ashley sleeping contently in his bed. She awoke late in the morning, stretching lazily across the mattress before rising to take a shower. She had just finished dressing when she heard light tapping on the front door. She peeked through the peephole. Standing there was an attractive young woman, clearly in her early twenties with short, dark hair. Ashley opened the door cautiously to offer her a friendly smile. "Hi," she said.

The girl appeared to be caught off guard by finding Ashley there. "Is Rick home?" she asked hesitantly, her eyes still wide with surprise.

"No, he's not here right now. Can I help you?" Ashley asked in a friendly voice.

She declined Ashley's offer with a shake of her head. "No, I guess not," she sighed. "May I leave a message for him?"

"Sure." Ashley volunteered willingly, watching the other girl fidget uncomfortably.

"Just tell him that Teri came by to say hello," she smiled nervously. "I'll be in town for a week or so."

Ashley nodded. "I'll tell him." The girl turned to go and Ashley watched with mounting curiosity as she got in her little red sports car and drove away, wondering who she was and what she meant to Rick.

She got her answer when Rick's sister Celeste dropped by to visit on her way home from her job as a legal secretary. Ashley was in the kitchen flipping through one of Rick's numerous cookbooks, determined to surprise him with dinner when Celeste's tenacious ringing of the doorbell summoned her.

"Rick has to work late and he asked me to come by and entertain you until he got here." Celeste stepped into the apartment, dressed to kill in pale-gray Ann Taylor and black pumps. She surveyed the room with a satisfied look on her face. "Spotless as always," she laughed. "Rick is by far the most anal-retentive man I've ever known."

"He is pretty neat and organized," Ashley agreed.

"That's an understatement," Celeste took off her charcoal wool overcoat and threw it over the back of a chair. "There! That ought to drive him over the edge," she declared triumphantly. Ashley laughed in appreciation. She really liked Celeste. Celeste and Rick were so opposite that it was hard for her to believe that they were related.

They moved into the immaculate kitchen and sat at the mahogany table, sipping freshly brewed coffee together. Ashley decided to ask Celeste about the girl who had appeared at the door earlier in the day.

"Who is Teri?" she inquired, leaning on her elbows as she observed Celeste's reaction.

Celeste blinked in surprise. "How did you know about Teri?"

"She came by earlier today."

"Teri was here?" Celeste was dumbfounded, gaping at Ashley in disbelief.

Ashley nodded enthusiastically in response to her question. "So, who is Teri?" she asked again, determined to get an answer.

"Teri is the girl who would have been my sister-in-law," Celeste answered, rising from her chair. She looked out the kitchen window, deep in thought, and Ashley continued to survey her with rising interest.

"What happened?" Now Ashley really wanted the whole story. Her curiosity was getting the better of her.

"Well, it's really a long story, and one that Rick should tell you himself," Celeste turned to advise her sternly.

"Oh, come on, Celeste. You know that I can't ask Rick about his former fiancée. I didn't even know *there was* a former fiancée. You can tell me."

Celeste sighed heavily, giving in. "I suppose you're right. But if I tell you, you can never tell Rick that you know about Teri. He would be pretty mad at me for telling you."

"I'll never tell, scout's honor."

Celeste refilled her cup of coffee and sat back down in her chair. She took a deep breath and began. "Teri and Rick met at Northeast, I guess it was seven years ago now. They were both freshmen, both in computer science, and instantly attracted to one another. I had never seen Rick so enamoured with any girl before Teri." Celeste's thoughts ventured back to a time gone by.

"They dated hot and heavy all the way through college. The longer they dated, the more Rick lived and breathed Teri. Teri was the most independent, free-spirited person I'd ever met. She had great ambitions of moving away and having a fabulous career on the East Coast. Rick, of course, wanted to settle down here in Monroe and get married."

Celeste paused, remembering the events of years past, clearly disturbed by some of the memories, judging by the pained look in her eyes.

"Rick wouldn't leave well enough alone. If he had given Teri time to think things over, I believe that she would have compromised and stayed here with him. I know that Teri loved Rick very much, but the more insistent Rick was about marriage, the more uncomfortable Teri became with him."

Celeste let out an unhappy sigh. "So finally, Teri took a job in New York. I remember the night that she broke the news to Rick. He was so furious with her that he frightened me, and flew into such a rage that I thought he would hit her."

Celeste noted the astonished look on Ashley's face and quickly ended her tale. "But he didn't hit her. Rick would never hit a woman," Celeste assured her with a gentle pat on her hand. "Teri moved to New York and left Rick heartbroken. And as far as I know, he has never heard from her again."

"Until now," Ashley spoke softly, chewing her lip thoughtfully as she absorbed the story of Rick and Teri. She could believe that Rick had exploded when Teri left him, remembering how violently he had reacted the night she'd gone out with the girls without telling him. She could only imagine how magnified his reaction to Teri's leaving him had been.

Before they could say more, Rick breezed in the front door, decked out attractively in his suit and paisley tie. The look Celeste shot her upon his arrival cautioned Ashley to remain silent about Teri.

Rick waltzed into the kitchen and kissed Ashley affectionately on the cheek. "Hello, sleepyhead. What time did you get up?"

"Not too late," she replied, smiling like a saint, bright and cheerful for his benefit.

"Did Celeste keep you entertained for me?" he asked. Celeste and Ashley looked at one another, nodding in unison.

Celeste declined Rick's offer to join them for dinner. "I promised Mother that I would go Christmas shopping for a little while this evening," she told him with a guilty smile. Only Ashley knew that it was a guilty smile. Rick didn't have a clue.

Ashley walked Celeste to the door while Rick changed out of his suit. "Not a word to Rick about our conversation," Celeste reminded her as she hastily pulled on her overcoat.

"I promised you I wouldn't, didn't I?" Ashley protested Celeste's lack of confidence in her silence. Celeste nodded as a co-conspirator in their mutual deceit of Rick.

"I will have to tell him that she came by, though," Ashley said as an afterthought. "She did ask me to tell him."

"You're nuts, Ashley. I'd just keep my mouth shut if I were you," Celeste shook her head dubiously as she cautioned her. "Good luck."

Rick and Ashley ordered Chinese take-out, eating on the living room floor and watching a movie that Rick had brought home with him. Ashley found it hard to concentrate on the film, her mind reeling at the prospect of telling Rick about Teri.

After the movie, Rick led her into his bedroom, casting aside her clothing before lifting her forcefully to his bed. Ashley kissed him passionately, determined to make love to him with such ardor that the memory of their night together would take away the sting of Teri being back in Monroe. She must have done a good job of it, she decided later, as she lay quietly watching Rick sleep, with a relaxed, peaceful expression on his face and a content smile on his lips. Ashley dreaded breaking the news to him about Teri but knew that she had no choice.

Rick let her sleep in again on Saturday morning. When she wandered out of the bedroom still clad in her pajamas, he was just returning from a workout at the gym.

"Good morning!" Rick said in a loud, lively voice, practically bouncing into the kitchen wearing gray sweat pants and a hooded sweatshirt, his face glowing with sweat from his vigorous workout.

Ashley winced at his cheerful disposition and poured a cup of coffee from the pot Rick had made for her, leaning against the counter as she sipped it, trying desperately to wake up.

"Breakfast?" Rick inquired.

Ashley shook her head while blinking her bleary eyes in an effort to focus them. "I don't do breakfast," she informed him, trying not to growl.

"You really don't like mornings, do you?" Rick teased her.

"I'd say that I'm more of a night owl. I'll be better after my shower." As her head began to clear, Ashley decided not to prolong the inevitable. "Rick," she began hesitantly, "Someone stopped by to see you yesterday," she told him as innocently as possible.

"Really?" Rick looked surprised. "Who?"

Ashley shrugged nonchalantly. "Someone named Teri."

Rick looked as though she had dropped a bomb in his kitchen, his smile fading instantly and his face losing all color. "What did she say?" Rick recovered from his shock nicely, forcing a casual smile onto his face.

"Not much. She just asked if you were here and when I told her no, she asked me to tell you that she had come by."

"Anything else?"

"She said that she would be in town for a week or so."

Rick nodded his head, deep in thought. "Her parents still live here. She must be home for the holidays," he said under his breath, more for his benefit than Ashley's.

Ashley decided that she should leave him to ponder the news on his own. "I'm going to take a shower," she said, kissing him on the cheek. Rick accepted her affection distractedly, still lost in his thoughts. Ashley took a long, hot shower while she contemplated what she should do or say next. That would depend on what Rick did.

When she got out of the shower, Ashley found that he was gone. He left a note for her on top of her makeup bag. "Dear Ashley," he wrote, "I had to go see someone. Please don't leave. I will return soon. Love, Rick."

Ashley plopped on the edge of the bed. So, Rick had gone to see Teri. She debated leaving for home right then and there, but voted against it. If Rick was upset when he returned from his encounter with Teri, he would need her comfort and support. She would stay.

She waited most of the day for Rick's return. Celeste called early in the afternoon for an update and Ashley told her that Rick had gone to see Teri.

"And you're still there?" Celeste was flabbergasted. "Unbelievable. You're a saint, Ashley Stewart. He doesn't deserve you."

"What else should I have done? If I left now, I would be the second woman to disappoint him. He doesn't need that right now," Ashley said democratically.

"You're too good to be true. Do you want me to come over and keep you company? Or maybe we could go grab a bite to eat or something."

"I guess not. There's no telling what Rick will be like when he gets home."

Rick arrived home just after five o'clock, deeply apologetic for deserting her and extremely grateful that Ashley hadn't retreated home in a huff. She tried to evaluate his mood, but he was cool, giving nothing away.

Ashley picked at her dinner wordlessly, dying to ask him what had happened. Rick was equally silent, not sharing his thoughts at all. Finally, Ashley lost her patience. "So, are you going to tell me where you were today?" she asked brusquely.

Rick looked at her sheepishly. "I went to see Teri," he said.

That much Ashley knew already. She wanted details. "And?"

"And what?" Rick glared at her, annoyed with her for prying.

Ashley returned his hot stare, annoyed with him for going to see another woman and not wanting to discuss it with her. "And are you going to see her again?"

"Yes, I'm sure I will. She's an old friend and will only be here for a short time," he said condescendingly. "I really don't see where it's any of your concern, Ashley."

Ashley knew that he was not being honest with her and that was her advantage. He had no idea that she knew exactly how good a friend Teri was to him "Then I guess I'll be going home." Ashley pushed back her chair and rose abruptly from the table. Rick followed her as she strode purposely toward the bedroom.

"I don't want you to go home," he protested, stopping her by pulling her into his arms.

"I'm not going to stay here and keep you from being with Teri tonight," Ashley thrashed in aggravation at his unyielding embrace.

"I don't want to be with Teri tonight. I want to be with you," Rick declared, kissing her deeply before she could protest. He pushed her gently down onto the bed, continuing to kiss her amorously and made love to her with such fervency that Ashley knew that he was thinking of Teri, wanting to punish Teri through her. She couldn't help but feel resentful.

After Rick drifted into a peaceful sleep, Ashley quietly pulled on jeans and a sweatshirt before leaving the room with the bag that she had packed earlier that day. She slipped soundlessly from the apartment and got in her car, pulling onto the highway and heading south for home.

CHAPTER EIGHTEEN

Ashley wailed most of the way to Pineville, because of her hurt pride and not her injured emotions. She wasn't really jealous of Teri. She was only mad for being put in second place behind Rick's old flame, and she certainly wouldn't put up with him thinking of Teri while making love to her. She hadn't bothered to leave a note for Rick when she left, knowing that he would figure out where and why she had gone when he awoke alone. She just didn't know how she would explain to her parents why on earth she was arriving home at three in the morning.

Ashley eased her car stealthily down the dark driveway, cutting the lights as she neared the house. She parked in front, cutting the engine. Not about to risk waking her parents at that ungodly hour, she elected not to go inside. Instead, she lay her seat back, covering up with her long wool coat. Tired and certainly irritable, she closed her eyes and drifted off to sleep.

An insistent tapping awakened her and Ashley opened her eyes, squinting through the window at her father. She unlocked the door and opened it for him. "Hi," she said casually as Remy wrinkled his brow in concern.

"Do you want to tell me what you're doing out here?" Remy asked, frowning sternly at her.

Ashley shrugged. "I got home a little earlier than I expected to and I didn't want to wake you all."

"When did you get here?"

"About three this morning." She swung her legs out and stood, stiff and sore from sleeping in the car. She indulged in a catlike stretch before giving Remy a hug. He continued to gawk at her with a look of utter disbelief on his face, bending down to retrieve the newspaper from the driveway before they strolled inside together.

Maggie, in her navy and white striped robe, stood at the kitchen counter pouring water into the coffeemaker. "Ashley! I wasn't expecting you until this afternoon." Maggie peered at the clock and quickly noted the time, aware that it was just before seven o'clock.

"She's been sleeping in the car since three o'clock," Remy informed her, scowling his displeasure to Ashley.

Maggie regarded her quizzically. "Any particular reason?" she questioned, although lately, nothing that Ashley did surprised her.

"I'm mad at Rick so I left early." Ashley leaned down, staring pathetically at the steady stream of coffee flowing down into the pot, desperately in need of a cup.

"Are you up for church?" Maggie let it go, deciding that her daughter would tell her all about her latest trouble with the already infamous Rick when she was ready. "Remy and I were planning on going this morning."

"I might as well, I'm already up," Ashley said, grumbling as she sat down at the kitchen table.

Maggie hovered over her, pouring some of the freshly brewed coffee. "So, what happened?"

"I don't want to talk about it."

Maggie sat in the chair opposite Ashley, noting the spasm of irritation that crossed her daughter's face. "That bad, huh?"

"I *said* I don't want to talk about it."

"Is he worth it?" Maggie said, forcing Ashley to look her directly in the face.

Ashley issued an unhappy sigh. "I don't know, especially right at this particular moment. I so wanted Rick to be the one to make me forget, but I just don't know if he's the one."

"Sometimes the one who makes us forget comes along when we least expect it," Maggie advised her with a distant smile.

"What would you know about it?" Ashley snapped, still edgy and irritable, and in need of a shower.

"You'd be surprised," Maggie said, meeting Ashley's exasperated gaze evenly.

Ignoring her, Ashley drained her coffee cup and jumped up to refill it. "I'm going to take a shower," Ashley told her, stalking from the kitchen and up the stairs to the bathroom.

Susanna was at church that morning and waved Ashley down enthusiastically after the service. "Kate said you wouldn't be here until tonight," she said, speaking first.

"No one seems to be glad that I'm home a little early," Ashley said in a strained tone, striving very hard not to lose her short temper.

"I just know you too well, chickadee. Something's up or you wouldn't have left Monroe one minute earlier than you had planned."

Ashley was hesitant to reveal all to Susanna. She was hardly in the mood for Susanna to call her a little princess again. Susanna sensed correctly that something was bothering her and took her by the arm. "Let's go to B.J.'s and grab a pizza."

After ordering their pizza and settling into a booth, Ashley reluctantly told Susanna the latest sordid Rick Tale and waited for Susanna to give her the standard speech about getting over herself and growing up. But Susanna pleasantly surprised her.

"What a total jerk," Susanna began with an outraged roll of her hazel eyes. "What a self-centered, inconsiderate, two-timing asshole! I *cannot believe* the absolute nerve of that guy. You did the right thing to come home. You should've come home the minute he left to go see her yesterday morning. You knew that's where he was."

"I know," Ashley sheepishly agreed with her. "I just wanted to see what happened with Teri. I thought that he might need me, but apparently he didn't."

"For God's sake, Ashley, didn't I teach you any better than that?" Susanna shook her head in frustrated wonder. "I'll just stay here in case Rick needs me," she mocked Ashley in a singsong voice, angry with her for being so stupid.

"You're a real comfort in my time of need," Ashley said wearily, scooping a cube of ice from her tea into her mouth and crunching it loudly to drown out Susanna's tirade.

"Well, at least you've started dating again," Susanna tried to cheer her up. "There are plenty of guys out there."

"Which is why you've dated so much since we graduated," Ashley spoke without thinking and immediately wanted to kick herself.

Susanna's face fell momentarily but she immediately salvaged her poise. "Always the true friend," she winked at Ashley to cover her deflated ego. "Thanks."

"I'm sorry, Suz. I didn't mean that. I've just had a rough night."

"I know you didn't mean it," Susanna said indifferently. "Let's eat and forget about everything else."

After Susanna dropped her off at the house, Ashley stood in the yard, admiring Remy's Clark-Griswald-like Christmas decorations. Kate spotted her and bellowed cheerfully from her back yard. "Hey!" she waved eagerly to Ashley, who trudged tiredly to meet her halfway.

"Hey yourself," Ashley approached her wearing a forced grin. "You go to church?"

"Yeah. There are a lot of people home for the holidays this year. I hear rumors of a New Year's Party at Scotty Jeansonne's."

"Good! I'll need *something* to do for New Year's."

"Trouble in paradise, so your mother tells me," Kate eyed her questioningly. "Says you slept in the driveway last night."

"I did sleep in the driveway but I didn't get there until three this morning," Ashley corrected her. "Kate, I can't tell the tale one more time today. Call Susanna, she'll tell you all about it."

"Touchy, touchy," Kate chided her, clucking her tongue disapprovingly.

"I just need a nap," Ashley apologized. "I'll talk to you tomorrow after I've had some sleep."

Ashley eased into the house and started up the stairs to take a nap just as Maggie called to her from the den. Ashley sighed tiredly, rolling her eyes, backtracking into the den to see what she wanted. She stood in the doorway and looked expectantly at Maggie, who sat needlepointing a Christmas stocking.

"Rick has called you twice." Maggie told her. Ashley scowled in exasperation.

"What does he want?"

"To apologize, I think. He was very concerned when you were gone this morning. You didn't even tell him goodbye?"

"There was no need." Ashley flung her drained body into Remy's recliner, flipping her legs angrily over the arm.

"Aren't you going to call him back?"

"I don't see why I should."

"I think you should."

"Why are you defending him again? You don't even know what happened," Ashley pointed out self-righteously.

"Yes, I do. Rick told me all about his old girlfriend, Teri, and the fact that he left you to go see her yesterday."

"And you still defend him?" Ashley turned a cold eye on her mother, in a huff over Maggie's betrayal.

"You haven't even heard his explanation, Ashley."

"Whatever it is, it can wait. I'm going to take a nap." She swung her legs to the floor, preparing to stalk from the room.

"Before you take that nap, I'd like to tell you something." Maggie patted the spot on the couch next to hers and Ashley begrudgingly sat down to hear what she had to say.

"You know, Ashley, you think I don't know what I'm talking about when I give you advice about Rick, but I have a little experience in this area myself."

Ashley glanced over at her, intrigued by her cryptic prologue.

"Remy isn't the only man I've ever loved," Maggie admitted quietly, her lovely eyes shadowed by uncharacteristic sadness. "There was another before Remy, and I loved him more than life itself. But I was childish, headstrong, and I wasn't as forgiving about things that happened between us as I should've been. I won't go into specifics because it no longer matters, but I eventually lost him and regretted it for a long, long time."

Ashley stared at her in surprise, unable to imagine that her mother had ever been in love with anyone other than her father. "Were you just heartbroken?"

Maggie nodded slowly with a faraway gleam in her eyes. "Yes, I was."

"How did you get over it?" Ashley was encouraged to know that Maggie Stewart had turned out to be a normal person after devastating heartbreak.

"I met your father," Maggie beamed at her, tightly squeezing her hand. "Remy Stewart waltzed into my life when I was least expecting it, and I fell head over heels in love with him."

"Wow," Ashley sighed in awe.

"So, now you know, Ashley. I do know a little something about the advice I give you," Maggie said with a teasing sparkle in her eyes, curbing her laughter and reaching out to smooth Ashley's hair back from her face. "You remind me so much of myself at your age. You are so independent, headstrong and hot-tempered. I feel for the man who really loves you."

"Gee, Maggie, thanks for the shining endorsement," Ashley said, unable to suppress the huge grin spreading across her face. "I can only hope my love life turns out as well as yours did. I want to marry someone just like Remy."

"Go take your nap," Maggie commanded her jokingly, pointing her finger toward the door. "You look terrible."

Ashley obediently trudged upstairs, but she didn't get the nap she longed for. Rick phoned her before she could go to sleep. "I was worried about you," he told her humbly. "I can't believe you left in the middle of the night like that. What if your car had broken down?"

"Well, it didn't and I made it safe and sound," Ashley reminded him coolly. "What do you want?"

"Look, Ashley, Celeste told me that she told you about Teri. I'm sorry that I wasn't straight with you."

"And that changes what?" Ashley maintained her icy position and sank, telephone in hand, onto the hardwood floor, staring out the window at the gray winter sky as she listened to his words.

"I had to see Teri to know for sure that I was over her," Rick confessed quietly. "When I first saw her, I was taken in by her all over again. But as I talked with her, I realized that she didn't mean the same thing to me anymore. I went back to see her again this morning to tell her I couldn't see her again."

Ashley listened wordlessly, enraptured by what he said and elated that she was hearing it. She waited breathlessly for him to go on.

"I don't want Teri or anyone else for that matter, Ashley. I only want you," Rick said, pausing for her response. "Say something, Ashley. Say anything."

"I'm sorry I left you in the middle of the night," Ashley said meekly. "I should've resolved this with you face to face."

"Tell me something," Rick, after recognizing that he had been forgiven, became more jovial. "Are you going to run home every time we have a misunderstanding?"

Ashley laughed. "If at all possible," she answered, a smile finally returning to her face.

Susanna gave Ashley hell for making up with Rick, starting the moment Ashley informed her of their reconciliation. "Jeez-us, Ashley! You are such a pushover," she said irately. "Little Ricky sweet talks you with a line of crap about you being the only one for him, and you go running back like nothing ever happened. How can you be so stupid? How can you believe anything he tells you after all that?"

"I have no reason not to believe him," Ashley defended Rick gallantly. "Weren't you the one who had such a fit the last time I got mad at him? Aren't you the one who accused me of being a prima donna and told me to grow up?"

"This," Susanna retorted with a haughty sniff, "is different. This is about another woman, the competition. The yelling episode was a whole 'nother ballgame."

"Teri is not the competition. She's an old girlfriend who lives on the East Coast and is no threat whatsoever."

"You're a pushover," Susanna repeated. "Ashley, have you ever thought that there's got to be something terribly wrong with Rick? A man who is that great looking, and that old, but not attached yet? Think about it, girlfriend! What deep, dark skeletons is he hiding in his closet?"

"Susanna, you're paranoid," Ashley dismissed her by turning her head, watching as a gang of small children scampered eagerly toward the mall Santa Claus, jumping up on his knee to excitedly whisper to him their heart's desire. Ashley stared wistfully, longing to have her greatest wish granted by jolly old Saint Nick. If it were only that easy, she sighed.

CHAPTER NINETEEN

When the doorbell rang on that crisp, winter afternoon, three days after Christmas, Ashley and Maggie spotted Rick through the kitchen window and raced one another for the door. Maggie won, sliding to a halt in the front entry, quickly smoothing her hair and swinging open the etched-glass front door to greet Rick, clearly liking what she saw.

"You must be Rick, come in!" Maggie welcomed him eagerly as Rick stepped into the front hall. Looking on, Ashley smiled, waving to him happily from the kitchen doorway.

"I'm Maggie Stewart, Ashley's mom," Maggie introduced herself and shook Rick's outstretched hand.

"It's nice to finally meet you," Rick smiled appealingly and although Doug would always be her sweetheart, Maggie's heart melted as she returned his dazzling smile.

"I know just how you feel," Maggie glanced at Ashley over her shoulder. "I thought Ashley was going to hide you from us forever," she whispered to Rick with a vivacious laugh.

Ashley made her way over to them, giving Rick a huge hug and a warm kiss on the lips. "Hi there, stranger," she smiled up at him and Rick returned her greeting with equal warmth, staring into her eyes like he hadn't seen her in weeks.

Maggie ushered them toward the den. "You two go visit while I make dinner."

"I could help you," Rick volunteered. "I'm a great cook."

"Don't be silly, Rick!" Maggie giggled like a little girl, flushing and batting her eyelashes flirtatiously. "You're a guest here."

"Brown noser," Ashley said, leading him into the den and depositing him on the couch, sitting next to him and watching as he surveyed his surroundings admiringly.

"I like the house."

"Thanks."

"I've missed you while you've been home," Rick squeezed her hand, his eyes warm with affection for her.

"I've missed you too," Ashley said, eyeing him cautiously. Rick LeNoir was still devilishly handsome on the outside. However, there was something distinctly different about his demeanor. Ashley studied him, trying to put a finger on it.

"I never want you to go away again," Rick said solemnly, putting his arm loosely around her shoulder.

"God, Rick, don't go getting all mushy on me. Why are you being so serious?" Ashley kidded with him. "It's the holidays, lighten up already."

"I didn't realize that I was being too serious. I was only telling you how I feel. Seeing Teri and remembering how much I hurt when I lost her made me realize how important you are to me. I never want to lose you, Ashley." Rick gazed adoringly at her with his huge blue eyes and Ashley wasn't sure how to react.

She quickly figured out what was different about Rick LeNoir. He was lacking the self-assured arrogance so characteristic of his personality. Ashley discovered over the course of Rick's stay in Pineville how profound an effect Teri's visit had on him. It was quite apparent that Teri had caused all of his buried insecurities to rise to the surface. Instead of the suave, confident man Ashley was crazy about, she found herself in the company of an unsure, doting stranger. And she didn't like it one bit. Ashley felt so smothered that she was almost breathless, and by New Year's Eve, she was ready to scream.

Kate and Susanna were going together to Scott's party, as neither of them wanted to take a date. Unfortunately, Ashley was obligated to bring Rick along. She felt guilty for the way she had dreaded having him around all week. She should have been more sympathetic toward him. After all, he'd just been through a reunion with the one woman in his life who had caused him so much pain. She should have been more understanding and tolerant of his clinging manner. But she couldn't. Rick was driving her insane.

Scotty Jeansonne's parents lived near the Fairchilds off Paper Mill Road, in a sienna stucco house with a lush green yard and kidney-shaped swimming pool. Ashley and Rick arrived at Scott's a little after nine-thirty to find the party in full swing. Scotty and Jeff Thomasee greeted them at the door and they tag-teamed Ashley with each of them planting a kiss on one of her rosy cheeks.

"Hello, Ice Princess!" Scotty said, needling Ashley affectionately.

Ashley beamed fondly at her old buddy, punching him lightly in the arm. "Hello Scott, hello Jeff." She motioned to Rick who had stepped to one side, observing the three of them with a slightly irritated frown.

"This is Rick LeNoir, from Monroe," Ashley introduced him as Rick stepped forward to shake their hands coolly. Scott and Jeff exchanged a puzzled glance at his standoffishness before excusing themselves to welcome Chris Alexander arriving behind Rick and Ashley.

"What was that all about?" Rick demanded as he and Ashley began to circulate through the crowded living room. Ashley glanced at his perturbed expression, rolling her eyes at him.

"Jeff and Scott are my friends," she informed him with an impatient shake of her head. "What *is wrong* with you?"

"I didn't like them all over you like that."

"I'm sorry if that bothered you, but you better get used to it," Ashley advised him. "You'll see similar encounters all night long."

Rick found out that she spoke the truth. Ashley and her friends had always been affectionate with one another and she wasn't going to act any differently for Rick's benefit. Naturally, he didn't mind the girls approaching Ashley in that manner, but he could scarcely deal with her male friends' zealous displays of affection. She dreaded bringing him and Doug together.

Ashley had the opportunity to introduce him to Susanna first, running into her and Kate near the pool table, where Susanna was giving Mitch Guidry a run for his money. Rick tried to be appealing to her, but Susanna regarded him coldly, still miffed over Ashley's account of the Teri episode.

"How much has she had to drink?" Ashley whispered to Kate as they watched Rick and Susanna interacting.

"Enough to make Rick sorry that he ever laid eyes on her," Kate cautioned her.

"That's all I needed to know." Ashley shielded Rick from the wrath of Susanna by linking her arm protectively through his, just as Susanna looked as though she was about to read him the riot act.

"Let's go this way," Ashley said, giving Susanna a warning glance, to which Susanna responded by sticking her tongue out. Ashley navigated Rick through throngs of partying ex-schoolmates and exited the house through French doors to the pool area where brightly colored Japanese lanterns swayed gently in the cool night air.

And there they encountered Douglas Fairchild, encircled in a group of guys who included Scotty and Jeff. Scotty saw them approaching and nudged Doug in the ribs, murmuring quietly to him. Doug turned to stare at them before he excused himself from the group and sauntered their way.

Doug had also been drinking, which was a rarity. Ashley couldn't remember the last time she saw him drink. He stopped directly in front of them, scrutinizing Rick with narrowed eyes. "So you're the guy who stole my best girl," Doug said to Rick, with just a hint of a challenge.

Oh shit, Doug, Ashley thought silently. Why of all nights would you pick this one to be so obnoxious?

"And you are?" Rick met Doug's challenge smoothly and Ashley had to hand it to him. Rick was definitely suave under pressure.

"Doug Fairchild," Doug extended his hand and Rick shook it firmly, each of them sizing up the other. Ashley wanted to punch them both.

"Rick LeNoir, nice to meet you," Rick gave the obligatory introduction as Kate, sensing the impending confrontation, moved smoothly through the crowd to join them.

"Kate, will you keep Rick company for a moment?" Ashley said, glad to see Kate come to the rescue. "I need to speak with Douglas."

Ashley grabbed Doug's arm and pulled him away from the group before anyone could object. Doug was chuckling loudly by the time Ashley got him alone beside the pool house, and his hearty laughter only served to annoy her more. She pushed him against the outer wall of the pool house, poking her index finger sharply into his muscular chest.

"So you're the guy who stole my best girl?" Ashley glared up at him with mounting irritation. "Really, Doug, couldn't you have come up with something more original as an introduction?"

Doug grinned broadly at her. "I thought it was pretty clever myself."

"You would."

"Well, he deserved it. The guy's an ass."

"Doug, will you please lighten up?" Ashley pleaded with him, crossing her arms fretfully across her chest. "Rick is not as bad as you all make him out to be."

"Says you. We just took an impromptu survey right after you arrived and it's unanimous. The guy's an ass."

"Doug Fairchild, what is wrong with you!" she said in a demanding tone, throwing her own back against the wall as Doug continued to push her buttons. "You're supposed to be my friend. Why can't you play nice with Rick?"

"Because I have no desire to play nice with him," Doug glanced over to forewarn her. "I don't like him."

"You just met him. How can you not like him?" Ashley said, resisting the urge to stomp her foot in anger.

"I've seen enough to know," Doug said, leaning into her as she stood against wall of the stucco pool house, his arm resting high above her head. His face was mere inches from hers and she could feel his warm, mint-and-alcohol-scented breath against her cheek. "I've been watching him since the two of you arrived. He is arrogant and overly possessive of you, and I damn sure don't like the way he's been treating our friends. I wish to God that Susanna had punched him."

Ashley laughed out loud in spite of herself. The visual image she had of Susanna decking Rick was too comical. She suppressed her humorous thoughts, forcing the somber expression back onto her face.

"Now, Doug, Rick is a guest here," she twirled her finger against his shoulder in a friendly gesture, hoping to win him over to her way of thinking. "Please be nice, just for tonight. Then tomorrow you can act any way you'd like."

"I'll act any way I'd like tonight," Doug was being unusually belligerent and Ashley knew that it was useless to try to reason with him. If she could only get them all to midnight without any brawling, she and Rick could leave unscathed and happy.

As Doug grinned devilishly after her, Ashley stalked off to reclaim Rick from Kate. She tried to be cheerful but, with the exception of Kate, she was very displeased with her friends' reception of Rick. She caught Doug's eye many times during the night as he watched them and turned her back haughtily to him, showing him exactly what she thought of his poor conduct.

Rick stayed close by her side all night. She finally managed to shake him loose long enough to go the bathroom, where she encountered Susanna outside the bathroom door.

"Well, he's certainly a handsome devil," Susanna said. "But his attitude stinks."

"How do you really feel about him, Susanna?" Ashley said bitterly, leaning against the wall beside Susanna to await her turn in the restroom.

"Oh, Ashley, you can't really like that guy," Susanna said with a scornful frown.

"I do like Rick, quite a bit actually."

"He's not your type. He's so full of himself that it's offensive."

"Susanna, are you trying to win friends tonight or what?"

"Hey, I'm entitled to my opinion," Susanna reminded her with an evil cackle.

"And I'm entitled to date whomever I please." Ashley was grateful that the bathroom became available to her at that moment and she left Susanna in a huff, slamming the bathroom door behind her.

After ringing in the New Year with glittery hats, obnoxious horns and sloppy kisses, Ashley ushered Rick toward the front door as quickly as possible, sidling hurriedly through the unruly crowd in hope of avoiding any further confrontation with Susanna or Doug. Success was hers, and she paused in the foyer to thank a confetti-covered Scotty for inviting them to his party.

"I sure am glad I got to see you again, Ice Princess," Scotty brushed some stray glitter from Ashley's hair as he kissed her cheek with great fondness. "Good luck with *him*," he whispered disdainfully in her ear. Ashley offered Scott one last weary look and led Rick out of the house.

Rick exploded immediately after getting into the car. "I'm glad Kate is your roommate and not that shrew, Susanna!" he said, throwing the car into gear and spinning out of the Jeansonnes' gravel driveway. "Why are you such good friends with her? She is so unpleasant."

Ashley didn't particularly care for Rick bashing one of her closest friends and jutted her chin out defensively. "You don't know her the way I do. She's not really unpleasant. She just comes across that way sometimes."

Rick grunted disagreeably. "And what about Doug Fairchild? Did you used to date him?" His irate interrogation of her was relentless, and Ashley turned away from him, too emotionally drained to face his cynicism.

"Doug and I are old friends too. We were never romantically involved." Ashley stared out into the darkness at the passing blocks of shadowed scenery, accented occasionally by the eerie blue glow of a dusk-to-dawn light.

"Did you date Scott or Jeff?"

Ashley shook her head tiredly as Rick continued his unreasonable tirade. "No, Rick."

"Ashley, I refuse to believe that you went through your entire adolescence without a single boyfriend. You had to have dated someone," Rick pointed out tensely.

"I did date someone," Ashley felt the familiar tug at her heart. Jimmy.

"Why didn't I meet him?" Rick said sarcastically. "Wasn't he there?

"No, he wasn't there."

Rick was too involved in his self-serving inquisition to notice the distinct sadness in Ashley's voice. "Why not? God knows everyone else you've ever known was there."

"He wasn't there because he's dead," Ashley answered woodenly, glancing back at him over her shoulder.

Rick jerked his head over at her, staring into her eyes to see if she was serious. "Dead?" he questioned in disbelief. Ashley responded with a solemn nod of her head.

"What happened to him?"

"He is not a topic for discussion," Ashley warned him. There was no way that she was going to tell Rick about Jimmy, especially while he was in his present state of mind. Jimmy was her special memory, and Ashley wouldn't have Rick belittle him.

They arrived at her parents' house and Ashley leapt from the car, striding purposely toward the veranda, several steps ahead of Rick. He hurried to catch up with her.

"Ashley," he caught her elbow. She paused, allowing him to walk beside her. "I'm sorry I was so hard on your friends." His apology was sincere and Ashley instantly forgave him.

"That's okay," she said with a burdened sigh, reaching out to open the front door. "Some of them were not particularly nice to you either." She kissed Rick goodnight in the foyer. "Happy New Year, Rick."

"Happy New Year, Ashley." He embraced her tightly. "I hope that it will be a good year for us."

"I hope so too," she prayed silently.

Rick retired to the downstairs guest room and Ashley ascended the stairs to her own bedroom, completely exhausted from running interference between Rick, Doug and Susanna all evening. She was ready for a good night's sleep.

The next afternoon, after bidding Maggie and Remy goodbye, Rick walked with Ashley out to his car. "Come back to Monroe with me, Ashley," he said, taking her into his arms and kissing her invitingly.

Ashley batted her eyelashes flirtatiously at him before graciously declining his request. "I'd love to but I'm not done visiting with my family and friends," she said with an apologetic smile. "Besides, you're leaving in three days to go to Oklahoma for a week and I'd would be stuck in Monroe all alone."

"I suppose you're right," Rick said, reluctantly agreeing with her. "I'll just miss you."

"We'll be together again before you know it," she said cheerfully, knowing she would miss Rick but glad she would have a couple of weeks without him to catch her breath. "Call me when you get back from Oklahoma," she told him as he got into his car and slid behind the wheel.

"I will. Enjoy the rest of your break, Ashley," he said, turning the key in the ignition. "I'll be glad when I get you back to Monroe where I can have you all to myself."

Ashley waved goodbye as Rick drove away, then sank wearily down onto the front steps, heaving a great sigh of relief.

She returned to Northeast to face a full class schedule that promised to leave her with very little spare time. She moved back into Slater Hall and readjusted to early mornings and late nights, supplemented by a steady diet of caffeine, chocolate and carryout pizza. Despite the relief she had felt when Rick left Pineville, Ashley found herself unable to wait for his return from Oklahoma. She had already forgotten the claustrophobia he had caused her. All she could remember were his irresistible eyes, his captivating smile and his warm, passionate kisses.

Rick returned to Monroe late on Friday afternoon. Ashley was just returning from a chemistry lab when the telephone shrilled loudly, beckoning her with its ring. When she picked up, Rick's voice rang over the line with enthusiasm. "I'm back!"

"Hi there!" Ashley welcomed him home, a radiant glow overtaking her face. "How was your trip?"

"The trip was fantastic," Rick sounded good, his voice radiating its customary level of confidence. "I can't wait to tell you about it."

"I can't wait to hear about it," Ashley said. "I'll be over in a flash."

As she hung up with Rick, she began shedding her clothes, changing into clean jeans and a pink cotton sweater. She pulled her hair from its ponytail, shaking her head from side to side until it fell loosely in soft waves down her back. She hastily scrawled a note to Kate, telling her that Rick had returned and not to expect her back to the dorm until Sunday night.

Rick flung open the door of his apartment before Ashley could reach the top of the stairs. "Come here, you!" he gestured to her with a broad smile and Ashley hurried toward him, throwing herself into his waiting arms.

"I missed you!" she told him truthfully, kissing him warmly as he pulled her into the apartment. She fell onto the couch with him, laughing happily, leaning on her elbow and looking up at him with dancing eyes. "Tell me all about your trip."

"Oklahoma City is wonderful," Rick began, his face brightening with excitement. "It's big, clean and sprawling, and compared to Monroe, Oklahoma City is absolutely bustling!"

"Okay, so you liked the city. How was your meeting with the big shots?"

"My meetings at corporate office went well. Naturally, they were pretty impressed with my abilities," he glanced at Ashley, pausing.

"And?" she pressed him to continue, sensing that there was something more.

"They offered me a promotion!" Rick said, grinning ear to ear with delight. Ashley squealed and threw her arms around him.

"Rick, that's terrific! I'm so excited for you. When do you get the promotion?"

"As soon as I move to Oklahoma City."

Ashley froze, his words hitting her like a ton of bricks. Move? How could he move? They had just gotten their relationship on track and things were progressing so beautifully. It was just her luck. She had finally started caring for someone again and now she was going to lose him too. Ashley certainly didn't want to rain on his parade, but she was profusely saddened at his news. Rick observed her in silence, waiting for some response.

"Oh," she said, giving the only response she could manage at that particular moment. "When will you be leaving Monroe?"

"Some time in May since my job starts the first of June."

"Well," she said, forcing herself to smile brightly at him. "At least we still have five months together."

Rick took her hands in his, squeezing them affectionately. "Ashley, I've really given this a lot of thought. I want to take this promotion, but I don't want to leave you behind."

"What do you mean?"

"I want you to come with me."

Ashley blinked incredulously, staring at him, taken aback by his unexpected request. "To Oklahoma City?" she said. "Rick, I can't go to Oklahoma City! What would I do about school? And what about my folks? They'd never go for that."

In response to her string of curious questions, Rick stood and crossed the room, returning with his briefcase. He opened it, removing a folder that he placed in her lap. "I've thought about the education part of it," he said, tapping the folder with his index finger. "Oklahoma City is home to the University of Oklahoma Health Sciences Center and the best pharmacy school in the state."

He opened the folder, revealing to her the colorful brochures and paperwork inside. "I brought home information about the school and an application for admissions. I was told if you were going to apply for the fall, you must mail the application soon. The college will interview applicants around the end of February."

Ashley stared at the papers in her lap and glanced up at him uncertainly as she debated the issue. She had prayed for God to send someone to help her forget Jimmy, and He had delivered Rick. She had wished for new surroundings in which to forget the past. Here was the answer: Oklahoma City was being offered to her on a plate, and yet she was still unsure that this was the thing to do.

Rick sensed her insecurity and patted her shoulder reassuringly. "You don't have to answer today, Ashley," he said gently. "Take some time to think it over and then we'll decide what to do next."

Ashley did think it over, she could think of nothing else. She returned to the dormitory on Sunday evening still having made no decision, and discussed it at length with Kate.

Kate's initial reaction was astonishment, followed by loyal understanding. "Well, it's a tempting offer, without a doubt," she said, running her long fingers through her silky blond hair, giving Ashley a slow, appraising glance. "How do you really feel about it deep down inside?"

Ashley paced to the window and stared out thoughtfully toward the bayou, contemplating the question wholeheartedly before responding. "I feel like this is the answer to my prayers," she admitted sincerely. "I need a new start so badly. This has got to be the way for me to forget the past."

Ashley sighed, pressing her face against the cool glass of the window and adding her true reservations. "But on the other hand, I can hardly bear the thought of leaving Maggie, Remy, and everyone else I love behind to move five hundred miles away."

"With Rick," Kate added unnecessarily, which Ashley acknowledged with a wry look.

"Well," Kate joined her beside the window, putting her arm around Ashley's shoulders encouragingly. "If you feel so strongly that this might be the thing for you to do, then fill out the application and mail it in. Applying to the college certainly won't hurt anything."

That was it! Kate was brilliant as always. That would be the way she would decide. She would apply to the College of Pharmacy in Oklahoma City. If she interviewed and was accepted, she would go with Rick to Oklahoma. If not, she would simply enjoy the time she had left with him, then wish him the best when he left, and move on.

Ashley spent the next several days rushing around campus, gathering her transcripts and obtaining letters of recommendation from her instructors. She prepared the application and, together with the other necessary paperwork, presented them to Rick.

Rick grinned ear to ear. "Does this mean what I think it means?"

"Don't go getting all excited," Ashley told him with a reserved smile. "It simply means that I'm applying to the college. I'll base my decision on the results."

"You do realize that I'm not asking you to go to Oklahoma City and shack up with me, don't you?" Rick asked her, regarding her seriously as he took her by the shoulders.

Ashley gazed up into his captivating aqua eyes and blinked in bewilderment. "Then what are you asking?"

"I guess what I'm trying to tell you is that Oklahoma is a two-part proposition," Rick said mysteriously. "If you decide to go to Oklahoma with me, I want you to go as my wife."

Once again, Rick had taken her completely by surprise, a fact that showed in her startled expression. "What's wrong with just shacking up?" she responded kiddingly, trying to make light of the weighty subject matter.

"I don't think that your father would approve of that idea."

"And you think that he will approve of my getting married just to move out of state?" Ashley asked skeptically.

"Just think about it for now," Rick said, confident that she would eventually agree to his plan. "You don't have to make any decision until you hear back from OU."

CHAPTER TWENTY

The letter for which Ashley waited arrived on a Friday afternoon, the third week of April, near the end of her second year at Northeast. She had applied to the University of Oklahoma College of Pharmacy and had flown up in February for applicant interviews. Rick bought a plane ticket, then put her on the plane to Oklahoma alone.

"Are you sure you won't come with me?" she asked him for the hundredth time on their way to the airport.

Rick shook his head and laughed. "No, Ashley, not this time," he said gently, squeezing her hand. "You should go alone and enjoy yourself. You'll like Oklahoma City, you'll see."

And he was right. Ashley loved Oklahoma City, finding it different from anything she had ever known. It was big, sprawling and clean, absolutely full of life and friendly people. As she rode in the taxi from the airport to her hotel, Ashley stared out the window, taking in the sights of the city stretching for miles and miles in every direction, feeling the excitement of being in a new place rise from deep within her. She could like it here with Rick, she decided. She could like it anywhere that allowed her to get away from the lingering memories of the past. Arriving at her hotel, she spent a quiet evening alone, embracing her surroundings while thinking of home, traveling the next morning to The Health Sciences Center near downtown Oklahoma City for her interview.

The University of Oklahoma College of Pharmacy was a three-story beige building, situated on the edge of the huge medical complex that was home to four hospitals, various specialty clinics, allied health colleges and academic buildings. Ashley leaned forward excitedly, viewing the campus from the back seat of a yellow cab, a thrill racing down her spine at the thought of actually going to school there. At the front of the school, she paid the driver then entered through a set of glass doors, checking in with the receptionist and pacing the corridor nervously until her name was called. Immediately following a lengthy interview with the admissions committee, Ashley left the college for Will Rogers World Airport and boarded a plane for Monroe.

As they waited for the letter, her relationship with Rick continued to flourish. Rick was thrilled about his promotion, along with his upcoming move to Oklahoma City, and Ashley was excited for him, knowing it would be a great boost for his career. The insecurities brought on by Teri's holiday visit had vanished. The suave, confident Rick LeNoir was back with a vengeance, much to Ashley's immense relief. Rick was wonderful with her concerning the move to Oklahoma. There was no pressure, no insistence that she give him a clue toward her inclination. The offer had been made and it was up to Ashley to decide. And so for the letter they waited.

Ashley spent most of her nights with Rick, but occasionally stayed at the dorm with Kate, Hillary and Melissa. She and Susanna had patched things up over the New Year's Eve fiasco. However, Ashley was unwilling to forgive Doug, still perturbed with him over his obnoxious behavior. He had called for her dozens of times since the beginning of the semester, leaving word with Kate for Ashley to call him back, but Ashley stubbornly refused.

At first, Kate found it rather amusing that Ashley was so furious with Doug, but as the months went on, she became irritated with their ongoing feud.

"Gracing us with your presence tonight, Princess?" Kate asked, her pencil clenched tightly in her front teeth, appearing quite intellectual in her horn-rimmed reading glasses as she looked up from her desk, flashing an annoyed stare at Ashley as she strolled in out of the blue one evening.

"I thought it might be a nice surprise for you," Ashley said, hanging her jacket in her closet. "Rick has a deadline to meet by the end of the week and I can be very distracting." She wiggled her eyebrows up and down suggestively, giggling and catching Kate off guard with her naughty insinuation.

"Well, good. While you have a little time on your hands, you might pick up that telephone over there and call Doug," Kate unclamped her pencil from her teeth, dropping it to the desktop as she swiveled in her chair to face Ashley. "He's been bugging me to death."

"Well, he can just get over it. I'm not calling him," Ashley said impatiently, glaring at Kate as she plopped down at her desk and slammed open her book to study. "I'm still pissed at him and I'm not calling him."

"I can't believe you're going to throw away fifteen years of friendship just because Doug drank too much and showed his butt a little New Year's Eve."

"Showed his butt a little? Please, Kate, he practically challenged Rick to a duel at sunrise."

"Oh, Ashley, boys will be boys," Kate's entertained laughter rang in her ears. "You should be flattered that Doug cares that much about you."

Ashley sniffed indignantly. "I'm not flattered," she said coolly. "And what about Doug telling me that Rick is an ass? How nice was that?"

"He's entitled to his opinion, Ashley."

"He can have his opinion." Ashley rose abruptly from her chair and flounced into the bathroom, eluding Kate's persistence by electing to take a shower. "But he doesn't have to share it with me," she added, bellowing loudly over the running water.

Now, with a pounding heart, Ashley carried the letter up the stairs of Slater Hall, turning it over and over in her hands, dying with anticipation, barely able to resist the temptation to rip open the envelope in the stairwell. Hurrying down the corridor and bursting into her room, she belly-flopped excitedly onto the end of her bunk, staring at the outside of the creamy white envelope one last time before ripping it open and deciding her destiny.

"Dear Ms. Stewart, It is my immense pleasure to inform you that you have been accepted to the University of Oklahoma College of Pharmacy...."

Ashley scanned the page quickly, inhaling sharply, scrambling to sitting position and dropping the creamy white letter into her lap. She had been accepted!

Kate breezed into the room, casually clad in jeans and a bright pink sweatshirt, her blond locks pulled high atop her head, whistling a happy tune as she closed the door lightly behind her. She glanced at Ashley sitting on the bed with the letter clutched to her chest.

"Hey, are you okay?" Kate asked, tossing her books on the floor and kneeling beside Ashley, her brow creased with worry.

Ashley didn't answer, only held out the wrinkled paper with a shaking hand. Kate grabbed the letter and checked over it quickly, snapping her wide eyes up to Ashley's stunned face. "You've been accepted!" Kate said, returning the crumpled paper to Ashley. "I guess congratulations are in order, if this is what you still want."

"What do you mean, if this is what I still want? Of course, I still want it. Why wouldn't I?"

"I don't know, Ashley. You just have that look on your face. You know, the one you get right before you throw up," Kate said, sitting down next to Ashley on the end of the bunk. "I don't care what bargain you made with Rick, it's not set in stone. Nothing is. Marriage is serious business and if you're not one hundred percent, tee-totally sure about it, you better not do it."

"What's with this fence jumping all of a sudden, Kate? You were pretty gung ho about this when we talked in January."

"That's because in January, I didn't really believe this would happen. Do you love Rick, Ashley?"

"What kind of stupid question is that?"

"It's an easy enough question, Ashley. Do you love him?"

Ashley wanted to give Kate the impression that she was sure of her love for Rick, but failed miserably, unable to even look her in the eye.

"That's what I thought," Kate nodded with satisfaction, shaking her head and sighing heavily. "Ashley, you really need to be in love with the man you marry."

Hearing the scolding cluck of Kate's tongue, Ashley spoke out, stopping Kate before she could launch into her standard speech about love and heartbreak.

"Leave me alone, Kate. I'm going!"

Ashley pushed away the voice of reason and jumped from the bed, crossing the room to the window and pressing her face against the glass, looking out across the parking lot toward the bayou, focusing thoughtfully on the shadowy outline of moss-draped cypress trees on the dusky horizon.

"I've already had my one true love, Kate." His dreamy milk-chocolate eyes, silky brown hair, his irresistible grin. Jimmy Moreau's image flooded Ashley's consciousness, breaking her heart in two. "And you know what they say: if you have true love once in your lifetime, you're lucky," Ashley looked back over her shoulder to Kate, offering her a sad smile. "To have it twice is almost impossible."

"Have you told Rick about the letter yet?"

Ashley shook her head fiercely. "Not yet."

"Then don't," Kate advised her, hugging her slender legs into her chest as she watched her best friend struggle with indecisiveness. "Go home for the weekend, Ashley. Think it over for a couple of days before you tell him anything."

Ashley turned away from her, gazing out the window reflectively. Kate was right, as always. She did need to go home for the weekend, if only to break the news to Maggie and Remy. Otherwise, it didn't really matter. Ashley knew exactly what she was going to do, regardless of whether she went to Pineville over the weekend or not. She was going to Oklahoma City, and she was going to marry Rick LeNoir before she went.

Before she left the next afternoon, Ashley hastily threw a few things into a bag, leaving Rick a short message on his answering machine and giving Kate a quick hug goodbye.

"Think long and hard about it before you do anything, Ashley." Kate called after her as she flew out the door. "Forever is a long time to be with someone, you know."

"Or without someone," Ashley thought ironically, heaving a sigh and closing the door behind her.

Ashley wheeled her car into her parents' circle drive, viewing the house through jubilant eyes. Having not been home since Christmas break, her homesickness had finally caught up with her. She bolted eagerly from the car, dashing up the front steps and bursting into the house, surprising Maggie and Remy with her unplanned arrival.

After having a light dinner and agreeing to go to work with Remy the next morning, Ashley tromped up to her room to unpack and to phone Susanna.

"Hey, you're home!" Susanna said. "Is *he* with you?"

"No, he is in Monroe, " Ashley replied, laughing at Susanna's intense dislike of Rick. "Susanna, why don't you like Rick?"

"Oh, come on, Ashley!" Susanna moaned loudly. "You know very well why I don't like Mr. Personality, but, just in case you forgot, let's review by going over a few things on my list. Number one, he's a smug, self-centered, conceited ass, who left you *all alone* in his apartment *all day*, while he went out to schmooze with his old girlfriend. Number two, he treated your friends like scum on New Year's Eve. Number three, and most importantly, he's just a total jerk. And besides the fact that he's a total jerk, I get a really weird feeling about him."

"What kind of feeling?" Ashley rolled her eyes and stopped unpacking, sitting on the edge of the bed, intrigued to hear what Susanna had to say.

"I can't really put my finger on it, I just don't like the way he is about you," Susanna said. "It's really bizarre, you know, the way he watches every move you make, and the way he doesn't like you going anywhere without him. It gives me the creeps."

"You're paranoid," Ashley said, stretching her legs out on the bed, snickering at Susanna's uneasiness. "You've only seen him a couple of times, Susanna. You wouldn't know anything about the way he is with me."

"You can laugh now, Ashley, but just mark my words. The man's one step away from a serial killer."

"So now you're a psychology expert."

"Let's just say that I'm a good judge of people," Susanna corrected her importantly. "It comes from working at the bank. I see a lot of psychos every day, and believe me, Rick LeNoir ranks right up there with the best of them." Susanna chuckled, amused with herself.

Ashley hurriedly changed the subject, growing tired of Susanna's Rick-bashing. "I'm working with Remy at the drugstore in the morning. Why don't you meet me there around lunch? I'll sneak out early and we'll go drink margaritas."

"Sounds good to me. I'll tell you all about the guy from the bank that I've been dating."

"The suspense may kill me," Ashley assured her before hanging up the phone. She finished unloading her duffel bag just as Maggie stuck her head in the bedroom door.

"Who was that?" she asked with a grin.

"Susanna. I called to tell her that I was here and made a lunch date with her for tomorrow."

"That sounds like fun." Maggie strolled casually into the room and sat down in the antique rocker next to Ashley's window, looking toward Ashley inquisitively. "Any particular reason you're here this weekend? And don't give me that homesick story. I don't buy it. You haven't been homesick a day since you met Rick."

"Well, I've got a couple of things to discuss with you and Remy, but I'd rather not go into them tonight. I'm pretty beat."

"Is it good news or bad?"

"Quit fishing! I'm not telling you anything tonight," Ashley scolded teasingly, pulling Maggie out of the chair. "Let's go downstairs and pester Remy for a while."

As they descended the stairs toward the den, the phone jingled noisily and out of habit, Ashley dashed for it, sliding around the corner, grabbing the extension in the kitchen.

"Hello?"

"Ashley, my pet," Rick's smooth voice filled her ear. "I do wish you would quit leaving town without telling me. It's really getting to be an annoying habit of yours."

His tone was light, but Ashley could sense the underlying irritation in his clipped speech. "I did tell you, silly," she replied playfully. "I left you a message."

"That's not what I meant, Ashley, and you know it. You know I don't like you traveling alone."

"Oh, you're such a worry wart. I got here just fine, like always."

"I could have come with you. I would've liked to see your mother again."

"Rick, this was a trip I wanted to make alone. I've been a little homesick and wanted to spend some quality time alone with the folks, that's all."

"What about your old high school flames?" Rick's subtle jealously amused her.

"My old high school flames are no longer here. I've told you that. The only person I'm going to see, other than my parents, is Susanna."

"Oh, joy." Rick's dislike of Susanna rang in his sarcastic tone. "That should be a ball."

"It will be for me," she giggled lightheartedly. "Now, aren't you glad that you didn't come along?"

"I suppose," Rick agreed with a reserved chuckle of his own. "When are you coming back?"

"Sunday afternoon. Do you want me to come over when I get back to town?"

"Do you have to ask?" Rick said, cheering up at the thought of their being alone. "I'll simply have to fill my empty hours with thoughts of your return."

"How very Shakespearean. I'll see you Sunday, okay?"

"I love you, Ashley," Rick said, his voice serious as he reminded her once more. "Remember that."

Ashley hung up the phone with an absent-minded smile before bounding into the living room to cuddle with her father on the couch.

"Rise and shine, Valentine!" Remy's jolly voice woke her early the next morning, and Ashley opened one sleepy eye as he called out to her from the doorway of her room.

She threw her pillow over her head and growled back at him, "Coffee! Bring me lots and lots of coffee!"

She rolled out of bed, unable to believe that she had given up a morning of sleep to work with Remy for free. However, getting to spend time at the store with Remy was worth losing a little sleep over. After a quick shower, Ashley threw on khakis and a denim shirt, pulling her damp hair up into a twist and shoving her feet into her well-worn loafers before joining Remy in his waiting pick-up.

Arriving at the store, Ashley was greeted heartily by the employees in the grill who were busily baking biscuits and brewing coffee for the Saturday morning breakfast crowd.

"Hallo, ma petit crawfish!" Mister Eddie bellowed to her from behind the counter, gripping an iron skillet in one hand and wearing a toothy grin on his face. "Don't you dare leave wid out comin' over to see me, ya hear?"

Ashley received a fond hug and kiss from Frannie, then joined Remy behind the prescription case, taking her place in front of the computer terminal, fielding questions and filling orders as the pharmacy became alive with ringing telephones and chattering customers. She was so busy and having so much fun that it was noon before she knew it.

"Hey, working girl! You ready for lunch?"

Ashley looked up to see Susanna standing in front of her, with her hands on her hips and a huge smile on her face. Dressed in a spring outfit of plaid shorts and Keds, with her unruly red curls shoved jauntily under the brim of a white baseball cap, Susanna looked closer to thirteen instead of nearly twenty-one.

"Hey yourself!" Ashley said, coming out from behind the prescription counter and surveying her quickly. "You look great, Susie Q. Banking must agree with you."

"Must be the company I've been keeping," Susanna winked, slyly alluding to the mystery man in her life.

"Let's go to lunch." Ashley turned to Remy, who had paused in his work, watching them with a broad smile on his handsome face. "Do you care if I go now, Remy?"

"I guess not, since I've already milked all the free labor out of you that I'm going to get today," Remy replied, winking and exhibiting a playful grin to his daughter. "Y'all have a good time."

Ashley followed Susanna out the heavy glass front doors of her daddy's drugstore and jumped into Susanna's little Chevy parked on the corner. "Mexican?" Susanna asked as she pulled away from the curb.

"Sure," Ashley said, curling her legs under her on the front seat before squinting curiously at Susanna. "So tell me about this guy."

"Well," Susanna's face glowed. "His name's Mark Lawrence. He works part time at the bank and part time in construction contracting. We've been going out since the first of the year."

"So you really like him?"

"Yes, I really do. He's a great guy."

"And he actually puts up with you?"

Susanna shot her a wry look. "Cute, Ashley," she said dryly, yet her cynical words couldn't wipe the enraptured look off her face. Ashley watched the rosy light washing over Susanna with amazement, realizing that Susanna was in love, really, truly head-over-heels in love. It was about time.

"Have you talked to Doug?" Susanna asked, offering her a naughty grin, knowing that she was pushing one of Ashley's buttons.

"No, I haven't talked to Doug," Ashley mocked her in a testy voice. "Not that he hasn't tried to get in touch with me. He has. I simply chose not to return his calls."

Susanna pulled up to Julia's, their Mexican restaurant of choice, and Ashley was glad to offer Susanna a distraction from her line of questioning.

"Here we are. Margarita Time!" Ashley called out, bolting from the car to make a mad dash for the door.

They took a table in the center of the room and Susanna snapped open her menu, looking mischievously over the top of it at Ashley. "So, what's up with Rick?" she asked, her eyes twinkling slyly.

"You aren't going to start bitching about Rick right off the bat, are you?"

"Not immediately, I've got to give myself a little time to warm up," Susanna said, chuckling as she flagged down their waitress.

"Rick's been offered a promotion in Oklahoma City," Ashley informed her casually after they placed their lunch order. She reached into the wicker basket in the middle of the table to retrieve a tortilla chip, dunking it into salsa and munching hungrily, suppressing a laugh as she watched Susanna's reaction.

Susanna set her glass on the table with a loud bang, her eyes wide with speculation. "Is he going to take it?"

Ashley nodded affirmatively. "I think so."

Susanna responded with a toothy grin. "Then this lunch date is really a celebration! Rick's leaving Louisiana is the best news I've had in a long time!"

Ashley chose to ignore Susanna's remark, idly fingering the edge of the tablecloth as she went on. "Yes, Rick is going to Oklahoma, and I'm thinking of going with him."

Susanna's celebratory facial expression froze and her mouth gaped open in shock. "What! You can't be serious."

"Sure, I'm serious." Ashley glanced down at her menu nonchalantly, enjoying, for once, being able to astound Susanna Robicheaux. "I think I'd like Oklahoma City."

"What about school?"

"Susanna, they have colleges in Oklahoma. It's not a wild open prairie, for God's sake. In fact, I've already been accepted to the pharmacy school at the University of Oklahoma."

"No kidding?" Susanna floundered for the appropriate words to express her distaste for Ashley's decision. "What do your folks say about this little move to Indian Territory to shack up with Rick, Chief Full of Bull?"

Within seconds, Susanna was right back on track. That hadn't taken long, Ashley thought with a grin. It was pretty tough to derail Susanna for very long. Her brief lack of cynicism had only been a temporary lapse due to overwhelming shock. "I haven't told them yet," Ashley answered. "I plan on telling them tonight."

"You know, your parents are pretty laid back, but they'll never go for you and Rick living together."

"Well I think they won't mind too much since I'm going to marry him before I go." Ashley swirled her frosty margarita with her straw and glanced up cunningly at Susanna, noting with pleasure that she had once again succeeded in sending Susanna into a complete tailspin. Susanna's eyes grew wider yet, processing what Ashley had just told her.

"I think I'm going to throw up!" Susanna's outburst drew stares from the other patrons, forcing her, against her will, to meekly tone down her response. "Ashley, you big dumb ass, you can't marry that creep."

Ashley raised her eyebrows, shooting Susanna an insulted glare, daring her to continue, which, of course, she did.

"You can't marry Rick because he's just not your type," Susanna bit her tongue, forcing herself not to be nasty. "You're easy-going and fun-loving, a real people person. Rick is overbearing, jealous and smothering, and I don't think he's capable of loving anyone but himself. I just don't see how it would work."

"You know what they say, Susanna, opposites attract. I think Rick and I'll be very happy together."

"You're nuts! I thought you were supposed to get *smarter* when you went to college. I think you're losing brain cells." Susanna dove into the chip basket, stuffing a handful into her mouth.

"Susanna," Ashley tried in vain to get a word in, but Susanna cut her off.

"What does Kate say about all this?" she demanded, talking with her mouth full, sputtering and angrily spitting chips. "Kate's opinion I trust, not yours."

"Kate'll back me up, just as long as she's sure this is what I really want. She likes Rick."

"Sure she does," Susanna snarled, leaning back in her chair, twiddling her thumbs as she considered the situation. "Does Doug know yet?"

Ashley shook her head. "Haven't talked to him, remember?"

"He's gonna shit," Susanna chuckled loudly, throwing her head back with glee. "I would *love* to be around for that conversation."

Remy and Maggie's reaction to her news wasn't much better. Returning from her lunch with Susanna, Ashley joined them on the screened-in back porch where they reclined, surrounded by greenery, Remy on the cedar divan and Maggie curled up at his feet, looking over the movie ads in the Saturday newspaper. Ashley sprawled on her back on the smooth, wooden floor, staring at the blades of the ceiling fan whirling above her head, gathering her courage before blurting out the news of Rick's promotion and subsequent move to Oklahoma City, along with her plans to go with him.

"You're doing what? Are you crazy!" Maggie shrieked hysterically, dropping the newspaper to the ground and sitting straight up, gawking as if Ashley had taken leave of her senses. "Have you *absolutely* lost your mind? Ashley, have you even given this idea one moment of serious thought?"

"Of course I've given it serious thought. How dumb do you think I am?"

"Pretty stupid, right at the moment," Maggie said, to which Ashley responded with an annoyed glance.

"That was a rhetorical question, Maggie. You didn't have to answer."

"What about school?" Remy asked, coming out of a speechless daze and eyeballing her skeptically. "Are you just going to drop out and wait tables, or what?"

"They really give me no credit at all," Ashley thought, fighting off the urge to lash out impatiently before trudging on with her well-rehearsed song and dance.

"That's a really valid question, and I'm glad you asked," she attempted to charm Remy, showing him her most winning smile. "I've really given this a lot of consideration, Remy. In fact, I flew to Oklahoma City in February to interview with the University of Oklahoma College of Pharmacy and I've been accepted. I got the letter yesterday."

"How is it that you ventured all the way to Oklahoma without our knowing about it?" Maggie asked suspiciously. "It costs a pretty penny to fly there."

"Rick bought my ticket," Ashley revealed with a soft smile. "He really wants me to go with him," she turned to her father to appeal to his professional side. "It would be great opportunity for me. The pharmacy school is on the grounds of a huge medical center near downtown Oklahoma City. Just think of the cutting edge clinical experience I could get there."

Maggie and Remy exchanged a perplexed glance, clenching their jaws and wisely biting their tongues as they contemplated their latest dilemma. Faced with their stony silence, Ashley fidgeted anxiously, looking from Maggie to Remy, waiting for one of them to say something.

"I'm not really happy about you moving away with Rick," Remy said finally, carefully choosing the words to express his displeasure. "Are you planning on getting your own place or are you planning to live with him?"

"Well, actually," Ashley hesitated, averting her eyes; knowing this would be the clincher. "I'm thinking of getting married before I leave."

"You'll do no such thing!" Maggie exploded, her bright-green eyes wild, calming slightly at the touch of Remy's hand on her arm. "You hardly know Rick well enough to marry him."

Ashley was saved by the bell. The pealing ring of the telephone offered a welcome interruption, cutting through the strained stillness of the Stewarts' back porch like a sharp saber. Ashley and Remy leapt from their respective places, racing across the floor and battling for the phone, each eager for an excuse to get out of the awkward discussion.

Remy won, beating Ashley by mere fractions of a second, smirking at her as he grabbed for the receiver. "Hello?" he answered, pausing as he listened to the caller.

"Hello, there! How are you doing? Are you in town this weekend?" Remy's mouth widened into a broad smile. "Great, that's just great. Let me get her for you." He gestured to Ashley, passing her the phone. "It's Doug."

Ashley beamed happily, until suddenly remembering that she was still peeved with Doug over New Year's Eve. She frowned at Remy, accepting the receiver reluctantly.

"Doug?" she said coolly.

"Still mad at me, I take it?" Amusement radiated from Doug's rich voice. "Well, I've cornered you now. You'll have to talk to me, if only for a minute."

"I haven't forgotten your behavior from New Year's Eve, if that's what you're asking," Ashley notified him in a huffy tone.

"Are you willing to call a truce long enough to go out to dinner or a movie?"

"Maybe I will and maybe I won't," she countered, unwilling to let him off the hook that easily. "How long are you in town?"

"I'm going back to Baton Rouge tomorrow afternoon. I just came home this weekend to visit Ma before we get started spring training and finals. How about you? When are you going back to Monroe?"

"Tomorrow afternoon. I have to study for an organic chemistry test."

"Spoken like a true scholar," Doug said with a teasing chuckle. "A far cry from Environmental Science."

He finally succeeded in breaking Ashley's icy barrier against him and she began to laugh. "How did you know I was home?" she asked, taking a seat on the edge of Remy's divan, feeling her parents' eyes drilling curious holes in her back.

"I have an annoying habit of driving by your house whenever I'm in town and I spotted your car. When are you going to replace that hunk of junk?"

"My little Corolla still holds her own," Ashley said, stoically defending her vehicle. "I'll replace her only when she dies a non-repairable death."

"So, give me an answer, Ash. You want to go out, or what?"

Ashley quickly weighed her options: On one hand, she could forgive and forget, go out with the gorgeous quarterback, and be the envy of thousands of adoring female fans. Or, on the other hand, she could stay home with Maggie to finish what she had started, and spend the evening listening to Maggie rant and rave over her rash decision to marry Rick LeNoir. Hmm, tough choice.

Once again, the handsome quarterback won out. "Sure, Doug, I'd love to," Ashley yielded happily, smiling into the phone.

"Pick you up at eight and don't be late?"

"That'd be great," Ashley giggled and hung up, turning to face her folks, catching their intent gaze.

"I'm going out to dinner with Doug," she said, acknowledging what they'd already heard while eavesdropping, rolling her eyes as Maggie grinned ear to ear.

"A date with Doug? How wonderful!" Maggie said brightly, tongue-in-cheek, knowing all too well how Ashley would respond to her giddy declaration.

"Doug and I are just friends, Mother!" Ashley reminded her, shaking her head as she rose from the divan and headed toward the stairs.

Remy stopped her before she left the room, putting a warm hand on her shoulder and looking into her face with a gentle pair of eyes. "I can live with you going to school in Oklahoma, Ashley, if that's what you really want to do," he conceded tenderly. Ever striving to be the peacemaker, Remy was clearly seeking a compromise. "But as for the rest of it, let's just leave that open for debate for the time being, shall we?"

"Thanks, Remy," Ashley smiled at him, tiptoeing up to give him a soft kiss on the cheek.

"Your father may be a pushover, but *I* am not," Maggie interrupted their tender moment, scowling her disapproval in Ashley's direction. "And as far as I'm concerned, this discussion is far from over. I want to talk more about you, Rick, and this Oklahoma thing before you go back to school tomorrow."

"Yeah, yeah, yeah," Ashley muttered and stalked out of the room, stomping up the steps to her room. She changed into jeans and a light green short-sleeved cotton sweater, electing to wear her hair down. She dabbed on a little perfume and brushed her teeth, reapplying her lipstick, and finally was ready to see Doug.

She peeked out her bedroom window when she heard him drive up, watching as Doug strode casually to the house, his blond hair catching the last rays of the late evening sunlight. A wheat-colored denim shirt covered his lean torso, and his long muscular legs were snuggly encased in dark blue jeans.

My, my, he's as handsome as ever, Ashley noted with an admiring twinkle in her eye. That was the great thing about Doug. His heart-stopping charisma didn't fade with time. Douglas Shawn Fairchild only got better with age. Ashley smiled, grabbed her purse and rushed downstairs.

Doug stood in the foyer, talking with her parents, looking up as he saw her on the steps. "Why, Ashley, it's so unlike you not to race your father for the door," he teased her, making Remy laugh and Maggie smile with delight.

"I'm getting too old to run down these steps," Ashley retorted with a smirk. "Besides, who says that you're worth running for anyway?"

Doug met her at the bottom of the stairs, taking her by the shoulders and planted a light kiss on her upturned lips. "You're looking good, Ash," he said.

"You don't look too bad yourself," Ashley said, punching his arm playfully. "For a dumb jock, that is."

"You two get out of here and go eat!" Maggie urged them, pushing them toward the door, receiving a look from Ashley that warned no matchmaking between her and Doug would be tolerated.

"Stay out as late as you want!" Remy said, grinning slyly as he opened the door for them. "Let Doug talk you out of going to Oklahoma, okay, Princess?" he teased quietly as Ashley sailed past him.

"You two are pathetic," Ashley said, whispering loudly over her shoulder to them, ignoring their insolent grins.

"Love you too, honey!" Remy said, continuing to terrorize her as he closed the front door.

"Apparently being quarterback is a little more profitable than being a pharmacy student," Ashley kidded Doug, admiring the new hunter green, four-wheel drive utility vehicle he was driving. "Nice car, Dougie," she acknowledged as he opened the passenger door for her, stroking the tan leather appreciatively as she settled into the seat.

"Thanks," Doug grinned widely at her, closing her door and walking around to the driver's side.

"Kind of conservative for you though, isn't it?" Ashley asked, thinking back to Doug's cherry-red Camaro, lost the same day that they lost Jimmy.

"It may not be fast, but it's so much better to take hunting and fishing," Doug educated her with an entertained twinkle in his eyes.

"At least there's logic behind your decision," Ashley laughed. "How's school?"

"School is good, considering I still have five years to go before I finish law school," Doug said, contemplating his statement before adding, "If I get in, that is."

"You'll get in, I have no doubt about that," Ashley reassured him with a fond smile. "How's the love life?"

"It's adequate," Doug said, amused by the question he had known she would ask.

"Translate 'adequate' for me, Doug." Ashley leaned back in her seat, eyeing him speculatively as she forced him to be more specific.

"Adequate means that I'm dating, although not a tremendous amount. And no, there's no one serious," he said, meeting her inquisitive stare with a grin. "Where do you want to eat?" he asked, changing the subject before she could start nagging him about women.

"Anything but Mexican. Susanna and I had Mexican for lunch."

"Catfish?" Doug suggested, and Ashley agreed with a nod of her head.

"And how is Susanna?" he asked, driving down Old Marksville Highway in the direction of Cajun Catfish, while Ashley gave him the details about her lunch with Susanna.

"So Susanna has a new man in her life!" Doug flashed a playful smile. "Good! Maybe a little hormonal release will mellow her out some."

"Doug!" Ashley burst into giggles, chiding him with a shake of her head. "That's not very nice."

"Don't take on that superior attitude with me, sister. You know exactly what I'm talking about. Susanna's attitude is the result of pent-up sexual tension."

"I don't think so, sweetie. Susanna's had the same attitude since we were seven. I hardly think she had any sexual tension then."

Doug cut his eyes to Ashley and, with a grin, pulled into the dirt drive leading to Cajun Catfish. The popular eatery, surrounded by a grove of tall trees and a gravel parking lot, was famous for its mouth-watering catfish, tasty hush puppies, and hot roasted peanuts, served still in the shell. The planked front of the restaurant sported a long veranda, packed tightly on most nights by eagerly waiting patrons.

Bypassing the crowd gathered around the entrance, Doug pulled open the front door, standing aside to let Ashley enter ahead of him. The room was busting at the seams, alive with the sounds of conversation and clinking dishes. Doug quickly surveyed the red and white checked tabletops for an empty seat.

"Hey, Darlene," he called out, waving to the well-endowed young hostess standing across the room. "You got a table for some old friends?"

Hearing her name, Darlene looked up, spotting Doug and beaming fondly at him. "Sure, Doug, I got a table right over here with y'all's name all over it."

She grabbed two menus and took Doug firmly by the arm, turning to Ashley with a grin. "Hey there, Ashley. How's life treatin' you up in Monroe, honey?"

Darlene led them to a wooden table in the corner, the familiar sound of crunching peanut shells under their feet echoing as they crossed the room. Once seated, Ashley ordered a beer, while the good athlete-in-training ordered water with lemon.

"Well, now that you've had your chance to interrogate me, let's talk about you, Ash. What's been going on in your life?" Doug asked, settling back comfortably in his spindle-back chair. "You've obviously been extremely busy since you haven't bothered to return any of my calls."

"Well, I've just been going to class, bumming around with Kate, you know, just stuff," Ashley answered, ignoring his cutting remark. "I did go to Oklahoma City in February," she added, watching the change in his facial expression with mischievous green eyes.

"Really?" Doug was intrigued. "What's in Oklahoma City?"

"You know, Doug," Ashley apprehensively twirled a lock of her mousy hair around her index finger as she began her explanation, "the University of Oklahoma has a great pharmacy school."

She got his attention. Doug leaned forward, lifting an interested brow, waiting for her to go on. "And?"

"*And* I went to Oklahoma City for an interview at the pharmacy school. I found out yesterday that I've been accepted."

"I see," Doug acknowledged softly, his disappointed face revealing his true feelings. "And what prompted this action?"

"Doug, my God, don't act like this is the end of the world. It really is a terrific opportunity for me."

"Northeast has a good pharmacy school," he reminded her indignantly, a faint scowl overtaking his handsome features.

"Yes, Northeast has a terrific pharmacy school, but I'm ready for a change. No, rephrase that, I *need* a change, Doug."

"Then come to Baton Rouge. It's a big city."

"Doug, I can't go to pharmacy school at LSU, you know that. They don't even have a program there for pharmacy. We've been through all this before."

Darlene brought their drinks and Ashley took a huge gulp of her beer, looking up from her mug to meet Doug's probing stare.

"What inspired you to apply in Oklahoma?" he asked again, sensing there was still more to the story than Ashley was admitting.

Now came the moment of truth. Ashley took a deep breath before spilling the beans, looking down uneasily at her hands. "Rick's being promoted and transferred to Oklahoma City, and I've decided to go with him."

"Just like that?" Doug's voice dripped with sarcasm. "You're going to pack up and leave with this guy just because he's getting a transfer? That's crazy, Ashley."

"No, Doug, it's not just like that." She reached across the table, taking his hand. "Rick wants me to marry him."

Doug flinched, drawing in his breath sharply, his eyes growing round and skeptical at her revelation. "Surely you're not going to marry him?"

"I'm seriously considering it," Ashley choked down more ice-cold beer, refusing to make eye contact. "Damn," she thought. Discussing this with him was worse than with Susanna and her parents combined.

"He's not right for you," Doug said, staring steadily into her nervous face.

"How do you know, Doug? You've only met him once."

"I've seen enough of him to know that he's not the one for you," Doug jerked his head in the direction of the kitchen. "Maybe I'll have that beer after all."

He flagged down Darlene and ordered a draft. She quickly returned with his order, and he drank it down smoothly before promptly requesting another.

"Are you going to be this way all night?" Ashley said after several minutes of his tense silence.

Doug responded with a surly frown. "Ashley, I just hate to see you do something so stupid. All right, I agree that Oklahoma City could be a lot of fun for you. Fine, go to OU. Finish school there. Just don't marry Rick."

He took her small hands into his much larger ones. "You don't love him, Ashley. I've seen you in love before, remember? You're not in love now, not with Rick. There's no light in your eyes when you talk about him, no excitement in your voice about being with him. Think about what I'm saying. You know I'm right."

"Douglas, you've just given the perfect description of infatuation," she spoke out irritably. "What I have with Rick is different."

"It's different, but it's not love," Doug said, sputtering in frustration as he ordered yet another draft from the lovely Darlene.

"It is too love," Ashley argued, jutting her chin out stubbornly, folding her arms firmly across her heaving chest.

"Bullshit, Ashley. All you're doing is running away. There's no love involved here, not for him anyway."

"What do you know about it, Doug!"

"Children, please," a voice interrupted their juvenile squabbling and they each shot an irritated sidelong glance to the person standing next to the table. Susanna, decked out in a bright turquoise pantsuit, stood fondly clutching the arm of a husky man with a shock of golden hair and round wire-rimmed glasses.

"Would the two of you tone it down a little? I could hear you before I even opened the door."

With an entertained grin, Susanna pulled up the chair next to Doug. "Move over, Douglas and we'll join you," she said, gesturing to her date. "Mark Lawrence, I'd like you to meet two of my dearest friends, Ashley Stewart and Doug Fairchild. Ashley and Doug, meet Mark."

She pointed to the chair next to Ashley, directing Mark with a nod of her head. "Sit with my good friend Ashley."

"A pleasure to meet you both," Mark, amused by Susanna's directness, grinned over her head to Doug and Ashley as he took his appointed seat at the table.

He's a perfect match for her, Ashley noted incredulously. An obvious foil to Susanna's every folly.

"Are you the Doug Fairchild who plays for LSU?" Mark turned to Doug, his bright, fascinated eyes shining behind his spectacles.

"That's me," Doug said with a friendly nod, clearly relieved to have a distraction from Ashley's earth-shattering bombshell.

Susanna gave them a withering glare and cleared her throat in exasperation. "Excuse me, boys, not to change the subject, but I gather that Ashley has told you her news," Susanna directed to Doug, her lip curled in visible disgust.

"What makes you say that?" Ashley said, narrowing her eyes in annoyance.

"That argument I jumped in the middle of wasn't about the menu, honey."

"The subject is closed, Susanna."

Susanna wasn't about to let it drop. "What did your parents say when you told them?" she asked snidely, not bothering to disguise her mocking smile.

"They thought it was wonderful news. Maggie's ready to plan the wedding."

"Yeah, I bet," Doug scoffed, and Ashley frowned at him, motioning to Darlene to refill her empty mug.

"We just saw the most incredible movie," Mark smoothly intervened, breaking the tension at the table by animatedly describing the film he and Susanna had just seen. Ashley offered him a grateful smile for successfully diverting Susanna and Doug from teaming up against her, and Mark returned her smile with a kind smile of his own, indicating that he sympathized with her awkward plight.

Doug ordered several more beers before dinner was over, then Mark helped Susanna guide Doug out to his car, while Ashley called Ms. Bobbie, advising her that Doug had one too many beers and she would be driving him home.

"If that's the case, I had better get his bed turned down!" Ms. Bobbie chuckled loudly as she hung up the phone.

Ashley drove down Paper Mill Road toward the Fairchilds' while Doug, three sheets to the wind, sang and lamented in the passenger's seat. "Oh, Ashley, Ashley," he slurred. "You're making one hell of a mistake."

"Douglas, you're one sloppy drunk!" Ashley said, teasing him as they pulled into his driveway. She jumped from the driver's seat to open his door while Ms. Bobbie bolted from the house to help get him out of the car.

"Boy, you are way too big for us to have to drag around!" Ms. Bobbie scolded him, hoisting his limp arm over her shoulder. "I'm taking you straight to bed while your father drives Ashley home."

"I want Ashley to tuck me in," Doug asserted in his drunken state, staring at Ashley with bloodshot eyes. Ms. Bobbie and Ashley exchanged an amused glance before Ashley nodded in agreement.

"Okay, Dougie, I will," she said, humoring him by following Ms. Bobbie to his bedroom.

Doug's room, decorated in navy and white, was a whimsical compilation of boyhood memories and collegiate accomplishments, with red Pineville High School pennants sharing precious wall space with the vivid purple and gold paraphernalia of LSU. Ashley grinned nostalgically at the framed photo of the old gang atop his maple chest of drawers. Adolescent versions of Scotty, Doug, Kate, Susanna and herself smiled back at her from the bow of Scott's old Ranger bass boat.

Ashley stepped carefully over the piles of clothing Doug had haphazardly deposited on the floor and helped Ms. Bobbie get him onto his bed. Ms. Bobbie removed his snakeskin boots before leaving Ashley alone with him, flashing a comical grin over her shoulder as she closed the door.

Ashley sat on the edge of the bed, shaking her head in amusement at his long body sprawled across the navy-and-white-striped sheets. Fondly, she reached up to smooth his wavy hair, caressing his temple with her fingers. "Doug, I'm going home now. I'll see you in May, after finals, okay?" she said, leaning down to whisper softly in his ear.

"Ashley, I love you. I do, you know." He rolled his head over, eyeballing her with unfocussed eyes.

"Dougie, you're very drunk!" she giggled, kissing his forehead affectionately. "I love you too, honey."

"Aw, Ash, give me a real kiss. Kiss me like you mean it," he said, his voice slurring a command. "Kiss me like that and then tell me that you're going to marry LeNoir."

"Okay, Doug, only if you promise not to throw up on me." Ashley pursed her lips flirtatiously, presenting him with a peck on the lips. Doug reached up with suddenly strong arms and pulled her closer, kissing her back longingly.

Ashley pulled away, oddly disturbed by his display of affection. "I've got to go."

She leapt from the bed and backed away, not liking the way the kiss had made her feel. It has to be the alcohol, she reasoned, turning the doorknob to exit into the hall.

"Now tell me that you're going to marry Rick." Doug struggled to lean on his elbows, his eyes daring her to deny the emotions welling up in her heaving bosom.

Ashley met his gaze unwaveringly, squaring her jaw with determination. "I'm going to marry Rick," she insisted before hurrying from the room and down the hall without a look back.

Nick Fairchild waited outside in Doug's car to drive her home. "How do you like Doug's new truck?" he asked proudly, resting his arm on the steering wheel as he turned to Ashley.

"I love it," she replied, distractedly, her mind still focused on Doug's stirring kiss.

"What happened to make him drink so much?" Nick asked, his expression full of curiosity. "He usually doesn't touch alcohol, especially after they start spring training. Coach Rachal will kick his butt."

"I'll let Doug tell you tomorrow," Ashley said as Nick pulled up in front of her house. She got out of the car, leaning against the doorframe, and flashed a sassy grin. "That is, if he remembers anything about tonight," she added with a laugh. "Good night, Mr. Nick."

"Good night, Ashley. Have a safe trip back to Monroe."

Ashley waved fondly as he drove away and bounded up the steps into the house, a reflective smile lighting her face.

CHAPTER TWENTY-ONE

Ashley returned to Monroe the next morning, escaping hours of endless lecture by vehemently promising Maggie that she wouldn't be too hasty in her answer to Rick's marriage proposal. She cranked up the faithful Corolla and popped her *Purple Rain* tape into the cassette player, allowing Prince to divert her mind from her tumbling thoughts. She had spent most of the morning thinking about Doug and the things he had said the night before. She couldn't seriously consider anything he had said to be sincere. He had been very drunk. Factoring Doug into the equation had not been her intent, but his kiss had stirred her.

Then there were her feelings for Rick. She really was crazy about him. His outstanding good looks and intellect attracted her like a magnet and he kept her constantly challenged by stimulating her mind and her body. Ashley sincerely wanted to go to Oklahoma with him, knowing that leaving Louisiana would be the best move she could make in her quest to forget the past and move into the future.

She arrived at Rick's apartment early in the afternoon and rapped eagerly at the door. Rick swung open the door, quickly pulling her into an enthusiastic embrace.

"My, I think you missed me," Ashley smiled vivaciously at him as she stepped inside the spotless apartment. Her cheerfulness pleased him and his face lit up with a radiant smile.

"I did miss you, Ashley," he said, removing her heavy backpack from her shoulder. His breathtaking eyes shone with unusual good humor. "Did you have fun with your little friends?"

Ashley rolled her eyes amicably as she smiled up at him. "Yes, I did have fun. It's always great to visit home."

"Are you hungry? We could get some lunch."

"Sure," Ashley nodded agreeably. "I'll get my books. You grab something to read and we'll have lunch down by the bayou."

After stopping for turkey sandwiches, Ashley and Rick settled on the grass beneath an old cypress alongside Bayou DeSiard. The spring afternoon was beautiful, with the sun shining brilliantly in a cloudless sky. The campus was littered with students, all out enjoying a laid-back Sunday afternoon. Ashley waved to Hillary, spotting her canoeing down the bayou with one of her many male conquests.

Hillary spied her on the grassy bank and waved back excitedly. "Hey, Ashley! When did you get back?"

"Just a little while ago!" Ashley yelled, cupping her hands around her mouth.

Hillary's date viewed them with amusement, cautioning Hillary to sit down before she turned the boat over in the water. The canoe wobbled precariously from side to side and Hillary obeyed his command, taking her seat dutifully inside the canoe.

"See ya!" she bellowed, waving again as they slowly floated away in the other direction. As their canoe disappeared from sight, Ashley turned back to Rick.

"Have you thought about my proposal?" Rick handed her a sandwich and Ashley accepted it, nodding in response to his question.

"Of course, how could I not?" She chewed her first bite of turkey, washing it down with sweet iced tea before revealing, "I got my acceptance letter from OU on Friday."

Rick's face lit up with a huge, incredulous smile. "That's great! Why didn't you tell me?"

"I wanted to discuss it with my folks first. They do pay for my education, you know."

"Not after we're married. We'll pay our own way," Rick advised her sternly.

"Now hold on, buddy. I haven't said yes to any of it."

"Yet," Rick stared at her authoritatively. "You know you will marry me, Ashley."

"Do I have no say so at all?" Ashley raised one brow speculatively, pursing her lips in mock irritation.

"Not as far as I'm concerned."

Without warning, Rick grabbed her, pinning her on the grassy bank and began to tickle her mercilessly, his uncommon playfulness taking Ashley by surprise.

"Say yes, Ashley. Say yes! I won't stop until you say yes," he told her as he continued tickling her ribs.

Ashley was laughing so hard that she could barely breathe, and she gasped nosily, yelling out, "Okay, Rick, YES!"

Rick stopped, holding her firmly by the shoulders. "Yes what?" he asked, looking deep into her merry green eyes.

"What do you want to hear? Yes, sir?" Ashley joked cheerfully. "Yes, Rick LeNoir, I will marry you." Ashley was relieved as soon as the words left her mouth. She had made her decision. To heck with all the naysayers she had encountered over the last few days. She felt comfortable with her choice.

"Really?" Rick was as excited as a little boy, and it was refreshing for Ashley to see him act that way.

"Yes, really," she assured him, allowing him to wrap her in a warm embrace before lifting her chin to accept his passionate kiss.

"Let's go back to my place and celebrate," Rick pulled away from their lip lock, eyeing her mischievously.

"Rick, I told you I have to study! Finals start in less than two weeks," she said, protesting weakly against his overwhelming persuasiveness. Rick simply smiled tolerantly at her objection, pulling her to her feet as he whisked the blanket from the ground. Ashley shook her head lightly in defeat, strolling cheerfully with him toward the car.

Ashley floated into the dorm room early in the evening, displaying an ecstatic smile to Kate as she looked up from her political science text. "Busy weekend?" Kate asked, leaning back casually in her chair, propping her feet up on the desk. "Your mother has called twice. She gave me a little background information."

"I'm sure she did," Ashley laughed, setting down her bags and made her way to the coffeepot, retrieving a steaming mug of stout coffee before settling in her own chair to face Kate.

"So, you took Doug Fairchild out and got him drunk, did you?" Kate eyed her humorously. "You shameless hussy. What have you got to say for yourself?"

"Number one, my being with Doug Fairchild is not to leave this room," Ashley said curtly. "All I need is for Rick to get wind of it. He's in a good mood right now and I'd like to keep him that way."

"Ms. Maggie said every duck in town tried to talk you out of marrying Rick."

"Yes, they did, and to no avail, I might add. I told Rick I'd marry him this afternoon."

Kate's jaw dropped, her mouth gaping wide in astonishment. She stared at Ashley, dumbfounded, until suddenly realizing she had lost her composure, and quickly pulled herself together.

"Are you sure that's what you want to do?" she asked, and Ashley nodded with confident certainty, sipping her coffee as she stared steadily at Kate's doubtful face.

Kate sighed, shrugging her shoulders indifferently. "You know what I always say, don't you? Just follow your heart. If your heart is set on marrying Rick, then it can't be wrong."

God bless Kate, always the loyal one. Ashley was glad for one ally. She was certain that Susanna would not be as supportive as Kate had been, and she wasn't sure that she even wanted to see Doug's reaction to the news.

As Ashley had anticipated, the impending nuptials received mixed reviews. Dominique and Celeste were delighted with the news, happily embracing Ashley and welcoming her into the family as Rick looked on, wearing a pleased smile.

After their initially strong objections, Maggie and Remy accepted their daughter's decision to marry Rick LeNoir, particularly after observing how happy Rick and Ashley appeared on their trip to Pineville to break the news. Maggie threw herself into the wedding plans, declaring that the wedding of her only child would be an event that the people of Pineville would never forget.

Susanna had given Ashley an earful of grief over the engagement.

"Well, I'm certainly glad that you took so much time to weigh the decision carefully before saying yes," Susanna blurted out sarcastically when Ashley phoned her, definitely not pleased.

"How much time does it take to say yes when you know it's what you want to do?" Ashley shot back at her, equally as cynical.

"Horse hockey," Susanna choked back stronger language. "I can't believe you're going to do this."

"I am going to do this," Ashley assured her. "Do you want to be a bridesmaid or should I look elsewhere?"

"Of course I'm going to be a damn bridesmaid," Susanna said with a hostile snarl. "I am one of the few people who belongs in the wedding party. The groom certainly doesn't."

"Goodbye, Susanna!" Ashley sang out her farewell. "I'm not fighting with you about this."

"Goodbye, Ash," Susanna sighed, calling a temporary truce. "You and I will have more words about this, I assure you."

"Of that I am certain," Ashley said, laughing as she hung up the phone.

Ashley and Rick's short engagement period proceeded happily and, as her feelings for Rick grew stronger, she became more confident that Rick was truly the one to make her forget the past.

Her upcoming marriage should have led Ashley Stewart down the path to a happy ending, to a new life in a new city with a great-looking, brilliant new husband. But it just wasn't in the cards. Little did she know, the hand of fate was once again working against her, and she could do very little to stop the events that were about to unfold.

Mid-May was a hectic time, with Ashley deeply engrossed in finals and Rick in the process of packing up his apartment in order to leave the following weekend for Oklahoma City. Ashley spent as much time with him as her schedule allowed, already filled with dread and loneliness over his leaving.

As finals week came to a close, Ashley began to feel drained and run down, with absolutely no energy whatsoever. At first, she chalked it up to finals and the rushed weekend trips to Pineville, throwing together her late June wedding with the aid of Maggie, Ms. Bobbie and Claire Robicheaux. But as the fatigue grew, coupled with crippling nausea and heavy aching breasts, Ashley began to suspect that there was much more to her condition than sleep deprivation.

She lay on her bunk in the dorm room, fervently trying to psych herself up to pack her things for the move out of Slater Hall. Kate busily stuffed her clothing into her overflowing metal footlocker, whistling happily as she anticipated going home. She glanced over at the unusually silent Ashley, her brow creasing with worry.

"You feeling okay, Ashley?" she said, peering at her inquisitively. "Ye gods, you look like hell."

"Thanks, Katie." Ashley wearily pushed herself up onto her elbows, turning slightly green as the room spun around her. "As a matter of fact, I *feel* like hell," she collapsed weakly back onto the lumpy mattress. "I'm nauseous all the time, and I'm tired and my chest hurts."

Dropping the crisp white shirt she was folding, Kate stared at her, wide-eyed with dismay. "Ashley, when was your last period?"

Ashley sprang from her bed, staring in horror at Kate as she tried to remember, counting back the weeks in her mind. "The end of March," she admitted, sliding her palm down her cheek, distressed at the sudden realization of the possible diagnosis of her symptoms.

"Oh shit, Ashley, you're pregnant," Kate plopped on the edge of her bed with a heavy thud, and Ashley joined her, light-headed with anxiety, unable to stand one minute longer on her rubbery legs.

"I can't be," Ashley gasped, heart in her throat, her eyes wide with denial and fear.

"Says who?" Kate grabbed her hand, and together they rushed to the all-night pharmacy to buy a home pregnancy test.

Returning to their little room in Slater Hall, Ashley took the test, looking apprehensively at Kate when the allotted time was up. "You look. I can't," she said, her stomach curling into queasy knots of anxiety as she watched Kate gingerly pick up the test and stare at the dark ring at the bottom of the test tube.

"Bingo." Kate's quiet voice echoed through the deadly silent room, vibrating hollowly through Ashley's stunned senses.

The night Ashley left Monroe was the darkest she could remember, pitch-black dark, with pea-soup fog from an adjacent bayou rolling across the highway, echoing her state of mind. She had bid Rick a fond farewell that morning as he left for Oklahoma City, forcing a brilliant smile on to her pale, haggard face as he kissed her goodbye. She hadn't spoiled Rick's departure, but now as she sank into the welcome serenity of her dark car and traveled Highway 165 toward home, Ashley allowed her troubling thoughts to overtake her consciousness, struggling to grasp the truth of her situation.

She was going to have a baby. How on earth could this have happened? They had been so careful, but obviously not careful enough. A baby. She would have it. She couldn't live with herself if she didn't.

"Rug rats," Rick's words echoed through her mind. Oh God, how would she tell him?

As she thought of her devilishly handsome fiancé, Ashley lifted her left hand, staring numbly at the huge round diamond on her ring finger. True, Rick didn't like children, but this was his child, his own flesh and blood. Surely, this child would be different.

The following morning she endured the long trip to Ville Platte for her dress fitting, surrounded by a vanload of giggling women when she could barely muster a miserable smile. She listened distractedly to the excited chattering of Maggie, Claire and Imogene while purposely avoiding Susanna's questioning stares. By the look on Ashley's face, Susanna sensed that something was wrong, but Ashley didn't confide in her. Only Kate knew the truth and it would remain that way for now.

Rick called several times over the weekend to say how much he missed her, and was filled with great enthusiasm over Oklahoma City and the move in general. He had spent his days sightseeing and house hunting, and chattered elatedly over the dozens of wonderful homes he had viewed with a Realtor.

Ashley listened in strained silence, chewing her bottom lip while her stomach churned, dreading the moment when she would burst his bubble and tell him her news.

On the third Monday in May, she went to see her gynecologist, Dr. Lisa Watson, who confirmed what Ashley already knew.

"Congratulations!" Dr. Watson, an attractive, thirty-something brunette with gold wire-rimmed glasses, beamed cheerfully as she came in the exam room. "The rabbit died."

Ashley's stomach flip-flopped as she turned several shades of green, and Dr. Watson observed her reaction, lowering her glasses and frowning slightly with concern. "What is it, Ashley? Morning sickness or something else?"

"Probably a combination of both," Ashley said, lying back against the pillows on the exam table.

"I take it that you weren't planning for this baby." Dr. Watson took the chair across from her as Ashley shook her head miserably. "You know, Ashley, they have these novel things called birth control pills. Perhaps you've heard of them?"

"It's a little late to lecture me about this, don't you think?"

"Aren't you getting married in June? I thought I read that in the paper."

"Yes, the end of next month."

"Well, I'd say that you're only six weeks pregnant, seven at the most. So you won't be showing yet," Dr. Watson advised her with a kind, sympathetic smile. "What does the perspective father say?"

Ashley sat up, looking at her with troubled eyes. "He doesn't have a clue, yet."

"So when do you plan to tell him?"

"Soon," Ashley said, shifting uneasily on the crinkled white tissue paper underneath her. "When will the baby be due?"

Dr. Watson reached into the pocket of her starched lab coat, pulling out her gestational chart, and studied it vigilantly. "Judging by the date of your last period, somewhere between Christmas and New Year's, I would say."

Ashley nodded, deep in thought. "We'll be living in Oklahoma City after the wedding. Can you recommend a good doctor for me there?"

"No kidding? Oklahoma City." Dr. Watson's kind face lit up with a broad smile. "I went to med school at OU. In fact, I have several classmates still practicing in Oklahoma City." She scribbled several names onto her pad of paper and, tearing off the sheet, handed it to Ashley. "Any of these guys would be great. You'll love it there, Ashley. I almost stayed there myself, but the Deep South kept calling me home."

Dr. Watson stood, patting Ashley's hand and preparing to exit the exam room. "I'll write you a prescription for prenatal vitamins, unless you would rather me just call it to your dad."

"No!" Ashley said, protesting loudly, and Dr. Watson stopped in the doorway, looking back over her shoulder, startled by Ashley's hostile reaction to her suggestion.

"I haven't told them yet either," Ashley said, offering a sheepish explanation.

After leaving the doctor's office with a list of recommended doctors and a prescription for prenatal vitamins, Ashley visited the florist to finalize the order for the wedding, grateful for a momentary distraction from thinking about the pregnancy.

"Everything looks perfect," Ashley praised the florist after inspecting the order, shaking her hand as she rose from her chair to leave. She started toward the door, then on impulse she turned back.

"May I have a bouquet of those mixed flowers?" she indicated the delicately hued bundles of spring flowers in the glass case. Ashley made her purchase and left the shop, setting out for a destination that she had sworn two years earlier never to visit again.

She drove along the back roads of town, turning onto an avenue lined with towering shade trees and entering the wrought iron gates of the cemetery. She located the grave with surprising ease, but hesitated inside her car, staring with despairing eyes at the slate-gray marble tombstone. Finally, she opened her door, forcing her leaden body to move, padding softly across the thick carpet of grass to kneel beside his grave, gently placing the spring bouquet beside his headstone.

Daniel James Moreau. Seeing his name chiseled in the stone brought it all back to her, and Ashley fell to the ground, her body wracked with uncontrollable convulsions of grief, and she lay weeping inconsolably, calling out his name.

"God, Jimmy, I miss you so much," she wailed broken-heartedly, wishing that he could hear her. "I never should've left you to go on that trip to Florida. If I hadn't, you would still be alive, and we would be happily living in Baton Rouge together. We had such great plans for our life. Why did you have to die?"

She lay against the cold headstone, her body trembling from violent sobs as she shed the pent-up tears of many long months without him. Finally, drained from crying, she wiped her eyes and lay motionless on the lush green grass, surrounded by peaceful stillness, staring up at the bountiful branches of green leaves above her head and sniffling sorrowfully.

"Oh Jimmy, I've made such a mess of things. Here I am, two short years down the line, pregnant, and about to marry a man I'm not even sure I really love." She closed her eyes, heaving a great sigh, picturing Jimmy's face in her mind. "You were the only man I ever wanted to marry. I want you back, Jimmy. I just want you back."

If she could only turn back the hands of time, everything would be perfect again. But, even in her unrealistic frame of mind, Ashley knew that she was asking for the impossible, yearning for something she could never have.

Ashley slowly rose to leave, gazing forlornly at the marker one last time, touching her lips to her palm before placing it tenderly against the smooth marble stone.

"Goodbye, Jimmy," her eyes misted over as she said her farewell, feeling the long-buried ache stabbing cruelly at her heart. "I'm not sure if I'll ever come here again. It just hurts too much. Even if you never see me again, just remember that I'll always love you, with all my heart."

Turning away, she walked deliberately to her car and got in, resting her throbbing head on the steering wheel until she felt calm enough to drive. Starting the engine, she drove away without looking back.

When Ashley arrived home, Maggie met her at the front door.

"Where on earth have you been!" she said, her voice shrill with emotion. "I've been so worried. I called the drugstore, I called Susanna at the bank. I called everyone I knew to call, and no one has seen or heard from you all day."

Ashley looked up in surprise as the grandfather clock in the foyer chimed five o'clock. The entire day had passed without her even being aware.

"I'm sorry, Maggie. I didn't know that you would be looking for me," she apologized guiltily "Time just got away from me. I went by the florist earlier to finalize the order and then I took flowers out to Jimmy's grave."

"Oh, honey, what in the world would make you go there? I can't imagine why you would want to make yourself so miserable."

"It was very therapeutic, actually," Ashley said quietly, lowering her eyes to avoid Maggie's fretful gaze. "Do you want help with dinner?" Maggie responded with a shake of her head. "Then I think I'll go lie down until Remy comes home, if you don't mind."

"Are you feeling okay, Ashley?" Maggie said worriedly and Ashley felt like a heel, consumed by guilt over not telling Maggie the whole truth behind her melancholy state.

"Yes, Mags, I'm okay. Just really drained from crying." She kissed Maggie's cheek and trudged slowly up to her room.

Ashley lay on her bed staring blankly at the wall before being summoned by the high-pitched ringing of the telephone.

"I see, judging by the engagement announcement my kind and wonderful mother saved for me, that our little dinner chat did nothing to change your plans." Doug's cynical voice rang clear over the line.

"Hi there, are you back in town?" Ashley said, choosing to ignore his invitation to spar. She was much too tired to fight a good battle against Doug.

"Just for a couple weeks. I'm going back to Baton Rouge the middle of June."

"How were finals?"

"Ashley, don't try the chit-chat with me. Where'd you run off to this afternoon? Your mother was frantic."

"I didn't realize that she had called you too," Ashley snapped, exasperated with him for demanding an explanation from her. "If you must know, I went out to Jimmy's grave."

"Oh." His tone became significantly more solemn. "Jeez, Ashley, I'm sorry for prying. I don't know why I feel the need to act as your keeper."

"That's okay, Doug. All my friends act that way lately."

"Why so glum, Ash? Something's up, I can tell by the sound of your voice."

"I'd rather not go into it right now." Ashley certainly didn't want to involve Doug in all her problems. She wasn't ready to deal with his reaction to her pregnancy. His harassment over the wedding was enough without adding the baby to his objections.

"Ashley, whatever it is, I want to help. I'm coming to get you after dinner and we'll go out and talk."

"There's nothing that you can do about this, trust me."

"We'll see about that. I can help, even it's only an ear to listen or a shoulder to cry on." Doug was being so sweet that Ashley gave into him.

"All right, but you may not have any alcohol," she attempted to joke with him.

"Fair enough, but neither can you."

"Don't worry," Ashley assured him silently. "It'll be at least nine months before I get a drink, though I could use one right now."

After dinner, Doug strolled in the front door, attired in gym shorts, T-shirt and Reeboks. He kissed a delighted Maggie hello, shook hands with Remy, and looked around expectantly for Ashley. He spotted her, descending the stairs at a snail's pace, her normally radiant face pale and colorless beneath a disheveled mane of brown hair. Regarding her appearance with disapproval, Doug decided that his intuition had been right on the money. Something was up with Ashley Stewart and that something did not appear to be good.

Taking Ashley firmly by the arm, Doug bade a cheerful goodbye to her parents, grinning broadly at their standard farewell, "Y'all stay out as late as you want!"

They drove aimlessly in silence, with Ashley staring forlornly out the passenger window and Doug glancing at her inquisitively, wondering what in the hell was the matter. Finally he asked, "Where would you like to go?"

"Preferably nowhere public." She wasn't in the mood to be a social butterfly. There was no way that she could manage to be nice to anyone given her present frame of mind.

"Then I know just the place." Doug wheeled his Jeep down the gravel road leading to the gently lapping waters of Ashley's lake. Surrounded by tall pine trees, their spot could barely be seen from the road, making it a perfect spot to hide from the world.

Getting out of the vehicle, Doug spread a blanket on the ground before pulling out a Thermos of cappuccino supplied by Ms. Bobbie. He filled Styrofoam cups with the steaming beverage and handed one to Ashley, then stretched out beside her on the ground.

It was a great night. The moon was almost full and shone brightly in silvery streaks across the calm water. "Nice night," Doug said, blowing on his coffee to cool it down before he sipped it.

"Yes," Ashley agreed, her dull eyes revealing nothing of what was on her mind.

Somewhat frustrated, Doug stared out at the water reflectively. "Do you remember how much fun we all used to have down here?" He reminisced with a jaunty grin, hoping to pull Ashley out of her deep funk.

She nodded, allowing herself to think back also. "Yes," she repeated lifelessly.

"This one-word answer stuff is so unlike you," Doug glanced over at her, his brow creased in worry. "What's wrong, Ashley? Is it pre-wedding jitters?"

"Well, it's jitters, but I don't know how much of it has to do with the wedding."

"Is it from being out to visit Jimmy?"

"No, visiting Jimmy broke my heart. This is something entirely different."

"Ashley, you're driving me crazy!" Doug looked into her eyes, begging for a straight answer. "Spit it out, Ash. Just tell me what's wrong."

"Oh, all right!" she cried out, aggravated by his prying. "I'm pregnant, Doug!"

"Excuse me?" Doug acted as if he hadn't heard correctly, but his eyes were wide with shock, indicating that he had heard exactly what she had said.

"I said I'm pregnant," she repeated, her quivering voice a little more subdued.

"That's what I thought you said," Doug said, attempting a jovial smirk. "Is it Rick's?"

Ashley rewarded his effort with a wry stare. "What do you think?"

Doug threw his hands up in the air, shrugging nonchalantly. "I was only hoping that I was drunker than I thought when I last saw you in April. You can't blame a guy for trying." His handsome face sobered. "What does Rick say?"

"Rick doesn't know yet."

"Then don't tell him!" Doug scrambled to his feet excitedly. "Marry me, Ashley. We'll elope tonight."

"Doug, are you insane?" Ashley snapped irritably at him, her green eyes flashing with fury. "What on earth possesses you to say things like that! This is serious."

Doug knelt in front of her, placing his hands gently on her shoulders and gazing at her with somber eyes. "I am serious. I love you, Ashley. I have for years. You'd be happy with me." His eyes searched her face, attempting to analyze her thoughts.

"Oh hell's bells, you do not love me! Not like that anyway," Ashley retorted with a scowl. "This is all you need. I can just see it now: 'LSU's starting quarterback, Doug Fairchild marries Ashley Stewart, former sweetheart of his dead best friend and pregnant mother of another man's child.' Wouldn't that be wonderful publicity for you?"

"I don't care what people say, you should know that by now." Doug sat back on his heels, studying her face with determined intensity.

Ashley shook her head indignantly. "There's no reason on God's green earth for you to marry me just because I'm pregnant."

"That's not the entire reason I'd marry you," he defended his motivation to her, carefully wording his thoughts. "I owe it to Jimmy. He'd roll over in his grave if he thought I'd stand by and let you marry a man you don't even love. The baby just adds weight to my argument."

"Oh, so that's it. You'd marry me for Jimmy's sake," Ashley raised her eyebrows doubtfully. "That's ludicrous, Doug. This conversation becomes more and more ridiculous with each passing moment," she told him hotly. "This baby is Rick's and he's entitled to know about it. And what makes you so sure that my telling Rick will change anything at all?"

"He just doesn't seem the paternal type." Doug stood, skipping stones off the water, enjoying some release of his increasing frustration with her stubbornness.

"That's true, he's not really crazy about kids, but he's never had his own."

Doug snorted indignantly. "Okay, let's make a deal. You tell Rick, see what he says, then let's have this discussion again," he said, glancing over his shoulder at her, catching the brunt of her angry glare.

"You really are nuts," Ashley said, too tired to argue the point any longer. "Why don't you just take me home?"

"Sure, if that's what you want."

Doug helped her gather their things, tossing them carelessly into the back seat of the Jeep as Ashley stomped in a huff around to her side of the car. She was highly irritated with Doug and didn't hesitate to show it.

"I'm only making this more difficult, aren't I?" he said, stealing a look at her as he pulled out onto the main road.

"Yes," she said abruptly, not wanting to say more for fear that she would be very ugly. She really just wanted to rip Doug to shreds for being so utterly aggravating.

Doug flashed his white teeth in a satisfied grin. "Good, that's exactly what I'm trying to do."

Ashley shot him a dirty look and he just laughed, amused with her reaction to everything he had said. Once in her driveway, Ashley flung open the car door, jumping out without a word and marched up the steps to the front porch.

"Aren't you going to say good night?" Doug called out, standing beside his door, leaning casually as he grinned at her.

"Good night, Doug!" Ashley pushed the front door open with a bang and stormed inside without a look back, hearing his hearty chuckling behind her as she slammed the front door.

Maggie sat at the kitchen table, painstakingly addressing the wedding invitations, and glanced up in surprise when Ashley burst into the kitchen.

"You're back pretty early. Did you have a nice time?" Maggie asked, smiling cheerfully at her.

"Peachy," Ashley said, reaching up in the cabinet for a glass and filling it with ice cold water from the refrigerator.

Maggie watched, placing her calligraphy pen on the delicate placemat before her and observing thoughtfully, "You know for a woman who's rarely speechless, you sure have given a lot of short answers the last few days."

"Right now, I don't have much to say." Ashley tried very hard not to lose her temper, especially since it seemed to her that she'd been forced to answer more questions than usual in the last several days.

"Would you please tell me what's wrong?" Maggie said gently. "If it's the wedding, it's not too late to call the whole thing off."

"The wedding is not the problem!" Ashley said, slamming her hand down on the countertop as she exploded. "The problem is that I found out this morning that I'm pregnant! Okay? Is that good enough?"

Maggie's face froze with shock, and she gaped at Ashley in silence for what seemed an eternity. "Well, I certainly wasn't expecting that," she said finally, blinking rapidly with astonishment.

"Yeah, well, that makes two of us," Ashley stared down at her feet, ashamed of her confession and hating herself for being so hard on Maggie.

"Have you told Rick?"

"No, I haven't. I'm scared to tell Rick," Ashley sighed. "But I have to tell him, soon. I owe him that much. I just can't marry him without telling him."

"How do you think he'll take the news?" Maggie leaned back in her chair, her uncharacteristically grave expression reflecting her disappointment.

Ashley shrugged unhappily. "I would imagine that he'll be none too happy about it but I honestly don't have a clue. We haven't really discussed having children."

"In your rush to get married, you two haven't really discussed much about marriage at all. Oh, Ashley, how could you let something like this happen?"

"Do you hate me, Maggie?" Ashley asked sadly, gazing up at her mother with puppy dog eyes, able to deal with anything but Maggie's disappointment.

"No! No, I don't hate you," Maggie reassured her, coming forward to embrace her, brushing the hair from Ashley's dismal eyes. "You're twenty years old, pregnant and unmarried. Sure, I'm disappointed in you. I'd be lying if I said I wasn't. And one day we'll discuss it at length, I assure you. But I don't think you need that tonight."

"Thanks, Maggie," Ashley smiled gratefully, returning her mother's warm embrace, wondering what she had done to deserve such a wonderful mother. "I love you."

"I love you too," Maggie said, patting her cheek softly with the palm of her hand. "Go on upstairs and get some rest. You've had a tough day."

Ashley escaped to the solace of her room, leaving Maggie leaning against the kitchen counter, hugging her arms to her chest, her holly-green eyes brimming with tears as she tried desperately to think of the best way to break the news to Remy.

Upstairs, Ashley changed into a cotton sleepshirt and slid open her window, deeply inhaling the cool night air as she leaned out into the darkness. From a distance, the familiar echo of croaking bullfrogs rang in her ears and she closed her eyes, resting her hot face against the windowsill. She rested, luxuriating in the solitude of the moment before being once more summoned by the telephone. Her eyes flew open in irritation and she stalked over to answer the annoying ring. "What?" she said, her tone more menacing than questioning.

"Hello, Ashley," Rick's lively chattering began immediately. "Just called to tell you that I found the most phenomenal house today. Two bedrooms with a study, in the best section of town, of course. It's absolutely perfect for us. I'm really sold on it, and I'm certain that you will be too."

Rick sounded so elated that Ashley hated to share her news with him, but since it had been such a lousy day for her anyway, now was as good a time as any.

"That's wonderful, Rick. I'm glad you had a good day." Ashley's heart pounded quickly in her chest as she went over her well-rehearsed speech in her head.

"What's wrong? A kink in the wedding plans?" Rick laughed, amused by what he thought was a little girl-like problem so typical of his young fiancée.

"That might be one way to put it," Ashley cleared her throat, deliberately beating around the bush, wanting to change her mind, but she had opened the door and there was no going back now.

"What is it? You make it sound so serious."

"Well, it is, I think so anyway. I'm telling you before the wedding because I don't think it would be right to surprise you with this. Not that I think it would change anything." Ashley struggled to control her trembling voice, immediately alerting Rick to the fact that whatever she was keeping from him was pretty significant.

alerting Rick to the fact that whatever she was keeping from him was pretty significant.

"Would you stop hedging? I hate it when you do that." His irritation with her was apparent as he snapped at her.

"Sorry," she apologized quickly, taking a deep breath. "Rick, I'm pregnant, I found out this morning."

The phone line resonated momentarily with dead silence, then came to life, crackling with the sound of Rick's labored breathing.

"Rick? Are you there?" Ashley chewed her lip, waiting for his response.

"I'm here," Rick said testily. "Just how pregnant are you, Ashley?"

"The doctor says six or seven weeks at the most."

He breathed a great sigh of relief. "Good, we can still take care of it," he said, instantly growing more cheerful.

"What do you mean by take care of it?"

"I mean, an abortion. You know what I mean. Get rid of the baby, Ashley, and we'll continue on like nothing ever happened."

Ashley felt sick as the room spun around her and her rubbery legs threatened to give out from under her. Get a grip, she told herself gruffly. This is no time for swooning.

Clutching the windowsill for support, she squared her shoulders purposely. "I will not have an abortion," she said hotly.

"Ashley, I do not like children. I do not want any children and I do not want this child." Rick was very blunt, in a voice so cold that Ashley barely recognized it.

"I *do* want this child," she said, suddenly defending the baby she had only known about with certainty for a few hours. "I will have this baby."

"If you have that baby, it will be without me."

Rick made his point perfectly clear and Ashley felt her face growing hot as her anger rose. "Oh, I see. You think you can bully me into an abortion by threatening to call off the wedding," she said, livid with fury. "Well, let me beat you to the punch. *I* am calling off the wedding!"

Her voice rose hysterically until she was shouting at the top of her lungs. "Rick LeNoir, you are a heartless, self centered bastard! Hell will freeze over before you ever lay eyes on me again!"

Ashley slammed down the phone and as it immediately began to ring again, she yanked the cord from the wall, flinging the phone angrily across the room. Remy ran up the stairs, taking them two at a time, and rushed into the room, grabbing Ashley and pulling her to him as she sobbed inconsolably. She rested her forehead on his chest, struggling with the undeniable urge to beat something with her fists. She looked up at her father with a tear-streaked face, tugging at his heartstrings with the forlorn expression in her eyes.

"Remy, the wedding is off," she said, her trembling voice barely above a whisper.

"So I heard, and I heard it all the way downstairs, I might add." Remy hugged her tightly, rocking her back and forth as they listened to the persistent ringing of the downstairs telephone, both knowing who was on the other end of the line.

"I will not talk to him," Ashley said adamantly, sniffing loudly as she wiped her eyes on the back of her hand.

"You don't have to talk to him, Ashley. You never have to see him again, if you don't want to," Remy reassured her, clenching his jaw squarely, and Ashley was grateful for his support. She had never before felt so empty and alone.

Maggie stuck her head in the door, assessing the situation with a swift look around the room, taking note of her daughter's tears, her husband's anger, and Ashley's telephone lying in a tangled heap at the base of the wall.

"Not that I don't know the answer to this already," she hesitated sheepishly as she quizzed Ashley. "But Rick is on the phone. Do you want to talk to him?"

Ashley's irate glare answered her question. "I thought not." Maggie retreated from the room, hurriedly descending the stairs to relay Ashley's message to Rick.

Remy and Ashley sat on her white eyelet coverlet and Remy reached out to smooth her hair back from her face. "So, I hear that we're having a baby," he said, trying to sound cheerful while his heart was breaking in two.

Ashley gave him a sad smile. "No, Remy, it looks like I'm having a baby, alone."

"You don't need Rick," Remy squeezed her hand consolingly. "I never thought that I would be saying this to you, but I'd rather see you with a baby alone than with Rick and miserable."

"He certainly showed his true colors tonight." Ashley hung her head, sighing heavily as she studied her hands, her diamond engagement ring feeling like the weight of the world on her finger. "I never knew that Rick could be so heartless and unfeeling."

"He may not give up on this," Remy said thoughtfully. "Rick may have acted like he didn't give a damn, but I wouldn't count on him letting you go without a fight."

Ashley lifted her head with renewed determination. "I will not have an abortion. I stand firm on that. Aside from that, I have no idea what I'm going to do. The rest of it I'll have to play by ear."

"Don't you worry, baby," Remy put a strong arm around her shoulder. "We'll manage just fine without Rick."

His unconditional love and support filled Ashley with guilt and she cast her eyes back to her lap where her fidgeting hands twisted her ring around and around her finger. "Remy, I'm so sorry. I know you're disappointed in me."

Remy tilted her chin upward, looking into her tear-filled eyes. "Yes, I'm disappointed," he acknowledged quietly, "but that doesn't mean that I love you any less."

Ashley threw her arms around his neck, embracing him tightly. "I love you too, Remy." It was then that she knew that everything was going to be okay, no matter what happened.

Ashley spent the next day at the drugstore with Remy to escape the dogged persistence of her ex-fiancé's telephone calls. None of the employees mentioned her upcoming nuptials. Maggie had resourcefully called ahead of Ashley's arrival to forewarn them that there might be no wedding. Even Mister Eddie remained silent, treating Ashley with subdued reverence, watching her as she worked diligently in the pharmacy, through sad yet compassionate eyes.

Near the end of the day, Susanna showed up at the pharmacy, swinging the door to the prescription counter open with a resounding bang. "Come on," she said.

"Where are we going?" Ashley said, protesting loudly as Susanna dragged her out from behind the counter. She was tired, cross, and she just wanted to go home.

"I'm taking you out to eat and then you may spend the night at my house. You are not going to be home tonight," Susanna informed her as she hauled her toward the front door.

"Why?"

"Why?" Susanna pulled open the door and pushed Ashley out onto the sidewalk. "Because I don't want that asshole Rick calling and upsetting you again, and I don't want you eloping with Doug Fairchild in a weak moment." She unlocked the passenger door of her car and shoved Ashley in, shutting the door firmly behind her.

"How do you know so much about all this?" Ashley regarded her quizzically as Susanna slid into the driver's seat.

"Comes from working at the bank," Susanna said, starting the car and pulling out into traffic.

Ashley laughed softly. "Susanna, everything in your life doesn't come from working at that bank."

"Sure it does. Those walls have ears." Susanna flashed a naughty grin in Ashley's direction. "No, to be honest, I've talked to both your mother and Doug today."

"Too much time on your hands at that job?"

"Not really. People just know where to find me. Your mother called me this morning and Doug called me this afternoon. Thanks for warning me about the baby," Susanna scowled unpleasantly. "Why is it that everyone knew about this but me?"

"I'm sorry, Susanna. I wasn't planning on the pregnancy becoming common knowledge."

"In this town? You've got to be kidding."

"Does Doug know what happened last night with Rick?"

"Bits and pieces, but I didn't give him the gory details. I just told him that something Rick said caused you to call off the wedding."

"What did Doug say when you told him?"

"There's not a chance in hell I'm telling you what Doug Fairchild said. For once, I won't do or say a thing to influence your decision-making." Susanna turned her head, giving Ashley a stern glare. "This ain't about a date to the prom, Ashley. This is another life we're talking about here, the life of your baby."

Thinking how unusual it was for Susanna to remain so unbiased, Ashley turned back toward the window, staring out at the incredible sunset streaking the dusky sky, stress lines forming on her brow as Rick's ice-cold comments replayed themselves over and over again in her mind.

Susanna crossed the river into Alexandria and pulled into the parking lot of the Holiday Inn on MacArthur Drive. "What are we doing here?" Ashley asked.

"Meeting Kate for dinner." Susanna parked the car then opened the door to get out.

"Why here?" Ashley joined her on the sidewalk, trotting to keep up with her as Susanna strode purposely toward the lobby door.

"Here we're less likely to run into anyone we know. After all, how many of our friends frequent the Holiday Inn?" Susanna laughed at Ashley's doubting expression. "Okay, okay, maybe one. But Rhonda doesn't live here anymore."

Kate met them at the entrance to the restaurant and instantly drew Ashley into a comforting embrace, her long, delicate fingers softly stroking the silky braid hanging down Ashley's back. "Everything will be just fine," she said soothingly.

"Oh shit, Kate, don't make her weak," Susanna said, berating her as they were seated at a table. "She's strong and she's standing her ground. If you make her weak, she'll give in and do something she'll regret."

"Such as?" Kate took her chair, raising an interested brow to Susanna.

"Such as marry Rick and abort her baby or elope with Doug and be reminded of Jimmy the rest of her life," Susanna sniffed haughtily, propping her sandaled feet in the chair between herself and Kate.

"Would the two of you please quit talking about me like I'm not here?" Ashley chimed in, glaring in irritation from Kate to Susanna. "This is my life, remember? Not yours."

"We can help you run it, can't we?" Susanna said.

"You always have. I don't know why you'd stop now." Ashley waved the waitress over and ordered coffee. "Regular, please, just black, and very strong."

"Don't you think you should have decaf?" Kate asked. "Caffeine may be bad for the baby."

Ashley impatiently counted to ten before answering. "Right at this moment, I would like to have a regular cup of coffee," she said through clenched teeth. "If everyone doesn't leave me alone, I'm going to scream."

"I say let her have her coffee," Susanna told the waitress, who was listening curiously, waiting for the argument to resolve.

"So," Kate glanced hesitantly at Ashley. "What are you going to do?"

"Over what time period? Tonight, for the next eighteen years, or the rest of my life?"

"Spoken like a true smart ass, Ashley," Susanna applauded gleefully, enjoying the fact that, for once, Kate was the one in the doghouse.

Ashley leaned her elbows on the table, twiddling her thumbs thoughtfully. "Well, to answer your question, Kate, tonight, I'm going to eat dinner, then I'm going home to my house to pack several bags and, what's tomorrow?" She paused, glancing at Kate.

"Wednesday?" Kate answered in bewilderment.

"Yes, Wednesday. Tomorrow, I'm going to load my bags into my car and drive to my parents' condo in Destin, *alone*. When I get there and stay there alone for a while, then I'll decide what to do with my life in the near future."

Ashley lifted her coffee cup and sipped her coffee, pleased with her spur of the moment decision. Yes, Destin would be just what the doctor ordered. She had run to Destin to resolve every other crisis in her life and she could think of no reason not to go there to resolve this one.

Susanna and Kate stared at her as if she'd lost her mind. "You can't just leave," Susanna told her indignantly.

"Oh yeah? Watch me," Ashley said, jutting her chin out stubbornly. "Now, if you two don't mind, the subject of what to do with my life is officially closed."

They ordered dinner and ate in a tense silence, with Susanna becoming quite huffy over Ashley's refusal to accept her advice. She finished her salad and stalked out, leaving Kate to drive Ashley home.

"Are you really going to Destin?" Kate quizzed her as they trekked through the streets of Pineville toward home.

"Yes," Ashley nodded adamantly. "I do my best thinking there."

"Then I'm going with you. I don't want you going alone."

"I don't need any nagging right now, Kate."

"I promise I won't nag you. I just want to go along in case you need me."

Ashley nodded again, this time in agreement. "Fine then, you can come with me."

"When do you want to leave?"

"Tonight." Ashley stared out the window with her arms folded tightly across her chest. The sooner she got out of town, the better it would be.

Kate dropped her at home, promising that she would be back as soon as she had packed. Ashley slipped quietly into the house and up the stairs to her room. Taking her suitcase down from the closet shelf, she tossed it on the bed and began throwing in articles of clothing without paying any attention to what she was packing. She didn't care. She only wanted to get away as soon as she possibly could.

Having heard Ashley come in, Maggie tapped lightly on the door and peeked into the room. "What on earth are you doing?"

Ashley looked back over shoulder, meeting Maggie's curious stare. "Do you mind if I use the condo for a few days?"

"In Destin?"

"Do you have another one I don't know about?"

"Why are you going to Destin?"

"I need time to evaluate my future."

"You can't do that here?" Maggie sat on the edge of the bed, wearing a look of puzzled uneasiness, watching Ashley stuff her suitcase with miscellaneous summer attire.

"If I stay here, do you know how many opinions I'll have to contend with?" Ashley stopped packing, glancing apprehensively at Maggie, silently pleading for her understanding. "I need to make this decision on my own."

"You can't be going to Destin alone."

"I won't be alone. Kate's going with me. She'll only offer advice if I ask for it."

"Remy and I have been very supportive, Ashley."

"Maggie, I'm sorry. That didn't come out right. You and Remy have been wonderful, especially under the circumstances. I was talking about Susanna and Doug, in particular."

"Rick called this afternoon."

Ashley whirled around, taken aback by Maggie's out-of-the-blue revelation. "What did he want?" she questioned, a little hopefully. Despite his harsh words and her hurt feelings, Ashley still cared for Rick deeply, and it bothered her not to have his support.

"He said that he was sorry for what he said last night."

Ashley sat next to Maggie on the bed, pondering the information skeptically. "Do you think he changed his mind about the baby?"

"He didn't say. He only said that he thought you two needed to talk."

Ashley shook her head fiercely. "Not yet. My feelings are still too hurt to talk to him right now."

"So, you still want to go to Destin?" Maggie asked as Ashley crossed the room to retrieve her purse from the dresser.

"Yes." Ashley lifted her suitcase and started toward the door, ready to make her getaway.

"You're going tonight?" Maggie followed her worriedly down the steps. "It's getting pretty late."

"It's only seven o'clock. We'll be there by three. I'm too full of nervous energy to sleep tonight anyway."

They reached the front foyer and stood together, their eyes meeting in mutual understanding.

"What should I tell Rick when he calls back?"

"Tell him I've gone out of town for a few days," Ashley told her with a wry smile. "And for God's sake, don't tell him where I am."

Kate bounded through the front door, suitcase in hand, wearing a wide-brimmed straw hat and floral Bermuda shorts. "I'm ready to go!" she announced cheerfully before glancing quickly from Maggie to Ashley, assessing the situation. "We are still going, aren't we?"

"Going where?" Hearing the commotion, Remy came out from the den, observing the suitcases beside the front door with a curious smile.

"The girls are going to Destin for a few days," Maggie said, warning him to silence with her stern glance.

Ashley smiled thankfully at her for giving her blessing then picked up her bag to leave. Maggie stopped her with a gentle hand on her shoulder. "Please let me know something soon. I have many things to cancel if you're not going through with the wedding."

Ashley wanted to protest that the wedding was definitely off, but after hearing that Rick had called to talk, she wasn't as certain of that now. She hoped that her perspective would be less jumbled after a few days away.

Instead, she embraced Maggie and Remy, promising to call the next morning and to make her decision as quickly as possible.

CHAPTER TWENTY-TWO

Kate and Ashley's journey to Destin was quick, with only two stops along the way, one in Slidell, Louisiana, to fill up with gas, and one at a truck stop outside Pensacola for a cup of coffee and bathroom break. Kate stayed awake for the entire trip, keeping Ashley entertained with small talk and humorous stories without allowing her any time to linger on the reason for the trip.

They arrived in Destin just after three in the morning, pausing at the locked gate of the condominium complex to obtain a guest pass. The security guard at the gate gave Ashley a peculiar gaze as she pulled to a stop. "It's either a very late night or a very early morning," he kidded as she accepted the guest-parking pass from him.

"A very late night," Ashley offered him a weary smile and waved as she drove away. Parking her car in the space in front of her parents' condo, she fumbled with the key and unlocked the front door, then she and Kate trudged inside, turning on the air conditioner and flopping face first on her parents' bed. Ashley was asleep before her head hit the pillow.

Kate let her sleep until eleven that morning before demanding that she get up. "Let's go to the beach!" she said in a booming voice. "It's a great day out there."

She opened the sliding door leading out onto the balcony, allowing a warm blast of ocean air to filter in and tickle Ashley's nostrils. Ashley moaned and rolled over, covering her head with a pillow as her usual morning queasiness welcomed her to Florida.

"I feel lousy," she mumbled from underneath the pillow.

Kate plopped down next to her, nudging Ashley with her elbow. "Here, I've got Sprite and crackers," she set them down on the night table. "Eat those and you'll be ready to go."

Ashley finally rolled out of bed around noon and rambled through her suitcase for a swimsuit. She rubbed on sunscreen, put on her sunglasses and grabbed a chair to join Kate on the beach. Ashley padded lightly through the cool sand, staring out at the Gulf of Mexico through dark sunglasses. As always, the beach was spectacular. The clear, blue-green waves crashing up onto the sugary white shore invariably took her breath away. She glanced up and down the coastline, shaking her head in amazement at the changes that had taken place since her last trip to Destin. The shoreline was rapidly changing with the addition of houses and high-rise condominiums. It was kind of sad. The secluded fishing village of Ashley's childhood was gone forever.

Weather-wise, mid-May was perfect, with crisp mornings and evenings, and warm, sunny afternoons just perfect for enjoying the sparsely populated beach. The weeks prior to Memorial Day were relatively quiet in Destin with only a few college students and graduating high school seniors vacationing before the official start of summer.

Kate glanced up with Ray Ban-covered eyes as Ashley neared her, flashing a bright smile from beneath the hot pink beach umbrella. "Welcome to the Land of the Living," she said, as Ashley opened her chair then flopped down beside her under the shade of the beach umbrella. They sat with their legs in the sun, observing their beautiful surroundings in easy silence.

The first couple of days they were in Destin, Kate and Ashley filled their days with sunbathing and beach walking, their evenings with dining out and watching movies. Ashley enjoyed her break from reality and, aside from her daily bout with morning sickness, managed to forget all her problems. Nevertheless, by Friday, her own nagging thoughts fought their way to the front of her mind, forcing her to begin what she'd come to Destin to accomplish.

Rising early on Friday morning, Ashley left Kate sleeping and strolled on the beach alone. She walked slowly at the water's edge, kicking the wet sand lightly with her toes, watching as the waves crashed dramatically onto the shore while turning ideas over and over in her head. If she kept the baby, she could go back to Northeast in the fall and get one more semester of school out of the way before the baby was born. After the birth would come the complications. Who would keep the baby while she went to class? Where would they live and how would she support the child?

Doug's proposal could not be considered a true option. Ashley loved Doug enough to dismiss his marriage proposal as the gallantry of a devoted friend. Then there was Rick. Considering his phone call to her mother, dare she hope that Rick might still be in the picture?

There were so many variables to consider. Her head was practically spinning by the time she returned from her walk. She found Kate awake and on the beach, patting the chair beside her as she offered Ashley a plastic cup of lemonade.

"Did you have a good walk?" she said in a motherly voice, and Ashley smiled, wondering what she had done to deserve such a wonderful friend.

"I did, I guess," Ashley said with a shrug of her shoulders. "I had a lot of things to think over." She accepted the cup, sipping the sweet lemonade gratefully as she took her seat in the warm sunshine.

"And so the great debate begins," Kate declared lightly, stretching her shapely legs out across the sand as she turned toward her best friend, eyeing her speculatively.

"Kate, if I got an apartment in Monroe, would you live with me and the baby? I wouldn't expect any babysitting out of you. I'd just want the company."

Kate's bubbly laughter filled the air, breaking Ashley's tension. "Of course I'd live with you and the baby. Auntie Kate would be just thrilled to help you out. Is that what you've decided to do?"

"No, I haven't made any decision yet. I've just been batting around some ideas." Ashley shaded her eyes with her forearm and stared into the distance, still debating her dilemma.

"Have you thought about Rick? Have you counted him out of your plans?"

"Yes, I've thought about Rick. I miss him. Even though I'm mad at him, my feelings for him haven't changed."

"Do you still want to marry him?"

Ashley considered Kate's question, creasing her brow pensively. "I guess that depends on what his stance is about the baby. I know how I feel about it and I'm not changing my mind."

Kate nodded in understanding and they sat silently sipping lemonade, watching as the crashing surf inched its foamy fingers closer to their spot in the sand.

"Did you know that Doug asked me to marry him?" Ashley broke the silence, lifting her sunglasses and glancing quickly in Kate's direction.

Kate met her gaze and sighed heavily. "I can't say that it surprises me," she admitted with a shrug. "Did he offer any logic behind this proposal?"

"Well, he said that he loved me," Ashley rolled her eyes skeptically. "And I told him that he didn't love me, not like that. Then he tried to tell me that he would marry me for Jimmy's sake."

"That's bull," Kate shifted in her chair, pulling her sun-kissed legs under the shaded protection of their umbrella. "Two years down the line, there is no reason to say that he's doing anything for Jimmy's sake."

"That's what I told him. I can't imagine what possessed him to propose to me." Ashley idly traced circles in the sand with her toes, thinking of Doug's tempting offer made under the silvery beams of Louisiana moonlight, and she smiled softly, touched once again by the unselfishness of his gesture.

"What else did you say to him?"

"I told him that he was being foolish, that I couldn't marry him." Ashley lifted her eyes to meet Kate's musing stare. "The offer was very sweet but Doug deserves so much more than a pregnant friend for a wife."

"I think that you're a very good friend to turn Doug down. He's a pretty good catch, especially for a scared, pregnant young woman. Not everyone in the same situation would have been so kind."

"I'm not saying that I wasn't tempted," Ashley said, chuckling lightly as she rested her head against the back of her beach chair, closing her eyes as she soaked up sunshine.

"At least you're keeping your sense of humor."

"That's about all I have going for me at the moment."

Their somber discussion was interrupted by the arrival of a group of rowdy students from the University of Alabama. With boom box blaring, they settled on the sand next to Kate and Ashley, making introductions as they unpacked their beach gear. After a lively afternoon in the sun with the guys and gals from Alabama, Ashley and Kate joined them for dinner at The Back Porch, a popular beachside restaurant on old Highway 98 in Destin. Ashley was glad for the company. It was a welcome distraction from the current events monopolizing her life.

After dinner and drinks that lasted late into the evening, Ashley and Kate declined the offer to go out dancing with the rest of the group, instead returning to the condo to plug a movie into the VCR. Ashley, garbed in an old T-shirt of Remy's, curled up in the corner of the couch to enjoy the video. Halfway through, Kate shook her awake.

"Ashley, go to bed." Kate gently prodded her off the couch and up the steps to Maggie and Remy's large open bedroom.

Ashley lay in the darkness, attempting to will herself back to sleep. She tossed and turned until she was crazy, then finally got out of bed and opened the sliding door to the balcony. Settling onto the porch swing, she propped her head onto a pillow and gently swayed back and forth, listening to the sound of the crashing waves echoing from the beach. She had come close to drifting off to sleep when she heard the door below her sliding open.

Kate must be coming out for a breath of fresh sea air, she thought, and was about to hail her when Ashley realized that Kate was talking to someone. She remained still and perked up her ears to listen.

"Get out here before you wake up Ashley!" Kate berated whoever was with her. "I can't believe that Ms. Maggie told you where we were."

"Ms. Maggie didn't have to tell me where you were." Ashley recognized Doug's pleasant voice immediately. "When I realized that you two had left town, I knew that you'd be here. Ashley always comes here during any crisis in her life."

"What are you doing here?" Kate demanded irritably, sounding none too pleased about Doug's arrival.

"I came to see how Ashley is."

"She's fine. Go home."

"I find that hard to believe." Ashley heard the downstairs porch swing groan under Doug's weight and the rusty chains began to squeak slightly as he swung slowly back and forth. "How is she really, Kate?"

"She's confused and she feels rejected. How else would you expect her to be?"

"What's she going to do?" Doug goaded her gently for more information.

"She doesn't know yet."

"Has she talked to that jerk since y'all have been in Florida?" Doug's contempt for Rick was reflected in the tenseness of his voice.

"No, she's not ready to talk to him yet. But I wouldn't count him out if I were you. Ashley really cares for him, you know."

"What did he say to her about the baby?"

"Ashley will tell you if she wants you to know." Ashley smiled broadly at Kate's never-ending loyalty.

"That bad, huh?"

"It wasn't pretty."

"Did she tell you that I asked her to marry me?"

"She did."

"Am I a contender?" Doug said, keeping his voice casual as he directed his eyes toward Kate.

"You can't be serious," Kate chided him irritably.

"I'm very serious, Kate. You know how I feel about her."

"Yes, I know how you feel about her. But as things stand right now, even if she wanted to, it would be a mistake for Ashley to marry you."

"Why? I'd be good for her. Better than *he* could ever hope to be."

"Yes, Doug, you would be wonderful. But Ashley's too good a friend to mess up your life by marrying you now."

"Why are you so against the idea of Ashley and me getting married? There's no way it could mess up my life," Doug argued, stopping the swing with a jerk and moving to stand next to Kate, leaning nonchalantly with his back against the balcony rail.

"Doug, Ashley cares about you, I know that. But she doesn't love you the way that you want her to. What if she married you and then, months or years from now, she falls in love with someone for real? Where would that leave either of you?"

"Kate, I appreciate your confidence in my charms," Doug said, chuckling quietly as he kidded with her. "I could make her love me."

"You can't make anyone love you. Don't push the marriage thing with her, Doug. Let it rest," Kate advised him kindly. "Ashley doesn't need that kind of pressure right now. She has enough to worry about."

Doug met her gaze thoughtfully, smiling broadly at her. "Kate, you are mature beyond your years," he said admiringly.

"I don't know if I'm all that mature. I'm just the only one out of all of us who displays one lick of sense."

"Very true," Doug laughed heartily. "How long are y'all planning to stay in Destin?"

"I don't know, but you aren't staying with us," Kate notified him coolly.

"Gee, Kate, your hospitality is lacking this evening. Can I at least spend the night?"

"I suppose so, but you're going back to Louisiana tomorrow. Ashley doesn't need you here clouding her judgment, and I don't trust you to behave." Kate slid the door open.

"Where am I sleeping?" Ashley heard Doug ask as they stepped back inside.

"Couch City, baby." Kate enlightened him, pulling the door closed.

Ashley lay in the swing, letting the ocean breeze cool her hot face as she pondered the conversation on which she had just eavesdropped. So much for her idea of Doug's unselfish gallantry. He had been sincere in his proposal after all, caring for her more than she could've ever known. She smiled sadly, closing her eyes and lying motionlessly on the swing. If she had only known how he really felt before now, things might have been different. There was no way that she could consider a relationship with him under these circumstances. It was a shame though. With those thoughts occupying her mind, Ashley felt herself relaxing, comforted by the knowledge that Doug was just downstairs.

The next thing she knew, the sun was shining brightly in her face and she sat up stiffly, looking around in bewilderment. She had slept all night on the porch swing. Moving slowly, she slid the door open quietly and slipped inside, biting back the bile rising in her throat. God, how she hated the morning sickness. The Captain's clock on the dresser chimed seven just as she pulled on a pair of boxers and a T-shirt and went downstairs.

Ashley padded noiselessly past Kate's closed door, not wanting to rouse her from sleep. She tiptoed into the living room, spying Doug on the tiny sofa, his long legs scrunched uncomfortably beneath him. Ashley smiled affectionately at his soundly slumbering form and turned to slip out the front door.

"Hey," Doug sat up suddenly, rubbing the sleep from his eyes.

Ashley stopped, looking back at him with a warm smile. "Hey yourself."

"You don't look too surprised to see me here," Doug said, suppressing a yawn.

"I'm never surprised about where you might turn up."

"Where're you going?"

"For a walk on the beach."

"Hang on and I'll go with you." Doug rolled off the couch and into the bathroom while Ashley leaned against the wall, waiting for him. He emerged wearing shorts, T-shirt and *the* khaki baseball cap, nodding that he was ready and they exited quietly out the front door.

They strode wordlessly down the shore while Doug took in his surroundings. "I just can't get over all the stuff they've built down here," he said with a disbelieving shake of his head.

"It's amazing, isn't it?" Ashley agreed, deciding that idle chitchat would be just fine with her. It sure beat fighting and she and Doug could really tie one on if the mood suited them. She reached into her shorts pocket, pulling out some saltines to nibble, hoping to ease her nausea.

"You feeling okay?" Doug said, his brown eyes softly reflecting his concern for her.

"Yeah, I'm okay. Just a little queasy. It gets better as the day goes on."

Doug nodded sympathetically, squinting at the water from behind the dark lenses of his aviator sunglasses. "We've had some good times down here too," he reminisced with a mischievous grin.

"Yeah we have." Ashley had to smile, remembering vividly the harem of bikini-clad admirers that had followed Doug relentlessly up and down the beach during one of their teenage trips to the beach with her parents.

"How much longer are you staying down here?"

"I haven't decided," Ashley said, with a shrug of her shoulders. "I have to go home some time."

"Why? You could spend the summer here. It'd be good for you, you know, down here away from all the stress and strain."

"I'd love to stay here all summer, but I need to go home and take care of some things."

"What kind of things?" Doug narrowed his eyes suspiciously, goading her to continue.

"I still haven't resolved everything with Rick," Ashley said quietly, leaning down to scoop a tiny white shell from the damp sand before the rushing surf could return it to the sea. She swished it gently back and forth in the water, holding it tightly between her fingers as she rinsed the clinging sand from its edges.

"What's left to resolve? I heard that you called off the wedding."

"I did, but I was mad when I did it. Rick said some things that hurt me and I called off the wedding. We haven't spoken since."

"Then I would say that it's resolved," Doug said, squaring his jaw stubbornly.

"Doug, I do have a child to consider. Rick is the father of this baby and he deserves to have a chance to say his piece."

"If he said things that hurt you bad enough to call off the wedding, I would say that he's said his piece," Doug ground his words between clenched teeth, struggling not to lose his temper with her.

"Rick was in shock when he said those things. I'm sure that he's had time to think things over and I'm interested in what he has to say."

Doug stopped in his tracks and turned to stare at her, his face flushing with indignation. "What is it about this guy that makes you put up with all this crap? He can't be *that* wonderful. I've never seen a woman act so stupid!"

Ashley crimped her mouth in annoyance, throwing her clenched fists onto her hips as the fighting commenced. "Did it ever occur to you that I might just love Rick and I might want to salvage what we have together?"

Doug rolled his eyes in exasperation. "Ashley, we've been through this before, you don't love the guy and you never will."

"Doug, this is none of your business. I don't even know why you're here!"

Ashley stomped off down the beach, leaving Doug standing in the surf staring after her. He sprinted effortlessly along the sand, quickly catching up with her.

"I'm sorry, Ash." He took her by the arm, his eyes pleading for forgiveness. "I should learn to keep my mouth shut. Kate's going to kick my ass."

Ashley suppressed an amused smile, knowing that Doug was right. Kate would be furious with him if she knew. It wasn't yet nine o'clock and they were screaming at the top of their lungs at one another on the beach. An unspoken truce was called and they continued their walk.

Ashley was just beginning to believe that Doug was going to let it rest when he spoke up, "Rick said that he didn't want the baby, didn't he?"

"Among other things," Ashley said, avoiding his probing eyes by turning her head away from him obstinately.

"Like what?"

"Doug!" Ashley glared at him, reducing him to a sheepish grin.

"Sorry, Ash. You can't blame a guy for trying." Doug glanced around uneasily, spotting The Whale's Tail, their favorite breakfast hangout from high school days. "I'll tell you what," he nudged Ashley playfully, "let's get Kate and I'll buy you breakfast."

After dragging Kate out of bed, they sat at an outside table on the upper deck of The Whale's Tail, overlooking the translucent emerald water of the gulf as they sipped hot black coffee and breakfasted on scrambled eggs, bacon and toast.

"Did y'all go walking?" Kate yawned widely, stretching her slender arms above her head.

"Yes," Doug and Ashley nodded enthusiastically, answering her in unison, their faces shining with identical angelic smiles.

"Did y'all fight?"

Doug and Ashley eyed one another conspiratorially, wondering how to respond without telling her a boldface lie. Kate watched as Doug's face took on a deepening hue of shame, instantly knowing the answer to her question.

"Go home, Doug," she said, shooting him a scorching look as he dropped his eyes sheepishly. "We were doing just fine without you."

"Now, Kate, at least let him stay overnight," Ashley said, winking at Doug flirtatiously. "He's not hurting anything, and I like having him here."

Doug flashed Kate a look that said I told you so, to which she glared impatiently in return. "Okay, big guy," she said indignantly, "you may have won that round, but first thing tomorrow morning, you're outta here."

Early the next morning, Ashley walked Doug out to his Jeep. He threw his duffel bag into the back seat and turned to her, holding her gently by the shoulders. "Call me when you get back to town," he said, kissing her forehead affectionately.

"Okay." Ashley smiled up at him, sad that he was leaving. His presence had brought some much-needed lightheartedness to her confused state of mind.

"My offer still stands," he said, revealing a winning smile.

Ashley cheerfully rewarded him with a saucy smile of her own, briefly reveling in the moment before her harmless flirtation with Doug was interrupted by Kate's irritated bellow. "Doug, go home!"

Doug laughed, grinning widely and shaking his head in amazement. "Kate, you've got the best ears I've ever had to reckon with," he said, calling over his shoulder to her as he got into the Jeep. "See ya, Ashley," he said, winking at her impishly.

"See ya, Doug," Ashley waved fondly as he drove away, regretting that she could not have something more personal than friendship with him. She joined Kate outside the door of the condominium, and Kate observed her downhearted expression, reading Ashley's thoughts without comment. Instead, she put her arm around Ashley sympathetically.

"I'm very foolish, aren't I?" Ashley leaned her head on Kate's shoulder, sighing contritely.

Kate shook her head, patting Ashley encouragingly. "You're doing the right thing for right now, Ashley. You've treated Doug with a great deal of consideration and I'm proud of you."

Kate smiled her sunniest smile, taking Ashley by the hand, pulling her toward the boardwalk leading to the glistening seashore. "C'mon girlfriend, let's hit the beach."

Kate and Ashley made their triumphant return to Pineville the following Wednesday, skirting into town on the wings of a sultry summer night. Maggie and Remy welcomed Ashley from the front porch swing, watching her expectantly as she climbed the steps to the veranda. She pulled up one of Maggie's high back rockers, sitting in front of them, smiling happily.

"I'm back," she said, looking from Remy to Maggie, hoping her cheerful face would ease some of their apparent anxiety.

"Glad to have you home." Remy reached out to touch her knee, patting it affectionately as he smiled at her. "I take it from that happy smile of yours that you've made some sort of decision."

"I have," Ashley said, rocking back and forth casually, feeling comfortable with her choice. "As it stands now, I've decided to keep the baby and go back to Northeast in the fall. Kate said that she would live with me."

"What about after the baby is born? You're hardly in any position to support and take care of the baby alone. You certainly can't work, go to school and take care of a baby," Maggie pointed out curtly.

"Why not? It won't be easy, but I think that I can manage." Ashley argued with the naivete of a child.

"I don't suppose you've talked to your fiancé?" Maggie said, eyeing her with an I-know-something-you-don't-know look.

"I think it would be safe to call him my ex-fiancé."

"Well, I would expect your *ex-fiancé* to show up at our door any time now. He has called every day since you've been away," Maggie said, her voice weary from the long hours spent consoling Rick over the telephone.

Ashley's heart skipped a couple of beats at the thought of seeing Rick. It had been almost three weeks since she had seen him and she didn't know how she would react. One look into his eyes would overpower all of her stubborn independence. She rocked in the muggy Louisiana night air, praying for a little time to brace herself before the arrival of Rick LeNoir.

Ashley was graced with only two days before Rick appeared, making his entrance back into her life early on Friday afternoon. He swung his car into the Stewarts' circle drive and Ashley watched from her bedroom window as he strode purposely toward the front steps, smiling in spite of herself. The sheer beauty of him was overwhelming, and Ashley hadn't realized how much she missed him until he mounted the steps and rang the front bell.

Resisting the urge to fly down the steps to greet him with open arms, Ashley waited in her room while Maggie let him in and sent him up the stairs. Rick tapped quietly on the door.

"Come in," Ashley called out casually, running her trembling fingers through her hair.

Rick swung the door open and stepped inside, his presence filling the entire room. "Hello Ashley," he smiled, slightly yet confidently as he leaned against the doorframe regarding her with his magnificent eyes.

"Rick." Ashley returned his greeting coolly, meeting his gaze with a haughty stare.

He approached her, taking a seat across from her at the foot of her bed, scrutinizing her physical appearance with an appreciative eye. "You look beautiful, Ashley. You must be feeling better."

"I'm okay," Ashley lied, not wanting any false sympathy from him. "Why are you here?"

"I came here to say that I'm sorry. You never gave me a chance to tell you."

"I didn't want to talk to you until I became more rational," Ashley said, averting her eyes from his piercing stare. "You really hurt me."

"I know that I did, darling. I shouldn't have said those things to you."

"I haven't changed my mind about the baby," Ashley said, standing her ground firmly.

"I didn't think that you had," Rick said, sighing in defeat. "Are you still going to marry me?" He took her hand, gazing adoringly into her lovely face.

"I don't think so." Pulling her hand away, Ashley squared her shoulders and looked him defiantly in the eyes. "I don't need you, Rick. I can take care of this baby alone."

Rick nodded absently, rising from his position at the end of the bed, pacing the length of the room as he stroked his chin reflectively. Ashley watched him with darting eyes, wondering timidly if his next move would be a violent one. Suddenly he stopped, turning slowly to face her with an icy glint in his emotionless eyes.

"I see," he said calmly, a smug smile forming on his lips. "So I take it your parents don't mind having a bastard for a grandchild?"

Ashley drew in a sharp breath as Rick's remark hit her like a ton of bricks. Leave it to Rick to bring up the one fact regarding their child that she hadn't considered. An angry flush crept over her face and she turned to him with livid eyes. "That's not a very nice thing to say," she told him through gritted teeth.

"Nice or not, my pet, it's true. The child you carry will be born out of wedlock and thus will be illegitimate. *That* should go over well in this community. Your parents will never be able to hold their heads up proudly in public again. And you, Ashley, will be to blame."

Ashley stared blankly at him as the color drained from her face and fought hard not to scream or cry. Rick sensed that she was having exactly the reaction for which he had hoped and sat next to her, taking her hand as he gazed complacently into her eyes.

"Ashley, I still want to marry you. I love you, and I want you to be with me."

"What about the baby?"

"I'll give the baby my name, just as its father should."

Ashley couldn't respond, feeling like a trapped animal. "I can't answer you now," she whispered, pulling away from him and moving woodenly to stare out the window, tears welling up in her eyes.

"Sleep on it tonight," Rick said, his face lighting with bitter triumph as he sauntered toward the bedroom door. "I'm staying in Alexandria at The Bentley. I will check with you tomorrow and see what you've decided."

Ashley did not turn to face him, but knew that he wore a self-satisfied grin as he exited the room. Rick had her where he wanted her and he knew it. She couldn't possibly present her parents with an illegitimate grandchild. Although she knew that they would support her without question, she also knew that it would break their hearts. Rick was right, the Stewart family would be the topic of conversation in their small southern town for years. After one very long, sleepless night, Ashley came to the conclusion that she simply had no choice in the matter. By dawn, Ashley determined that the only option she had was to marry Rick after all.

CHAPTER TWENTY-THREE

Her wedding day dawned clear and sunny, and for that Ashley was thankful, hoping it was a sign that everything was going to be all right. The preceding four weeks had been sheer hell for her. As an actress, she had been put to the test; her role being that of the happy bride-to-be, hell-bent on convincing her family and friends that she was ecstatic to be marrying to Rick LeNoir. Nothing could've been further from the truth.

Convincing Maggie and Remy had been difficult. It took all she had to persuade them that she knew exactly what she was doing in marrying Rick and was thrilled to be doing so. She had forced herself to smile brilliantly at her father as he eyed her doubtfully, knowing that he would never stand for her to marry out of a sense of obligation, especially to save his standing in the community. Although she protested at first, persuading Maggie had been a little easier. The soft spot Maggie held in her heart for Rick made her an easy mark.

Kate had been tough, logically putting up an argument to Ashley's every statement. "So what did he have to say for himself?" she asked, demanding of Ashley an explanation for Rick's forgiveness.

"He apologized profusely and admitted that he was wrong," Ashley said, forcing her voice to be light, glad that over the telephone, she didn't have to face Kate's knowing eyes. "He told me he loved me and begged for my forgiveness. I decided that it was best for all involved to forgive him and forget it ever happened. We're getting married just as planned."

"Did you allow yourself to be included in the circle of people for which this is best?"

"Yes, Kate."

"And you really feel like you're doing the right thing? Marriage is a little more serious than wearing someone's class ring."

"Of course, I feel I'm doing the right thing."

"Don't 'of course' me, Ashley Stewart. This is Kate whose eyes you're trying to pull the wool over. I know you as well as I know myself."

"Kate, I do not intend to go into this again. I'm marrying Rick and that's the end of it," Ashley had abruptly ended the conversation, cutting Kate off as she tried to rationalize with her. She didn't want to listen to Kate's voice of reason. She had made her decision and was sticking to it.

Susanna had been tougher. Upon receiving news of the on-again wedding, Susanna had been livid, bursting into Ashley's bedroom with frantically smoldering eyes, her russet red hair standing wildly on end. She accosted Ashley in the center of the room, angrily speaking her piece and calling Ashley every name for stupid that she could come up with.

"Ashley, you're crazy! Why are you doing this?" Susanna protested weakly, close to defeat after arguing with Ashley for more than half an hour.

"Damn it, Susanna," Ashley had listened patiently for the first thirty minutes of Susanna's furious tirade, but she would be damned if she were listening to any more of it. "You want the truth? Okay, sister, here's the whole ball of wax.

Number one, I don't want to humiliate my parents by giving them a bastard grandchild. Number two, I don't want Doug Fairchild to feel any obligation to try to marry me and ruin his life. I want him to move on and find someone who will make him happy. Number three, I'm scared to have this child alone. Rick is the baby's father and I'm going to marry him. That's the truth of the matter. Are you happy now?"

"No, I'm not happy now," Susanna said, mocking her in a sniveling singsong. "You're marrying Rick for all the wrong reasons."

"I was going to marry him before I found out I was pregnant."

"You weren't marrying him for the right reasons then either."

"You make me tired," Ashley sank into a heap on the floor, resolving not to argue with Susanna one minute longer.

"That's what I'm here for," Susanna said, chuckling slightly as they had reached a stalemate and she knew it. "You're not going to change your mind, are you?"

"No, Susanna, I'm not."

Susanna sighed in frustration, falling ungracefully to land beside Ashley on the hardwood floor. "Then I'll be a true friend and stand by your side to support you through this fiasco," she proclaimed loyally.

"Thank you, Susanna," Ashley smiled warmly at her, acknowledging her sacrifice.

"However, I won't hesitate to say I told you so, if the situation ever presents itself," Susanna added smugly, flashing an evil grin.

The toughest to tell had been Doug. Ashley could not bring herself to call him, no matter how badly she wanted to talk to him. She could face anyone's anger but his. She had a feeling that Kate or Susanna had already told him the news, and if he wanted to talk to her about it, Ashley felt sure that he would find her.

On Sunday, less than two weeks from her wedding day, Ashley attended church with Maggie and Remy and spotted Doug sitting across the aisle. During the service, she felt his eyes on her several times but just couldn't look at him. Finally, during the sermon, she glanced his way, meeting his eyes and agreeing to his signed invitation to meet after church. She met him on the front sidewalk, smiling nervously as he strode toward her, his wavy blond hair reflecting the morning sunlight. He was almost irresistible. Her heart pounding, Ashley looked expectantly at him, waiting cautiously for him to make the first move.

"Hi," Doug greeted her awkwardly, his lips pursed tightly in a stony line of suppressed irritation.

"Hi," Ashley said softly, twisting the hem of her lace blouse in her hand as she stared up at him with a forced smile.

"Go to brunch with me." Doug took her by the hand, pulling her alongside him down Main Street. They walked in tense silence, neither wanting to bring up the subject weighing heavily on their minds.

After an almost wordless brunch, they strolled past Remy's store, pausing in the small garden park across from city hall to rest together on a stone bench. Ashley kept her eyes downcast, anxiously clasping and unclasping her sweaty palms. Doug watched her, clearing his throat uneasily before he spoke.

"So, I heard that you're really going through with this thing."

Ashley lifted her eyes, nodding affirmatively. "Yes, I am."

"I can't talk you out of it? My offer still stands," he said, coercing a lighthearted smile to his face. "I hear you already have a dress."

"Doug, you know I can't marry you. It wouldn't be right."

"Marrying me is as right as marrying Rick would be." Doug leaned forward and clasped his hands together pensively, his brown eyes clouded with sudden sadness.

"Doug, please." Ashley rolled her eyes, looking away to hide the tears streaming down her cheeks.

"If I can't talk sense into you," Doug leaned back against the bench, closing his eyes, "then, I'll just tell you goodbye. I'm going back to Baton Rouge."

Ashley gaped at him, stunned. "Will you come back for the wedding?" she asked, studying his handsome face as he opened his eyes to regard her with forced aloofness.

"Nope." He straightened his shoulders, shaking his head with a sardonic smile. "No, Ashley, I won't be at your wedding."

"Doug, don't do this to me. You are one of my best friends. You have to be there."

"Ashley, ordinarily, I'd do anything in the world for you, but I won't do this."

"Please, Doug, please! I need you," Ashley said, pleading with him, aware that she was being not only unreasonable but also extremely unfair.

"No, Ashley, I won't be there. I won't watch you marry Rick LeNoir. It's a mistake, and since I couldn't talk you out of it, I won't watch you make it."

Ashley began to cry, her tiny body convulsing with violent sobs until finally, Doug wrapped his arms around her and rested her head on his chest. Ashley lay there sniffling, listening to his heartbeat and finding it strangely comforting. In that moment all she wanted was to remain locked in his strong embrace forever. Overcome with guilt, she sat up abruptly, pulling away from him with reluctance. Doug reached in his pocket and handed her a tissue.

"Thanks," she smiled gratefully to him and wiped her bloodshot eyes. Doug stared off in the distance, sullen and close-lipped.

"Susanna and Kate behaved much more graciously about this than you have," she touched him lightly on the arm, taken aback as he jerked his arm away with a growl.

"I'm not Susanna or Kate." He leapt abruptly from the bench, stalking off in the direction of the church and his waiting car. Ashley followed him, carefully keeping her distance, allowing Doug to walk alone and vent some of his obvious frustration.

After an equally distressing drive home, Ashley glanced hesitantly at him as he pulled into the drive. "Do you want to come in?" she asked hopefully, not wanting to leave things the way they were.

Doug cut his eyes toward her, shaking his head adamantly. "No, I'd rather just say goodbye now. It may be a long time before I can see you again."

"Will you call me?"

"No." Doug refused her request but impulsively cupped her face in his hands, kissing her longingly. Ashley returned his kiss, not wanting to let him go, but knowing she had no choice. It was too late for them.

She pushed him away and bolted from the car. "Goodbye, Doug, I'll miss you," she turned as she reached the top of the front steps, looking back at him with brimming eyes.

"Have a good life, Ashley." He backed out of the driveway and Ashley watched him roar away, waving as tears coursed uninhibitedly down her face. She had done it. She had forced Doug to move on with his life. She only wished that she had felt more pleased about it.

Yes, Ashley reflected, sinking into the antique rocker in front of her open bedroom window, telling Doug had been the hardest thing she had ever done. And seeing Rick again had been almost as painful.

Rick had arrived in Pineville two days beforehand on Thursday night, followed by Dominique LeNoir and Celeste on Friday morning. Claire Robicheaux and Imogene Ducote hosted a luncheon in their honor, inviting family and close friends to a banquet fit for a king at Lee J's on the Levee.

Rick's presence made Ashley's acting role almost impossible. Publicly, Ashley clung possessively to his arm, playing her part as the jubilant bride, but privately she avoided him, resenting him immensely for forcing her hand. At Lee J's, an amused Rick observed as Ashley, dressed to the nines in a champagne-hued linen sheath dress with her long hair pulled into a French braid, worked the room, visiting happily with luncheon guests as she skirted away from him. He managed to get near her after lunch was served, his warm breath tickling the nape of her neck as he leaned down to whisper in her ear.

"After tomorrow, staying so far away from me won't be quite so easy for you, my pet." Ashley cringed at his words, looking back into his mocking eyes with a frown.

Over lunch, Dominique chattered excitedly with Maggie about the wedding. The future mothers-in-law appeared to be getting along famously, much to Ashley's relief. Dominique had yet to mention Ashley's pregnancy, so Ashley surmised that Rick had not told her and kept silent, sure that Rick would tell her later when the time was right.

However, Celeste knew everything, as Ashley learned when Celeste cornered her in the ladies room at Lee J's. "Finally, a moment alone," Celeste said with a friendly smile. "How are you feeling, sister-in-law-to be?"

In answer to Ashley's questioning glance, she replied, "Rick told me all about the baby."

"How do you feel about it?" Ashley leaned against the bathroom wall with her hands behind her back, waiting for Celeste's opinion.

"I think babies are wonderful," Celeste said with a gentle smile. "However, I do know that grumpy old brother of mine is not too crazy about children. How have the two of you resolved your differences regarding this child?"

"Rick was pretty mad at first, but he apologized for his hasty words and we decided to go ahead with the wedding," Ashley summarized, deciding to omit the subtle emotional blackmail Rick had used to secure her hand in marriage. Celeste would have been sure to let Rick have it, and Ashley didn't have the energy needed to survive one of Rick's tantrums.

Celeste sighed, patting Ashley's shoulder reassuringly. "Be patient with Rick, Ashley. I know that he loves you. A baby will just take a great deal of adjustment on his part, that's all."

Ashley nodded, respecting Celeste's devotion to Rick and appreciating that she would have an ally in the family. God knows she would need one.

Rehearsal went off without a hitch, as did rehearsal dinner, hosted by Dominique and Celeste at Tunk's Cypress Inn on Kincaid Lake. Afterward, Ashley bid Rick and the LeNoir women farewell and rode home with Maggie and Remy, savoring her last night alone with them.

Now, on her wedding day, Ashley rose from the rocking chair, pulling her robe over her thin cotton chemise, and padded downstairs to join Remy, the early riser, for coffee. He sat at the table, handsome in his navy robe and reading glasses, studying the headlines of the *Town Talk* as he sipped heavily creamed coffee.

"Hi, Remy," Ashley tiptoed up behind him, wrapping her arms around his neck and kissed his cheek affectionately. He looked back at her, surprised to see her out of bed.

"Hi, baby. What are you doing up so early?"

"I couldn't sleep," Ashley shrugged nonchalantly, refilling his coffee cup as she poured some for herself. She took the chair next to him, realizing with regret that this would be the last morning that she would be at home as Remy's little girl. The next morning, she would be a married woman, hundreds of miles away from the only home she had ever known. That thought made Ashley a little sad—a little sad and very apprehensive.

"How are you feeling?" Remy took off his reading glasses and examined the odd look on her face with concern.

"Nervous," Ashley peered over the edge of her coffee cup with an uneasy smile on her lips.

"How about physically?"

"Tired and nauseous. But I'm almost to the end of my first trimester, so this too shall pass. That's what they tell me anyway," she laughed lightly, hoping to keep the mood upbeat.

"You going to be okay today?" Remy's eyes met Ashley's and were so full of love that she thought she might cry. Of all the men on Earth, Ashley knew she would always love her father most.

"Remy, I'll be fine," she reassured him, reaching across the table to clasp his hand tightly.

"I'm really going to miss you," Remy said, his voice cracking as he blinked away tears.

"I'm going to miss you too, Remy." Ashley moved to hug his neck tightly. "I love you," she whispered, glad that she had gotten up early to share this private time with him. It would be one of their last quiet moments all day.

The normally calm Maggie was a wreck and spent the entire morning flying around the house in a nervous frenzy. Remy and Ashley found it in their best interest to keep quiet and stay out of her way. At half past noon, Kate and Susanna chauffeured Ashley to the beauty salon, which was alive with talk of the wedding and subsequent reception at The Hotel Bentley. Ashley listened to the chatter absently, watching with dread as the clock on the wall ticked closer to her inevitable union with Rick.

After having her hair done, Ashley had three hours to kill before her six o'clock wedding. The mothers left for the church to meet the florist while Kate drove Ashley home to pick up her dress. The house was empty when they arrived. Remy had gone to play golf with Rick and the groomsmen before picking up his tuxedo and going directly to the church. Ashley wandered deliberately through the house, storing all its precious details in her memory. She climbed the hardwood stairs, moving down the hall to her room, and sank onto the bed, gazing around reflectively. So many memories lingered within the walls of her white eyelet bedroom.

She had grown up in the same house and slept in the same bed for almost twenty-one years. In this room, she, Kate and Susanna had played dolls and had shared their most intimate secrets. This bedroom held the remembrances of the great joys and disappointments of adolescence. She had spent hours in this room on her pink princess telephone with both friends and sweethearts. She had climbed from the window of this room to share one of the first kisses she received from the boy she would love forever.

This was not the wedding day Ashley dreamed of as a small girl. Never once while picturing the most wonderful day of her life did she pretend that she would marry out of a sense of obligation. Not one time did she think about being married because of an unplanned pregnancy. She lay back on the mattress, blinking away her disappointed tears as Kate entered the room.

"Come on, Ashley, cut it out." She tugged playfully at Ashley's outstretched arm. "If you don't stop that silly reminiscing, you'll ruin your makeup."

"Oh Kate," Ashley pushed herself up and sat at the end of her bed. "This is not at all what I imagined my wedding day would be like." Kate sat down next to her, slipping a caring arm around her as Ashley leaned her head on Kate's shoulder. "I always imagined this big, white lace dress with a huge train and yards and yards of tulle veil. I envisioned you and Susanna in gaudy, bright colored dresses, hating every minute you had to wear them."

"Thank God you changed your mind about those dresses," Kate said, rolling her eyes comically.

"The very worst part about it is that I thought I'd be ecstatic on my wedding day, ecstatic and head-over-hills in love with my groom. I guess I always thought I would marry the great love of my life," Ashley revealed sadly. "This is not what I had in mind at all."

"Ashley, Ashley," Kate said soothingly, squeezing her tightly. "You can still back out if you want to. No one would hold it against you, honey."

Ashley raised her head in disbelief. For the first time in her life, Susanna had kept a secret. Kate didn't know the real reason behind her decision to marry Rick, and Ashley decided to let it remain that way.

"No, Kate, I've just got the pre-wedding jitters." Ashley forced a smile and leapt to her feet, pulling Kate up with her as she lied to her for the very first time. "Let's go to the church."

"Stubborn to the end, aren't you?" Kate looked at her sternly, her brow wrinkling as she frowned her disapproval.

"Have you ever known me to be any other way?" Ashley took one last look around the room, then descended the staircase one last time as Ashley Stewart. It was a strange feeling to be leaving her childhood home, knowing that she would never live there again.

At the church, they found Maggie working diligently with the florist. In her fitted dress, simple yet stylish and made of turquoise organza, Maggie looked lovely and much too young to be the mother of the bride. She smiled at Kate and Ashley as they approached with garment bags draped cumbersomely over their arms. Ashley handed her dress to Kate and reached into the florist's box to pick out Maggie's corsage of ivory roses.

"You look gorgeous," Ashley whispered solemnly as she pinned on the corsage.

With shining tears in her holly-green eyes, Maggie embraced her tightly, never wanting to let her go. "I love you, Ashley." Maggie smiled tenderly at her only child. "Be happy, honey, please be happy."

Off the sanctuary, Ashley dressed in the bride's room, gawking in pleased wonder at the reflection in the floor-length mirror. In front of her stood a bride, dressed in an eggshell-hued gown covered in lace and seed pearls, with an off-the-shoulder bodice, full skirt and short train. Her upswept brown hair was adorned with a long veil, her headpiece a simple band of delicate magnolias.

Ashley sighed appreciatively. "Wow! I've never looked like this before!"

Susanna strolled through the doorway, looking on with mixed emotions. "Well, don't get used to that look," she said, slipping into her bridesmaid dress, a long sheath of creamy melon. "You're only supposed to do this once, although I wouldn't count on that in your case."

Ashley located Susanna in the mirror's reflection, scowling a warning in her direction. "That's not a very nice thing to say on my wedding day."

"I only call it like I see it," Susanna said, plopping down on a gray metal folding chair, sliding her dyed-to-match pumps over her stocking feet.

"That's enough, Susanna," Kate was a lovely referee with her upswept blond hair and identical bridesmaid dress. A spasm of irritation crossed her pretty face as she admonished Susanna, humbling her momentarily.

"Sorry," Susanna said, before a wicked smile lit her face and she eyed Ashley devilishly, "but it's not too late to change your mind." She got one last punch in before Ashley turned away and ignored her.

Ashley clutched her bouquet of pale pink roses as the photographer snapped pictures, smiling and posing woodenly with Susanna and Kate, each holding long-stemmed roses trimmed with greenery and ivory ribbons. As the guests began to arrive, Dominique and Celeste LeNoir came back to sneak a peek at Ashley in her dress.

"You're just lovely!" her mother-in-law to be beamed happily as Ashley shyly kissed her cheek.

"Thank you," Ashley whispered faintly, feeling somewhat queasy. The butterflies turning cartwheels in her stomach were starting to get the better of her.

Celeste, beautiful in seafoam green, was next in line to embrace her. "I wish you all the happiness in the world," she spoke very softly into Ashley's ear. "Be patient with Rick, Ashley. He loves you."

Ms. Bobbie breezed in just as the LeNoir ladies were leaving, and stood just inside the doorway with an enraptured expression on her face. "You're a beautiful bride!" she hugged Ashley robustly. "But I never doubted that you would be."

She tilted Ashley's chin up with her index finger and looked squarely into her wide, frightened eyes. "Be happy, Ashley girl. Life is what you make it, kid." Ms. Bobbie flashed one final grin and left, leaving Ashley longing for a wedding day under vastly different circumstances.

As she waited to be called to walk down the aisle, Ashley stood beside the window and stared out, twisting the silver band on her right hand, allowing her thoughts to drift back to Jimmy just one more time before she married. He was the groom she had dreamed of all those years. Jimmy Moreau should have been the great love to grace her ideal wedding day. If things had gone as planned, she and Jimmy would have been preparing to spend the rest of their lives together as husband and wife. To Ashley, fate had been cruel.

Suddenly Kate was there, tapping her gently on the shoulder. "It's time, Ashley," she said, whispering softly in her ear.

The sensation of dread Ashley had suppressed all that day surfaced, and she whirled around to face Kate, feeling as if she was being led off to execution. Before she knew it, Ashley was on Remy's arm, preparing to walk down the aisle. The rest of the ceremony was a blur.

Remy, breathtaking in his black tuxedo, gently supported her arm as they walked down the aisle. In a dreamlike state, Ashley smiled at some of the guests, then stared saucer-eyed at an elegant Rick LeNoir as he watched her walk slowly toward him.

"Oh God, I think I'm going to be sick," Ashley thought while, with quaking knees, she took her place at the altar, gazing woefully at Remy as he presented her trembling hand to Rick.

As the minister asked if there were any objections to this man and this woman being joined in holy matrimony, Ashley hoped for a fleeting moment that Doug would jump out of some clandestine hiding place, object, and whisk her away to parts unknown. But, true to his promise, Doug was absent and the minister began to recite their wedding vows. There, before her friends and family, Ashley Stewart promised to love, honor and cherish Rick LeNoir until the day she died.

Suddenly, the minister pronounced them man and wife and Rick lifted her veil, kissing her with undeniable passion.

"Oh my God, it's over already," Ashley's mind reeled as she reluctantly returned Rick's kiss. It hadn't taken very long at all to change her life forever. They left the church for the reception in a limousine with champagne chilling in the back. Rick popped the cork and filled a glass, handing it to Ashley.

"I really shouldn't," she said, protesting as she pushed the glass away.

"Take it, Ashley," Rick said, giving her a withering stare. "Take it and drink it. One glass will not hurt you. You have to toast to our marriage."

At Rick's insistence, she accepted the glass, deciding it was best not to start the marriage fighting on the way to the reception. Rick smiled his approval and they clicked their glasses together. "To my bride and one hundred years of wedded bliss."

"I'll drink to that," Ashley said, gulping champagne. The champagne somewhat helped to calm her nerves and Ashley began to wish that she could guzzle the entire bottle.

Arriving at their reception, they were greeted by gleeful cheers and catcalls from the rowdy crowd of family and friends. Ashley held tightly onto Rick's arm, smiling radiantly until her face ached. She endured all the obligatory reception requirements: cutting the cake, toasting, and posing for hundreds of photographs. After dancing her first dance with Rick and spinning around the floor in Remy's skillful arms, Ashley finally got a break, separating from Rick to socialize with her friends.

She located Susanna with Mark Lawrence, chattering obnoxiously with Hillary, Melissa, Kate, Mitch Guidry and Scott Jeansonne. Nearby were Cheryl Moreau, Kimberly Seaton and Jeff Thomasee, drinking champagne and eating stuffed mushroom caps. It was almost a high school reunion, although one person was prominently missing. Ashley wasn't certain if she could ever forgive him for deserting her when she needed him most. She missed Doug more than words could describe and longed for his comfort and reassurance.

Even Rick noticed Doug's absence and didn't hesitate to mention it to Ashley. "Wherever is your buddy Doug?" he said scathingly into her ear as he passed by her. "I can't believe that he would desert you on the happiest day of your life."

Ashley smirked at him as he walked past, resisting the childish urge to stick her tongue out at his back. "Who says this is the happiest day of my life, anyway?" she taunted him silently.

All too soon, it was time to leave for her honeymoon night in Dallas. Maggie, Susanna and Kate ascended the grand staircase with Ashley to help her out of her wedding gown and into an ivory going-away dress. The time had come to say goodbye and Ashley hesitated, not wanting to leave.

"Thanks for being here for me today." Ashley hugged Susanna tightly and Susanna got a little teary-eyed in spite of herself.

"That's okay," Susanna said, gruffly, swiping at her eyes with the back of her hand. "You'll need all the support you can get, believe me."

Ashley turned to Kate, embracing her next. "You've been the best friend a girl could ever have. I'm really going to miss you." She used a lace handkerchief to wipe her misty eyes. "I love you, Kate."

"I'm only a phone call away," Kate squeezed Ashley's hands as she moved toward the door with Susanna. "I love you too, honey. Good luck and Godspeed."

Their departure left her alone with a very solemn Maggie. "Well, this is it," Ashley sighed, looking at Maggie, who squared her shoulders and tried to smile. "No crying," Ashley warned her with a small smile.

"Take care of yourself, Ashley. You're expecting a baby and you shouldn't wear yourself out. You make Rick be good to you."

"Maggie, I'll be fine, I promise you. You and Remy raised a fighter. I can take care of myself and my baby."

Pleased with her feisty response, Maggie rewarded Ashley with a sincere smile, pulling her into a warm embrace as Remy tapped lightly on the door.

"They're waiting for you, Ashley," he said, as he opened the door and stepped inside.

Ashley flung herself into his arms, kissing him fiercely. "I love you, Remy," she held onto him tightly as he kissed her forehead, his eyes sad at the loss of his little girl.

"I love you too, baby," he said, taking her hand, and they walked together down the hallway to the landing at the top of the stairs. A crowd gathered at the foot of the staircase as someone yelled out, "Throw the bouquet, Ashley!"

Ashley stepped up to the rail and turned her back to them, glancing over her shoulder once to locate her target and tossed her bouquet over the rail. It landed, as she had planned, in the arms of Susanna Robicheaux, who held it up and cheered loudly.

And with that, the newly married Ashley LeNoir sprinted down the steps to take Rick's hand before they raced through a shower of birdseed to their waiting car. Rick appeared elated, although Ashley didn't understand until much later that it wasn't newly married bliss fueling his pleased smile. It was the fact that he had won the battle. She now belonged exclusively to him.

Arriving in Dallas in the wee hours of Sunday morning, Ashley and Rick checked into their hotel and rode the glass elevator up to their room. Ashley peeked over at him shyly. Rick was exhilarated while she was scared to death. Although she had spent most of the last year with him, it felt so strange to be alone with Rick. Their relationship had taken on a whole new dimension. Ashley no longer felt that she could revel in her independence. Adjusting to her new title of Mrs. Richard Emile LeNoir would take some effort on her part.

Rick unlocked the door to their room, sweeping Ashley effortlessly into his powerful arms, carrying her over the threshold to set her down on the carpeted floor. She smiled timidly and took her bag from his hand, retreating to lock herself in the bathroom.

As she changed into her white satin negligee, a wedding gift from Celeste, Ashley swallowed nervously, wondering incredulously at her newfound shyness. God knows she had slept with this man numerous times in the last nine months and she was expecting his child. But it seemed different now, as if it were out of her hands. Being with Rick was no longer her choice. It was what was expected of her.

Reluctantly she left the protection of the bathroom, padding softly on bare feet across the carpet. Rick watched her with smoldering eyes, meeting her in the center of the room and reaching down to remove the pins from her upswept hair. The thick brown mane tumbled down and lay in shining curls across her shoulders. "I love your long hair," he murmured, gathering the fragrant locks in his fingers. Ashley leaned against him, allowing him to play with her hair, luxuriating in the relaxation his fingers provided. She lifted her face to him, kissing him warmly as he led her to their bed.

There in Dallas, at three o'clock in the morning, Ashley and Rick consummated their marriage. Throughout the night, Rick took her again and again, not so much for his pleasure, but to remind Ashley that she belonged only to him. Finally, as the sun began to rise on the horizon, Rick closed his eyes, holding her tightly in his arms as he drifted off to sleep. Ashley studied his chiseled good looks with uneasy eyes, praying that she could find happiness with Rick LeNoir.

Ashley had wanted change and she got it. Life in Oklahoma City was different from anything she had ever known. She arrived in Oklahoma on a Sunday in early July, welcomed by sunshine, low humidity and temperatures soaring near one hundred.

"It's so hot here," she said to Rick, stepping from the car as he filled the tank with gas.

"And this is not yet the hottest month of the summer," Rick said, smiling as Ashley fanned herself with a magazine. "Just wait until August."

As they reached the outskirts of Oklahoma City, Ashley perked up, pressing her face against the glass of the car window and staring eagerly at her new surroundings. She found the modern architecture appealing, awestruck by the skyscrapers, sparkling brilliantly as the rays of afternoon sunshine reflected off thousands of windows above the streets of downtown.

She was fascinated with the highway system, interstate connected to interstate by way of bypass loops and bridges, with very few lazy two-lane roads by which to travel. Astonished by the sheer volume of traffic, Ashley gawked in horror at the speeding cars around her.

"Will I ever learn my way around here?" she said, tearing her eyes away from the heavily populated roadway to stare doubtfully at Rick.

"By the time school starts in August, you'll be an old pro at driving around town." Rick laughed as he reassured her. "I have faith in you, Ashley. After all your midnight drives down those foggy Louisiana highways, this should be a piece of cake."

Ashley settled into their northwest Oklahoma City home, delighted with Rick's choice in houses. The LeNoir residence, located in a cozy neighborhood of patio homes just off one of the main drags, was a small two-story of gray brick, adorned by tall windows that allowed soft light to spill abundantly into their living space. Just inside the stenciled glass front door was a tiled foyer that lead to a great room with a stone fireplace in one direction, and to the master bedroom and bath in the other. Off the great room was a large kitchen with a red brick floor, equipped with a center island and tiled countertops of dove gray.

Upstairs were Rick's office, another bathroom, and a small bedroom with a skylight, which Rick begrudgingly agreed could serve as the nursery. Rick had already filled the house with many of his expensive antique furnishings and accessories, turning the starter home into a small-scale showplace.

"I'll leave the bed linens and towels up to you," Rick said, watching Ashley roam through the house, opening cabinets and peeking into closets. "But show some good taste, Ashley, and promise me that you won't do anything too prissy and feminine." He teased her with a slight twinkle in his eye, leaning against the wall of his office, surrounded by his computer equipment and office furniture, looking so devilishly handsome that Ashley tiptoed up to kiss him playfully.

"Do you like the house, Ashley?" he asked, draping his arm around her shoulder as they descended the light gray-carpeted steps into the great room.

"Yes, Rick, I love it! It's just perfect," Ashley beamed up at him. She did love the house and was beginning to feel a little more comfortable with her new life. Ms. Bobbie had told her that life is what you made it and Ashley was determined to make her life with Rick wonderful.

As Rick brought the suitcases in from the car, Ashley stood in the living room by the sliding door, studying their back yard and the open fields surrounding them.

"What would you like for dinner?" Rick came up behind her, sliding his arms securely around her waist. "I won't make you cook on your first night home."

"That's awfully diplomatic of you," Ashley said laughingly. "Let's do something easy. How about a pizza?"

Over dinner, Rick presented Ashley with a map of the city, sliding it across the table to her. "This will help you find your way around tomorrow."

"My way around?" Ashley lifted a surprised brow. "Where am I going?"

"You should go by financial aid at the college and get your loans finalized," Rick reminded her.

"But I thought you would take me to do that."

"Ashley, I have to work. You are a married woman now and it's high time you started acting like one."

"What if I get lost?" she argued with him, not particularly caring for the idea of driving around a strange city alone.

"Then you'll ask for directions," Rick said, tossing his crumpled napkin onto his empty dinner plate and scowling at her impatiently. "Honestly, Ashley, I never thought that you could be so timid. I thought I was marrying someone with an independent streak."

"You did." Ashley lifted her chin to him defiantly, insulted by his suggestion that she was chicken. "I'm not timid, I'm just a little intimidated by trying to find my way around."

"Well, you'll have to get over that or you will be spending a lot of time here at the house alone. I have too much to do at the office to baby-sit you."

Ashley picked at her pizza silently, pouting, unused to being dismissed in this manner. Remy had never been this way with her or with Maggie. Recognizing that he had hurt her feelings, Rick gently lifted her chin with his finger and met her sullen gaze with a look of sparkling amusement.

"You'll be fine," he assured her with a smile. "I wouldn't set you loose on this city if I didn't believe that you could take care of yourself."

Ashley tried to smile as he moved toward her, pushing away her tremendous feeling of homesickness as he lifted her up from the chair and kissed her inviting mouth passionately before leaving a trail of hot kisses down the length of her throat.

"I love you, Ashley," Rick said, murmuring in a husky voice as he gazed provocatively into her eyes. "Let me show you how much." He carried her easily into their bedroom and they christened their new home by making love between the crisp sheets of their sleigh bed before falling asleep wrapped snuggly in each other's arms.

Rick was an early riser, leaving for work every morning promptly at seven thirty and never returning before seven every evening. On their first morning in the new house, Ashley rolled out of bed with him, sipping coffee as he dressed for work then walked him to the front door to kiss him goodbye.

"What are you making for dinner tonight?" she asked him, straightening his tie and kissing him affectionately. "You know I don't cook."

Rick tapped her nose lightly with his index finger, smiling down at her teasingly. "You had better learn. You have to do something to justify your existence here."

"Isn't being your wife enough to justify my existence?"

"Almost," he kissed the top of her head and pulled on his suit jacket, leaving her alone to fend for herself.

Ashley spent the summer battling homesickness, pushing away her longings for the sultry Louisiana days of summer by learning her way around the city by way of her trusty map, tracing her routes and getting lost dozens of times but never telling Rick that she had done so. She wouldn't dream of giving him the satisfaction of knowing that she had really lost her way. Sticking close to home, she became familiar with the northwest side of town, finding grocery stores and specialty shops, studying cookbooks and recipes as she settled into a routine of lonely domestication.

She blocked all thoughts of Doug. After years of close friendship, his renouncement of their relationship was the ultimate betrayal. Yet, she yearned to talk to him, missing him tremendously every single time he came to mind, so she pushed away his image, storing it in the back of her mind with the other things too painful to remember.

Ashley enjoyed frequent phone calls to her parents, entertaining them with her tales of the big city. Maggie and Remy were relieved that she seemed happy. Ashley didn't tell them how much she missed home, only that she missed them. She painted for them a picture of newly wedded bliss, wanting to convince them with her words as much as she wanted to convince herself.

Kate was a poor correspondent but Susanna called habitually, via the 800-number at the bank. She shared hometown gossip, keeping Ashley abreast of the important events in Pineville and the surrounding areas. She didn't buy Ashley's act of absolute exhilaration. Instead, Susanna demanded the truth of Ashley's domestic situation.

"Don't bother to lie to me, *Mrs. LeNoir*," she said gruffly. "I know a line of bullshit when I hear it. I want the truth and I want it now. Don't make me come up there." Ashley would laugh at Susanna's idle threats, insisting that she and Rick were fine, that all was peachy.

For the most part, in the beginning, Rick *was* wonderful, and he and Ashley got along very well. However, as the summer progressed, Ashley discovered that there were two sides to Rick, and those sides were as different as night and day.

On one hand, when Rick wanted to be with her, he was terrific: warm, attentive and charming. During their first week in Oklahoma City, Rick took Ashley to his office, proudly introducing his lovely bride to his new coworkers. In the evenings after work, he showed her around town in an effort to make her more comfortable with her new surroundings, frequently taking her to dinner, a movie or to a coffeehouse to enjoy her favorite gourmet coffees. On the weekends they visited the Omniplex, the space and science museum, the Oklahoma City Zoo and later, Remington Park, the state-of-the-art race track, attending the horse races after Ashley's twenty-first birthday the end of July. Ashley enjoyed being with Rick when his mood was good. He was again the man who captured her heart in Monroe, entertaining her with his charm and intelligence and making love to her with accomplished skill and passion. When Rick was happy, Ashley was happy.

But on the flip side, there was the preoccupied, ultra conservative, anal retentive, overbearing workaholic that Ashley had to contend with. Whenever Rick was working, which became more and more frequent as time went on, there were to be no interruptions under any circumstances. If Ashley even dared to attempt conversation him on those occasions, the reaction she received varied from clear annoyance to the ranting and tantrums of a small child.

Ashley tried not to get her feelings hurt. She knew that Rick's new job put a great deal of pressure on him and speculated that when he was more settled in his new position, he would have more time to spend with her. She would just have to be more patient.

Rick was a stickler when it came to his household, expecting everything to remain neat and orderly at all times. The house was to stay immaculate, the laundry to be done daily, and the meals served in a timely fashion. He, of course, was not a participant in this obligation to his obsession, and it was Ashley's duty as his wife to run his household and earn her keep. Ashley had a real problem with this side of him, her independence and pride greatly insulted by his male chauvinism. He had no right to be so hard on her. After all she was a twenty-one-year-old child trying to adjust to being the wife of a man of twenty-six.

Their real troubles surfaced as Ashley began losing her figure and her once flat tummy began to swell ever so slightly. The more pregnant she appeared, the less interest Rick showed in her. Still hating the idea of a child, Ashley's pregnancy annoyed Rick to no end, and he became obsessed with keeping her pleasing to his eye. He nagged her daily to exercise, dragging her to the gym with him to walk on the treadmill while he lifted weights, and monitored her caloric and fat intake, eyeing her irritably if she ever strayed from his healthy diet plan.

"I'm only doing this for you," Rick told her, standing beside her at the gym, wearing gray wind pants and a tank top, his brow glistening with perspiration, watching his pregnant wife pant as she walked briskly on the treadmill. "I wouldn't push you so hard if a good diet and exercise weren't so good for the baby."

"Like you care what's good for the baby," Ashley grumbled silently. That was the first time Rick had mentioned the baby since they had been in Oklahoma. Her feelings were hurt and she wondered if they would ever again have the relationship that they once had.

As summer drew to a close, it seemed that Rick no longer welcomed affection from her, and became more and more short tempered with her and whatever he considered to be her shortcomings. The more irritated Rick became, the harder Ashley tried to please him. She dressed beautifully for him, wearing delicate silks and linens, allowing the heavy weight of her hair to flow loosely past her shoulders, ignoring the stifling summer heat to give him free access to run his fingers through it if he so desired. She spent long hours in the kitchen, covered from head to toe in flour as she scanned his cookbooks, preparing elaborate meals in an effort to remain in his good graces. She kept the house spotless, just the way Rick liked it, scrubbing and vacuuming for hours on a daily basis. She received little thanks for her efforts and quickly became discouraged.

From the list of doctors given to her by Lisa Watson, Ashley chose Tim Bergen, an obstetrician practicing at nearby Baptist Hospital. At sixteen weeks pregnant, she checked in with the receptionist for her first doctor's appointment in late July and was whisked from the waiting room by Dr. Bergen's nurse, Sarah, for her weight and blood pressure. Sarah showed her to an exam room, giving her a tissue paper gown to change into as she waited for Dr. Bergen.

Following a short wait, Tim Bergen, a robust teddy bear of a man, breezed into the exam room wearing blue hospital scrubs, carrying her chart wedged under one sturdy arm as he extended his free hand to her. "Tim Bergen," he introduced himself with a jovial smile. He was a young doctor, early forty-something, with straight sandy hair and round glasses. His warm disposition and frequent hearty laughter endeared him to Ashley immediately.

"Ashley LeNoir," Ashley shook his hand, greeting him comfortably as Dr. Bergen raised an intrigued eyebrow.

"Judging by that accent, I'd say that you're not from around here, are you?" he asked in reference to her Louisiana drawl. He took the chair opposite her, scanning quickly through the pages of her medical record, his face breaking into a broad smile. "Lisa Watson! Is that who sent you to me?"

"Yes, she's my doctor in Louisiana."

"So she's in Louisiana now?" Dr. Bergen laughed fondly. "I haven't seen Lisa in years. She was my favorite classmate and one feisty cookie."

"If that's the case, she hasn't changed much," Ashley said with a wink.

"That's what I was afraid of," Dr. Bergen said, still grinning ear to ear as he lifted his stethoscope from his lab coat pocket. "I may just have to call her and thank her for the referral."

Ashley discovered love that day, falling head over heels for the child within her womb as, through Tim Bergen's stethoscope, she listened to her baby's heartbeat for the very first time, making the child more real to her, and not just an imaginary little person.

"Amazing," Ashley said softly, gazing up at Dr. Bergen with wide green eyes.

"One of God's greatest gifts," Dr Bergen agreed, patting her kindheartedly on the shoulder. "Ashley LeNoir, you're doing just great. Get with Sarah and set up your next appointment. Until then, just continue what you have been doing." After asking if she had any questions, he moved to the door. "Then I'll see you in four weeks," he flashed a friendly grin and opened the door to exit.

"Thank you, Dr. Bergen," Ashley said and he turned to look back at her.

"Call me Tim. All my patients do."

That evening, Ashley climbed the stairs to Rick's office and made an effort to discuss her doctor's appointment with him, but Rick showed little interest, ignoring her for the most part as he continued to plug away on the computer keyboard. Disappointed, she went back downstairs and picked up the telephone to share her news instead with Maggie and Remy.

CHAPTER TWENTY-FOUR

In late August, three days after her second doctor's appointment with Tim Bergen, school finally started. Ashley left for the Health Sciences Center early, just after six-thirty that morning, kissing Rick affectionately as she ran out the front door, backpack in hand, feeling as excited as a kindergartner. After two long months of sheer boredom, she was hungry for both knowledge and human contact.

Plagued with a heavy load and seven o'clock classes, the eighteen hours Ashley was required to carry would not be easy. Anatomy, physiology, pharmaceutical calculations, medicinal chemistry, therapeutics. Ashley studied the names of her classes, shaking her head in wonder. "Good lord!" she exclaimed, feeling a little overwhelmed. "No more blow-off classes for me. I've hit the big time."

There were seventy-seven in her class, the majority of which were Oklahomans, but other regions of the southwest were represented by students from Texas, Kansas, Arkansas and Missouri. Ashley held the distinction of being the only Ragin' Cajun from Louisiana and quickly noted that most of her classmates were close to her in age, but unlike her, most were single. There were a few married students, but Ashley was definitely the only pregnant one.

The first-year class at the College of Pharmacy was a likable crew, and out of seventy-seven students, there were six who became especially close friends.

Ashley met Eleanor Holman almost immediately. Ellie was an attractive, twenty-year old brown-eyed blond, born and raised in Oklahoma City. A lifelong tomboy and avid athlete, Ellie engaged in league play of softball and volleyball, and absolutely lived to water ski. She was vivacious and outgoing with contagious energy and zest for living, and Ashley felt an instant kinship to her.

Ashley became acquainted with the others over lunch at The Painted Desert, a southwest-style café where Ellie waited tables in the evening. Seated to her left was Ava Ryder, twenty-five and married, with one son and a degree in biochemistry. She and her husband Michael lived near Ashley on the northwest side of town and after several years of working for a local oil company, Ava returned to school to pursue her degree in pharmacy. With high intelligence and a sweet disposition, Ava served as the group's cheerleader and mother hen, keeping them on the straight and narrow path toward graduation.

Seated next to Ava was Greg Benning, Mr. GQ, a smooth talking, Porsche-driving Casanova from Little Rock. Greg's best buddy was Sean Farmer from Missouri, the incredibly handsome son of an independent pharmacy owner, notorious for turning the head of every female within a twenty-mile radius.

And enjoying an icy cold Corona with his cheese nachos was Matt Whitford, the rowdy OU party boy with an adolescent grin and a mouth that would put Susanna to shame. Having done his pre-pharmacy studies at the University of Oklahoma in Norman, he was the very epitome of how Ashley pictured the typical fraternity guy—attractive in a disheveled sort of way, usually attired in torn, faded jeans and a T-shirt boasting some inappropriate slogan or statement.

It was with Matt that Ashley, acting on a tip, secured her pharmacy intern job at University Hospital, one of the teaching hospitals on the Health Science Center campus. As interns, they were required to earn fifteen hundred hours of on-the-job training before being allowed to take state board exams, some of which came from curriculum but much that had to be obtained on their own. As the others already had leads on jobs, Ellie suggested that Matt and Ashley check with the student secretary, Sheila, for possible job openings. Sheila Banks worked in the front office on the first floor of the pharmacy school and served as the fountain of information for students and faculty alike.

"Why, as a matter of fact, I do," Sheila smiled, answering Ashley's inquiry about a job. She reached into the filing cabinet behind her desk and pulled out a file folder. "I had a call from Patricia Wallace over at University Hospital. She has openings for three freshman interns. You might want to go over and talk with her."

After getting directions to University, Ashley left the office hurriedly, almost colliding with Matt in the hall. "Hey, what's your hurry?" he said with a grin, steadying her as she wobbled, thrown off balance as she avoided running him down.

"I have a lead on some available jobs," Ashley told him. "Do you want to go with me to talk to the Director of Pharmacy at University?"

"Yeah, that'd be great. Let me stop by my car and change shirts," Matt said, taking Ashley by the arm as they walked together to the parking lot. Unlocking his rusted out Chevy Nova, Matt leaned into the back seat heavily littered with crumpled fast food sacks and aluminum soda cans, yanking a button-down oxford shirt from its hanger. Stripping off his fluorescent yellow T-shirt, he flung it carelessly back into the car and pulled on the starched dress shirt, buttoning it quickly as he and Ashley walked down the sidewalk in the direction of the hospital.

Ashley viewed the entire process with an entertained smile, shaking her head slowly. "Do you always keep spare starched shirts in the back seat of your car?" she asked, hiding the laughter rising in her throat.

Matt shot her a mischievous grin, the corners of his cobalt blue eyes crinkling with mirth as he shrugged nonchalantly. "Sure, I do," he said. "You never know when you might have a date with some hot babe."

Reaching their destination, Matt and Ashley rode the crowded elevator to the inpatient pharmacy, located on the fifth floor of University Hospital. Sheila had phoned ahead to let Ms. Wallace know that they were coming and, after ringing the bell outside of the thick metal door, they were admitted by one of the pharmacy technicians and led down the long corridor leading to the paper-cluttered office of Director of Pharmacy Patricia Wallace.

She was a handsome woman in her mid-fifties with a short blond bob, dressed immaculately in a blue power suit. After shaking hands in introduction, Ms. Wallace directed Matt and Ashley to take seats and, after obtaining some background information from them, launched into a concise description of the available intern jobs.

The pharmacy interns worked the weekend shifts during the school year, combined with weekdays and evenings during school breaks and summer. The weekend hours were from seven o'clock a.m. to three-thirty p.m. or two-thirty to eleven p.m. on Saturday and Sundays, rotating shifts every other weekend. The general job description included filling the medication carts with the medications ordered for patients, learning how to prepare sterile intravenous medications, delivering orders to the hospitals floors, and putting away medication shipments. She concluded her speech by drawing a deep breath and asking, "Does that sound like something either of you would be interested in?"

Matt and Ashley exchanged an eager glance then answered in unison, "Sure."

Ms. Wallace seemed pleased by their enthusiasm and extended her hand to Ashley, then to Matt in congratulations. "Then it looks like you've got yourselves a job."

"You are not going to work every weekend!" Rick exploded, not at all pleased at the news of her newly acquired intern position. Ashley eyed him apprehensively, watching as he paced their living room like a caged animal, agitation written all over his face. She waited before replying, anxious to hear what he would say next.

"I'll never see you." He stopped pacing to sit next to her on the sofa, his face relaxing as she put a soft hand on his thigh.

"I know, Rick, but it's not really as bad as it sounds," she said, soothing him gently with her reassuring tone. "I'll only work eight hour shifts. You can work while I work, then, when I get home, we can spend the rest of the day together," she smiled, regarding him persuasively with flirtatious green eyes.

His stubborn heart melted slightly as he glanced down at her and he almost gave in to her, but not quite. "I just don't think that you should have to work and go to school," he said. "That's just ridiculous."

"Rick, I have to work these hours in order to sit for the state board exam. It does me no good to finish pharmacy school if I can't get a license." Ashley laid it on the line for him, battling tenaciously with him until finally, after lengthy protests and justifications, Ashley convinced him to let her take the job.

She started her job in September, on the early shift, yawning outside the door as she rang the bell. Steven Schneider, one of the second-year students she recognized from school, let her in, giving her the combination to the lock so that she didn't have to keep ringing the bell. The inpatient pharmacy consisted of a substantially-sized central room, off of which was a large storeroom for drugs and IV fluids, a locked vault housing narcotics, a sterile room for preparation of intravenous medications and a long corridor leading to the break room and administration offices.

Taking Ashley by the arm, Steve guided her to the far side of the room, introducing her to one of the day pharmacists, Sam O'Brien. Sam was seated at a desk in front of a row of windows that overlooked the brick wall of the adjacent building, telephone cradled against his shoulder as he took orders from a physician in ICU. He was slender and middle-aged with thick salt-and-pepper hair and a pencil-line mustache above a satirical grin. Sam was the anchor of the day crew, spending long hours holding down the fort while entertaining the interns with great off-color stories and some of the dirtiest jokes Ashley had ever heard.

In charge of the IV room was Meg Hall, a petite woman in her thirties with severely short black hair and round blue eyes behind copper-rimmed glasses. When Ashley entered the room with Steve, Meg stood beside one of the vented hoods, supervising an intern who was manufacturing an IV. Ashley watched with great interest, peeking through the Plexiglas window of the hood as the student drew medication from a tiny glass vial, measuring it precisely with a syringe, and injected it into a bag of dextrose.

"You'll learn how to do all this after you've been here for a while," Steve told her before calling out to Meg. "Hey, Meg, meet Ashley."

Meg smiled warmly, introducing herself to Ashley and rolling her eyes in Steve's direction with a playful grin. "I just hope that these guys, especially Steve here, won't be bad influences on you."

"You know that we will be," Steve joked with her, slinging his arm around Ashley's shoulder mischievously. "This little girl right here needs to be corrupted."

Ashley's first duty of the day was to help Steve deliver the med carts to the hospital floors. They moved to the fill area where another intern, Roseanne

Shapiro, a transplant from Brooklyn, busily filled patient orders, smacking gum obnoxiously as she sang to the blaring radio.

"I fill 'em and you deliver 'em!" she barked out to Steve, pushing the six-foot high cart toward him. She nodded her wiry head of dark hair enthusiastically as Steve acquainted her with Ashley. "Glad to meet you. Hope you catch on quickly," she told Ashley with a saucy grin.

Up on the floor, Steve showed Ashley the ropes, exchanging carts in the med rooms of various nursing stations. Steve was a flirt and knew all the nurses, hailing them by name as he and Ashley pushed their carts past them.

"Hey, Stevie," called a cute nurse from behind her cubicle at the ninth floor nurses station. "Where's Jack?"

Steve's robust laughter echoed loudly along the hallway as he rolled his eyes wickedly at her question. "Evenings, Sandy, evenings," he reminded her, grinning as he wheeled the cart out of the med room.

Ashley scurried behind him, trotting to keep up as he sent the cart racing on its wheels around the corner toward the elevator. "Who's Jack?" she asked curiously, stepping onto the elevator, helping Steve pull the empty cart safely past the closing doors as they rode down to the pharmacy.

"Jack Chambers, one of the evening pharmacists," Steve said. "Avid sportsman and best damn poker player I've ever known."

Ashley was surprised how quickly the day passed, noting the time in astonishment when Matt's image appeared on the screen monitoring the front door, ringing the bell as he arrived for the evening shift.

"How is it?" he asked cautiously as Ashley let him in the door.

"Oh, it's fine," she assured him with a smile. "You'll fit right in."

She brought him inside, leading him to the desk where the day crew surrounded Sam, laughing as they listened to one of his crude anecdotes. As with Ashley, they welcomed Matt with open arms, putting him at ease with their cheerful introductions and repartee.

Ashley was seated across the desk from Sam, sorting patient orders when the front door opened again, admitting a tall, athletically framed figure dressed strikingly in starched Ralph Lauren, his tie flying over his shoulder as he breezed into the room.

"Hey, Jack!" Ashley did a double take as the day crew hailed him, staring as he crossed the floor on great-looking legs, almost as great as Mitch Guidry's.

"Hey, guys! How's it going?" he responded with a grin and Ashley craned her neck to watch as he strolled casually down the corridor toward the break room. So, this was Jack Chambers. No wonder the nurses inquired after his whereabouts.

"My God," Ashley said under her breath, shaking her head in wonder.

Roseanne, hands on her broad hips, stood watching her expression, smirking at Ashley's astonished face. "He'll be back," she said, laughing as Ashley blushed guiltily under her knowing gaze.

Roseanne patted her hand reassuringly. "It's okay, honey. We all look at him like that. Married, unmarried, gay or straight, every woman I know is in awe of Jack. The nurses up on the floor fight over him, I swear to God."

An extremely attractive man, Jack appeared to be around the same age as Rick, with a head full of softly curling hair in the most unique shade of cinnamon, almost the color of tarnished pennies. Ashley gaped admiringly as he came back up the hall, pausing as Steve introduced him to Matt Whitford. Jack had a terrific smile, engaging with straight rows of pearly white teeth, and breathtaking eyes of rain forest green, surrounded by an abundance of thick dark lashes. Jolting herself back to reality, Ashley buried her head in her work, forcing her eyes to stay averted from Jack's charismatic persona. She listened with keen ears to his laughter, hearing the rumblings of their deep voices as Jack, Steve and Matt exchanged dueling male-bonding stories.

"Hey, you're new too." Ashley looked up with a start to find Jack standing there, smiling down at her as he watched her work.

"Hi, I'm Ashley." Sounding calmer than she felt, Ashley casually extended her small hand to him.

Jack took her hand and held it warmly, his eyes enchanting her as he spoke, "Hi, Ashley, I'm Jack Chambers."

"Yes, I know. Your reputation precedes you," Ashley told him, managing to tear her gaze away from his incredible eyes. Jack Chambers was quite captivating.

He threw his head back in surprised laughter, intrigued by her witty comeback. "Oh yeah?" he said with mirthful eyes. "And what did my fine colleagues tell you about me?"

"Only that you're a great sportsman and the best poker player around."

Jack dismissed her notion with a nonchalant gesture of his hand. "Ah, that's nothing, I come from a long line of overachievers." He sat on the edge of the desk, leaning his face closer to hers. "But did they mention that I love women? All women, young, old, fat, thin, I love 'em all."

Ashley snickered, ducking her head to hide her amused grin.

"Well, you're obviously happily married," Jack said, observing the wedding band on her left ring finger.

"Well, I'm married anyway," Ashley said with a shrug of her shoulders.

Jack noted her reluctance to elaborate on her marriage and quickly changed the subject, not wanting to make his newly found friend uncomfortable. "How was your first day?"

"It was fun."

Jack raised a skeptical brow. "Fun?" he looked at Sam quizzically. "Sam, what's been going on around here? Ashley here says she's having fun."

Sam grunted doubtfully. "Sounds like Ashley needs a life," he said, a bit cynically.

Jack glanced pointedly down at Ashley's protruding stomach. "Seems to me that Ashley may have more of a life than we do, Sam."

Ashley blushed profusely with embarrassment while Matt, who walked up in time to hear the end of their conversation, busted out laughing. "That was great!" he chuckled to Jack.

Ashley rolled her eyes at them, turning her back so that they couldn't see her grinning ear to ear, delighted with their good-natured teasing.

Yes, she decided as she drove her Corolla down the Centennial Expressway toward home, this job just might turn out to be her salvation. Her home life was a joke. With each passing day, her pregnancy became more and more obvious and Rick became more and more withdrawn. She was lonely, hungry for companionship. With Ellie, Matt and the gang at school she had found friendship and was now pretty certain that she would have good friends at work too. She had enjoyed her first day with the high-spirited pharmacy staff and looked forward to working with them again the following weekend.

Her ultrasound was scheduled for the middle of September and once again, Ashley asked Rick if he wanted to come to the ultrasound appointment with her, foolishly hoping that if Rick saw his child, he might be able to feel something for it.

Rick was upstairs in his office, scowling in frustration as he stared at his computer screen, perplexed by some sort of problem. He glanced impatiently at Ashley as she stood beside him, snarling in response to her question. "Why would I?"

"Why wouldn't you want to see the first picture of your baby?"

"Ashley, I've told you before, I have no interest in children." He turned away from her, focusing his eyes back onto the screen. "I wish that you would quit pushing it on me the way that you do."

Ashley, particularly hormonal and emotional that afternoon, felt the hot tears flood her eyes as Rick's remarks got the better of her. "Why did we get married then?" she said, shooting daggers at him with her look. "I thought we settled this before the wedding. I never would've married you if I'd known that you didn't want the baby." She sobbed, her voice quavering as she covered her face with her hands.

Rick looked up, rolling his eyes, clearly exasperated with her show of emotion. "Ashley, I never told you that I wanted that baby," he said caustically. "I wanted you, that's why we got married. You are my wife and you are mine. That baby is yours. I want no part of it. Giving it my name should be enough, even for you."

Ashley lowered her hands to glare at him, hating him so much at that moment that she couldn't speak. If she didn't get out of there, she would be tempted to slap his arrogant face. Deciding that would probably be a bad idea, she swallowed hard, gulping back her lingering sobs, and held her head high in defiance.

"I'm going for a walk," she told him hotly.

"That's an excellent idea," Rick said, his icy stare unwavering as he dismissed her, watching her through narrowed eyes as she flounced angrily from the room.

Ashley marched down the stairs and out of the house, slamming the front door resoundingly behind her. She walked quickly down the street and onto the next block, turning the corner before her frustrated, angry tears returned, choking her as she cussed Rick LeNoir for every inch of his life. She vented loudly, calling him every name in the book before realizing how she must look, stomping down the road, fuming to herself. She wiped her eyes, stopping her furious tirade before the neighbors had her committed, and paused to rest, panting heavily as she caught her breath.

"Hey, sexy pharmacy student!"

Startled, Ashley glanced around for the source of the voice and spied Jack Chambers getting out of his Suburban in front of a house one street over from her own. "Jack?" she said, calling out to him in surprise.

Jack strolled over to where she stood, becoming alarmed as he studied her tear-streaked face. "Hey, Ashley, are you okay?" he asked, putting his arm around her shoulder. "What in the hell happened? Are you hurt?"

"No, I'm not hurt," she said, running her fingertips under her eyes to remove her streaked mascara. "Just had a fight with my husband, that's all."

"That's all? You look like your heart is breaking in two. Must've been one helluva fight."

"It was," Ashley sighed heavily and Jack took her by the elbow, guiding her across the street toward his red-bricked, two-story house.

"Come over to the porch and sit down. I'll get you something to drink and you can tell me all about it." He took her around back and settled her into a deck chair underneath the arbor on his back porch then entered the house through French doors, returning with a cold glass of lemonade that he placed into her outstretched hand.

Ashley sipped the lemonade, eyeing her surroundings appreciatively as she drank. "I like your house," she said, smiling up at him as she set her glass on the redwood patio table beside her.

"Thanks, I'm pretty fond of it myself." Jack sat down in the chair next to hers, observing her with kind eyes as he leaned back in his chair, leaning his chin against his clasped hands as he studied her contemplatively.

Ashley peeked at him shyly, liking the way he looked in casual clothing. He wore a navy-and-gray-striped rugby shirt, snug Levi's and white leather tennis shoes, appearing totally different from the starched shirt, pleated pants, loafer-wearing pharmacist she had met on Saturday. He looked different, but he still looked great.

"You must live close by," he observed.

"What, you don't think this roly-poly body can make it very far on foot?" she teased him slyly. "Actually, yes, I live one street over, on Redbud Court."

"Cool," Jack nodded pleasantly, crossing his ankle over the top of his knee as he shifted in his chair. "Do you want to tell me about that fight?"

Ashley didn't know why, but she found herself telling Jack Chambers about her history with Rick, including the fight that they'd had when she found out she was pregnant and how she'd thought that the baby situation had been resolved before they had married. "So now, I'm six months pregnant and Rick isn't any closer to wanting this baby. How could anyone not want his own child?" she said, looking Jack's way.

Jack shook his head, his eyes flashing angrily. "That lousy bastard," he said, muttering his opinion bitterly. Ashley blinked at him, taken slightly aback by his blunt declaration, and Jack glanced at her sheepishly. "I'm sorry. That was out of line," he said.

Over the shock of his impassioned statement, Ashley found herself agreeing with him. "No, you weren't out of line. I've wanted to call him that many times over the last several months," she confessed with a small chuckle.

"I just can't believe that he coerced you into marrying him and now is treating you this way."

"I should've known better," Ashley said thoughtfully. "But what could I do? An illegitimate child is an illegitimate child."

"True, but having a child outside of marriage isn't exactly uncommon these days. The last I'd heard, we'd left the Dark Ages, Ashley."

"Not in the Deep South they haven't," Ashley said with a small giggle, meeting Jack's amused gaze.

"So what will you do?"

Ashley shrugged her shoulders extravagantly. "Nothing before the baby comes. I still want to have this baby in wedlock. Then I'll decide what to do," she said, hoisting herself up out of the chair. "I better go before he starts looking for me. I wouldn't want him to find me here with you."

Jack pretended to be hurt, pushing out his bottom lip in an exaggerated pout. "Thanks a lot."

"No offense," Ashley laughed, patting his shoulder comfortingly as she started to walk away. "It's just that Rick has a bit of a jealous streak, regardless of the fact that I look like a baby whale. Finding me with another man after the fight we've had would not make for a pleasant evening."

"I understand," Jack said with a cynical smile. "I'm divorced myself."

Ashley turned, casting a doubtful look at him from over her shoulder. "I find it hard to believe that any woman would leave you."

Jack shrugged, forcing a cheerful expression onto his face. "That's a long story for another time," he said nonchalantly.

Ashley nodded, accepting that there was more to Jack Chambers than met the eye. "Thanks for listening, Jack," she said, grateful to have a friend in whom to confide. She barely knew him, but there was something about him that drew her to him. She felt like she could confess anything to Jack Chambers.

"Any time, Ashley. I'm always here for you." Jack watched her as she walked away, his concern for her leaping into his eyes. Ashley looked back at him, grinning widely as she waved, rounding the corner for home.

Rick was waiting for her when she came in the front door, pacing the great room angrily, his eyes smoldering, his fists convulsing with suppressed rage. He glared at her as she walked into the room, clipping his words as he spoke. "Where have you been, Ashley?"

"Walking," she said curtly, refusing to look at him as she kicked off her shoes, leaving them in the middle of the floor to annoy him.

"Where did you walk?" Rick narrowed his eyes suspiciously. "You've been gone a long time."

"Around the neighborhood. What does it matter, really?" she sighed, not wanting to discuss anything with him, and started across the foyer toward the bedroom.

"Don't give me that attitude," Rick said sharply, gritting his teeth as he suppressed his fury.

Ashley should have kept her mouth shut, but was too angry, empowered by her heart to heart with Jack. "I'll give you any attitude that I want!" she said, her voice rising hysterically. "How dare you deceive me! Why did you force me into marrying you? Why didn't you just let me go when I broke off our engagement, you bastard!"

His face changed from red to purple and in two quick strides, Rick was across the room, grabbing a handful of Ashley's hair and yanking her head toward him. Ashley screamed out in pain as his palm streaked smartly across her cheek.

"Stop it now," Rick said, his eyes seething rage as he wrapped her hair more tightly in his hand. Ashley, frightened by his crazed look, abruptly stopped screaming, and stared into his stony expression with wide intimidated eyes.

"I told you earlier, I married you because I wanted you," he said, his voice lowering to a stern drawl. "I wanted to marry you no matter what. You're mine now and you will show me proper respect."

He abruptly let go of her hair, pushing her down onto the couch with a powerful shove. Ashley never took her eyes from his face, not trusting him enough to turn her back on him. "You will never speak to me that way again, you got that?" he leaned down into her face, leering at her arrogantly. "That's not rhetorical, Ashley. Answer me. You got it?"

"I got it," Ashley said, whispering hoarsely as she watched him grab his car keys from the kitchen countertop.

"I'm going out." Rick stalked out of the house without a second look back, slamming the door with a thunderous bang. Ashley stared at the vibrating glass in the front door, raising her hand to gingerly touch her smarting cheekbone, loathing Rick LeNoir with every fiber of her being.

Ashley had seen him angry before, but never like this. This man wasn't the man she had known in Monroe. She found it so hard to believe that the man who had been so charming to her in the beginning had turned out to be such a monster, making her wonder if she had gotten the real story behind his break up with Teri. If Rick had behaved anything like this with Teri, Ashley certainly didn't blame her for running as far away from him as she could.

Only three more months until the baby came, she reminded herself as she walked slowly into the kitchen to put ice on her throbbing cheek. Just three never-ending, nail-biting, nerve-racking months and she could walk away from Rick and their hellish nightmare of a marriage.

The next morning Rick acted as if nothing had happened, embracing and kissing Ashley affectionately as she left for school while Ashley resisted very hard the urge to cringe when he touched her. As far as she was concerned, nothing Rick had done the evening before had been forgiven.

She arrived alone for her doctor's appointment, managing a slight smile as Tim Bergen came in to perform the ultrasound. "Hi, Ashley LeNoir," Tim offered her a light-hearted greeting, patting her shoulder as he sat down on the swivel stool next to the exam table.

"Hi, Tim."

"Husband joining us for the picture show?" Tim said, glancing around for the absent Mr. LeNoir.

"No, he's not coming," Ashley said quietly, her overwhelming melancholy written all over her face.

Tim nodded his silent understanding, his facial expression momentarily distressed before he forced himself to smile cheerfully at his patient. "Okay. Well, let's get this show on the road, shall we?"

The ultrasound was the most fascinating thing Ashley had ever seen. She lay spellbound, watching the monitor as Tim pointed out the rapid beating of the baby's tiny heart before moving to show the baby's face, arms, legs, fingers and toes. Ashley gaped in amazement as the baby yawned and sucked its thumb, smiling softy, in love with the small being on the video screen. Her baby, hers and hers alone, so it would seem.

"Would you like to know the sex?" Tim asked as he studied her enraptured expression.

Ashley shook her head. "No, surprise me."

"Everything looks wonderful. The baby appears to be right where it should be for twenty-four weeks," Tim said, helping her into sitting position. "Anything we need to talk about?" he asked, giving her the chance to elaborate on her relationship with Rick.

"No. Everything is fine," she said, lying gracefully. Tim was aware that she was lying, but let her off the hook, this time.

In late October, Ashley drove to work for her Saturday evening shift dressed in black leggings and a light sweater, enjoying the cooler temperatures of fall. The autumn-like weather had altered the scenery around the city, changing the green leaves on the trees to brilliant shades of russet, amber, orange and gold. She rolled her window down, letting the crisp breeze whip through her hair as she sang aloud to Whitney Houston. She was in a good mood when she entered the pharmacy, hearing rowdy cheers and finding Sam, Matt, Steve and Jack gathered around a portable television, watching college football. She grinned, waving to them as she passed by, strolling to the break room to put her things into her metal locker.

"Hey, Ashley, I bet you know some of these guys!" Matt called out to her as she returned down the long corridor and into the main pharmacy.

"Which guys?" she glanced at him inquisitively, craning her neck to see the television.

"These guys playing for LSU."

"LSU is on?" Ashley sprinted to the television eagerly, pushing Matt out of the way so that she could see the tiny screen. "When did the game come on?"

"It just started," Jack said, grinning at her unusual enthusiasm. "I've never seen you spark up like this before, Ashley. I didn't realize that you were such a football fan."

"Do you know anyone?" Matt repeated persistently while Ashley studied the tiny screen, squinting in concentration. As he came into view, Ashley's heart skipped a beat and she pointed at the middle of the screen to the helmeted figure throwing a pass.

"Just this one," she said softly, her voice barely more than a whisper as she stared at Doug longingly. She hadn't realized the extent to which she had missed him until the moment he appeared before her eyes, and she reached out, touching the screen as if she could feel the warmth of him through the glass.

"You know Doug Fairchild! How cool!" Matt said, much more excited than Ashley had ever seen him. "I'm a huge fan!"

"I grew up with him," Ashley replied, never taking her eyes from the screen. She felt a nudge against her back and turned to find Roseanne standing with her hands on her hips, a surly frown upon her disapproving face.

"You gonna work today or what?" she said to Ashley, rolling her eyes at the men lounging in chairs, their eyes fixed in a trance on the ongoing game. "It's bad enough that I gotta deal with these clowns without you being mesmerized by football too."

Ashley reluctantly began filling medication carts, all the while peeking around the corner at the microscopic television, hoping to catch glimpses of Doug. Unbeknownst to Ashley, Jack studied her inquisitively throughout the first half of the game, realization coming over him in waves as he observed her glowing face. He waited until halftime, then invaded her privacy by joining her in the fill area, leaning against the counter as she reached up to retrieve a drawer.

"So, Ashley, just who is Doug Fairchild to you?"

Ashley felt the warmth flood her face as she became flustered, avoiding Jack's eyes as she responded. "Doug is a very good friend of mine," she said, stammering noticeably. "We've known each other since kindergarten. I used to hang upside down on the jungle gym with him," she explained with a mischievous grin.

"He must be a great friend to account for lighting up your face that way," Jack said, regarding her skeptically. "That's the most color I've seen in your cheeks since I met you."

The deafening roar from the crowd at Tiger Stadium resonated through the pharmacy as the game came back on, and Ashley snapped her head around the corner to view the players taking the field. Jack threw his head back and chuckled knowingly.

"Well, at least now I've figured it out. All I needed was the missing piece of the puzzle," he said, speculating over his shoulder as he went back to work. "Rick LeNoir may be your husband, and an asshole, but Doug Fairchild is the one who holds the key to your heart."

Ashley rolled her eyes, ignoring him as she stood transfixed, forgetting her duties and watching the game. LSU won and an ecstatic Ashley dropped into a chair in front of the screen, glowing as Doug was interviewed after the game. Ashley's tears began to flow the instant she heard his voice, listening as Doug told the reporter how excited he was that LSU had played such a great game and how lucky he was to have such talented teammates.

He always was too modest. Ashley smiled, thinking of Doug fondly as she walked away from the television. But at least he gave credit where credit was due. She sighed regretfully, her aching heart heavy in her chest, wishing that she could call him and tell him what a good game he had played.

Jack strolled over and handed her a tissue. "Here, Kiddo, blow your nose," he said, smiling kindly, for once holding his tongue and not offering anything clever. "Cheer up, will you? I promise, I'll tape the rest of the LSU games for you."

He walked away, leaving Ashley staring after him in bewilderment. Jack was highly intuitive, already knowing things about Ashley's feelings that she didn't know herself.

Just as Ashley's relationship with Jack Chambers blossomed, so did her close friendship with Ellie Holman. A camaraderie that started as struggling students chatting casually in the lounge between classes quickly progressed to devoted study buddies, enjoying each other's company while putting their heads together to stay above water.

The Holmans were a tight-knit bunch, residing in a historical neighborhood near downtown, with Ellie living in a compact apartment above her parents' garage, and Ellie's brother, Scott, living next door with his wife Corrine and their two golden retrievers, Beau and Luke. Ashley felt at home there, spending many evenings with Ellie, ducking out of the house after Rick went upstairs to his computer and driving like a mad woman to the garage apartment for a relaxing night of studying and girl talk.

Ellie was her anchor, her reminder that life was good. Even though they had only officially met once, Ellie quickly became fed up with Rick's pompous and demanding attitude, making up her mind to bring some fun back into Ashley's life.

"How much laundry could you possibly have to do?" Ellie asked indignantly, pulling Ashley down the sidewalk toward her waiting car, purposely ignoring yet another declined invitation for an afternoon of carefree entertainment. "No two people could wear all the clothes you wash in one week."

Ellie never took no for an answer, coercing Greg and Sean to chauffeur Ashley to The Painted Desert, slipping her out from under Rick's nose to sip coffee while they drank beer. Their intent was to study together while Ellie waited tables, but more often than not, the trio would end up swapping stories, with Greg doting on the very pregnant Ashley, and Sean, scowling and shaking his head, bringing Greg back to earth by impatiently reminding him that Ashley was married.

When she wasn't working, Ellie conned Ashley to forget about her household chores, dragging her shopping, or to Charleston's to review notes over a plate of fries loaded sinfully with gobs of cheddar cheese and bacon bits, a caloric nightmare that would have sent Rick LeNoir right over the edge.

Instead of Rick, it was Ellie who cooed over the ultrasound pictures, fingering the shadowy image of the baby tenderly. "I can't wait until the baby's born. I just love babies," she told Ashley with a big smile. "I'm not about to get married and give birth, and since Scott and Corrine can't have children, I've been waiting forever to have an honorary niece or nephew to spoil."

Since Rick wanted nothing to do with any of it, Ellie became Ashley's obvious choice for her labor coach, and they attended childbirth classes once a week for six weeks, finishing up right after Thanksgiving. Ashley began to prepare diligently for the birth of her child, putting her name on a highly recommended daycare's waiting list and decorating the small upstairs bedroom, painting the walls mint-green and furnishing the sunny room with a white crib and pastel bedding.

Maggie and Remy planned to arrive in Oklahoma City on December twentieth, to stay for Christmas and the birth of their first grandchild, due on December twenty-third. Ashley reluctantly broke the news to Rick over dinner a week beforehand, wincing painfully as he exploded.

"I'm your family now! Why are they coming?" he said, slamming his fist thunderously onto the antique dining table. Ashley flinched as the table shook from the force of his blow.

"Rick, please don't be unreasonable," she said wearily. She was in her ninth month of pregnancy, was tired, irritable, and did not feel up to fighting with him. "Maggie and Remy are my parents, and this baby is their first grandchild. They have every right to be here for its birth."

She remained calm in the face of his ranting, reminding herself that this was the last Christmas she would have to listen to him. After the baby came, she would leave him, return to Louisiana with Maggie and Remy, and reestablish her original plan of action to live with Kate in Monroe.

Her last final was on the afternoon of December twentieth, the same day her parents were due to arrive, and the same day as her weekly appointment with Tim Bergen. She saw Tim first thing that morning, yawning from sleep deprivation as she lay back on the table for her examination.

"Well, Ashley, you're dilated to a two. It could be today or it could be two weeks from now," Tim said matter-of-factly after he finished her exam, pushing the swivel stool across the floor and standing to offer his hand to Ashley, pulling her into sitting position.

"Tim, I knew that already. What do I need you for?" she said, snapping at him irritably and apologizing immediately after noting his shocked expression. "Sorry, I didn't mean to sound so bitchy. I guess I'm a little touchy today. I haven't slept much this week with finals and all."

"That's okay," Tim said, smiling reassuringly. "I'm used to patients slapping me around right at their due date, even the normally pleasant ones. At least you have a good excuse to offer."

After her last final, Ashley hurried home to welcome her parents, meeting them in the driveway as they pulled in, their minivan loaded down with luggage, baby gifts and Christmas presents. Giving hugs and kisses, Ashley leaned into the door of the van, attempting to help Remy bring in the Christmas packages.

"You shouldn't be carrying anything at all," Maggie said, scolding her and taking the box Ashley held in her arms. "You should be resting."

"I feel fine!" Ashley said, unused to someone making a big deal over her being pregnant. Rick certainly didn't care what she lifted or carried. She begrudgingly gave in to Maggie, sitting on the stairs as they unloaded the van, then showing Maggie the newly decorated nursery as Remy stretched across Rick and Ashley's bed to catch a catnap before dinner.

Rick was not yet home so Ashley could enjoy some quality time alone with Maggie. Maggie eyed her daughter speculatively as she unpacked her suitcase. Ashley played it up, acting like the appropriately blissful new bride, but Maggie didn't buy it. She had a sneaking feeling that something was not quite right, although she was unable to put her finger on exactly what.

"Everything's okay with the baby?" Maggie asked, glancing up inquiringly from her suitcase.

Ashley smiled back sincerely, recognizing that Maggie was on a fishing expedition. "Yes, Mags, the baby is fine," she said, shaking her head at Maggie's intuitive paranoia. "And before you waste your breath asking, I'll just go ahead and tell you. Yes, I'm fine too."

Maggie rolled her eyes in exasperation, then dug into her bag, spying the white envelope peeking out from underneath her silk underwear. She pulled it out, handing it to Ashley with a flourish. "Here."

Ashley took the envelope, turning it over in her hands. The outside of the envelope was blank without writing or return address. She looked up at Maggie, curiosity blazing in her eyes. "What is it?"

"I don't really know. Bobbie brought it by the house yesterday and asked me to bring it to you."

Thinking it a best-wishes-with-the-baby letter from Ms. Bobbie, Ashley tore open the envelope and unfolded the letter within. But to her surprise and delight, Doug's bold handwriting leapt from the page.

"Okay, Ashley," he wrote and she could hear his voice leaping off the page. "I've tried to act like you don't exist, but it's not working. I'm ready to call a truce because I miss fighting with you. I'm sorry I was an ass. I should've been there for you. Write soon and let me know that you're all right."

Ashley held the letter tightly to her chest and looked up at her mother, happy tears flooding her eyes. "It's from a letter from Doug."

"Hallelujah," Maggie smiled. "It's about time. I was wondering how long it would take y'all to make up."

"I know. I've been miserable without him. I miss him so much."

"I know you do, honey. I'm sure it's been tough on you. Doug's been your friend for more years than I can remember."

Maggie didn't know the half of it, Ashley thought wickedly. She had never told Maggie of Doug's marriage proposal. Maggie would faint dead away to know that Ashley had turned down a chance to make Doug her son-in-law.

Ashley took the letter downstairs to lock it in her cherished little cedar chest before Rick came home. As she and Maggie leaned against the center island in the kitchen, discussing what to make for dinner, Ashley felt a great gush of water flow down her legs and glanced down quickly before looking up at Maggie in surprise.

"Oh my," Ashley said, gasping loudly. "I think my water just broke."

Maggie looked down at Ashley's legs, the registered nurse in her kicking into high gear. "I would say so," she said, and began barking orders. "Remy!"

He appeared from the bedroom, his hair disheveled, rubbing his bleary eyes as he looked to his wife inquiringly. "Get Ashley's suitcase. You do have your bag packed, don't you?"

Maggie directed her question to Ashley, who nodded vigorously. "Okay, good. You call labor and delivery and tell them that you're coming in so they can alert Dr. Bergen. Do we need to call Rick?"

Ashley considered her answer only for a brief moment before shrugging indifferently. "We'll leave Rick a note. We'll call Ellie. She's my birth coach."

Ellie was more nervous than Ashley was. "Oh my God!" she said, squealing in a high-pitched voice. "I don't know if I'm ready!"

"Ellie, don't you dare freak on me," Ashley said gruffly. "Just pull yourself together and meet me at Baptist Hospital."

Ashley hung up the phone, watching as Maggie and Remy scurried around gathering items for the hospital and she scrawled Rick a short note:

> "Rick,
>   My water broke and I have gone to the hospital to have my baby.
>   You may join us if you would like.
>   Ashley
> P.S. I will be at Baptist Hospital—I'm sure you didn't know that."

She signed the letter, leaving it on the center island in the kitchen, knowing there would be hell to pay later for her sarcastic note, but she didn't care. Mere hours from now, her baby would be born, and she would be free of Rick LeNoir forever.

The contractions began on the way to the hospital, starting out mild and light. After her arrival at labor and delivery, Ashley's labor nurse settled her into a birthing suite across the hall from the nurse's station identical to the one Ashley and Ellie had toured during childbirth classes. It was spacious, with cherry-wood floor and furniture, including the usual hospital bed and a foldout couch, normally used by new fathers, although Ashley was certain that Rick would not be gracing the mattress of this particular couch. She would be lucky if he showed up at all.

Remy checked out the room, letting out a low whistle. "I've never seen a hospital room like this in my life," he said to Maggie, grinning broadly. "This is impressive, Mags. They've sure come a long way since Ashley was born."

Maggie laughed, beaming in amusement as she ushered him out to the waiting room, allowing Ashley to undress in privacy. Tiffany, the labor nurse, helped her into a hospital gown, then did a quick determination of Ashley's progress, estimating that she was dilated to four. "Are you going to want an epidural?" she asked.

"Oh, yes ma'am!" Ashley said emphatically, and Tiffany smiled, entertained by Ashley's strident declaration.

"Then I'll need to page the anesthesiologist. I'll be right back." Tiffany left the room, sending Maggie and Remy back to be with Ashley, trailed by Ellie, the excited labor coach.

"Have you all met?" Ashley asked as they came through the door.

"Yes, we introduced ourselves in the hallway," Maggie said.

Ashley watched Ellie with interest, grinning as she unloaded her bag, pulling out a stopwatch for timing contractions and fluorescent green tennis balls for massaging Ashley's lower back. "Ellie, I don't think you're going to need all that junk," Ashley told her. "I'm having an epidural, remember?"

"A good coach is a prepared coach," Ellie said, wagging her finger and lecturing Ashley pompously.

"I hope I didn't interrupt any potential beer brawl you were planning for tonight."

"Well, I was going to Sean and Greg's apartment for a party since they are going home for Christmas tomorrow. But we can drink when they get back from break. Drinking I can do any time. This is a once in a lifetime event," Ellie said, taking a seat on the couch next to Maggie.

Tiffany returned with Dr. Christopher Grace, the anesthesiologist. Maggie and Remy decided to walk down the hall for a cup of coffee while Ellie remained by Ashley's side, watching in fascination as Dr. Grace inserted the epidural. The epidural was heaven on earth and Ashley felt absolutely none of the contractions. She was smiling and laughing, lying on her side in bed, talking to her parents and Ellie when Rick arrived, three hours after she had been admitted to the hospital.

He smoothly greeted everyone, shaking Remy's hand and embracing Maggie fondly, then came to Ashley's bedside, leaning down to kiss her forehead as he whispered, "You could have called me. Are you trying to make me look bad in front of your parents?"

Ashley batted her eyelashes at him, as if he had just paid her the nicest compliment. She reached for him, wrapping her arms around his neck and whispered back to him, "Don't start acting like you give a damn now." She dropped her arms, smiling sweetly as Rick's face hardened and a muscle twitched dangerously in his jaw.

He stepped back from the bed, leaning against the wall as he regarded her critically. "You don't appear to be in much pain."

"That's because I've had an epidural, you moron," Ashley bit her tongue before she could blurt out what she thought. Instead, she used considerable self-control and replied, "I've had an epidural block for the pain."

Rick regarded her quizzically, pretending to be concerned. "Why would you do that? Isn't that harmful to the baby?"

"Let me answer that," Ellie spoke up, unable to resist the opportunity to put Rick in his place. "If *you* had bothered to attend childbirth classes with your wife, *you* would know that the epidural isn't harmful to the baby in any way."

Rick turned a cold eye toward her. "Eleanor, what exactly is your function here this evening?"

"*I* attended childbirth classes with Ashley. *I'm* the birth coach, so *I'm* staying," she smirked, standing up to him while Ashley, suppressing a pleased smile, silently applauded her.

Maggie and Remy observed their exchange with great interest. They had not known that Rick didn't go to childbirth classes and didn't have any idea that he and Ashley had come to the understanding that they had about the baby. They looked from Rick to Ellie then to Ashley, questioning her with their bewildered stares. Maggie appeared to enjoy Ellie's sparring with Rick as much as Ellie did, but Remy seemed uncomfortable, hating confrontations of this type.

"Rick, if you're going to stay in the room, I'm going to have to ask you not to fight with the birth coach," Ashley piped up, joining in on the terrorization of her husband. "I need her total concentration."

Rick's mouth tightened into a stubborn line and he stormed out of the room. Ellie and Ashley exchanged a triumphant glance, bursting into gales of laughter.

"What in the hell is going on here?" Maggie demanded an explanation, growing tired of being left in the dark.

"It would take too long to explain, Maggie," Ashley said apologetically. "I can fill you in on the last three months later."

"I think we have plenty of time *right now* to hear that explanation. I'm sure you'll be in labor for a while."

"Not now, Maggie," Ashley said insistently. "Rick may have stormed out, but he won't stay gone for long, trust me."

Tiffany returned to check the fetal monitor strapped around Ashley's large belly. The baby's heartbeat was steady and strong, just as it should have been.

Tiffany then checked her cervix and sat down on the stool beside the bed, clipboard in lap, charting her observations.

"This is going pretty fast," she said, glancing up at Ashley. "You're a little over seven, it won't be long now."

Rick wandered in and out of the room periodically, sullen and silent, avoiding the puzzled stares of Maggie and Remy. Tiffany regarded him curiously. "Your husband?" she asked of Ashley, wrinkling her brow as Ashley nodded. "Doesn't he want to be in here?"

"I'm sure he doesn't," Ashley said, observing the odd expression on the face of her labor nurse. "It's a complicated tale."

Just before eleven p.m. Tiffany checked her cervix again. "Well, I believe it's time to push. I'll call Dr. Bergen and we'll get started," she told Ashley as she left the room.

Maggie rose and kissed Ashley on the forehead. "Remy and I are going to the waiting room, before he faints on me. We'll be right out there if you need us." She started out the door, then stuck her head back in. "I'll keep Rick with us," she added, smiling broadly as she took Remy from the room.

Tim Bergen came in around midnight. "Hey, Ashley, I told you it could be today!" he kidded her as he slipped a gown over his scrubs. "By the way, I met *Mr.* LeNoir out there. It was mighty nice of him to show up for the birth, don't you think?"

Tim had understood perfectly all along. Ashley was grateful that she didn't have to offer him any further explanation for Rick's odd behavior.

With Ellie by her side, timing contractions and holding her hand, Ashley pushed, anxious to complete her first phase of motherhood, started nine long months beforehand.

At 12:53 a.m. on December twenty-first, Molly Michelle LeNoir came into the world, kicking and screaming as Tim Bergen held her high in the air.

"It's a girl!" he announced, grinning ear to ear at his elated patient. "Would you like to do the honors?" He turned to Ellie, motioning her to join him at the foot of the bed. Ellie, delighted with the privilege, cut the umbilical cord, thereafter considering Molly to be half her baby.

Tim gave the baby to Tiffany, who quickly wrapped her in a blanket and presented her to Ashley. Ashley gazed at her newborn daughter lovingly, her sparkling eyes moist with joy. Molly was the most beautiful thing she had ever laid eyes on, absolutely perfect from the top of her bald head to the tips of her tiny toes.

Tim finished his work with Ashley, while Tiffany took the baby to perform a postnatal exam. Tim rose, coming to stand at Ashley's side. "You did great, Ashley. I'm very proud of you," he took her hand, squeezing it tightly. "I have the feeling that you can handle whatever your future brings."

"Thanks Tim," Ashley said, beaming at him, her face flushed with happiness.

"My pleasure," Tim returned her smile, letting go of her hand as he moved toward the door. "I better tell the new grandparents the happy news before they jump out of their skins. Should I also inform Mr. LeNoir of the birth of his daughter?" he asked, lifting a skeptical eyebrow, offering Ashley a lopsided grin as he pulled the door open, exiting the room.

"What an odd thing for him to say," Ellie commented, sitting on the edge of Ashley's bed with a tired smile on her face.

"No it wasn't," Ashley said. "He understands how things are between Rick and me. He was giving me a thinly veiled pep talk."

Her parents burst into the room, trailed by Rick. They had been by the nursery and had seen the nurses checking the baby. "She's just beautiful." Remy squeezed Ashley's hand, leaning down to kiss the top of her head affectionately.

"I think she looks just like you," Maggie declared, cutting her eyes toward her son-in-law, trying to gauge his reaction to her words. Rick remained silent, offering no response or congratulations. "What are you going to name her?" Maggie asked.

"Molly Michelle."

"I don't think so," Rick said, speaking up with disapproval, and all eyes turned toward him as he leaned sullenly against the wall, his fists shoved deeply into the pockets of his pleated slacks. "I don't like it."

Ashley gave him a withering stare, jutting her chin out defiantly. "My baby, my name," she said, cleverly reminding him of his stance on her child.

Rick's eyes narrowed with contempt, glaring at Ashley as he snatched his navy wool overcoat from the corner chair, pulling it huffily over his work clothes. "I'm going home," he said in a brisk business-like voice. "But don't believe that this discussion is over, Ashley. I will be back later this morning and we'll talk further, resolving this matter once and for all." He stalked out of the room and Ashley breathed a deep sigh of relief.

"I should go too," Ellie said, rising from the edge of the bed and suppressing a yawn. "I haven't slept for days now, between finals and childbirth." She turned to Ashley. "Congratulations, Ashley, and thanks for letting me be a part of such a phenomenal experience. Molly's a beautiful baby."

Remy insisted on walking Ellie to her car, more to protect her from Rick than from any potential rapist. After their departure to the parking garage, Maggie sat on the edge Ashley's bed, reaching up to brush a lock of limp hair from Ashley's eyes. "Things are not good at all between you and Rick, are they?" she asked, her brow creased in worry.

"That's an understatement," Ashley sighed, falling back against the elevated head of her hospital bed.

"Maybe you and Molly should come back home with us."

"Maybe we should give Rick a chance to bond with his child before we start packing my bags." Ashley shocked herself with her sudden declaration, not at all certain why she felt Rick deserved a chance. However, Molly was his child and Ashley still held fast to the belief that maybe she could make a difference between them.

Maggie and Remy stayed with her all night, sleeping on the foldout bed in her room. The nurse brought Molly in around four o'clock for a feeding and Ashley held her elatedly in her arms, staring down at her with lovestruck awe. Molly

Michelle LeNoir was a gorgeous baby with a perfectly round head, cherub cheeks, a small button nose and sweet little mouth. Her eyes were round and incredibly blue, and although most newborns had blue eyes, Ashley felt certain that Molly would be blessed with the same dramatic aqua eyes as her father.

The flowers and balloons began arriving at noon, bright pink balloons attached to a huge white teddy bear from Kate and Susanna, a bouquet of pink and white carnations from Matt, Sean and Greg, and a huge pink poinsettia from Ellie and Ava. Jack sent pink roses and Molly's grandparents decorated Ashley's door with banners and a pink wreath declaring proudly, "It's a girl."

The last to arrive were red roses, an even dozen arranged with greenery and baby's breath in a large crystal vase. Ashley beamed happily, believing that Rick had finally come to his senses as she reached for the attached envelope. Blinking incredulously, she was taken aback by the message written on the card: "Congratulations, Ash! Love, Doug." She shook her head in wonder. Doug had sent the roses. Who'd have thought?

She completed the birth certificate before Rick returned to the hospital, making the baby's name officially Molly Michelle LeNoir. The way Ashley saw it, after his behavior of late, Rick was lucky that she had acknowledged him on the birth certificate at all.

He came up to her room that afternoon, appearing shortly after Maggie and Remy had gone for lunch. Ashley sat in the rocking chair holding Molly, giving her a bottle and looked up expectantly as Rick entered the room. He sat on the edge of the hospital bed, glancing quickly at the flowers and balloons filling her room.

"Word traveled fast, I gather," he said, craning his neck to peek over the top of the blanket at Molly while Ashley watched him hopefully, trying to read his thoughts.

"Would you like to hold her?" Ashley offered optimistically, praying this would be the moment Rick bonded with his child.

"No." His answer was simple and his uninterested gaze unwavering. His indifferent reaction to Molly was enough to show Ashley that she had been foolish. Nothing between them was ever going to change. Ashley sighed heavily, lifting her weary eyes to meet his watchful stare. "Rick, you know, I can't imagine where our relationship is going."

"What are you talking about, Ashley?" he asked. "This doesn't change anything," he added, gesturing impatiently at Molly.

"This, as you call her, is my daughter. She changes everything."

"Not for me she doesn't."

"Rick, why don't we just admit that we made a mistake and call it quits?" Ashley said a quick prayer, hoping he would listen to the voice of reason. Molly had his name now, and they could both be free.

"Who made a mistake?" he said, regarding her critically. "I'm perfectly happy."

"How can you say that? You work eighteen hours a day. We never spend any time together. Whenever we are together, all we do is fight. How can you be perfectly happy?" Ashley said shrilly, her eyes wide with indignation.

"Chère, I married you for better or for worse. I am absolutely content to wait until you come around and accept my way of doing things. You can't fight me forever." He sat back, crossing his legs casually as he flashed a superior grin.

"How can you be so sure that I'll ever do things the way you want me to?" Ashley said angrily. "Why do you have to change me? I don't want to change."

Rick crossed his arms, assuming a posture of superiority as he calmly shaped his statement. "Ashley, my dear, you may leave if you like," he said, sniffing haughtily. "But Molly stays with me. Because you have no real income and are independently incapable of providing for her, no judge in the land would award custody of Molly to you over me."

Ashley stared at him, blinking back scorching tears of rage and disbelief. "Why would you do that to me? You don't even want her. You've said so yourself, a thousand times."

"It's simple, really," Rick leaned forward with a victorious gleam in his eyes. "As long as I have Molly, I know you will never leave."

Ashley lifted her chin, her eyes flashing rebelliously. Rick may have won this round, but she was tired of bowing down to him. And even though he had blown Plan A out of the water, she would find another way to win this impossible situation. It might take until she finished school but she would win, she had no doubt.

Dr. Bergen entered the room after tapping lightly, regarding the battling couple cautiously while sensing that he had interrupted something significant. He smiled warmly at Ashley, noting her red, swollen eyes with dismay, and acknowledged Rick with a curt nod before ignoring him. "You look just terrific and the baby is doing great," Tim said after a quick check of Ashley's shrinking uterus and stitches. "You can go home tomorrow morning, if you'd like."

"Yes, I think going home would be a very good idea," Rick spoke up and Tim dismissed him with an abrupt sidelong glance.

"Ashley, you're the patient," Tim said. "What do you say?"

Ashley sighed, unprepared to return to the real world with Rick, but could find no good reason to remain in the hospital. "Tomorrow morning will be fine, Tim," she said

"Then I'll come by in the morning and write your discharge orders." Tim peeked at Molly, beaming with delight. "Beautiful baby," he said, patting Ashley's shoulder before he strolled out of the room.

Rick rolled his eyes disdainfully, then stood up. "I'm going back to work, Ashley," he said, draping his coat over his forearm. "I assume we've resolved this little matter?" he smiled triumphantly as she nodded in a subdued manner. "Good, so we *are* clear on things now?"

"Crystal clear," Ashley shot back at him, glad that he was leaving. She loathed the sight of him. She cringed as he leaned down to kiss her, turning her head so that his lips brushed only her cheek instead of their intended target. Rick straightened abruptly, smiling arrogantly as he turned on his heel then chuckled lightly as he strode from the room.

Ashley rose wearily from the rocker, laying the peacefully sleeping Molly into her bassinet before retreating to the bathroom to splash cold water on her hot face. After changing into a fresh nightgown and robe, she returned to her chair, rocking back and forth reflectively as she swallowed the bitter disappointment of the most recent turn of events.

The afternoon brought visitors to cheer her, with Ellie and Ava arriving just before three. They took turns holding Molly, cooing and making all kinds of ridiculous noises, and Ashley watched them play with the baby, losing count of how many times Ellie told Ava that she had cut the umbilical cord.

Jack, still in starched shirt and tie, surprised her by dropping by on his way home from working a rare day shift at University. Ashley introduced him to Ellie and Ava, smiling humorously as she observed their open admiration of him. Ashley had seen women interact with Jack before. His effect on them was astounding.

Jack scooped Molly away from Ellie and cuddled her, peeking at her tiny face under the receiving blanket. "Well, Ashley, there's no doubt that she'll be a real beauty like her mother," he said, winking as he grinned at her.

"Why, thank you, Jack!" Ashley giggled, flirting outrageously with him as Ellie and Ava exchanged a speculative look. She wanted to tell them that it wasn't anything like what they were thinking, but decided to let them wonder just for fun.

Ellie and Ava gathered their things to leave, thinking that it might be an opportune moment for them to depart for the mall to finish their Christmas shopping. "It was nice to meet you," Jack told them, flashing his charming smile.

"Likewise," Ellie said, beaming radiantly at Jack, batting her eyelashes vivaciously. Ashley was entertained by their exchange, seeing Ellie flirt with Jack was a novelty. Ellie usually didn't express much admiration for men in general.

"I'm glad to have met you too," Ava stepped between them, blocking Ellie's view of Jack. "Come, Ellie." Ava took her by the wrist and pulled her toward the door, while Ellie continued eyeing Jack appreciatively as she went.

Jack still held Molly, rocking her gently in his arms. "Now that's how a father should act," Ashley thought wistfully. As if reading her thoughts, Jack asked, "So where's Asshole?"

Ashley looked startled, peering at him inquisitively. "Who, Rick?"

"If the shoe fits." Jack looked at her over the top of Molly's head.

"Where else? He's working."

"Did he come to the hospital for her birth?"

"Yes, he was in the waiting room."

"What a fool." Jack leaned over to place Molly into Ashley's arms before pulling up a chair to sit beside her. "You look terrific, Ashley. Motherhood suits you, even though you would never know you'd just had a baby by looking at you."

"Thanks, Jack. You're a great friend," Ashley smiled at him. "Thanks for the gorgeous flowers," she acknowledged the soft pink rosebuds in the windowsill with a nod of her head.

Jack rose out of his chair, leaning down to brush her cheek softly with his lips. "My pleasure, Kiddo. When are you coming back to work?"

"Not until after school starts next semester."

"Have a Merry Christmas, Ashley." Picking up his brown leather jacket, Jack started toward the door, glancing at his watch. "Gotta go, I have about a hundred women to buy Christmas presents for," he flashed a toothy grin over his shoulder to her, pulling open the door to her room.

"Merry Christmas to you too, Jack," Ashley smiled as she watched him leave, grateful to be able to count Ava, Ellie and Jack among her many new friends.

Christmas was uneventful. Rick behaved as a perfect gentleman the entire holiday. He was pleasant and charming, almost irresistible, making Ashley remember why she had been attracted to him in the first place. Late in the night as everyone slept, Ashley slipped out of bed and into the living room, pulling out her stationery and painstakingly composed a letter to Doug.

"Dear Doug,

"I received your letter, and I was so happy to hear from you. My life hasn't been quite the same without your overprotective sarcasm. All kidding aside, I understand why you couldn't be at the wedding. It was unfair of me to ask you to be there. I'm glad that you're no longer mad at me, because I miss you too."

She paused in her writing, chewing the end of her pen and contemplating what to say next. She wanted to lie, to tell him that everything was perfect but she couldn't do it. Instead, she wrote,

"I can't wait for you to see Molly. She's a beautiful baby. Having her is the best thing I've ever done."

She signed the letter and sealed it, quickly stashing it for safekeeping until she could pass it on to Maggie for secure delivery. Rick would be livid if he discovered that she was renewing her friendship with Doug Fairchild.

Ashley and Molly were faring well together at home, so Maggie and Remy left the day after Christmas, planning for Maggie to return in mid-January to care for Molly until she was old enough to start day care. Ashley walked with them out to their minivan, embracing them lovingly and thanking them profusely for everything they had done to help her.

"You don't have to thank us, Ashley," Maggie said, kissing her cheek. "We do what we do because we love you. Are you sure you won't come home with us?"

Ashley shook her head, forcing a convincing smile onto her face. She hadn't told them of her conversation with Rick in the hospital room, thinking it better to work things out in her own way. She couldn't tell them the truth. If they'd had an inkling of the way that Rick had become, they would've never left her and the baby there alone with him.

Molly was a fantastic baby. She slept well and rarely cried. Ashley moved upstairs to the nursery, sleeping on the guest bed so that Molly didn't wake Rick when she awoke for her nighttime feeding. Rick, jubilant that the pregnancy was over, concentrated on getting Ashley's figure back, holding her feet down nightly as he made her do sit-ups. After work, he sent Ashley out into the cold night air to walk, not caring if it was pitch-black dark and freezing out. Getting Ashley back in her own clothes was much more important to him than her safety. Soon she was wearing jeans again, giving Rick something over which to be pleased.

"Now you look like my wife again," he said, praising her and nodding with approval when she emerged from their bedroom wearing a pair of nice-fitting Levi's and the new oxford shirt he had given her for Christmas. He crossed the room with panther-like grace, stopping her in the foyer to kiss her with renewed passion, pulling her by the shoulders up against his hard, muscular body.

Apparently, Rick thought that because he now desired her again, their relationship would automatically revert back to the way it had been before they married. Ashley had news for him. The damage had already been done. His verbal and physical abuse, together with his rejection of Molly, had killed any fond feelings she'd ever had for him.

CHAPTER TWENTY-FIVE

Susanna phoned on New Year's Day, to hear all about Molly and to chatter excitedly about holiday parties and get-togethers. She tried hard to be nonchalant and managed to carry on a decent conversation for about two minutes before she threw in the towel.

"Oh hell, I can't stand it anymore," Susanna said, bursting at the seams. "I'm engaged, Ashley! I'm getting married."

Ashley squealed with her, jumping up and down with glee in the middle of the kitchen floor. Rick jerked his head around from the great room to stare at her, looking at her like she had finally lost her mind, and listened with a keen ear to find out what was causing his wife to behave so childishly.

"Engaged!" Ashley said breathlessly, stopping her bouncing to plop down on the couch next to Rick. "To who, Mark?"

"God, Ashley, yes to Mark," Susanna said impatiently. "Who else?"

Grinning ear to ear with happiness for Susanna, Ashley grabbed her calendar from the end table. "When's the wedding?" she asked, flipping open the leather cover of her planner, waiting for Susanna to reveal the date.

"The wedding is the first Saturday in June. That's why I'm calling you. Get your figure back, girlfriend. I need a matron of honor!"

"I'd love to be your matron of honor, Susanna," Ashley said, ignoring Rick's annoyed glance. "I only hope that I can offer to you the same encouraging support that you gave to me at the time of my wedding," Ashley added, tongue-in-cheek.

"I'm going to pretend that I didn't hear you say that," Susanna said. "I think I was incredibly gracious considering the fine catch you married."

Happy for Susanna and Mark, and thrilled to know that she would be going home for their wedding, Ashley listened to Susanna babble ecstatically for more than twenty minutes before finally getting off the phone. She turned to face Rick who was drumming his fingers impatiently on his leg.

"So, the shrew is getting married," he said cynically. "I assume you are going to the wedding?"

"You heard me tell her that I would be her matron of honor."

"I suppose you will be going to Louisiana for more than just the weekend."

"I'll be out of school, so I think I'll go for the entire week," Ashley said, looking down at her open calendar, tracing the week of Susanna's wedding with her index finger.

"You will be taking the child with you when you go?"

"Of course," Ashley suppressed a smile at the double meaning of her answer. *Of that you can be sure, Rick LeNoir. When I do finally leave here, Molly will be with me.*

Ashley's first act of open rebellion was the shearing of her long mane of hair, the very same luxurious, silky locks of which Rick was so fond. Classes at the pharmacy school had resumed in mid January, filling Ashley's already busy schedule with another round of challenging classes. She made it through the first week of the new semester no worse for wear, finally refining her lifestyle to some sort of organized routine. Upon hearing Ellie offhandedly mention that she was going for a haircut, Ashley was inspired, glancing at her boring mop of hair in the plate-glass window as they strolled out of the building to the parking lot.

Ashley followed Ellie to the beauty salon, and emerged two hours later looking completely different, glancing shyly into the rear view mirror at her changed appearance as she drove home. Gone were the heavy locks of mousy hair, replaced by a side-parted, one-length blunt cut to her chin, shining with blond highlights, accenting her high cheekbones and her wide, green eyes.

Rick's car was in the driveway when she pulled in, and she gathered her courage before getting out of the Corolla and strolling casually up the front sidewalk. She opened the front door, finding Rick and Maggie in the great room, seated on the couch, sipping wine while Molly dozed in her swing near the patio door. Their conversation stopped as she breezed into the room and they stared at her in astonishment, offering their opinions simultaneously.

"What have you done to your hair!" Rick said, appalled at her appearance. Ashley saw immediately that he did not like it, but she didn't care. Mission accomplished.

"I love it!" Maggie's opinion rang out, outweighing Rick's in Ashley's eyes. "It's darling on you, Ashley, just perfect."

"Don't encourage her, Maggie," Rick said, sternly. "She's growing it back out."

"Not any time soon," Ashley told him. "My schedule can no longer support maintaining all that hair."

"Then stay at home. A mother belongs at home with her child," Rick said, crossing his arms across his chest in irritation. "There's no need for you to have a college degree anyway."

"Don't even think about quitting school," Maggie shot Rick a scorching look before turning to Ashley. "Everyone needs a college degree to get a decent job."

"And while we're on the subject of your working," Rick said, refilling his glass with white zinfandel, "what are you planning to do with Molly while you work weekends at the hospital? I'm certainly not going to keep her; there's no way that I can work and watch a baby." He lifted his eyes, looking at Ashley smugly.

Maggie was oddly silent, with displeasure written all over her solemn face, leading Ashley to believe that she and Rick had already been discussing the issue. Ashley plopped into a chair at the kitchen table, weighing her options. Once again, Rick had pulled from his hat a point that she hadn't considered. The daycare center would not be open on Saturday and Sunday when she worked at the hospital. With Rick's refusal to help out with Molly, she would have to find an additional source of childcare, and she had only two weeks to find someone she trusted with her baby. Ashley didn't know where to start.

Ellie solved the problem for her, calling later that evening to find out what Rick's reaction had been to Ashley's haircut. After she heard Ashley's predicament and had finished cursing Rick for being such an ass, Ellie got off the phone, stating that she would check on something and call right back.

In fifteen minutes, Ellie was back on the line. "Problem solved," she announced cheerfully, returning a smile to Ashley's face. "My sister-in-law Corrine would love to watch Molly for you."

"Are you sure?" Ashley couldn't believe her good luck.

"Remember, I told you that Corrine loves babies, but hasn't been able to get pregnant," Ellie said, reminding her of a previous conversation. "And my brother Scott is as big a workaholic as Rick is, working seven days a week, eighteen hours a day. He's never home and Corrine is lonely, with a lot of time on her hands. Trust me, Ashley, you'd be doing her a favor too. You and Corrine would be helping each other out, only in different ways."

"Tell Corrine that I love her for this," Ashley thanked Ellie gratefully and hung up the phone. Later, as she lay in the bed next to Rick, she smiled gleefully into the darkness, recognizing that Ellie had once again foiled Rick and knowing that when she had revealed the solution to her dilemma, Rick had silently cursed, ruing the day that Ashley met Eleanor Holman.

When Molly turned two months old, Maggie returned to Louisiana, boarding the airplane with tears in her eyes as she kissed Ashley and Molly good-bye. By the end of February, Ashley had her routine down to an art. She dropped Molly off at the daycare each weekday morning, no later than six thirty, and picked her up in the afternoons between three-thirty and five, depending on her class schedule. Ashley and Molly ran errands before going home and Ashley prepared dinner while Molly sat in her infant seat watching, her big blue eyes following her mother's every move, a smile lighting her angelic face.

Rick came home for dinner at seven, leaving afterward for the gym or to retreat upstairs to work. Ashley bathed Molly, fed her, and put her to bed by seven thirty, then did the dinner dishes and sat down to study until midnight before turning in. She rose every morning at five to start over again.

On weekends, Ashley took Molly to Corrine. Corrine Holman, shy with a sweet disposition, was a lifesaver and was absolutely devoted to Molly. The adoration between them was mutual. As time went on, Molly came to love Corrine as a second mother, never uttering one cry of protest whenever Ashley left her with Corrine.

The spring went by quickly and, with the glaring exception of ignoring Molly, Rick behaved rather well, without harassing, dominating or making ridiculous demands of Ashley. Ashley made it easy for him to be reasonable, living her life by his rules instead of her own, because at that point, it had been easier to do it Rick's way than to defy him. She didn't need any additional pressure while trying to balance motherhood with school and work. Her mastering this balance of marriage, motherhood, school and work was definitely working to Rick's disadvantage. What he didn't realize was that by insisting that she do it all alone, Ashley was becoming quite proficient at being a one-woman show, thus growing up and regaining her independence. Ashley, without a doubt, neither wanted nor needed Rick in her life. Her only goal was to figure out a way to leave him and take Molly with her.

Sometimes, during rare idle moments, Ashley would relax, letting down her guard, and think back to Jimmy, picturing him in her mind's eyes: handsome Jimmy, artistic, witty and intelligent, with a heart of solid gold. Her eyes misted over as she mourned him, missing him and remembering how much he had meant to her. He had been gone for so long that it began to seem as though he had only been a dream, a wonderful, pleasant dream. But the love Ashley had for Jimmy was still present, burning passionately, locked securely in her heart, and was as real to her as the silver band she still wore on her finger.

When she thought of Jimmy, her thoughts inevitably turned to Doug and her disconcerting feelings for him. As Jack Chambers had so ineptly pointed out, what Ashley felt for Doug was much more than friendship although she didn't know precisely how to define it. She only knew that she thought of him frequently, missed him tremendously and couldn't wait until she could see him again.

Ashley worked with Jack every other weekend. Their evening shifts together gave them a lot of time to talk, and their friendship grew as the year continued. Ashley could confess anything to Jack, exchanging with him tales of childhood and teenage romantic escapades. She told Jack about her hometown and her friends in Louisiana, even telling him about Jimmy, and she had told no one about Jimmy, not even Rick. It felt so good to talk about Jimmy to someone, and with Jack, she was free to express her true feelings without fear of ridicule or persecution.

Jack, in turn, shared his childhood in Colorado with Ashley, and always kept her advised of his newest romances, accepting her opinion of his romantic conquests with easygoing laughter. Jack had an army of girlfriends from all walks of life, a schoolteacher from Edmond, a ballet dancer in Dallas and a CPA in Oklahoma City. However, his foremost passion was nurses, dating four of them from University alone.

Ashley enjoyed her friendship with Jack. They liked each other tremendously but never romantically, and were of like mind and temperament. Ashley felt secure around Jack, certain that she could count on him for anything that she ever needed. Jack enjoyed Ashley's company, finding her dry wit and bubbly personality exhilarating, liking her immensely while feeling oddly protective of her, and hating how unconsciously miserable he sensed that she was.

The last Saturday in May arrived, and Rick took his wife and daughter to Will Rogers World Airport in Oklahoma City, putting them on a flight bound for Louisiana. As the plane touched down on the runway in Alexandria, Ashley quivered with anticipation, so excited that she could scarcely wait for the plane to come to a complete stop before leaping from her seat. Scooping up her carry-on bag and juggling Molly on her hip, she bolted down the aisle, clamoring down the metal stairs of the prop plane to the walkway below. She had five days at home alone with Maggie and Remy before Rick arrived, and she wasn't wasting a minute of it.

Maggie and Remy waited for them. Ashley spotted them immediately, standing just inside the door as she and Molly deplaned. Remy pushed open the double glass doors to greet them, taking the heavy carry-on from her shoulder while Maggie plucked Molly from Ashley's hip, holding her close as she covered her tiny face with multiple kisses.

"Gee, I remember when I used to be your favorite!" Ashley said, kidding Maggie as she watched her shower Molly with grandmotherly love. "Did you miss the baby?"

"Look how big she's gotten," Maggie continued to kiss and coo with Molly as Ashley flung her arms around Remy in a fond embrace.

"Hi, Remy!" she said, linking her arm through his as they strode to the baggage claim, grinning at his scrutiny of her changed appearance. "Well? You like?"

"I like," Remy said, nodding, his eyes raking her from head to toe. "You look very different, but I like it."

"Do I look grown up?" she asked, teasing him as he rescued her garment bag and suitcase from the revolving belt of the baggage carousel.

"Ashley, no matter where you go or what you do, you'll never look grown up to me."

Sunny and warm was the forecast of the day, and the air was already quite sticky, unusually so even for late May. Ashley inhaled deeply as she walked across the parking lot toward Remy's new sports utility vehicle, reveling in the scent of fresh green pine. As they traveled from the airport, Ashley pressed her nose against the window, taking in all the sights around her hometown, missing it as she remembered it, filled with nostalgia for an adolescence gone by. She peered out, smiling sentimentally as they passed the drive-in before crossing over the Red River into Pineville. The cheers of the Friday night football crowd echoed through her senses as they topped the hill overlooking Pineville High School's stadium. In her mind's eye, she longingly envisioned herself on the track, in her red and gray uniform, leading cheers and socializing with Kate and Susanna, all while keeping an eye on her two favorite players, Jimmy and Doug.

Remy wheeled his Jeep Cherokee into the circle drive of her childhood home, and Ashley sprang from the car without waiting for her three car companions, running up the front steps and through the freshly painted front door. Once inside, she took the stairs two at a time, sprinting down the hallway and bursting into her old bedroom.

It was exactly as she had left it, brightly lit by the large picture window draped in white lace, with walls of pale yellow adorned with school pennants, framed group photos and plaques of award. Her wrought iron bed remained catty-cornered at the far end of the room, with sheets trimmed in white eyelet and her grandmother's patchwork quilt spread across it like a protective cloak. Ashley couldn't resist, bounding across the room and falling backward onto the feathery mattress, sighing with elation at the familiar feel of her own bed. Hearing laughter, she lifted her head to see Maggie standing in the doorway with Molly on her hip, giggling at the comical sight of her overly excited daughter rolling atop the bed.

"I'm going to have a play date with my granddaughter," she said with a light-hearted grin. "If you're done wallowing on the bed, why don't you run next door and see Kate?"

Scampering across the yards separating the two homes, Ashley banged loudly on the Ducotes' door, squealing delightedly as Kate swung open the door. "Kate!" Ashley threw her arms around her best friend, bear-hugging her as Kate patted her affectionately on the back.

"Welcome home, stranger!" Kate said, her pretty face radiating vivaciously as she held Ashley at arms' length to get a better look at her. "Your hair, I love it!" she reached up to bounce the ends of Ashley's shortened hairline with her palm, grinning with approval. "And look at you, you skinny thing! I can't believe that you've had a baby."

She pulled Ashley into the house smelling of apple pie and roses, depositing her on the floral divan in the living room. "By the way, where is Molly? I'm dying to meet her."

"She's with Maggie. Good luck if you think you're going to get anywhere near her for the next day or two. Grandma is already monopolizing her."

Kate was as lovely as ever, dressed in olive shorts and a cream camp shirt, her light hair brushing her shoulders in a shining pageboy. She looked relaxed and happy, her cheeks rosy and her grass-green eyes sparkling cheerfully as she curled up on the opposite end of the sofa from Ashley.

"You look terrific, Kate," Ashley said. "You must've had a good year at Northeast."

"It was nothing really special," Kate admitted with an indifferent shrug. "No big parties, no great romance. I just went to class. My roommate was very sedate and she studied a lot."

"She sounds fascinating," Ashley said sarcastically. "Are you rooming together again next year?"

"Nah, for my senior year I thought I'd find a man to shack up with," Kate teased. "I'm thinking of going co-ed and moving to Hudson Hall."

"Please, why would you want to live that close to a man? I'd rather find a good female roommate." Ashley said, a wise smile on her face. "How are Hill and Melissa? Do you ever see them?"

"Hillary and Melissa are still my suitemates, thank God. They were my only saving grace last year. They're fine. They miss you, though, just like I do," Kate punched her arm fondly and Ashley beamed, glad to know that, although she was no longer with them in Monroe, she had not been forgotten.

"You know, Kate, it wouldn't kill you to drop me a line every once and a while."

Kate rolled her eyes guiltily. "I know, I know, I'll try to do better, I promise," she said with a sheepish grin, vowing to write more often, despite the fact that both she and Ashley knew that she wouldn't.

"Are you still seeing Mitch?"

"Off and on. I go out with him and some other guys too. There's nothing really special going with any of them."

"I always thought you'd end up marrying Mitch," Ashley said, baiting her speculatively, and Kate burst into entertained laughter.

"Marriage to anyone, particularly Mitch Guidry, is the last thing on my mind," she said. "I leave that department to you and Susanna. Speaking of, tell me, how was your year?"

"Well, it certainly wasn't dull, I'll put it that way," Ashley shifted uncomfortably, resisting the urge to scowl by coercing a bright smile onto her face. "How is Susanna? Have you seen her since you've been home?"

"I saw her briefly last week but only for a minute. She couldn't sit still long enough to carry on a conversation. Susanna is awfully scattered. This wedding has thrown her for a loop," Kate said, just as the doorbell rang interrupting their conversation. Before Kate could rise to answer the door, Susanna blew in like a tornado.

"Susanna!" Ashley said. "We were just talking about you."

"Sure, visit Kate first! Don't come see the bride!" Susanna strode purposely toward the couch to hug Ashley, then glanced up, regarding Ashley's new hairstyle with a sardonic smile. "Well, hell, there goes my idea for matching wedding hairstyles."

"Blew that French twist idea for you, did I?" Ashley teased her good-naturedly.

"Yeah, but that's okay. That cut is great for you. It brings you one step closer to being somewhat attractive." Susanna plunked down between Kate and Ashley on the sofa. "It's much better than that old brown mop pulled back in a ponytail."

"You better quit while you're ahead, Susanna," Kate intervened, letting Susanna know that she was just about to cross the line, not wanting to see Ashley and Susanna begin to brawl within the first few minutes of their reunion.

"I'll tell you what," Susanna slapped Ashley's knee, shooting her a naughty grin. "Let's blow this Popsicle stand. We'll go for your dress fitting then stop off for drinks."

They ended up at Julia's for nachos and margaritas, taking a large corner booth, their gossip commencing the minute they sat down. "Rhonda Williams is getting married in July," Susanna revealed with a wry grin, eyeing Ashley for her reaction as she reached across the table for the basket of tortilla chips.

Ashley raised a cynical brow. "Who's the lucky fellow?"

"Some guy she met in Texas at school," Susanna elaborated on Rhonda's wedding plans, commenting on Rhonda's poor bridal etiquette. "Can you believe that *Rhonda* is wearing white? It's sacrilege, I'm telling you."

"Aren't you wearing white?" Kate said, tongue-in-cheek, laughing at Susanna's offended expression.

"I have every reason in the world to wear white," Susanna said huffily. "I'm as virginal as the rest of you are or were."

"Tell me about your flowers," Ashley said, shooting a sidelong glance to Kate to see if she found Susanna's reasoning as comical as she did.

"I'm using calla lilies, tulips, roses and irises," Susanna counted the varieties off on her fingers, rolling her eyes upward with recollection.

"I should've known that you would pick out-of-season flowers for your wedding. Poor Ted, this must be costing him a fortune." Ashley laughed.

Susanna stuck her tongue out in reply. "Whatever. I'm worth it. My wedding will be most gorgeous wedding you've ever been to."

"Of that I am sure," Ashley said, her eyes dancing playfully.

The three friends chattered loudly, each tripping over the words of the other, as they exchanged anecdotes and stories of the past year. As the margaritas began to take effect, Ashley's reserve melted away, and she finally broached the subject most dear to her heart.

"So what do you hear from Doug?" She tried to be as nonchalant as possible, her eyes downcast as she stared into the lime green slush of her margarita, swirling it around casually with her straw.

Susanna snickered, regarding Ashley knowingly. "I wondered how long it would take you to bring him up. You surprised me. It took much longer than I thought it would."

"What?" Ashley said, lifting her eyes innocently to Kate and Susanna as they stared at her. "I'm just asking about my good friend Doug."

"Sure you are," Susanna continued to cackle, waving the waitress over for another pitcher of drinks.

"I hear he has a girlfriend," Kate said, dipping a chip into the thick, gooey queso and lifting it to her mouth, catching the dripping cheese with the palm of her hand.

Ashley's wide eyes darted to Susanna for confirmation, and Susanna curbed her laughter, nodding at her solemnly.

"Yeah, he does, and one humdinger of a girlfriend she is," she said. "Her name's Camille Rabalais and she's the governor's niece."

"Which governor?" Ashley blinked at her, still trying to grasp that Doug really had a girlfriend.

"Which governor? *The* governor, Ashley. The governor of the great state of Louisiana," Susanna rolled her eyes scornfully. "She's in pre-law with Doug at LSU."

Ashley's heart grew heavy with regret. "Is she pretty?" she asked soberly.

"Get a grip, Ashley," she scolded herself sternly. "Next thing you know, you'll be babbling and sobbing into your drink."

"I heard she's quite a beauty, although I haven't seen her personally," Kate said, stretching her lightly tanned legs comfortably across the red leather seat of the booth. Ashley nodded somberly in acknowledgment, letting it slowly sink in, her emotions written all over her face.

"Does it hurt not to be the center of the universe anymore, Ashley?" Susanna questioned her teasingly, meeting the ill-tempered glare Ashley gave her with an amused smirk.

"What's that supposed to mean?" Ashley said, her cheeks and tone of voice growing hot.

"You know as well as I do that, up until now, you've always had Doug's undying affection. I was just wondering how it feels to know that he has found someone else?" Susanna said devilishly, her evil streak emerging.

Ashley continued to stare angrily at her, ready to retaliate with something really nasty when Kate quickly interrupted them. "Let's talk about something else," she said, striving to keep the peace. "I've heard enough about Susanna's wedding. Ashley, tell us all about school and your job."

Ashley filled them in on life at the college of pharmacy, then described with a light-hearted narration her weekends at University Hospital with the very witty and charming Jack Chambers. She finished by painting a vivid picture of her hectic daily routine of juggling Molly, school and work.

"Whoa, whoa, wait a minute," Susanna interrupted her, raising her hand in protest. "Where exactly is Rick during all this running, cooking, cleaning and studying? What is his role as a father?"

"To put it as simply as possible, Rick serves no function as a father," Ashley said brusquely.

Kate and Susanna stared at one another, exchanging troubled looks. "What's his problem? Other than his usual personality, I mean?" Susanna demanded, sputtering indignantly.

"He's never wanted Molly and he's made that perfectly clear for quite some time now."

"Might I take this moment to utter 'I told you so'?" Susanna mumbled under her breath, her hazel eyes flashing bitterly.

"You poor kid," Kate reached across the table to pat her hand sympathetically before Ashley hastily snatched it away.

"I don't want your pity, Kate. You'll only make me cry," Ashley said, her voice quavering, filled with sadness and regret. "I only want to enjoy this week without talking about Rick or any of my other problems. I just want to enjoy the short time that I have here at home."

"Time to go!" Susanna announced, rising abruptly from her seat, wagging her finger in Ashley's face. "You may not drink anymore this entire week if you are going to get sloppy or mean."

Ashley raised her hand in a mocking scout's honor salute. "I promise not to pout for the rest of the week."

"That's better," Susanna smiled vibrantly and threw her arm around Ashley's shoulder. "Let's talk about my favorite subjects: Mark and the wedding."

Rick's flight landed in Alexandria late Friday afternoon and Ashley avoided his arrival at her parents' house by leaving with Kate for Susanna's wedding rehearsal. As Susanna's stand-in, Ashley stayed occupied, holding Mark Lawrence's hand at the altar as he practiced his wedding vows, missing Rick's grand entrance into the dimly lit sanctuary of the church. As rehearsal ended, Ashley caught a glimpse of him sitting on the back row of the church, deeply engrossed in conversation with Susanna, devilishly handsome in tan slacks and light blue button-down shirt, his thick hair falling just above his collar. In spite of their mutual dislike of one another, Rick and Susanna appeared to being playing nice together, with Rick refraining from being pompous and Susanna refraining from reading him the riot act.

Taking a deep breath, Ashley strolled as casually as possible toward Rick, dreading her reintroduction to life as Mrs. Rick LeNoir. "Hello," Ashley said, greeting him with as much warmth as she could muster.

Rick looked up, seeing Ashley standing before him, stunning in a little black dress, and smiled mockingly. "Ah, so you do remember that you have a husband," he tormented her lightly. "I was beginning to wonder."

"How could I forget?" she asked him, smiling as sweetly as sugar, carefully keeping her distance from him, hoping to avoid any direct contact.

Sensing that an argument could ensue at any moment, Susanna cleverly stepped between them. "You all know how to get to the restaurant? Will you give Max a ride over for me?" she asked, setting into motion her plan to keep Rick and Ashley from tearing each other apart during her wedding festivities.

Ashley enjoyed the rehearsal dinner. Fifty of Susanna's closest friends and family attended, many of whom she had not seen in years. Rick stuck to Ashley's side like glue the entire evening, making it impossible for her to mingle. As the dinner came to an end, Susanna approached them with a well thought-out purpose in mind.

"Now Rick," she addressed him first, offering him her most enchanting smile. "You know as matron of honor, Ashley is required to spend the entire day with me tomorrow. It's part of the rules."

"And who will be taking care of her child while she is with you?" Rick questioned Susanna, but for the answer, he looked to Ashley, regarding her with a lofty expression.

His arrogance was almost more than Susanna could bear, and she scowled bitterly at Rick, nearly biting her tongue in half as she struggled to keep her opinion of him to herself.

"Maggie will keep her until time to leave for the wedding," Ashley said, responding quickly to keep Susanna from going absolutely ballistic. "Then Kate's cousin Simone is coming over to baby-sit, just as she is tonight."

For a split second, Rick appeared visibly relieved before regaining his usual air of self-importance and Susanna stared at him with barely concealed distaste.

"Good," she said, dismissing him with a curt nod and turning to Ashley. "Then I'll see you around nine in the morning," she reached over to hug Ashley goodnight.

"That son of a bitch," Susanna whispered softly in her ear, growling her disapproval before she walked away.

Rick was unusually subdued on the way home from rehearsal dinner, making Ashley a little nervous, wondering if her clear evasion of his phone calls over the past week was the reason behind his reserve. She hated when he was this way. At least when he was scolding or lecturing, she knew what he was thinking. His cool silence gave her no clue where she stood with him.

Simone Ducote, Kate's lanky teenage cousin, met them at the door when they arrived home, hailing them with a metal-mouthed grin, her shiny braces flashing as she informed them that Molly was sound asleep. "Thanks for letting me baby-sit. Molly is a great baby," Simone said as Ashley walked with her out on to the veranda. "I'll see y'all tomorrow night."

Ashley watched as Simone bounded down the steps and jumped in the driver's seat of her little white Nissan pickup, smiling at her adolescent light-heartedness. She waved as Simone drove away, then turned to gaze longingly at the front porch swing. "Oh what the hell," she reasoned. Rick could wait a little longer to be alone with her. She curled up onto the comfortable wooden swing, relaxing with her head against the steel chain, swaying back and forth as she listened peacefully to the sounds of the summer night.

Everyone had gone upstairs when she tiptoed back inside. Rick waited in her bedroom, bare-chested, sitting on the bed in silk sleep shorts with his powerfully sculpted legs stretched out in front of him. Ashley thought it strange to find his virile body on the pristine altar of her bed, hating that he would be the first man to sleep in her old room.

"Are you ever going to let your mother take down this shrine to your adolescence?" he asked as she entered the room, his eyes fixed on the teenage paraphernalia littering the pale yellow walls.

"Nope," she answered curtly, crossing the room and leaning over the crib to kiss Molly good night. Molly's hair was growing in, curling in soft blond ringlets around her angelic face, and Ashley stroked her rosy cheek tenderly, her eyes misting over sentimentally as the overwhelming love she felt for her daughter tugged at her heart strings. Sighing, she reluctantly changed into gym shorts and a T-shirt then joined Rick in bed.

"That's sexy," Rick said sarcastically, lifting a critical brow at her attire.

"Were you expecting leather and lace?" she said. "Surely you can't be thinking about sex with my parents across the hall?"

"Why not? You are my wife, Ashley."

"True enough, but I can't relax knowing my folks are across the hall from us," she told him, her purpose to get out of her wifely duty.

Rick reached out to put his finger in her face, tapping her nose lightly as he advised her, "Enjoy this weekend, Ashley. On Sunday, you return home with me, to our life, and you won't be escaping again any time soon."

Ashley met his gaze evenly, his stern final statement echoing through her brain. The idle threat was Rick's way of letting her know that things would be no different for her when they returned home to Oklahoma. She would be expected to return to doing things Rick's way and she dreaded it. Having glimpsed life with freedom from Rick, Ashley was reluctant to let it go.

Promptly at nine the next morning, Ashley pulled up in front of the Robicheaux's red brick home, getting out of Maggie's Buick and striding up the sidewalk to tap lightly on the door. Susanna answered with tousled hair, clad in chartreuse baby-doll pajamas, swinging the door open widely as she yawned.

"Good morning," she grumbled, not truly awake yet.

"I thought you wanted me here at nine," Ashley said, observing Susanna's sleepy appearance as she stepped into the planked entryway.

"I did. I wanted to get you away from Rick as early as possible," Susanna said. "My matron of honor must remain cheerful, which would have been next to impossible if you had stayed home with *him* all morning," she yawned again, stretching lazily. "Go in the kitchen with my folks and get some coffee while I shower."

Ashley wandered down the paneled hallway toward the kitchen. Passing the living room, she spotted Max flat on his back, sleeping soundly on the beige carpeted floor, the remote control still clutched in his hand. "Late night," she guessed as she grinned at his dozing form. She and Susanna had spent many nights sprawled out on that very carpet, snuggling deep into cozy sleeping bags and watching horror movies until the wee hours of the morning.

She found Claire and Ted sitting at the kitchen table reading the Saturday newspaper, sipping their morning caffeine out of steaming oversized mugs. Ashley stopped by the coffee pot, pouring herself some coffee and joined them at the table. "Morning," she smiled as she pulled out a chair, taking a seat across the pine table from Claire.

"Well hello, Ashley," Claire Robicheaux returned her greeting cheerfully, glancing up from the Women's section of the paper. "You're out and about early."

"I'm on matron of honor duty," she said, chatting idly with Claire until Susanna reappeared, dressed in walking shorts and a white blouse, significantly more alert as she sat down next to Ashley, coffee mug in hand.

"It's my last morning as a single woman!" she said loudly, winking slyly at her father. "You better ground me now because after tonight, your chance is gone forever," she teased him.

Ted Robicheaux peered at her over the top of his newspaper, eyeing her skeptically and wearing a wry smile on his face. "Oh, you think so?" he challenged her. "Just watch me."

Ashley listened to their happy-go-lucky heckling with a pleased yet astonished smile. After all the years of butting heads, Ted and Susanna had finally come to a peaceful understanding and actually seemed to enjoy one another's company. It was about time.

After the bridesmaids' luncheon, a trip to the beauty salon, and by the Robicheaux's to retrieve the dresses, Ashley and Susanna drove in Maggie's car to the church, picking up Kate along the way.

Tramping into the sanctuary of the Methodist church, they found the florist hard at work, draping the pews with greenery and bows under the careful direction of Claire Robicheaux. Susanna stopped in the back of the church, appraising with a critical eye the arrangements of pink tulips, sterling silver roses and daisies on either side of the altar. Huffing loudly, she unloaded her garment bag onto Ashley's outstretched arms before flying down the center aisle of the church, her upswept hair teetering precariously as she went, skidding to a halt at the front of the chapel to consult with the florist.

Ashley shot Kate a dry look, rolling her eyes and shaking her head in wonder. "C'mon Kate," she said, jerking her head toward the adjacent exit. "Let's get changed."

Donning matching long sheaths, sleeveless and emerald green, Ashley and Kate chatted gaily, reapplying their makeup and unpacking Susanna's gown while they waited in the bride's room for the bride. They heard her coming before they saw her and with Claire at her heels, Susanna rushed into the room, her eyes flashing irately.

"I just thought my way would be better!" Susanna said to Claire, protesting loudly.

Claire looked exasperated, her patience worn severely thin after months of dealing with Susanna and her nuptials. "Susanna, you paid the florist to do the flowers. Leave the woman alone and let her do her job. I assure you that she knows what she's doing."

Kate turned her back, giggling discreetly at Susanna's indignant pout and Ashley smirked, unable to resist harassing Susanna just a little, even if it was her wedding day.

"Susanna, lighten up already. Tomorrow morning you won't even remember the silly flowers."

With a haughty roll or her eyes, Susanna childishly stuck her tongue out and unzipped her walking shorts, dropping them into a crumpled pile onto the floor as she stepped out of them and reached for her wedding dress.

Susanna was a beautiful bride, radiant in a simple gown made of silk and unadorned by anything other than a lovely strand of pearls, her wedding gift from Mark. A cathedral-length veil topped her fiery upswept hair, and a lift of her full skirt revealed white satin pumps and a garter of blue. After applying soft pink lipstick, Susanna lifted the lid of the florist's box, pulling out her nosegay of roses and handing Ashley and Kate each a spray of calla lilies and delicate tulips.

"Let's go take pictures," she said, bolting out the door ahead of them, her silk train trailing down the glossy tiled corridor as she moved hurriedly toward the church parlor.

Again, Ashley shook her head, glancing dubiously at Kate, agreeing with her statement of Susanna from the previous Saturday: "Definitely scattered."

In the church parlor, they posed for formal portraits. Ashley admired the shot of Susanna and Claire, so alike with flaming red hair, and open, friendly smiles, yet so different in temperament. Claire was gentle and kind. Susanna, without a doubt, was Ted Robicheaux's daughter in every sense of the word. As Susanna stood in front of the camera, her arms linked through those of Kate and Ashley, the florist appeared, beckoning frantically to Claire. Claire leaned her head toward that of the florist, wrinkling her brow fretfully before pulling Ashley quickly to the side.

"There's a small problem that I have to attend to," she whispered to Ashley. "Keep Susanna calm and come get me when they're ready for me."

Ashley nodded and smiled reassuringly at Susanna, who was viewing them with rising curiosity. "What's the matter?" she questioned in a panicky voice, her face paling with uncharacteristic anxiety.

"Nothing that your mother can't take care of," Ashley said, rejoining them in front of the backdrop. "Just relax and smile for the camera."

Max and Ted slipped into the room for family portraits and Ashley scurried to the sanctuary to find Claire. After sending Claire, Ashley took her time going back to the parlor, strolling down the hallways of the church building, trailing her fingertips along the creamy textured walls and hearing the laughter of children as she recalled the days of Sunday School and Vacation Bible School. She smiled whimsically, killing time as she retraced her steps, pausing to look at plaques and framed photographs along the corridor.

"Ashley?" she startled at the sound of his voice echoing down the empty hallway, recognizing it instantly, and allowed herself a slight smile as she gathered her courage and turned to face him.

"Hello Doug," Ashley smiled softly at him, regarding him with open fondness as she reached for him, her heart melting the moment their hands touched. She looked up, gazing adoringly into the twinkling brown eyes that she remembered so well. Doug looked wonderful, strikingly handsome, especially so outfitted in a camel double-breasted suit.

"God, are you a sight for sore eyes," Doug said, grinning as he studied her appreciatively. "But I swear, Ash, I wouldn't have known you if I hadn't been looking for you. I love the new look."

"How have you been?" she asked him, struggling to control the nervousness in her voice as her heart thumped wildly.

"I've been great, just great. And you?"

Ashley hated their measly game of chitchat, wanting so badly to tell him the truth. She was miserable and wanted to come home. Instead, she let her pride get in the way and lied.

"I'm just terrific. I love living in Oklahoma City," she said simply, managing a cheerful lilt in her voice as she smiled at him. "School and Molly are keeping me out of trouble."

"I saw Molly earlier this afternoon. She's a cutie," Doug revealed with a wink.

"Where did you see Molly?"

"At your house, naturally. I went by to see you this afternoon but Ms. Maggie said that you were already gone with Susanna."

"Oh, I'm sorry I missed you," she said, scorching him with her intense green eyes, absorbing every feature of his handsome face, well aware that she was staring at him, yet unable to force herself to look away.

"I've found you now. God, how I've missed you," Doug gazed at her earnestly, searching her face for a clue to her thoughts. "Really, Ash, how are things? Is that jerk good to you? I need to know the truth. I've been worried about you."

His eyes pleaded with her, and they stood staring deeply at one another, neither able to look away. He squeezed her hand, urging her to say something, and Ashley would have told him the truth right then and there had they not been interrupted.

"There you are, you sneaky boy. I've been looking for you everywhere." Ashley heard the sensuous, southern drawl of a woman and glanced down the hall to see her moving toward them with feline grace, very tall and very lovely in an expensive, clinging-in-all-the-right-places ivory silk dress. Surveying Ashley curiously, she strolled up to them and hooked her arm through Doug's possessively.

"Who have we here?" she asked, glancing up to Doug with thickly lashed jade-green eyes as he looked, flustered, from her to Ashley, involuntarily dropping Ashley's hands as he hurriedly introduced them.

"Camille, this is Ashley Stewart. Ashley, Camille Rabalais."

So, this was Camille Rabalais. Ashley assessed her quickly. Camille was the picture of a true southern belle, elegant like a magnolia, with long, shiny auburn hair, a creamy, flawless complexion and an exquisite smile that lit her entire face. Camille was breathtakingly beautiful, and Ashley hated her.

Camille, in turn, studied the petite woman before her, speaking first as she stared at Ashley with jealously flashing eyes. "So you're Ashley Stewart," she said. "Doug speaks of you often, but only when he drinks."

She leaned forward, so close that Ashley could smell her flowery perfume, putting her face directly into Ashley's, "So I quit letting him drink." She affected an evil smile, leering at Ashley as she returned to a more poised stance.

Ashley stepped back from her, too much of a lady to spit in her face, and blinked in astonishment, caught off guard by Camille's spiteful disposition and unsure of how to respond.

"Ashley! *Where* are you?" Ashley was rescued as Susanna's nasal whine resonated down the corridor. "We have to finish taking pictures!"

Ashley and Doug glanced in the direction of the parlor, smiling broadly and exchanging a look of reciprocal amusement. "The bride summons me," Ashley said, her eyes dancing with good humor.

"So it would seem," Doug suppressed a chuckle, grinning naughtily at Susanna's customary boorish behavior.

"I'm glad I got to see you," Ashley told him sweetly, gazing with eyes meant only for him.

"Likewise," Doug's manner was more reserved than usual, because of the hellcat on his arm, and he continued to squirm uncomfortably in the company of both women.

Impulsively, Ashley stood on her tiptoes, kissing his cheek affectionately, then turned to Camille. "It was a pleasure meeting you, Camille," she fibbed while smiling graciously. "Will I see you at the reception?"

"Oh, I'm betting on it," Camille narrowed her eyes with disdain, watching as Ashley walked away in the direction of the parlor.

"And *I'm* betting that ol' Camille won't be letting Doug partake in any champagne drinking tonight," Ashley thought with a smirk, laughing softly as she sashayed down the corridor away from them.

As Susanna had promised, the wedding was beautiful. Ashley stood by Susanna, holding her bouquet and watching with delight as she became Mrs. Mark Lawrence. Susanna was absolutely radiant, gazing adoringly into Mark's eyes. Mark grinned ear to ear, regarding his bride with love-struck passion.

So this is what love looked like, Ashley sighed dreamily as she observed them before the candle-lit altar. What a blessing it was to be so sure of your vows, and to truly be in love with the one you married. She supposed she would never know.

Susanna and Mark left the church in a vintage Rolls Royce, bound for the reception at the Dubois Plantation thirty miles outside Alexandria, belonging to a distant relative of Frannie's. Ashley met up with Rick and her parents at the reception, finding them sipping punch in front of an ornate swan ice sculpture, conversing idly and partaking in people-watching while eyeing the reception crowd. Rick looked quite dazzling in his light gray summer-weight suit and Ashley told him so, complimenting him as she adjusted his tie.

Rick looked pleasantly surprised, smiling genuinely at her, putting his arm around her waist as they watched Susanna and Mark at the bride's table, cutting their elaborate cake for the camera and toasting one another with crystal goblets of champagne.

Glancing discreetly around the room, Ashley spotted Camille and Doug next to the champagne fountain, talking with the old high school gang. Ashley watched as Camille enchanted all those around her, holding their attention with her bubbly laughter and smiling eyes. The one exception, other than Ashley, was Kate. She stood encircled in Mitch Guidry's warm embrace, eyeballing Camille critically, later telling Ashley, "I didn't like her, not at all. She's a redheaded Rhonda Williams, I swear to you. Her evil twin separated at birth."

The feeling that had washed over Ashley as she watched Camille was one that she had not experienced in quite some time. She was jealous of Camille. Not only jealous, but also envious of what Camille had that she could not. Camille had Doug.

Recruited by Claire and Susanna to oversee the catering, Mister Eddie Thibodeaux approached Ashley as she nibbled wedding cake, laughing heartily as he bear-hugged her.

"Hallo, ma petite crawfish," he kissed her noisily on the cheek before spying Rick next to her. "This be yo' husband, chère? Don' be rude, honey, introduce ol' Mist' Eddie."

Ashley introduced them and they shook hands with Mister Eddie regarding Rick dubiously. "I thought my gal done married her a Cajun boy. You sure don' sound like no coon ass."

Remarkably, Eddie Thibodeaux amused Rick and he smiled generously at him, humoring him with his reply. "I may not sound like one, but I'm a coon-ass where it really counts," he patted the spot on his chest over his heart, "Right here."

Eddie chuckled, patting Rick on the back, missing Rick's scowl of disdain, telling him in a jolly voice, "Go dance wid your wife, boy." He pushed them with massive arms toward the dance floor, cackling mischievously.

On the dance floor, Rick took Ashley in his arms and she grew cold, stiffening slightly at his touch before making herself relax and enjoy the music. Doug and Camille were several couples over, smiling and talking softly as they danced, and Ashley watched them discreetly over Rick's shoulder, aching with envy and inner longing. The striking couple did not go unnoticed by Rick, who commented on Camille immediately.

"Who's that babe with Fairchild?" Rick asked admiringly. "She's a real peach."

"Shut up, Rick," Ashley said, snapping in irritation. Even her own husband was in awe of Camille.

Rick quickly picked up on the fact that she was jealous of Camille, and used that information to terrorize her. "Poor Ashley," he glanced down at her, smiling condescendingly as he pretended to be sympathetic. "You're no longer the belle of the ball. You're just an ordinary married woman with a kid now."

It was just like Rick to spoil the only pleasant moment they had experienced together in months. Ashley glared bitterly at him as he threw back his head, laughing devilishly.

"It's a good thing that you have me, Ashley," he said mockingly. "Who else would want you now? Why have used goods when you could have someone as luscious as she is?" He nodded in Camille's direction, relishing the fact that Ashley was miserable. Ashley held her tongue, not wanting to brawl with him in the middle of the dance floor. She and Rick would remain civil at Susanna's wedding. She owed that much to Susanna.

The music stopped and Ashley stalked off the dance floor, hoping to lose Rick and mingle with old friends. She found Kate and Mitch beside the hors d'oeuvre table, snacking on crudités. Ashley stood with them, enjoying Kate's take on the wedding and reception when she overheard, "Why, are you Ashley's husband, Rick?"

Camille's sexy drawl drifted over to Ashley and she turned to see Camille with Rick, fingering his lapels lightly as she looked at him with flirtatious eyes. "Why on earth would a handsome thing like yourself marry a mousy little thing like her?"

Ashley scowled unpleasantly, observing as the appropriately flattered Rick asked Camille to dance with him, rolling her eyes at Kate as they strolled onto the dance floor together. "For the love of God," Ashley said, muttering in disgust.

"Well, I've got to hand it to you, Fairchild," Ashley startled guiltily when she realized from Mitch's words that Doug had joined them, cutting off her opinion of Camille in mid thought while Mitch finished his statement. "It may have taken you forever to find a girlfriend, but man, is she worth the wait."

Ashley wrinkled her brow in vexation, wanting to stick her tongue out at Mitch for his unsolicited opinion. Before she could say or do anything, she felt a warm hand on her shoulder. "Would you like to dance?"

Ashley spun around, brushing against Doug's hard chest as he stood behind her. Flushing with happiness, she gave him her hand as Kate looked on, carefully keeping a pleased smile under wraps.

"I'd love to," Ashley accepted and Doug led her to the dance floor, putting his arm around her waist. The warmth of his arm through her thin dress burned like fire against her back and she looked up at him, meeting his smiling eyes.

"So, Ash, what do you think of Camille?" he asked and Ashley pondered, searching for a suitable response before answering.

"She's a jewel," she replied, trying to keep the sarcasm out of her voice. "How long have you two been going out together?"

"A little under six months. We met at a Christmas party."

"She goes to LSU?" Ashley knew the answer, but acted as if she knew nothing about Camille whatsoever. She wouldn't dare let Doug know that Camille had been the topic of any conversation in which she had participated.

"Yes, she'll be in law school with me in the fall."

"How nice for you two to have classes together," Ashley murmured softly, glancing over to Camille dancing with her husband. They were laughing and talking elatedly, their faces lit in mutual admiration. Ashley frowned, shaking her head slightly at Camille.

"Does she not remind you of Rhonda?" she asked seriously, looking up at Doug with a dubious expression on her face.

Doug chuckled good-naturedly. "Well, I guess she does a little," he admitted with a smile. "I think it's because Camille is a little jealous and possessive."

"A little? She could be Rick's soul mate."

"Rick can't have a soul mate, Ashley. The man has no soul."

Caught off guard by Doug's bluntness, Ashley laughed out loud in spite of herself. Not that she minded if Doug bad-mouthed her husband. It was just a shock to be around someone, other than Susanna, who gave such an unadulterated opinion of Rick.

As the music ended, a throng of single women formed as Susanna threw her bouquet, aiming and almost knocking Kate out cold with it. Susanna and Mark left for their honeymoon at midnight, running through a rain of birdseed and cheers wishing them well. Ashley caught one final glimpse of Doug and Camille as they left, descending the front steps of the great plantation house arm in arm, smiling at one another affectionately. Ashley watched through melancholy eyes as they climbed into Doug's car, driving away into the foggy night. She sighed heavily, returning inside to locate Rick and her parents.

On the drive back to Pineville, Ashley listened begrudgingly to Rick's arrogant oration. He'd had a wonderful time at the reception, charming every woman there, and was very proud of it.

"I think Camille should have caught the bouquet," he said wickedly, cutting his eyes to Ashley. "I think we'll be attending a wedding for her and Fairchild before much longer." Rick goaded Ashley smugly and received in return a look from her that quickly let him know how much she appreciated his thoughts.

"She's a pretty girl," Remy noted from the front seat and Ashley rolled her eyes haughtily. "Great," she thought, "betrayed by my own father."

"Yes, and truly a fine catch for Doug Fairchild," Rick said, agreeing with Remy and needling Ashley again with his words.

"Well, she may be pretty, but I think Doug could do better," Maggie said, expressing her opinion doubtfully. "She was just a little unpleasant, if you ask me."

"Thank you, Maggie," Ashley silently applauded her, flashing her a pleased smile.

When they finally reached home, Ashley sprang from the car, striding quickly into the house before the others, not only to pay Simone for babysitting but also to escape any further talk of Camille. Rick followed her into the house, chuckling devilishly, and enjoying seeing her that way.

Rick, Ashley and Molly left Louisiana on an early afternoon flight the next day and Rick hardly waited for the wheels to leave the ground before he began tormenting Ashley. "Did you have fun with your friends, Ashley?" he asked, looking up from his in-flight magazine, regarding her inquisitively.

Ashley had been staring absently out the window, reflecting back on the night before. Hearing his question, she glanced back over her shoulder, meeting his eyes. "Yes, of course, I did," she said with a genuine smile.

Rick nodded, wearing a purposely-smug mask on his face. "That's good, my pet. I'm glad that you did, since that's the last time you'll see any of them for a very long time."

The smile disappeared from Ashley's face as he sneered at her, and she turned away from him. "Just remember, Ashley," she felt his breath on her ear as he rested his chin on her shoulder, "I'll never let you go."

His underlying threat may have been veiled, but Ashley understood him perfectly, knowing then that her road to freedom would be hard fought.

As life in Oklahoma returned to what had become normal, Rick and Ashley entered their second year of marriage shortly after Susanna's wedding.

Over the summer, Ashley worked for vacationing employees, spending weekdays as well as weekends at the hospital. With her knowledge and duties expanding, Ashley found her job to be both interesting and challenging. Jack took her on rounds with him up on the hospital floors, visiting each floor to check patient medications, and to stop by the various nurses' stations.

"Hello Jack!" The nurses flirted scandalously with him and Jack ate it up, leaning nonchalantly on the counter, feeding them lines and charming them with his dazzling smile while he shopped for new women to date.

"When are you going to settle down and marry one of those women?" Ashley asked him one evening as they walked the floors.

Jack lifted a skeptical brow. "Been there, done that," he commented cynically. "I do not regard marriage as something I want to do again."

"How can you say that?"

He turned his head to stare at her, grinning at her mockingly. "That question comes from you, Ashley? You, who are so happily married in your own right?"

"Touché," Ashley applauded his quick wit. "Tell me about your wife," she urged curiously, taking the opportunity to find out the story behind his former marriage since the subject had been broached.

"My ex-wife," Jack abruptly corrected her with a slight frown, leaning against the wall adjacent to the stairwell, averting his eyes from Ashley's inquiring gaze.

"Okay, then, tell me about your ex-wife."

"My ex-wife, Samantha, was in dental school while I was in pharmacy school. She met, fell in love with, and left me for one of her fellow classmates."

Jack kept the explanation simple, yet Ashley could tell by the pained look in his eyes that, even after many years, his deep hurt prevailed. She placed a comforting hand on his arm. "I'm sorry, Jack," she said sincerely.

He laughed, forcing a jolly tone back into his voice. "Oh hell, don't be sorry. She was a bitch anyway."

"But you still loved her."

"Yes, damn it, I loved her," he said gruffly, scowling at Ashley as he conceded. "Can we please change the subject now? Or will I be forced to make you discuss Doug Fairchild?"

Ashley flounced away from him, clearly to avoid any debate about Doug, and could hear Jack chuckling behind her. "Why don't you just cut your losses and leave?" Jack called out, sprinting to catch up with her as she took long strides down the hospital corridor. "Just take Molly and go back home."

"I wish it were that simple," Ashley said, sighing heavily while Jack eyed her peculiarly.

"It is that simple, Ashley. Nothing could be more simple."

Ashley shrugged, not having any desire to get into it with Jack. Jack was a smart guy and everything he said always made sense, until the same advice was applied to Rick. With Rick, it all took on different consequences. And Ashley knew that Rick would never let her just waltz out of his life. Not without a fight anyway.

"Shut up, Jack." Frustrated, she punched the elevator button, jumping on when the doors opened.

Jack followed her onto the elevator, studying her acutely as they descended to the fifth floor pharmacy, wishing he knew what really motivated her to stay married to Rick LeNoir.

Summer ended, and Ashley's second year of school began, with her classes expanding to specifically drug-related classes. She and Ellie spent countless hours quizzing one another, finding their course content sometimes overwhelming. Her routine was much the same as it had been the year before. She juggled Molly with school and work, ran a household in tip-top fashion, and dealt with a husband who, although unreasonably possessive and passionately jealous, remained distant and cold. Ashley spent more and more time away from the house, taking Molly nightly after dinner to find solace with Ellie and Corrine. At that point in time, it didn't bother Rick if she left to study in the evenings. He didn't care what she did, just as long as she had Molly with her.

As the semester continued, Rick became increasingly impossible to deal with. Over Christmas break, they celebrated Molly's first birthday, with Remy and Maggie journeying to Oklahoma for ice cream and cake. Molly was thrilled with her cake, smearing icing from head to toe. Ashley cheerfully snapped photos with the Kodak, letting Molly demolish her cake as she laughed with glee. Rick found little amusement in any of it.

"Good, Ashley, good," he cheered her sarcastically, scowling unpleasantly from his position in the kitchen. "Teach her that it's funny to play with her food."

"Oh, Rick, lighten up," Ashley said, frowning slightly at him. "It's her birthday, for heaven's sake."

Without a word, Rick stalked upstairs to his office, slamming the door thunderously as he went inside, not caring what Remy or Maggie thought of his behavior. He rarely even pretended to care for Molly for her parents' benefit anymore. He was smug and arrogant, sure in his position because he knew that he had Ashley where he wanted her for now. His threats alternated between taking Molly away from her, and reminding Ashley that he would never let anyone else have her.

Ashley remained subdued and tried to ignore him. She certainly didn't argue with him. There was no justice to be gained from arguing with Rick. She had learned that he would not hesitate to become physically abusive with her.

No, with Rick, it was in Ashley's best interest to bide her time and finish school. After that, she could get away when the time was right.

For Christmas, Jack presented Ashley with a set of videotapes, each labeled "Doug Fairchild's Finest Moments in College Football," and grinned as she shrieked with delight.

"That's a hell of a reaction from someone who's only a friend," Jack said, winking mischievously as Ashley hugged the tapes ecstatically to her chest.

She sneaked by Jack's house as often as she could to view a few stolen moments of Doug on the tapes, watching him with adoring eyes glued to the set, and a blissful smile on her pretty face. Jack observed her emotions, never directly commenting on the depth of the attraction he sensed she had for Doug. He only insinuated what he thought, and teased her mercilessly about her insistence that Doug was just a good friend, confident that sooner or later the truth would come out.

Finally, in a weak moment, Ashley broke down and told Jack the truth about her feelings for Doug, recalling for him how Doug had proposed to her when he found out she was pregnant with Molly, and how she had turned him down for his own good.

"You regret it, don't you?" Jack asked rhetorically, already knowing the answer.

"Every day of my life."

Approaching her final year of college, Ashley could at last see the light at the end of the tunnel. She was one year away from graduation, and would no longer have to live in fear of Rick taking Molly from her. Her goal was in sight, her mission almost complete. As she anticipated emancipation, her temporarily clipped self-confidence soared once more.

And that's when the transformation of her husband became so unbelievably complete.

CHAPTER TWENTY-SIX

Ashley couldn't pinpoint the exact moment when Rick snapped. Dramatic though it was, it couldn't have happened all at once. He must have been steadily heading in that direction over time, becoming worse in so subtle a manner that she didn't notice until it was too late. Whatever the case, by the end of the summer before her senior year of college, Rick had become a complete and utter psycho, making her final year of school by far the most frightening year of her life.

Where Rick had been distant and aloof before, he was suddenly concerned with every hour of her day, wanting her complete class, clinical rotation and work schedules, and recording the mileage on the Corolla, holding her responsible for any discrepancies from the norm. Ashley sensed that he knew every move she made, spotting him at various times of day, camped in his car outside the pharmacy school or in the parking lot of University. With all his following, watching and stalking of her, Ashley didn't know how Rick managed to remain employed. He couldn't be getting much work done. Every time she turned around, he was lurking nearby, never discreet about his presence, not caring whether she saw him or not.

Rick became insanely jealous, not only of every man Ashley knew or had ever known but also of her girlfriends, Ellie in particular. He would tolerate no mention of Eleanor Holman, flying into a rage whenever he heard her name, and Ashley thanked God daily that Rick knew nothing of her friendship with Jack.

The final downward spiral in their relationship began one evening shortly after the fall semester started. Ashley had an exceptionally hard day on her hospital rotation and came home dragging, literally worn to a frazzle from the day's events. She unlocked the front door, immediately spotting Rick anxiously pacing the living room. It was going to be one of those nights. Taking a deep breath, she breezed inside, setting Molly down to play with her toys on the living room floor and proceeded, without a word to Rick, into the kitchen to start dinner.

Rick crossed the living room floor, taking great strides, coming into the kitchen and blocking her path from the refrigerator to the stovetop with his rock hard physique. "Where did you have lunch today?" he asked, staring down into her face with suspiciously narrowed aqua-blue eyes.

Ashley met his stare with unwavering eyes, pushing past him to add spaghetti noodles to the boiling water on the range. "I had a burger at Johnnie's," she said, keeping her answer simple, because with Rick these days, the less she elaborated, the better, never knowing what minute detail might set him off.

On this night, however, simple didn't satisfy him. "With whom did you dine?"

"Ellie and Ava."

He slammed his fist onto the countertop, his eyes smoldering angrily. "I should've known you would be with *her*," he said acidly, a spasm of irritation crossing his face as he leaned closely into hers, his nose almost touching the tip of her own. "What about Sean and Greg? Did they go with you?" His fiery eyes searched hers, watching for any flicker of deception.

"Sean and Greg were not with us," Ashley responded quietly to his interrogation, turning her back to him and hoping he would go away if she jumped headlong into dinner preparations. Again, she was wrong, feeling his hot breath against her ear.

"No lying, Ashley, no lying," he murmured, caressing her earlobe with his tongue before tracing a line to the nape of her neck with his lips. He nuzzled her there, smiling victoriously as she scrunched her shoulder involuntarily. "Such an interesting pressure point, don't you agree, my pet? A place which can offer so much pleasure, yet give so much pain."

He reached up, clamping his hand so hard against the nape of her neck that Ashley feared he might bruise her. She flinched in response to his painful grip but refused to give him the satisfaction of uttering the slightest whimper.

"You better not be lying to me, Ashley. If I ever find out differently, I will make you very sorry," he said, threatening her as he released her neck and sauntered out into the living room, glaring with contempt at his daughter, who played on the floor at his feet.

Ashley's hands shook as she finished dinner, but her face revealed no emotion. She was careful not to show Rick that he intimidated her in any manner. She hoped that she was making the right decision in remaining with Rick until May. She just couldn't give up, being so close to the end. She had to stick it out and play the game with him until she could support Molly on her own. She couldn't lose her, no matter what she had to sacrifice to keep her.

"The courts will never give custody to a mother who cannot support her own child. Molly would be mine if you ever left." Rick had used those words to taunt her hundreds of times over the course of their two-year marriage—just another instance of the emotional blackmail at which he had become so accomplished. He had used the same kind of blackmail to ensure that Ashley married him, and he continued to use it to ensure that she stayed married to him.

When he wasn't saying incredibly nasty things to belittle her, Rick would stare at Ashley peculiarly, as if he were trying to get inside her head, covetous of her every thought. His behavior made Ashley very nervous. She never knew what he was thinking or what he would do next, and she constantly tried to second-guess whether his next move would simply be bizarre, or turn violent. Ashley dreaded his black moods. Rick's insane rages had sent her crashing into a wall more times than she could count.

True to his promise after Susanna's wedding, Rick did his best to keep Ashley isolated from the rest of the world. She hadn't been home to Louisiana in well over a year, and she missed Kate, Susanna and Doug like mad. At Rick's insistence, Maggie and Remy's visits to Oklahoma City had become less and less frequent, and Rick had long since banned Celeste and Dominique from seeing them, after Celeste had tried to offer him some unsolicited marital advice. Ashley hated being cut off from Celeste. She genuinely liked Rick's sister and had enjoyed her visits. Celeste had been distraught over losing contact with her only niece. She was crazy about Molly, but was too frightened of Rick to dare defy him.

Ashley became bitter and discouraged. She rarely slept, seldom ate, and had transformed into an anxious, cowardly shadow of her former self. She didn't like the person she saw in the mirror's reflection every morning. There was no light in her eyes and no hope in her heart. The light-hearted days of her youth had vanished, and the only emotions Ashley LeNoir felt now were fear and insecurity.

But Rick couldn't isolate her completely, and that was Ashley's saving grace. From her friends and colleagues, she received great moral support. Ellie pushed her to be independent of Rick and not to be afraid of him. Having seen Rick's true colors at the time of Molly's birth, Ellie did not like Rick, nor did she trust him, and she wanted nothing more than to get Molly and Ashley away from him for good.

"Don't ever give that SOB the satisfaction of knowing that you're afraid of him," Ellie advised her time and time again.

"I quit wearing my heart on my sleeve long ago, Ellie," Ashley told her, trying to make light of Ellie's concerns. "In fact, I think I've mastered a pretty decent poker face."

"That's all good and fine, Ashley, but let me tell you, you're not fooling me any. I see right through you."

"Only because you have the inside track."

"Maybe, or maybe you're just transparent as hell."

"Thanks, that's encouraging," Ashley told her with a wry smile. "I'll tell you one thing, Ellie. If I ever get out of this mess, I'm never marrying again."

Ellie chuckled at Ashley's determined expression. "Yeah, sure. Tell me another one," she said. "Don't let Rick ruin your opinion of wedded bliss, Ashley. Not all marriages are hell on earth. You just happen to be in one of the worst of them."

"You think I don't know that? Believe it or not, there was a time in my life when I had something very special. Knowing what I know now, I'll never settle for less again."

"You're setting your standards a little high, aren't you?"

"Apparently not. I married Rick, didn't I?"

"True, but look at it this way. Starting at rock bottom like this, your choices can only get better, right?"

Ashley shook her head stubbornly, dismissing Ellie's suggestion with a wave of her hand. "You think I'm kidding, but I'm not. I never want a man running my life again. I'm going to be my own person."

She would just make it her policy to avoid future commitment like the plague, adopting Jack's unwavering philosophy on marriage: been there, done that, never again.

But in as much as she confided in Ellie, Ashley never told her the complete truth about her home life. She kept it all inside, never revealing how psychotic and obsessive Rick had become. She believed her poker face to be perfect, never thinking that the dull look in her eyes would give away her secret.

When all was said and done, the only thing that kept Ashley going was Molly. Molly LeNoir lived in an extremely turbulent household, but fortunately never showed one sign of being affected by it. At almost two years of age, Molly was more sunny and beautiful than Ashley could have ever imagined, with a peaches and cream complexion, curly blond hair and sparkling, bright aqua-blue eyes, the one characteristic she had inherited from Rick. Molly rolled with punches like a pro, traveling with Ashley to and from daycare or Corrine's house every day of the week, at ungodly hours of the day and night, never uttering a complaint.

Molly's bubbly laughter was contagious, and she made every day that Ashley struggled to get them out of their situation more bearable. Ashley loved Molly with her entire heart and soul, never regretting for one day her decision to have Rick's child. Her only wish was that she had gone it alone. Enduring family disgrace and single parenthood would have been a piece of cake next to enduring Rick.

Ashley thought of all the amazing milestones that Molly had sailed through in the two years of her life: her first tooth, her first words and her first steps. Ashley believed all of these accomplishments to be wondrous, but Rick hadn't commented on them at all, astounding her by, in essence, ignoring his only child.

As December arrived, and she was forced to manufacturer yet another excuse explaining to Maggie why she couldn't come home for Christmas, Ashley was struck with a bad case of the blues. In days past, she had loved the holidays, but now she hated them. With Rick, they were meaningless. Terribly melancholy, she dragged around for days, needing to share her fears and feelings with someone before she went insane. Out of all the people she knew, there were only two logical choices in whom to confide—Jack or Ellie—and she chose Jack.

Ashley picked an evening shift at the hospital to unload her problems onto Jack's broad shoulders, confiding in him as they filled med carts together in total seclusion, shielded from the rest of the pharmacy by the high walls of medication bins. "Jack, he reads my mail, he screens my calls, he follows me. I have absolutely no privacy whatsoever."

Jack ceased working, staring in amazement at her nonchalant description of Rick's behavior. "What do you mean 'follows you'?" he asked suspiciously. "Around the house like a puppy, or from place to place like a stalker?"

"I mean from place to place," Ashley studied her hands, fidgeting uncomfortably as she described Rick's strange actions. "And I never know when he'll be there. Sometimes he's in the parking lot at school when I leave class, and sometimes he's in the parking garage at night, waiting for me to come out of the hospital. I've even spotted his car parked down the street from Corrine's house when I pick Molly up after work."

Jack sank numbly to the chair next to her, a sick knot growing in his stomach, staring into her gaunt face and sunken eyes as if seeing them for the first time.

"My God," he said, his tone bordering on guilty. "I didn't realize that things had gotten so bad." The poor kid looked like hell. Her horrible marriage was taking its toll on her youthful good looks.

He took her gently by the shoulders, forcing her to look at him. "Ashley, you listen to me and listen good. You've got to get away from that guy," he said, his brow creased with worry. "He's progressed from just being an ass to being obsessed with you, and that, kiddo, could be dangerous."

"Do you honestly think I don't realize that? But I can't leave him, not until I graduate," she said, finally admitting the truth about why she stayed with Rick. "I wouldn't be able to provide for Molly, and the courts would take her away from me and give her to Rick."

Jack's eyebrows shot up in surprise and his eyes grew wide with disbelief. "Is that the line of shit he's been feeding you to keep you here?" he asked incredulously. "That's why it wasn't simple just to walk away? Why didn't you tell me that was the reason? I would've straightened you out months ago!"

"How was I supposed to know that Rick was lying?"

"Why the hell would you think Rick would tell you the truth? He hasn't been honest with you since the day you met him," Jack said, shaking his head in frustration, then chuckling in response to an afterthought, "Well, I'm glad to know that you didn't stay with Rick due to stupidity alone."

"I must say that I can always depend on you to be perfectly blunt," Ashley said, flashing a rare, humorous smile in his direction.

"Ashley, damn it, this is serious. Don't try to get out of this by acting cute with me," Jack said, giving her an annoyed scowl. "Get out of that marriage now.

No judge in the land would take Molly from you, and we can come up with ways to get you by until graduation."

"That may be very true," Ashley's voice trembled ever so slightly. "But you don't seem to understand. There's no way Rick will let me just walk out on him. Trust me, he's told me that plenty of times, and I fully believe he's capable of stopping me if I tried. My leaving will have to be carefully planned, right down to the smallest detail." She reached out, patting his arm reassuringly. "It won't be that bad, Jack. I only have six more months to play his game, then I'll be free."

He contemplated her ashen face, noting the shadow of fear in her eyes. "You're afraid of him, aren't you?"

"Yes, I'm afraid of him, but as long as I stick to my schedule and come home on time with Molly, I feel pretty confident that I'll be fine."

"Is that all? I can't believe that you're dealing with this like a normal, everyday situation."

"It is a normal, everyday situation for my marriage."

"Ashley, one of us is going to have a nervous breakdown before graduation, and with my luck, it'll probably be me," Jack smiled, putting a friendly hand on her shoulder, his face reflecting how much he cared for her. "Listen carefully, kiddo, and remember this, if you're ever in trouble, no matter what time of the day or night, just call me and tell me that you need me," he stared into her face, reiterating his sincerity with unwavering eyes. "I'll come and get you."

"Oh yeah? You and what army?" Ashley teased him, trying to get him to lighten up a little.

"I do have connections, Ashley," Jack said, finally rewarding her comical effort with a reluctant smile. "My friend, Dan Little, is an undercover cop. He, of course, has friends who can help us with anything we need."

"Oh, Jack, I seriously doubt that it will ever come down to that."

"Ashley, honestly, I don't know what it's going to come to. I just wish to God that I could make you leave him now. Do you have a death wish or something?"

"What are you going to do about it? Take me over your knee?" Ashley flashed him a naughty grin, making him laugh for the first time that evening.

"The thought has crossed my mind on more than one occasion," Jack winked at her, rising from his chair as he was paged to the telephone. Walking away from her, the troubled cast returned to his face, and he knew that he would worry about her until the day she got enough guts to walk out on Rick LeNoir.

As things became more and more tense in the LeNoir household, friends and family began calling Ashley during her shifts at University Hospital.

"Ashley! It's for you again!" Matt Whitford bellowed deafeningly after intercepting another one of her calls, facetiously belly-aching as he handed her the receiver. "You would think I was your damn answering service, for crissakes."

Maggie called Ashley so often that Matt had taken to calling her "Ma," developing a fond kinship with her over the telephone.

"That Matt is such a darlin'," Maggie said, praising him to Ashley.

"You would think 'darlin' if you could hear the vocabulary that boy knows and uses," Ashley said, giggling as she enlightened her.

"He has always been a perfect gentleman on the phone with me."

"My mother loves you," Ashley informed Matt as he sauntered by her chair, covering the mouthpiece of the telephone with her hand to keep any of Matt's inappropriate responses from reaching Maggie's ears.

Matt lifted his eyebrows with good humor, flashing Ashley a roguish grin. "They always do, until I corrupt their daughters." His eyes sparkled devilishly as he winked at her, chuckling in amusement as he left the room.

Ashley shook her head, smirking as Matt disappeared through the doorway. "And that man is going to be someone's physician some day," she thought, "what a scary notion."

Beneath his crude vocabulary, Matt Whitford was truly a remarkable guy, and with him, Ashley had developed a special bond of friendship during their time at the hospital together. Matt became like a brother to her, a very protective big brother who had he known, would not take very kindly to the treatment Ashley was receiving at home. Matt and Jack were also big buddies, playing poker or golfing on the weekends, throwing in a little womanizing if the opportunity arose. They never lacked for female companionship, and Jack even seemed to actually welcome having a little competition from Matt for the nurses' affections.

Because Rick felt it his place to open and read her mail, Ashley rented a post office box and managed to keep in touch with Kate and Susanna, receiving a letter from one of them every couple of weeks. Susanna and Mark had relocated to Dallas and loved it, with Susanna still in banking and Mark in construction contracting. They had a son, Eric, and were expecting another child in July of that year. Susanna frequently invited Ashley and Molly to visit her in Dallas. Ashley would have loved to go, but Rick wouldn't even consider it, still loathing Susanna as she did him. Therefore, Ashley being allowed to associate with her was out of the question.

Kate had become a much better correspondent, and had graduated from Northeast the previous spring with a degree in criminal justice, moving back to Pineville and taking a job with the district attorney's office in Alexandria. She and Mitch had finally called it quits, and the name of Todd Richardson began to pop up repeatedly in Kate's letters. Ashley read between the lines, quickly suspecting that there might be something serious developing between Kate and this mystery man, and kept her fingers crossed, forever hopeful for Kate's romantic happiness.

Still making her heart leap were the faithful letters from Doug that Ashley still received monthly. She had not physically seen Doug since Susanna and Mark's wedding. The previous year she had used every chance available to watch LSU football games, getting her Doug fix, if only via the television screen, but it had been over a year since Doug had played football and Ashley missed seeing her favorite quarterback on college football Saturdays.

In one of his letters, Doug mentioned that his father, Nick, was still in an uproar because Doug had chosen law school over the option to play professional football.

"Just what Louisiana needs is another lawyer!" Doug had animatedly described his father's bellowing and Ashley had laughed, entertained with the mental image she had of their discussion. Doug's football career had been his father's obsession and Ashley was certain that Nick was sorely disappointed that Doug's football days were over.

Doug never mentioned Camille in his letters, nevertheless, Ashley had heard from Kate and Susanna that he was still dating her and she wondered when they would marry. She still cared greatly for Doug. Consequently, she wanted only the best for him, and marrying into one of the richest political families in Louisiana would be great for him and his future career as an attorney. Besides that, once you got past her holier-than-thou personality, Camille was a truly beautiful woman and Ashley sensed that Doug cared for her deeply. She only hoped that Camille could give him the happiness that he deserved.

Ashley wrote back to Doug religiously, falsely portraying in her letters a happy, carefree lifestyle. She wrote only of safe subjects: school, her job and Molly, never mentioning Rick and the way that he had become. To tell Doug would only make him worry about her, and Ashley would never admit to Doug that she had made the wrong decision in marrying Rick. She may have lost her self-confidence, but never her foolish pride.

CHAPTER TWENTY-SEVEN

Another New Year came, and life continued on as Ashley concentrated on humoring Rick. As always, she played the game, never giving him any reason to believe that she was leaving him. She kept up her role as the good wife and tried not to cringe when Rick touched her, though any form of intimacy with him was nauseating to her. Nevertheless, she went through the motions to avoid raising his suspicions.

Unbeknownst to Rick, Ashley began slipping small, personal items from the house, secretly storing them in Jack's attic for safekeeping. Ashley was careful to take only things that would go unnoticed, limiting her choices to the things that were irreplaceable. Among the few treasures she entrusted to Jack were Molly's baby book, and her magnolia-etched cedar chest full of memories, given to her by Jimmy Moreau on a memorable day of Christmas past.

Ashley made it peacefully from the first of the year until the beginning of March, and often looked back on that time in her marriage as the calm before the storm. The brief period of tranquility ended when, on Thursday night of the first week in March, Ashley received a rare call at home from Maggie.

"Hi, Mags, what's up?" Ashley took the call in the kitchen and greeted her mother cheerfully, surprised that Maggie had called while Rick was home. Maggie was not in the habit of risking a conversation with her son-in-law. Any goodwill between the two of them had long since disappeared.

As if on cue, Rick rushed from the living room to monitor Ashley's phone call, leaning against the kitchen counter mere inches from her, his trained ears ready to eavesdrop on her conversation. Ashley pointedly ignored his overbearing presence, focusing instead on the sound of her mother's strained voice.

"Honey, I've got some bad news," Maggie said hesitantly, and for a moment, Ashley panicked.

"What is it?" she asked, her heart in her throat. "Please don't let it be my father," she prayed, "I couldn't bear it."

"Honey, Frank Ducote passed away this morning. He had a massive heart attack and died in his sleep."

"Oh no!" Ashley gave a startled gasp, as hot, scalding tears welled up in her eyes. She ignored Rick's questioning stare, turning her back to him so that she could talk to her mother in peace.

"How's Kate?" Ashley's heart immediately went out to her best friend. Kate had always been such a daddy's girl. She must be devastated.

"Pretty upset, needless to say."

"When is the funeral?" Ashley scrambled for a pen and paper, scribbling as Maggie filled her in on the details.

"The funeral is Saturday morning. Remy and I have already booked a plane reservation for you and Molly. We knew you'd want to come."

"What time is the flight?" Ashley asked, hearing Rick's labored breathing and knowing without looking at him that he was gearing up to have a fit.

"You leave Oklahoma City at five-thirty tomorrow night."

Ashley wrote down the airline and flight number, then hastily folded the piece of paper and stuffed it into her pocket before Rick could snatch it away. After hanging up with Maggie, she dialed the number to the pharmacy at University Hospital, speaking with Meg and canceling her shifts for the weekend. Then slowly, she replaced the receiver, turning to face Rick.

He was livid, his lips pursed tightly with suppressed fury, regarding her with a stony expression etched across his chiseled features. Ashley backed against the kitchen's center island, gripping the edge and digging her fingernails into the wood, bracing herself for another of his incensed tirades.

"Just where do you think you're going?" he asked, his voice dripping with spite. "You are not going to Louisiana, not without me, and I cannot go. I have an important program to finish up over the weekend."

"Rick, I *am* going." Ashley glared at him defiantly. She was not backing down this time, not caring what kind of grief it caused her. She would not miss the funeral. Her being there was too important to Kate.

"Kate is one of my best friends. I loved her father and I'm going to his funeral."

"I see no need for you to make a five-hundred mile trip for two short days."

"I'm going to the funeral, Rick," she said firmly, yet calmly, meeting his venomous look with steady eyes. "And that's final."

Discovering that he was dealing with the old Ashley, Rick ceased his ferocious bellowing, remembering that it did no good. "Okay, fine, Ashley, go!" he said, snapping bitterly. "But Molly stays here with me."

Ashley wanted to sputter angrily back at him, but waited, tactfully forming her reply, keeping the upper hand by remaining calm. "Rick, you just said that you have to work all weekend," she reminded him gently. "You haven't kept Molly a day in her life. There's no reason in the world that I should leave her here with you this weekend."

"As long as Molly is here, I know that you'll be back." Rick sounded so pitiful that Ashley almost felt sorry for him, then realized that it was just one of his deceitful ploys for her sympathy and countered cynically.

"Rick, don't be ridiculous. Of course, I'm coming back. I'm only going to a funeral."

The thought of not coming back from the funeral had not entered Ashley's mind. It was an ingenious idea. She only wished that she had thought of it herself.

After a grueling night of persuading, pleading and justifying, Ashley finally succeeded in getting Rick to agree that she could attend Frank Ducote's funeral and take Molly with her.

"You'll have to find your own way to the airport. I can't take you. I have meetings all afternoon," Rick said after yielding to her.

Ashley rolled her eyes impatiently. His refusal to take her to the airport was just another way for him to be difficult. "That's fine. I'll just leave my car at Ellie's, and she can take us to the airport."

She took her suitcase from the hall closet, and Rick followed her into the bedroom, watching as she packed, doubtfully eyeing the amount of clothing she was taking. He still didn't trust her to go, and his eyes followed her every move, watching her with suspiciously narrowed eyes as she pulled her black suit from the closet, along with jeans and a couple of shirts.

She closed her suitcase, setting it beside the bedroom door, then went up to Molly's room to gather some of her things. Rick did not follow her to the nursery, choosing instead to pace around his office, muttering unpleasantly under his breath. Ashley blocked him from her mind and peeked over the crib railing at Molly. She was sleeping peacefully.

My little angel, she thought as she gently stroked her cheek. It won't be for much longer, sweet girl. I promise.

Ashley finished packing their bags and returned to the kitchen to phone Ellie, with Rick nearby listening to every word she said.

"You're leaving now!" Ellie asked excitedly after Ashley's request for a lift to the airport. "Isn't this freedom flight seven weeks premature? What about graduation?"

"I'm going to Louisiana for a funeral," Ashley covered marvelously, wincing at the volume of Ellie's voice. Don't blow this for me, Ellie, she pleaded silently, hoping Rick had not overheard Ellie's gleeful jubilation. "My best friend's father's funeral."

"Rick's standing right there, isn't he?" Ellie asked sheepishly, suddenly understanding the reason behind Ashley's wooden-voiced reply.

"That's right," Ashley told her, managing to keep a straight face. Rick studied her keenly, watching as always for signs of deceit. It was times like this that Ashley's best poker face came in handy.

"Sorry, Ashley, I lost my mind there for a second. Sure, I'd love to drive you to the airport. I'll meet you after rotations tomorrow afternoon."

Ashley called Jack from school the next afternoon before meeting Ellie, not wanting him to be alarmed when she didn't show up for work. "Why come back, Ashley?" he asked. "This is the perfect getaway. You couldn't ask for a better cover than this."

"Leave now and piss away five years of education seven weeks shy of graduation? I don't think so, Jack," Ashley said, hardheaded as ever; knowing in the back of her mind that he was right.

"You can always go back to school," he snapped irritably. "This isn't a game, Ashley. Who's going to be a mother to Molly when he kills you?"

"Gotta go, Jack!" she sang out, trying to ignore him. "See ya!"

"Damn it, why do you always run away when I'm trying to talk some sense into you? I've never met a more stubborn woman in my whole life. Just do me one favor. Take thirty measly seconds to think about what I said before you board that plane to come home!" Aggravation rang out in Jack's voice, echoing sharply through her head as Ashley replaced the receiver on the pay phone.

Riding to the airport, Ashley filled Ellie in on their conversation. "He's right, you know," Ellie said "This is a perfect get away. You'd be nuts to come back."

"Thank you, *Ellie*, for that vote of support," Ashley said defensively. "Nothing would give Rick more pleasure than to see me do something so drastic just to get away from him," she mused aloud. "I'll just bide my time and do it my way. I'm going to win this time."

Ellie shot her a doubting look. "I just hope you know what you're doing."

"Of course I don't know what I'm doing," Ashley said, laughing cynically. "Obviously I never have, which is how I ended up in this mess in the first place."

Maggie and Remy waited impatiently at the airport in Alexandria, battling to be the first to get to Molly when Ashley carried her through the double glass doors. Remy won, sliding cleverly past Maggie and scooping Molly up into his arms, hugging her tightly.

"Just look at my big girl!" he marveled, and Molly rewarded him by giving him a huge kiss on the mouth.

"Kiss-kiss!" She smacked her rosy lips against his, successfully wrapping her grandfather around her little finger, batting her eyelashes and staring up at Remy with huge aqua-blue eyes, showing him that at the young age of two, she was already a charmer.

Ashley happily embraced her parents, kissing them and holding on for dear life, still unable to believe that it had been almost two years since she had been back. Inside Remy's Jeep, she savored the drive through town, a tide of joy washing over her as she took in the familiar sights of home.

Thank God, good old Pineville was still the same. Ashley smiled, watching the slide show of evergreens and small-town southern architecture flash outside her back seat window. It was as if nothing had changed in her absence, as if time had stood still.

At home, Remy strolled around the yard with his huge Coleman flashlight, holding Molly's hand and humoring her as she wandered the vast boundaries of her grandparents' property, looking up in awe at the tall pine trees that seemed to reach infinitely into the dark sky. Ashley watched them from the front porch, giggling softly as Molly trampled through Maggie's prize flowerbed, picking spring flowers and presenting them sweetly to her delighted grandfather. As they spotted her, Ashley smiled broadly, waving to them as she opened the front door and stepped into the house.

Maggie's chocolate-chip cookies and rose-petal potpourri, the smell of home rushed to the foyer to welcome her, taking her back in time. Ashley's heart soared. It felt so good to be back. She picked up her bags and dashed up the staircase to her room.

She stood in the doorway, her gaze drifting from one side of the room to the other, her weary mind returning to a much happier era. She entered the room slowly, moving to her bed, distractedly fingering her white-eyelet bed linens as she glanced around the room.

Her eye caught the glare of light reflecting off an ocean of glassed frames above her bed, and she focused on the hodge-podge of pictures, grinning at her childhood pals, captured forever in their awkward adolescence. Standing out in the crowd was a pretty young girl with long brown hair, lively eyes, and a vivacious smile. Ashley stared at the girl she had been in those pictures.

"My God," she thought deliriously, "I don't even know that girl anymore." That Ashley was a complete stranger to her now.

Maggie drifted into the room and sat on the edge of the bed, staring disapprovingly at her exceedingly thin daughter. "You look terrible. When was the last time you slept?"

Ashley looked over her shoulder, her brow wrinkled in mock concentration. "Hmm, let's see. How old is Molly?" she asked lightly, tapping her index finger against her chin as she teased her mother. "I probably haven't slept more than three or four hours a night since Molly was born."

"Really, Ashley, you're so thin and pale, and those circles around your eyes are worse than a raccoon's," Maggie said, frowning her concern. "This is more than child-related sleep deprivation. It's Rick, isn't it? What's going on with him now?"

"You really know how to welcome a girl home, don't you?" Ashley continued to make light of Maggie's fretfulness, insistent upon keeping the conversation casual. She saw no reason to give Maggie anything to lose sleep over, especially so early in their weekend together. They had plenty of time later to rehash her miserably failing marriage.

"I think I'll go over and see Kate," Ashley cleverly skated around the issue and marched purposely toward the door. "She may need a shoulder to cry on, and God knows, she's been there enough for me over the years."

"I'm not done with you yet," Maggie said, in hot pursuit behind her as Ashley hurried along the hallway and down the stairs. "We *will* discuss this before you go back to Oklahoma City!" she called from the front doorway, watching her daughter bolt across the shadowy field toward the Ducotes' house.

Ashley rang the Ducotes' front bell and waited until Kate's older sister, Debbie, opened the door. She was solemn and pale, the profound grief she felt written all over her face. Ashley reached out to embrace her gently, hoping to offer whatever comfort she could.

"I'm so sorry about your daddy," Ashley spoke softly, consoling Debbie with her words. "We'll all miss him."

"Thank you, Ashley," Debbie said, offering her a somber smile. "And thank you for coming. Kate's in her room, she'll be so glad you're here."

Ashley made her way through the kitchen, bypassing the countertops overflowing with covered-dish casseroles and foil-wrapped dessert plates, offerings of condolence from loving friends and neighbors. She proceeded quietly down the carpeted hallway, passing the closed bedroom door of Ms. Imogene, and tapped lightly on Kate's door.

"Come in," Kate's solemn voice beckoned from inside and Ashley twisted the doorknob, sticking her head just inside the door.

"Hey, Katydid," she said, greeting Kate with a gentle smile.

"Ashley!" Kate leapt from the bed, bear-hugging her tightly, her blood-shot eyes round with surprise. "I didn't know that you were coming in this weekend."

"You had to know that I'd move heaven and earth to be here for you."

"I'm so glad you came," Kate confessed, with tears flooding her already-swollen eyes. "I just can't believe that you had to come home for Daddy's funeral." She lowered her head and began to weep.

Her tears tugged at Ashley's heart and she put her arms around Kate, holding her as she sobbed. It seemed so strange to see Kate cry. She was always so in control of her emotions. Ashley couldn't recall ever seeing her break down this way. But heaven knows she had good reason. Her father was her world.

After getting the latest round of tears out of her system, Kate wiped her eyes and sank onto the bed, pulling Ashley down to sit beside her, and, in true Kate-like fashion, tried to be more cheerful. "Where's Molly?" she asked. "I can't wait to see her."

"Next door with Maggie and Remy. They're getting their grandchild fix," Ashley laughed softly.

"And Rick? Is he over there too?"

"No, Rick's in Oklahoma City. I came alone."

Something in Ashley's voice gave her away, immediately rousing Kate's suspicions. She leaned forward, studying Ashley more closely. "What's going on with you two? Are things still pretty rotten?"

The time had finally come to let Kate in on her dirty little secret. Without omitting one grim detail, Ashley began to tell Kate the real truth about Rick and the way that things had been. Kate's facial expression changed with Ashley's every sentence, transforming from supportive and nonjudgmental to bewildered and appalled, until finally she was staring at Ashley in open-mouthed disbelief.

"Good Lord!" she said. "This is much more serious than his not wanting Molly. Why didn't you tell me what was really going on?"

"I don't know, foolish pride I suppose," Ashley said, looking down and twisting her hands anxiously, relieved that at last Kate knew the truth.

"It's more like stupidity," Kate retorted. Ashley jerked her head up, taken aback by Kate's unusual harshness.

"Well, Ashley, it is. I can't believe you'd put yourself in such a dangerous position. How could you be so asinine? I can't lose you too. Losing Daddy was enough."

"You're not going to lose me, Kate," Ashley fidgeted uncomfortably under Kate's worried stare and quickly changed the subject. "So, tell me about this Todd Richardson," she requested with a knowing grin.

"Oh, Todd is just wonderful!" Kate's face lit up radiantly like a lovesick schoolgirl. "He's twenty-six and went to school at LSU. In fact, he knows a lot of our friends. He was a couple years ahead of Doug in law school."

At the mention of Doug's name, it was Ashley's turn to light up, feeling the rosy, warm sensation as her cheeks flooded with color. Fortunately, Kate didn't notice her giddy reaction. She was much too wrapped up in telling Ashley all about her new beau.

"Todd works in the district attorney's office right now, but hopes some day to go into private practice."

Since Kate had opened the door, Ashley couldn't help but ask a few questions about Doug. "Is Doug still dating Camille?" she asked nonchalantly, gazing at Kate with wide, angelic eyes.

"The last I heard they were still together," Kate peered at her suspiciously. "Why do you ask?"

"I was only inquiring out of curiosity for the well-being of a good friend."

Kate raised an eyebrow skeptically, not buying it for one minute. "Bull, Ashley. The thought of Doug with Camille still bugs the hell out of you."

"You're starting to sound just like Susanna," Ashley said, laughing abruptly. "I think Camille will be an asset to Doug, and to his career. I just don't think that she'll ever make him happy."

"From what I've heard, she seems to be doing a good job so far."

"What's wrong with you, Kate? What happened to the friend that used to stand by me and support my feelings?"

"I'm still that friend," Kate said, meeting Ashley's indignant glare. "I just want you to be realistic about your feelings. You had the opportunity to marry Doug. You chose Rick. You wanted Doug to get on with his life. He's moved on. You just can't expect things to go back to the way they were before, even if you are leaving Rick."

"I'm not leaving Rick because of Doug. I hope you know that."

"Ashley, I know you're leaving Rick because he's clearly disturbed, and you're clearly miserable. Susanna and I both tried to warn you years ago that Rick would eventually smother the life out of you. You were just too obstinate to listen," Kate reminded her with a reproachful glance.

"You didn't take enough time to get over losing Jimmy before you plunged head first into marriage with Rick. You never finished grieving for him. You just pushed him out of your mind, squared your shoulders, and foolishly pressed forward. I told you it would eventually come back to haunt you."

Ashley bit her tongue and struggled to contain her anger. After all, Kate was going through a tough time. "Kate, Jimmy's been gone for almost five years. He has nothing to do with this."

"I don't know why you always use that as some sort of crutch. It doesn't matter how much time has passed. Jimmy has everything to do with this, he always has. You thought being with Rick would erase the pain you felt when you lost him. Now, years later, you've woken up to the fact that you don't love Rick, and you never have," Kate assessed her soberly. "I can see why you're miserable."

"What about Rick's bizarre behavior? Doesn't that count for some of my misery?"

"Rick's behavior is just icing on the cake."

"Since when are you a licensed therapist?"

Kate smiled slightly, finding humor in Ashley's sarcasm. "I'm sorry to come down so hard on you, Ashley, but I can't be strong for you today. You have to take some responsibility for your own situation."

"A fine friend you've turned out to be," Ashley told her, sulking, appalled by Kate's lack of support.

Kate leaned over and hugged her fiercely. "Don't go getting all bent of shape," she said, giving Ashley a gentle smile. "You know I love you. And I'm glad you've come home to be with me."

Ashley softened, forgiving her instantly. "Well, if anything, I've kept your mind off the funeral."

"Yes, you certainly have," Kate agreed with a soft chuckle. "You know, there is motive behind my madness."

"What's that?" Ashley asked, scratching her head and shooting Kate a lopsided grin. "And it had better be good since you just ripped me to shreds."

"One day, you'll have to face all the things you've conveniently tucked away in the dark corners of your mind," Kate said seriously, ignoring Ashley's grin. "You'll have to face losing Jimmy, you'll have to face your marriage to Rick and his rejection of Molly. And you'll have to face your mistake of letting Doug go."

"Doug is just my friend," Ashley protested lamely.

"Save it, Ashley. I know how you feel about him. And it's too late."

Ashley lay awake for a long time that night, watching the moonlight dance through the lace curtains of her bedroom window and thinking about all Kate had said. Kate was right. She had been so foolish for so long, and she might end up regretting many things for the rest of her life. She had waited too long to finally realize her true feelings for Doug, and now it was too late to resolve anything between them. He had Camille, and Ashley had to let him be.

If anything, she would have to grow up and not expect the world to revolve around her wishes. It was good that Kate had been so hard on her, opening her eyes to a lot of things. She only wished that Kate had been so harsh with her years ago. Nevertheless, the end result was the same. Kate had finally matured enough to tell Ashley the truth, and Ashley had finally matured enough to listen to her.

The next morning Ashley opened her eyes, finding herself in her own bed, her chest growing heavy with sorrow when she remembered why she was there.

"Another black dress, another funeral," she thought as she solemnly reached for the simple linen garment hanging in her closet. She pulled the dress over her head and shouldered into its matching black jacket, stepping into her pumps before leaving the house, going in the direction of the Ducotes' to see if there was anything she could do before Frank's funeral that afternoon.

In answer to her knock, Kate opened the door and yanked Ashley into the house with a glad smile, indicating that their heated discussion the evening before was all but forgotten. "Mama, look, Ashley's home!"

Imogene Ducote crossed the room and gently embraced her, keeping her arm around Ashley's shoulder as she whispered softly into her ear, "Thank you for coming, honey. Kate'll need a friend today."

With a motherly hand, Imogene brushed Ashley's hair back from her face and frowned. "Is everything all right, baby?" she asked fretfully. "You look like a ghost."

Ashley smiled and chuckled softly. Apparently, she looked pretty awful. "Yes, Ms. Imogene," Ashley was quick to assure her. "Everything's going to be just fine."

She glanced around the room crowded with close friends and Ducote relatives and spotted a stranger, an attractive man about the same age as Kate relaxing on the couch. Ashley cocked her head to one side, perplexed.

He didn't look like any of the Ducotes she could remember, and she'd been to enough family reunions with Kate over the years to know them all. He had sandy hair, soft light-colored eyes and a nice build. "Now where did he come from?" Ashley wondered, continuing to assess him with open curiosity.

Feeling her eyes upon him, he turned to look at her, catching her scrutinizing stare. Ashley quickly cast her eyes downward in embarrassment, studying the toe of her shoe with great interest as he rose from the couch and moved across the room, standing next to Kate and placing a fond hand on her shoulder.

Kate cleared her throat insistently, elbowing Ashley in the ribs until she lifted her eyes. "Ashley, I want you to meet Todd Richardson," Kate said, gazing at him adoringly. "Todd, this is my best friend, Ashley LeNoir."

Ashley raised her eyebrows in surprise, looking from Kate to Todd with delight as she grasped Todd's extended hand. So, this was Todd Richardson. No wonder Kate was head over heels in love. He was charming.

"I approve," she told Kate later, drawing her to the side as she prepared to leave with Maggie and Remy for the funeral.

"I'm glad," Kate smiled, squeezing Ashley's hand.

"Like it would matter if I didn't," Ashley let go of her hand and headed toward the door, beaming discreetly back at Kate. "It's too late for my opinion to make any difference. You're already sunk."

Frank's service was held at the same funeral home where Jimmy's had been, and Ashley stared at the building bleakly. This would not be a good day.

Remy parked the Jeep behind the mortuary and got out, opening Ashley's car door and offering his strong arm for support, sensing that she might need a few moments to regain her composure. Maggie walked silently beside them, shooting small discreet glances in Ashley's direction, still waiting for some explanation for her haggard appearance.

Once inside, Ashley pulled away from Remy. "I'm okay," she insisted, smiling reassuringly at his worried look. "I'm going in to see Mister Frank."

Frank Ducote seemed to be sleeping, looking just as he had on many a Sunday afternoon, kicked back in his old gray corduroy recliner, nodding off during the New Orleans Saints game and snoring loudly enough to shake the rafters.

Ashley gazed into his open casket. Gosh, it didn't seem possible that he was gone. How they all would miss him. He had been such a loving, giving individual, much like his younger daughter. Ashley reached out, touching the shoulder of his navy suit.

"My God, which one of you is the corpse?"

The shrill voice cut through Ashley's thoughts like a knife, startling her, and she shook her head in wonder. There was only one person who could ask anything so unrefined. She whirled around to face a very pregnant Susanna Robicheaux Lawrence.

"You're so lacking in social graces that it's terrifying," Ashley scolded her as they embraced.

"Why don't you eat a sandwich or something? You look like a damn skeleton."

"I'm glad to see you too, Susanna."

"Well, it's the truth, Ashley. You look absolutely dreadful," Susanna shot back abrasively. She was dressed in a black maternity dress, her red hair appropriately subdued by a barrette, and stood fanning herself furiously with her hands.

"Hormonal?" Ashley asked.

"Hell yes, I'm hormonal. Don't you remember being pregnant?"

"I try to block out all memory of being pregnant."

"In your case, I can understand why," Susanna looked around the room. "Where's Rick the prick? I haven't seen him lurking around here anywhere. Should I expect him to pop out of a closet or something?"

"I came to Louisiana with Molly. Rick is at home."

"I'll be damned," Susanna cackled, grinning broadly. "He let you out of his sight. Amazing." She hooked her arm through Ashley's, pulling her toward the door. "Let's mingle."

"What makes you act this way?" Ashley asked her crossly. "This is a funeral, Susanna, not a cotillion."

They sidled through the crowd, meeting up with Mark outside the chapel door. Ashley said hello to him with a hug, silently thanking God for sending such a wonderful soul to contend with Susanna. Mark Lawrence had definitely earned his spot in heaven. The man was a saint.

As the small chapel began to fill, Mark suggested that they find somewhere to sit. "Susanna will never let us hear the end of it if she has to stand through the entire service," he whispered to Ashley, winking at her, wearing an expression of feigned horror.

Ashley giggled in agreement, pushing through the crowd and finding Remy and Maggie near the front. Sitting between Susanna and Remy, Ashley inspected the mob of people packed into the pews, finding the faces of many childhood friends and acquaintances. She spotted Mitch Guidry across the aisle with Scotty Jeansonne and Jeff Thomasee and waved a discreet greeting to them, thinking how sweet it was of Mitch to drive all the way from Vicksburg. Mitch had moved to Mississippi after graduating from Northeast, but had remained very close to Frank Ducote even after he and Kate split up. Ashley watched his sad eyes move to the front pew of the chapel, lingering on the blond head of the girl he once called his own.

"How does he do it?" she wondered. "How can Mitch just sit there and watch Kate with someone else without his heart breaking in two?" He appeared unruffled, complacent at best, as if Kate had never meant anything to him at all. However, Ashley knew better. Mitch was to be congratulated on his facetious air of nonchalance. It was a feat she could never pull off as gracefully, of that she was sure.

After the touching service, Ashley stood on the steps outside, enjoying the sunshine and fresh air, leaving Remy and Maggie inside to visit with friends before driving out to the cemetery for the graveside service and burial. She removed her wide-brimmed hat and shook out her chin-length bob, closing her eyes and lifting her face gratefully into the warm rays of the sun, thankful for five minutes of peace and quiet.

"Hello Ashley," his voice hailed her quietly, taking her by surprise. The thrill that ran up her spine told her who it was even before she turned around.

"Hello, Doug," she smiled brilliantly at him, overjoyed to see him again.

"God help me," she thought as she stared into his captivating brown eyes. "I still love him, despite Rick and Camille."

"How are you, Princess?" he asked as he studied her face, clearly not at all pleased by what he saw. "You look frazzled."

"So I've been told, countless times I might add," Ashley said, annoyed by his comment on her appearance. "You really know how to compliment a girl, Douglas."

He looked spectacular, of course, and had not changed at all, except to become more handsome, if possible. He was leaner and more muscularly defined, and his blond hair reflected the bright sunlight, giving him the appearance of a Greek god. Ashley stared at him, mentally slapping herself, resisting the overwhelming urge to reach out and finger the curly locks brushing just above his collar.

Doug's eyes sparkled brightly as he took her hands, squeezing them affectionately. "When did you get to town?" he asked, trying to make amends for his tactless critique.

His touch brought her to life, filling Ashley with surging warmth that flowed from her fingertips and flooded her entire body. She held his hand loosely, giving nothing away, managing to affect a casual smile. "I got in last night. How about you?"

"I came in early this morning."

"Where is Camille?" Ashley said, glancing around, wondering how she could have missed the auburn-haired bombshell.

"Camille's in Baton Rouge. She doesn't do funerals."

In the spirit of old times, Ashley couldn't resist asking him, "What exactly does 'Camille doesn't do funerals' mean, Doug?"

"It simply means that this isn't the type of event Camille would enjoy," Doug laughed. "She chose to pass on this one."

"That figures," Ashley thought unkindly. "Self-centered little debutante."

"Would you like to ride out to the cemetery with me?"

How could you ask me that, Doug? How could you ask me to be alone with you when I've resolved to get over you? She debated with her inner demons, longing to go with Doug but knowing that it would be best if she rode with Maggie and Remy.

"I should ride with my folks. I haven't seen much of them in the last year." She did the right thing and declined his offer, kicking herself as she did so. Resisting him was so hard.

"Would you mind if I came by the house later to see Molly? I haven't seen her since she was little bitty. I bet she has grown a bunch since then."

"I would like that a lot," she said, just as she spied Maggie and Remy coming out the front door of the mortuary.

Having absolutely no willpower and unable to resist him any longer, she impulsively kissed his cheek, then hurriedly walked away without looking back, missing the astonished look on Doug's face as he lifted his hand to caress the spot she had kissed.

Molly was having a fabulous time playing with Candace Cooper, babysitter extraordinare, peering over the mountain of toys on the den floor as Ashley and her parents came in from the funeral.

"Mommy!" Molly yelled, scampering to Ashley with outstretched arms, her blond curls bouncing wildly as she careened across the floor. Ashley scooped the little girl up into her arms and hugged her tightly, smiling over the top of Molly's head to Candace, thanking her for doing such a wonderful job watching Molly.

"She was no trouble, really. She's very well behaved," Candace said with a shy smile, pushing herself up from her spot on the floor. "Your husband called while you all were gone. I told him when the funeral would be over and he said that he'd call you back."

Ashley tried not to scowl at the mentioned of Rick's name and, after Candace left, went upstairs to change out of her suit and into a pair of jeans and a T-shirt. While brushing her hair, she heard the doorbell ring.

Maggie answered and was tickled pink to find Doug standing there. Ashley could hear her babbling happily to him as she started down the steps. Doug glanced up as he heard her boots on the wooden stairs, and Ashley met his gaze with a smile, happy that he had come by, and motioned him to follow her into the den.

They found Molly playing with Legos on the floor and Doug looked upon her with open fondness. "She's lovely, Ashley, but where did she get that blond hair? Are you sure she's not mine?"

Ashley smiled broadly at his clever question, wishing silently that Molly were his. "I'll never tell," she said teasingly. "You did have an awful lot to drink that night."

"Surely I would have remembered something that earth-shattering," he said with a mischievous twinkle in his eyes.

"Now Doug, you are staying for dinner, aren't you?" Maggie stuck her head into the den, thrilled at having her favorite guy back in the house.

Doug gladly accepted, although he was sure that his mother would be miffed about him missing her usual pot roast dinner. "But she'll get over it," he told Maggie with a grin. "If you've had one Bobbie Fairchild pot roast, you've had them all."

Ashley smiled at his laughter, relieved that he seemed so happy. Life, along with Camille, must have been treating him well. She had never seen him look better.

Maggie bellowed out the kitchen door for Remy, and they sat down for dinner. The telephone pealed loudly just as Ashley slid into her chair, and she excused herself to answer it, sure that it was Rick. She was right.

"Hello, Ashley," he mocked her, even over the phone line. "I've just called to remind you that you have a husband."

"I don't have to be reminded," she replied scathingly.

"I know how you tend to push me from your mind whenever you're down there."

"Trust me, I haven't forgotten about you."

"Are you having fun, darling?"

Ashley could picture his acidic sneer and tried to keep the contempt she felt for him out of her voice. She knew it showed on her face. "Rick, I am not here for fun. I am here for a funeral."

"Sure, sweetheart, and I'm certain that you have not seen any of your old friends. It's probably a regular high school reunion down there this weekend," he continued to drip sarcasm. "Enjoy it, my pet, because you are coming home."

She wanted to scream but maintained her cool stance. "Yes, I am coming home," she responded dully. "Rick, is there some point to this?"

"What time is your flight back tomorrow?" he asked abruptly, finished with his game of cat and mouse now that the mouse would no longer play.

"I should land at Will Rogers around three o'clock. Will you be there to pick us up?"

"I wouldn't dream of letting anyone else get you," his reply was pointedly double-edged. "And if you aren't on that flight tomorrow, I'll be down to get you."

Ashley hated him more with each passing day, wondering what kind of state of mind he would have to be in to continuously torment her the way he had for so many months. She desperately tried to remember what drew her to him in the first place. There had been a time when she could recall what a charming man he had once been, but that time was past. Now all she could see when she thought of Rick was the horrible person he had become.

After Rick's phone call, Ashley felt drained and weak, staunchly resisting the urge to curl up in fetal position and cry. She had lived with Rick's taunts and threats for so long that her nerves were shot. His invasion of her parents' home, the only place where she felt safe, was almost her breaking point. She sank back into her chair at the dinner table, her face pale and drawn, with three pairs of eyes glued to her.

"Sorry for the interruption," she apologized, knowing what they had overheard. "That was Rick."

"So we gathered," Remy said gruffly, frowning with his dislike of the situation.

Ashley reached across the table and squeezed his hand. "Let's not let Rick ruin the short amount of time we have to spend together this weekend," she said. "In fact, let's not bring him up again, okay?"

Remy smiled grimly at her, a very troubled look shadowing his face. Ashley was not doing as well at disguising things this time as she had in the past, making Remy even more certain that there was something terribly wrong with her marriage.

Maggie pressed her lips together in disapproval, dying to express her opinion, stopped only by the fact that they had a dinner guest.

Doug appeared thoughtful, processing everything he had seen and heard. They finished dinner in tense silence, none of them knowing quite what to say. Rick had succeeded in putting a damper on Ashley's weekend home. He would have been very pleased with himself had he known.

After dinner, Doug played with Molly while Ashley helped Maggie with the dishes. Molly took well to Doug, an amazing feat considering the small amount of exposure to men she'd had in her short life. Ashley delighted in watching Doug and Molly together and hated having to return her to life with Rick. Molly was entitled to a much happier home life and Ashley was determined to give her one very soon.

"I really want to know what is going on in Oklahoma," Maggie muttered under her breath, joining Ashley at the sink and interrupting her thoughts.

"I don't want to get into that right now," Ashley said insistently. "We have company."

"Doug is not company, and I'm sure that he would love to hear an explanation as much as Remy and I would."

"Maggie, not now," Ashley glanced at her watch, noting the time. "I really should go see Kate before it gets any later."

Doug offered to walk her to Kate's house, and Ashley took him up on it, strolling across the yard with him in comfortable silence, enjoying the cool night air and Doug's company. Her serenity was short-lived. Doug's natural curiosity got the better of him and he looked over at her, studying her inquiringly.

"What's going on with you and your husband?" he asked, his eyes burning a hole in her hotly glowing face.

"It's really none of your business," she said, protesting and walking a little more quickly, thinking she could make it safely to Kate's without having to answer his question.

Doug caught her arm, stopping her. "Talk to me, Ash. You can trust me. I'm still your friend."

"I don't want to discuss this with you."

The light from Kate's front porch suddenly lit their path and Ashley sprinted away from him, up the driveway full of cars, letting herself in the Ducotes' front door, and wandered through a sea of people in search of Kate. Doug followed Ashley inside, shaking his head in frustration at her maddening stubbornness. It was the only trait Ashley possessed that drove him completely crazy.

Finding Kate and Todd at the kitchen table, Doug and Todd retreated to another room, leaving Kate and Ashley with some much-needed privacy. "How are you holding up?" Ashley asked, clasping Kate's hand. "You going to be okay?"

Always the trooper, Kate nodded graciously. "Yes, I'll be fine. This is all just so surreal to me, you know?" she dabbed at her eyes with a crumpled tissue. "I can't imagine what life will be like without Daddy."

Kate's face was scarlet and swollen from days of crying, and was etched with sorrow that would fade, but never be erased. "I just keep waiting, hoping to see Daddy walk through the front door," she said in a voice barely above a whisper.

Ashley nodded in quiet sympathy and understanding, she too had been in a similar position not so very long ago.

"It took a long time for me to stop expecting to see Jimmy or listen for his laughter to ring out across a room," she admitted softly, tearing up as Jimmy's image filled her mind. It did seem like she had missed Jimmy forever, and there were still moments when she caught herself thinking of him, wishing that she could see him just one more time.

Ashley stayed with Kate and her family until most of the other visitors had cleared out before deciding that she too should go home and spend what was left of the evening with her parents. She found Doug with Todd on the back porch and bid them good night.

"I'll walk you back," Doug offered.

"That's really not necessary," she said. "I've walked across this yard a million times in the dark. You stay here and finish talking."

"I'll see Todd again soon," Doug said, getting up from the wicker divan. "Who knows when I might see you again?" He took Ashley insistently by the arm, showing her that he had won. He would be walking her home.

Kate accompanied them as far as the front door, hugging Ashley tightly and whispering quietly in her ear, "You be very careful, Ashley. I really believe that this situation with Rick has gone too far to be safe."

"I promise I'll be careful," Ashley whispered back to her. They held one another at arms' length and Kate studied Ashley's face fretfully, not wanting to let her go.

"I'll see you *soon*," Ashley told her, and only Kate understood exactly how soon she meant.

Doug and Ashley walked wordlessly through the night toward her house. Doug whistled a cheerful tune, staring up at the star-filled skies, while Ashley's thoughts were a million miles away, anticipating the future. Life would be good again. She only had to get past the one obstacle of leaving Rick. If only that weren't such a hellacious barrier.

"Penny for your thoughts," Doug said, breaking the silence. He had stopped whistling and had been observing her for quite some time.

"Just wondering what the future will bring," Ashley smiled as she answered him, forgetting about Rick, light-hearted to be with Doug, if only for a short time longer.

They reached the front steps of her home and stopped, a moment of awkwardness forcing itself between them. Ashley shoved her hands in her pockets and looked down at the ground, kicking the dirt with the toe of her boot, not wanting him to go, but unsure of what to say next.

Doug cleared his throat and stole a glance at his watch, looking back at her regretfully. "I should go now, I guess. It's getting late."

"I'm glad that I saw you, Doug. You've been a sight for sore eyes," Ashley gazed up at him and smiled sentimentally, using one of his favorite expressions.

"I'm glad that I saw you too," he said softly. "I worry about you, you know."

Their eyes met, betraying carefully concealed emotions, and Ashley lifted her hand to gently stroke his cheek with her index finger before she realized what she was doing. Doug caught her hand, pressing it tenderly to his lips, and they stared at one another passionately, their gaze never wavering, until Ashley came to her senses and pulled her hand away.

"Good luck with the rest of law school, and with Camille," she said, breathlessly, averting her smoldering eyes, feeling obligated to remind him of his girlfriend, even if she didn't care to remember her husband.

Doug leaned down and kissed her cheek softly. "You've always been too damn concerned with my love life," he chuckled lightly. "See ya, Ashley."

"See ya, Doug." She watched as he crossed the driveway and got into his car, loving him so much that it hurt, glad that it was pitch-black dark so that he couldn't see the tears welling up in her eyes. "Goodbye."

CHAPTER TWENTY-EIGHT

Remy drove Ashley and Molly to the airport the next morning. Maggie walked them out to the Jeep, embracing Ashley tenderly as she climbed into the car.

"We'll see you for graduation," she said, and it was unclear to Ashley whom she was reminding, herself or Ashley.

Maggie opened the back passenger door and leaned into the car to kiss Molly. "Bye, sweet Mollykins," she said, waving her hand at Molly.

Molly returned her wave sweetly. "Bye-bye, Grandma," Molly said, enchanting her grandmother with her bright smile.

Anxiously chewing her nails and feeling guilty over keeping secrets from her family, Ashley made the decision to come clean with Remy on the way to the airport. "Remy, how would you like for me to come work with you at the drugstore after I graduate?" she asked, smiling innocently.

Remy looked at her out of the corner of his eye, caught off guard. "I'd like that very much, sweetie," he said, cautiously. "What does Rick think about that?"

Ashley cleared her throat, taking a deep breath before blurting out the truth. "Remy, I'm leaving Rick. Things have never been right between us and I think that it would be better for Molly and me to make a life for ourselves."

"Does Rick know about your plans?"

"Do you think Rick knows about my plans?"

"Ashley, I just want straight answers, okay?" Remy was uncharacteristically abrupt with her, snapping irritably at her unwise attempt at humor.

"Sorry," she apologized sheepishly. "No, I haven't told Rick of my intentions yet."

"When were you planning to tell him?"

"I can't go into much detail on this, Remy," she said evasively. "I'm going to leave some time after graduation, but I can't say exactly when yet."

"I'll be glad to have you and Molly back home, but I do hate that your marriage hasn't worked out."

"Me too," Ashley admitted, feeling defeated. She'd never been a quitter and hated failing at anything. But this was different. It couldn't really be counted as a failure. Life with Rick LeNoir was a whole new ballgame.

She pleaded with him not to tell Maggie anything, and Remy reluctantly agreed, cursing himself, certainly not for the first time, for raising Ashley to be so infuriatingly independent.

"Why don't you at least let me come up there and help explain things to Rick?" he suggested, looking for some way to make the inevitable easier on her.

"Now Remy, don't be silly. That's hardly necessary. I've got it all under control," she reassured him with a forced smile, wishing she felt as confident as she sounded.

As he promised, Rick was waiting for her at Will Rogers. He leaned against the wall across from the gate, his hands stuffed deeply into the front pockets of his jeans, looking very handsome, but mocking her with his sarcastic smile. His eyes were cold and calculating, watching her as she approached, carrying Molly on her hip.

"Hi, honey," Ashley said, mustering all the acting experience she had to greet him cheerfully.

"Hi, *Darling*," Rick was equally insincere, and they didn't bother to continue the charade by kissing or embracing. He stalked off ahead of Ashley and Molly, leading the way to baggage claim to recover their luggage. On the drive home, Rick glared at her unpleasantly, spouting cynical, off-the-cuff remarks in response to anything she said. His marked belligerence indicated that she would pay dearly for attending Frank Ducote's funeral against his wishes.

Ashley made dinner and told him about the funeral, carefully omitting any reference to Doug.

"Sounds like the social event of the season," Rick said, regarding her with disdain. "Sorry I missed it."

Ashley shot him a withering look. "It was just nice to see everyone again, that's all," she responded with a deep sigh, not knowing why she bothered to tell him anything. But she just couldn't stop talking to him. That was against the rules of the game. She would just have to do everything in her power to remain pleasant.

"If I pull this one off," she thought as she carefully disguised the disgusted look in her eyes, "I'll deserve an Academy Award."

May found Ashley with mixed emotions, but not second thoughts. It seemed like a lifetime had passed since she had moved to Oklahoma with Rick, and yet her time at school and the hospital had flown by. She had not changed her mind about leaving Rick but found herself already missing those she had come to love in Oklahoma.

Maggie and Remy arrived in town the Thursday night before graduation, electing to stay in a hotel instead of at the house with Rick and Ashley.

"I'd rather not stay in the same house with Rick," Maggie admitted uncomfortably. "He just makes me feel unwelcome."

Ashley didn't argue with her, aware that Rick *didn't* want them there and would certainly not go out of his way to be hospitable.

Her college graduation was far more exciting for Remy than for Ashley and he beamed proudly, grinning ear to ear as Ashley accepted her diploma. Ashley wished that she were more ecstatic over achieving such a milestone, but her anxiety over things to come overpowered any sentimental feelings she might have had. Afterward at a reception for the graduates, Ashley effervescently introduced Maggie and Remy to her friends.

"Ma!" Matt Whitford flashed a toothy grin, embracing Maggie with delight as they finally got to meet in person.

"Matt, you're as much a doll as I imagined you'd be," Maggie told him, pinching his cheek affectionately. "And you're going to be a doctor too," she cast a sidelong glance at Ashley as she kidded him, "If you'd only met my daughter sooner!"

Matt busted out laughing. "Trust me, Ma. It'd never work. Ashley's too much of a class act for this old dog. She'd never put up with me."

Ashley smirked at Matt's flattery, punching his arm fondly as she intercepted his playful wink. Rick viewed their exchange with great interest, his fiery gaze burning a hole in Ashley's back. She turned, cringing as she caught his eye, thinking of the fury that he might unleash over her harmless flirtation with Matt. "Thank God Maggie and Remy are here," she thought with a nervous shudder.

Back at the LeNoir house, all appeared forgotten as Ashley opened her graduation gifts. Rick provided the biggest jolt by producing a diamond solitaire pendant on a gold chain, fastening it around Ashley's neck with a flourish and kissing her warmly on the lips. Ashley felt a slight tinge of guilt as she observed the genuinely affectionate sparkle in his remarkable blue eyes, but the feeling was short lived when she put their entire relationship into prospective. In her eyes, Rick's extravagant present didn't alter a thing. There wasn't a diamond on earth that could make up for what he put her through.

Her parents left Sunday morning, and Ashley returned to University Hospital the next evening, breezing through the pharmacy's front door, struck by a sudden sensation of melancholy when she realized this would be her final week to work with Jack.

Ashley drifted nonchalantly to the break room, finding Jack making a fresh pot of coffee, looking particularly sharp in a freshly starched shirt and paisley tie. Ashley peeked around the corner, ensuring that the coast was clear. Satisfied that they were completely alone, she sat on the countertop in front of Jack, leaning against the palms of her hands as she told him of her plans.

"Well, this is it, our last week together," she said with coerced brightness.

Jack snapped on the coffee maker and looked at her, sadness flickering briefly in his eyes. "Finally," he said, forcing a wry grin, mocking her to disguise the emotion in his voice. "It's about time. I've only been trying to get you to go for a year."

"You certainly don't have to act so happy about it. I can see how much I'll be missed around here."

"You want me to say it? Okay, I'll say it. I'll miss you, Ashley."

Ashley laughed and slipped her arms around his neck in a fond embrace. "I'll miss you too, Jack. But look on the bright side, you'll still have Matt here to play with."

Jack rolled his eyes in irritation. "Being with Matt is not like being with you," he informed her. "Matt tries to steal my dates away from me."

"And I just try to discourage them from going out with you in the first place."

Jack filled two Styrofoam cups with coffee, giving one to Ashley, then took her by the shoulders, gazing into her eyes with genuine concern. "I'll be off work this weekend," he said solemnly. "You call me if you need anything."

"Yes, Jack," Ashley answered obediently, jumping off the countertop and grabbing his clipboard from the break room table. "Let's make rounds."

Ashley made the most of their stroll through the hospital, knowing that it would be one of their last. She always got a kick out of seeing Jack in action, watching as he paused at each nurses' station, flirting outrageously with the girls on duty. He mesmerized them, even with Ashley standing behind him, shaking her head, warning them all that he was full of it. She couldn't believe that they hadn't caught on to him yet. She'd heard all of his lines by now, and they only served to amuse her.

"What will these poor women do when I'm not around to warn them about you?" Ashley teased Jack as he finished checking out the tenth floor.

"I just might be able to get a date once I've got you out of the way," he said kiddingly. "You won't be around to give away all my good lines."

"I'm the least of your worries. You better concentrate on using your really good lines before Matt steals them," she laughed.

"Matt? Matt's only an amateur. He's still learning from The Master," he answered with a roguish grin. "What about you, Miss Ashley? What happens when you get back to Pineville?"

Ashley considered this for a moment before replying. "Nothing. I'll just go on with my life with Molly and my folks."

"Sounds pretty sedate for a young divorcee," Jack's eyes were bright with amusement. "How about dating a little?"

"Why would I want to do something stupid like that? I'll just be getting rid of the man I have now. Why would I want another one?"

"What about Mr. Fairchild? He might be interested in knowing that you'll be available again."

"Mr. Fairchild has someone else," Ashley told him through gritted teeth.

"I bet she's a sad second compared to you."

"I certainly wouldn't say that if I were you. You haven't even seen her."

"But I've seen you," Jack smiled at her fondly and Ashley rolled her eyes in response.

"Shut up, Jack," she said irritably, jumping onto the next available elevator, leaving him standing on the tenth floor, grinning ear to ear.

Saturday morning, Ashley rose early, padding softly into the kitchen to make coffee. Her duties at University Hospital had ended, but she cleverly led Rick to believe that she was working the evening shift both Saturday and Sunday. She spent the day trying to study some notes for her upcoming board exams but couldn't concentrate, feeling as if she might throw up at any moment. It was all she could do not to stand up and pace the floor.

Ashley was changing into work clothes, thinking of where she could go to kill eight hours, when Rick entered the bedroom. "You work two-thirty to eleven tonight, right?" he asked, checking her schedule for the tenth time that morning and marking it in his ever-present black day planner.

"Right," Ashley said, her heart thumping so loudly that she feared that Rick would hear it.

"Okay, I'm going out for a while," he said, touching her bare shoulder and kissing her absentmindedly. "I'll be here when you and that child return."

"Okay," Ashley said, as casually as possible, holding her breath as she watched him go out the front door.

As soon as his car left the driveway, Ashley sprang into action, throwing on the rest of her clothing and retrieving some cash she had stashed in her underwear drawer. She quickly changed Molly's disposable training pants then stuffed her diaper bag with extra clothing, snacks and plenty for her to drink.

She went over her mental checklist one more time. She had plenty of gas, as she kept her tank filled at all times now. She had plenty of cash, plenty of things for Molly. That was it. Everything else had been taken care of weeks beforehand. She inhaled deeply, with every nerve ending in her body tingling with anticipation. She was ready.

She gazed around the house for a last time, filled with some regret for the years she had spent there. It was such a neat little house, and Ashley wished that she'd had happier times in it. But those walls had seen too many temper tantrums and insane rages. It was time for her to go.

Pausing by the front door, she remembered one last thing. She removed the diamond necklace and her wedding rings, placing them purposely on the center of Rick's antique dresser. Smiling victoriously, Ashley scooped Molly up, giving her a big kiss on the cheek, then swung open the front door to walk out into freedom.

To her horror, Rick was striding up the sidewalk toward the house, his eyes blazing murderously. Ashley stopped in her tracks, chewing her lip anxiously as he approached.

"Where are you going, Ashley?" he demanded, shoving her back into the house with a rough hand to her chest.

"To work, Rick, where else?" she said fluidly. She had become so smooth at telling him lies.

"Wrong," Rick leered at her, smiling viciously. "You know, my pet, things had been going so well for us lately that I decided to surprise you with a little post-graduation getaway. I called the hospital this afternoon to find out what your schedule was for the next week so I could make some plans. Guess what, Ashley? You don't work there anymore. Yesterday was your last day. What do you think about that?"

A cold chill of realization spread over Ashley's body and her face lost all color. The cat was out of the bag. She could no longer lie to him. The truth had to be told.

"I'm leaving Rick," she said, setting her jaw determinedly, even though her heart was racing like a jackrabbit's.

Rick nodded, smirking cynically as he stroked his chin. "We've established that, Dearest. Where are you going?"

"I'm leaving for good, Rick."

"Why are you leaving, Ashley?" he said, playing cat and mouse with her, watching her with a fixed level stare.

Molly began to whimper in Ashley's arms, so Ashley set her down on the living room carpet, kissing her small forehead reassuringly. She straightened, squaring her shoulders bravely as she turned back toward Rick.

"I'm leaving because we have no marriage," she said.

He lunged at her, pushing her up against the wall in the entryway, holding her there with a bruising palm to her chest. "We have no marriage because you never wanted a marriage," he roared, his breath hot against her face, the veins in his neck standing out in livid ridges.

"That's not true, Rick," she stared undauntedly into his bulging eyes, working hard to keep her composure. "That's it, Ashley, stay calm," she told herself. "Keep the upper hand. He wants you to get upset."

"I wanted our marriage to work," she said, her cool gaze unwavering. "If you had only cared for me, if you had only tried to care about Molly, things might have worked out for us."

"If I only cared for you?" Rick laughed maliciously, mocking her in a sniveling singsong. "I loved you with all my heart and we would have been happy forever if you hadn't been so insistent on keeping that child. She ruined everything for us."

"Molly is the only good thing I ever got from you," she said, her eyes raking him frigidly.

"Liar! You used me, Ashley, first to get over some dead nobody, and then to pay for your education. And now that you don't need me anymore, you're leaving!"

His remarks struck a nerve and Ashley lost her edge, giving him a piece of her mind. "Rick LeNoir, you were the one who used dirty, underhanded mind games to get me to the altar," she reminded him hotly. "And you did not pay one penny toward my education! I have thousands of dollars in student loans to repay. What do you think I did with that money? I paid for my tuition, my books, Molly's childcare and her upkeep. You did nothing to provide for my schooling!"

"I put a roof over your head and fed you, didn't I?"

"Rick, I was your wife. Where else did you expect me to live?"

"You are still my wife," Rick pointed out smugly, smiling wickedly at her.

"That is very temporary, I assure you," Ashley said with feisty self-confidence, proud of herself for standing up to him.

"What man are you leaving me for, Ashley? Is it Matt Whitford?" Rick erratically switched gears, goading her in a tone thick with insinuation. "Have you been having an affair with him? Is that why you're leaving?"

"In what moment of spare time would I have had an affair?" she asked him, chuckling incredulously and shaking her head. "No, Rick, I'm not leaving you for another man. I'm leaving you for me. For me and for Molly."

"You're not leaving," he said, his eyes narrowing with contempt. "You're not going anywhere."

"Yes, Rick, I am," Ashley said, and with that, every emotion she had repressed for three long, turbulent years exploded to the surface.

"I cannot stay here any longer," she said, her voice rising hysterically. "Don't you understand? *I hate you, I loathe you, and I despise you!*"

She should have seen it coming but she didn't. Ashley didn't know that Rick had punched her until her head hit the corner of the wall and she slid to the floor. Wearing the crazed look of a mad man, Rick kicked her in the side with all his might, slamming her to the tile with the force of his assault. Before she could recover from the blow, he was on top of her, shaking her and beating her in the face.

From the living room, she could hear Molly screaming, terrified as Rick put his hands around Ashley's throat and began choking her. She stared into Rick's grotesquely contorted features. He was livid, screaming at her, his face growing scarlet and swollen from shouting, but Ashley could no longer comprehend what he was saying. She could no longer get any air.

"My God, he's going to kill me," she realized as she lay beneath the weight of his body, numbed by terror. "Please don't let me die," she pleaded for her life to the only One who could hear her. "Please God, for Molly's sake, don't let me die."

Then everything went black.

Ashley awakened slowly to the feeling of someone frantically patting her cheeks. She lifted her heavy eyelids, squinting as light from the entryway window filtered into her swollen eyes. Rick leaned over her, his face still possessing a deranged look, and he peered into her face, wild-eyed. Seeing her stare blankly from the narrow slits representing her eyes, he appeared visibly relieved.

"Good, you are alive," he said, straightening to pick up Molly, who sobbed uncontrollably. He sneered down at Ashley, his face lit with bitter triumph.

"See," he said, flashing a superior grin. "I told you that you weren't going anywhere. I'll never let you go, Ashley."

He turned, opening the front door with his free hand while balancing Molly with the other. "I'm taking the child out for ice cream," he announced, glancing back at her over his shoulder. "I would suggest that you clean up this mess you made before I return."

Rick continued to smile smugly as he closed the door behind him.

Ashley lay in fetal position on the tile beside the front door, with a backdrop of her blood splashed against the crisp white walls of the entryway. Her head was heavy and pounding, and she could feel the hot blood seeping from the wound in the back of her head, soaking through her clothing.

Even in this state, Ashley knew that she didn't have much time. She had to move now or never. Wincing in agony, she dragged herself across the floor to the telephone on the end table. Clenching her teeth, she pulled herself up, leaning against the wall, painstakingly dialing the number she had memorized, just in case. "Please be home," she prayed.

He answered, his cheerful voice rising above the laughter in the background. "Jack's pool hall."

"Jack," Ashley's voice was raspy. She struggled to clear her throat, trying again, "Jack."

"Yes," he said, shushing the voices around him and listening carefully.

"Jack, I need you," she said, her voice barely above a hoarse whisper, confirming the reason for her call.

"Ashley, where are you, at home?"

"Yes." It was sheer torture to draw her breath and speak loudly enough for Jack to hear her.

"I'll be there in two minutes. Open the back door, if you can, honey. I'll come in that way, in case he's watching the house."

Ashley dropped the receiver and crawled by whitened knuckles to the patio door, unlatching the lock, but did not have the strength to slide the glass open. She collapsed onto the carpet in front of the door, waiting for Jack.

She must have blacked out again, because suddenly Jack was there next to her, kneeling to touch her face. "Holy Mother of God!" he said, muttering in anger and disgust. "Ashley, can you hear me, honey? Open your eyes," his voice was gentle yet commanding.

Ashley managed to open her eyes to small slits and squinted at Jack. He was not alone. Surrounding them were four others, including Matt Whitford. "Jack," she whispered deliriously, "how did you get all this help so fast?"

Jack smiled slightly. "Well, kiddo, it happened to be my night to host the monthly poker game. Not only do I have Dan Little, the uncover cop I told you about here, but I also have his partner, Mike," he explained, gesturing to the men around him. "And you remember Dr. Tom Brandon, from the hospital?"

On cue, Dr. Brandon crouched beside her. "I won't hurt you, Ashley," he reassured her soothingly, lifting her wrist to take her pulse. "I just want to get a closer look at you."

Dr. Brandon checked her over while Dan and Mike questioned her about the events of the evening, examining the entryway wall and taking notes. Matt paced the floor, ashen and very angry, feeling helpless, not knowing what to do or say. Seeing Matt Whitford speechless was a first for everyone present.

Recalling the details of what had transpired, Ashley suddenly remembered Molly's whereabouts. "Jack," she said, clutching his arm weakly. "We've got to find Rick. He has Molly! What if he hurts her or runs away with her?"

Glancing quickly toward the front entryway, Jack exchanged a troubled look with Dan Little. Dan snapped to attention, picking the telephone receiver up off the floor and calling for assistance. Ashley gave him a description of Rick's little black M.G. and as much of its license plate number as she could remember, while Dan instructed the police dispatcher to put out an all points bulletin for the car.

"Jack, we really should get Ashley to the hospital," Dr. Brandon pulled him to the side, advising him wisely. "That head laceration needs stitches. In addition, we're probably dealing with some broken ribs and, judging by the bruising around her throat, maybe a fractured esophagus. I want to get some X-rays."

Jack nodded in agreement. "Let's do it," he said, kneeling down to lift Ashley off the floor.

"I won't leave without Molly!" Ashley clung to Jack, begging him not to take her away, thinking only of her child. "She'll be scared and she'll need me."

Jack pondered the predicament, his brow wrinkled in concentration. "I've got it," he said with an enlightened smile, snapping his fingers. "What's the phone number of that crazy friend of yours? You know, Ellie."

Glad that at last he could be helpful, Matt pulled out his wallet, producing Ellie's phone number and giving it to Jack. "If she's not there, try The Painted Desert," he said.

"We'll have Ellie come over here to be with Molly," Jack reassured Ashley as he lifted her into his strong arms. "She'll be fine with Ellie."

After having Ellie paged at The Painted Desert, Matt quickly relayed to her what had happened. She was horrified and instantly agreed to help.

"I'm on my way," she told Matt, then tossed the phone to the nearest patron and rushed from the restaurant, squealing out of the parking lot in her little Mustang like a bat out of hell.

Followed closely by Tom Brandon, Jack carried Ashley out the back door and to his house by way of the fields separating their two streets. Placing her gingerly in the back seat of Jack's Suburban, they went immediately to the hospital.

Ashley later learned from Ellie what took place over the next two hours.

Rick finally arrived back home after dark, with a sleeping Molly in his arms. He walked in, glaring venomously at the bloodstained wall in the entryway.

"Ashley!" he bellowed thunderously, waking Molly, sending her into terrified wails. He stared down at her impatiently and transported the shrieking toddler to the master bedroom, tossing her onto the bed and rushing back down the hallway in a rage.

"Ashley! God damn it, woman, I told you to clean up this mess before I got back! Where are you, you bitch!"

Ellie told Ashley that Rick was raving like a lunatic, with a face so purple that she thought he might have a stroke, too furious to even notice the two men sitting in the darkness of the living room, watching him and waiting.

Ellie sunk deeper into the couch, afraid, staring at him in fascinated horror. She couldn't believe her eyes. Ashley had told her that Rick was crazy, but to see him in action was something else all together.

"Did you not get enough of a beating the first time?" Rick screamed, continuing to rant as he moved toward the lamp on the end table. His eyes raked the room as he flipped on the light, and he could have turned to stone when he discovered that he had an audience.

Dan Little rose from his chair, proceeding cautiously toward Rick.

"Rick LeNoir?" he asked the sputtering man before him, while his partner Mike opened the back door and gestured for the waiting backup officers.

Rick regarded him haughtily, cocky enough to continue to act like an ass. "Yeah, that's me," he said, harshly. "Who the hell are you, and where is my wife?"

"Rick LeNoir, you're under arrest. You have the right to remain silent.." Dan Little began reading Rick his rights, smoothly clicking a pair of handcuffs around Rick's wrists.

Rick furiously wrestled with the cuffs and required some restraining from the policemen present. During the struggle, he spotted Ellie.

"I should've known that you would be here!" he shouted at her. "You've never been anything but trouble!" He lunged at her, stopped only by the powerful grip of Dan Little and his crew of backup officers.

Matt stepped protectively in front of Ellie, glaring at Rick, disgusted with him after seeing what he had done to Ashley.

Rick returned his stare evenly, wearing an arrogant sneer. "You still can't have Ashley, Whitford," he barked at Matt. "She'll always be my wife."

Caught off guard, Matt stared at him, dumbfounded, struck speechless and unable to respond. Ellie lifted her eyebrows, looking to Matt in surprise.

"What on earth is he talking about?" she muttered, questioning Matt under her breath. Neither could have possibly known about Rick's delusional accusation.

Molly, still crying, came out of the bedroom, watching the whole chaotic scene through wide, frightened eyes. Ellie ran to her and lifted her up, cradling her tightly in her arms.

"Come on, Molly, I'm taking you to your mommy," Ellie told her in a soothing whisper, stroking the little girl's blond curls. She and Matt whisked Molly away just before Rick was escorted to the waiting police car.

Ashley had finished her X-rays by the time Dan brought Matt, Ellie and Molly to the emergency room. Two of her ribs were broken, and the gash to her head required fourteen stitches. Luckily, her esophagus had not been crushed and none of her vertebrae had been fractured. Her face and throat were severely bruised, and her eyes were swollen from Rick's fists and bloody from the pooled blood collected in them, a result of being strangled. Ashley heard the doctors' descriptions, but had not seen a mirror. She didn't think she wanted to.

Sitting with her feet dangling off the edge of the hospital bed, Ashley let out a cry of joy when Ellie appeared, pulling back the edge of the curtain around Ashley's cubicle and coming forward with Molly. Molly looked tired and frightened, her little head rested on Ellie's shoulder and her tiny arms hooked in a death grip around Ellie's neck.

With a reassuring whisper, Ellie loosened her grip and sat Molly in Ashley's lap, and Ashley embraced her, holding her tight and kissing her thankfully. Then Ashley cried. She cried with relief for Molly's safe return, and she cried from the fear that had welled up inside of her. She never thought that she would make it out alive. God had some unknown purpose for her life. That had to be the reason. Otherwise, she should have been dead.

Dabbing at her tender eyes with a tissue, Ashley found Ellie staring in disbelief at her appearance. "That bad, huh?" Ashley asked, trying to joke with her.

Ellie nodded solemnly. "You look pretty rough," she said. "But you're alive, Ashley, and that's all that matters."

Jack reappeared, sipping coffee from a Styrofoam cup, and smiled broadly when he saw Molly with Ashley. "Thank God," he said, winking at Ashley before pulling Dan outside of the exam room to get the details of Rick's arrest.

"What did Rick say?" Ashley asked Ellie, her voice gravelly and hoarse.

Ellie shook her head somberly, "You don't want to hear about that right now."

Matt spoke up from his position in a corner chair, appearing to be over the initial shock from the evening's events with some color finally returning to his face. He leaned forward, regarding Ashley with fiery eyes.

"I can't believe that son of a bitch did this to you, Ashley," he growled angrily. "How long has this been going on?"

Ellie discouraged Matt's line of questioning with another shake of her head. "Later Matt," she told him, pursing her lips sternly.

Jack stuck his head back into the room, directing the gaze of his extraordinarily green eyes toward Ashley. "Ashley, I'm going to call your parents and then I'm going to call an attorney friend of mine."

Ashley managed an amused smile. "Jack, I am constantly amazed at your vast circle of friends," she told him, and that night she was thankful for every one of them.

Jack phoned her parents and, after establishing who he was, explained as calmly as he could what had happened. He assured them that Ashley was going to be fine, that she just looked much worse than the extent of her injuries. He made it clear that Molly was safe, and that Rick had been arrested and told them that he and Tom Brandon would take Ashley and Molly to his house to await their arrival from Louisiana.

"I'll take good care of them," he promised.

"It sounds as though you already have," Remy, still in shock, thanked him profusely. "I can't thank you enough for taking care of my daughter."

"She means a lot to me," Jack told him sincerely. "I wish I could have done more to keep this from happening at all."

Ashley was finally released from the emergency room at ten o'clock, and sent home with a prescription for a tranquilizer and pain medication. After being strapped securely into the passengers' seat of Jack's Suburban, Ashley embraced Ellie, who awaited Tom Brandon for a lift back to her car. "Thank you for everything," Ashley whispered in her ear. "I mean everything, Ellie, everything you've done for me since day one."

"You're welcome, Ash," Ellie said, looking completely exhausted. "I'm just glad it's finally over."

Jack drove Ashley to his house with Molly snoozing peacefully against the back seat. Ashley glanced over her shoulder, shaking her head in wonder at her amazing daughter. Once more, Molly displayed what a little trooper she was, appearing completely unscathed by the irrational actions of her father.

Jack glanced at Ashley while they were driving, evaluating her with a long, searching look. "You okay?" he asked.

"I'm going to be," she reached over to squeeze his hand. "You really came through for me tonight, Jack. I would've died in that house if it hadn't been for you."

Jack didn't answer. He only held on to her hand tightly until they pulled into his driveway. Jack carried Molly inside, then led Ashley, holding her firmly by the shoulders to enable her wobbly legs to climb the stairs to his bedroom. He tucked her tired and abused body in next to the fast-asleep Molly, kissing her lightly on the forehead before he left the room.

Some time during the night, Ashley woke screaming, her tormented dreams filled with visions of Rick's distorted, furious face. Hearing her screams, Jack came to her, taking her into his strong arms, holding her as Ashley's violent sobs wracked her body. She shed all the tears she had held back for so many months, for the tension, for the abuse and for the fear.

Jack held her until she quieted, sniffling softly against his shoulder as he gently stroked her hair. Exhaustion took over and Ashley dozed off. Jack gingerly laid her back on the pillows, tucking the sheet high under her chin and softly touching her lips with his own.

She awoke to yellow sunlight shining brightly through the wooden blinds on Jack's bedroom window. She blinked in confusion as she focused her swollen eyes, trying to grasp her surroundings. Then she remembered, and she remembered it all. She reached to the other side of the bed for Molly and discovered that she was gone. As she sat up with a start, she heard Molly's tinkling laughter drifting up the stairs, followed by the melodic hearty chuckle of Jack.

Rolling carefully from bed, Ashley showered and changed into the clean hospital scrubs Jack had laid out for her. Hesitantly, she wiped the steam from the bathroom mirror to reveal her shocking reflection. Both of her eyes were scarlet with blood and outlined with purple welts. Her lip was split and there were perfect purple finger marks around her throat. Ashley could feel tears welling up in her eyes, as memories of the night before came flooding back.

"Stop it," she told the girl in the mirror irritably. "You survived it and you'll be okay. Now suck it up and go on."

She straightened her shoulders as well as she could with her aching ribs, forcing a brave look onto her face. Kate would've said that she was burying things in the dark corners of her mind again, but that's how she had always dealt with the worst, by steeling herself against it and moving on.

She descended the staircase stiffly, finding Molly seated at the kitchen table, eating cereal with Jack, Ellie and Tom. Seeing her mother enter the room, Molly looked up at Ashley, regarding her curiously.

"You face," she observed. Even at two and a half, she knew that Ashley didn't look quite right.

Ashley went to her, putting her arms around the sunny little cherub. "Mommy's face will be better soon, Molly," Ashley assured her, before glancing at the others around the table. "Good morning."

"Coffee?" Jack asked, rising to get a cup for her. Ashley accepted and sipped it gratefully, noting by the clock above the kitchen sink that it was close to nine o'clock. Remy and Maggie would be arriving at any time.

"I've called my attorney friend, Kevin Ford," Jack advised her over coffee. "He's going to come by this afternoon and do whatever you need done."

"You mean, my divorce and custody of my child?"

"Whatever you need."

The arrival of Remy and Maggie brought more tears. Jack welcomed them at the door, introducing himself, hoping to soften the blow before they saw their only daughter. As he brought them into the kitchen, Maggie gasped, the color draining from her lovely face, and Remy stared in stunned disbelief. They rushed to Ashley's side, embracing her tightly, and Remy thanked Jack, Ellie and Tom repeatedly while Maggie wept, holding Ashley's hand tightly in her own.

"No thanks needed," Jack told him. "Like I said last night, I just wish I could have done more to prevent it. I just couldn't convince her to leave him any sooner."

"Ashley is too stubborn and independent for her own good sometimes," Remy told him, shooting Ashley a stern look.

"Endearing qualities, sometimes, but not in this case," Jack said, teasing Ashley with his smile.

Molly grew tired of being ignored and began to demand a little attention from her grandparents. She climbed into Remy's lap, kissing him with her sweet little girl kisses, offering him some comfort in the hour of what could've been his worst nightmare.

Later in the morning, Dan Little called to advise them that Rick was still in jail, but would be released on bail early Monday morning. Jack, Remy and Ellie returned to the LeNoir house to retrieve the remainder of Ashley and Molly's personal items and to bring Ashley's faithful Corolla to Jack's.

Alone in Jack's house, Ashley and Maggie settled onto Jack's bed, using their private time for a heart to heart.

"Oh Ashley, why didn't you tell me what was going on up here?" Maggie scolded her gently, with tears filling her sad green eyes. "I begged you and begged you to tell me what was going on."

Ashley was instantly filled with guilt. Maggie had pleaded with her time and time again, and she had been too stubborn to confide in her or to depend on her and Remy for help. Her obstinate attitude had almost cost her life.

"I'm sorry, Maggie," Ashley said humbly. "I thought I could take care of everything without having to make you worry."

"Well, I hate to tell you this," Maggie smiled grimly at the irony of it all. "I've worried anyway. I knew that things were not right up here."

"But they haven't always been this extreme. If they had, I would have never been able to stick it out as long as I did. The last eight months have been hell."

"Ashley Stewart, nothing is worth dying over!" Maggie burst out in frustration. "No amount of pride, stubbornness and certainly no college degree is worth risking your life for. Whatever were you thinking!"

"It's a long story," Ashley sighed. "But it all had to do with keeping Molly. I would never have married Rick, or stayed with him, if it hadn't been for Molly."

"Do you want to explain what you mean by that?"

"Well," Ashley hesitated, knowing that her explanation would sound so ridiculous now, in light of the last twenty-four hours. "Three years ago, when I returned from Destin and had decided to raise Molly alone, Rick reminded me that Molly would be illegitimate. He said that you and Remy wouldn't be able to hold your heads up in public with a bastard for a grandchild."

Ashley glanced over to Maggie, who was listening intently, not wanting to interrupt her. "So I married him to give Molly a name. After she was born and I was still in the hospital, I asked Rick why we didn't just cut our losses and get divorced. He said that I could leave but that he was keeping Molly. He had me convinced that he would automatically be awarded custody of her since I had no means of supporting her."

"That's absurd!" Maggie said. "I can't believe that you fell for that, Ashley. You're much smarter than that."

"I was a child, Maggie. A scared, lonely child, and I didn't know what to do. And yes, I was stupid to have too much pride to tell y'all the truth. I was wrong. I can't go back and change all that now. I left Rick as soon as I thought I could and still keep Molly."

Ashley's remorseful tears streamed down her face and Maggie drew her into her comforting arms, stroking her hair and letting her cry, forgiving her for her stupidity.

"It's all right now, honey," she said soothingly. "It's all over now and everything will be just fine, you'll see."

Ashley met with the attorney, Kevin Ford, that afternoon and liked him immediately. Kevin was young, bright and gung ho, truly outraged when he saw what Rick had done to her, and vowed to help her make everything right. They agreed to file her divorce the following morning and obtain a victim's protection order against Rick. However, they had a difference of opinion when it came to marital dividing assets.

"I don't want anything," Ashley told him.

Kevin Ford's mouth dropped open in disbelief. "But you're entitled to personal property, to bank accounts, to child support," he argued, filled with frustration over Ashley's refusal to take her fair share.

"He can have it all," Ashley answered with a determined smile. "All I want is Molly. The rest is unimportant."

Ashley left Oklahoma on Wednesday morning. She told Ellie goodbye on Tuesday, making promises to write and call, expressing gratitude for all the support she had given for the past three years.

"I owe you my sanity," Ashley said, smiling at Ellie through sentimental tears.

"No one ever said that you were sane to begin with," Ellie said gruffly, hugging Ashley tightly to hide her own tears. "And don't think that you won't be seeing me again. You have to keep in touch. Remember, Molly is really half my baby."

The night before she left, Maggie and Remy went to bed early, taking Molly with them. Jack and Ashley sat on the couch, reminiscing about their times together, both good and bad.

"I'm really going to miss you, Jack. You're one of the best friends I've ever had," Ashley said tearfully.

"Do you think that I'm going to drop off the face of the earth just because you're moving home?" Jack asked her with a merry twinkle in his eye. "I happen to love Louisiana and plan to visit frequently. With all that hunting and fishing that goes on down there, you won't be able to keep me away!"

"Did I thank you for saving me?" Ashley asked, squeezing his hand tightly.

"You can thank me by getting your life back, Ashley. Move on, be strong. You're a survivor."

The following morning, Ashley climbed into the Jeep with Molly and Maggie, leaning out the window to give Jack a fond kiss goodbye. "Call me soon," she said with a warm smile.

"You are staying here when you come back for the big divorce, aren't you?" Jack said.

Ashley offered him a dubious grin. "Only if Dan Little can stay here with us."

"Dan can stay, but you won't need him. Rick won't be able to get near you with a ten-foot pole, I promise you that," Jack said sternly, his voice growing hard with loathing at the mention of Rick.

Remy drove the Corolla, loaded down with boxes, while Maggie, Molly and Ashley followed him in the Jeep. Ashley stared out the passenger side window, taking in the beauty of Oklahoma City one last time, remembering her excitement when she had arrived only three years beforehand. Oklahoma would always hold many memories for her, both good and bad. She still loved the city, but she was glad to be going home.

CHAPTER TWENTY-NINE

"Never let it be said that you can't go back home again," Ashley thought as Maggie steered the Jeep through the streets of Pineville. She rolled down the window and inhaled, letting fresh air and the lingering scent of pine fill her senses. The tall trees, lush green grass and swampy bayous welcomed her back with open arms. She even loved the sweltering humidity. Coming home, knowing that she never again had to return to Rick, was heaven on earth to her.

Ashley spent a lot of time wandering aimlessly around town those first weeks home, revisiting old haunts and hangouts, and thinking back to better days.

"How could anyone be so stupid?" She beat herself up relentlessly over the predicaments she'd gotten into over the last five years. It was a nonproductive process. Thinking back and remembering did her no good whatsoever, but she did it anyway.

Obviously, life in Pineville was not the same as it had been during her childhood. As Rick had so deftly pointed out, she was no longer the belle of the ball, surrounded by devoted pals. Most of her friends had moved away. Only Kate remained out of the gang she grew up with. And Ashley was no longer a light-hearted teenager with no responsibilities. She was now an adult woman with a small child to care for.

Still, even with all that to consider, for Ashley, there was no other place in the world like home.

Not to say that everything was automatically wonderful the minute she stepped foot back in Louisiana. She had her share of emotional baggage to deal with, waking many nights, crying out from the vivid images haunting her dreams. She still saw Rick's enraged face above her own, still felt his hands around her throat and his fists striking her face. She couldn't shake the fear that his attack had instilled in her, and she had never been afraid of anything before in her life.

Ashley resented Rick greatly for the change in her. Gone was the vivacious, carefree girl she had been before her marriage. She had become a much quieter, more solemn version of her former self. Ashley didn't like her transformation, but she couldn't go back to the way she had been before. Too much had happened and she was changed forever.

Kate showed up at the Stewarts' the day after Ashley's arrival, her knees buckling at her best friend's battered appearance. After the initial shock wore off and Kate seemed able to stand, Maggie sent the two young women outside with a pitcher of iced tea, settling them on the front porch swing.

"I shouldn't have judged you so harshly when you were here for Daddy's funeral," Kate reflected solemnly, pushing the swing back and forth slowly with the tip of her shoe. "I was wrong to let you have it the way I did."

"Kate, you weren't wrong. You said what needed to be said," Ashley replied quietly, staring out in the direction of the lake as she thoughtfully sipped her tea. "I was acting like a child and you made me realize that there are other lives to consider than my own. You, of all people, had every right to say those things to me. You've put up with me for a long time."

"I almost lost you, didn't I?" Kate's voice quivered, suddenly overcome with emotion. "Rick came close to killing you, didn't he?"

Ashley sighed, shrugging indifferently, "I don't know if he would've actually killed me, but he did succeed in smothering the fire out of me."

"Don't you ever say that again!" Kate said, suddenly feisty with anger. "Don't you ever give him the satisfaction of thinking he crushed your spirit. That's what he wanted. You'll be okay. You've just been through a lot this past year."

"Who are you trying to convince, Kate, me or you?"

"I'm not trying to *convince* anyone, Ashley. I just know how you are. You deal with difficulty and loss better than anyone I've ever known."

"Maybe, but not this time, Kate. This time is tough."

"You've been through worse."

"True, but that's when I could rely on my trusty defense mechanism. You said I couldn't continue tucking things away in the corners of my mind. You said I had to start dealing with them."

"And you picked now to start listening to me?" Kate asked, staring in exasperation, bringing the swing to a halt with her foot. "Did it ever occur to you that I might not be as wise as everyone thinks? Forget what I said, Ashley. You do whatever you need to do to get through this."

Ashley turned away, laying her head against the back of the swing, feeling weak and vulnerable. Kate was right. She had been through worse. She could do this. She would block it all out and gain back her life, coming out on top, absolutely invincible.

It had worked for her before. Maybe it would work again.

By summer's end, Ashley's marriage was officially dissolved. Rick had hired one of the best criminal attorneys in the state of Oklahoma, and had received a deferred sentence for assault and battery. Ashley dreaded seeing him in divorce court.

She returned to Oklahoma City with Remy, meeting up with Kevin Ford at the county courthouse for the proceedings. Her blood turned to ice water when Rick entered the courtroom. He was cool and smug, pointedly ignoring her, and Ashley couldn't bring herself to look at him. Her physical wounds were healing, but psychologically, it would be many years before she recovered from the trauma of their marriage.

Rick did not contest the divorce or her sole custody of Molly. He asked for no visitation, getting in one final jab when the judge questioned him about it.

"Your Honor, I do not want visitation because I'm not even sure the child is mine," Rick said, mocking Ashley with his words.

Ashley was appalled and stared indignantly at Rick, stunned by his hatred for her. Feeling her heated stare, Rick looked her way, smiling wickedly, taunting her one last time.

After their divorce was granted, Ashley left the courtroom, fueled by an overwhelming sense of liberation. Taking Remy's arm, she ignored Rick's attempt to make eye contact and held her head high, sailing past him without a second glance, walking out of his life forever.

Ashley sat for pharmacy boards in June, and in July received confirmation of something she had known would happen all along. She sat at the kitchen table with Maggie, reading the Sunday newspaper. She flipped open the community section and was slapped in the face with an engagement announcement. Doug and Camille Rabalais were officially engaged to marry.

Ashley gawked at Doug's smiling face, feeling the bile rising rapidly in her throat. "Damn," she cursed, laying down the paper.

Maggie looked over at her, startled by her outburst. "What's the matter?" she asked curiously.

Ashley slid the paper across the table. Maggie glanced down at it, then back to Ashley with eyes full of compassion, "I'm sorry."

Ashley shook her head stubbornly. "Don't be sorry. He deserves to be happy. This is what I've always wanted for him."

"You are *such* a liar," Ashley's head snapped upward as Kate's voice boomed into the kitchen. "I was hoping to get here before you saw that," Kate said, nodding toward the engagement announcement.

"How long have you known about it?" Ashley asked her suspiciously.

"Just about five minutes longer than you have. I just saw it myself and ran over here to cushion the blow."

"There's nothing to cushion me from. I've known all along that Doug would marry Camille. I'm just surprised that it's taken this long."

"Does it say when the wedding will be?" Maggie peered at the announcement interestedly. "It only says here that the happy couple plans to marry at the completion of law school."

"That would be next spring," Kate said, patting Ashley on the back sympathetically.

Ashley pretended that it didn't bother her, yet she couldn't help being disappointed by the news. Doug's engagement was just one more way of showing her that things would never revert to the way they used to be. Life would continue to move forward and Ashley would have to move forward with it.

Ashley received her state board results the first week in August, passing her exam and becoming a bona fide registered pharmacist. She began working full time at the store as the pharmacist while Remy continued the accounting and bookkeeping.

Ashley and Frannie spent their first days alone in the pharmacy in the midst of a power play. Frannie wasn't at all sure that she was comfortable with Ashley running the show. She had been in charge of Remy and the business for too many years to hand over the reins without a fight. After their first full day of tug of war, Ashley decided that it might be in her best interest to let Frannie think she was boss for the time being, then take control later, a task that would soon prove to be easier said than done.

After Doug had left home for LSU, Ms. Bobbie Fairchild found that she no longer needed to remain home to be at his beck and call. She went to work with Nick, decorating new homes built by his company. Nick Fairchild's office was just down from the drugstore on Jackson Street and Ms. Bobbie dropped in from time to time to visit with Ashley and Frannie.

The first few times she visited, Ms. Bobbie was careful not to mention Doug, Camille, or their upcoming nuptials out of respect for Ashley, clearly unsure of how she might react. But as time went on, Ms. Bobbie could no longer stand it. Ashley looked up one afternoon to find Ms. Bobbie standing across the counter from her, hands on her hips, studying her with a perplexed expression.

"Is something wrong, Ms. Bobbie?" Ashley asked, stopping her work and smiling warmly.

"I'm just watching you," Ms. Bobbie answered, her mouth shaping into a wide grin. "You would've made a fine daughter-in-law."

Ashley's smile turned shy, and she lowered her eyes in embarrassment. "What brought that on, Ms. Bobbie?"

"Just been wanting the answer to a question that has been bugging me for years. Why didn't you marry my boy when he asked you?"

Ashley glanced up with a start, meeting the inquiring stare of Ms. Bobbie's wise dark eyes." You know about that?"

"Yes'um, of course, I know about it. Doug made no secret of how heartbroken he was when you married that man from Monroe. Took him a long time to get over that, if he ever has."

Ashley leaned against the counter, crossing her arms loosely against her chest, her eyes taking on a faraway look as she remembered Doug's marriage proposal of long ago. Another "what if" in her life full of "what if"s. She sighed, shaking her head slightly, returning to the present and Ms. Bobbie. Frannie stood by the register, her ear cocked to one side, dying with curiosity to hear the answer to Ms. Bobbie's question.

"I didn't marry Doug because, when he asked me, neither the time nor the circumstances were right for either of us," Ashley sighed as she admitted the truth, regret hanging heavy on her words.

Ms. Bobbie raised a skeptical eyebrow, "Any time would've been right. The boy loved you for years."

"Well, that's neither here nor there," Ashley replaced the yearning on her face with what she hoped was a cheerful smile. "I don't even know why we're discussing this. It's all water under the bridge anyway. Doug is engaged to Camille, and soon they'll be happily married."

Ms. Bobbie flashed a grim smile as she leaned forward to whisper to Ashley, "That may be true, but it doesn't make it right." She pinched Ashley's cheek fondly, "and it sure doesn't mean that he's any happier right now than you are."

She grinned knowingly as she turned to leave, waving goodbye as she walked confidently down the health and beauty aisle, whistling a merry tune as she went. Ashley shook her head, hoping to clear the conversation with Ms. Bobbie from her mind, and met Frannie's mirthfully dancing eyes. Ashley scowled at her, not at all happy that Frannie overheard the entire exchange.

"Don't you say a word," she shook her finger good-naturedly at Frannie's broad smile. "I don't want to hear one word from you about any of that."

In October, Ashley bought a house up the road from her parents. It was a small house—single story with three tiny bedrooms and one bath, nestled just on the other side of the lake. Her favorite things about the house were the veranda that wrapped cozily around the front, and the window seat in front of the dining room window. It was a comfy spot that offered her an unhampered view of the lake and the thick groves of cypress and pine surrounding it.

Maggie protested greatly over her moving out of their house again.

"Did you think Molly and I were going to live with you forever?" Ashley kidded her. "I am a grown woman, you know."

"I know," Maggie agreed sadly. "I just love having you at home with us, that's all."

"You love having Molly at home with you. Me you could do without."

"That's not true, Ashley," Maggie tried to deny it, but couldn't hide her mischievous grin. She was crazy about her granddaughter.

"Maggie, I'll just be up the street, for heaven's sake. And I'm going to need lots of help fixing up the place, so I'm sure you'll see more of me than you really want."

Ashley decorated her house in sunny pastel shades of yellow, soft pink and green, using floral patterns and white lace for window treatments, and painting the woodwork and wood blinds white. When she and Maggie finished decorating, the house was cheerful and full of light. Ashley was pleased. She had not only a house, but a home of her own.

"This is such a great house!" Kate went from room to room, checking things out, pausing in Ashley's bedroom, taking in the quilt-covered bed, antique rocker, and large, light-filled windows draped in white lace.

"Very feminine!" Kate said, turning toward Ashley with a teasing grin. "Are you rebelling from all those years of paisley and plaid with Rick?"

"I'm rebelling against everything I had with Rick," Ashley said, laughing lightly.

Ashley packed up her room at her parents', bringing everything to her new house. When she came to The Box, she took it into her bedroom and unloaded it onto her bed. As she lovingly caressed the treasured items covering her quilt, laughter, music, moonlight and kisses sprang forth from the dark corners of her mind, and she smiled, opening her heart, just a little, as she looked over Jimmy's things. She came across a picture of them together, taken by Lana in front of the Moreaus' house by the lake, and she reminisced, gazing at the wonderful boy in the photograph and thinking of how she had loved him so completely.

"Oh, what I wouldn't give just to see him one more time."

She sighed, blinking back sentimental tears, and returned most of the items to the box, keeping out only her locket from their Christmas together, and the framed portrait of her that Jimmy had sketched, hanging it in a place of honor on her bedroom wall.

Ashley felt at peace in her new home. In the evenings, while Molly slept, she curled up on the window seat to read or to play on her new computer, a housewarming surprise from Remy. It was during such an evening that Ashley made an amazing discovery. She could write again. Her creative side, which had shut down after Jimmy died, had suddenly reopened and she began to write short stories and poetry as she had in what seemed like another life.

After a long hard road, Ashley was finally content.

Ellie, lively and giddy with happiness over her budding romance with Dr. Tom Brandon, was Ashley's first visitor to Louisiana, followed shortly thereafter by Jack.

Jack arrived for his first visit at Thanksgiving, driving down in his Suburban loaded full of camouflage and camping gear. Deer season had just begun and Jack hoped to get in a little hunting. Ashley granted Jack's wish by introducing him to Todd Richardson, waving cheerfully as Todd kidnapped Jack and drove the Suburban off in the direction of the hunting lodge.

When he finally returned from his expedition, Ashley and Jack enjoyed Thanksgiving dinner with Maggie and Remy. Jack fit in perfectly with the Stewarts, keeping them in stitches with jokes and stories all during dinner. And Ashley didn't miss the shining looks of admiration flashed at him by her mother.

After a filling Thanksgiving feast, Jack and Remy retired to the den to watch football while Maggie and Ashley cleared the table.

"You know, Jack would be good husband material," Maggie casually tossed out a hint as Ashley rinsed the dishes.

"You only like him because he saved my life."

"Well, that alone shows he cares for you, making him *perfect* husband material."

"Maggie, please," Ashley scowled at her, rolling her eyes indignantly. "The ink isn't even dry on my divorce papers yet."

"I didn't say that you had to marry him today," Maggie said, batting her eyelashes innocently. "It was just a suggestion for future reference."

"You're wasting your time. I'm never going to marry again," Ashley declared firmly, closing the dishwasher door with an emphatic slam.

Maggie's gales of laughter filled the kitchen and Ashley gave her a dirty look. "Ashley, never is a long time. You're only twenty-four years old. I think you'll probably marry again before you die."

"Well, if I do, it won't be Jack. We're just friends."

"Why do you keep all the good ones as 'just friends'?" Maggie sighed disappointedly.

"Because I've had much better luck with friends than husbands."

"But you've only had one, and he doesn't count."

"Enough, Maggie."

"Well, all I can say is never say never," Maggie sang out knowingly, ignoring Ashley's irritated frown, slipping from the kitchen to deliver a tray of banana pudding and pumpkin pie to Jack and Remy.

Jack and Ashley returned to her house later that evening, tucking a sleeping Molly into bed and making hot chocolate to sip in front of the fireplace. The glow from the flames enhanced the cinnamon sheen of Jack's hair, catching Ashley's eye with its brilliance, and when she glanced at Jack, she found him watching her, smiling softly over the rim of his cocoa mug.

"What?" she asked him, grinning as she met his admiring gaze.

"You look so good," Jack said. "There's something different about you now."

"Could it be the lack of fear and stress in my life?" she asked kiddingly, stretching out on the rug to enjoy the toasty warmth of the fireplace.

"No," Jack said, shaking his head as he studied her more closely. "It's something else."

"I think it's just old-fashioned, small town living. My life is so simple now. It's just Molly and me, and we're perfectly happy this way."

"Don't you miss having a man in your life?"

"Like Rick?" Ashley tossed him a saucy grin, laughing heartily as Jack scowled and narrowed his eyes unpleasantly.

"No, not like Rick," he said, repeating her mockingly. "I meant male company that you might enjoy."

Ashley stared into the flickering orange flames of the fire, reflecting solemnly. "The men I've had in my life have brought me nothing but profound sorrow, in one way or another. I don't feel the need to bring any of that upon myself again."

"Ashley, you can't close your heart off completely. There's someone special out there, just waiting for you to find him."

"Oh, stop it! The next thing I know you'll have me singing *Some Day My Prince Will Come.*"

"I only want to see you happy."

"I am happy, Jack. I promise." Ashley sat up, hugging her knees tightly to her chest as she gave him a genuine smile. "I don't need a man to make me happy."

"That's a very healthy statement," he said. "You've grown up a lot since I met you."

"Did I have a choice?"

"You done good," Jack said, his voice full of admiration. " I'm proud of you."

"I couldn't have done a lot of it without you, Jack."

"I was glad to be of service," he said, reaching out to clasp her hand affectionately. "Having you for a friend has made a difference in my life too. I sure miss having you around."

"Well, you always have an open invitation here."

"Even after you take on another Cajun husband?" Jack grinned tauntingly, chuckling good-naturedly as Ashley rolled her eyes.

"*Especially* if I take on another Cajun husband," she laughed. "I'll need *someone* around to keep him in line."

Jack loaded his gear into the Suburban on Saturday morning, ready for his trip back to Oklahoma City. He kissed Ashley's cheek fondly, promising he would return soon.

"After all," he said, climbing into the truck and flashing a naughty grin, "duck season is just around the corner."

CHAPTER THIRTY

Kate married Todd Richardson on December fifteenth, ten days before Christmas and six days before Molly's third birthday. Shortly after the New Year started, Ashley began to date again, much to her mother's delight, going out with friends of Kate and Todd, and socializing with colleagues of Dr. Lisa Watson, with whom she had become friends since returning home. Ashley had fun, but did not want to pursue more than a friendly relationship with anyone, becoming more and more content with just being alone with Molly.

"You could show a little gratitude, especially after Katie went to all the trouble of parading the pick of the litter by you," Susanna told her, offering her unsolicited opinion over the telephone during her weekly call. "They may not be much, but you could at least have the common courtesy to go out on a second date with one of them."

"Why do you feel the need to make this your business?" Ashley replied indignantly. "I thought marrying you off and banishing you to Texas would get you off my back."

"Oh please! It'll take much more than that to get rid of me."

"Susanna, this isn't junior high. I'm perfectly capable of arranging my own social calendar."

"Okay, but don't blame me when Molly flies the coop and you're nothing but a lonely old spinster woman."

"For heaven's sake!" Ashley snapped in exasperation. "I haven't even been divorced a year. I think I have plenty of time left before Molly flies the coop."

"All the good men will be dead or gone by then."

"Then that's a chance I'll have to take."

"Why *are* you so dead set against another commitment in your lifetime?" Kate asked later, sipping hot apple cider on the window seat alongside Ashley.

Ashley sighed, pressing her face against the window and peering out at the trees, watching a cyclone of dead leaves swirl against the gray winter skies. "Kate, you know as well as I do that there's only one man on earth that I'd give up my newly found freedom for."

Ashley glanced over, gathering from Kate's expression that she knew exactly to whom she was referring. "And he's marrying Camille Rabalais."

The endless round of engagement parties and wedding showers for Camille and Doug had begun. Ashley saw smiling photographs of them in the *Alexandria Daily Town Talk*, taken at various celebrations held in their honor. She studied the pictures, pointedly ignoring Camille, focusing instead on Doug's handsome face, and she had to admit that he looked happy.

Kate and Todd had gone to Baton Rouge on Valentine's Day for one such engagement party, an elaborate ball given by Camille's uncle, Governor Rabalais, and the First Lady. Ashley, in fact, had surprisingly been issued her own invitation to the elegant affair, but had respectfully declined. She hadn't seen Doug in close to a year and although her feelings for him remained unchanged, not seeing him helped her deal with his marrying Camille. To be in the same room with him, even for one moment, would destroy all the progress she had made in getting over him.

Kate came over the next afternoon to share the juicy details with her. "It was spectacular!" she admitted to Ashley with a huge grin. "Everyone who is *anyone* was there, along with *tons* of people we graduated with. You really should've gone. You would've had a great time, in spite of the reason for the party."

Ashley offered her a thin smile. "How was Doug?"

"Well, in light of your new approach to handling all this maturely, I'll be perfectly honest with you. Doug looks wonderful and happy." She glanced Ashley's way and proceeded with caution, "I think he really loves Camille, Ashley, and I think he's really going to go through with the wedding."

Ashley nodded thoughtfully, letting Kate's latest tidbit of information soak in, and tried not to appear disappointed. Realistically, she knew the wedding would go off as planned. However, she carried in the back of her mind the hope that some small miracle, some Divine Intervention, would stop Doug from committing permanently to Camille.

Ashley leaned on the counter, staring out at the warm April sunshine. It was such a lovely afternoon and she had spring fever. It would have been a great day to play hooky and take Molly to the park.

She sighed. She had a lot on her mind, and work was the last place she wanted to be. She was preoccupied with Doug's approaching wedding, fed up with Susanna's constant nagging, and now she had Remy's retirement looming over her head.

"I'm going to sell you the business, Ashley," Remy had dropped the bombshell on her earlier in the afternoon, catching her completely off guard.

"Maggie and I have finally come to the conclusion that you've grown up enough to leave you on your own, and hope that you can stay out of trouble."

So now, Remy and Maggie were going to drop everything, hit the road and become world travelers, trusting her not to run his thriving business into the ground in their absence. What was the world coming to?

"May I help you, sir?" Frannie's voice drifted from the cough and cold aisle, breaking into Ashley's thoughts.

"Darn, a customer," Ashley looked up, glancing at the clock in annoyance. "And at closing time too."

She peeked out from behind a display of vitamins, hoping to discourage the last-minute shopper with her irritated scowl. Instead, she let out a huge yelp of surprise. Will Moreau stood at the cash register wearing the same look of astonishment on his face as Ashley wore on hers.

"Will!" Ashley vaulted over the counter into his waiting embrace. Frannie viewed them with wide-eyed fascination. This was the most enthusiasm for a man she had seen Ashley display in a long time.

Will hugged her tightly, then held her at arm's length to get a better look. "Ashley Stewart, you've grown up on me," he declared with a huge grin.

"Will, what are you doing here?" she asked him in amazement, staring at him with adoring eyes. It had been six years since she'd last seen him, but he looked much the same, a little older maybe, but still devilishly handsome.

"I was in Shreveport for a couple of days and as I drove back through Alexandria, I decided to stop in and say hi to your daddy. I never expected to find you behind the counter!"

"Can you stay for dinner?"

"Sure, where would you like to go?"

"How about I make dinner for you?" Ashley laughed as he raised a doubtful eyebrow. "I assure you that it will be nowhere near the caliber of one of your mother's dinners, but I won't poison you either."

"Then it's a deal," Will smiled warmly and waited as she finished closing the store and put in a call to Maggie.

Will followed Ashley to her house in Pineville. He nodded and smiled as he viewed her little home. "It suits you," he said.

"Thanks," she unlocked the front door and led him inside, settling him on the window seat so that he could talk to her as she made dinner.

"So, where do you live now?" she asked, handing him a tall glass of iced tea.

"Down in south Louisiana, around Metairie. I married a girl from there and we settled near her family."

"Is she a nice girl?" Ashley teased him.

"Very nice," he nodded. "We've been married almost three years."

"That's wonderful. Any kids?"

"Not yet. We're not quite ready for that," Will laughed.

"You should. You'd love it."

"What about you? I thought you got married several years ago," Will glanced at her inquisitively, observing her dark frown.

"I did, but we divorced last year."

"What happened?"

"It's a long story. Let's just say that it didn't work out." She didn't want to spoil their reunion by talking about Rick. "I do have a wonderful daughter named Molly."

"I heard about her through the grapevine, right after she was born," he said, leaving the window seat to pick up a framed picture from the bar. He studied Molly's face with an appreciative smile. "She's a beauty," he declared, looking back at Ashley.

"Thanks, she's my pride and joy," Ashley bragged, sliding dinner into the oven and joining him on the window seat.

"What made you go into pharmacy? Not that I don't think it's a great choice, but I thought your heart was set on journalism?"

"I developed a severe case of writer's block after Jimmy died," Ashley revealed solemnly. "It was senseless to pursue a degree in journalism when I couldn't even write."

Will regarded her thoughtfully and Ashley hated that their conversation had shifted to a subject so tender to them both, but it was inevitable that they would have to discuss him.

"How did you cope, Ashley?"

Ashley sighed, her heart heavy with sentiment. "I guess I didn't cope very well. I spent the first year hiding in my dorm room, and the second year I married on the rebound."

Will's gaze shifted from the sadness in her eyes to the shiny silver band on her finger. "I notice that you still wear the ring Jimmy gave you," he said quietly.

"I've worn it since the day he gave it to me," she said with a soft smile, twisting the ring reflectively around her finger. "Jimmy gave it to me to remember his hugs and kisses," she looked over at Will. "And I do. He'll always be a part of me."

Will reached over and squeezed her hand. "Jimmy loved you so very much. I'm glad that you remember him this way."

The timer went off, breaking the graveness of the moment. Ashley wiped away her tears and hurried to retrieve dinner from the oven. She joined Will at the table, wanting desperately to liven up the mood.

"Tell me how Lana and John are doing," she requested with a cheerful smile.

Will seemed just as grateful to have something more light-hearted to discuss. "They're fine," he said. "They're still down in south Louisiana with Gram. Dad still travels quite a bit and Mother spends most of her time with hobbies and trying to con me into giving her some grandchildren."

Ashley smiled, trying to envision Lana Moreau as a grandmother. She definitely didn't look the part and probably never would. "Please give them my love."

"You should come down and see them some time. They would love to see you."

"I'll try," Ashley said noncommittally, not wanting to make promises she might not be able to keep.

"What do you hear from Doug?" Will asked.

"Nothing lately. I saw his engagement announcement in the newspaper last summer and received an invitation to his engagement ball last month. But I haven't personally heard from him."

"Have you met his fiancée, Camille Rabalais? He had started seeing her right before I moved from Baton Rouge."

"Yes," Ashley tried not to growl, and Will regarded her with an amused smile.

"Don't you like her, Ashley?"

"I don't have to like her. I don't have to live with her."

"I'll take that as a no," Will laughed, helping himself to seconds. "You did learn how to cook. I'm astonished."

"I've mastered lots of things. Anything domestic, I can do it."

"I'm going to pretend I didn't hear you say that. The Ashley Stewart I knew would never admit to anything so mundane," Will clutched his chest, his brown eyes twinkling comically.

Ashley laughed, punching his arm playfully. It was so good to be with Will again. His warmth and good humor cheered her, relieving her tension and lightening her spirits, taking her back in time to regain some of her lost vivacity.

After dinner, Will followed Ashley to her parents' house to say hello, but declined Remy's offer to come inside. "I better hit the road. I've still got quite a drive," he said regretfully.

He told them goodbye and walked with Ashley to his car.

"I'm glad you came by," she said, smiling up at him happily.

"I hope I didn't open up too many painful memories," Will took hold of her hand, his eyes filled with compassion and concern.

"No, on the contrary, you made me remember the very pleasant ones," Ashley said sincerely, kissing his cheek. "Give my love to your parents."

"I will. Mother will be thrilled that I saw you." Will opened his car door and slid into the driver's seat. "I'll stop by again," he promised as he started the car. "I go to Shreveport a few times a year."

"I'd like that," Ashley blew him a kiss and waved as he drove away, then walked back toward the house to collect Molly, wearing a thoughtful smile.

Will's visit triggered an explosion, releasing a firestorm of repressed memories and emotions. Ashley fought them off bravely, but by week's end found herself drawn to the one place she swore she'd never go again.

She sat in the grass, tracing his name with her fingertip, seeing his face, hearing his laughter, feeling his kiss. "Hi, Jimmy," she whispered softly, her voice blending with the serenity of her surroundings.

She leaned against the cool marble of his headstone, yearning for him with every beat of her heart. She sensed his presence, feeling the warmth of his arms around her and his breath against her skin. She closed her eyes and remembered, basking in the glow of Jimmy's love.

She pulled away and sat back on her heels, studying the delicate band of silver she had worn for so many years, knowing what she had to do. She twisted the ring from her finger and placed it next to his grave, covering it carefully with soil and grass. She stood, her heart pounding wildly as she stared at the shadowy vision before her, seeing him just one more time.

"Jimmy," she reached out to him, wanting him to be real. "I love you and will miss you until the day I die, but I have to let you go. I know you understand."

With one last brush of his lips, the image faded, leaving her filled, not with sadness but with tranquility. She blew a small kiss toward heaven and walked away, knowing she had finally let go of the great love of her life. The pain was gone. All that remained were sentimental thoughts and treasured memories.

She was ready to move on.

Jack checked in on her often. His visits progressed from an occasional trip to hunt or fish until soon he was coming down to celebrate the change of each season. By the end of spring, Jack was showing up so frequently that Ashley converted her frilly, feminine guest room into a masculine shrine for him. Jack's visits were a ray of sunshine into her life of quiet contentment. He was so captivating, so vibrant and full of energy that Ashley found herself actually counting the days until he was with them again.

Jack liked fishing with Todd. They went to Toledo Bend, hauling Todd's new bass boat behind Jack's Suburban, loaded down with the finest fishing equipment for days of power fishing. It was exhilarating, and in Todd, Jack had found a kindred spirit.

But there was something very special about fishing with Ashley. Ashley always took Jack to her sentimental lake to fish with cane poles from Remy's old metal boat. It was usually just the two of them, facing one another from opposite benches, their fishing poles loosely in hand, spending hours and hours talking and laughing as the waters of the lake lapped peacefully against the sides of the boat.

Jack understood about the lake. For Ashley, it was a very special place with memories of ecstatic young love and passion with Jimmy, and of long walks, pep talks and a sincere proposal of marriage from Doug. And now, Ashley hoped to make happy new memories there, fishing alone with Jack.

"You know, I could very easily leave Oklahoma City and move down here with you all," Jack told her as they fished together one sunny afternoon.

Ashley glanced at him, surprise written all over her face. "What about Matt? And all those nurses?"

Jack laughed. "Hell, I could find more nurses, Ashley. They're pretty prevalent in our society," he replied with a devilish grin. "And Matt would just have to move down here or deal with me being gone."

"Todd Richardson would be in hog heaven, seeing how you're obsessed hunting buddies and all, but I suspect that Kate might not be as enthusiastic about having you here, since you steal her husband for days on end."

"What about you, Ashley Stewart?" Jack winked at her. "How would you feel about me being here all the time?"

Ashley shrugged with feigned indifference. "I suppose I could put up with having you around again," she nudged him playfully and flashed a teasing grin.

She adored Jack and hoped he was sincere about relocating to Pineville. He would make a welcome addition to the community, and seeing him around town everyday would certainly give the women something to look forward to.

It took all of Ashley's strength to cope the day she received her engraved invitation to the May fourteenth nuptials of Camille Rabalais and Doug Fairchild. It arrived in the mail exactly four weeks before the wedding, as was dictated by proper etiquette. Ashley walked from the mailbox, turning the calligraphy-addressed envelope over in her hands, knowing very well what was inside and not wanting to open it. To see it this way made Doug and Camille's inevitable wedding even more realistic.

She opened the envelope and stared at the creamy white invitation and its delicate embossing, reading the names and dates over and over again. And she wept. She wept for all the foolishness she had displayed over the years, and she wept for letting Doug slip through her fingers like fine white Destin sand.

Act stupidly, she reminded herself severely, and you will eventually suffer the consequences. And losing Doug forever was one of the most difficult consequences she was forced to face.

Friday, the thirteenth of May was the day before Doug and Camille's wedding. Kate and Todd left for Baton Rouge on Thursday to participate in rehearsal dinner on Friday evening and all the activities planned afterward.

Ashley had declined her invitation to the Fairchild-Rabalais wedding, regardless of the fact that it was *the* social event of the season. She just couldn't go. She couldn't watch Doug marry Camille. She'd rather have teeth pulled or be shot through the heart by a firing squad.

Kate understood her reasoning perfectly, but Susanna gave her hell over her decision not to go to Baton Rouge.

"If you had any guts at all, you'd go to this shindig!" she protested loudly over the phone. "Do you want that hog Camille to think that she got the better of you?"

Ashley rolled her eyes for Susanna's benefit, even if Susanna couldn't see her. "Susanna, at this juncture, I don't care *what* Camille thinks, or anyone else for that matter," she said tensely, clenching her jaw in frustration. "I'm not going to the wedding to protect my own feelings. That's all I'm concerned about."

"I can't believe you still carry a torch for him after all this time."

"I'll always carry a torch for him. Doug will always hold a special place in my heart."

"You're making me sick! God, Ashley, sometimes you're worse than a greeting card," Susanna said, bellowing in disgust. "I'll tell you what, while we're all in Baton Rouge drinking champagne, and you're in Pineville, carrying your torch for Doug, why don't you drink, say, about a case of quality tequila, cry a little, and get this all out of your system? You're so much more fun when you're not sulking."

"Goodbye, Susanna."

Ashley replaced the receiver, listening to the eerie silence filling her house. She didn't even have Molly to keep her company. Maggie and Remy had taken her to San Antonio for the weekend.

"Just because you declined the invitation doesn't mean you can't be rude and go anyway," Maggie had suggested before leaving on Friday afternoon. "I'm sure no one would notice if you slipped in."

"I've already made my choice, Maggie. I'm not going," Ashley said, pulling her toward the car. "You better get going. Remy and Molly are waiting for you."

"I was only telling you, in case you change your mind."

"I won't, trust me." Ashley sent her off with an annoyed look, kissing Maggie's cheek and shoving her in the passenger door of the car, then leaned into the back seat to tell Molly goodbye.

"Have fun at Sea World, Molly. Tell Shamu hi for me," Ashley teased her with a smile. Molly returned her grin, gazing at her with beautiful aqua-blue eyes.

"I will, Mom!" she giggled, and Ashley watched them drive away, waving until they turned out of the driveway and onto the street.

So, there she was, deserted by both family and friends, and all alone on the eve before Doug's marriage to Camille. The only thing that kept her from running to Destin was the fact that she had to work the next morning. This was one crisis she could not take to Destin to solve. Ashley tried not to think about it, but when that proved to be useless, she decided to take Susanna's advice. She retrieved a bottle of wine from the refrigerator and took it, along with a glass, out to the front porch swing. She was going to drink, drown her sorrows and let the tears fall where they may.

It had grown quite late when she saw the dark green four-wheel drive pull into her driveway. At first, she thought that it might be a drunken hallucination, but she'd only had two glasses of wine. No, it really was Doug Fairchild, she decided, and he was climbing the steps to her front porch.

She watched him, her heart pounding, her palms growing damp around the stem of her wine glass. Hallucination or not, this was much too good to be true. What was he doing here?

Doug paused at the top of the stairs, melting Ashley's heart with his smile, and their eyes met, sending shock waves of longing across the length of the veranda. They stared in passionate silence, exchanging smoldering looks for what seemed like forever until Ashley spoke up.

"Am I mistaken, or don't you have a wedding to attend?"

Doug plopped down in the rocking chair across from her. "I don't know what happened," he said, scratching his head in a puzzled manner, endearing himself to her more. "One minute I was at rehearsal dinner, toasting with Camille, and the next I was heading up I-49 toward Pineville. And you."

"Well, you have to go back," she scolded him. "They'll be looking for you."

He shook his head stubbornly. "Let them look. I'm not going back until I say what I came to say."

"Would you like a drink?" Ashley asked him, holding up her bottle of wine. She pushed the swing back and forth with her toes, observing him cautiously.

"Nah, I better pass," he said, grinning sheepishly. "I've never been much of a drinker. I always end saying things that are better left unsaid."

He leaned back in his chair, inspecting her with admiring eyes. "You look good," he declared. "Much better than the last time I saw you."

"Thanks, I should certainly hope so." She waited, suspecting that he had plenty to get off his chest.

"I'm sorry I haven't come to see you before now. Kate told me what happened with Rick."

He stared off in the distance, his eyes clouded with anger and contempt for her ex-husband. "I didn't come to see you then because I couldn't bear to see you that way. I've thought about you, though.

"Hell, that's an understatement," he shook his head, laughing at the irony, shifting his gaze to look directly in her eyes. "The truth is, I can't seem to get you out of my head. And as hard as I've tried to go through with all this, I don't know if I can marry Camille now that you are free again."

Ashley could feel the eerie sensation of disbelief overcoming her and she simply stared at him, wide-eyed and speechless. Was the Divine Intervention she had prayed for at work?

"I've kept up with you through mutual friends, mainly Kate and Todd, but I couldn't see you again, not until I knew you'd be receptive to me," he paused, carefully choosing his words. "The way I see it, this is an opportune time to come back into your life. You're not engaged, pregnant or married. You've healed amazingly well from your experience with Rick."

His look softened. "And I feel pretty confident that I'm no longer competing with memories of a dead man," he added quietly.

Ashley brought the swing to an abrupt halt, color flooding her face. This really can't be happening, she thought deliriously. It was too surreal for words.

"I'm no longer interested in being just your friend," Doug said, leaning forward, his expression serious, watching her closely for further signs of a reaction. "I want it all, Ashley, the whole shebang. The way I see it, I love you, you love me, and we're great together. Why shouldn't we be together?"

"Didn't you say something like that to me a long, long time ago?" she finally spoke, flashing a soft smile, thinking about the way he had asked her to the homecoming dance.

"Yes, I believe I did," Doug remembered immediately, his twinkling eyes meeting hers. "So what do you think, Ashley?"

Ashley's heart was in her throat, her emotions a quivering mound of jelly, her mind swirling so wildly that she couldn't think straight. She caught her breath, giving herself a quick pep talk, then held up her empty bottle of wine.

"I think I need another drink." She effectively danced around his question, rising abruptly to go into the house. "Entrée," she beckoned playfully, holding the door open for him. "Welcome to Chez Ashley."

Doug came inside and looked around, nodding in approval. "Nice place, Ash. You've really done a lot."

"Thanks."

She walked away, leaving him standing in the middle of the living room, retreating to the kitchen for another bottle of wine. As she searched for the corkscrew, she felt him come up behind her, wrapping his arms around her waist. She tensed involuntarily, trembling at his touch. Life with Rick had left its mark on her, and despite what she felt for Doug, she was still notably skittish.

Sensing her reluctance, Doug leaned his head into hers, whispering softly in her ear. " I promise, I would never hurt you, Ashley. You know that. Relax." He kissed the top of her head gently.

"Let's have that drink!" Ashley wiggled out of his embrace, picking up the wine glasses, skirting out of the kitchen and away from him. Doug watched her intently, following her with an amused look on his face.

They settled onto the couch. Ashley took one end, kicking off her shoes, curling her feet beneath her, and Doug lounged in the opposite corner, his long legs stretched out in front of him, uttering not a word, waiting for her to make the next move. Ashley uncorked the wine, filling both glasses. She handed one to Doug, then drained her own glass, quickly refilling it. Doug threw his head back, laughing heartily.

"What?" she asked indignantly.

"How long are you going to continue to fight this? You've been fighting your feelings for me for years."

"Doug, what makes you so sure that I'm in love with you?" she asked him, her irritation level mounting.

"Remember, Ashley, I've seen you in love before. You loved me before you married Rick and you love me now."

"You're pretty confident," Ashley declared coolly. "Just how do you know that?"

"I see it in your eyes," Doug said. "No matter what your mouth says, your eyes give it away. They always have."

Ashley tried to think of a comeback, looking down at her hands, wanting to deny it but knowing she couldn't. She peeked up at him through her eyelashes. Doug was eyeing her knowingly, an entertained smirk on his face in anticipation of Round Two.

"Okay," she conceded. "Suppose I do love you. What makes you think that you still love me? You don't even know me anymore. I'm not the same girl you fell for, trust me."

"Oh," he leaned closer, examining her soberly. "The girl I love is still in there, only now she's the new, stronger, independent version. That only makes me want you more."

He winked at her, depositing his half-empty wine glass on the coffee table, and strolled over to the window, pulling aside the lace curtain and gazing out at the soft summer moonlight. With his back to her, Ashley let down her guard, regarding him with open affection, her heart singing, remembering all the things she loved about him most.

Doug let her stew, giving her time to sort out her thoughts, then dropped the curtain and turned around. "Aren't you tired of arguing with me yet?" he teased, chuckling at the testy look on her face. "Didn't anyone ever tell you that it's futile to argue with an attorney? You'll never win."

"Just because you have a law degree doesn't mean that I can't win an argument with you," she said, offended. "I've been holding my own against you for years."

He laughed heartily, his face lit by a jovial smile, glad to know that nothing between them had changed. He moved across the room with confidence and determination, diving onto the couch and taking Ashley into his arms before she could object, kissing her deeply.

Ashley remembered this kiss. This was the kiss that seared through her body like fire, turning her to jelly and leaving her feeling bewildered for days. She tried not to enjoy it, fighting her desire for him as rationally as she could.

"This is wrong," she thought, battling to stay in control of her emotions. Doug was engaged, on the very threshold of committing his life to Camille. She had to put a stop to this before it was too late. She argued with her inner demons, trying to resist him, but she couldn't. She'd waited too many years for this. She gave up, relaxing against him and kissing him back.

She lay alongside him on the couch, her head against his chest, listening to the steady rhythm of his heart as she thought back, reflecting on their long relationship together.

"I love you," Doug said, brushing her hair back from her face with a gentle sweep of his hand.

"How long have you known?" she asked him.

"How long have I known I love you? Hmm," Doug pondered, his brow creased in concentration. "I feel like I've known it my whole life, but I guess I first realized it in Environmental Science. Suddenly you weren't that goofy little girl I'd known forever. You changed overnight. I thought you were very cute and very witty." He winked at her, grinning at the memory.

"But as luck would have it, about the time I got up enough courage to ask you out, Jimmy moved to town and you went absolutely bonkers for him. Not that I have to remind you of that," he cut his eyes to her, smiling comically. "I asked you to homecoming anyway, hoping that my vast charm and wit would lure you away from him. That didn't work."

"After Rhonda came close to sabotaging everything that night at B.J.'s pizza, Jimmy was devastated. I could see how much he cared for you, and knew how much you cared for him, so I decided to put my desires aside and be the good guy. I made it my mission to patch things up between you two."

Ashley beamed at him thankfully, wondering how anyone could be so giving and selfless. "That was very sweet," she acknowledged softly.

He accepted her gratitude with a nonchalant nod. "Anyway, you were so terrific together. I don't think I've ever seen two people more in love. The more time I spent with the two of you, the more I wanted what you had. It didn't take me long to figure out that it wasn't what you and Jimmy had that I wanted. It was only you."

"I was your ideal," Ashley spoke out loud, realizing what Jimmy had meant so many years ago.

"What?" Doug looked down at her, bewildered.

"That was something Jimmy said. I wanted so badly to find the perfect woman for you, but Jimmy said that I could forget it. You had some ideal in mind and wouldn't rest until you had her."

"He was right. You were exactly what I wanted."

"Did he know how you felt about me?"

"I didn't think so then, but looking back on it, I'm sure he had a pretty good idea. But Jimmy was too good-hearted to be bitter about it. He knew I'd never do anything to hurt him."

"He was wonderful, wasn't he?" Ashley reflected with a wistful smile.

Doug nodded, "Yes, he was." He rolled onto his side, propping up on his elbow, a pensive expression overshadowing his handsome features. "And I'm sure he trusted me to take care of you if anything ever happened to him."

He laughed cynically. "And what a *fine*, fine job I've done of it! I left you alone to grieve your heart out, stood by while you ran off to Monroe, then just sat back and watched you marry Rick, knowing what a catastrophe it would be."

"You did everything in your power to stop me, short of kidnapping me," Ashley said. "None of that was your fault. I was the one who made a complete mess of everything. I was so headstrong and so determined that I was going to be fine that I wouldn't listen to anyone."

"How bad was it?"

This was the first time Doug had come right out and asked her anything about her marriage to Rick and Ashley felt obligated to tell him the truth.

"It didn't start out so badly," she confessed with a sheepish grin. "Even you have to admit that Rick is one great looking man. He was so charming and so unlike anyone I had ever met. I guess I allowed myself to be swept away by him and didn't even consider the consequences.

"I should have realized early on that he was also an overbearing, hot-tempered, control freak that I could never be happy with. But I chose to ignore all that, even when it was most obvious.

"We may have been okay, if not for my pregnancy. As you are well aware," she smiled at Doug, "I ran to Florida and hid from him. That only made it worse, because then he was hell-bent on having total control of me. He tricked me into marrying him by reminding me that Molly would be illegitimate if I didn't."

She hesitated, noting Doug's grim face, "Are you sure you want to hear all this?"

"You bet I do," he answered soberly. "If you're still willing to talk about it."

"It all went downhill after we got to Oklahoma and Molly was born. Rick never really wanted Molly. I've been totally responsible for her since the day she was born. Rick never touched her, fed her, changed her or spoke to her. And I resented him, but not for that reason alone."

Ashley stared at the ceiling, flinching as the haunting images flashed through her mind. "Rick was verbally abusive most of the time, and sometimes even physically abusive."

"That son of a bitch," Doug growled under his breath, tightening his arms around her protectively. "Kate said he damn near killed you. Is that true?"

Ashley nodded, shuddering involuntarily. "Yes, it's true. I decided to leave him, and he wasn't going to let me go." She simplified the details greatly for Doug's benefit, offering him a slight smile. "And the rest is history."

"Why didn't you marry me when I asked you?" Doug inquired softly into the semi-darkness of the room. "I was sincere, I promise."

Ashley gazed up at him, her face illuminated by the pale light of the moon. "I know you were. I overheard you and Kate out on the balcony that night in Destin. I didn't want you to marry me because I was pregnant. I only wanted the best for you."

"Which is exactly why you should have married me."

"I know that now, but by the time I figured out how I felt about you, you were already with Camille." She eyed him curiously, searching for a polite way to phrase her next question. "I'm not being ugly, Doug, I promise, but what do you see in her?"

"You mean other than the fact that she's very rich and very beautiful?"

"You're so clever," Ashley smirked, rolling her eyes sarcastically. "But she's so Rhonda-like."

"She really isn't that way," Doug defended his fiancée. "Camille has always been very sweet to me. Her problem is with you. As she pointed out, I tend to let my thoughts wander to you a little more often than she would like. Camille knows that you're the only other girl I've ever loved and that I still have great feelings for you. That's why she treated you as badly as she did."

They lay awake, talking late into the night, asking all the questions they'd always wanted to ask and confessing all the feelings they'd kept bottled up inside. As his eyes grew heavy, Doug wrapped his arms around her, pulling her tightly against him.

"Everything's going to be okay now, Ashley," he said, pressing his lips to her forehead. "I'm here, and no one will ever hurt you again."

Ashley fell asleep in the crook of Doug's arm and awoke just as the sun was peeking over the horizon. She lay on her side, watching him sleep, instantly recalling everything they had said. She watched his chest rise and fall in peaceful slumber, loving him more than ever, coming to the heartbreaking realization that what was happening between them wasn't right.

It's not me he loves, she recognized sadly, but the memory of me.

The Ashley Doug loved was gone, dead to all those around her. She was no longer the vivacious young teenager that Doug remembered in his heart. She was a different person now. She reached up, fingering the blond hair curling irresistibly around his ear, sorrow washing over her in waves.

There was no way that he was prepared to deal with the nightmares and periods of melancholy she experienced. Doug hadn't lived through Ashley's ordeal with her, but he had just as much reason to hate Rick. Rick had robbed him, in more ways than one, of the girl he loved.

More than that, Ashley knew the real truth. Doug truly loved Camille, more than he was consciously aware. Ashley sensed it from the times she had seen them together, from the way he spoke of her, with a soft glow on his face and light shining in his eyes. Yes, he loved her, and even though Ashley would never like her, Camille was more right for Doug than the person she had grown up to be.

"I've got to be crazy, absolutely insane," she closed her eyes, her head spinning with disbelief. "I've spent most of my adult life wanting him, and now I'm going to send him away."

As the first rays of sunshine streaked across the sky, Ashley gazed adoringly into the face of the man she had wanted for so long. She tenderly kissed his lips, thinking one last time about what she prepared to do, knowing in her heart that her decision was the right one. She kissed him again, then gently shook him awake.

Doug was surprised to see her face before his, then smiled broadly, remembering how and why he slept on Ashley Stewart's living room sofa. "Hi," he murmured sleepily, drawing her into his embrace.

Ashley didn't stop him. She wanted one last moment to cherish before she let him go. She savored the familiar warmth that flooded through her, knowing this would be the last time she would experience this sensation in the arms of Doug Fairchild.

Doug regarded her with dancing eyes, tracing her cheek with his fingertip. "Well, today should be an exciting day," he said teasingly.

"It sure will," Ashley said, forcing a cheerful lilt into her voice. "It's not every day that a guy gets married."

"I tend to think that's off now, in light of the last few hours."

"Not necessarily," Ashley pulled away from him, sliding over the couch cushions to put some distance between them. She turned sideways, looking into his puzzled face.

"Doug, you know I love you, " she said, her tender expression reflecting her obvious affection. "I've loved you for such a long, long time."

"I love you too," Doug interjected.

Ashley pursed her lips, putting up her hand to stop him. "Shut up, Doug, I have something important to say. Don't interrupt me or I'll never get through it."

"You're getting ready to fight with me again, aren't you?"

"Doug!"

He closed his mouth, folding his arms across his chest, and she continued.

"You were drinking last night, and I'm aware that when you're drinking, the ghost of Ashley Stewart often visits you from the deep dark corners of your mind. And you love her, I know that you love her," Ashley leaned forward, taking his face in her hands, gazing deeply into his brown eyes, "But Ashley Stewart doesn't exist anymore. She's now a memory, and a memory only."

He began to sputter and protest, and Ashley covered his mouth with her hand.

"You and I will always love one another and share a sentimental bond that no one can ever break, but we waited too long. The two people who fell in love are gone forever."

Ashley blinked back tears, scolding herself for letting them come at all. To cry in front of Doug would spoil everything she was trying to accomplish. She swallowed hard and looked over at him. He was listening to her, thoughtfully and incredulously, absorbing every word she said.

She reached over, touching his face, her fingers lingering on his tightly clenched jaw. "You'll always have the memory of the happy-go-lucky girl who loved to argue with you, just as I will have the memory of the gallant boy who offered to marry his pregnant best friend," she sighed, her chest heavy with regret. "But we aren't those people anymore, and never will be again."

Ashley couldn't stand it any longer. She sprang from the couch, pulling Doug up with her before she changed her mind. "It's time for you go back to Baton Rouge. It's your wedding day."

Doug stared at her. "I can't believe you're doing this, especially after last night. I thought we finally got everything straight."

"Come on, Doug," she persisted, ignoring the tugging at her heart, urging her to take back everything she had said. "You know everything I've said is true. I know that you love Camille. You know it too."

Doug lowered his eyes. "I do love Camille," he confessed quietly, "but I don't want to let you go."

Ashley put her arms around him, pulling his face even with hers. "I'm not going anywhere," she teased him with a smile. "I'll always be your dear friend, and you can count on me for anything. But you belong with Camille Rabalais, not Ashley LeNoir."

He cupped her face in his hands, kissing her long and hard. As the kiss ended, their eyes met and he winked at her. "I'll always love you," he said, his tone much more upbeat.

Ashley knew then that he had accepted the truth and would return to Baton Rouge to marry Camille.

"And I'll always love you," she said, pinching his cheek fondly. "My heart has room for lots of love."

Ashley made coffee while Doug took a quick shower. As he entered the living room, she admired the sheer beauty of him. Doug was indeed a spectacular man, both inside and out. She handed him a mug of coffee and shooed him toward the door. Before he opened it to leave, Doug bent down, embracing Ashley one last time.

"See ya," he said, finding it impossible, as always, to say goodbye to her.

Ashley nodded and smiled brightly. "See ya," she answered in return.

She opened the door and sent him on his way, watching as he drove out of her life. She moved out onto the porch into the early morning sun and sipped coffee, thinking about what she had just done, and suddenly came to realize that she had done for Doug what he had once done for Jimmy and her. She had put aside her own wants and desires so that he could find happiness with Camille.

Doug did marry Camille that evening in a candlelight ceremony, which Kate admitted was to die for. She called Ashley Sunday morning after she and Todd returned from Baton Rouge. "It was truly lovely, Ashley," Kate sighed dreamily. "You really should have come."

"I'm rather glad I passed on the trip to Baton Rouge," Ashley replied in a faraway voice, thinking of the way she had spent Friday night.

"There was a period of time when we all thought Doug had chickened out," Kate revealed mysteriously. "He disappeared right after rehearsal dinner and didn't reappear until early Saturday afternoon. He was nowhere to be found."

"Really?" Ashley tried to sound convincingly surprised as she responded to Kate's news. Dear Kate immediately became suspicious.

"You wouldn't happen to know anything about where he was, would you?" she interrogated Ashley lightly.

"How could I possibly know where Doug might have gone?" Ashley answered with a small laugh.

Invariably capable of reading her like a book, Kate knew that Ashley was lying to her. But she also knew that Ashley wasn't going to tell her what she knew. It was their secret, Ashley's and Doug's, and they would take it to their graves.

Ashley hung up the phone and lay back on the window seat, deep in thought. Letting go of Doug meant letting go of her last link to the Jimmy Era, and although some sadness lingered, Ashley felt an odd sense of relief.

As she stared out at the lake, watching the sunset behind the tall cypress trees, a knock sounded on her front door. Ashley crossed the room and swung open the door to find Jack leaning against the doorframe, fishing pole in hand.

"Hey, kiddo," he said, flashing one of his most charming grins. "How about some night fishing?"

EPILOGUE

Ashley's life didn't end the day Doug wed Camille in that lavish ceremony in Baton Rouge. Instead, that's the day her life started over again.

Years later, she returned to Destin, accompanied by Kate and Molly.

Molly had grown to be even more extraordinary—bright, tall and slender, with a head full of thick blond curls, and two best friends who Ashley hoped would be to Molly what Kate and Susanna had been to her: too good to be true. Molly was happy and content, barely remembering Rick and that fateful night so long ago. And for that, Ashley was glad.

Doug had become quite the man around the state capital of Baton Rouge and the latest rumors were that he was being groomed for a possible senate position in the near future. He and Camille remained blissfully wed, and although she still did not like her, as long as Camille continued to make Doug happy, Ashley had no problem with her.

Maggie and Remy traveled extensively, thoroughly enjoying their retirement together. Ashley thought that Frannie might quit her job when she learned that Remy was retiring. She and Remy had worked together for so many years and Frannie didn't think she would be able to work with anyone else. But she changed her mind about leaving the moment she laid eyes on Jack.

Unable to resist the lure of unlimited hunting and fishing any longer, Jack moved to Pineville shortly after Doug and Camille married. At twenty-five,

Ashley hadn't yet gained the experience needed to run the business all alone so she enticed Jack to come to work for her. It was the shrewdest business decision she could have ever made.

Jack took over and worked his magic, charming them all, from Frannie to Ms. Bobbie to Dr. Lisa Watson. It seemed that Jack would always have that effect on women. Undeniable attractiveness radiated from him like some sort of aura. Even now, it never failed to astonish her.

Mister Eddie Thibodeaux thought the world of Jack, and told Ashley so on numerous occasions. "Now, der's da man for you, chère," he flashed his toothy grin every time Ashley walked into the grill with Jack.

Ashley rolled her eyes, glaring at him impatiently. "Don't you even try that with me," she told him. "I remember only too well what happened the last time I listened to you."

Jack was the one who brought customers to the pharmacy in droves, so Ashley left the social aspect of the business to him while she retired to the office to handle the accounting. As the months went on, Ashley watched Jack from her office window, and as he captivated the customers, he, in turn, captivated her. Ashley fell more deeply in love with Jack Chambers with each passing day. However, she was unwilling to sacrifice another great friendship to romance, so she kept her feelings to herself. It was well over a year before Ashley learned how Jack felt about her.

She was in the office, finishing the end-of-the-month paperwork, so engrossed in her work that she had lost all track of time until Jack stuck his head in the office door.

"Ready to go?" he asked her. She glanced up at the clock, realizing that it was closing time.

"Hang on," she replied. "I'm just finishing up."

Jack peeked over her shoulder at the spreadsheet on which she scribbled furiously. "How's business?" he inquired curiously.

"Couldn't be better," Ashley declared with a playful smile. "Which only goes to show you that sex sells. Just keep charming the customers and we'll be set for life."

Jack grinned and lounged in the chair next to her desk, studying her face as he spoke. "Ashley, I've known hundreds of women in my lifetime and this is the first time that I've ever been at a loss," he said mischievously.

"What are you talking about?" Ashley didn't look up at him and wrinkled her brow as she tried to concentrate.

"I've been knocking myself out for months and I still don't know how to get your attention."

Ashley dropped her pencil, turning her head to gaze into the depths of his incredibly green eyes. "It's too late to try to figure that out now," her eyes danced with amusement as she teased him. "You've had my attention for quite some time."

Jack smiled broadly at her confession. "Don't you think it might've been helpful for me to be privy to that information?"

"Why? So you could add me to your collection of conquests?"

"Hell no," Jack leaned forward in his chair. "You're in a league all your own, Ms. Stewart. I think I could even have a meaningful relationship with you."

"Why, Jack," Ashley slid her arms flirtatiously around his neck. "What's gotten into you? This talk of commitment is so unlike you."

"Maybe I've just finally met my match," Jack conceded, and when his lips finally met hers, Ashley knew that Jack's kiss was the one she had waited for all her life.

Jack chuckled as their kiss ended. "So, does this mean that I don't have to play that whole seduction game with you?"

"Even if you did, it wouldn't do you any good," Ashley pointed out to him with a saucy grin. "I already know all your best lines."

Ashley and Jack married six months later in a double Las Vegas ceremony, sharing the spotlight with Ellie Holman and Tom Brandon. Maggie had been horrified when Jack and Ashley eloped.

"Stop whining, Maggie," Ashley told her, amused by the look on her face after she and Jack had broken the news. "I married Jack. You should be happy."

"You could have at least had a wedding," Maggie said, pursing her lips disapprovingly.

"No thank you," Ashley replied, making a face. "I've had enough pomp and ceremony to last me a lifetime."

"But Ashley, did you have to elope? And to Las Vegas, of all places? I can think of nothing more tacky than being married by Elvis!"

This trip to Destin had been good for Ashley. She enjoyed a week of relaxation and covered a lifetime of memories. Kate would be so proud of her. She'd spent the entire morning cleaning out those dark corners in her mind.

"Kate's been right all along," Ashley decided, digging her toes blissfully into the cool white sand. "I do feel much better now that I've relived it all."

She had looked back, reliving each situation with rational eyes, and could finally answer the question she had posed to herself earlier.

What, if anything, would she change?

Would she give back the time she had with Jimmy? Losing him had been the most devastating thing she'd ever experienced and it had taken years to get over it. Such anguish she would wish upon no one, particularly herself. Nevertheless, she couldn't replace her time with Jimmy, not even if she had tried.

Jimmy had been her first love, and the days she spent with him were among the best days of her life. He had deep warmth and great humor, and had given her the giddy, unbridled, overwhelming feeling that all was right with the world and nothing would ever change. His positive outlook on life had brought out the best in her. Jimmy made Ashley know what it was to truly be in love and her love for him would remain forever, locked safely in her heart.

Nor did she regret how things turned out with Doug. Doug remained one of her closest friends, and had supported her through the best and worst of times, guiding her out of her grief after Jimmy's death and setting her back on the path toward happiness.

As her love for Doug grew, Ashley was tormented by wanting him yet not being able to have him, first because of Rick, and then because of Camille. Yet, even then, Ashley had been rewarded with how wonderful she felt when their eyes met, and the warmth that spread over her entire body each time they touched. And the special night they shared on the eve of his wedding to Camille was one she'd never forget. In her own way, she would always love Doug. He too would forever hold a special place in her heart.

Then there was the matter of Rick. Out of all the things Ashley could consider to change, to have never met Rick LeNoir should have ranked number one on the list. He was a horrible person, and their marriage had been a disaster, almost costing Ashley her life, and leaving such a scar on her that she was forever changed. However, through Rick LeNoir, Ashley had gained so many extraordinary people in her life. She couldn't imagine what her world would be like without ever having known them. Dear, dear Ellie, Matt and Jack—they had restored her lost self-confidence, keeping her aloft, giving her the courage to believe in herself again.

But most importantly, Rick had given Ashley one of the most wonderful gifts that life had to offer. Rick gave her Molly, her beautiful, amazing daughter. Molly was her greatest treasure, and Ashley loved her more than she could've ever known was possible. She would have gladly endured it all again, if only for Molly.

The domino effect of Jimmy's death, combined with the fickle hand of fate, triggered the events in her life that led Ashley to Jack. And in the end, it was with Jack that Ashley found real happiness. It was only fitting that the two "been there, done that" kids would find true love together. They had been right there for one another all along, never realizing what a perfect match they were.

With Jack, Ashley had great friendship and deep love. She could laugh with him and cry with him, and Jack comforted her, as no other could, when she awoke from the disturbing nightmare that sometimes revisited her in the middle of the night.

In spite of knowing all she'd had to endure to arrive there, with Molly and Jack, Ashley had everything. What would she change? She smiled, lifting her face into the warm rays of Florida sunshine.

In light of how wonderfully her life had been blessed, Ashley could honestly say that she wouldn't change a thing.

THE END